The Edinburgh Companion to British Colonial Periodicals

Edinburgh Companions to Literature and the Humanities
These single-volume reference works present cutting-edge scholarship in areas of literary studies, particularly those which reach out to other disciplines. They include volumes on key literary figures and their interaction with the arts, on major topics and on emerging forms of cross-disciplinary research.

For a complete list of titles in the series, please go to
https://edinburghuniversitypress.com/series/ecl

The Edinburgh Companion to British Colonial Periodicals

Edited by David Finkelstein, David Johnson and Caroline Davis

EDINBURGH
University Press

Edinburgh University Press is one of the leading university presses in the UK.
We publish academic books and journals in our selected subject areas across the
humanities and social sciences, combining cutting-edge scholarship with high
editorial and production values to produce academic works of lasting importance.
For more information visit our website: edinburghuniversitypress.com

© editorial matter and organisation, David Finkelstein, David Johnson and
Caroline Davis, 2024
© the chapters their several authors, 2024

Published with the support of the University of Edinburgh Scholarly Publishing
Initiatives Fund.

Edinburgh University Press Ltd
13 Infirmary Street
Edinburgh EH1 1LT

Typeset in 10/12 Adobe Sabon by
IDSUK (DataConnection) Ltd, and
printed and bound in Great Britain

A CIP record for this book is available from the British Library

ISBN 978 1 3995 0063 0 (hardback)
ISBN 978 1 3995 0064 7 (webready PDF)
ISBN 978 1 3995 0065 4 (epub)

The right of David Finkelstein, David Johnson and Caroline Davis to be identified as
the editors of this work has been asserted in accordance with the Copyright, Designs
and Patents Act 1988, and the Copyright and Related Rights Regulations 2003
(SI No. 2498).

Contents

List of Illustrations	ix
Acknowledgements	xiii
Introduction: British Colonial Periodicals in Context *David Finkelstein and David Johnson*	1

Part I: Creating and Contesting the Colonial Public Sphere

1. Authorship and Collective Self-Fashioning in Pre-Confederation English Canada
   Cynthia Sugars and Paul Keen — 37

2. Early Colonial Periodicals in Nineteenth-Century Canada: *The Literary Garland* in Context
   Fariha Shaikh — 51

3. The Afro-Caribbean Press and the Politics of Place in Jamaica and Barbados: *The Watchman and Jamaica Free Press* and *The Liberal*
   Candace Ward — 66

4. Mofussil versus Metropolis, Subalterns versus Seniors: The Rise and Demise of *The Meerut Universal Magazine*
   Graham Shaw — 81

5. Writing the 'Wooden World': Periodicals and Settler Environmental Knowledge in Colonial New Zealand
   Philip Steer — 97

6. British Missionary Magazines at Home and Abroad: Southern Africa as Topic and Southern Africans as Readership
   Lize Kriel, Annika Vosseler and Chantelle Finaughty — 112

7. The Sydney *Bulletin* and the Settler Colonial Subject
   Tony Hughes-d'Aeth — 127

8. Periodicals and Australian Federation
   Sam Hutchinson — 139

CONTENTS

9. The *South African News* and the Anglo-Boer War of 1899–1902   154
   Jonathan Derrick

10. The Weekly *West Africa*: Commerce, Empire and Decolonisation   168
    Jonathan Derrick

Part II: Women and Colonial Periodicals

11. Transnational Reprinting and the Colonial Women's Magazine:
    The Montreal Museum, 1832–4   185
    Honor Rieley

12. The Birth of the Australian Women's Magazine: The *New Idea*, 1902–11   201
    Michelle J. Smith

13. Women's Writing and Reporting on Women in the Ghanaian and
    Nigerian Press, c. 1880–1930s   213
    Katharina A. Oke

14. Indian Women's Pre-Independence Periodicals in English: *The Indian
    Ladies' Magazine*, *Stri-Dharma* and the Indian New Woman   228
    Deborah Anna Logan

15. *Marriage Hygiene* and the Internationalisation of Eugenical Sexology
    in the 1930s   242
    *Tanya Agathocleous, Ruwanthi Edirisinghe, Jessica Lu, Jaïra Placide
    and Sarah Schwartz*

Part III: Language and Colonial Periodicals

16. Making Māori Citizens in Colonial New Zealand: The Role of
    Government *niupepa*   255
    Lachy Paterson

17. Language and the Making of the Colonial Modern: Periodicals from
    Late Nineteenth-Century Kerala, India   272
    G. Arunima

18. Simple Letters? British and Pacific Literacies in the Victorian Missionary
    Periodical   285
    Michelle Elleray

19. Interrogating the Imperial Factor and Convoking Black South Africa:
    The Cape African Newspaper *Izwi Labantu*, 1897–1909   300
    Janet Remmington

20. Colonial Government Periodicals in 1920s East Africa: *Mambo Leo*
    and *Habari*   317
    Emma Hunter

21. Print Networks and Linguistic Interaction in the Early Yoruba Press   330
    Karin Barber

22. Colonial Entanglements: Black South African Periodicals and the Colonial Printsphere, 1920s–30s 343
Corinne Sandwith and Athambile Masola

Part IV: Trans-Colonial Connections in Colonial Periodicals

23. Samuel Revans and Company: Colonial Commercial Trade Newspapers in the Age of Responsible Government 361
Melodee H. Wood

24. Colonial Trade Identity and Labour Information Exchange in the International Typographical Trade Press, 1840–1910 375
David Finkelstein

25. The Anglo-Zulu War in the *Friend of India*: Mediation, Meaning and Authority 390
Andrew Griffiths

26. British Anarchism and the Colonial Question: The Case of *Freedom*, 1918–62 404
Ole Birk Laursen

27. The Atlantic Charter in British Colonial Periodicals 418
David Johnson

28. Citation and Solidarity: Reporting the 1955 Asian-African Conference in African Newspapers and Periodicals 432
Christopher J. Lee

29. Non-Alignment and Maoist China: *Eastern Horizon* in the Era of Decolonisation, 1960–81 446
Alex Tickell and Anne Wetherilt

Part V: Anti-Colonialism in the Colonial and Postcolonial Public Sphere

30. For Illustrative Purposes: Nana Sahib, Jotee Prasad and Representation in British and Anglo-Indian Newspapers 463
Priti Joshi

31. The Indian Newspaper Reports of British India: 'A Kind of Periodical Press' 477
Sukeshi Kamra

32. The Anti-Colonial Periodical between Public and Counterpublic: *The Beacon* and *Public Opinion* in the Interwar Years 493
Raphael Dalleo

33. 'Not a Newspaper in the Ordinary Sense of the Term': The Geopolitics of the Newspaper/Magazine Divide in the Nigerian *Comet* 505
Marina Bilbija

34. Africa in Jamaica: W. A. Domingo, George Padmore and *Public Opinion* 519
Myles Osborne

35. Citizenship, Responsibility and Literary Culture in the University Periodical in Eastern Africa: Spaces of Social Production in *Busara* and its Networks 531
    Madhu Krishnan

Notes on Contributors 542
Index 550

Illustrations

Plates

Plate 1   Frederick Stack, *View from the Ranges, overlooking the entrance to the Manukau Harbour, Auckland*, 1862, hand-coloured lithograph, 203 x 405 mm. The forested landscape of the Auckland province was generally seen as an encumbrance to settler agriculture. Courtesy of Auckland Art Gallery Toi o Tāmaki, purchased 1989.

Plate 2   George O'Brien (1821–88), *View of Otago Heads and Port Chalmers from Signal Hill near Dunedin*, c. 1866, watercolour with pencil & opaque white on paper, 288 x 634 mm. The relative absence of forest in the landscape of the Otago province. Courtesy of Hocken Collections Uare Taoka o Hākena, University of Otago, 7,302.

Plate 3   *Eastern Horizon*, December 1967, cover. Courtesy of the authors.

Plate 4   *Busara*, 3.4, 1971, cover. Courtesy of the author.

Plate 5   *Busara*, 3.4, 1971, table of contents. Courtesy of the author.

Figures

Figure 1.1	Cover of *The Literary Garland and British North American Magazine*. Courtesy of the authors.	45
Figure 2.1	'Combination Borders' advertisement, from the *Specimen*, 1846, p. 132 of 258. Creative Commons Licence, courtesy of www.archive.org.	61
Figure 5.1	*Scene on Henderson's Creek, Auckland. Illustrated New Zealand News*, 13, 4 August 1884. Ref: S-L-1764.01. New Zealand periodicals' use of lithography assisted in disseminating ideas of local natural beauty. Courtesy of Alexander Turnbull Library, Wellington, New Zealand.	102
Figure 5.2	Alexander Walker Reid, *Mountain with road and clearing farms of trees*, c. 1890–1900, gelatine half plate glass negative. The extent of deforestation in the vicinity of Taranaki Maunga by the end of the nineteenth century. Courtesy of Puke Ariki, New Plymouth, PHO2007-301.	108
Figure 6.1	*Wesleyan Missionary Notices*, January 1904, p. 1. Courtesy of the author.	119
Figure 6.2	*Foreign Field*, 1, cover, 1904–5. Courtesy of the author.	119

LIST OF ILLUSTRATIONS

Figure 6.3	A 'snap shot' of readers of the *Foreign Field* as seen in the *Foreign Field* ('The Business Side of the Magazine', 1907, p. 118). Courtesy of the author.	119
Figure 8.1	'Cartoon: What about trade unions federation?', *The Worker*, 2 February 1901, p. 1. Courtesy of the author.	149
Figure 8.2	'Cartoon: The Curse of Queensland', *The Worker*, 12 January 1901, p. 4. Courtesy of the author.	150
Figure 9.1	The *South African News*, weekly edition, 12 December 1900. Courtesy of the British Library.	154
Figure 10.1	'Arrival of West African Editors in Britain', *West Africa*, 14 August 1943, p. 704. Courtesy of the author.	175
Figure 11.1	Title page, *The Montreal Museum*, 1, 1832–3. Courtesy of the Canadiana Collection of the Canadian Research Knowledge Network (*canadiana.ca*).	185
Figure 11.2	'The Queen of the Belgians', *The Montreal Museum*, 1.1, December 1832. Courtesy of the Canadiana Collection of the Canadian Research Knowledge Network (*canadiana.ca*).	187
Figure 11.3	'Fashions for October 1832', *The Montreal Museum*, 1.1, December 1832. Courtesy of the Canadiana Collection of the Canadian Research Knowledge Network (*canadiana.ca*).	187
Figure 12.1	The *New Idea*, 1 August 1902, masthead. Courtesy of the author.	203
Figure 12.2	The *New Idea*, 6 July 1909, masthead. Courtesy of the author.	203
Figure 14.1	*The Indian Ladies' Magazine*, July 1901, front cover. Courtesy of the author.	231
Figure 15.1	*Marriage Hygiene*, 1.2, November 1934, cover. Courtesy of the authors.	243
Figure 15.2	*Marriage Hygiene*, 1.2, November 1934, advertisement for contraceptives and table of contents. Courtesy of the authors.	247
Figure 16.1	*Te Karere o Nui Tireni* (The Messenger of New Zealand), 1 January 1842, p. 1. This was the first issue of a Māori-language newspaper. The nameplate sports the crown's coat of arms, and the statement 'Na te Kawana i mea kia taia' (Printed under authority of the Governor). The first article explains the purpose of the paper, such as providing information on law and government procedures. The rest of the page relates to the capture and imminent trial of Maketū, a Māori who murdered a Pākehā settler family. Courtesy of Hocken Collections – Uare Taoka o Hākena, University of Otago.	257
Figure 16.2	Instructions to Māori voters and potential candidates on how the first election for the Eastern Māori seat will proceed. *Te Waka Maori o Ahuriri*, 19 March 1868, p. 9. Courtesy of Hocken Collections – Uare Taoka o Hākena, University of Otago.	264
Figure 16.3	Notification of candidates for upcoming election. *Te Waka Maori o Niu Tirani*, 11 January 1876, p. 5. Courtesy of Hocken Collections – Uare Taoka o Hākena, University of Otago.	266
Figure 17.1	Nineteenth-century Malayalam periodical *Bhashaposhini*. Courtesy of Sree Chithirai Thirunal Library, Trivandrum, Kerala.	274

Figure 17.2	Nineteenth-century Malayalam periodical *Vidyavinodini*. Courtesy of Sree Chithirai Thirunal Library, Trivandrum, Kerala.	276
Figure 18.1	Title page, volume 1, the *Juvenile Missionary Magazine*, 1844. Courtesy of the author.	286
Figure 18.2	Aperaamo's letter, the *Juvenile Missionary Magazine*. Courtesy of the author.	286
Figure 18.3	Cover page, *O le Sulu Samoa*, 1839. Image reproduced with kind permission of Special Collections, State Library of New South Wales.	287
Figure 19.1	*Izwi Labantu*, 27 August 1901, p. 2. Courtesy of the National Library of South Africa, Cape Town.	307
Figure 19.2	*Izwi Labantu*, 18 February 1908, p. 1. Courtesy of the National Library of South Africa, Cape Town.	312
Figure 20.1	Cover of *Habari*, 4.4, April 1925. Reproduced by kind permission of the Syndics of Cambridge University Library.	318
Figure 21.1	'Impertinent newsmonger!' Adeoye Deniga's open letter to the *Nigerian Advocate. Eko Akete*, 18 August 1923, p. 3. Courtesy of the author.	333
Figure 22.1	*Umteteli wa Bantu*, 1 May 1920, p. 3. Courtesy of the National Library of South Africa, Cape Town.	349
Figure 22.2	*Bantu World*, 9 April 1932, p. 5. Courtesy of the National Library of South Africa, Cape Town.	354
Figure 23.1	The first issue of the *New Zealand Gazette*, printed in Wellington on 18 April 1840. Courtesy of the National Library of New Zealand.	368
Figure 24.1	*The Australian Typographical Circular*, 1, January 1858, p. 1. Courtesy of the print collection of the British Library.	377
Figure 24.2	'J. Farrell: First President of S.A.T.U.', *South African Typographical Journal*, 4.39, January 1902, p. 13. Courtesy of the print collection of St Bride's Library, London.	381
Figure 25.1	The *Friend of India and Statesman*, 14 February 1879, p. 1. Courtesy of the British Library.	392
Figure 25.2	The *Friend of India and Statesman*, 14 February 1879, p. 136. Courtesy of the author.	397
Figure 26.1	*Spain and the World*, 13 October 1937, p. 1. Courtesy of the British Library.	407
Figure 27.1	'Cartoon: Freedom for All', *Hindustan Times*, 18 August 1941, p. 1. Courtesy of the British Library.	424
Figure 28.1	'Editorial: The Spirit of Bandung', *The Ethiopian Herald*, 24 April 1985, p. 2. Courtesy of the author.	433
Figure 28.2	'From Bandung to Algiers', *Daily Nation*, 17 June 1965, p. 6. Courtesy of the author.	442
Figure 29.1	Distribution list, *Eastern Horizon*, December 1967, back cover. Courtesy of the authors.	453
Figure 30.1	'Nana Sahib', *The Illustrated London News*, 26 September 1857. Courtesy of the author.	464

Figure 30.2	'Nana Sahib (From a picture painted at Bhitoor, in 1850, by Mr. Beechy, Portrait painter to the King of Oude.)', *The Illustrated Times*, 26 September 1857. Courtesy of the author.	465
Figure 30.3	'Nana Sahib', *The Lady's Newspaper and Pictorial Times*, 28 November 1857. Courtesy of the author.	467
Figure 30.4	'Nena Sahib's Turn-out.--p. 115', frontispiece of John Lang's *Wanderings in India and Other Sketches of Life in Hindostan*, 1859. Courtesy of the author.	471
Figure 31.1	Title page of a 'Newspaper Report', p. 1 of report, IOR/L/R/5/14. Courtesy of the British Library.	478
Figure 31.2	Typical page of a Newspaper Report with (translated) extracts from multiple Indian-language newspapers. Proceedings of the Home Office (Oct 1891, prog. 260), P/3880, IOR. Courtesy of the British Library.	485
Figure 31.3	Example of the standardised tabular statement of Newspaper Reports. Among information produced by the table is 'tone' of the Indian-language press. Proceedings of the Home Office (Oct 1891, prog. 263, IOR). Courtesy of the British Library.	486
Figure 32.1	*The Beacon*, March 1931, p. 1. Courtesy of the University of the West Indies Library.	497
Figure 32.2	*Public Opinion*, 20 February 1937, p. 1. Courtesy of the British Library.	499
Figure 33.1	The *Comet*, 22 July 1933, p. 1. Courtesy of the author.	506
Figure 33.2	Ovaltine advertisement, the *Comet*, 11 May 1935. Courtesy of the author.	509
Figure 34.1	*Public Opinion*, 16 March 1957, p. 1. Courtesy of the British Library.	520

Tables

Table 4.1	Military v. civilian readers of *The Meerut Universal Magazine* (*M.U.M.*)	91
Table 4.2	Breakdown of military readers of the *M.U.M.*	92
Table 4.3	Breakdown of civilian readers of the *M.U.M.*	93

Acknowledgements

THIS VOLUME EMERGED from a series of conversations started by Caroline Davis, who set our project in motion, and developed it into what you see in the pages to follow. We are most grateful to her for her initial insights and drive that ensured our path to completion was clear and well defined. Due to a serious accident, Caroline was unable to complete the full editorial journey with us. We dedicate this volume to her.

We also thank Jackie Jones, senior commissioning editor at Edinburgh University Press, whose belief in this project led to its inclusion in EUP's groundbreaking list in Periodical Studies History. Elizabeth Fraser at EUP was patient and ever-helpful in guiding us through EUP's production process, Cathy Falconer was the most scrupulous of copy-editors, and Rachel Goodyear completed the index with great skill.

Our contributors to the *Companion* have been exceptional in all respects, meeting deadlines, replying to endless emails, adapting to the changed production schedules imposed by Covid and lockdown, and, most importantly, embracing and sharing fully the ambitions of the project and producing work of the highest quality.

Along the way we have been helped by several critical friends. Our thanks to the anonymous reviewers who offered helpful insights into areas of development for the volume, to Anne Wetherilt for her keen-eyed editorial help as we processed the manuscript, and to our friendly readers Andrew Griffiths, Ole Birk Laursen, Alex Tickell (and Anne Wetherilt), whose comments on our Introduction were extremely helpful in shaping our thinking and steering us clear of any grave mistakes. Warm thanks are due too to Clair Durow for transforming many of the images into high-definition versions suitable for press use.

Sincere thanks are due to the Open University, which funded the two-day international conference on British Colonial Periodicals in January 2021 that generated early versions of many of the chapters subsequently developed for the volume. Philip Steer acknowledges the support of the Marsden Fund Council for grant funding enabling the work for his volume contribution (grant no. MFP-19-MAU-022), managed by Royal Society Te Apārangi.

We are grateful to the following individuals who have supplied images from their private collections for use in the volume: Tanya Agathocleous, Marina Bilbija, Michelle Elleray, David Finkelstein, Andrew Griffiths, Sam Hutchinson, David Johnson, Priti Joshi, Paul Keen, Lize Kriel, Madhu Krishnan, Christopher J. Lee, Deborah Anna Logan, Honor Rieley, Michelle J. Smith, Cynthia Sugars, Alex Tickell, Anne Wetherilt and Melodee H. Wood.

We are also grateful to the following institutions and holdings who have provided permissions and access to several images featured in this volume: www.archive.

org; Alexander Turnbull Library, Wellington, New Zealand; Auckland Art Gallery Toi o Tāmaki; The British Library; Syndics of Cambridge University Library; www.canadiana.ca; the Hocken Collections – Uare Taoka o Hākena, University of Otago; National Library of South Africa, Cape Town; Puke Ariki, New Plymouth; Sree Chithirai Thirunal Library, Trivandrum, Kerala; St Bride's Library, London; Special Collections, State Library of New South Wales; University of the West Indies Library.

Finally, we are grateful to our readers, current and future, for seeking out this volume in whatever form it arrives on your desk or screen. We hope you enjoy its contents as much as we as editors have enjoyed working with our great collaborators to bring it to fruition.

David Finkelstein and David Johnson

For Caroline

Introduction: British Colonial Periodicals in Context

David Finkelstein and David Johnson

Surveying Britain's expanding Empire in 1836, the *Friend of India* noted, 'Our Empire in India is an empire of opinion' (Anon. 1836, *Friend of India*: 1). Underpinning this observation was an acknowledgement that Britain's authority in India (and by extension in other imperial spaces) was secured in great part by newspapers and periodicals. Britain's political power in India – and in the rest of the Empire – rested on managing the flow of information, monitoring content, imposing legal restrictions, and censoring offending publications.

Twenty-five years later, reflecting on how little capital was required to enable the colonial press to play an effective role in shaping public discourse, Mountstuart Elphinstone, the one-time Governor of Bombay, commented presciently:

> The Press is a great system of circulation, of which the types and printing machines form only a part. When the art is once understood, a very small quantity of printing even in a language not more generally understood than English in India, is enough to furnish material for a great quantity of manuscripts, as well as of declamation, conversation, dissemination of rumours and alarms. (Wilson 1861: 105n)

Those who oversaw the Empire recognised the need to maintain control of the flow of information, using newspapers, newsletters, magazines, journals and periodicals to reinforce colonial norms, while restricting through legal, political and economic means the dissemination of the ideas of those challenging such norms. Individuals and groups who fought against colonial structures nonetheless appropriated and adapted the resources provided by the colonial press in order to address their constituents, to criticise colonial rule, while striving at all times to avoid censorship. For British émigrés, expatriates, administrators, military personnel and civilian workers, by contrast, the magazines and journals in the colonies created a shared sense of identity that connected them to each other, to other settler/colonial communities, and to their homeland.

The history of the British colonial press over two centuries of colonial expansion and contraction is therefore one of contestation, negotiation, accommodation and interpretation. It is a history of the acquisition and utilisation of the tools of print communication for a range of purposes, including the circulation of colonial knowledge across imperial networks; the communication of information about economic activities and political events; the dissemination of metropolitan culture; the provision of entertainment; the creation of communities of readers; the constitution of individual and group identities; and the mobilisation of collective resistance to colonialism.

The *Companion*

Showcasing original research on British colonial periodicals by leading scholars in the field, the thirty-five chapters in the *Companion* analyse the crucial role played by colonial periodicals in legitimising as well as contesting the economic, political and cultural hegemony of the British Empire from its inception to its end. British colonial periodicals have conventionally been treated primarily as sources of information by scholars writing the social, political, cultural and literary histories of Britain's colonies. Seldom the subject of in-depth scholarly analysis themselves, periodicals have instead been treated as transparent and unmediated repositories of facts about colonial societies. The ambition of the *Companion* is to rescue the many hitherto invisible and taken-for-granted colonial periodicals from such scholarly neglect by placing them centre stage and analysing them in their own terms. By examining the multiple histories of Britain's colonial periodicals, we seek to understand how they functioned under colonial rule.

A wide range of colonial periodicals are discussed in the *Companion*. There are chapters focused on periodicals produced in Britain for colonial consumption and ones produced throughout the Empire, including West, East and Southern Africa, the British Caribbean, Australia and New Zealand, the Pacific, British North America, the Indian subcontinent and Southeast Asia; periodicals produced for readers in individual colonies, as well as ones aimed at a transnational readership across the colonial world; and periodicals published in many different languages (and in combinations of languages), notably Māori, Hindi, Urdu, Malayalam, Odia, Swahili, Yoruba, isiXhosa and isiZulu and English.

A methodological commitment sustained in all the chapters is to locate the colonial periodicals under discussion in their respective historical contexts. While certain habits of British colonial rule were repeated across the Empire, the historical specificities of the different colonies meant that the editors, journalists and print workers, the production processes, the circulation, the reception and the social impact of the periodicals differed markedly from colony to colony. With each chapter paying careful attention to the relationship between periodical(s) and its/their colonial context(s), the *Companion* captures the diversity of Britain's colonial periodicals. Clearly a single volume such as this one cannot be comprehensive; the hope is that the thirty-five chapters pose challenging new questions about the meaning and significance of British colonial periodicals, and in so doing provoke fresh research into the many more periodicals not examined within these pages.

With regard to the scope of the *Companion*, our definition of 'British colonial periodicals' is deliberately porous and capacious. We reject the inherited division between 'the press' (defined as daily and weekly newspapers, geared to reporting on current events, politics and social mores) and 'the periodical press' (defined as print outputs of less immediate currency or frequency, such as monthlies and quarterlies, geared to chronicling and circulating cultural and literary commentaries, and trade or niche interests). In many colonial contexts, as a number of the chapters in the *Companion* argue, this division collapses, with some 'newspapers' publishing intermittently and providing an abundance of opinion and commentary, and some 'periodicals' appearing regularly and publishing extensive reportage. By adopting a definition broad enough to accommodate the full range of such publications, the *Companion* admits the widest range of publications to the conversation.

The Infrastructure of Colonial Print Communication

Developments in print production technology in the nineteenth century were the basis for the expansion of press activity first in the British Isles and then in the colonies. A key moment was 29 November 1814, when the owners of *The Times* of London imported and installed Koenig (named after its German inventor Friedrich Koenig) steam-powered, flat-bed cylinder press machines to drive forward production of the next morning's edition. Churning out copies of the newspaper at 1,000 impressions an hour, within a few hours 4,000 copies of the newspaper were on their way out for distribution. As the editors would crow in the next editorial, it was a revolutionary moment: 'Our journal of this day presents to the public the practical result of the greatest improvement connected with printing since the discovery of the art itself' (Anon. 1814, *The Times*: 1). The Koenig press would be supplemented a decade later by more efficient engines created by Augustus Applegarth and Edward Cowper, and by the late 1830s, large printing operations in Britain as a matter of course invested in steam presses at the expense of hand presses to power their production needs.

In addition to the development of steam-powered machinery and cheaper paper and ink production methods, new processes enabled widespread and increasingly sophisticated methods of reproducing illustrations at low cost, notably the invention of lithographic printing processes and, in the second half of the century, new photographic processes, such as half-tone and photogravure. Illustrations in the press became more numerous, although colour printing remained too complex and expensive in the periodical trade.

The nascent colonial presses benefited from such new machinery, technologies and skills, which were brought in initially to support government and missionary interests. As demand expanded, many presses began operating across two separate communication spheres: one working to service the needs of the colonial government, missionary societies and commerce (issuing directives, proclamations, official documents, newsletters and official journals), and another producing print outputs for the emerging reading communities in the colonies. Lithographic printing allowed such presses to reproduce indigenous language material not enabled by the standard lead typefaces of the early hand and steam-driven presses still in wide use in the colonial print landscape.

A good example of such dual positioning was the success of the Naval Kishore Press of Lucknow, which was founded in 1858 and used iron presses to produce press material for government use, and a combination of iron and lithographic presses to support printing of Urdu and Islamic texts and newspapers in the North-West Oudh province, including the Urdu newspaper *Avadh Akhbar*, which was founded in 1859 and modelled closely on *The Illustrated London News* (Stark 2007: 351–84). Steam presses would not significantly feature in the Naval Kishore Press arsenal until 1885, when the Press ordered and installed several as part of a major expansion and modernisation programme (Stark 2007: 178–9). *Avadh Akhbar* was issued first as a weekly, and then from 1877 as a daily, circulating widely across India and outlasting most of its rivals until its cessation in 1950.

A second example of British print infrastructure being redirected to address alternative communities of (non-English-language) readers occurred in Malta, which had become a British protectorate in 1800. Evangelists of the Anglican Church Missionary Society (CMS) in Malta imported a printing press and Arabic type from London, and in 1826 began to issue Arabic and Turkish texts and newspapers for consumption across the whole region. Between 1827 and 1842, it is estimated that the CMS press produced over 150,000 copies of Arabic and Turkish books, and 6,800 newspaper copies, which were distributed and read across Arabic Mediterranean and peninsular circuits that included Egypt, Lebanon, Syria, Palestine and Iraq (Ayalon 2016: 26–7).

The Naval Kishore Press and CMS press in Malta used communication networks creatively to find new reading communities for their periodicals and newspapers. These examples challenge the contemporary understanding of colonial press interactions, which assume a model of the colonial press configured as a simple sequence of binaries, with Britain as the central hub ('home') and the colonial world as peripheral extensions ('abroad'). However, as the Naval Kishore Press, the CMS in Malta, and many other examples in this volume demonstrate, the communication infrastructure enabling and sustaining colonial press production in the nineteenth and twentieth centuries was much more complex. Communication links connecting different parts of the colonial world often cut London out of the loop, with news and information flowing through channels, circuits and networks sustained by alternative sources of financial support, distribution nodes, and trained personnel committed to providing the labour necessary for the writing, production and dissemination of the print material. (A point we develop in several chapters of the *Companion* is that for all its advances, the infrastructure of colonial print cultures could never guarantee accurate trans-colonial intercommunication in all instances; miscommunications, silences, blockages, and breakdowns in communication were as frequent and as likely as instances of efficiently functioning systems and networks.)

Intrinsic to the British Empire's trans-colonial systems of communication were its polymathic personnel. Many who worked on colonial periodicals combined the roles of owner, editor, reporter, literary contributor and opinion writer. Two examples from the nineteenth century illustrate both the mobility and the versatility of the producers of British colonial periodicals. Thomas Pringle (1789–1834) performed several different roles on different continents: in 1817, he was co-editor of the first six monthly issues of the Edinburgh-based *Blackwood's Magazine*; in the 1820s, he was the founder of Cape Town's first library; and in 1824, he was the co-owner and editor of the Cape Colony's first independent periodical, the *South African Journal*, and its first newspaper, the *South African Commercial Advertiser*. The *Advertiser* was banned in its first two years of operation by the Cape Colony's Governor Lord Charles Somerset because of its criticism of government policy and Pringle's campaigning on behalf of the indigenous Xhosa people (Shum 2020: 9–132; Elbourne 2021). A second example was John Lang (1816–64), an Australian-born novelist and irrepressible social campaigner, who founded the Indian *Mofussilite* periodical in 1848, and for decades shuttled between India and Britain, editing numerous newspapers and journals, and contributing articles on Indian themes to Charles Dickens's *Household Words* (Joshi 2021: 173–200). Thirdly, working in conjunction with those who produced the content for colonial periodicals were the many skilled print workers who travelled the Empire providing the essential technical infrastructure for print production. Print specialists trained in Britain, Europe and North America answered the needs of new colonial settlements, with press operators, compositors and skilled artisans transforming 'raw' news into published form and delivering it to expanding colonial reading communities (Finkelstein 2018).

Finally, in surveying the infrastructure of British colonial periodicals, it is essential to emphasise the sheer number of newspapers and periodicals that emerged in the nineteenth century and continued to proliferate in the twentieth. John S. North's authoritative *Waterloo Directory of English, Irish and Scottish Newspapers and Periodicals, 1800–1900* has published evidence of over 3,900 Irish titles, 7,300 Scottish titles, and over 100,000 English titles still extant in archival collections that were produced over the course of the nineteenth century (North 1986; 1989; 1997).

The colonies saw a similar expansion in the numbers of newspapers and periodicals in the nineteenth century. The examples of three colonies – India, British North America and New Zealand – illustrate the trend.

In India, over 14,000 new newspapers and periodicals in forty different languages were published in the nineteenth century (Dhawardker 1997: 126). Many of these remain widely unknown, although recent scholarship has made a start in exploring their significance (Agathocleous 2021; Bayly 2007; Joshi 2021; Khan 2009; Logan 2017; Mann 2017; Otis 2018).

In British North America, newspapers and periodicals emerged in three provinces. Between 1760 and 1840, over 120 periodical publications appeared in Quebec and Lower Canada, ranging from magazines and reviews to specialised papers and newspapers (Laurence 2004: 233). In the Atlantic and Upper Canadian regions, over 170 newspapers were launched between 1801 and 1840 (Decook 2004: 229–33). By 1840, the introduction of new printing technology allowed newspaper production to expand, though by contrast magazine production during this period was subject to high rates of attrition and failure (Distad 2004: 293). Matters improved in the second half of the nineteenth century, with cheaper postal rates, quicker access to overseas news and communication, and automated developments in typesetting reducing labour and production costs, enabling easier entry into periodical and press management. In 1873 Canada had forty-seven daily newspapers and forty-one monthly journals, and by 1900 this had increased to 112 and 202 respectively. Taking stock of the whole century, the increase in the numbers of newspaper and periodical publications is especially impressive, as the total in Upper and Lower Canada rose from twenty-one in 1801 to 314 in 1900 (Decook 2004: 229; Distad 1991: 156).

In New Zealand, newspapers and periodicals were consumed by a small but highly literate population of European descent. Between 1840 and 1889, over 350 newspapers were established, with '28 newspapers founded between 1840 and 1848 for a European population of 59,000; 181 newspapers founded between 1860 and 1879; 150 founded between 1880 and 1889' (Traue 1997: 109). Between 1850 and 1962, more than 129 periodicals of literary interest were founded, and were distributed by the newly established postal system. While some publications endured, many suffered a swift demise, due to commercial failure, the lack of a large regional base of paying readers, the shifting concerns and political ambitions of owners, or the inadequacies of transport and postal networks (Finkelstein 2003: 105).

Postal systems capable of distributing the increasing number of publications also developed apace. Driven in the first instance by the demands of colonial officials and merchants for accurate information about trade, commerce and political events in their regions, publications providing such information were circulated internally via coach, postal couriers and paid messengers, or externally via sailing ships and steamships plying the maritime routes. Before the advent of telegraphy in the mid-nineteenth century, steamships were vital conduits for moving print media not only across the Empire, but also across South Asia, the Antipodes and the Pacific, linking the western coast of India to China and Japan via the Bay of Bengal and the China Seas (Bonea 2010: 278–83). With the formalising of imperial mail services via seabound routes in the second quarter of the nineteenth century, friends and family routinely posted press material through parcel services, and publishers developed networks of subscribers willing to pay for overseas shipments. Print also circulated from the British Isles to the colonial world through British and Irish émigrés sailing to foreign shores with numerous copies of books, newspapers and periodicals for leisure and communal reading, and in some cases also through the production of shipboard newspapers en route for passenger entertainment (Bell 2021: 41–76).

The number of newspapers and periodicals circulated by steamship grew exponentially as the century progressed. In the mid-1840s, over 320,000 'printed sheets', mainly newspapers, were posted each year between Britain and Canada, with some Canadian readers individually, or as part of a larger community, paying to receive bundles of forty to fifty newspapers at any one time (Potter 2017: 282). In 1872, the Canadian dominion post office system was handling over 24.5 million newspapers and periodical mailings, and by 1900 press and periodical items in postal circulation had reached 100 million (Rutherford 1982: 3). In the early 1860s, Australia and New Zealand customs was handling over 176,000 British newspapers shipped via the Peninsular and Oriental (P&O) Steam Boat Company (Potter 2017: 282). By 1885, a New Zealand settler population of just over 500,000 was sending and receiving 14,233,878 newspapers within and across its borders (as well as 35,829,855 letters and 1,774,273 telegrams) (Blackley 2001: 26). Such postal items, while linking 'remote and insecure communities such as Wanganui with other colonial outposts, also maintained colonists' communications with their homelands' (Blackley 2001: 26). The distribution of newspapers and periodicals was never simply one-way, as many publications produced in the colonies were transported to Britain by steamship: by 1912, for example, 140,000 newspapers per week were arriving on British shores from India, Canada, South Africa, Australia and New Zealand (Potter 2017: 282).

Following the laying of a successful submarine telegraph cable between Dover and Calais in 1851, moves were made to develop this new technology for transnational communication. A patchwork of transatlantic cables was laid down over the final third of the nineteenth century, linking Britain to its colonial possessions. British telegraphic connections to Ireland were established by a cable run between Scotland and Portpatrick in 1853. After initial failures, transatlantic cables were successfully laid between Ireland and Newfoundland in 1866. Cables laid down between 1868 and 1870 linked Cornwall, Gibraltar, Malta, Egypt, Suez and Bombay, enabling continuous telegraphic communication via transoceanic means between Britain and India for the first time. London would be linked directly to Australia by cable in 1872, and New Zealand would be plugged into the imperial cable system via Australia in 1876. By 1902, following the laying of a trans-Pacific submarine cable linking Vancouver to Fanning Island (part of what is now Kiribati in the Central Pacific), Fiji and Norfolk

Island, Britain completed the circuits needed to bind its dominions and colonies into a worldwide seamless telegraphic communication network, labelled the All Red Line (Kennedy 1971).

Such transoceanic telegraphic routes, combined with the development of overland telegraphic cable routes, established connections between the remotest regions of the British Empire. As a contemporary press commentator noted in the *African World Annual* of 2 December 1903, 'As a bond between kindred and kin scattered in the uttermost parts of the earth [the cable] is unsurpassed. It has been one of the greatest factors in the realisation of the Imperial idea . . . it defies time and annihilates space' (quoted in Potter 2003: 29). Press organisations sprang up to provide succinct telegraphic summaries of international news for the English-language press via these cables. Among the best known of these were Reuters, founded in 1851, and the Press Organisation, founded in 1868. An immense network of telegraph operators versed in transmission became woven into the newsgathering fabric of English-language press operators in colonial spaces. Though expensive to use, thus limiting the amount of information conveyed at any one time, by the start of the twentieth century, telegraph systems connecting the local, regional, national and international presses of the world had become commonplace.

Part I: Creating and Contesting the Colonial Public Sphere

A sense of the reach and the content of nineteenth-century colonial periodicals is conveyed in fictional form in Joseph Conrad's 1897 short story 'An Outpost of Progress'. Two colonial traders, Kayerts and Carlier, are consigned to a remote post up the Congo River, and come upon copies of the 'home paper' left behind by their dead predecessor:

> They also found some old copies of a home paper. That print discussed what it was pleased to call 'Our Colonial Expansion' in high-flown language. It spoke much of the rights and duties of civilisation, of the sacredness of the civilising work, and extolled the merits of those who went about bringing light, and faith and commerce to the dark places of the earth. Carlier and Kayerts read, wondered, and began to think better of themselves. Carlier said one evening, waving his hand about, 'In a hundred years, there will be perhaps a town here. Quays, and warehouses, and barracks, and – and – billiard-rooms. Civilisation, my boy, and virtue – and all.'
> (Conrad 2002: 9)

Our opening section examines not only the kinds of (British) 'home papers' Kayerts and Carlier might have read, but also the many other variations available. A key argument in Part I is that although a substantial percentage of nineteenth- and early twentieth-century colonial periodicals may well have served imperial ideology, the picture was more complicated, with several chapters pointing to striking examples of publications which were written against the imperial grain.

Investigating how public spheres were created and contested in different colonial settings – Canada, Jamaica, Barbados, India, New Zealand, South Africa, Australia and West Africa – the ten chapters in Part I introduce periodicals serving and/or criticising different kinds of colonial societies, from settler colonies to communities only just liberated from slavery. The chapters on the settler colonies (Canada, New Zealand,

Australia and South Africa) demonstrate how periodicals represented and narrated the conquest and seizure of land, the violent subjection of indigenes, and the mass arrival of British immigrants for permanent settlement (Banner 2007; Belich 2009; Darwin 2009; Free 2018). Early nineteenth-century periodicals in such settler societies were derivative, following the formats, styles and conventions of imported British journals such as the *Edinburgh Review*, *Blackwood's Edinburgh Magazine* and the *London Magazine*. However, as the chapters on Canada's emergent public sphere demonstrate, early literary periodicals in settler societies were also characterised by debates about forging a 'national' identity independent of Britain. These debates involved negotiating a new Canadian identity that insisted upon maintaining strong connections with Britain while simultaneously fostering an independent settler colonial identity. The chapters on New Zealand, Australian and South African periodicals later in the nineteenth century provide variations on how settler colonial identities were negotiated in other colonial public spheres.

Beginning in Canada, Cynthia Sugars and Paul Keen examine the rhetoric of Canadian periodicals produced in the first half of the nineteenth century, notably *The Acadian Magazine* (Halifax, 1826–8), *The Literary Garland* (Montreal, 1838–51), *The Montreal Museum* (Montreal, 1832–4) and *The Canadian Literary Magazine* (York, 1833). These periodicals provide an invaluable window on nineteenth-century Canada as they created a public sphere characterised by dialogical relationships between the periodicals and their readers. Sugars and Keen observe, 'In the years immediately prior to 1867, when the British North American colonies united into what would become the new Dominion of Canada, debates about Canada's "national" identity and culture dominated the popular press' (37). A central element in the discursive forging of Canada's national identity in these periodicals was the search for domestic literature that could serve both as a vehicle for personal enlightenment and as the means of imagining an independent Canadian identity. Especially important in these discussions was the periodicals' desire to cultivate a strong sense of civic responsibility in their readerships. Complicating the efforts to create a community of readers united by a new sense of collective (national) identity were the residual weight of British cultural norms and the competing presence of both indigenous and other emigrant communities. Sugars and Keen note that the fostering of local literature was often undertaken at the expense of addressing directly political relations between Canada's competing settler communities and the colonised, but suggest that 'the periodicals may have played a more effective political role precisely to the extent that they *did* disavow politics: contributing to the ideological consolidation of a colonial hegemony by naturalising and strengthening a sense of settler community' (48).

Picking up on Sugars and Keen's concerns, Fariha Shaikh expands upon the role of the colonial public sphere in creating settler colonial identity in a chapter focused on the Montreal-based *The Literary Garland* (1838–51), edited by the Irish emigrant John Lovell. Framing her research on *The Garland* as a contribution to the broader body of recent research investigating 'the foundational part that periodical culture played in the formation of settler colonies' (52), Shaikh sets out the central role *The Garland* played in constituting anglophone Canadian identity. In demonstrating how *The Garland* performed this role, Shaikh describes how the editors of the early periodicals propagandised on behalf of the emigration schemes and promoted settler colonial migration. In a close reading of *The Garland*, Shaikh proceeds to analyse how the periodical provided its middle-class readers with a model of colonial settlement based upon the cultivation of genteel literary tastes and pursuits. Shaikh underlines her argument with an extended discussion of the contributions of Susanna Moodie, *The Garland*'s most famous and prolific contributor. Periodicals like *The Garland* afforded women writers such as Moodie the opportunity to articulate the place of women within settler communities, in the process self-fashioning an identity as distinctively Canadian authors. Moodie's sketches of emigrant life for *The Garland* – later collected in the bestselling work *Roughing It in the Bush* (1852) – would prove integral to forming a tradition of 'local colour' fiction centred upon female experience of emigration and settlement in Canada.

The histories of the colonial public sphere in settler colonies like Canada contrast sharply with those of the periodical press in the former slave colonies of the Caribbean. In Candace Ward's chapter, the Jamaican-based *The Watchman and Jamaica Free Press* (founded in 1829 by Edward Jordon and Robert Osborn) and the Barbadian newspaper *The Liberal* (started in 1837 by Samuel J. Prescod) are the focus of analysis. Produced by Black editors in the years leading up to and immediately following Britain's Act of Emancipation in 1833, these two publications have since become key elements of Jamaican and Barbadian national memorialisation, as they represent an emergent Black public sphere which countered the plantocracy press of the West Indies. The two periodicals exemplify the appropriation and remediation of print technology to provide a public platform for those representing the disenfranchised colonial subject. Both *The Watchman* and *The Liberal* grappled with slavery and its immediate aftermath, 'acknowledging the degree to which British (and other European) colonies of the Caribbean were bound together by its legacies' (67). Yet while there was acknowledged solidarity and commonalities in approach, these periodicals also differed in their focus on how their local conditions affected the transition from enslaved to free states. Ward describes the two periodicals' attacks on plantocracy interests, showing how *The Watchman* and *The Liberal* laid the foundation for a proto-nationalist public sphere that would a century later shape anti-colonial efforts in the region. Edward Jordon and Robert Osborn's election in 1835 as members of the newly constituted Assembly presaged a change in tone and editorial focus in their oversight of *The Watchman* and its successor *The Morning Journal* (founded in 1838). Ward tracks how the changed status of the lead editors was reflected in their absorption into the mainstream of political society, which in turn led to a shift in their publications from active opposition to compromised accommodation.

Graham Shaw turns our attention to a contemporaneous Indian-based journal addressing a marginal colonial readership which was seeking a space within India's colonial public sphere. An early example of a periodical aimed specifically at a readership on the periphery of Empire, *The Meerut Universal Magazine* (*M.U.M.*) (1835–7) was the first periodical published in the provincial hinterland (mofussil) of the Bengal Presidency, 880 miles north-west of Calcutta, and far from British India's centres of power and influence. *M.U.M.* was created and edited by Henry Miers Elliot and Henry Whitelock Torrens, two junior subalterns who would later become senior members of the East India Company. During the two years of its publication, *M.U.M.* attracted a European readership drawn from civil and military ranks, mostly occupying subaltern positions, scattered in isolated stations across Upper India. Frustrated at being ignored and unrepresented in Calcutta as a result of their remote provincial station postings, the editors of *M.U.M.* set it up as a counterweight to the newspapers and periodicals emanating from Calcutta, such as the *Englishman*, *Calcutta Courier* and daily *Bengal Hurkaru*. *M.U.M.* survived on subscription sales, which numbered around 300 and were spread geographically across thirty-nine different provincial locations. Virulent in its condemnation of Company policies, *M.U.M.* promoted an 'Orientalist' accommodation of Indian social, cultural and religious traditions and practices in opposition to the increasingly inflexible 'Anglicist' approach that was to become the hallmark of British rule over India from the middle of the nineteenth century. The criticisms voiced by *M.U.M.*, however, did not aim to change the status quo; rather, they expressed the frustrations of a British subaltern class and their readership stuck in regional backwaters (as they saw it) and complaining about their distance from the colonial centres of power.

How settler colonial concerns were articulated in the environmental sphere is the subject of Philip Steer's chapter on periodicals and settler environmental knowledge in colonial New Zealand. Steer examines a range of periodicals published between 1860 and 1900 to gauge how nature and the environment were represented during a significant period of New Zealand's colonial development. His analysis takes in gazettes and monthlies such as *The Southern Monthly Magazine* (1863–6), *The Saturday Review* (1864–71) and *The Illustrated New Zealand Herald for Home Readers* (1868–83), religious periodicals such as *The New Zealand Tablet* (1873–1996), and scientific publications such as *Transactions and Proceedings of the New Zealand Institute* (1868–). Colonisation in New Zealand was dominated by conflicts over the settlement and use of land, with the periodicals hosting fierce disagreements on the subject. On the one hand, in the period 1860–80, the argument was made that clearing natural habitats and forests for farmland was an acceptable price to pay for creating a modern agricultural society; on the other, from the 1880s onwards, a nascent cultural nationalist argument emerged which insisted that New Zealand's remaining 'primeval' forests represented key markers of local settler colonial identity. Steer notes the range of such arguments, drawing attention to how forest legislation was actively discussed in religious publications and professional magazines, and how Māori forest knowledge was remediated in literary magazines, with scientific journals publishing pieces suffused with literary references derived from a mix of Māori folk tales and European Romantic literature. Steer emphasises the irreconcilable nature of the disagreements between those perceiving New Zealand's forests as a commodity to be husbanded, managed, harvested and renewed, and those who favoured deforestation as an inevitable step in 'progressing' towards sheep and cattle ranching. Close examination of New Zealand settler periodical writing reveals that while some drew on Māori environmental knowledge to offer powerful arguments in support of the preservation of environmental assets, Steer concludes that such insights were often 'diminished and dismissed through its framing as a "mythopoetic" expression of an earlier mode of society' (109). These debates significantly shaped New Zealand's settler colonial history, with colonial periodicals utilised to narrate settler identity in relation to land, space and environmental management.

While these periodicals reproduced settler colonial discourse primarily for a New Zealand audience, periodicals in other parts of the Empire during this period were preoccupied with representing colonial societies to British (and secondarily to colonial) readers. This was particularly true of missionary periodicals, whose editors described colonial territories to readers in Britain through missionary lenses. Lize Kriel, Annika

Vosseler and Chantelle Finaughty provide a contextualised comparison of British missionary periodical reportage on Southern Africa for a British readership (the 'home' audience), and missionary periodicals produced for a Southern African readership (the audience 'abroad'). Periodicals published by British missionary presses for circulation in Southern Africa were further divided between those aimed primarily at white settler elites, and those aimed at the African Christian communities founded by British missionary societies. Religious journals formed a significant proportion of British periodical production at the turn of the twentieth century – about 40 per cent of all periodicals published in Britain. As Kriel, Vosseler and Finaughty note, 'The missionary periodical was the bearer of a communication network which, over the span of the nineteenth century, became increasingly multi-directional as far as places of publication and intended audiences were concerned' (112). Focusing on Methodist missionary journals aimed at British readers (*Wesleyan Missionary Notices* and *The Chronicle of the London Missionary Society*), periodicals developed for white South African readers (*The Christian Express*), and later journals produced for Black South African readers (*Isigidimi Sama-Xosa*, *Mahoka a Becwana* and *Inkanyiso yase Natal*), Kriel, Vosseler and Finaughty examine how the concepts of 'home' and 'abroad' were articulated in the pages of these periodicals between 1813 and 1890. They note a significant shift: early missionary periodicals encode white colonialist interpretations of 'abroad' for readers at 'home', but later periodicals source material from 'abroad' (Britain, the United States, India) for the different (white and African) colonial audiences in South Africa. As they conclude, '[T]he South Africa-based periodicals imagined an audience far more complex than the periodicals designed for British readers: fellow black African, white South African, fellow Christian readers in the Global South as well as British readers "abroad" in the metropole were addressed' (123–4).

The Sydney *Bulletin* (1880–2008), one of the best-known Australian magazines to have shaped Australian identity and settler colonial-nationalist aspirations, is the focus of Tony Hughes-d'Aeth's chapter. Launched as an eight-page weekly journal for the working man, the *Bulletin* offered a mix of original journalism, cartoons, poetry and short stories by the likes of Henry Lawson, A. B. 'Banjo' Paterson, Barbara Baynton, 'Steele Rudd', Stella 'Miles' Franklin and Joseph Furphy. The *Bulletin* appeared alongside a substantial number of daily newspapers circulating in Sydney and New South Wales. Starting with an initial circulation of 3,000, by 1900 the *Bulletin* was selling over 100,000 copies per week, though its sales and its influence waned significantly after the First World War. Racist and masculinist, the *Bulletin* announced itself as representing the interests and views of white Australian working men. Its efforts to speak for this constituency were especially to the fore in the run-up to the establishment of the Australian Federation of 1901, when Britain's Australian colonies constituted themselves as a federated nation. The *Bulletin* stridently advocated unification in tones that were anti-establishment, denigrated women, indigenous inhabitants, Chinese and other non-white foreigners, and were scornful of what they characterised as effete, class-ridden British rule which had exploited Australia as a holding pen for its convicts and surplus population of waifs and strays. The *Bulletin* was anti-colonial insofar as it ceaselessly demanded independence from Britain, yet at the same time very seldom deviated from the tropes of British settler colonial ideology. As Hughes-d'Aeth notes, the settler colonial mentality expressed in its pages was that of white Australian men, 'vital and no-nonsense souls, transvaluing values and overhauling the rotten substrate of their source culture' (135). The colonial frontier was an empty space that was there to be conquered, tamed and dominated. Those best suited for the task were 'bushmen', 'tempered on the settler frontier, hardened by hardship and surreptitiously indigenised' (135). Such rhetoric was intrinsic to settler colonial ideology, with the *Bulletin* its most zealous advocate in Australia's periodical press.

Australian Federation is also the theme of Sam Hutchinson's wide-ranging survey of periodical literature produced during the political period that preceded its implementation on 1 January 1901. Federation formally established a single Australian nation, unifying the previously separate provinces. The Australian newspaper and periodical press were vigorous participants in shaping public perceptions of Federation, as they provided abundant commentary on the accommodation of competing regional interests, changes to institutional and political arrangements, and the building of a consensus as to what constituted 'national' values and policies. Hutchinson explores the responses of prominent Australian periodicals of varying ideological persuasions to the events preceding and culminating in Federation, surveying periodicals ranging in outlook from the aggressive settler colonial stances of the *Bulletin* (1880–2008) and *The Worker* (1890–1955) to the pro-imperial Anglocentric positions of the *Sydney Mail* (1860–1938), *The Queenslander* (1866–1939) and *The Australasian* (1864–1946), and the anti-Federation opinions aired in the radical labourite weekly the *Sunday Times* (1897–1902). The extension of the franchise that followed Federation was accompanied by restrictions on immigration that discriminated against Chinese labourers. The extensive coverage of anti-Chinese sentiment, labour and suffragette protests, and severe economic hardship rubbed uncomfortably against the national narrative of progress that 'was both quantitative (growth in material affluence and tangible advancements) and qualitative (the nation had arrived at a level of maturity sufficient to play its proper part in global affairs)' (152). Whereas the mainstream press glossed over the difficult social issues, outspoken journals such as the *Bulletin* and *The Worker* disrupted the optimistic national narrative of the new Australian nation.

Settler periodicals publishing at the turn of the twentieth century in other parts of the Empire also challenged the social fabric of white colonial society. The *South African News* (1899–1915), introduced by Jonathan Derrick in the next chapter, was a white liberal colonial daily and weekly paper published in the Cape Colony, which provided a voice for those campaigning against British government policies during the Anglo-Boer War of 1899–1902, as well as for those opposed to Sir Cecil Rhodes and the mining magnates. Well-known liberal figures who supported or wrote for the *South African News* included the novelist Olive Schreiner, her brother William Schreiner (who became Premier in 1898 and invested in the paper), and Albert Cartwright (1868–1956), an English-born journalist, who had edited two other South African newspapers and took on the editorship of the *South African News* in its early years. An initial daily circulation of about 1,300 in 1902 increased to 4,000 by 1907, and the *South African News* retained a loyal readership through to its cessation in 1915. Derrick contextualises its position within the landscape of the South African press, as he discusses the competing papers produced during this period for English, African and Afrikaans readerships. Anti-imperialist in tone, the *News* attacked British policies towards the Boers and the Randlords' exploitation of mine-workers. Such criticisms did not, however, extend to fully developed arguments for a modern and inclusive democratic polity; rather, the *News* lobbied for self-government along Australian and

Canadian lines, that is, as white settler colonial government with very limited political representation or participation for Africans. As Derrick concludes, while not entirely indifferent to African demands, the *News* – much like its Australian contemporary the *Bulletin* – spoke on behalf of an anti-colonial and even anti-capitalist white settler colonial constituency which only very rarely stretched its political sympathies to embrace black South Africans.

The focus in the final chapter of Part I shifts from South Africa during the Anglo-Boer War to twentieth-century West Africa. The link between the *South African News* and the periodical *West Africa* (1917–2003) was editor and journalist Albert Cartwright, a figure like Pringle and Lang who worked on colonial periodicals in different parts of the British Empire. Jonathan Derrick outlines how *West Africa* started out in 1917 as a weekly journal published in London documenting general and commercial news relating to the West African colonies of Nigeria, the Gold Coast, Sierra Leone and the Gambia. For the first thirty years of its existence, *West Africa* was primarily a magazine for Britons living and working in these regions, with readers drawn from colonial officials in those countries, businesses and their staff, teachers and missionaries. The independence of Ghana (1957), Nigeria (1960), Sierra Leone (1961) and the Gambia (1965) heralded widespread changes in education, trade and business, literature and the arts, as well as the forging of new Pan-Africanist political alliances. Derrick explains how *West Africa* negotiated these changes in order to accommodate and address the transformed political landscape. *West Africa* successfully reorientated itself to address a postcolonial audience, becoming a respected chronicler of the commercial and political transitions in progress. In its post-independence phase, *West Africa* extended its coverage to report extensively on anti-colonial struggles in the African colonies of the other European powers (like Algeria), to cover West African arts and cultural events, and to review books and exhibitions of interest to West African readers. Though broadly conservative in political approach, *West Africa*'s factually informed coverage of African politics attracted a substantial African readership from the 1950s to the 1980s, attesting to its successful transition from a 'colonial' to a 'postcolonial' periodical.

Part II: Women and Colonial Periodicals

Following the emergence of aristocratic ladies' journals in the late eighteenth and early nineteenth centuries, British women's magazines evolved into spaces enabling women to engage fully in all aspects of press and periodical production. One historian sums up the significance of women in Britain's press industry during this period as follows:

> A study of women's spaces in the nineteenth-century press opens a window onto an exciting intersection of industrialisation and domesticity, where women editors, authors, readers, correspondents, proprietors, illustrators, needlework designers, columnists and a host of silent female workers in print production participated in the expansion of the women's press, as well as the larger press throughout Britain. (Ledbetter 2020: 688)

Such endeavours were replicated in the colonies in the nineteenth and twentieth centuries, though the dynamics of women's engagement in colonial public spheres were often complicated, as the politics of gender intersected in contradictory ways with colonial relations of power. At different stages and in different contexts, women participated in colonial societies variously as colonisers, as settlers, as missionaries, as colonised subjects, and as citizens of emerging nations. Gendered identities in colonial spaces were contingent, fluid and hybrid, as the women who produced and consumed periodicals were subject to the economic, social and political relations of individual colonies, and complicit with and negotiating between the demands of British settler colonial interests, competing settler communities (like the French in Canada, Afrikaners in South Africa), and representatives of the colonised (like the Māori in New Zealand).

Such contending contextual pressures could produce complex identities and affiliations, as in the case of Welsh Presbyterian female missionaries based in India, whose Welsh-language contributions to missionary journalism were featured in Welsh periodicals between the 1880s and 1920s. Their work uneasily addressed two audiences simultaneously, that of the mission field in India, and that of Welsh readers in Britain learning about British colonies in Welsh vernacular texts. While ostensibly representing a religious mission seeking to convert those in India, Welsh women reporters also served as agents of communication creating links between the two worlds. Their publications introduced cross-cultural bonds that filtered into Welsh social spaces to the extent that '[i]n the interwar years, there are reports of pupils in Welsh primary schools being taught to sing folk songs in Bengali. Women's only meetings in chapels were known as zenanas, and poems and hymns were composed that eulogized the special relationship between the people of Wales and of northeast India' (Jones 2003: 262). This example demonstrates the hybrid nature of colonial press production, as do several more of the examples discussed in Part II, with women involved in colonial periodicals displaying 'hybridity as a sense of cultural ambidexterity' (Finkelstein and Peers 2000: 15).

In nineteenth-century Canada, Mary Graddon Gosselin edited *The Montreal Museum*, a monthly journal that ran for fifteen issues between December 1832 and March 1834. Honor Rieley highlights that *The Montreal Museum* was the first periodical in British North America to be edited by a woman and to be aimed at a female readership. *The Montreal Museum* took as its model its London predecessor, *The Ladies Museum*, which had flourished between 1798 and 1832. As chapters in Part I have noted, *The Montreal Museum*, like many of its Canadian contemporaries, was proto-nationalist, seeking to cultivate a taste for literature in Canada and to provide a venue for the 'development of native genius, and the increase of national respectability' (188). Unlike its Canadian counterparts, however, it was written for women, with original content 'largely typical of such metropolitan publications as *The Ladies Museum* or *La Belle Assemblée*, mixing poetry and fiction with didactic pieces on female education and deportment, and snippets of writing on popular science, travel and nature' (186). Rieley argues that in addition to copying British women's magazines, *The Montreal Museum* also looked for inspiration to women's periodicals in the United States, functioning as a 'colonial women's magazine as equally closely entwined with the American periodical scene' (188). Rieley documents how the journal engaged in 'scissor and paste' or 'exchange journalism', whereby original material was interspersed with material reprinted from other regional and overseas journals. Over the course of its existence, material was culled and reproduced from the pages of the London *Athenaeum* and *The Penny Magazine*, the New York-based *Family Magazine, or Monthly Abstract of General Knowledge*, the Philadelphia-based *Greenbank's Periodical Library*, and the Scottish-based *Berwick Advertiser*, which in 1832 had published the popular Scottish border tales of John Mackay Wilson in literary columns which were subsequently reprinted in *The Montreal Museum*. The periodical also included translations of material from French-language journals such as *Le Corsaire* and *Le Voleur*, exemplifying cultural ambidexterity by encoding references to the colony's French colonial past in a discourse of the local, the domestic and the feminine.

In the 1880s, several decades after *The Montreal Museum*, the first Australian magazines for women began to appear. Focusing on the monthly magazine the *New Idea*, one of Australia's most successful mass-market publications for women readers, Michelle J. Smith describes its founding in 1902 and its consolidation and extension of the pioneering efforts of earlier publications, such as the *Australian Woman's Magazine and Domestic Journal* (April 1882–September 1884) and *The Dawn: A Journal for Australian Women* (May 1888–July 1905). Like *The Montreal Museum*, the *New Idea* followed closely Anglo-American magazine conventions, publishing regular features and columns about society news, housekeeping, child rearing, health and beauty, dress, humour, and short and serial fiction. The *New Idea* nurtured a female reading community by publishing fiction and non-fiction by amateur Australian writers and by offering competitions for its readers. Preoccupied with the place of women within Australia's national identity, female contributors were central to the discursive construction of Australian womanhood in the magazine's early years. As Smith notes, 'The *New Idea* stands in marked contrast to other Australian women's magazines of the period for its deep interest in the place of women within the nation and regular publication of Australian women writers' (201). The formula was a success, as within two years of its launch, the *New Idea* had achieved a monthly circulation of 40,000 subscribers, rising to 250,000 by 1908 (an estimated 10 per cent of the white Australian female population of the period). One of the ways in which the *New Idea* constructed Australian national identity was through portraits of Australian women, particularly celebrities and prominent figures in the community. These profiles reinforced a vision of Australian women as sophisticated, refined, and capable of making contributions to national and international life. At the same time, the magazine also strove to document the lives of all classes of (white) Australian women so as to 'foster a sense of the collective contribution of women to home and the Commonwealth' (211).

From the settler colonial public spheres of Canada and Australia, Katharina Oke moves the focus to the West African public spheres of the 1920s. Carefully contextualising the multiple pressures Ghanaian and Nigerian female journalists confronted in the Gold Coast press landscape of the period, Oke examines the work of Mabel Dove Danquah, who contributed many articles (including ones under the pseudonym 'Mabel Mensah') to the *Times of West Africa* and the *West African Times*. In their many articles and opinion pieces, these West African pioneer women journalists wrote extensively about the social, economic, political and cultural issues of the day. According to Oke, Dove Danquah was able to take advantage of new opportunities for expression that were opening up for women journalists, as 'the public sphere [was] becoming, from the 1920s, more accessible to the public beyond the African educated elite, and more open to textual experimentation' (215). Oke demonstrates how women from 'the outskirts' gradually became more prominent in the West African press, 'as authors of texts, but also as objects and means of negotiating and responding to colonial gender ideologies, codes, values and social change' (216). Read in a longer twentieth-century context, the work of exemplars such as Dove Danquah, Oke concludes, led to the greater representation of female voices and perspectives in the Ghanaian and Nigerian public spheres in later decades.

Roughly contemporaneous with Dove Danquah's groundbreaking journalism in West Africa were the publications in India of the Madras (Chennai)-based *Indian Ladies' Magazine* (*ILM*, 1901–18, 1927–38) and *Stri-Dharma* (1918–36), two women's journals created to express a range of women's voices in pre-independence India. As Deborah Anna Logan notes, both journals were part of an '"upliftment" of Indian womanhood [that] was reflected in the proliferation of woman-centred periodicals in English and the vernacular, offering a safe platform for women to express themselves, to educate themselves in the absence of formal schooling, and to access news of female activities, achievements and accomplishments, in India and throughout the world' (229). The *ILM* and *Stri-Dharma* addressed Indian, British and Anglo-Indian readers, advocating social unification, religious tolerance and cultural cooperation. The two diverged, however, with regard to the appropriate means for defining modern Indian womanhood in the context of the Raj. The *ILM*, edited by Kamala Satthianadhan, synthesised traditional Indian and British positions, promoting late-Victorian views of domestic femininity as the appropriate model for a modernising Indian womanhood. The *ILM* campaigned for universal women's education and featured columns highlighting the achievements of women on the international stage, yet, like its Australian counterpart the *New Idea*, its proto-nationalist Indian discourse included traditional representations of women in the domestic sphere. By contrast, *Stri-Dharma*, edited by Margaret Cousins and Dorothy Jinarajadasa and sponsored by Theosophists (led by Annie Besant), was expressly feminist and anti-colonial in its support for women's participation in the Indian Nationalist movement. *Stri-Dharma*'s promotion of modern Indian womanhood nonetheless also retained a residue of conservative values that sought to keep women tied to home and family, ostensibly as a means of preserving Indian culture from western influence. Both periodicals documented the major social and political changes in India, but Logan believes they were unique among Indian journals 'in that they aimed to establish productive links between English speakers throughout the world and Indians newly literate in English language and literature' (230). Neither periodical was able to withstand the global economic impact of the Great Depression, with *Stri-Dharma* ceasing publication in 1936 and *ILM* in 1938.

Tanya Agathocleous, Ruwanthi Edirisinghe, Jessica Lu, Jaïra Placide and Sarah Schwartz conclude this section with a chapter on *Marriage Hygiene*, an Indian-based journal focused on gender and sex education, edited by A. J. Pillay, a prominent doctor involved with several influential eugenics initiatives in India. Transnational and comparative in outlook, during its first incarnation (1934–7), *Marriage Hygiene* published controversial articles by Indian writers and prominent European writers, including Havelock Ellis and Norman Himes, on topics ranging from contraception to eugenics to sex education and Hindu marriage reform. Positioning itself as forward-thinking, scientific, educational and international in outlook, *Marriage Hygiene* attracted widespread interest among Anglo-American circles. At the same time, the periodical aligned itself with the anti-colonial, nationalist impulses of the period, framing arguments about birth control and family planning in ways that provided 'a large-scale counter-argument to colonial sexological discourses that fed into racist narratives about Indian sexual depravity and civilisational backwardness, that in turn served as an apologia for colonialism' (245). Katherine Mayo's notorious travelogue about Indian marriage and child-bearing customs, *Mother India* (1927), which alleged 'degenerate' Hindu customs and 'backward' Indian cultural norms, provoked particularly vigorous counter-arguments in *Marriage Hygiene*. As Agathocleous et al. conclude, such eugenics-focused sexology ideas published in *Marriage Hygiene* 'reshaped the synonymity of woman with the nation that underwrote both the idealised figure of "Mother India" in early anti-colonial discourses, and the abject figure of Mayo's book, by transforming her from traditional and passive to modern and progressive' (246). The result was 'a subject whose growing autonomy was crucial to the liberal imagination of the postcolonial state' (246).

Part III: Language and British Colonial Periodicals

As the British Empire spread, so too did the English language. The close historical connection between political economy and the globalisation of English has recently been reiterated by John P. O'Regan, who argues 'that English has acted as a vehicular free rider upon capital, and that by means of capital's global spread English has become in an almost default manner "structured in dominance" in the world-economy and system' (O'Regan 2021: 5). Characterising the 'free riding of English on capital more as a type of symbiosis or even parasitism', O'Regan locates the beginnings of the simultaneous expansion of capital and the English language in the sixteenth century, followed by a sharp acceleration in the middle of the nineteenth century:

> The vast sums which were being dispensed around the world from the City of London, along with the movement of British products for trade, and the importation of raw materials for infrastructure projects, such as real estate development and railway building, gave an enormous boost to the spread of English globally as it caught a ride on the octopus tentacles of capital. (O'Regan 2021: 8, 83)

The agents facilitating the spread of capital and the English language included Christian missionaries; British sailors and soldiers; anglophone merchants, traders and speculating companies; and artisans, industrial workers and farm labourers escaping poverty in Britain. English functioned as the Empire's lingua franca in trade agreements and financial contracts; in government and political communications; in legal and administrative documents; in the colonial education system; and in the everyday encounters of domestic and commercial life. A crucial element in securing the hegemony of the English language within the formal and informal Empire was Britain's emerging colonial public sphere, as the vast majority of colonial periodicals, newspapers and pamphlets were published in English. In the terms of O'Regan's metaphors, English-language colonial periodicals provided the free vehicles/the parasitic forms/the octopus tentacles enabling English to traverse the globe.

Such metaphors have their limits, however, as English-language periodicals did of course on occasion themselves host anti-colonial and anti-capitalist critique, and, further, the supremacy of the English language in colonial periodicals was often moderated. Arguably the best-known historical example of colonial administrators adjusting their English-first policy was the drawn-out tussle between the Orientalists and Anglicists in India (see Zastoupil and Moir 2000). Alastair Pennycook concludes his summary of the clash between those British administrators promoting English and those promoting Indian vernacular languages by observing that strategic considerations ultimately trumped cultural-imperialist zeal: the 'dominant view . . . was one that favoured vernacular education. This was . . . a pragmatic Orientalism, that on the one hand acknowledged the superiority of English and Western knowledge, but on the other sought to develop and control India through as efficient and practical education as possible' (Pennycook 1998: 83). After surveying several more histories of colonial language policy, notably in China and Africa, Pennycook argues that in colonial contexts what mattered more than installing English in every area of colonial rule was protecting and promoting the material interests of British capital. If the dogmatic insistence upon English ever threatened the political and economic stability of a colony, concessions to vernacular languages invariably followed. An important corollary was that vernacular languages could as readily be deployed in colonial periodicals to consolidate and further British imperial interests. Pennycook accordingly wraps up his survey of English versus vernacular language policies within the Empire by insisting upon the importance of attending closely to the context(s) of each specific colony, and by warning against lazy assumptions based upon ahistorical projections:

> One of the lessons we need to draw from this account of colonial language policy is that, in order to make sense of language policies we need to understand both their location historically and their location contextually. What I mean by this is that we cannot assume that promotion of local languages instead of a dominant language, or promotion of a dominant language at the expense of local languages, are in themselves good or bad. Too often we view such questions through the lenses of liberalism, pluralism or anti-imperialism, without understanding the actual location of such policies. (Pennycook 1998: 126)

With respect to colonial periodicals, it would therefore be a mistake to assume automatically a pro-colonial politics in those periodicals published in English, and an anti-colonial politics in those published in vernacular languages. Even the most cursory attention to individual colonial periodicals and their contexts explodes any such dichotomy; accordingly, in Part III, all seven chapters assiduously locate each periodical's choice of language (or combination of languages) 'within the broader social, political and economic structures and ideologies that they support' (Pennycook 1998: 128).

In the first chapter in Part III, Lachy Paterson foregrounds the nineteenth-century colonial history of New Zealand to explain how the British in New Zealand aspired to provide a model of how European colonial settlement might benefit the indigenous people, beginning in 1840 with the Treaty of Waitangi, an agreement by which Māori became British subjects with the same rights and privileges as the incoming Pākehā settlers. In this context, the colonial government sought through its *niupepa* (Māori-language periodicals/newspapers) to promote the integration of Māori into the new colony, socially, politically and economically. Undertaking close analyses of the major *niupepas*, Paterson demonstrates how the first *niupepa*, the Auckland-based *Te Karere o Nui Tireni* (1842–63), propagandised the benefits of British rule, exhorting its Māori readers to engage sympathetically with colonial laws and government institutions, a message repeated and reinforced in the *Waka Maori* series first published in Napier for local Māori by the Hawkes Bay Provincial Council from 1863 to 1871, and then as a national Māori paper from Wellington until 1877. As to the crucial question of how

Māori readers responded to the *niupepa*'s pro-colonial ideology, Paterson concludes that they were cynical about the *niupepa*'s promise that parliamentary politics would advance their standing as citizens, remaining acutely conscious of 'how *niupepa* discourses of engagement and inclusion [were] aligned to the government's own colonial needs and aspirations' (268).

In contrast to the colonial ideology expressed in the New Zealand *niupepa*, the late nineteenth-century Malayalam periodicals in Kerala, India, articulated an independent collective identity rooted in Malayali language and society. G. Arunima's chapter introduces such themes as expressed in the Malayalam periodicals *Bhashaposhini* [Language Advancement], started in 1892 by Kandathil Varghese Mappilla and printed by the Manorama Press, and *Vidyavinodini* [Knowledge as Pleasure], started in 1889 by C. P. Achyutha Menon and published until 1903 by the Vidyavinodini Press. Reaching readers well beyond the educated elite, these secular periodicals hosted vigorous debates on social, cultural and political issues alongside poems, essays and short stories. Arunima emphasises how central the debates about language in the pages of these periodicals were to the constitution of a collective Malayalam identity: they 'were integral to reimagining Kerala residents as a linguistic community. The "Malayali" – or the one who speaks Malayalam – could belong to any caste, religious community, or region of Kerala – but was linked to others through a linguistic kinship' (278). Unlike North India, where language reinforced religious difference, with Urdu identified with Muslim subjects and Hindi with Hindu subjects, in Kerala Malayalam speakers were imagined as one linguistic and political community that transcended all divisions. Attitudes towards English were complex. Intellectuals like Mappilla saw the introduction of English in Kerala as beneficial in that it liberated Malayalam from its subordinate status in relation to Sanskrit. At the same time, none of the contributors to the periodicals ever wanted to abandon Malayalam for English; rather, they sought to nurture and develop the Malayalam language and its literature so that it could emulate the achievements of the English language and its literature.

The focus shifts next to Oceania, as Michelle Elleray undertakes a contextualised close reading of a translated letter from Aperaamo, a Samoan convert, which was published in January 1845 in the London Missionary Society's *Juvenile Missionary Magazine* (1844–87). Elleray first reproduces Aperaamo's letter as it appeared in the *Juvenile Missionary Magazine*, explaining the exchange underpinning the publication of such letters: British missionaries in the Pacific sent content (like the letter) to the children's periodical, and child readers made donations to the continuing missionary endeavour in the region. What does this specific letter mean in the context of the *Juvenile Missionary Magazine*? Elleray argues that in terms of the *Magazine*'s hegemonic English-evangelical discourse, the letter 'performs the convert's alphabetic literacy as a sign of the capacity to read the Bible and engage in the LMS's print culture networks; at the same time, the stilted or ungrammatical phrasing reinforces extant assumptions that Samoan society is less complex and knowledgeable than British society' (291). As a corrective to this partial reading, Elleray outlines the history of the contemporaneous *O le Sulu Samoa*, a Samoan-language missionary periodical which was first published in 1839. Although the early issues have been lost, Elleray argues that *le Sulu* represents the Samoans' appropriation of the missionary periodical genre to record their own histories and concerns, and to express in textual form the Samoan articulation of interpersonal relationships. By juxtaposing texts and contexts of the English *Juvenile*

Missionary Magazine and the Samoan *le Sulu*, supplemented by recent scholarship, Elleray demonstrates the capacities of Oceanian languages to disrupt the 'simple' Anglocentric reading of Aperaamo's letter, and draws attention to the register, allusions and import of Aperaamo's choice of specific Samoan words and phrases in his letter, and the extent to which these are erased by its translation into English.

Unlike *O le Sulu Samoa*, which was published exclusively in the Samoan language, the Cape Colony publication *Izwi Labantu* appeared in a combination of languages – isiXhosa, Sesotho and English. As Janet Remmington explains in her contribution to this volume, the Cape Colony's emergent African-language public sphere at the end of the nineteenth century faced formidable political and economic obstacles: the erosion of the African franchise, encroachment on African land, and British- and Boer-ruled polities fighting for control over the subcontinent. The two major African publications – *Imvo Zabantsundu* [Native Opinion] (1884–1997) and *Izwi Labantu* [The Voice of the People] (1897–1909) – competed for readers, income and political influence. Focusing on the latter, Remmington outlines how *Izwi Labantu* 'choreographed a complicated dance between invoking imperial belonging, signalling Christian values, critiquing colonial practices, negotiating African factionalism, and promoting black activist efforts across the South African stage' (301). *Izwi*'s trilingual content served its overlapping readerships: all three languages were on the front page; isiXhosa on the whole of page two; and page three was divided between Sesotho and English. Remmington draws out the subtle differences in emphasis between articles in isiXhosa, Sesotho and English, but emphasises that they nonetheless collectively strove to engage the different African reading publics scattered across Southern Africa, producing in the process an imagined community united in the struggle for full citizenship under the banner of the British Empire.

From South Africa, the focus shifts to East Africa in the 1920s, with Emma Hunter examining *Mambo Leo* and *Habari*, two African-language periodicals published by colonial governments for African readerships. Hunter argues that such periodicals played an important part in East Africa's colonial public sphere. On the one hand, they were explicit attempts to establish colonial power and legitimacy. On the other hand, they were forums in which African writers could participate and on occasion develop anti-colonial critiques. Introducing *Mambo Leo*, published by Tanganyika's Department of Education from 1923, and *Habari*, published in Kenya from c. 1922 to 1931, initially by the Department of Native Affairs and then by the Education Department, Hunter contextualises both publications in relation to their respective local political, linguistic and economic conditions, and proceeds to delineate their similarities and differences. Both periodicals carried many articles on health advice and agricultural practices; both stressed the benefits of British rule; both published folk stories; and both invited readers to think of themselves as citizens of a British Empire. As to the differences, *Mambo Leo* had the larger circulation (9,000 as against 3–5,000 for *Habari*), largely because Kenya's Swahili-language missionary and government publications were more developed and therefore competed for readers. *Mambo Leo* was also published entirely in Swahili, whereas *Habari* published two columns, one in English, the other in Swahili. Although both invited reader contributions, *Mambo Leo* gave far more space to contributors who were in no sense formally employed by the newspaper, particularly in the sections 'Habari za Miji' [News of the Towns], the poetry section and the letters' pages. Challenging the assumption that government

African-language publications like *Mambo Leo* and *Habari* always reproduced colonial ideology, Hunter argues that both periodicals (to contrasting extents and in different ways) 'succeeded in building a community of readers who in turn shaped the contents of the pages' (319).

During the same decade, emerging newspapers and periodicals for African readers flourished in West Africa, as the 1920s heralded the appearance of nine new predominantly English-language and five new predominantly Yoruba-language publications. In Chapter 21, Karin Barber notes that English- and Yoruba-language periodicals have in recent years been consigned to separate sub-disciplinary silos (Nigerian nationalist historiography and Yoruba literary studies) but argues that only by reading them in intimate dialogue with each other can one appreciate their significance. Focusing primarily upon the weekly Yoruba papers – *Eko Akete* (1922–9), *Eleti Ọfẹ* (1923–53), *Iwe Irohin Ọsọsẹ* (1925–7), *Eko Igbẹhin* (1926–7) and *Akede Eko* (1928–53) – Barber provides vivid examples of how the two languages interacted at many levels: between newspapers; within the same newspaper; and within the same articles. Managed, edited and authored by enterprising individuals on the fringes of the Lagosian elite, these newspapers reached a growing public who could read (or be read to) in Yoruba but not in English. Achieving in several cases readership figures in the thousands, they reached well beyond Lagos into the interior, and maintained vigorous exchanges not only with each other but also with other African and English periodicals. Barber's close reading of exemplary extracts establishes the close symbiotic interaction of Yoruba and English, as the newspapers quoted, emulated, traduced, evaluated and translated one another. Far from a case of glottophagia – English the imperial language killing off the local vernacular languages – Barber concludes that the cohabitation of Yoruba and English in 1920s Lagos 'was fashioned into a conscious art in the pages of the local press, [and] seems to have acted as a stimulant to creativity. The sense that Yoruba was being sidelined by those who foolishly only valued English gave rise to vigorous counter-attacks and exhilarating displays of Yoruba linguistic virtuosity' (340).

In a third chapter on African periodicals of this period, Corinne Sandwith and Athambile Masola focus on two multilingual South African periodicals financed by white capitalists but edited and written by black journalists. *Umteteli wa Bantu* (launched in May 1920) and *Bantu World* (launched in April 1932) are examined with an eye to how they delivered their didactic but far from univocal messages in distinctive newspaper forms. Operating on the margins of an inhospitable, settler-dominated public sphere, even moderate black publications like *Umteteli wa Bantu* and *Bantu World* were regarded with suspicion and subject to routine state scrutiny. Attending to the layout, typography, headlining and font styles, Sandwith and Masola emphasise the significance of the newspapers' multilingual format, which featured front pages dominated by English, followed by isiZulu, isiXhosa, Sesotho and Setswana sections. Rejecting the characterisations of 'the docile black editor and the dominant white funder', Sandwith and Masola argue that power relations in *Umteteli wa Bantu* and *Bantu World* were under constant negotiation, a process reflected in their 'polyvocality and multilingualism: many interests were represented in these papers' (344). In the case of *Umteteli wa Bantu*, its critical assaults on radical black political organisations and its repetitive articles encouraging obedient conduct alternated with attacks in English on white South African politicians, officials, clerics and newspapers, as well as irreverent and subversive insertions in its African-language sections. In the case of *Bantu World*, it functioned as a kind of moral guide, prescribing appropriate political behaviour in a variety of genres, but it also contained subversive elements, notably in the isiZulu sections, which constituted a sub-community of readers who generated political critique and debate.

Part IV: Trans-Colonial Connections in Colonial Periodicals

As the limitations of analysing the history of the British Empire exclusively in terms of core-periphery models have been exposed, historians of colonialism have highlighted the hitherto neglected connections linking different parts of the Empire. Since the 1990s, many historical studies have accordingly conceptualised the Empire as connected not only by ties to the imperial-metropolitan centre but also by the widest range of trans-colonial connections. Sanjay Subrahmanyam has noted that 'Nationalism has blinded us to the possibility of connection', and that as an antidote, historians should proceed by seeking out 'fragile threads that connected the globe' (Subrahmanyam 1997: 761–2). Frederick Cooper has counterposed traditional imperial-colonial historiography which reduces 'time into linear pathways, privileges state building over other forms of human connection, and tells a story of progress that inevitably leaves Africans and Asians on the side' and the new global histories which provide 'an analytical idiom sensitive to the multiple forms and degrees of commonality and connectedness, and to the widely varying ways in which actors (and the cultural idioms, public narratives, and prevailing discourses on which they draw) attribute meaning and significance to them' (Cooper 2005: 14, 76–7). The lead article in a recent special issue of the *Journal of Colonialism and Colonial History* makes a vigorous case for '"connected histories of empire" that seek to uncover links that operated across the formal borders of imperial formations and that deploy novel spatial frameworks', thus striving to dislodge once and for all the inherited view of the Empire as 'one homogenous monolith directed from London with a single overarching objective' (Potter and Saha 2015). The advantages of dispensing with an imperial historiography starting and ending in London are enthusiastically expounded in the Introduction to one of the many recent collections on global history:

> It is easy to re-imagine a borderless globe populated not by states but by a pullulating mass of networks: administrative, commercial, financial, religious, migrational, scientific, educational, and military – all bound together by investments, remittances, bills of exchange, reports and despatches, telegrams, letters, parcels, newspapers and books, as well as by soldiers and sailors, merchants and salesmen, indentured labourers and slaves, peripatetic officials, wandering scholars, journalists, travellers, and tourists. (Belich, Darwin and Wickham 2016: 17)

Such encouragement provides the impetus for the volume section on trans-colonial connections in colonial periodicals, the spur to look beyond the relationship between Britain and its colonies, and to seek out alternative connections/ communities/ affiliations/ collectives/ systems/ networks within and across the formal and informal Empire. The guiding question is: how have colonial periodicals functioned across the national-colonial political borders drawn in London?

The question is addressed by attending closely to the historical specificities of individual periodicals in their respective contexts, with each of the section chapters foregrounding the roles played by historical actors, as well as the conditions of production, distribution, circulation, reception and readerships. In line with the historicising emphasis of the *Companion*, currently fashionable theoretical terms which describe contemporary transnational connections – pre-eminently 'network' – are themselves subject to critical scrutiny. The briefest consideration of how the meaning of 'network' has mutated historically gives cause to hesitate before deploying the term to describe how colonial periodicals communicated and functioned across the Empire, especially in the nineteenth century. The Oxford English Dictionary lists seventeen meanings of 'network', of which the great majority relate to later knowledge systems and formations – electrical engineering; broadcasting; computing; interconnected groups of businesses or people; and mathematics (OED 2003: 'network'). Less predictable, more open-ended, often inconclusive and inefficient, and dogged by miscommunications, the connections linking colonial periodicals across national-colonial boundaries often bear only the faintest resemblance to contemporary communications networks. Accordingly, the failures and limits of trans-colonial connections are noted along with the instances of smoothly functioning 'networks' of communication.

The first of the chapters in this section focuses on an exemplary individual whose career unfolded in two settler colonies at opposite ends of the Empire. Melodee H. Wood provides a critical overview of the work of the editor and journalist Samuel Revans (1807–88), who was responsible for newspapers in different colonies – the Montreal-based *Daily Advertiser* in Canada and the Wellington-based *New Zealand Gazette*. Wood carefully locates the two publications in their respective political and economic contexts to correct misperceptions about their ideological priorities and commitments. Noting that *The Advertiser* in Canada has routinely been characterised as sympathetic to the radical Reform Party, and the *Gazette* as a mouthpiece of the pro-establishment New Zealand Company, Wood looks beyond the two periodicals' political articles to read both in their entirety, and in relation to Revans's personal writings and correspondence. Her conclusion is that underlying the different political causes Revans pursued in Canada and New Zealand, he was consistent in serving the economic interests of the settler colonies in both contexts. Although Revans's political positions in Canada and New Zealand were at odds with each other, his publications in both colonies always provided comprehensive trade information in order to inform and thus promote the expanding settler colonial economies: 'Revans consistently supported the development of colonial markets, the engagement of colonists in global trade, and the improvement of government to better support free enterprise and reward hard work and good character' (372).

David Finkelstein examines the typographical trade journals that emerged across the globe in the nineteenth century – in Britain, the United States, South Africa, India, New Zealand and Australia. Finkelstein analyses the London-based *Compositors' Chronicle* (1840–3), the *Typographical Circular* (1854–8), the Melbourne-based *Australian Typographical Circular* (1858–60), the Edinburgh-based *Scottish Typographical Circular* (1857–), the *South African Typographical Circular* (1898–), the *Australasian Typographical Journal* (1870–1916) and the *Indian Printers' Journal* (1895–6, 1912–13). Finkelstein demonstrates how the earliest of these journals conjoined literary with professional material to inform, entertain, educate, and support the development of a cooperative and shared professional trade identity, while later variations shifted to become more focused on trade knowledge and information dissemination. These periodicals fulfilled overlapping functions: as guardians of historical craft memory; as chroniclers of contemporary labour concerns; and as the discursive expression of a trans-colonial trade brotherhood. In colonial settings, however, these periodicals' rhetoric of an egalitarian trade brotherhood foundered as '[p]rint unions in colonial spaces invariably emphasised colonial divisions of race, identity and trade skills. Official labour union rhetoric, particularly in South Africa and Australia, emphasised a trade identity that was overwhelmingly white, male and colonialist in intention' (383). Contrasting the histories of Chinese, Indian and African print workers in different settler colonial contexts, Finkelstein notes how strict racial barriers prevented cross-racial social connections outside workspaces, and how the periodicals dutifully reported upon and upheld such barriers. The typographical journals thus fed into the wider, trans-imperial discourses of colonialism, generating a trade identity consistent with and integral to a racially exclusive, trans-global British settler identity.

The transmission of news and opinion across colonies is the subject of Andrew Griffiths's study of how a military conflict in the Southern African colony of Natal was communicated in an Anglo-Indian colonial periodical. Using the Calcuttan *Friend of India*'s coverage of the 1879 Anglo-Zulu War as a case study, Griffiths demonstrates the limitations of conventional models of imperial news circulation, which assume linear flows of information, centrally controlled by news agencies, commercial interests and governments, and moving primarily between London and British territories overseas. Attending closely to the Calcutta context of the *Friend of India*, Griffiths shows how this widely circulating Anglo-Indian periodical's coverage of the Anglo-Zulu War was shaped less by British-imperial discourse, and more by the agenda of its editor, Robert Knight, and by the regional concerns of its Indian readership, most notably the contemporaneous war in Afghanistan. The *Friend of India*'s stringent criticisms of Governor Bartle Frere's conduct of the war, based upon his unhappy record in India, and the sympathetic paraphrases of attacks on Britain's military belligerence are two of many examples of how the political context of Calcutta – as opposed to the political context of London – determined the content of the periodical. Highlighting how difficult it was for the *Friend of India* to acquire up-to-date information on the war, Griffiths argues that the periodical was forced to run 'an informal newsgathering and analysis operation outside mainstream news networks, which nonetheless competed for authority with better-connected publications' (390–1). Working around silences, miscommunications, mistakes and blockages in the flow of information, and focused upon commentary rather than reportage, the *Friend of India* confounded the limitations of the imperial communication system to deliver a distinctive and outspoken critique of imperial policy in Africa.

The focus shifts to the twentieth century in Ole Birk Laursen's critical survey of a long-running anarchist anti-colonial periodical issued from London. The English-language *Freedom*, including its short-term incarnations *Spain and the World* (1936–8), *Revolt!* (1939) and *War Commentary* (1939–45), provided a forum for dialogue between British anarchists and anti-colonial intellectuals from across Britain's Empire. The chapter examines how specific events across the colonial world – Irish and Egyptian freedom, the Amritsar massacre, the Arab Revolt in Palestine, the Italian invasion of Ethiopia, Gandhi's civil disobedience movement, labour strikes in the West Indies, and the Mau Mau uprising – were reported, and how ongoing debates about colonialism and freedom, nationalism and transnationalism, state-building and anti-statism, terrorism and non-violence, and racism and anti-racism were conducted. Laursen argues that personal/political/intellectual connections were forged between anarchists and anti-colonialists in the pages of *Freedom*, as they exerted a reciprocal influence upon each other: British anarchists 'raise important questions about the true meaning of freedom and open a window on to anarchism's reach into the colonial world. At the same time, such conversations illuminate the ways in which anti-colonial resistance influenced British anarchist thinking about freedom' (404). Publishing articles by anti-colonial figures from across the Empire, notably George Padmore, C. L. R. James, Jomo Kenyatta, Chris Braithwaite, M. P. T. Acharya and N. J. Upadhyaya, *Freedom* disseminated radical ideas to an international readership who were critical not only of colonial rule, but also of the neo-colonial regimes which seized power after political independence.

Laursen's analysis of the several decades of *Freedom* is followed by David Johnson's discussion of how British colonial periodicals debated the Atlantic Charter – the statement issued by Winston Churchill and Franklin D. Roosevelt on 14 August 1941 setting out the common principles upon which Britain and the United States would build the post-war world. Summarising Clause Three, which committed the two major Allied nations to '"respect the right of all peoples to choose the form of government under which they will live"' (418), Johnson surveys the divergent interpretations of the Clause in colonial periodicals. Far from evidencing a coherent and unified British colonial public sphere, the disagreements over Clause Three demonstrate parallel but fragmented colonial and anti-colonial public spheres, which only sporadically display traces of meaningful communication within and between each other. Johnson identifies three broad interpretations expressed in colonial press commentary during this period. One view saw Clause Three as only applying to European nations under Nazi rule, so it was not an independence charter for the colonies (the *Bulletin* in Australia; the *Tanganyika Standard* in East Africa; the *Ashanti Pioneer* in West Africa; and the *Trinidad Guardian*). A second stance viewed Clause Three as extending to Nazi-occupied European nations and British colonies alike (*Current Notes on International Affairs* in Australia; the *Comet* in West Africa; *Inkundla ya Bantu* in South Africa; and the *Hindustan Times* in India). A third position argued that not just Clause Three but the Atlantic Charter in its entirety was a false promise peddled by the two leaders of the capitalist world (the *New Leader* in London; the *African Morning Post* in West Africa; the Jamaican *Public Opinion*; the *Modern Review* in India; and the *Bulletin* in South Africa). Johnson concludes that notwithstanding the many miscommunications and silences, 'anti-colonial periodicals circulating in the counterpublic spheres of the 1940s . . . inspired their readers with radical alternatives to the Atlantic Charter, visions of post-independence futures invariably anti-capitalist, in some cases anti-Stalinist, and in other cases rooted in collectivist non-western political traditions' (429).

Moving into the post-war period, Christopher J. Lee attends closely to the periodical coverage of another iconic event in the history of twentieth-century anti-colonialism: the 1955 Asian-African Conference in Bandung, Indonesia. Lee's contribution addresses how the Bandung Conference was reported in African newspapers and periodicals over an extended period, and how in the process Bandung became mythologised in the global public sphere. The chapter focuses on the wide-ranging symbolic circulation of the event across Africa, notably in *The Ethiopian Herald* (Ethiopia), the *Daily Nation* (Kenya), *Africa South* (South Africa) and *New Age* (South Africa). Lee captures participants' and observers' immediate impressions of the Bandung Conference by analysing Richard Wright's account in *The Color Curtain* (1956) and the 1955 reports in the South African periodicals *New Age* and *Fighting Talk*. Emphasising the subsequent myth-making power of the Final Communiqué agreed by the Bandung delegates (the ten principles known as the *Dasasila Bandung*), Lee traces how the idea of Bandung, an amalgam of Third Worldism, internationalism, non-alignment, anti-colonialism and tri-continental solidarity, was nurtured and promoted in periodicals and newspapers like *Africa South* (1958), *The Ethiopian Herald* (1960–5) and Nairobi's *Daily Nation* (1964–5). In so doing, Lee demonstrates that although the Bandung Conference took place in Southeast Asia, it became a constant reference point and source of inspiration in Africa during the decolonisation period, and concludes that 'newspaper and periodical accounts [played a crucial role] in producing and sustaining this political vision of intercontinental solidarity and anti-colonial internationalism that would last in idea and spirit until the end of the Cold War' (434).

The themes of non-alignment and internationalism are picked up by Alex Tickell and Anne Wetherilt, who analyse the radical Hong Kong-based periodical *Eastern Horizon*, which was founded in 1961 at the height of the Cold War and continued to appear for two decades. Started by Liu Pengju, a journalist previously employed on Chinese Communist Party newspapers, *Eastern Horizon*'s long-term editor was Lee Tsung-Ying, with the well-known author Han Suyin also an influential presence and frequent contributor. *Eastern Horizon* consistently supported Communist China, as well as the Bandung ideals of Third World solidarity, non-alignment and decolonisation. Support for the Chinese Communist Party in the pages of *Eastern Horizon* continued until Mao Zedong's death in 1976, after which its editorial policy became less celebratory. The contents of *Eastern Horizon* were wide-ranging: opinion pieces and reviews by writers sympathetic to Mao, such as Rewi Alley and David Crook; articles on culture and politics in Asia and Africa; artworks and poems; and literary criticism by intellectuals who would later contribute to postcolonial theory (notably E. San Juan Jr). *Eastern Horizon* occupies a paradoxical position in that its Hong Kong location makes it in temporal terms a colonial periodical, but its vigorous support for decolonisation and Maoism fit more readily within a dissident anti-colonial public sphere. Tickell and Wetherilt trace the subtle shifts in the editorial policies of *Eastern Horizon* through three phases: (1) the early years; (2) the Cultural Revolution (1966–76); and (3) after Mao (1977–81). Taking stock of *Eastern Horizon*'s twenty-year archive, they emphasise the periodical's ability to function successfully in a late British colonial outpost such as Hong Kong, and 'to flourish as an international publication critical of old and new imperialisms and supportive of the revolutionary Maoism of neighbouring Communist China' (456).

Part V: Anti-Colonialism in the Colonial and Postcolonial Public Sphere

If periodicals helped Conrad's fictional colonial officials, Kayerts and Carlier, 'to think better of themselves' (Conrad 2002: 9), other kinds of periodicals challenged the assumptions of colonial rule and lifted the morale of the colonised. Peter Abrahams describes the impact of his encounter with the periodical *Bantu World* in 1930s segregationist Johannesburg:

> One day a slim, neatly dressed, collar-and-tie young man stopped for coffee and fatcakes. While he ate he read a paper. I saw the paper's name: *The Bantu World*. I knew the names of all the Johannesburg papers because I sold them. But I had never come across *The Bantu World*. I twisted my body to see better. Yes, the pictures on the front page were of black people! All the papers I sold only had pictures of white folk. I tried to read what it said about the black people's pictures. (Abrahams 1954: 187)

For Abrahams, this chance encounter with *Bantu World* is transformative, as the 'collar-and-tie young man' initiates a conversation with him about this periodical published for African readers (though financed by white businessmen), and then goes on to direct him to the Bantu Men's Social Centre, where he is supported and guided in his efforts to become a writer (see Sandwith and Masola's discussion of *Bantu World* in Chapter 22).

For anti-colonial intellectuals, the periodical press has always functioned as a vital resource in disseminating radical ideas. For example, Indian activists launched the multilingual periodical *Ghadar* [Mutiny] in San Francisco in November 1913, which soon reached a global readership: '*Ghadar* was carried with the mails across the Pacific to Manila and the treaty ports of China, and then via Singapore and Penang to India . . . [Copies] turned up in Indian garrisons across the great arc of the Indian Ocean, in East Africa, Sudan and the Middle East [and] as far as Morocco' (Harper 2021: 184). In parallel with individual periodicals reaching different diasporic reader constituencies, individual activist-intellectuals published their anti-colonial arguments in a wide variety of periodicals. Again, examples abound. Shapurji Dorabji Saklatvala, the Communist member of the British Parliament and tireless fighter for Indian independence in the 1920s, left no monographs or collated body of work, but made 'journalistic contributions to a range of political organs, including the *Labour Leader*, the *Labour Monthly*, the *Daily Worker*, and the *Anti-Imperialist Review*' (Gopal 2019: 220). A decade later, C. L. R. James published articles in anti-colonial periodicals in Trinidad (*The Beacon* and *Trinidad*), Britain (*Africa and the World*, *African Sentinel*, *International African Opinion*, the *New Statesman and Nation*, the *New Leader*, *The Keys* and *Fight*), and the United States (the *New International*) (Høgsbjerg 2014: 6, 25–30, 67–70, 94–9, 108–14, 198).

After the Second World War, during the decades of decolonisation and the Cold War, the number of anti-colonial periodicals and newspapers proliferated. Although many suffered censorship and banning, collectively they represented, narrated, and sought to hasten the end of the Empire. Notwithstanding their contributions to the ultimate achievement of political independence, such popular publishing initiatives always had their limits. For example, in British colonies in Africa, where nationalist print cultures gave unstinting support to independence struggles, 'the building of nationalist movements across the continent was overwhelmingly oral work [and] efforts to transform political consciousness could only contain and ameliorate – rather than eliminate – abiding divisions based on region, generation, class and religion' (Brennan 2013: 496).

Many of the individual chapters in this volume discuss periodicals which published articles expressing opposition to colonial rule. To take an example from each section at random: in Part I, Ward demonstrates how in the Caribbean of the 1830s, *The Watchman and Jamaica Free Press* and the Barbadian newspaper *The Liberal* constituted a Black public sphere countering the white planter press; in Part II, Oke's analysis of women's publishing activity in 1930s Ghana and Nigeria establishes that 'periodicals were one space in which women could participate in negotiating social, economic, political and cultural change' (215); in Part III, Arunima explains how in 1890s Kerala, the Malayalam periodicals – *Bhashaposhini* [Language Advancement] and *Vidyavinodini* [Knowledge as Pleasure] – forged connections between language (Malayalam), region (Kerala) and ethnic identity (Malayali), thus shaping an early and distinctive form of anti-colonial nationalism; and in Part IV, Laursen demonstrates how *Freedom*, the London-based anarchist periodical, brought European anarchist thought and anti-colonialism into productive dialogue from 1918 to the 1960s.

The chapters in our final section elaborate further examples of periodicals in the British Empire which articulated criticism of colonial rule, either implicitly or directly. All public spheres have been associated with the expression of criticism – political, aesthetic, cultural, economic, literary. In Jürgen Habermas's pioneering history of the European bourgeois public sphere, Britain in the late eighteenth century saw the emergence of 'the new, large daily newspapers like *The Times* (1785) [and] other institutions of the public reflecting critically on political issues' (Habermas 1989: 65). The European bourgeois public sphere anatomised by Habermas is but one of many historical instances of public spheres, with an expanding critical-theoretical vocabulary attuned to describing the distinctive varieties available: Europe's 'proletarian public sphere' (Negt and Kluge 2016: 54–95), 'counterpublics' (Warner 2002: 65–124), and 'the black public sphere in the United States' (Baker 1994: 4). The many different colonial and anti-colonial public spheres inhabited by the periodicals discussed in the *Companion* represent yet further historically distinctive public spheres, and accordingly, the question as to how anti-colonial ideas expressed in British colonial periodicals might be conceptualised is answered case-by-case in relation to the historical specificities of each periodical and its context(s).

The periodicals and newspapers of the 1850s and 1860s discussed by Priti Joshi in her contribution are by no stretch 'anti-colonial', but in reporting on Indian resistance to British rule, they bear witness to how the Uprising of 1857 was represented – and, more significantly, misrepresented – in the colonial public sphere. Joshi examines how images of Nana Sahib, 'the arch-villain of Indian Mutiny', mutated across space and time. Joshi provides a scrupulously historicised reading of the visual images of Nana Sahib in the *Illustrated Times*, *The Illustrated London News* and *The Lady's Newspaper and Pictorial Times*, arguing that the contrasting images (one a false representation) vied for primacy in the public sphere, with the ultimate winner conditioned by expectations of how Britons wanted 'their' Indians to look. Explaining how an image of Jotee Prasad (a wealthy but innocuous Marwari banker) had been inserted as an image of Nana Sahib (a Maratha nobleman) in *The Illustrated London News*, and how John Lang, the opportunistic lawyer, journalist and 'old India hand', had represented Prasad (successfully) in court and (inaccurately) in the press, Joshi concludes that '[f]or those willing to look, the case shed light on the deception that undergirded the colonial regime [and] also signalled resistance, an Indian using the courts to clear his name' (473). The image-and-text of the British and Indian presses cannot provide unmediated access to the voice of Indian resistance, but by reading them simultaneously and in active conversation, Joshi disrupts colonial stereotyping, challenges the misrepresentations of colonial discourse, and thus gives due weight to the agency of Indian actors.

Sukeshi Kamra's contribution on the nineteenth-century Indian periodical press examines how resistance – and news in general – was (mis)represented in the Native Newspaper Reports (NNRs). Kamra describes the vital role played by the NNRs, which were weekly compilations of passages from articles in the Indian press published in periodical form by the colonial government from the 1870s to 1910. Noting the scholarly consensus that the Indian-owned press in this period contributed to a growing anti-colonial print nationalism, Kamra proceeds to examine the NNRs both as a substitute for the Indian-owned press and as a form of surveillance commissioned and read by the colonial bureaucracy. Providing vivid examples from the NNRs, Kamra exposes how the 'government translator' (the editor/compiler of the NNRs) selected the extracts from the Indian press so as to exaggerate the number of sensationalist and emotive passages and to diminish the reasoned and carefully argued ones. In the process, Kamra argues, 'a heterogeneous press [is flattened in the NNRs] into a homogenously inflammatory one' (482). The selections assembled in the NNRs accordingly provided immediately accessible evidence of the kind of insurrectionary language actionable under the colonial government's sedition laws. Kamra emphasises that the Indian-owned periodical press did not acquiesce in the NNRs' misrepresentations of its content; rather several Indian journalists and editors argued that it was the NNR version of the Indian-owned press which echoed the melodramatic excesses of Victorian sensationalist newspapers, not the Indian-owned press itself. Kamra's historicist against-the-grain reading of the NNRs thus illuminates the vigorous contestation in the Indian periodical press over how resistance should be represented in print culture.

From nineteenth-century India, the next two chapters shift to the Caribbean and West Africa in the 1930s. In the first instance, Raphael Dalleo examines two publications from the Caribbean that illustrate the challenges colonial rule posed for periodicals which aspired to speak to and for their local context. The periodicals discussed in the chapter, the Trinidadian *Beacon* (1931–9) and Jamaican *Public Opinion* (1937–74), enjoy a prominent place in Caribbean literary history, as the editors and journalists associated with both of them became nationalist leaders in the era of decolonisation. Drawing upon the theoretical vocabularies of Jürgen Habermas, Michael Warner, Saidiya Hartman and Houston Baker, Dalleo characterises the two periodicals as 'a site of tension between a nationalist position allowing it to speak in the name of a public and a subaltern space of critique' (495). Analysing *The Beacon* and *Public Opinion* in their respective contexts, Dalleo identifies their key differences and their similarities – most strikingly, the important place literature played in both periodicals. Providing examples of 'yard literature' by writers like C. L. R. James and Alfred Mendes, Dalleo argues that in representing the Caribbean poor, these short stories simultaneously voiced a critique of Trinidad society and pointed out the dangers of unchecked gossip. At all stages of their respective histories, Dalleo emphasises, the relationship between the political and literary content of *The Beacon* and *Public Opinion* was complex, as literary intellectuals integrated their writing as part of an anti-colonial movement, but ultimately never resolved all the tensions, which have resurfaced more forcefully in the new independent nation states.

In the second chapter focusing on the 1930s, Marina Bilbija examines the history of the popular anglophone Lagos weekly newsmagazine the *Comet*, founded and edited from 1933 by Duse Mohamed Ali, Egyptian-born editor and businessman, which would go on to become one of Nigeria's longest-running periodicals. Firmly differentiated from the Nigerian daily newspapers, the *Comet* juxtaposed local and international news stories, providing extensive coverage of disputes within the League of Nations, the rise of the Fascist powers in Europe, racial politics in United States, and concerns dominating Pan-Africanist forums – pre-eminently the Italian invasion of Ethiopia in 1935. Crucially, such stories about occurrences from well beyond West Africa were framed as events directly concerning Nigerian readers, a mode of address which both disrupted and mediated between the local-global division of news stories. Ali thus created a unique niche for the *Comet* within the Nigerian print culture of the 1930s. Contrasting the *Comet*'s political message with the radical anti-colonialism of Ali's earlier London-based periodical the *African Times and Orient Review* (1912–14; 1917–20), Bilbija suggests that 'the function of the *Comet*'s condensed reviews and editorials was to map global political and economic trends and underline recurring issues as they related to West Africa' (507). Finally, Bilbija emphasises the long-term influence of the *Comet*, as it informed the ideas of the younger generation of Nigerian nationalists who ultimately became the political leaders of independent Nigeria.

In the final two chapters of this volume section, the focus shifts to the end of Empire – the moment of decolonisation and its immediate aftermath. Myles Osborne turns our attention to the Jamaican *Public Opinion*, analysing the periodical's history in the 1950s and 1960s, and highlighting its role in supporting Jamaica's transition to independence and its coverage of anti-colonial struggles in Africa. Osborne explains how *Public Opinion* built upon earlier twentieth-century Pan-Africanist movements – Marcus Garvey's Universal Negro Improvement Association, Rastafarianism, the Ethiopian World Federation, and the Afro-West Indian Welfare League – to locate Jamaica's struggle for independence in close synchrony with contemporaneous African anti-colonial struggles. Quoting from articles in *Public Opinion* by George Padmore, W. A. Domingo, Roger Mais and Paul Robeson, Osborne shows how the periodical hosted, publicised and animated debates about Jamaican politics, posing such questions as 'should the island be an African satellite, a wholly independent nation, or part of the West Indies Federation? And what role should larger, global movements like Pan-Africanism or socialism play, with their promises to leave the nation behind in search of a brighter future?' (519–20). Osborne conveys the range of anti-colonial opinions expressed in *Public Opinion*, notably Padmore's Marxist internationalism versus Domingo's Garveyite Africanism, as well as the complicated attitudes towards the Soviet Union, which juggled appreciation of its support for anti-colonial movements and disapproval of its Stalinist authoritarianism. The reception of *Public Opinion* in Jamaica, Osborne argues, was also complicated: middle-class readers were in broad sympathy with its moderate Pan-Africanism, whereas poorer Jamaican readers were drawn to the violent anti-colonial struggles of the Mau Mau in Kenya. Far from diminishing the significance of *Public Opinion*, its hosting of such debates over anti-colonial strategies and postcolonial futures has ensured the periodical's continuing relevance.

The final chapter examines an East African periodical which had its political and intellectual roots in the anti-colonial struggle, but which first appeared after independence: the Kenyan literary periodical *Busara* [Wisdom in Kiswahili] (1967–75). Madhu Krishnan locates *Busara* in the immediate postcolonial context of East African print cultures, arguing that the periodical played a central role in framing the literary and political discourses of the new nation. Drawing contributions from East Africa, the United States and Europe, and featuring work by well-known figures such as Ngũgĩ wa Thiong'o and Taban Lo Liyong, as well as a significant number of women critics, *Busara* published literary-cultural articles debating the extent to which East African literature should break with European aesthetics, and political articles grappling with ideas of citizenship, culture, race, gender and class in the post-independence context. Krishnan argues that from 'this relatively small, localised literary magazine ... comes a far larger statement about the role played by cultural production in the forging of a post-independence African reality' (536). *Busara*'s short stories, poems, reviews and comments sat alongside features of important debates between key African intellectuals, such as the one between Atieno-Odhiambo and Albert Ojuka on the role of the intellectual and art in society, and one initiated by Ellen Mae Kitonga on racism in Joseph Conrad's fiction. Read in the context of post-independence East Africa, *Busara* therefore constituted a significant site for debating conflicting visions of social responsibility and identity, giving expression to ideas and perspectives which challenged the dominant discourses of the time.

Conclusion

In the early decades of the British Empire, colonial officials were convinced that the circulation of imperial ideology via books and periodicals was vital in securing colonial rule because 'our Empire' was an 'empire of opinion'. At the dusk of Empire, the government agents of the United States, Britain's successor as global super-power, held very similar views. A report by the US Central Intelligence Agency (CIA) in 1961 identified the dissemination of (US-funded) books and periodicals as fundamental to combating Communist ideology during the Cold War. Accordingly, through proxy organisations, the Congress of Cultural Freedom and the Farfield Foundation, the CIA funded over twenty prestigious magazines worldwide, including several influential African literary and political periodicals – such as *Black Orpheus, Transition, The New African, Africa South* and *The Classic* (Spahr 2018: 85–109; Shringarpure 2019: chapter 4; Kalliney 2022: 51–82). A formal analysis of the content of these publications reveals little overt evidence of direct CIA involvement, or at most a mild but consistent anti-Communism, but the publication histories of the magazines disclose that in Africa by the late 1960s, the 'apparently decolonised network of [African] literary publishing had the US government, and specifically the CIA, at its centre' (Davis 2020: 88).

The examples of the *Friend of India* in 1836 and the CIA policy statements of 1961 communicate the message that to imperial powers, at least, colonial periodicals matter, that securing control over the circulation of ideas in colonial and postcolonial public spheres is always a strategic priority. At the same time, as many of the chapters in the *Companion* attest, imperial ideology has also been contested, disputed and discredited in the pages of colonial periodicals. By examining exemplary periodicals in their respective historical contexts, the *Companion* has attempted to treat British colonial periodicals with the seriousness they deserve by delivering analyses that give due weight to the complex congruences and contradictions between their content, form, economics and political ideologies.

Bibliography

Abrahams, Peter (1954), *Tell Freedom*, London: Faber.

Agathocleous, Tanya (2021), *Disaffected: Emotion, Sedition, and Colonial Law in the Anglosphere*, Ithaca and London: Cornell University Press.

Anon. (1814), *The Times*, 29 November, 1.

—— (1836), *Friend of India*, 27 October, 1.

Ayalon, Ami (2016), *The Arabic Print Revolution: Cultural Production and Mass Readership*, Cambridge: Cambridge University Press.

Baker, Houston A., Jr (1994), 'Critical memory and the black public sphere', *Public Culture*, 7.1, 3–33.

Banner, Stuart (2007), *Possessing the Pacific: Land, Settlers and Indigenous People from Australia to Alaska*, Cambridge, MA: Harvard University Press.

Bayly, C. A. (2007), *Empire and Information: Intelligence Gathering and Social Communication in India, 1780–1870*, Cambridge: Cambridge University Press.

Belich, James (2009), *Replenishing the Earth: The Settler Revolution and the Rise of the Anglo-World*, Oxford: Oxford University Press.

——, John Darwin and Chris Wickham (2016), 'Introduction: The prospect of global history', in James Belich et al. (eds), *The Prospect of Global History*, Oxford: Oxford University Press, 3–22.

Bell, Bill (2021), *Crusoe's Books: Readers in the Empire of Print, 1800–1918*, Oxford: Oxford University Press.

Blackley, Roger (2001), *Stray Leaves: Colonial Trompe l'oeil Drawings*, Wellington: Victoria University Press.

Bonea, Amelia (2010), 'An imperial ideology of news: News values and reporting about Japan in Colonial India', in David Finkelstein (ed.), *The Edinburgh History of the British and Irish Press, Volume 2: Expansion and Evolution, 1800–1900*, Edinburgh: Edinburgh University Press, 278–83.

Brennan, James R. (2013), 'Communications and media in African history', in John Parker and Richard Reid (eds), *The Oxford Handbook of Modern African History*, Oxford: Oxford University Press, 492–509.

Conrad, Joseph (2002) [1897], 'An Outpost of Progress', in *Heart of Darkness and Other Tales*, Oxford: Oxford University Press, 1–25.

Cooper, Frederick (2005), *Colonialism in Question: Theory, Knowledge, History*, Berkeley: University of California Press.

Darwin, John (2009), *The Empire Project: The Rise and Fall of the British World System, 1830–1970*, Cambridge: Cambridge University Press.

Davis, Caroline (2020), *African Literature and the CIA: Networks of Authorship and Publishing*, Cambridge: Cambridge University Press.

Decook, Travis (2004), 'The spread of newspapers in British North America', in Patricia Lockhart Fleming, Gilles Gallichan and Yvan Lamonde (eds), *History of the Book in Canada, Volume 1: Beginnings to 1840*, Toronto: University of Toronto Press, 229–33.

Dhawardker, Vinay (1997), 'Print culture and literary markets in Colonial India', in Jeffrey Masten, Peter Stallybrass and Nancy J. Vickers (eds), *Language Machines: Technologies of Literary and Cultural Production*, London and New York: Routledge, 108–36.

Distad, Merrill (1991), 'Review: *The Monthly Epic: A History of Canadian Magazines, 1789–1989* by Fraser Sutherland', *Victorian Periodicals Review*, 24.3, 154–7.
—— (2004), 'Newspapers and magazines', in Yvan Lamonde, Patricia Lockhart Fleming and Fiona Black (eds), *History of the Book in Canada, Volume 2: 1840–80*, Toronto: University of Toronto Press, 293–303.
Elbourne, Elizabeth (2021), 'Rights, interpersonal violence and settler colonialism in early nineteenth-century South Africa: Thomas Pringle and Scottish colonialism at the Cape, 1820–34', *Journal of Indian Ocean World Studies*, 5.2, 185–214.
Finkelstein, David (2003), '"Jack's as Good as His Master": Scots and print culture in New Zealand, 1860–1900', *Book History*, 6, 95–107.
—— (2018), *Movable Types: Roving Creative Printers in the Victorian World*, Oxford: Oxford University Press.
—— and Douglas M. Peers (2000), '"A Great System of Circulation": Introducing India into the nineteenth-century media', in David Finkelstein and Douglas M. Peers (eds), *Negotiating India in the Nineteenth-Century Media*, Basingstoke: Macmillan Press, 1–22.
Free, Melissa (2018), 'Settler colonialism', *Journal of Victorian Culture*, 46.3–4, 876–82.
Gopal, Priyamvada (2019), *Insurgent Empire: Anticolonial Resistance and British Dissent*, London: Verso.
Habermas, Jürgen (1989) [1962], *The Structural Transformation of the Public Sphere*, trans. Thomas Burger, London: Polity.
Harper, Tim (2021), *Underground Asia: Global Revolutionaries and the Assault on Empire*, Dublin: Penguin.
Høgsbjerg, Christian (2014), *C. L. R. James in Imperial Britain*, Durham, NC: Duke University Press.
Jones, Aled G. (2003), 'Welsh missionary journalism in India, 1880–1947', in Julie F. Codell (ed.), *Imperial Co-Histories: National Identities and the British and Colonial Press*, Madison, NJ: Fairleigh Dickinson University Press, 242–72.
Joshi, Priti (2021), *Empire News: The Anglo-Indian Press Writes India*, Albany: State University of New York Press.
Kalliney, Peter J. (2022), *The Aesthetic Cold War: Decolonization and Global Literature*, Princeton: Princeton University Press.
Kennedy, P. M. (1971), 'Imperial cable communications and strategy, 1870–1914', *The English Historical Review*, 86.341, October, 728–52.
Khan, Nadir Ali (2009), *A History of Urdu Journalism (1822–1857)*, Delhi: Idarah-i-Adabiyat-I Delhi.
Laurence, Gérard (2004), 'The newspaper press in Quebec and Lower Canada', in Patricia Lockhart Fleming, Gilles Gallichan and Yvan Lamonde (eds), *History of the Book in Canada, Volume 1: Beginnings to 1840*, Toronto: University of Toronto Press, 233–8.
Ledbetter, Kathryn (2020), 'The Women's Press', in David Finkelstein (ed.), *The Edinburgh History of the British and Irish Press, Volume 2: Expansion and Evolution, 1800–1900*, Edinburgh: Edinburgh University Press, 688–708.
Logan, Deborah Anna (2017), *The Indian Ladies Magazine, 1901–1938: From Raj to Swaraj*, Bethlehem, PA: Lehigh University Press.
Mann, Michael (2017), *Wiring the Nation: Telecommunication, Newspaper-Reportage and Nation Building in British India, 1830–1950*, Oxford: Oxford University Press.
Negt, Oskar, and Alexander Kluge (2016) [1972], *Public Sphere of Experience: Analysis of the Bourgeois and Proletarian Public Sphere*, trans. Peter Labanyi, Jamie Owen Daniel and Assenka Oxiloff, London: Verso.
North, John S. (ed.) (1986), *Waterloo Directory of Irish Newspapers and Periodicals, 1800–1900*, Waterloo, ON: North Waterloo Academic Press.

—— (ed.) (1989), *Waterloo Directory of Scottish Newspapers and Periodicals, 1800–1900*, Waterloo, ON: North Waterloo Academic Press.

—— (ed.) (1997) *Waterloo Directory of English Newspapers and Periodicals, 1800–1900*, Waterloo, ON: North Waterloo Academic Press.

O'Regan, John P. (2021), *Global English and Political Economy*, London and New York: Routledge.

Otis, Andrew (2018), *Hicky's Bengal Gazette: The Untold Story of India's First Newspaper*, Chennai: Tranquebar.

Oxford English Dictionary (2003), 'network', https://www.oed.com/dictionary/network_n?tab=meaning_and_use#34657811 (accessed 15 June 2023).

Pennycook, Alastair (1998), *English and the Discourses of Colonialism*, London and New York: Routledge.

Potter, Simon (2003), *News and the British World: The Emergence of an Imperial Press System, 1876–1922*, Oxford: Clarendon Press.

—— (2017), 'Journalism and Empire in an English reading world: The *Review of Reviews*', in Joanne Shattock (ed.), *Journalism and the Periodical Press in Nineteenth-Century Britain*, Cambridge: Cambridge University Press, 281–8.

—— and Jonathan Saha (2015), 'Global history, imperial history and connected histories of Empire', *Journal of Colonialism and Colonial History*, 16.1, Spring.

Rutherford, Paul (1982), *A Victorian Authority: The Daily Press in Late Nineteenth-Century Canada*, Toronto: University of Toronto Press.

Shringarpure, Bhakti (2019), *Cold War Assemblages: Decolonisation to Digital*, Abingdon: Routledge.

Shum, Matthew (2020), *Improvisations of Empire: Thomas Pringle in Scotland, the Cape Colony and London, 1789–1834*, London: Anthem Press.

Spahr, Juliana (2018), *Du Bois's Telegram: Literary Resistance and State Containment*, Cambridge, MA: Harvard University Press.

Stark, Ulrike (2007), *An Empire of Books: The Naval Kishore Press and the Diffusion of the Printed Word in Colonial India*, Ranikhet: Permanent Black.

Subrahmanyam, Sanjay (1997), 'Connected histories: Notes towards a reconfiguration of Early Modern Eurasia', *Modern Asian Studies*, 31.3, 735–62.

Traue, J. E. (1997), 'But why Mulgan, Marris and Schroder? The mutation of the local newspaper in New Zealand's colonial print culture', *Bibliographical Society of Australia and New Zealand Bulletin*, 21.2, 107–15.

Warner, Michael (2002), *Publics and Counterpublics*, New York: Zone Books.

Wilson, John (1861), 'Short Memorial of the Honourable Mountstuart Elphinstone, and of his Contributions to Oriental Geography and History', *Journal of the Bombay Branch of the Royal Asiatic Society*, 6, 97–111.

Zastoupil, Lynn, and Martin Moir (eds) (2000), *The Great Indian Education Debate: Documents Relating to the Orientalist-Anglicist Controversy, 1781–1843*, London and New York: Routledge.

Part I

Creating and Contesting the Colonial Public Sphere

1

Authorship and Collective Self-Fashioning in Pre-Confederation English Canada

Cynthia Sugars and Paul Keen

In the inaugural issue of *The Canadian Magazine*, launched in Toronto (then known as York) in January 1833, William Sibbald expressed concern that the newly arising Canadian periodicals, including his own, might not be a match for their British counterparts. His apparent hesitation had an obvious rhetorical purpose, for he ultimately persuaded readers of the contrary by refuting the reservations he had raised. Yet in some form, Sibbald's statement would find echoes in the many magazines and periodicals that were springing up throughout the British North American colonies in the early nineteenth century.[1] On the one hand, Sibbald worried that the Canadian colonies might not offer the same 'food to the craving mind' that established British and European traditions provided (Sibbald 1833a: 1), a lack that was caused not only by the dearth of experienced authors in the colonies but also by the mundane realities of colonial living conditions. How could one make Canadian topics of sufficient 'literary' interest to garner the public's attention? On the other hand, the fault seemed to lie with the intended readership rather than the magazine itself. In Britain, the appearance of each new issue was met with 'anxiety and excitement . . . as the moment of delivery approaches' (Sibbald 1833a: 1–2). In Canada, well . . . not so much.

And so, Sibbald issued an invigorating call to arms to the Canadian public, inciting them to show a bit of pluck and remember their ancestry: 'Have your Friends, Brethren, Countrymen, passions and propensities diametrically opposite [to their British forebears]?' The answer to his own question – again rhetorical – was emphatic: 'No! no, you have not forgot!' (Sibbald 1833a: 2). Having recognised the need for colonial self-affirmation and the promise of the current age of literary magazines, a combination that heightened the heroic nature of his mission, Sibbald's magazine, like so many others before and after his, was set to respond to the epic challenge it had posed.

This example provides a good snapshot of the dilemma – and the often contradictory responses it inspired – that confronted new Canadian magazines in the colonies. In the years immediately prior to 1867, when the British North American colonies united into what would become the new Dominion of Canada, debates about Canada's 'national' identity and culture dominated the popular press. Commentators on both sides of the issue argued for or against the merits – even the mere existence – of a new national culture. However, these passions were not unique to the Confederation debates. Canadian periodicals from as early as the late 1820s were ardently committed to the task of colonial self-definition and the fostering of a local civic sensibility, both of which would come about, the magazines attested, through the development of a local literature.

However frequently these periodicals may have aligned the prospect of their success (a confidence that was almost always belied by their relatively short lifespan) with a vision of the individual and collective improvement of their readers, information about who these readers were or even about circulation numbers remains obscure. As Mary Lu MacDonald points out:

> It is almost impossible to know who read these periodicals. Editors wrote of their 'many respectable subscribers,' but their testimony is unreliable because editors were always trying to prove that their subscribers were numerous and respectable in order to encourage others to subscribe. Literacy rates for 18th- and 19th-century Canada are the subject of vigorous debate among social historians. (MacDonald 1993: 223)

Thomas Brewer Vincent, Sandra Alston and Eli MacLaren agree that subscription figures remain 'hard to determine', though, as they also note, '"five hundred copies" is mentioned by several editors' (Vincent, Alston and MacLaren 2004: 249). The 20 July 1833 edition of the Hamilton-based *Canadian Garland*, for instance, referred with evident pride to producing 'five hundred numbers of the Garland' on the very spot on which just 'a century ago the solitary forest stood undisturbed' (Smyth 1833: 183). But like most periodicals of the day, *The Canadian Garland* struggled to cope with costs in an era before economies of scale made production more efficient. Having noted that 'on a paper such as ours, the postage amounts to nearly one third the price of subscription', *The Canadian Garland* added, 'we hope that each subscriber will promptly pay up his respective debt' (Smyth 1833: 183).

It was an uphill battle from the start. The challenge, apart from these financial pressures, was to convince readers, and prospective local writers, that the colonies were 'ready' for such local literary productions. Periodicals such as Nahum Mower's *Canadian Magazine and Literary Repository* (1823–5), John Kent's *Canadian Literary Magazine* (1833) and John Lovell's *The Literary Garland* (1838–51) promoted themselves as both a leading cause and a sure sign of a wider sense of progress. For most of them, the extraordinary growth of the past few decades – culturally, economically, and in broader forms of civic improvement – was the most noticeable feature of their age. Edmund Ward's Halifax-based *British North American Magazine, and Colonial Journal*, which first appeared in February 1831, took inspiration from 'the first Nova Scotia Magazine' (John Howe's Halifax-based *Nova-Scotia Magazine* which ran from 1789 to 1792), but even more so from this broader sense of historical progress which had fundamentally altered the challenges faced by periodical writers and publishers: 'What an encouraging contrast, does the present state of the Province, make with what it was then? At that time even decent types could not be procured at Halifax; and what was more, liberal education was but just dawning' (Ward 1831: 2).

D. C. Harvey's description of Nova Scotia in the years between 1835 and 1848 as a period of 'intellectual awakening' applied to other regions equally well (Harvey 1933: 2). It was a time of considerable unrest but also of cultural and intellectual fermentation; a time when writers from a range of cultural and political perspectives raised important questions about the public worth of a domestic literature, the status of the authors who produced it, and the challenges involved.

Periodicals frequently hailed their own success as a clear sign of this intensifying momentum which fused economic, cultural and institutional advances, from the most material details (access to decent types) to the most indirect (the supporting role of an educational infrastructure). The mid-century saw an explosion of periodicals in all these British colonies: Upper and Lower Canada, Nova Scotia, and the other Atlantic provinces. Many were general or more consciously literary, such as *The Literary Garland* (Montreal, 1838–51), *Barker's Canadian Monthly Magazine* (Kingston, 1846–7), *The Canadian Magazine* (York, 1833), *The Canadian Casket* (Hamilton, 1831–2), *The Montreal Museum* (Montreal, 1832–4) and *The Scribbler* (Montreal, 1821–7). Some had an explicitly denominational focus, such as *The Evangelical Pioneer* (London, 1847), *The Canadian Presbyterian Magazine* (Toronto, 1851) and *The Canadian Baptist Magazine and Missionary Register* (Montreal, 1837). Others were regionally based, such as *The Gaspé Magazine, and Instructive Miscellany* (New Carlisle, 1849), *The Acadian Magazine* (Halifax, 1826–8) and *L'Abeille Canadienne* (Montreal, 1818–19); aligned with specific demographics such as *The Youth's Monitor and Monthly Magazine* (Toronto, 1836), *Weekly Miscellany: Devoted to the Intellectual and Moral Improvement of the Young* (Halifax, 1863–4) and *The Life Boat; A Juvenile Temperance Magazine, in the Interest of the Cadets, and Other Youthful Associations of a Like Nature* (Montreal, 1853); or targeted to economic sectors, such as *The Canadian Quarterly Agricultural and Industrial Magazine* (Montreal, 1838), *The Canadian Agriculturalist* (Toronto, 1849), *The Canadian Merchant's Magazine and Commercial Review* (Toronto, 1857), *The Saturday Evening Magazine* (intended for working men; Montreal, 1833–4) and *The City Magazine: Devoted to the Interests of Young Men in Commercial Pursuits* (Montreal, 1847). Most of them lasted only a year or two, but collectively their presence reinforced *The British North American Magazine*'s claim that earlier hardships had been overcome, though they continued to characterise this progress as tenuous, and their own success as being wholly reliant on locals' support as both subscribers and contributors.

It is no accident, then, that many of these periodicals described themselves as crucial shapers of Canada's destiny, even as early as the 1820s. In the opening remarks in his 1826 *Acadian Magazine*, Jacob Cunnabell declared that he had been 'induced to hazard an undertaking, which, if successful, will advance the literary standing of the Country' because 'the public interest imperatively demands, that something of this nature should be attempted', if only 'to efface the impression which has been far too prevalent abroad, and particularly in the mother Country, that we were comparatively ignorant and barbarous' (J. Cunnabell 1826: i). In doing so, he added, he was riding a larger wave of multifaceted cultural progress that included a growing number of literary and educational initiatives and institutions whose mutually reinforcing contributions were laying the groundwork for the literary field within which periodicals operated. One decade after *The Acadian*, *The Pearl: Devoted to Polite Literature, Science, and Religion* (Halifax, 1837), which was published by Cunnabell's young brother William, made strikingly similar claims, both about 'the new and important era' of modern periodicals generally and about its own local significance. 'Few publications of the age are more popular and influential than those which are entitled, periodical and miscellaneous,' it declared. But 'although Nova Scotia is not behind her sister provinces in the variety and general excellence of her periodical publications, yet to this hour she does not possess a single respectable journal devoted chiefly to the diffusion of literary and scientific information', an 'urgent want' that its presence would do much to rectify (W. Cunnabell 1837: 8).

This sense of the literary magazine's ability to serve and promote the needs of the emergent colonial communities was nowhere better expressed than in Nahum Mower's Montreal-based *Canadian Magazine and Literary Repository* (1823–5), which articulated a seemingly contradictory purpose: both to represent colonial culture and to conjure it into being. This 'if you build it they will come' scenario is pursued by the magazine in its figuration of Upper Canada as yet in its infancy, a metaphor which positioned the magazine as nurturer and instructor. While the editor claimed that the colony of Upper Canada 'still bears the impress of infancy on her brow, and the stamp of uncultivated wildness on her forehead', he anticipated 'the time . . . when her present condition will be remembered no more' (Mower 1823a: 5–6).

By the completion of the first volume of the magazine, it appeared that this fantasy had been accomplished, in part, one is to assume, through the intervention of *The Canadian Magazine* itself. The Preface appended to the conclusion of the first volume, dated 31 December 1823, issued a thank you to its readers for supporting the magazine through 'this early period of its progress' (Mower 1823b, n.p.). Its goal, the editor proclaimed, was to 'develop the moral and physical history of this vast colony. . . . the only British CONTINENTAL Colony in the Western hemisphere, which has yet made any progress in settlement and cultivation'. Apparently, Mower felt confident that the magazine had achieved the goals set out in the Introduction to the inaugural issue of July 1823. Not only was the progress of the colonies a sign of great things to come, but he foresaw a time when 'Canada' would become the centre and repository of knowledge. With a surge of hyperbolic euphoria, Mower set the stage for the glorious future of the colonies:

> [A]s we know not the secrets of futurity, would it not be proper to invite a portion of all those triumphs of the mind to our own distant shores. . . . Nations, who now give jurisprudence and learning to all the habitable parts of the earth, were once Colonies of a more extended Empire. . . . [W]ho knows but that the wild and unpeopled provinces of this modern Continent may become the refuge of the sciences and the mother of the arts? (Mower 1823a: 4)

As this fantasy of manifest destiny would have it, Canada would become the new centre (and preserver) of British intellectual achievement, surpassing the mother country in the same way that Britain itself had once eclipsed the Roman Empire.

The epic tone of *The Canadian Magazine and Literary Repository* would be picked up by periodicals in subsequent decades. A. Crossman's *The Canadian Casket*, for example, included a remarkable piece entitled 'Canadian Literature' in June 1832, in which the editor lamented the fact that 'Canadians have resembled more than a century past, persons who have been removed in childhood from the city to a desert, and forgetful of the illustrious home and parentage from which they sprung' (Crossman 1832: 119). Similar to Sibbald's call for Canadians to stand up and embrace their literary-cultural pedigree, *The Canadian Casket* envisioned its audience as living in a kind of trance: 'Regarding themselves as a new race of beings, they have slumbered in the dream of neglectful self-distrust' and have been 'long awaking to a sense of intellectual duty'. If the inhabitants of the colonies are thus infected by a form of colonial somnambulance, the invigorating presence of a literary magazine, and an editor perspicacious enough to perceive what ails his community, will provide the 'incentives to provoke the exertion of their powers' (Crossman 1832: 119).

Such thoughts were echoed in Wyllys Smyth's *Canadian Garland* (1832–3),[2] which thanked the 'enlightened community' whose 'fostering care' had nurtured it into existence, and stood 'in unison', it claimed, alongside this 'young, free, and rising country ... in the triumph of perseverance and industry' (Smyth 1833: 183). The editor proceeds to align the history of *The Garland* with the progress of Canada, in a story of epic triumph and conquest: 'As the army of Hannibal on the flowery plains of Italy, gazed with undaunted eyes on the bleak and snow-clad cliffs of the Alps, ... so may we ... look back on our journey of editorship.' The editor hails his contemporaries whose publications 'f[e]ll in battle', while *The Garland* has 'trod on their ruin to triumph and renown'. And then, reaching a pitch of enthusiasm, Smyth situates *The Garland* at the very centre of the epic, by focusing the reader's imaginative view on the literal location of his printing shop in Hamilton, Upper Canada:

> Is it not curious to remember that a century ago the solitary forest stood undisturbed where now we enjoy all life's luxury? Then the wild deer stood in wild fixedness ... or snuffed in the distance his foe, the wolf; then the golden-plumaged turkey gambolled on the prostrate ancient trees ... on the spot where we now strike five hundred numbers of the Garland. (Smyth 1833: 183)

The culmination of this civilising momentum, the article continues, is that 'We yet may become great in Literature and Fame' (Smyth 1833: 183).

William Sibbald's *Canadian Magazine* (1833) struck an equally heroic note that fused an emphasis on the importance of the broader historical context with a dramatic evocation of his own extraordinary personal devotion, seizing on the present moment as an ideal opportunity to move history forward, even if the task remained a daunting one. In 'The Editor's Address, to the Inhabitants of Upper and Lower Canada', Sibbald declared that 'this country, with its Churches, Houses, Shops, Signs, names, and manners, is no longer "the Land of Strangers" – it is Europe, with only one difference – means to gratify a love of reading, and intellectual acquirement' (Sibbald 1833a: 1). The Canadian provinces might not offer the same 'food to the craving mind', Sibbald allowed, but the conditions that would redress this lack were changing rapidly as a direct result of '[t]he stream of emigration [that has] continued to flow, and encreased until it has become a mighty flood. ... Echoes are crying from the rocks, while all is bustle, life, and joy' (Sibbald 1833a: 1). Sibbald posited his magazine as the perfect venture to fill the gap, acting as both voice and ear – and resident genie – to the fledgling communities he served:

> Such I have been informed are your wishes and your wants. – They came to my ear in *our* native land: to gratify those wishes, and supply your wants, – friends, kindred, – all are forsaken! I have left my country – my home, for your amusement and mental entertainment. – To satisfy your angelic passion for knowledge am I come; and will try to gratify your every wish, by pleasing all ages, all ranks, and

all palates. This Magazine shall contain whatever is useful, amusing, instructive, 'lovely, and of good report'. (Sibbald 1833a: 2)

If this seemed like a lot to ask of one man, the anticipated results were worth it, as Sibbald's inspiring magic would have transformative potential:

> The boy as he reads will exclaim 'oh! was I only a man,' '[t]he courage of the soldier will be heightened,' the seaman will find new sources of strength and inspiration, '[t]he sinner will be horrified, and forever forsake the sin with which he was most grievously beset.' – The heart of the mild and elegant shall flutter, tears coursing down the delicate cheek. (Sibbald 1833a: 2–3)

Few accounts matched Sibbald's rhetoric of elevated sacrifice, yet his emphasis on the importance of his task, in terms of both the challenges he faced and the potential benefits involved, was a widely shared feature of periodicals' accounts of their own role within these colonies. Indeed, by the fourth issue of *The Canadian Magazine*, Sibbald's notice to his readers articulates his sense that his ambition has been accomplished. Not only has he fostered the work of local authors and sought to 'amuse, instruct, and benefit the community . . . and the contributions of valued friends' (Sibbald 1833b: 381), but he has achieved 'his first object': 'to promote the cause of Canadian Literature' (Sibbald 1833b: 382).

The editor of *The Montreal Museum* (1832–4), Mary Gosselin, likewise sought to overcome derogatory representations of cultural life in the colonies, proclaiming herself 'severely wounded by the sarcastic remarks of uninformed strangers, on our defective education, our slight acquaintance with literature' (Gosselin 1832: 1). Because such critics have attributed this state of affairs to the fact that 'in the Canadas there is not a single Literary Journal' (Gosselin 1832: 1) – an assertion whose inaccuracy was belied by the sheer number of journals that made this sort of claim – the editor establishes it as her mission to administer to these needs by 'open[ing] a field to literary adventurers' by and for their Canadian readers (Gosselin 1833: 128). *The Museum*'s professed object was not only to facilitate 'the advancement and happiness of their native or their chosen land' (Gosselin 1832: 2), but also to create a literary predisposition among readers themselves. This circularity, by which 'educating' readers would bring those readers (as writers) into being, is a common thread in many of these accounts. In the case of *The Montreal Museum*, Gosselin announced her hope 'that a taste for letters may . . . be confirmed, by furnishing a medium through which the young aspirant to Literary honour shall become distinguished from his less gifted contemporaries, and . . . incite him to such exertions as may ultimately lead to excellence' (Gosselin 1832: 2). In order to accomplish this dream of literary greatness, of course, the magazine required writers, even embryonic authors who didn't know themselves to be authors – who were yet untried and unaware that 'the reward of an undying fame' lay within their grasp (Gosselin 1832: 2). Thus, *The Montreal Museum* launched its appeal at the conclusion of its opening introduction for 'the Ladies and Gentlemen of Canada to aid us in our labours by sending us the fruits of their leisure hours' (Gosselin 1832: 3).

The Canadian public's intellectual torpor, figured as being in need of robust editorial intervention, was also invoked by *The Canadian Garland*, which, in its notice 'To the Public' in September 1832, expressed its goal 'to call into action the literary energies of the Canadas ... [which have] for a long time laid in sluggish inactivity, merely for the want of an emenating [*sic*] medium' (Smyth 1832a: n.p.). Establishing its crucial role in securing the literary future of the colonies, *The Canadian Garland* asserted that 'many a polished author is compelled to ... remain in obscurity' for want of a magazine to reawaken their dormant talents: 'To expiate this and to elide the rock that has long concealed the diamonds of our country, we now protend [*sic*] our proposals to a generous public' (Smyth 1832a: n.p.). Like *The Canadian Magazine* and *The Canadian Magazine and Literary Repository*, *The Canadian Garland* saw itself as being at a pivotal moment in history, when 'the progress of science, and the cultivation of literature has had considerable effect in changing the manners of our nation ... [W]e have now arrived at that state of society, in which those faculties of the human mind that have beauty and elegance for their objects, begin to unfold themselves' (Smyth 1832b: 7). The magazine was set to capitalise on these hidden resources, even though 'perfection ... is not the work of a day', by which it would 'cherish the original talent of our country' and achieve the more weighty task to 'sustain *Canadian* Literature' (Smyth 1832b: 7).

It is not surprising, then, that in 1852, Mary Jane Kratzmann's *The Provincial: or, Halifax Monthly Magazine* (1852–3) featured an opening address that brushed aside the fear 'that no purely literary undertaking will succeed in Halifax' (Kratzmann 1852a: 2). It followed this with an 'Editorial Colloquy' between the editor and a fictionalised local sceptic named 'Snaffle'. Snaffle taunts the editor by mocking the 'mad scheme' and doomed venture of founding a magazine in the colonies and alludes to the local context (in this case Nova Scotia) as an intellectual backwater: 'So you are actually going to try your hand at a Literary Magazine. ... [T]he difficulty will be, to persuade the woods and forests, or the denizens thereof to become subscribers' (Kratzmann 1852b: 3). Undaunted, the editor gamely points out that while *The Provincial*'s content may not be 'equal to *Blackwood* or the *Edinburgh Review*', nevertheless contributions by 'distinguished Colonists' will possess deep interest to local inhabitants. As she puts it, 'among these forests there are a million and a half of human hearts, not unwilling to be either instructed or amused, if we can only reach them' (Kratzmann 1852b: 3).

This conjunction of an uphill battle and auspicious timing elevated editors' sense of the larger value of their public role in helping to nurture the cultural health of the colony. The opening address of John Kent's Toronto-based *Canadian Literary Magazine* expressed similar thoughts about the challenges and potential success of periodicals in a colonial context in its first number of April 1833. Reflecting on his own 'preconceived ideas', the editor insisted that he had not arrived in the colony expecting 'to find the Canadians an ignorant people, plunged in mental sloth and intellectual darkness', but even so, he had been happily surprised. 'I find them advanced in civilisation, beyond my expectations. In the remotest woods I behold the conveniences and comforts of life gathered together, from all the four quarters of the globe' (Kent 1833: 1). The settlers' struggle with adversity may have imbued them with a practical spirit, but this, he insisted, should not be mistaken for literary and cultural indifference.

For Kent, Canadians were essentially diamonds in the rough, who retained an ancestral predisposition to literary sensibility:

The severe trials of an early settler, and a daily warfare with mental and physical difficulties, may have superinduced a crust of roughness over the outward man; but the same feelings which the settler brought with him from his native land, or which the Canadian-born inherits from his parents, exist, though perchance it may be, in a latent state. (Kent 1833: 1)

The fledgling state of this readership, in which an intrinsic literary thirst (carried with them from their imperial home) was covered by the 'crust' of often daunting pragmatic challenges, heightened the role of local periodicals as vehicles uniquely capable of bringing writing into the broader public domain. Brimming with an intrinsic curiosity beneath this pragmatic crust, these settlers, Kent argues, will 'welcome with pleasure any honest chronicler who . . . will rescue from oblivion's stream those floating fragments, which some Canadian Hume or Robertson will hereafter search for, when composing the annals of his country' (Kent 1833: 1).

It may have been premature to look for great national historians like the British writers David Hume and William Robertson, though this did not lessen the importance of rescuing the 'fragments' that would one day become the primary material of future historians' epic national tales. Nevertheless, Kent is insistent that Canadian locations have literary potential, asserting that 'the events which have characterised the infancy of this extensive country afford ample materials for the Historian, the Poet, and the Novelist' (Kent 1833: 1). For Kent, as for others, it was the role of the literary magazine to collect these local fragments, but he reminded his readers that this embrace of the local would necessarily be a collective effort, dependent on 'the support of every individual who feels a desire that Canada should possess a Literature of its own' (Kent 1833: 2).

A similar archival impetus animated Mower's *Canadian Magazine and Literary Repository*. As he announced in the preface to the fourth volume in 1825: 'Periodical publications are the germs of historical details. They catch events as they rise' (Mower 1825: n.p.). Like *The Canadian Literary Magazine*'s anticipation of 'some Canadian Hume or Robertson', Mower insisted that periodicals constituted 'an archive for giving permanency to literary and scientific pursuits' (Mower 1823b: n.p.), furnishing future historians with 'data' that had both an immediacy and a 'fidelity' which the 'future compiler of history' could never hope to equal (Mower 1825: n.p.). Still too early to be epic, Canada's history-in-progress was being compiled in real time by those in the literary community who were willing to help.

But this participatory emphasis highlighted the importance of periodicals' related task of nurturing the literary communities (both readers and authors) who were to play this role. Like *The Canadian Literary Magazine*, it insisted that periodicals' greatest value lay in their ability to 'diffuse a spirit for reading and research' in contemporary readers by serving as 'the epitomes of the literature, arts, and sciences of the days in which they appear' (Mower 1825: n.p.). In doing so, they also intensified the age's spirit of intellectual fermentation by fostering broad public debate about new theories and discoveries which guaranteed that 'no new position is advanced without mature deliberation' (Mower 1825: n.p.). If, it continued, 'the patronage such publications have met with in any country has been considered as a pretty sure criterion of the estimation in which it holds literature, and the degree of civilisation to which it has reached', then the attention that it had itself received from both 'readers and contributors' must be welcome evidence that 'this Colony will soon rank for the encouragement of periodical publications as high as any part of the favoured empire to which it belongs' (Mower 1825: n.p.).

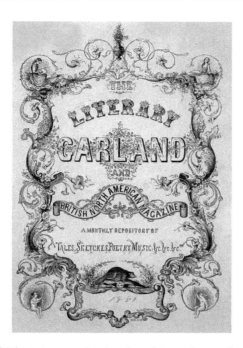

Figure 1.1 Cover of *The Literary Garland and British North American Magazine*. Courtesy of the authors.

These kinds of sentiments were nowhere better expressed than in John Lovell's *The Literary Garland*, the longest-running and most successful of Canada's pre-Confederation literary magazines (see Figure 1.1). In his view, the refinements of the day demanded the support of a literary magazine that would answer the intellectual and cultural needs of the burgeoning local communities. 'Every day furnishes additional evidence', the introduction to the second volume agreed, 'that, in the Canadian Provinces, literature, and the more elegant refinements of the age, are forcing themselves into that position . . . which their importance to its enlightened character warrants them to hold' (Lovell 1839d: 1).

Echoing the accounts of other editors in the need to overcome disparaging notions of colonial education and literature, *The Literary Garland* addressed this prejudice head on: 'We have been often told that Canada is not a literary country—that the people have neither leisure nor inclination for the pursuits of literature,' Lovell mused in the Introduction to its New Series in January 1843 (Lovell 1843: 1). Like the *British North American*'s memory of an earlier, more difficult era, *The Garland*'s forward-looking account allowed that 'there was a time—perhaps some twenty years since—when such an assertion might have been truly made; when the poor emigrant, yielding to the stern laws of necessity, was forced to devote his time and energies to obtain a provision for his family. That time has gone, and we hail a new era, more favourable to the diffusion of polite and useful literature' (Lovell 1843: 1). *The Garland* offered its own considerable success as 'ample proof' that people were seizing on their new-found leisure as an opportunity 'to cultivate their mental powers. . . . The fact that it has been sustained from original sources is proof sufficient that the germ exists among us, and that it requires but careful cultivation ultimately to produce abundant and tempting fruit' (Lovell 1843: 2).

The Literary Garland's ability to nurture local authors and 'original' submissions was hailed as a unique feature of its contribution to local literary culture, although this aim was paramount in most of the Canadian magazines of the period. Thus, at the core of *The Garland*'s grandiose visions of cultural progress was an urgent emphasis on periodicals' important role in soliciting local submissions. They had launched the magazine, *The Garland* reminded readers at the close of the fourth volume, 'as an experiment . . . with the intention of fairly testing the problem, whether such a work could be sustained by resident or native writers' (Lovell 1842b: 579), an experiment 'in which all who are friends to literature in Canada are interested' (Lovell 1842b: 580). Nor was the success of this 'experiment' always a given. 'Only a very few years ago, when speaking of the probabilities of success, in favour of a magazine entirely devoted to literary subjects,' it reflected in its April 1842 edition, 'the most frequent remark was that writers could not be found, able and willing to contribute to its original contents. Well-founded as, at the time, the opinion seemed, we have lived to see it most pleasingly disproved' (Lovell 1842a: 240).

The Literary Garland was easily the most successful literary magazine of the period, but this sense of a collective mission, 'calling out the energies of *our* country' (Lovell 1843: 4), was widely shared throughout the provinces. Announcing in its first number that 'Progress is the motto of the age and the Province of New Brunswick is quite alive to its importance', *The Guardian, A Monthly Magazine of Education and General Literature* (St. John, 1860), edited by two young teachers, Edward Manning and Robert Aiken, devoted itself to 'afford[ing] an opportunity for those, who wish to improve themselves by writing, to bring their works before the public' (Aiken and Manning 1860: 1–2). The opening number of *The Canadian Literary Magazine* had similarly declared that 'the aid of numerous and talented contributors, male and female', would be crucial, though it warned that it would 'reject all outrageous embellishments and tinsel trimmings . . . in the fashion of "spectre-mongering" Monk Lewis' or the sorts of '[r]eligious and political controversy' that would 'interrupt the peaceful pursuits of Literature' (Kent 1833: 2). 'Original communications from correspondents are respectfully solicited, which shall be carefully attended to,' *The Gaspé Magazine and Instructive Miscellany* (1849) declared, though it reminded its readers that as a 'literary undertaking', it too would 'studiously avoid any participation in the Politics at present engrossing public attention' (Anon. 1849, *The Gaspé Magazine*: 1).

Again and again, editors and readers would insist on the need to include local writers, and, more specifically, identifiably local subject matter. A letter to the *Cabinet of Literature* (Toronto, 1838–9) from 1839, for example, asks the editor to establish 'a department devoted to local *Literature* . . . [which would] elicit much literary talent that would otherwise lie dormant' (Stephens 1839: 192). *The Canadian Casket* regretted the absence of original Canadian submissions and in December 1831 established a prize (three pounds currency) 'to the writer of the best *Original Tale*, written expressly for the Casket, and having its scene laid in Canada' (Crossman 1831: [29]). Likewise, many journals, such as *The Canadian Magazine and Literary Repository*, insisted that their pages would 'contain *original* matter' of local character to appeal to their target readers (Mower 1823a: 8). To encourage local submissions – and claim the interest of local readers – many periodicals established regular sections devoted to Canadian topics, from *The Canadian Review and Magazine*'s regular feature of 'Canadian Legends' to *Barker's* 'Legends of the Early Settlements' to the *Cabinet*'s 'Border Tales' to *The Canadian Casket*'s 'Select Canadian Tales', which opened each issue from May 1832 onwards and which bore as its epigraph 'To hold the mirror up to Nature'. It is no coincidence, then, that in the subtitle of every issue of Montreal's *The Scribbler* is an assertion of its dedication to 'local subjects'.

These concerns are echoed in *The Montreal Museum* as it launched its case to solicit the work of local authors. 'As we cannot draw upon the legendary lore of ages past', the second issue asserts, 'imagination must be invoked to supply the deficiency, and that creative faculty of mind, would, if so directed, invest with an intense interest, scenes of a less romantic shade, than those to be met with in Canada' (Gosselin 1833: 128). *The Museum*'s sense that Canadian material needed to be *invented*, and the mundane details of geography and other 'uninteresting' subjects be transformed by imagination's 'witching wand to enliven and animate the scenes' (Gosselin 1833: 128), echoes Sibbald's self-description as a presiding genie over Canada's cultural future.

The Literary Garland cited its ability to offer these sorts of 'original sources' as a sign of the colonies' growing cultural maturity, but it also embraced the duty of proactively cultivating this local body of contributors as one of its most important tasks. The role of periodicals, it suggested, was not just to provide a showcase for local writers but to actively promote these literary resources. Insisting that 'the richest ground yields not its fruits untilled', *The Garland*'s opening address embraced its double role as both an archive and an inspirational presence. Providing a public venue for these 'native gems' simultaneously 'preserv[ed] them from oblivion' and 'assist[ed] in fostering the spirit of literary enterprise' by 'urging the authors themselves, to produce something still more valuable than any that have hitherto appeared' (Lovell 1838: [4]). Likening the contemptuous taunt of a British reviewer – 'Who reads an American book?' – to an 'Enchanter's Wand' that 'called spirits from the deep [so that]. . . . [p]oets and novelists sprang into being as if by magic', *The Garland* insisted that its central purpose remained 'to assist in calling out the energies of *our* country. And it is by united exertion only that we can succeed' (Lovell 1843: 3–4).

Nor was this determination to 'nurture and cultivate the infant literature of our country' mere rhetorical posturing (Lovell 1843: 4). Both *The Canadian Garland*'s and *The Literary Garland*'s brief 'To Correspondents' section at the end of each number actively encouraged contributors to submit, even though they may be forced to wait to see their works in print, or to revise in cases where they had been initially unsuccessful. 'We are under many obligations for the favours we have received in the shape of contributions, in prose and poetry, to the pages of *The Garland*,' the latter acknowledged, 'and if some of them occasionally remain unnoticed, we trust that none of our correspondents will look upon themselves as overlooked' (Lovell 1839a: 240). Sometimes individual authors needed specific encouragement. 'Although we beg to decline the acceptance of the lines of "Maria"', it noted at the end of one number, 'we must express our conviction that the pen which produced the latter piece, requires only a little practice to become an ornament to our Canadian literature' (Lovell 1839b: 336).

For many of these literary journals, this self-assumed responsibility to nurture local talents extended from a desire to encourage native authors to the more ambitious goal of founding a collective body of literature: not just encouraging a set of individual contributors but helping to establish a recognisable national (or, before Confederation, provincial) tradition. This aim was anticipated early on, in 1826, when *The Canadian Review and Magazine* (Montreal, 1824–6) published an entire piece entitled 'Writers and Literature of Canada' (Anon. 1826, *The Canadian Review*: 189). By 1833, 'The Editor's Address to the Public' in the opening number of *The Canadian Literary Magazine* closed by appealing for 'the support of every individual who feels a desire that Canada should possess a Literature of its own' (Kent 1833: 2). Six years later, the final number of *The Literary Garland*'s first volume opened by expressing their own hope 'that through our humble exertions might be laid a corner-stone to Canadian literature' (Lovell 1839c: 537). In a review of Susanna Moodie's new publication, *Enthusiasm and Other Poems*, later in the same number, it hailed the news that Moodie had decided 'to publish a new edition, for circulation in the Canadian Provinces ... as another "sign of the times", [which] cannot fail to afford much gratification to all those who desire to elevate the standard of our Colonial literature' ('Our Table' 1839: 579). 'It can scarcely be doubted', it added, 'that in these Provinces, literature will rapidly advance and permanently flourish. There is no community, either in the old or new world, in which there is a greater comparative degree of talent and useful knowledge' ('Our Table' 1839: 579). For *The Literary Garland*, this 'long struggle in aid of Canadian literature' was a very self-conscious task (Lovell 1850: 586). 'A Word at Parting', in its final number after a fourteen-year run, offered a 'pleasurable' retrospective glance at the success with which it had approached 'the design for which the Garland was established—that of fostering and encouraging the growth of Canadian literature' (Lovell 1851: 572).

In 'A Few Words to Our Readers' at the beginning of its second volume, *The Provincial* proudly reflected on the success that its first volume had met with despite its own 'considerable hesitation' at the outset. Supported by the contributions of 'ladies and gentlemen ... known and unknown', it could revel in its status as a fine example of 'the almost universal feeling in favour of the rise and progress of a native literature', not just in Nova Scotia but in 'Canada, New Brunswick and the other Colonies' (Kratzmann 1853: 1). This provincial sense of affiliation was reinforced by an underlying sense of their shared identity as British North American colonies, a level of identification that was consolidated by their mutual (and sometimes anxious) relations with the United States. Periodical writers dedicated themselves to what they repeatedly described as the neutral goal of avoiding politics while fostering a local literature, and in doing so strengthening the links that Benedict Anderson has cited between nineteenth-century print culture and a burgeoning sense of national identity. Ironically, periodicals may have played a more effective political role precisely to the extent that they did disavow politics: contributing to the ideological consolidation of a colonial hegemony by naturalising and strengthening a sense of settler community. As we have seen, *The Provincial*'s themes reverberated in the many periodicals appearing throughout the various parts of British North America. Like many others, it aspired to be a glorious example and a driving force in a rapidly developing proto-national literature within a closely linked set of colonies that were still years from Confederation.

Without a doubt, the metaphor of manifest destiny and enchantment in many of these periodicals bore material results. The community of writers and readers in early Canada certainly sustained and encouraged literary expression in the pre-Confederation period, launching the careers of such figures as John Richardson, Catharine Parr Traill and Susanna Moodie, who would become celebrated authors of the time. By the time the early debates about Confederation began, from the early 1860s onwards, the ground was well set for the nascent British North American sensibility to take hold. In a sense, Sibbald, Kent and many of the editors of these early ventures achieved what they set out to do.

Gosselin closed the first issue of *The Montreal Museum* in December 1832 by explaining the symbolism of the frontispiece to their magazine, encapsulating the spirit of the new Canadian age which these early adventurers into periodical publication felt themselves to be sustaining and creating:

> [T]he pillar represents the country yielding its support to literature, the figures at the base, emblematic of the arts and sciences are entwining their ornamental wreaths around it, whilst genius at the summit has broken through the surrounding clouds of prejudice and indifference. We are too much interested to offer an opinion on the excellence of the execution, but it possesses one merit . . . it is the production of Canada. (Gosselin 1832: 1)

If the pillar represents the country and the figures are the arts and sciences, the implication was that it is the compiler of all of these elements, the magazine itself, which enables genius to break through. While the editors applaud the illustration as 'the production of Canada' – not of a *Canadian*, but of *Canada* – this could be said of all these early periodicals, which saw themselves as mediums not only for Canadian readers and authors, but for a projected future 'Canada' that was about to materialise.

Notes

1. The three colonies that would merge to form the Dominion of Canada in 1867 were Nova Scotia, New Brunswick and Canada, the latter made up of what, prior to 1841, had been Upper and Lower Canada (today the Canadian provinces of Ontario and Quebec). Because we are discussing anglophone periodical publications that range from the 1820s through to the 1850s, the designation 'Canada' can refer to slightly different political boundaries depending on where the publication is based. Nevertheless, many of the editors of these publications regarded the colonies to be united in spirit – and often say so directly – with similar goals and cultural affiliations.
2. This periodical is not to be confused with *The Literary Garland* (1838–51), discussed later in this chapter and in greater detail by Fariha Shaikh in Chapter 2.

Bibliography

Aiken, Robert, and Edward Manning (1860), 'To Our Readers', *The Guardian, A Monthly Magazine of Education and General Literature*, January, 1–2.
Anderson, Benedict (1991), *Imagined Communities: Reflections on the Origin and Spread of Nationalism*, London and New York: Verso.
Anon. (1826), 'Writers and Literature of Canada', *The Canadian Review and Magazine*, September, 189–96.
—— (1849), *The Gaspé Magazine, and Instructive Miscellany*, August, 1–2.
Crossman, A. (1831), 'Literary Premiums', *The Canadian Casket*, 3 December, [29].
—— (1832), 'Canadian Literature', *The Canadian Casket*, 16 June, 119.

Cunnabell, Jacob (1826), 'Preface', *The Acadian Magazine*, July, i–ii.
Cunnabell, William (1837), 'The Pearl: A Select Literary, Scientific, Religious, and Miscellaneous Journal', *The Pearl: Devoted to Polite Literature, Science, and Religion*, 3 June, 8.
Gosselin, Mary (1832), 'To the Readers of the Museum', *The Montreal Museum, or, Journal of Literature and Arts*, December, 1–3.
—— (1833), 'To Readers, and Correspondents', *The Montreal Museum, or, Journal of Literature and Arts*, January, 127–8.
Harvey, D. C. (1933), 'The Intellectual Awakening of Nova Scotia', *Dalhousie Review*, 33, 1–22.
Kent, John (1833), 'The Editor's Address to the Public', *The Canadian Literary Magazine*, April, 1–2.
Kratzmann, Mary Jane (1852a), 'Our Address', *The Provincial: or, Halifax Monthly Magazine*, January, 1–2.
—— (1852b), 'Editorial Colloquy', *The Provincial: or, Halifax Monthly Magazine*, January, 3–7.
—— (1853), 'A Few Words to Our Readers', *The Provincial: or, Halifax Monthly Magazine*, January, 1–3.
Lovell, John (1838), 'To Our Readers', *The Literary Garland*, December, [3–4].
—— (1839a), *The Literary Garland*, April, 240.
—— (1839b), 'To Correspondents', *The Literary Garland*, June, 336.
—— (1839c), 'To Our Readers', *The Literary Garland*, November, 537–8.
—— (1839d), 'To Our Readers', *The Literary Garland*, December, 1–2.
—— (1842a), 'Our Table', *The Literary Garland*, April, 240.
—— (1842b), 'To the Readers of The Garland', *The Literary Garland*, November, 579–80.
—— (1843), 'Introduction to the New Series of The Garland', *The Literary Garland*, January, 1–4.
—— (1850), 'The Close of the Year: To Our Readers', *The Literary Garland*, December, 586.
—— (1851), 'A Word at Parting', *The Literary Garland*, December, 572.
MacDonald, Mary Lu (1993), 'English and French-language periodicals and the development of a literary culture in early Victorian Canada', *Victorian Periodicals Review*, 26.4, 221–7.
Mower, Nahum (1823a), 'Introduction', *The Canadian Magazine and Literary Repository*, July, 1–8.
—— (1823b), 'Preface', *The Canadian Magazine and Literary Repository*, July, n.p.
—— (1825), 'Preface to the Fourth Volume', *The Canadian Magazine and Literary Repository*, January, n.p.
'Our Table' (1839), *The Literary Garland*, November, 579–80.
Sibbald, William (1833a), 'The Editor's Address, to the Inhabitants of Upper and Lower Canada', *The Canadian Magazine*, January, 1–4.
—— (1833b), 'To the Subscribers for The Canadian Magazine, and to the Public', *The Canadian Magazine*, April, 381–3.
Smyth, Wyllys (1832a), 'To the Public', *The Canadian Garland*, 15 September, n.p.
—— (1832b), 'To Our Patrons', *The Canadian Garland*, 15 September, 7.
—— (1833), 'Canadian Garland, Second Volume – Enlarged', *The Canadian Garland*, 20 July, 183.
Stephens, W. A. (1839), 'To the Publisher of the Border Tales', *Cabinet of Literature*, June, 192.
Vincent, Thomas Brewer, Sandra Alston and Eli MacLaren (2004), 'Magazines in English', in Patricia Lockhart Fleming, Gilles Gallichan and Yvan Lamonde (eds), *History of the Book in Canada, Volume 1: Beginnings to 1840*, Toronto: University of Toronto Press, 240–9.
Ward, Edmund (1831), 'To the Public', *The British North American Magazine, and Colonial Journal*, February, 1–2.

2

Early Colonial Periodicals in Nineteenth-Century Canada: *The Literary Garland* in Context

Fariha Shaikh

Introduction

In December 1838, a new periodical, *The Literary Garland*, announced its arrival on the Canadian literary scene. As its name suggested, literary pursuits were at the heart of the journal's ambitions. The editor, John Gibson, declared in the opening address that '[We] have no hesitation in contending, that with the true prosperity of every country, its literature is indissolubly associated' ('To Our Reader' 1838: 3). Accordingly, the aim of the journal is to 'look upon the literary garden' to find 'native gems', and to 'foster' 'literary blossoms':

> Be the task ours, to gather up of these the most beautiful, and by giving them a 'local habitation and a name,' in the pages of the GARLAND, as well as preserve them from oblivion, as assist in fostering the spirit of literary enterprise, and, it may be, aid in urging the authors themselves, to produce something still more valuable than any that have hitherto appeared. ('To Our Reader' 1838: 4)

In making these claims, Gibson was aware of the problems that faced the production of a new literary journal. While he candidly 'acknowledged' the 'many' 'difficulties to be surmounted' in launching such a periodical, he was determined to have 'no fear' in the face of those who 'deem, that in a country yet in infancy, with little storied or traditional love, the sphere of our action must be circumscribed, and that our efforts like those of our predecessors, will end in failure'. Taking the decision to commit to the project 'for one year at least' during which 'our efforts will not be relaxed', Gibson states that if after this time the 'GARLAND shall not have fathered a stem sufficiently powerful to support itself, it must fall and wither, as has been the fate of a more beautiful and classic wreath' ('To Our Reader' 1838: 3). However, *The Garland* outdid both Gibson's and its readers' expectations, and ran monthly from 1838 before finally folding in 1851.

The Literary Garland's print run of thirteen years made it unique in a periodical marketplace where most Canadian periodicals lasted for only a few years. Canadian printing culture through much of the early nineteenth century was dominated by gazettes and heralds. Such gazettes and heralds were necessary to the governance and infrastructure of the developing colony. As Henry Gundy notes, from the mid-eighteenth century onwards, almost 'all books and pamphlets published in Canada . . . were produced to meet the needs of government, of the law courts, the church and the schools. It was not until the early years of the nineteenth century that a reading public emerged, interested in general literature and capable of supporting independent bookstores' (Gundy 1965: 31).

By the late 1820s and early 1830s, periodicals were beginning to emerge that supported the development and growth of a local literary scene. The editor of *The Canadian Literary Magazine*, for example, John Kent, invited 'the support of every individual who feels a desire that Canada should possess a literature of its own' ('The Editor's Address to the Public' 1833: 1). This push towards a distinctly literary trend within periodical publishing was partly due to the conjoined phenomena in the 1820s of the rise of middle-class settler colonial emigration and the growth and importation of printing presses from Britain.[1] As Carole Gerson argues, the '[m]obility of editors and writers has always been a significant feature of Canadian literary history' (Gerson 1989: 9).

Reflecting on the rising literary interest in the colony in the mid-century, Susanna Moodie, one of the most prolific contributors to nineteenth-century Canadian periodical literature, writes that '[t]wenty years ago Canada was not in a condition to foster a literature of her own' as the country was '[p]eopled almost entirely by U. E. [United Empire] loyalists, or poor emigrants from the mother country [who] had no leisure for the study of books, and no money to spare for the purchase of them' (Moodie 1853: xi). However, sustained efforts over a few decades through various emigration schemes had 'strengthened the British foundation of literary endeavour' (Klinck 1976: 159).

This chapter explores how this growth in literary interest and pursuits in early nineteenth-century Canadian periodical culture was embedded in discourses of settler colonialism and emigration. A growing number of scholars have argued for a re-examination of the integral relationship between periodical culture and settler colonialism over the last few years. Rather than focusing on the novel as a genre of mobility, critics have begun to reorient our attention to the foundational part that periodical culture played in the formation of settler colonies. As Jason Rudy argues, '[i]n early nineteenth-century colonial cities around the world', it was 'first newspapers and then magazines [that] were largely responsible for establishing and maintaining a sense of literary culture' (Rudy 2017: 46). Jude Piesse points to the ways in which periodical culture propagated 'ideologies of "settlement" – which stressed the importance of domesticity, affective place, and links to the metropolitan centre', while at the same time 'struggled to contain an uneasiness about the destabilizing, unruly and emotionally disorienting acts of migration with which it engaged' (Piesse 2016: 3–4). From even before emigrants arrived in the colonies, the production of periodicals on the voyage out transformed the journey into a space where emigrants could practise a provisional form of settlement prior to the actual task of settling in the colonies (Shaikh 2018: 63–94).

Despite this resurgent interest in the connections between the British Empire and periodical studies, little has been done to frame early nineteenth-century Canadian literary periodical culture within the framework of settler colonialism.[2] Focus on Canadian periodicals has tended to come within the scope of these studies alongside other genres such as poetry and novels, to fall under categories as broad as 'literary publishing' (Gundy 1976: 188–202), or the broader print culture of the colony

(Gerson 1989).[3] As Carl Ballstadt notes, these 'persistent and constant search[es] for a distinctive Canadian literature in the nineteenth and early twentieth centuries' were undertaken by 'writers who displayed serious concern for the tendencies and possibilities of literature in Canada, often within a context of literary movements elsewhere as well as within the context of English literary traditions' (Ballstadt 1975: xiv, xii). While this provides an important context for how the periodical marketplace coexisted alongside broader literary publishing trends in nineteenth-century Canada, these historical surveys neither focus solely on periodicals, nor focus on the attendant logic of settler colonialism. By contrast, while it is important to recognise that the growth of periodical publishing was at the 'heart of the dialogue', 'encouraging literary endeavours and in the general improvement of the cultural climate', it is also worth acknowledging the crucial role that literary periodical culture played in fashioning settler sensibilities as they emerged and developed over the course of the first half of the nineteenth century (Ballstadt 1975: xiv).

This chapter aims to uncover this relationship between early nineteenth-century Canadian periodical culture and settler colonialism through three interlinked approaches. Firstly, it will place the short-lived nature of precursors to *The Literary Garland*, such as *The Canadian Magazine and Literary Repository* (1823–5), the *Canadian Review and Literary and Historical Journal* (1824–5) and *The Scribbler* (1821–7), within the context of contemporary colonial and transatlantic publishing landscapes. Secondly, by uncovering the connections the editors of these earlier periodicals had to emigration schemes and societies, the chapter will demonstrate how these periodicals acted as propaganda for settler colonial migration. Thirdly, it will explore the ways in which *The Literary Garland* offered its middle-class readers a model of colonial settlement through its attempts to cultivate genteel literary tastes and pursuits. By attending closely to the work of Susanna Moodie, one of the periodical's most famous and prolific contributors, the chapter ends with an exploration of how periodical culture afforded such women the opportunity to shape the cultural and literary sensibilities within the context of their settler communities.

Copyright and Competition

In 1823, David Chisholme, a Scottish emigrant who had arrived in Lower Canada the previous year and had taken on the editorship of the Montreal-based *Canadian Magazine and Literary Repository*, wrote in the 'Preface' to the periodical's first issue that

> All we would wish to advance on the present occasion is simply that, a Magazine, from its very nature, is better calculated, not only for giving stability and permanency, but spirit and enterprise to literary pursuits, than the ordinary political Journals of the day. ('Preface' 1823: n.p.)

The Canadian Magazine and Literary Repository was one of the earliest nineteenth-century literary periodicals to be published in Canada. The magazine's desire to shift the periodical marketplace from the 'ordinary political Journals of the day' to more 'literary pursuits' speaks to emerging attempts in the 1820s to cultivate a specifically literary culture within the colony. Despite its aspirations to 'giv[e] stability and permanency' to the 'spirit and enterprise' of 'literary pursuits', *The Canadian Magazine and Literary Repository* lasted only two years. A year after starting, Chisholme stated frankly the difficulties faced by editors of Canadian periodicals:

> the conductor of a periodical in Canada, has a heavier task to perform than in older countries, where he can have the assistance of men whose leisure time and independent situations admit of their turning their undivided attention to literary pursuits ... a writer who undertakes a periodical publication in Canada is more dependent upon his own talents and resources. ('The Canadian Review' 1824: 113)

Chisholme was not speaking solely of *The Canadian Magazine and Literary Repository*, but of the fate of most Canadian periodicals, which in the nineteenth century were short-lived, with an average lifespan of around two to five years. The Ontario-based *Christian Recorder*, for example, ran from 1819 to 1820, the Montreal-based *Literary Miscellany* ran from 1822 to 1823, and the Halifax-based *Acadian Magazine or Literary Mirror* ran from 1826 to 1828.

There were a number of factors that contributed to the difficulty of sustaining a literary periodical for long periods of time. Editors and publishers had to be sure that their periodicals would sell: in order to do so, they often resorted to subscription publishing, a method whereby purchasers were invited to pay for all or part of the cost of each periodical's issue or run.[4] As Gundy notes, '[b]oth newspapers and bookstores, in the early period, protected themselves against financial loss by declining to publish until an advance subscription list guaranteed enough sales to cover the printing costs' (Gundy 1965: 10). The principal difficulty that publishers had in selling their work, however, was competition from America, which flooded the Canadian market with their own works as well as cheap pirated copies of British literature. Even as late as the 1890s, copyright laws meant that firms had to wait three months between the publication of work in England and copyrighting it in Canada, which gave the American market plenty of time to produce pirated editions ('The Copyright Question' 1892: 6).

As a result of the Copyright Act, Canadian publishers resorted to publishing in Britain or in America (Gundy 1976: 196). These problems were well registered by Canadian editors and contributors to periodicals. Moodie, writing in 1853 shortly after the closure of *The Literary Garland*, writes of the sheer abundance of '[t]hese American monthlies', which were 'got up in the first style, handsomely illustrated, and composed of the best articles, selected from European and American magazines, [and] sold at such a low rate that one or the other is to be found in almost every decent house in the province. It is almost impossible for a colonial magazine to compete with them' (Moodie 1853: xvi). The editorial of the final issue of *The Literary Garland* ends on the 'hope that the day will yet come, when Canada will be able to support, not one but several periodicals ... at present the abundance and cheapness of foreign publications, render it either very difficult, or altogether impossible to compete successfully with them' ('A Word at Parting' 1851: 572).

The sheer difficulty caused by the copyright issue of maintaining a periodical written by settler emigrants for settler emigrants was felt by many editors to be a hindrance to the development of a local literary culture. For example, *The Montreal Museum* noted that

> The extraordinary facility with which American Works may be obtained, and their multiplicity, goes far to confirm this prevailing indifference towards the development

of native genius, and the increase of national respectability. Many of our friends in representing to us the hazards of our enterprize [sic], have dwelt on the cheapness, and superior execution of American Works, over any publication likely to be produced here. (Anon. 1832, *The Montreal Museum*: 1–2)

Rather than using the brief runs suffered by many Canadian periodicals to highlight the difficulties of the periodical literary marketplace (a recurring point that has already been well made), taking a longitudinal view across the careers of certain editors suggests instead a more concerted effort to promote and support the growth of a literary and national culture within early nineteenth-century Canada. This shift in perspective is important because it allows us to reframe the beginnings of Canadian periodical culture from being a series of aborted attempts to a sustained effort to drive forward literary endeavours in the colony. David Chisholme's career is a particular example of this. His emigration from Scotland to Canada afforded him career opportunities in periodical publishing and editing throughout his lifetime. A year after his arrival, he took on the editorship of the *Montreal Gazette* and *The Canadian Magazine and Literary Repository*, leaving both in 1824 to edit both the *Montreal Herald* and the *Canadian Review and Literary and Historical Journal* for two years, between 1824 and 1826 (Ballstadt 2003). From 1837 until his death in 1842, he reoccupied the editorship of the *Montreal Gazette*.

Despite Chisholme's short bursts of editorship at each of these journals, a longer history of the editorship of these journals suggests a growing network of editors in the colony. For example, Alexander James Christie, another Scotsman who had emigrated to Canada in 1817, had been the editor of the *Montreal Herald* in 1818, before Chisholme. When Chisholme stepped down from the editorship of the *Montreal Gazette* and *The Canadian Magazine and Literary Repository* in 1824, Christie took over for a short while, before moving on to become the editor of the *Bytown Gazette* from 1836 to 1843. The two men knew each other, and were initially on good terms: Chisholme invited Christie to contribute to *The Canadian Magazine and Literary Repository* while he was the editor. Under Chisholme's editorship, *The Canadian Magazine and Literary Repository* arranged material according to 'Original Papers' and 'Selected Papers'; this was a format that Christie kept when he took over in March 1824. In fact, Christie seems not to have wanted to make much of an editorial intervention when he took over: very little seems to have been made of the fact that the magazine had changed editorship apart from just a line notifying readers that 'Communications for the CANADIAN MAGAZINE, addressed to Dr. Christie, the Editor, at Mr Nickless, the Publisher, will meet with respectful attention' ('Contents of No. IX' 1824: n.p). Nevertheless, when his relationship with Chisholme fell apart, he used the magazine as a mouthpiece for denigrating Chisholme's work at the *Canadian Review and Literary and Historical Journal*, questioning in *The Canadian Magazine and Literary Repository* 'how far this writer [Chisholme] is either by talents or acquirements fitted for [the] undertaking' of the work of an editor ('The Canadian Review' 1824: 113).

Editors and Emigration Schemes

Despite personal differences between editors, both *The Canadian Magazine and Literary Repository* and the *Canadian Review and Literary and Historical Journal* were edited similarly in tone and content, aspiring to present literary content and cultivate a sense of place and pride in Canada, although not always achieving this. Colonial emigration played a significant part in this cultivation of a sense of place. This is not least because the editors themselves actively worked in supporting emigration schemes. Christie, for example, was involved in promoting settler colonial emigration through early Canadian emigration schemes, developing early settlement infrastructure, and writing emigrant guides. Christie was the Secretary of the Emigrant Society of Montreal and 'felt himself called upon, from his situation, to use every diligence in acquiring such information as would be useful for the strangers on their first arrival in this Country' (Christie 1821: iii).

The result was an emigrant guidebook, *The Emigrant's Assistant* (1821), which, like other guidebooks of the time, aimed to educate readers who may have been interested in knowing what Canada was like as a possible place to resettle. Christie was well aware of the power of 'booster literature' in promoting emigration, from emigrants who have 'carried home flattering accounts of the country, and sent many works from the press, which are loud in the praise of its superior advantages' (Shaikh 2018: 31–62; Belich 2009: 153). The 'dissemination of these reports and writings, has excited a general desire for emigration . . . and has been the cause of bringing numbers to settle in the Canadas, who will in time draw forth the immense resources the country possesses' (Christie 1821: 21). These sentiments found their way into *The Canadian Magazine and Literary Repository* during the course of his editorship.

Christie was friends with Samuel Wilcocke, the editor of *The Scribbler*, Canada's first satirical periodical. The aim of *The Scribbler* was to 'produce a weekly paper, assuming the form of essays, light, desultory and amusing . . . with now and then a lash at the follies, the inconsistencies, and the abuses of the times, of fashions, of manners'. The paper was to be only 'occasionally directed to literary enquiries' and 'sometimes to matters of public utility, and domestic economy, sometimes also to local matters of praise or of reprehension . . . avoiding as much as possible, all intermixture of party-politics, and of religious controversy' (Anon. 1821a, *The Scribbler*: 3). Much of the paper, however, ended up being a veiled diatribe against the Hudson's Bay Company and their disagreements with the Scottish North West Company over the establishment of a colony on the Red River. As Mary Lu MacDonald notes, 'it requires a vast and detailed knowledge of English Montreal between 1821 and 1827 to decipher much of the text of the *Scribbler*' (MacDonald 1976: 48).

Although *The Scribbler* was different in tone and content to the more mainstream *Canadian Magazine and Literary Repository*, Wilcocke was on good terms with Christie while he was the editor. Wilcocke himself had come over to Canada to publicise the North West Company settlement on the Red River, and was familiar with emigration schemes. Likewise, this preoccupation with emigration seeps into *The Scribbler* as well. He writes of an 'account' in the 'Quebec Mercury' of 'a poor woman just landed from Ireland, who, after lying on a wharf for part of two days and a night, actually died on the spot from the want of any place where they would admit a sick emigrant . . . What, because you have not received the arrears of your salary . . . the forlorn and suffering stranger is to be allowed to die on the wharves, and infection to be communicated to the whole population' (Anon. 1822, *The Scribbler*: 116–18). Furthermore, Wilcocke also favourably reviewed Christie's guidebook *The Emigrant's Assistant* in *The Scribbler*, commenting in passing on 'the latest work that has appeared on this (locally) interesting subject' in which 'the accuracy and plain intelligence of the accounts' can be 'pursued by . . . various classes of emigrants' (Anon. 1821b, *The Scribbler*: 29–30).

In *British Settler Emigration in Print*, Jude Piesse argues that the periodical's 'dependence upon new technologies of motion and transport, transnational range, and fluid formal dynamics' both contributes to the periodical's 'circulatory drives' and makes possible a 'new way of understanding it as an intrinsically migratory form' (Piesse 2016: 2). The Victorian periodical was 'an inherently mobile form', with 'an unrivalled capacity to register emigration'. The editorial priorities of these early Canadian periodicals, however, suggest that literary periodicals did not just contain an ability to 'register' emigration, but to actively shape the debates and politics around it in the early nineteenth century. The close connections and disagreements between these three editors, as well as the culture of reviewing each other's work inside their own periodicals, suggest that we can take these three as illustrative examples of an emergent literary scene in early nineteenth-century Canada.

Colonial emigration formed a key part of these early periodicals' literary sensibilities. In *The Canadian Magazine*, for example, an extremely short-lived periodical edited by William Sibbald, the very first item after the Editor's address is a letter to the editor from a generic 'Sincere Friend, and most humble Servant, THE EMIGRANT', who presents a 'plain and unvarnished tale' of 'what has been seen, felt, enjoyed, or endured, since my arrival in this land of Lairds'. The letter is an introduction to an article on 'The Emigrant', prefaced with a reproduction of the second stanza of the Scottish poet Robert Gilfillan's 'Emigrant's Song' ('The Editor's Address, to the Inhabitants' 1833: 5). Like *The Canadian Magazine and Literary Repository*, *The Canadian Magazine* also contained information to encourage people to emigrate: the literary sensibilities that these early periodicals aimed to cultivate within their reading publics was intertwined with an emigrant sensibility.

This can especially be seen in editorial discussions around the effect that colonial emigration was having on the shape and formation of different communities in Canada. The 'Editor's Address' of *The Canadian Magazine*, for example, notes wryly that 'It will soon be a matter of wonder and astonishment in other lands, should a vast territory, where "Red men hunted and paddled the light came" – where the people . . . settled a colony: – then English, Irish, and Scots, leaving the Rose, Shamrock and Thistle, crossed the Atlantic for successive years, and in almost countless numbers – present no food for the craving mind' ('The Editor's Address, to the Inhabitants' 1833: 1). In other words, Sibbald is of the opinion that emigration should provide an ample resource for aspiring local authors.

Thus, perhaps in part because of their editors' connection with emigration schemes, these early periodicals acted as emigration guides, or offered social and political commentary on poorly run emigration schemes. This is where *The Literary Garland* set itself apart from its predecessors: even though its editor was not directly involved with an emigration scheme, the periodical, at the same time as cultivating an interest in emigration by soliciting the works of authors such as Susanna Moodie, through its form and content, also aspired to cultivate a middle-class literary taste.

The Literary Garland: Cultivating Literary Sensibilities

Like *The Canadian Magazine and Literary Repository* and the *Canadian Review*, *The Literary Garland* aspired to be, above all, a literary periodical, focusing on developing the literary talent within Canada. The periodical was published by John Lovell, and edited by his brother-in-law, John Gibson. Lovell had moved with his family to Lower Canada in 1820 from Ireland. His career in periodical publishing began in 1823, when he was apprenticed to Edward Vernon Sparkhawk, who owned and edited the *Canadian Times and Weekly Literary and Political Recorder*. While *The Literary Garland* was his most successful periodical, he also branched out into other areas of publishing, including but not limited to map-printing, school textbooks and anthologies of poetry, as well as printing other periodicals. By the 1860s, he had established a name for himself as one of a small number of 'Canadian celebrities':

> Canada is indeed largely indebted to him for his indefatigable spirit in aiding in the advancement of its general progress, and in giving to the world a graphic compendium of its varied and numerous characteristics. He is the true patriot of his adopted country, the friend and patron of native talent and literature, the encourager of home-manufacturers, and the liberal supporter of every good cause in which the temporal and spiritual welfare of the people is involved. (Spedon 1863: 211)

When *The Literary Garland* announced its intention to concentrate on publishing original content by Canadian authors, it was not the first magazine to do so. There were precursors that held similar aspirations, although the marketplace may not have supported such a venture. Lovell and Gibson were realistic about their aims, as noted in an editorial to readers:

> it will afford us much pleasure to lay before the public such original literary tales and sketches as it may be in our power to procure, but our principal dependence must be, for a time, at least, that we can borrow from minds so much richer than our own, that many will deem it a waste of space to devote the pages of the Magazine to our own outpourings. ('To Our Reader' 1838: 4)

Mary Markham Brown points out that such claims that something was 'new' or 'original' did not always mean what we think it meant: while much of the work in both *The Literary Garland* and its predecessors was marked 'original', in fact many items were often extracts and items culled from British and American periodicals as part of well-established 'scissor and paste' journalistic practices of the time (Brown 1962).

While early Canadian print culture might have reproduced and drawn upon British sources of poetry and fiction for inspiration, such re-assemblages also encouraged and underpinned movements towards a distinctive Canadian identity in the early nineteenth century, rather than a reliance on British literary traditions (Rieley 2017). In the case of *The Literary Garland*, for example, such borrowing was often strategic. The frequent inclusion of poetry by British authors Letitia E. Landon, Felicia Hemans and Lydia Sigourney was less a move suggesting a reliance on British and American literature, and more a strategic inclusion for signalling to the reader the 'models of taste' that the periodical aspired to, as these were 'writers who could measure out excitement and instruction in acceptable proportion' (Klinck 1976: 159).

Despite its occasional borrowing of such material, however, *The Literary Garland* was unique in the landscape of periodical publishing at the time for the sheer number of new pieces that it managed to secure, often from a core body of contributors. In so doing, the periodical tried to make writing in and about Canada into a legitimate literary profession. The task Lovell had before him was a hard one, as he well knew:

> My father was perhaps the first Canadian bookseller to move in the matter, for he paid a visit to try and induce English publishers to give Canadian firms a chance. This mission was a complete failure. The English firms do not consider that the returns from Canada would be a sufficient off set to the loss of business if a firm like the Appletons or Harpers, in New York were to be antagonised. The upshot was that they simply threw in Canada when they were selling in copyright to an American firm, and do so still. When he pointed out to the McMillans the injustice of this, they simply laughed at him and said they would not be dictated to by colonists. ('The Copyright Question' 1892: 6)

The throwaway comment about the lower status of 'colonists' illustrates the extent to which it was difficult for colonial periodicals to be taken seriously at times, to generate any kind of identity as a distinctly colonial production in its own right. Undeterred by his father's failures, Lovell was adamant that *The Literary Garland* would be dedicated to supporting local authors. One of the ways in which he attempted to do so was by paying a body of regular contributors. Susanna Moodie, one of *The Literary Garland*'s most famous contributors, recalled the relief that payment brought in the straitened circumstances of bush life:

> Several other American editors had written to me to furnish them with articles; but I was unable to pay the postage of heavy packets to the States . . . Mr L— . . . offered to pay the postage on all manuscripts to his office, and left me to name my own terms of remuneration. This opened up a new era in my existence . . . it seemed to my delighted fancy to form the nucleus out of which a future independence for my family might arise. (Moodie 2007: 281)

Moodie grasped this rare financial opportunity with both hands, becoming such a 'consistent contributor' to the periodical that 'it was the rare issue that did not contain her work' (Moodie 1993: 79). From the moment that she first contributed through to the periodical's closure, she steadily produced for it a wealth of poetry, sketches, short stories and serialised original fiction.[5] Gerson argues that *The Literary Garland* 'became a site of convergence that helped forge a sense' among Canadian readers 'of common social, aesthetic, and political values' (Gerson 2010: 37), but it is perhaps more accurate to state that the periodical meant different things to different people, at different times. For example, while Lovell's vision was to cultivate a local literary scene, Moodie used it not only for this purpose, but also to generate income, to navigate the difficulties of settling in the bush, to write herself into the Canadian environment, and to create an identity for herself as a distinctly Canadian author. She regularly used the periodical as a testing ground for her longer works: thus it was not just her best-known work *Roughing It in the Bush* that appeared in *The Literary Garland* in a provisional form, but also her novels such as *Mark Hurdlestone* (1853) and *The Monctons* (1856).

Much of her work for *The Literary Garland* centred on her experiences of emigration, the most famous of which were the six sketches that would eventually form the nexus of *Roughing It in the Bush*, a semi-autobiographical account centred specifically on female experiences of emigration and settlement. These sketches were integral to forming a tradition of local colour fiction that centred the female experience of emigration and settlement in Canada. In her sketch 'The Walk to Dummer', she writes critically:

> [The] government's grants of land, to half-pay officers [which] have induced numbers of this class to emigrate to the backwoods of Canada, who are totally unfit for pioneers; but, tempted by the offer of finding themselves landholders of what, on paper, appear to them fine estates, they resign a certainty, to waste their energies, and die half-starved and broken-hearted, in the depths of the pitiless wild. (Moodie 2007: 299)

These earlier sketches are also transparent about the struggle that Moodie faced in cultivating an affective attachment to Canada. For example, in 'Tom Wilson's Emigration', while she laments the loss of 'Dear, dear England' and longs to be 'permitted to return and die upon your wave-encircled shores, and rest my weary head and heart beneath your daisy-covered sod at last', she also apostrophises, 'Canada! thou art a noble, free, and rising country . . . The offspring of Britain, thou must be great, and I will and do love thee, land of my adoption, and of my children's birth!' (Moodie 2007: 49).

Her poetry, however, often displayed a much more positive attitude towards emigration. 'The Emigrant's Bride', for example, casts itself as a 'Canadian Ballad' that allegorises the relationship between Britain and Canada as a harmonious marital one (Moodie 2007: 106; see also Moodie 1840: 218), while 'The Otanabee', an ode to the 'Dark, rushing, foaming river' that 'shakes with thundering force / The vale and trembling mead', is a celebration of the Canadian environment (Moodie 2007: 181; see also Moodie 1839: 275). Thus, while Lovell may not have been connected with emigration schemes in the same way that other editors of literary periodicals such as Christie and Wilcocke were, his solicitation of such material from contributors such as Moodie suggests that he, too, saw *The Literary Garland* as a means of channelling important debates over emigration and the cultivation of a settler community.

In addition to coming up with a viable financial model to ensure longevity of contributors as well as readers, and the development of a sensibility in Canada, Lovell and Gibson were also interested in cultivating an appreciation for the art of printing. For *The Literary Garland*, where the 'literature of a country is the *measure* of its progress towards refinement' (Holmes 1840: 432), it was not only the content, but also the periodical's materiality that was given careful attention. In 1846, Lovell published a *Specimen of Printing Types and Ornaments* that aimed to showcase the wide variety of fonts and artistic borders available at Lovell's publishing house: 'L. & G. respectfully acquaint the Public, that they have received . . . a Splendid Assortment of New and Elegant Plain and Fancy Type . . . By which they are enabled to execute every description of Printing in a Superior and fashionable style' (Lochhead 1975: 4). As Douglas Lochhead writes, this move placed Lovell and Gibson as exemplars of 'progressive, imaginative printers and publishers' offering a 'most impressive array, constituting a financial investment', and showcasing to printers in Canada and beyond that 'fine printing could be done in Canada', and was 'clearly designed to improve standards and to widen the range of printing practices amongst Canadian printers and publishers' (Lochhead 1975: 7, 1, 3).[6]

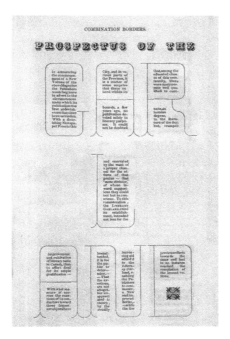

Figure 2.1 'Combination Borders' advertisement, from the *Specimen*, 1846, p. 132 of 258. Creative Commons Licence, courtesy of www.archive.org.

Within this *Specimen*, there are references to *The Literary Garland*, which suggests the close association that Lovell and Gibson saw between the periodical and aspirations of middle-class literary fashionability. The most prominent example is on the first page advertising 'Combination Borders' (Anon. 1846, *Specimen*) (see Figure 2.1). Intertwined in between the word 'Garland' is the announcement of 'a New Volume' of *The Literary Garland*: 'it is a matter of some surprise that there existed within [the City until] a few years ago, no publication devoted solely to literary purposes'; *The Literary Garland* was established 'for the improvement and cultivation of literary taste in Canada' (Anon. 1846, *Specimen*). In other words, the periodical aimed to model a form of 'genteel colonialism' through its attempt to curate a delicate sensibility amongst its readers, and a cultivation (or continuation) of good taste (Klinck 1976: 159).

The Literary Garland's distinct target audience opened up other avenues for periodical ventures on the broader literary scene. Realising the possibility of making an income from the periodical marketplace, Moodie and her husband, John, took on the editorship of their own magazine, the *Victoria Magazine*, in 1846. Her intention was to supplement her income from *The Literary Garland* through the *Victoria Magazine*. Anxious not to set themselves in competition with *The Literary Garland* and ruin her relationship with Lovell, they aimed the *Victoria Magazine* at a working-class readership, as the 'hope of inducing a taste for polite literature among the working classes . . . first stimulated us to accept the editorship of the Magazine' (Moodie and Moodie 1968: xii. 287). While *The Literary Garland* 'may command a certain circulation, in reference to its size and price, another periodical, such as the "Victoria Magazine" is intended to be, of a smaller size, and at a very low price, should, of course, be expected to obtain a much wider circulation, to enable the proprietor to secure an adequate remuneration'. The 'class of readers' that *The Literary Garland* aimed itself towards could 'afford to give two or three dollars a year for a magazine', but a 'much more numerous class can afford to pay only one dollar an annum' (Moodie and Moodie 1968: I.i.1). While they managed to solicit material from local authors, many of the contributions were written by themselves: two remaining sketches that resulted in *Roughing It in the Bush* were first published in the *Victoria Magazine*. Other material, such as the serialised story 'Rachel Wilde', also featured emigration as a topic.

A comparison between *The Literary Garland* and its competitors, however, indicates that the periodical may have aspired to high-brow literary sensibilities – at least in terms of printing – rather than actually realising them. *The Literary Garland* was based on British and American giftbooks and annuals. One of its literary models was the Philadelphia-based *Godey's Lady's Magazine*. In contrast to *The Literary Garland*'s slightly cramped print, spread over two columns with very few, if any, engravings, *Godey's* print was generously spread across one column, and each issue included coloured fashion plates and engravings. *Godey's* was itself based on British women's periodicals such as *La Belle Assemblée* and the *Lady's Magazine*. These literary models and precedents perhaps indicate why over half of the content in *The Literary Garland* was produced by women, with '55 percent of its poetry and 70 percent of its fiction' written by women (Gerson 2010: 37). In addition to Moodie, *The Literary Garland* was instrumental in launching the careers of many prominent female Canadian authors, such as Moodie's sister Catharine Parr Traill, Anna Jameson, Frances Brooke, Sara Jeanette Duncan, Mary Ann Madden, Rosanna Leprohon and Isabella Valancy Crawford.

Indeed, one of the reasons why Moodie became such an avid contributor to *The Garland* had origins in her writing career in England, where she had got her start contributing to ladies' magazines, annuals and giftbooks, including *La Belle Assemblée* (Shaikh 2018: 94; Ballstadt 1997). Her work and that of others coming through in this period were part of an important shift in the gendered contexts of these periodicals across the first half of the nineteenth century. While earlier periodicals had included male-dominated experiences of colonial emigration, *The Literary Garland* afforded female authors space to produce their own experiences of settler colonialism through their own experimentation with literary styles and forms. In a mutually symbiotic relationship, it relied – and capitalised – on these women's contributions to bolster its genteel, middle-class credentials.

The conjoined emergence of periodical culture, literary taste and settler colonialism from the 1820s to the 1850s is part of a larger story of 'the development of national print infrastructures' in nineteenth-century Canada (Finkelstein 2018: 3). This chapter has explored some of the ways in which the cultivation of a literary sensibility within early nineteenth-century Canadian periodicals was embedded in the practices of settler colonialism. Whether this was because of editors' participation in the emigration schemes, as in the case of Christie, Chisholme and Wilcocke, or because of the editors' active solicitation of content relating to emigration from contributors, as in the case of Lovell and Moodie, the periodicals discussed here strove towards placing literary concerns at the heart of settler emigrant communities. Despite the obstacles they faced with colonial copyright laws and competition from pirated American periodicals, these periodicals aspired towards cultivating a literary sensibility that was distinctly local to the experiences of settling in early nineteenth-century Canada.

Notes

1. For more on the importation of printing presses from Britain, see Parker 1985 and Fleming 2004.
2. See Vann and VanArsdel 1996; Potter 2003; Kaul 2006; Tusan 2016; Korte and Lethbridge 2018; Joshi 2021; Atkin 2021.
3. One notable exception which does focus on periodical culture is Meyer 1983.
4. For more on subscription publishing, see MacDonald 2004: 78–80.
5. While no complete bibliography of Moodie's contribution to Canadian periodical culture exists, Mary Markham Brown's *Index* (1962) and John Thurston's bibliography of Moodie's published works in *The Work of Words: The Writings of Susanna Moodie* (1996) provided invaluable starting points.
6. Lovell and Gibson's commitment to developing printing as a fine art carried through into the 1890s. Gibson was invited to, although could not attend, the Annual Banquet of the Employing Printers' Association in 1890. See 'The Printers' [*sic*] Dine' 1890: 9.

Bibliography

Anon. (1821a), *The Scribbler*, 28 June, 1–8.
—— (1821b), *The Scribbler*, 19 July, 29–31.
—— (1822), *The Scribbler*, 22 August, 116–18.
—— (1832), *The Montreal Museum, or, Journal of Literature and Arts*, December, 1–2.
—— (1838), *The Literary Garland*, December, 4.
—— (1839), *The Literary Garland*, May, 275.
—— (1840), *The Literary Garland*, April, 218.
—— (1846), *Specimen of Printing Types and Ornaments in Use at the Printing Office of Lovell and Gibson, St Nicholas Street Montreal*, Montreal: Lovell and Gibson.
Atkin, Lara (2021), *Writing the South African San: Colonial Ethnographic Discourses*, Basingstoke: Palgrave Macmillan.
Ballstadt, Carl (1975), 'Introduction', in Carl Ballstadt (ed.), *The Search for English-Canadian Literature: An Anthology of Critical Articles from the Nineteenth and Early Twentieth Centuries*, Toronto: University of Toronto Press, xi–l.
—— (1997), 'Editor's Introduction', in Susanna Moodie, *Roughing It in the Bush, or, Life in Canada*, Ottawa: Carleton University Press, xvii–lxix.
—— (2003) [1988], 'Chisholme, David', in *Dictionary of Canadian Biography*, vol. 7, Toronto: University of Toronto Press and Université Laval, http://www.biographi.ca/en/bio/chisholme_david_7E.html (accessed 4 January 2022).
Belich, James (2009), *Replenishing the Earth: The Settler Revolution and the Rise of the Anglo-World, 1783–1939*, Oxford: Oxford University Press.
Brown, Mary Markham (1962), *An Index to The Literary Garland, Montreal, 1838–1851*, Toronto: Bibliographical Society of Canada.
'The Canadian Review and Literary and Historical Journal' (1824), *The Canadian Magazine and Literary Repository*, August, 113–24.
Christie, Alexander J. (1821), *Emigrant's Assistant: or, Remarks on the Agricultural Interest of the Canadas*, Montreal: Nahum Mower.
'Contents of No. IX' (1824), *The Canadian Magazine and Literary Repository*, March, n.p.

Cooper, Elena (2018), 'Copyright in periodicals during the nineteenth century: Balancing the rights of contributors and publishers', *Victorian Periodicals Review*, 51.4, 661–78, https://doi.org/10.1353/vpr.2018.0048 (accessed 23 January 2022).

'The Copyright Question' (1892), *Books and Notions*, October, 6.

'The Editor's Address, to the Inhabitants of Upper and Lower Canada' (1833), *The Canadian Magazine*, January, 1–4.

'The Editor's Address to the Public' (1833), *The Canadian Literary Magazine*, April, 1.

Finkelstein, David (2018), *Movable Types: Roving Creative Printers of the Victorian World*, Oxford: Oxford University Press.

Fleming, Patricia Lockhart (2004), 'First printers and the spread of the press', in Patricia Lockhart Fleming, Gilles Gallichan and Yvan Lamonde (eds), *History of the Book in Canada, Volume 1: Beginnings to 1840*, Toronto: University of Toronto Press, 61–70.

Gerson, Carole (1989), *A Purer Taste: The Writing and Reading of Fiction in English in Nineteenth-Century Canada*, Toronto: University of Toronto Press.

—— (2010), *Canadian Women in Print, 1750–1918*, Waterloo, ON: Wilfrid Laurier University Press.

Gilfillan, Robert (1851), *Poems and Songs*, 4th edn, Edinburgh: Sutherland & Knox.

Gundy, H. Pearson (1965), *Book Publishing and Publishers in Canada Before 1900*, Montreal: Bibliographical Society of Canada.

—— (1976), 'Literary publishing', in Carl F. Klinck (ed.), *Literary History of Canada: Canadian Literature in English*, 2nd edn, vol. 1, Toronto: University of Toronto Press, 188–202.

Holmes, James (1840), 'To the Editor of The Literary Garland', *The Literary Garland*, August, 432.

Joshi, Priti (2021), *Empire News: The Anglo-Indian Press Writes India*, Albany: State University of New York Press.

Kaul, Chandrika (ed.) (2006), *Media and the British Empire*, Basingstoke: Palgrave Macmillan.

Klinck, Carl F. (1973), 'Samuel Hull Wilcocke', *Journal of Canadian Fiction*, 2, 13–21.

—— (1975), 'The world of the Scribbler', *Journal of Canadian Fiction*, 4, 123–48.

—— (1976), 'Literary activity in Canada East and West: 1841–1880', in Alfred G. Bailey et al. (eds), *Literary History of Canada: Canadian Literature in English*, 2nd edn, 3 vols, Toronto: University of Toronto Press, vol. 1, 159–76.

Korte, Barbara, and Stefanie Lethbridge (2018), 'Introduction: Borders and border crossings in the Victorian periodical press', *Victorian Periodicals Review*, 51.3, 371–9, https://doi.org/10.1353/vpr.2018.0028 (accessed 24 January 2022).

Lochhead, Douglas (1975), 'Introduction', in *Specimen of Printing Types and Ornaments in Use at the Printing Office of Lovell and Gibson, St Nicholas Street Montreal*, Toronto: Bibliographical Society of Canada, 1–7.

MacDonald, Mary Lu (1976), 'The literary life of English and French Montreal from 1817 to 1830 as seen through the periodicals of the time', MA thesis, Carleton University.

—— (2004), 'Subscription publishing', in Patricia Lockhart Fleming, Gilles Gallichan and Yvan Lamonde (eds), *History of the Book in Canada, Volume 1: Beginnings to 1840*, Toronto: University of Toronto Press, 78–80.

Meyer, Bruce (1983), 'Literary magazines in English', in William Toye (ed.), *The Oxford Companion to Canadian Literature*, Oxford: Oxford University Press, 455–63.

Moodie, Susanna (1839), 'The Otanabee', *The Literary Garland*, May, 275.

—— (1840), 'The Emigrant's Bride: A Canadian Ballad', *The Literary Garland*, April, 218.

—— (1853), 'Introduction', in *Mark Hurdleston, the Gold Worshipper*, London: Richard Bentley, vii–xxxii.

—— (1993), *Susanna Moodie: Letters of a Lifetime*, ed. Carl Ballstadt, Elizabeth Hopkins and Michael Peterman, Toronto: University of Toronto Press.

—— (2007) [1852], *Roughing It in the Bush*, London: W. W. Norton.

—— and J. W. Dunbar Moodie (eds) (1968), *Victoria Magazine 1847–1848*, repr., ed. and intro. William H. New, Vancouver: University of British Columbia Press.

Parker, George L. (1985), *The Beginnings of the Book Trade in Canada*, Toronto: University of Toronto Press.

Piesse, Jude (2016), *British Settler Emigration in Print, 1832–1877*, Oxford: Oxford University Press.

Potter, Simon (2003), *News and the British World: The Emergence of an Imperial Press System 1876–1922*, Oxford: Oxford University Press.

'Preface' (1823), *The Canadian Magazine and Literary Repository*, July, n.p.

'The Printers' [*sic*] Dine' (1890), *Books and Notions*, July, 9.

Rieley, Honor (2017), '"Every Heart North of the Tweed": Placing Canadian magazines of the 1820s and 1830s', *Studies in Canadian Literature*, 42.1, 130–53.

Rudy, Jason R. (2017), *Imagined Homelands: British Poetry in the Colonies*, Baltimore: Johns Hopkins University Press.

Shaikh, Fariha (2018), *Nineteenth-Century Settler Emigration in British Literature and Art*, Edinburgh: Edinburgh University Press.

Slauter, Will (2019), *Who Owns the News? A History of Copyright*, Stanford: Stanford University Press.

Spedon, Andrew Learmont (1863), *Rambles Among the Blue-Noses: Or, Reminiscences of a Tour Through New Brunswick and Nova Scotia, During the Summer of 1862*, Montreal: John Lovell.

Thurston, John (1996), *The Work of Words: The Writings of Susanna Moodie*, Montreal: McGill-Queen's University Press.

'To Our Reader' (1838), *The Literary Garland*, December, 3–4.

Tusan, Michelle (2016), 'Empire and the periodical press', in Andrew King, Alexis Easley and John Morton (eds), *The Routledge Handbook to Nineteenth-Century British Periodicals and Newspapers*, London: Routledge, 153–62.

Vann, J. Don, and Rosemary T. VanArsdel (eds) (1996), *Periodicals of Queen Victoria's Empire: An Exploration*, Toronto: University of Toronto Press.

'A Word at Parting' (1851), *The Literary Garland*, December, 572.

3

The Afro-Caribbean Press and the Politics of Place in Jamaica and Barbados: *The Watchman and Jamaica Free Press* and *The Liberal*

Candace Ward

THIS CHAPTER EXPLORES the cultural work and legacy of two newspapers published and edited by people of colour in the years leading up to and immediately following the British Parliament's Act of Emancipation. *The Watchman and Jamaica Free Press*, established by Edward Jordon and Robert Osborn in 1829, and *The Liberal*, a Barbadian newspaper edited by Samuel Jackman Prescod, first printed in 1837, represent the construction of a black public sphere, born of a desire to counter the dominance of the white planter press in the British West Indies and to provide a political platform from which to challenge the 'rule of the Great House' (Beckles 2004: xiii).

Although an exact demographic profile of the two newspapers' local readers is impossible to construct, it is certain that both circulated on their respective home islands, delivered to readers in urban centres like Kingston, Montego Bay and Bridgetown as well as in the countryside, as Johanna Seibert describes in her account of distribution practices and challenges (Seibert 2022: 39–41). It is as certain from each paper's correspondents and contributors, and given the papers' editorial missions to address racial injustices, that readers crossed colour lines – from sympathetic white planter-politicians like Augustus H. Beaumont in *The Watchman* to emerging political leaders of the black and brown voting classes like Price Watkis in Kingston and Thomas Harris, Prescod's early partner in Bridgetown. Less clear is the breakdown along the lines of male and female readers. Correspondents using gendered pen names like 'A Man of Colour' in *The Watchman* and 'A Countryman' in *The Liberal* suggest a predominantly male readership – hardly surprising considering the disenfranchisement of women in public-facing colonial politics. That said, the political activities conducted in more 'domestic' spaces, like the election meeting of coloured and black freeholders to be held at Robert Osborn's house, or the breakfast party at which the American abolitionists James Thome and Horace Kimball were entertained by the newly married Samuel Prescod and his wife ('liberally educated in England'), attest to the likelihood that women like Mrs Osborn and Mrs Prescod were intimate with and active readers of *The Watchman* and *The Liberal* (Anon. 1825, *The Watchman*: 2; Thome and Kimball 1838: 301).

As an examination of the editorial pages of these two publications reveals, the West Indian colonial space was shaped not only by the centuries-old practice of chattel slavery but also by the protracted resistance to it waged by enslaved people, their local allies and their descendants. Both *The Watchman* and *The Liberal* engage with slavery and its aftermath, acknowledging the degree to which British (and other European) colonies of the Caribbean were bound together by its legacies. One of the most pernicious after-effects, which I discuss more fully below, was 'Apprenticeship'. According to the British Parliament's Act for the Abolition of Slavery passed in 1833 (effective from 1 August 1834), all enslaved people over the age of six would become 'Apprentices', bound to their enslavers for a period of six years for praedial field workers and four years for non-praedial labourers. With the exception of Antigua and Bermuda (where full emancipation took place in 1834), planters in Britain's colonies embraced the new system. Anti-Apprenticeship activists, including the Apprentices themselves, however, launched a campaign that eventually ended the system, and full emancipation for all went into effect 1 August 1838.

Even as publishers and editorialists like Jordon, Osborn and Prescod understood the significance of the shared history and lived experience of slavery for colonial subjects across the region, they also recognised slavery as a global system that impinged on and was shaped by local conditions – particularly in the transitional period from enslaved to free. The complicated nature of the negotiations between colonial subjects' sense of solidarity in the fight against the long tail of plantocratic rule, of the transatlantic currents of capital and labour plotted out by metropolitan interests, and of localised political responses to the immediate demands of place, shaped an emergent anti-colonial, sometimes proto-nationalist public discourse that would in turn shape Caribbean subjectivities in later periods.

The spaces opened and occupied by newspaper artefacts like *The Watchman* and *The Liberal* are marked by their simultaneously ephemeral and static character. Both papers appeared bi-weekly, providing readers of each issue with highly topical news, thereby exhibiting what Benedict Anderson describes as the 'obsolescence of the newspaper on the morrow of its printing' (Anderson 2006: 35). But even as Jordon and Osborn in Jamaica and Prescod in Barbados supply readers with ephemeral content like local birth and death announcements, mercantile advertisements and shipping news, their highly political editorial content purposefully guides readers backwards and forwards in time, alluding to past events and laying out future prospects for people of African descent.

Such temporal moves contribute to *The Watchman*'s and *The Liberal*'s complicated status as artefacts. For even at the moment of their printing, the moment the type was set and the pages laid out, the writings of Jordon and Osborn and of Prescod became fluid, unmoored from the date and place of their publication: newssheets were picked up at the printing office or circulated across Jamaica and Barbados to be read by local residents, or distributed across the Caribbean and beyond via mail packets and steamships, delivered to subscribers, reading rooms and newspaper offices in other colonies and in the metropole; editorials and news reports reappeared months after debuting in *The Watchman* and *The Liberal*, to be extolled or decried in other newspapers and periodicals, those publications in turn collected (sometimes solicited from subscribers for the purpose) and bound together for posterity; entire runs of surviving issues appeared again in the century following, still-but-dynamic microfilmed images spooling across reader screens; and now, pages of *The Watchman* (if not *The Liberal*) are resurrected yet again nearly 200 years after first leaving the printing presses in Kingston and Bridgetown, as digitised, recommodified visual objects available to a new, 'live' generation of readers via institutional or individual database subscription services.

As important as it is to acknowledge these afterlives of *The Watchman* and *The Liberal* as artefacts, it's also important to recognise how their reputations as engines of reform and vehicles of resistance have contributed to that longevity. Certainly, a consideration of the two papers in this *Companion* places them squarely in our present-day project of decolonising the archives, a project that has gained urgency in recent years as scholars like Christina Sharpe have challenged us to 'become undisciplined' from traditional research practices and engage in new 'method[s] of encountering' a 'past that is not past' (Sharpe 2016: 13). Sharpe's call has been echoed by the editors of a recent special issue of *Victorian Studies*, which observes that our contemporary climate of anti-blackness 'extends well beyond the wake of the slave ship and continues to structure our lives and symbolic [and material] economies' (Chatterjee et al. 2020: 369).

Such calls are indisputably compelling and necessary. However, even as we respond to them, we must also acknowledge that they are hardly new. Indeed, I would argue that the editors, contributors and subscribers involved in the production of *The Watchman* and *The Liberal* laid the foundation for the work we are currently engaged in, explicitly identifying the past as not past and challenging the colonised and colonising archive almost two centuries earlier.

News of the Past-Not-Past: Jordon, Osborn and *The Watchman*

Two letters submitted to *The Watchman*, the first on 7 December 1831, and the second ten days later, illustrate these earlier confrontational strategies. Signed 'Cato', the letters respond to the passage of Jamaica's 'Brown Privilege Bill' of 1830, which gestured toward greater, if not fully implemented, civil rights for free people of African descent in Jamaica.[1] As a number of scholars have noted, from Mavis Campbell to Gad Heuman, Alpen Razi and most recently Johanna Seibert, the push against the disenfranchisement of free people of colour was central to *The Watchman*'s inception in 1829. Less has been said, however, about the ways that particular fight was waged in order to wrest control of a historical narrative that, as Cato declares, had been used for 167 years – from 1663, when Jamaica's legislative body was established to the 1830 bill – not only to entrench the system of slavery but also to oppress Jamaica's free people of colour, perfecting the strategy of '*Divide et Impera*' and shoring up 'that ridiculous *colonial* prejudice, the . . . aristocracy of the skin' (Cato 1831b: 6).

Tellingly, Cato's desire to trace the 'true cause' of that prejudice constitutes a (succinct) reassessment of Jamaican colonial history, a re-presentation in sharp contrast to works like the Rev. George Bridges' *Annals of Jamaica*, parts of which had been serialised in the pro-planter *Jamaica Journal* prior to its two-volume publication in London in 1828. As Campbell points out, Bridges' *Annals* was not merely favoured by the pro-planter press, which lovingly predicted in the pages of the *Jamaica Journal* that the work, written by the sitting Rector of St Ann's parish and a slaveholder himself, would contribute 'more important services to our cause than anything which ever issued from the press'; the House of Assembly subsidised its publication with a grant of 700 pounds, ensuring its quasi-official status and its distribution well beyond the readers of the *Jamaica Journal* (Campbell 1976: 138).

Insisting that his version of Jamaican history adheres 'to the truth of history' and contains 'authentic facts alone', Bridges assures readers that his enquiries are 'pursued without prejudice or partiality' (Bridges 1828: I, ix). He concedes, however, that his work will doubtless have detractors, not least of whom will be the 'false philanthropists' in England governed by anti-slavery zeal and, more insidiously, the radical missionaries and their allies in Jamaica. Applying the tortured logic often found in pro-planter writings of the period, Bridges conflates critical readers with

> those whose purpose is to bring ruin and desolation on these devoted colonies; and with whom no authority, however great, no testimony however respectable, has any influence, unless it tend to the advancement of their own visionary projects. . . . To such persons the page of history is uselessly unfolded. (Bridges 1828: I, xi)

Clearly Bridges' work conforms to the pro-slavery line, which plots the unfolding pages of Jamaican history as a narrative of improvement, extending over a period that has witnessed the 'gradual melioration of [slavery's] early conditions' to the present moment marked by the 'comparative lightness of its bonds'; contrary to the claims of Emancipationists, Bridges insists, enslaved workers in Jamaica labour in an 'evanescent servitude' that stands as proof of the wise policy and governance of Jamaica's ruling planter class (Bridges 1828: I, xi–xii).

Such assertions by Bridges were challenged immediately on numerous fronts, including in the pages of *The Watchman*, which dismissed the *Annals* as the work of a 'Reverend though "mendacious" historian sending forth statements to the world so void of truth' that they could not be taken seriously (Anon. 1831a, *The Watchman*: 5). The denunciation of Bridges' history is in keeping with the paper's identification of him as the embodiment of all that was corrupt in the established colonial clergy and those of its members who, unlike the anti-slavery missionaries then allied with *The Watchman*, were firmly invested in resisting any reforms to slavery, let alone doing away with it altogether – even while gesturing to the clichéd pro-slavery concession that the inherited system was 'repugnant to the spirit of the times' (Bridges 1828: I, vii).[2] As for *The Watchman*, the newspaper was unsparing in its indictment of Bridges, referring to him as 'the champion of slavery', sparing 'neither pains or trouble to extenuate [its] offences against the pre-requisites of his station, by a sycophantic adulation of the powers that be'; his devotion 'to the perpetuation of a beloved system, to the disguise of all its deficiencies' was, in the eyes of one *Watchman* contributor, a betrayal of his liberal university education, of his respectable family back in England, and, most damningly, of his Christian duty as an ordained clergyman (Anon. 1831b, *The Watchman*: 2; Anon. 1831c, *The Watchman*: 1).

For *The Watchman* and its advocates, Bridges' defence of the plantocracy's 'beloved' system was part and parcel of his prejudice against Jamaica's free people of colour, a class he had alienated thoroughly by his commentary in volume 2 of the *Annals*. Describing events of the 1820s, and even as he anticipated the eventual success of their push for greater civil rights, Bridges bitterly complained of what he saw as the presumptuous demands made by the free people of colour, who appeared to forget that, 'while the blood of pagan Africa still flowed thick and darkly in their veins', they were not entitled to full civil rights, regardless of their 'free' status (Bridges 1828: II, 371).

As reprehensible as Bridges' language is – condemned as such then and now – it also points to the means by which a rhetoric of consanguinity was reappropriated by activists working to dismantle the 'aristocracy of the skin' that was inextricably bound up in the socio-political operations of the colonial plantocracy. As Cato's letter makes clear, Jamaica's free people of colour were well aware of the constructed nature of these systems and of the political manoeuvring by which assembly houses across the British Caribbean shored up their power. Pointing to 1733 as a crucial date in Jamaican legislative history, the beginning of the 'era of Private Bills', Cato describes the 'Machiavellian policy' that allowed free people of African descent to petition the House of Assembly as individuals to be granted (or denied) greater rights. For Bridges, such private bills, 'discreetly and liberally granted, to such as maintained a character that merited distinction', were necessary to maintain proper social order (Bridges 1828: II, 372). For Cato, the practice was a 'component part' of slavery, constituting 'a piece of political charlatanism', the most pernicious effect of which was the codification of the cynical policy of 'Divide et Impera'. Not only did such a policy ensure divisions between enslaved and free, between free Blacks and free people of colour, it also drove a wedge between 'privileged' and 'not privileged' people of African and European ancestry, easing the way for the ruling class 'to perpetuate the colonial system' (Anon. 1831d, *The Watchman*: 6).

The new era Cato sees heralded in by the 1830 bill – in addition to correcting the trajectory embedded in the historical narrative laid out by Bridges and eradicating the feelings of 'distrust and suspicion' between free black and brown people – sets the stage for even greater liberty and justice. 'The coloured man,' insists Cato, 'by having shaken off these shackles *he never justly* bore, . . . has given a death-blow to the *future existence* of slavery, and has paved the way for the chains to *fall* from the body of his darker brother' (Cato 1831a: 7).

Such optimism on Cato's part was hard-won. A year previously in December 1830 *The Watchman* had denounced an earlier version of the Brown Privilege Bill, exposing the hypocrisy of the Assembly as it sought to continue the disenfranchisement of freed people of colour under the guise of reform. Like Prescod, who would wage a similar fight as chair of the Committee of Free Coloured and Black Inhabitants of the Island of Barbados, Jordon and Osborn understood, to use Prescod's words, that 'without great exertions on their part, the benefits' of 'Brown Privilege Bills' 'would never be any more than nominal': 'that coloured man who could believe' that colonial assemblies 'would, without a struggle,' grant full civil rights to free people of colour 'must have very little knowledge of human nature' ('Public Meeting' 1833: 2).[3] This well-justified and politically astute scepticism ultimately expressed itself in the awareness, as expressed by Cato above, that the political fortunes of all people of African descent in the West Indian colonies – regardless of their so-called privileges – were inextricably bound up with the abolition of slavery and, later, the end of Apprenticeship.

The resultant rallying cries for unity between people of African descent in the fight for emancipation appeared routinely in the pages of *The Watchman*, including in one of the most often-cited passages of the newspaper's history, first recorded there in an editorial of 7 April 1832. Referring to the 1830 July Revolution in France, the editorialist issues a clear challenge to the plantocracy:

> The streets of Paris have recently flowed with blood, and it may not be long before the streets of Kingston may witness a similar sight. . . . [W]e shall be happy . . . to

give a long pull – a strong pull – and a pull altogether until we bring the system down by the run – knock off the fetters, and let the oppressed go free. (Editorial 1832, *The Watchman*: 6)

The power of this passage was not confined to its initial appearance in print. Rather, the words reverberated. Immediately after its publication, Jamaican authorities seized on its (to them) incendiary tone, using the Island Act of 1823 to charge Jordon – identified on *The Watchman*'s masthead as the paper's editor – with 'constructive treason'.

I have described Jordon's trial and *The Watchman*'s coverage at the time elsewhere (Ward 2018), but here I want to point to the event's residual power, its archival afterlife. From the faded but still visible handwritten note by a contemporary reader of the editorial ('Treasonable Language!') to vivid accounts of Jordon's trial, Osborn's refusal to incriminate himself on the witness stand, and his partner's acquittal appearing decades later in works like Henry Bleby's *Death Struggles of Slavery* (1853) and the *Anti-Slavery Reporter*'s celebratory profile when Jordon was awarded the honorific Companion of the Order of the Bath in 1861, to W. Adolphe Roberts's inclusion of Jordon in his *Six Great Jamaicans* (1952), to the 1970s-era short film *The Watchman: The Story of Edward Jordon*, this event has enshrined the reputation of Jordon and Osborn and *The Watchman* as unquestioningly heroic.

As important as it is to acknowledge the power of celebrating such victories in the anti-slavery war, it's also important to challenge any tendency towards hagiography, recognising – as did Cato and as did Jordon and Osborn routinely in *The Watchman* and Prescod in *The Liberal* – the ways historical figures and events are appropriated and deployed politically. One need only consider the thirty-minute educational film produced by the Jamaica Film Institute in the first decade of Jamaican independence, distributed by the Jamaica Information Service. Part of a series dedicated to building civic and national pride in the early postcolonial era, *The Watchman: The Story of Edward Jordon* operates as an archival through-line connecting the Emancipation and Independence periods, exemplifying an act of (re)memorialisation tying together past and present struggles for sovereignty and self-rule at key junctures of Caribbean history.[4]

Drawing from *The Watchman*'s archived editorials, the filmscript portrays Jordon and Osborn as fitting models for Independence-era leaders. When, for example, a passionate Osborn confronts a planter class dedicated to erasing the role of enslaved labourers in generating colonial wealth, he proudly asserts a 'double claim' of Jamaican subjecthood. 'This is *my* country!' he insists:

> I have in my veins the blood of the people who took this island from the Spaniards and gave their guts to build up its wealth. I also have in me the blood of the people who were forced to give their bodies and souls to tear the wealth out of the soil of Jamaica. I have a double claim to this country! (Anon. n.d., *The Watchman*: n.p.)

Here the film's pointed rejection of white supremacy is in perfect keeping with the moment of its production. Like the fiery language of Michael Manley's speeches, the politically charged music of Bob Marley, the theoretical interventions of Sylvia Wynter, and the creative energy of *Savacou*, the journal of the Caribbean Artists Movement, *The Watchman: The Story of Edward Jordon* articulates for its Jamaican viewers the decolonising imperative to forge a new national identity as Afro-Jamaicans.

In so doing, the film demonstrates the seemingly paradoxical dual role of the colonial archive – as expansive catalogue of colonial violence and oppression but also as trove of source material for a postcolonial national mythos. In other words, the archive represents a site from which the script of oppression and resistance can be retrieved and re-enacted, the latter overcoming the former. As the filmmakers understood, *The Watchman*'s editors and contributors like Cato had already identified 'the disabling repressive harms of colonial power' and provided a foundation for the 'justificatory narrative of resistance' that characterised early postcolonial activism but that had been anticipated much earlier with Jordon and Osborn's embrace of the '*black* and *white* blood flowing in our veins' (Scott 2014: 799; Cato 1832: 5). Just as contemporary readers of *The Watchman* were encouraged to reject the 'aristocracy of the skin' upheld by laws, social practices and, not least, the 'force of habit' that taught them to 'abhor all who boast not a complexion so amazingly bright and pure' as that of the white ruling class, so too were newly independent Jamaicans being warned about the dangers of denying 'that part of themselves which was made out to be the primary cause of their deprivation', that is, their African ancestry (Nettleford 1990: 18).

The very fact of the film's production in the 1970s reveals the perceived need to re-confront the 'disabling harms' wrought by slavery and the colonial system and called out in *The Watchman* nearly a century and a half earlier. It also reveals the powerful impulse to lionise Jordon and Osborn. The film, after all, focuses exclusively on *The Watchman*'s most radical period, the early 1830s, when Jordon and Osborn battled for the enfranchisement of free people of colour and soon after linked that fight to abolishing slavery. In the wake of the Sam Sharpe Rebellion of 1831–2 they maintained their radical position, condemning the violent reaction of the planter class – institutionalised by the formation of the Colonial Church Union, supported by Bridges – in charged language that led to Jordon's arrest and trial.

The film does not, however, depict the last years of *The Watchman*, a period characterised by an editorial reorientation that coincided with Jordon's and Osborn's entry into Jamaica's political power structure – the same power structure they had challenged previously. The paper's increasing conservatism did not go unnoticed by its readers, as Campbell, Heuman and Seibert note in their discussions of the tensions and schisms between political aspirants in the years between the beginning and end of Apprenticeship, from 1834 to 1838. Campbell, whose book is quite contemporary with the film, is damning in her reading of the perceived shift by Jordon and Osborn. Whereas *The Watchman* 'was a fearless, bold paper that was always forthcoming in exposing abuses', she describes *The Morning Journal* as one that quickly became 'the dullest paper on the island', a commercially – rather than politically – oriented paper. As for Jordon, Campbell writes that his 'only aim from this period was to acquire offices for himself and his mulatto friends', his new conservatism representing an abandonment of the newly emancipated class (Campbell 1976: 191, 188–9). Heuman, in sharp contrast to Campbell, attributes the shifting positions of Jordon and Osborn to their commitment to local, 'creole' governance, even if that meant making (temporary) alliances with the planter majority in order to fight parliamentary interference. Jordon, writes Heuman, was willing to oppose the Government in certain cases 'because he believed it was better to fight for an Assembly that was open to coloureds than to have no Assembly [and thus no representatives of colour] at all' (Heuman 1981: 110). Although these scholars disagree about the cause of this shift, it was formally marked on 10 April 1838 by the appearance of Jordon and Osborn's new publishing venture, *The Morning Journal*.

Paraphrasing *The Morning Journal*'s prospectus, Roberts describes the 'temperate language' with which Jordon and Osborn communicated the need for a new daily in Jamaica, a need they would address: 'the WATCHMAN would cease publication but its spirit would live in its successor, with modifications as befitted a calmer period' (Roberts 1952: 18). For many contemporaries, however, this prognostication proved wrong on both counts. Several months after *The Morning Journal*'s first issue appeared, the *British Emancipator* provided coverage of the contentious debates in the Jamaican House of Assembly over ending Apprenticeship on 1 August 1838 for all Apprentices, rather than only non-praedial labourers as stipulated in the 1833 Abolition Act, signalling a tumultuous beginning to the post-Emancipation period. According to the 1833 Abolition Act, the period of Apprenticeship was to end on 1 August 1838 for non-praedial workers – that is, domestic and skilled workers – and 1 August 1840 for praedial, or unskilled, field workers. The status itself was highly problematic. In theory, an individual's classification as praedial or non-praedial was to be determined by their role as indicated in the slave registries. In practice, the matter was more confused, particularly as individuals were shifted between categories according to immediate needs of estate management. As for the planters, their best interests – that is, prolonging the period of Apprenticeship – were served by classifying as many people as possible as praedial workers.

Of particular concern for the *British Emancipator* were remarks made by Osborn as the sitting member for St Ann's parish, an office he had occupied since his election to the House in 1835. Osborn's statement that both Apprentices and planters needed more time 'to look about them' and better prepare for the transition to wage labour was interpreted by the *British Emancipator*'s editor as a betrayal: '[A]s the editors of the Jamaica Watchman', he wrote, Jordon and Osborn had distinguished themselves as 'undaunted champions of liberty in Jamaica'; with the transition to *The Morning Journal*, however, not only did they 'change the *title* of their journal', but 'its principles' as well:

> We have no fear of Messrs. Jordan [sic] and Osborne's [sic] ever becoming the enemies of liberty, but it is much to be lamented that they should cease for a moment to be its open and fearless advocates. We are not without hopes that they will ere long retrace their footsteps. (Editorial 1838, *British Emancipator*: 5–6)

Although the *British Emancipator* was a metropolitan production, it provides an important link in what Seibert identifies as the 'cross-island and generational shifts in the landscape of Black newspapers in the Anglophone Caribbean', part of the 'ongoing history of Black archipelagic newspapers' (Seibert 2022: 278). Printed 'Under the Sanction of the Central Negro Emancipation Committee', the radical wing of the Anti-Slavery Society, the *British Emancipator* first appeared on 27 December 1837. Its *raison d'être* was laid out 'in the broadest and most unequivocal terms' in its first issue: to bring about '*the entire extinction of the system of Negro Apprenticeship*, and the concession of absolute, unabridged, and unconditional freedom to the Negro, on or before the 1st of August, 1838' (Anon. 1837, *British Emancipator*: 1).

The editor, A. L. Palmer, had witnessed the abuses of the Apprenticeship system while serving as a special magistrate in Jamaica, appointed per the terms of the 1833

Abolition Act to adjudicate cases between Apprentices and estate proprietors and management. Declaring that the British public had been bamboozled by the Abolition Act to the tune of 20 million pounds paid to the planters as recompense for their lost 'property' and deluded into thinking that the enslaved had been emancipated in 1833, Palmer and the *British Emancipator* prepared to set the record straight: '*Slavery has not been abolished!* – the Demon has but changed its name' (Anon. 1837, *British Emancipator*: 1). This fact needed to be broadcast as loudly and widely as possible and to that end subscription notices were sent to sympathetic newspaper offices across the English-speaking world, including to Samuel Jackman Prescod's office in Bridgetown, Barbados, where copies of the *British Emancipator* could be obtained.

'Too Troublesome': Prescod's *Liberal*

The alliance between Prescod as editor of *The Liberal* and Palmer, first as editor of the *British Emancipator* and two years later as editor of the Jamaican-based *Colonial Reformer*, isn't surprising.[5] Like *The Watchman* in its early days, Prescod's *Liberal* relied on metropolitan publications to help circulate its on-the-ground coverage of colonial affairs and gain support in Britain for ending Apprenticeship. Signed letters by Prescod, written specifically for the *British Emancipator*, appeared routinely over the course of its two-year run, as did extracts from *The Liberal*. Similarly, *The Liberal* reprinted commentary from the *British Emancipator* and the *Colonial Reformer*, including another lengthy condemnation of 'Messrs. Jordon and Osborn' in early June 1839.[6] Through this mutually beneficial relationship, Prescod earned admiration and respect in anti-Apprenticeship circles, whose members identified him as 'able' and 'high spirited' (Anon. 1838, *British Emancipator*: 6). Whether he was exposing wrongdoing 'emanating from the government house or originating in the colonial assembly', wrote US abolitionists James Thome and Horace Kimball, Prescod was undaunted by Barbados's powerful planter class, determined in his pursuit of 'Truth and Justice' – the title he gave to *The Liberal*'s editorial columns (Thome and Kimball 1838: 301). Before launching *The Liberal*, Prescod had served as editor of the *New Times*, a newspaper described by Thome and Kimball as

> the first periodical and the only one which advocated the rights of the coloured people, and this it did with the utmost fearlessness and independence. It boldly exposed oppression, whether emanating from the government house or originating in the colonial assembly. The measures of all parties, and the conduct of every public man, were subject to its scrutiny, and when occasion required, to its stern rebuke. (Thome and Kimball 1838: 301)

As Jordon and Osborn had earlier in Jamaica, Prescod gained a reputation as a vociferous opponent of the plantocracy of Barbados, a reputation that led to his election as the first Afro-Barbadian delegate to the House of Assembly in 1843 and even later to his memorialisation as one of Barbados's ten national heroes in 1998.

Given the treatment of Afro-Caribbean subjects in this period, Prescod's repudiation of the planter class is hardly surprising. He had himself been the object of derision and contempt as the son of a free woman of colour, Lydia Smith, and a wealthy white planter, William Hinds Prescod (1775–1848), who, in an 1833 petition to the Colonial

Secretary seeking to prevent passage of the Abolition Act, described himself as 'the largest proprietor of both land and slaves' in Barbados. Writing from his English country seat in Gloucester, Prescod's father warned of the ill effects that would attend abolition, not least the sudden loss of the planters' paternal benevolence (Prescod 1833: 3).

According to the Legacies of British Slavery database, Prescod's planter father was born in Barbados but educated in England, graduating from Trinity College Cambridge in 1799. He returned to Barbados to work for his uncle, William Prescod; between 1806 and 1812 he fathered four children by Lydia, the eldest of whom was Samuel Jackman Prescod. On the death of William Prescod in 1815, William Hinds inherited Barry's Plantation as owner-in-fee and became tenant-for-life for a number of other estates. The 1822 Levy Book for St James parish lists William Hinds Prescod as owning 352 enslaved people and 794 acres of land, likely to be the combined acreage and labour force of the various estates he owned. In a letter to Edward George Geoffrey Smith Stanley (later Lord Stanley), the Colonial Secretary, William Hinds Prescod refers to his 'plantation accounts' to establish his credentials. For the year 1831, on one estate he records '389 slaves'; on another, 424; on a third estate, 143; and on a fourth, 248. He assures Stanley that '[t]hese accounts . . . are open to your inspection' (Prescod 1833: 3). Contemplating abolition, he wrote, 'Permit me . . . to enquire where, and by whom' the suddenly abandoned 'sufferers are to be provided with shelter during sickness, and from the inclemencies of a tropical climate? . . . [A]re the sick, the diseased, and the decrepit to crawl on the highways and byways, and there perish?' (Prescod 1833: 3). Prescod Senior's language is all too common in pro-slavery discourse up to 1833, from its humanitarian claims to the well-worn comparison between enslaved West Indians and Irish and English agricultural labourers 'to whom the ordinary comforts of the negroes would be a luxury' (Prescod 1833: 3). The fact that Prescod's father did not extend that concern to Lydia Smith's children compounds the ironies of the address he proudly offers up on behalf of the West India planters and the labourers under their 'care' – less than a month after his unacknowledged son presented an address to the Governor of Barbados on behalf of 'His Majesty's Free Coloured and Free Black Subjects', containing their 'grievances' over injustices perpetrated by ruling-class whites. At the time Prescod was serving as the Chairman of the Committee of Free Coloured and Black Inhabitants of Barbados, the members of which thanked him for 'the manner in which he had met the wishes of his Coloured and Black brethren on the drawing up' of the address ('Public Meeting' 1833: 2). While Prescod Senior was living the life of an absentee proprietor in Gloucester, garnering prizes at the Cheltenham Horticultural Society show for strawberries 'of a prodigious size and exquisite flavour' ('Cheltenham Horticultural Society' 1832: 3) and attending social events like the annual fancy dress ball in the Cheltenham Assembly Rooms, dressed as a 'Spanish nobleman' ('Grand Fancy Dress Ball' 1833: 2), his son was laying the foundation for a public career that would span decades.

A less obvious but crucial irony resides in the implicit threat contained in Prescod's father's suggestion that previously enslaved people will lose the 'shelter' once provided by planters if/when slavery ends. Certainly, by the time Prescod and his then partner Thomas Harris launched *The Liberal* in June 1837, that threat was realised in the form of Trespass-Complaint Nuisance bills, part of the expansive legislative manoeuvrings performed by colonial assemblies across the region in their attempts to regulate people's movements, to ensure an oversupply of labour, and – once the payment of wages became required – to keep those wages depressed. Bills like the 'Tumult and Riot Bill' (which Prescod referred to as the 'Death Bill'), which made 'unlawful' assembly a capital offence, 'maximum wage' and anti-emigration bills all came under Prescod's scrutiny, his reporting of them in *The Liberal* presented as due diligence. 'We shall not go back', he pronounced in February 1838, 'even a few brief years'; 'who in his senses can doubt', he asked, that such bills were anything more than an obvious attempt 'to bring back the halcyon days of old slavery in all things but the name?' (Anon. 1838a, *The Liberal*: n.p.).

In this liminal period – the end of Apprenticeship in sight but not immediately assured – Prescod emphasised his editorial priorities, at times interrupting his own reporting to address 'subjects of more pressing importance.... We are seeking JUSTICE for the poor of every class, and are therefore, addicted to quarrel with the law, when law is opposed to justice' (Anon. 1838d, *The Liberal*: n.p.). Prescod's quarrels did not stop at simply challenging hurriedly enacted legislation but extended to demands for positive laws to protect the rights of Apprentices and future free labourers, including the 'RIGHT TO DOMICILE' – a right, rather than the boon to be granted at the whim of planters like Prescod Senior.

Prescod's battle for this right was provoked by the multitude of trespass complaints brought against Apprentices by plantation management, complaints most often upheld and resulting in evictions. One such case was covered in a series of 'Truth and Justice' columns in February and March of 1838. On 28 February, in a column subtitled 'Blessings of the Apprenticeship System', Prescod named the complainant – Joseph Rock, a newly employed overseer on the large Walker's Estate – and the defendants, Margaret Rose and Elizabeth, two women whose husbands, King Green and Henry Callendar, respectively, worked as Apprentices on Walker's.

Prescod's description of Rock's cruelty in trying to evict the two women – sarcastically referring to his 'tender mercies' – and the sentence imposed (thirteen days in the workhouse in lieu of a fine they were unable to pay, despite the fact that Margaret Rose was seven and a half months pregnant) provided ample evidence of the planters' determination to wield the same powers they held over enslaved workers prior to the 1833 Act. Prescod, pointing to the 'savagery' of the laws, demanded counter-legislation:

> *A law must be enacted to protect the Apprentice* NOW, *and the free labourer* HEREAFTER, IN ALL HIS RIGHTS OF DOMICILE.... If our local Legislature will not do it, *the Imperial Parliament must do it for them*.... For the house in which [the labourer] dwells, is, for the time being, his, of right.... Who dares gainsay this? (Anon. 1838b, *The Liberal*: n.p.)

Rock, unsurprisingly, dares to gainsay Prescod's assertions, printing a furious letter of response in another Bridgetown newspaper, *The West-Indian*. And, equally unsurprisingly, Prescod replies just as quickly and just as angrily. In his column for *The Liberal* of 7 March 1838, Prescod cites Rock's letter, using the occasion and his antagonist's own words to reassert the demand for imperial action ensuring Apprentices' 'RIGHTS OF DOMICILE', to castigate the authors of bills like the newly passed trespass and vagrancy laws, and – as importantly – to challenge the crude but proprietary claim over colonial history with which Rock closes his letter, specifically through his allusion to what is now known as Bussa's Rebellion of 1816.

Crucially, Rock's letter does not refer to Bussa, today the most famous of the rebels, but to a lesser-known figure, a free man of colour named Joseph Pitt Washington Franklyn. Surely, Rock asks, Prescod has not 'forgotten the fate of FRANKLYN, the chief of the rebels in the year 1816 . . .? The gray-headed apprentice at *Walker's* [Henry Callendar] is happier while subject to my "tender mercies" than *he* would be if subject to the "rude grasp" of the Hangman' (cited in Anon. 1838c, *The Liberal*: n.p.). The threat of violence behind Rock's message is clear, one that Prescod addresses head on in his response:

> One word on 'the fate of FRANKLYN' . . . There are some very respectable people who believe, even to this day, that FRANKLYN was no more concerned in the rebellion of 1816 than the man in the moon. He was a man of bold independent spirit and therefore greatly disliked by those who then ruled the country with rods of iron – the opportunity to get rid of him was too good a one to be lost, so he was hung. (Anon. 1838c, *The Liberal*: n.p.)

The version of history invoked by Rock and the planter class, as relayed in Robert Schomburgk's *History of Barbados* (1847), represents Franklyn quite differently, most damningly for his radical leanings and his allegiance as a free man of colour, not to the planter elite, but to the enslaved. According to Schomburgk, Franklyn was 'a person of loose morals and debauched habits', given to 'reading and discussing before the slave population those violent speeches which were at that period delivered against slavery in the mother country; nor is there any doubt that he conceived and planned the outbreak which spread such desolation over the island' – that is, Bussa's Rebellion of 1816 (Schomburgk 1847: 395).

Not only does Prescod reject the planter version of history that Schomburgk recirculates a decade later, but he also inserts himself into the past, claiming kinship with Franklyn: had he been old enough in 1816, he assures Rock, he would have been proud to 'have been hung for the same reason that hung FRANKLYN – *We are too troublesome*' (Anon. 1838c, *The Liberal*: n.p.). Conceding the differences between 1816 and 1838, Prescod acknowledges that although a court of law – even in Barbados – would need more evidence in 1838 to hang an Afro-Barbadian troublemaker, there was always the possibility of extra-judicial 'punishment': 'We may be *lynched*, assassinated, but we are not likely to be hung for rioting or rebelling, or for killing a negro with *happiness*' (Anon. 1838c, *The Liberal*: n.p.).

Whose Emancipation? History, Memory and Identity

Reading Prescod's editorials, produced in the same period that saw *The Watchman* give way to *The Morning Journal*, it's tempting to privilege *The Liberal*'s emancipatory work over the (re)alignment of Jordon and Osborn with the planter class. Situating such a comparison in the context of the politics of place, of questions about local and global, and the emergence of proto-nationalist and postcolonial discourses, however, helps emphasise 'the complexities and conflicts of their perspectives', as Melanie Newton encourages us to do, to focus instead on the historiographical work being performed by and within the archives, including by and in the editorial work of these founding figures of the Afro-Caribbean press (Newton 2008: 286). Whether or not Jordon and Osborn's post-*Watchman* conservatism was wrought by a belief in Jamaican self-rule, a desire for local rather than imperial governance, as Heuman suggests, and whether or not Prescod's push for imperial legislation suggests he prioritised workers' rights regardless of which legislative body wrote the laws, remain important questions – but not because we need definitive answers. Rather, we need to explore them with the same kind of scrutiny we apply to our own moment of grappling with a past-not-past.

As Allan Megill suggestively argued a quarter of a century ago, 'in a world in which opposing certainties come into frequent conflict with each other and in which a multitude of identity-possibilities are put on display, insecurity about identity is a possibly inevitable by-product'. Prescod, Jordon and Osborn lived in such a world, as do we still, subject to the 'rule' Megill postulated about the relationship between history, memory and identity: 'where identity is problematized, memory is valorized' (Megill 1998: 39–40). I suggest, however, that, as evidenced in this necessarily brief examination of *The Watchman* and *The Liberal*, we can productively alter Megill's 'rule' to embrace the 'where' and the 'when' of problematised identities, and ask the 'where', the 'when' and, crucially, the 'why' of valorisation.

Notes

1. For a detailed analysis of this bill and *The Watchman*'s role in the debate, see Campbell 1976: 118–53 and Heuman 1981: 21–53.
2. Bridges' notoriety comes from his role in establishing the Colonial Church Union and inciting mob violence against missionaries and their congregants and anyone suspected of being involved in the Sam Sharpe Rebellion of 1831–2. For a detailed account of the CCU's activities, see Turner 1998: 166–73.
3. For more on the Barbadian context of the Brown Privilege Bill of 1831, see Newton 2008: 125.
4. There is no date marked on the filmstrip, and staff at the National Library of Jamaica have no information about its production or release date, although, according to Jamaican film scholar Rachel Moseley-Wood, the production values date the film to the early 1970s.
5. Although Palmer's name never appears on the masthead of the *British Emancipator*, a notice announcing the launch of the *Colonial Reformer* identifies Palmer as the 'late editor of the (London) *British Emancipator*' (Anon. 1839, *Palladium*: 2).
6. The occasion for Palmer's dissatisfaction was *The Morning Journal*'s editorial campaign to deny British Parliament's authority to suspend Jamaica's constitution if it refused to recognise the Prison Act, legislation intended to reform West Indian prisons. Like the earlier 'crisis' over a threatened suspension of Jamaica's constitution in 1836 (see Seibert 2022: 276–9), this imperial legislation too threatened the Jamaican House's ability to self-govern.

Bibliography

Anderson, Benedict (2006) [1983], *Imagined Communities: Reflections on the Origin and Spread of Nationalism*, London: Verso.
Anon. (1833), *The Barbadian*, 15 May, 2.
—— (1837), *British Emancipator*, 27 December, 1.
—— (1838), *British Emancipator*, 16 May, 6.
—— (1838a), *The Liberal*, 24 February, n.p.

—— (1838b), *The Liberal*, 28 February, n.p.
—— (1838c), *The Liberal*, 7 March, n.p.
—— (1838d), *The Liberal*, 10 March, n.p.
—— (1839), *Palladium, and St. Lucia Free Press*, 27 April, 2.
—— (1825), *The Watchman*, 26 December, 2.
—— (1831a), *The Watchman*, 17 September, 5.
—— (1831b), *The Watchman*, 24 September, 2.
—— (1831c), *The Watchman*, 29 October, 1.
—— (1831d), *The Watchman*, 17 December, 6.
—— (n.d.), *The Watchman*, n.p.
Beckles, Hilary McD (2004), *Great House Rules: Landless Emancipation and Workers' Protest in Barbados, 1838–1938*, Kingston: Ian Randle.
Belle, George A. V. (2001), 'Samuel Jackman Prescod', in Glenford D. Howe and Don D. Marshall (eds), *The Empowering Impulse: The Nationalist Tradition of Barbados*, Mona, Jamaica: Canoe Press, 56–101.
Bridges, George (1828), *Annals of Jamaica*, 2 vols, London: John Murray.
Campbell, Mavis Christine (1976), *The Dynamics of Change in a Slave Society: A Sociopolitical History of the Free Coloureds of Jamaica, 1800–1865*, Rutherford, NJ: Fairleigh Dickinson University Press.
Cato (1831a), 'Letter', *The Watchman*, 7 December, 7.
—— (1831b), 'Letter', *The Watchman*, 17 December, 6.
—— (1832), 'Letter', *The Watchman*, 6 June, 5.
Chatterjee, Ronjaunee, Alicia Mireles Christoff and Amy R. Wong (2020), 'Introduction: Undisciplining Victorian studies', *Victorian Studies*, 62.3, 369–91.
'Cheltenham Horticultural Society' (1832), *Cheltenham Chronicle*, 5 July, 3.
Editorial (1838), *British Emancipator*, 25 July, 5–6.
—— (1832), *The Watchman*, 7 April, 6.
'Grand Fancy Dress Ball' (1833), *Cheltenham Chronicle*, 28 February, 2.
Heuman, Gad J. (1977), 'Robert Osborn: Brown power leader in nineteenth-century Jamaica', *Jamaica Journal*, 11.1–2, 76–81.
—— (1981), *Between Black and White: Race, Politics, and the Free Coloureds in Jamaica, 1792–1865*, Westport, CT: Greenwood Press.
Megill, Allan (1998), 'History, memory, identity', *History of the Human Sciences*, 11.3, 37–62.
Nettleford, Rex (1990), 'Freedom of thought and expression: Nineteenth-century West Indian creole experience', *Caribbean Quarterly*, 36.1–2, June, 16–45.
Newton, Melanie (2008), *The Children of Africa in the Colonies: Free People of Colour in Barbados in the Age of Emancipation*, Baton Rouge: Louisiana State University Press.
Phillips, Glenn O. (1982), 'The beginnings of Samuel J. Prescod, 1806–1843: Afro-Barbadian civil rights crusader and activist', *The Americas*, 38.3, 363–78.
Prescod, William Hinds (1833), *Morning Post*, 8 June, 3.
'Public Meeting' (1833), *The Barbadian*, 15 May, 2.
Roberts, W. Adolphe (1952), *Six Great Jamaicans: Biographical Sketches*, Kingston: Pioneer Press.
Schomburgk, Robert H. (1847), *The History of Barbados, Comprising a Geographical and Statistical Description of the Island; a Sketch of the Historical Events Since the Settlement; and an Account of its Geology and Natural Productions*, London: Longman.
Scott, David (2014), 'The tragic vision in postcolonial time', *PMLA/Publications of the Modern Language Association of America*, 129.4, 799–808.
Seibert, Johanna (2022), *Emancipation Enterprise: Archipelagic Media and African Caribbean Newspapers in the Early Nineteenth Century*, Leiden: Brill.
Sharpe, Christina (2016), *In the Wake: On Blackness and Being*, Raleigh: Duke University Press.

Thome, James A., and J. Horace Kimball (1838), *Emancipation in the West Indies: A Six Months' Tour in Antigua, Barbadoes, and Jamaica in the Year 1837*, New York: American Anti-Slavery Society.

Turner, Mary (1998), *Slaves and Missionaries: The Disintegration of Jamaican Slave Society, 1787–1834*, Kingston: The Press University of the West Indies.

Ward, Candace (2018), '"An Engine of Immense Power": *The Jamaica Watchman* and crossings in nineteenth-century colonial print culture', *Victorian Periodicals Review*, 51.3, 483–503.

The Watchman: The Story of Edward Jordon (n.d.), filmscript, Kingston: Jamaica Information Service.

4

Mofussil versus Metropolis, Subalterns versus Seniors: The Rise and Demise of *The Meerut Universal Magazine*

Graham Shaw

Peace! *M. U. M.*'s the word, – a star's gone out,
A shining light expired,
Unhallowed rogues will jeer and flout
'Tis what they've long desired

'Bob Balaam' 1837: 575

These lines penned in late 1837 marked the demise after just three years and sixteen issues of *The Meerut Universal Magazine*, known affectionately to its readers as *M.U.M.*, the first periodical (as opposed to newspaper) to be published in the Bengal Presidency outside the Calcutta metropolis. Ever since the 1780s, the publishing of books, magazines and newspapers catering for the expatriate European community in North India had been confined to Calcutta as the headquarters of the East India Company. But in the 1830s, a number of English-language newspapers sprang up outside the metropolis at, for instance, Delhi (the *Delhi Gazette*) and Kanpur (the *Cawnpore Examiner*, *Cawnpore Omnibus* and *Cawnpore Free Press*). At Meerut *M.U.M.*'s creators had earlier also started a newspaper, the *Meerut Observer*, but not a single copy has been recorded as extant. Ironically all that is known of its contents are the extracts which appeared in the Calcutta press. Happily, sets of *M.U.M.* have survived, and this chapter explores its importance in breaking the metropolitan information monopoly to provide a public space for junior-ranking soldiers and civilians stationed in the mofussil ('up country') to express their opinions and discuss their interests, concerns and aspirations (independent of Calcutta), in a more expansive, leisurely and reflective way than was possible through the pages of a newspaper.

Mofussil versus Metropolis

When *M.U.M.* ceased publication in 1837, Calcutta's European population was estimated to be 3,138 (Sykes 1845: 50). It was truly the metropolis of British India as the seat of the senior echelons of the East India Company's Bengal government and of its military command, the headquarters of the judiciary and police, and the hub of the Company's commercial activities and of private trade. Additionally, there was a support population of non-official residents: artisans, tradesmen and service-providers of all kinds from boot-makers and coach-builders through to apothecaries and jewellers, engineers and undertakers. In origin mofussil was simply a geo-administrative term:

> 'The provinces' – the country stations and districts, as contra-distinguished from the 'Presidency'; or, relatively, the rural localities of a district as contradistinguished from the 'Sudder' or chief station, which is the residence of the district authorities. Thus if, in Calcutta, one talks of the *Mofussil*, he means anywhere in Bengal out of Calcutta. (Yule and Burnell 1886: 435)

But among the expatriate European community, mofussil took on a pejorative tone, the equivalent of 'out in the sticks'. New recruits to the East India Company, civil or military, fervently hoped to secure a post in Calcutta itself and avoid the mofussil altogether. As one anonymous versifier wrote in the *Government Gazette* in 1822:

> Reader adiew! – when next I court thy eye
> Th' amusements of the city I'll recite
> For which alas! I daily pine and sigh,
> Lamenting I'm a poor Mofussilite
> Nailed to a station which gives me no delight.
> Would I could get a sick certificate,
> I'd hasten down and renovate my sight,
> With all Calcutta charms, but helpless fate,
> Denies the hopes and keeps me here to vegetate. (Kopf 1969: 223)

Those unfortunate enough to be stationed in that perceived social, cultural and intellectual desert could exert no influence over the Company's policies and practices, except through the refracting filter of the Calcutta press over which they had no control, subject to any censorship and editing Calcutta interests deemed fit.

M.U.M.'s creators took a romantic view of their situation, characterising themselves and fellow mofussilites mischievously as 'Baratarians'. For them the mofussil was akin to the island in Barataria Bay, Louisiana, the hideout of the French pirate Jean Lafitte. The mofussil was the remote, untamed lair of independently minded young men who could use their position on the periphery, their 'mantle of marginality' as a recent study of mofussil newspapers in the 1840s has called it (Joshi 2021: 15), to snipe unchecked at all forms of central authority. In an atmosphere of mutual animosity, those in the mofussil disparagingly dubbed Calcutta 'the Ditch', and its inhabitants 'Ditchers', after the defensive work carried out in 1742 as protection against marauding Maratha cavalry. The ditch itself symbolised the intellectual as well as physical gulf between the metropolis and not only the surrounding presidency of Bengal but all of British India. *M.U.M.* repeatedly accused the Calcutta press of arrogant insularity and self-interest: 'You [in Calcutta] are a deuced bad jobbing set, you desire all India should be sacrificed to the Ditch . . . Doing as you do, it is impossible the interest of India and Calcutta can be united' ('Ourselves and Retrospects' 1837: 591). Unlike the Europeans concentrated within Calcutta, those in the mofussil were scattered at multiple locations. By 1831, for instance, there were over 800 indigo factories in 'Upper India', each with its isolated European overseer(s) (Ray 2011: 223). The largest mofussil numbers were to be found at places such as Meerut,

880 miles north-west of Calcutta, the largest military cantonment in the Bengal Presidency after Kanpur and an important administrative hub (Fane 1842: I, 103). When *M.U.M.* first appeared, its subscription list showed five regiments of the Company's Bengal Army stationed at Meerut together with two of the British Army, providing a local pool of several hundred potential readers.

M.U.M.'s Subaltern Creators

M.U.M. was created by two precocious subalterns: Henry Miers Elliot and Henry Whitelock Torrens, who both obtained writerships in the East India Company's Bengal Civil Service, in 1827 and 1828 respectively. The early part of their careers brought them together at Meerut for two periods: first for eighteen months between July 1830 and January 1832, and secondly for twelve months between April 1834 and March 1835. Each period saw Elliot and Torrens jointly take a bold journalistic initiative, establishing the *Meerut Observer* in the first and planning *M.U.M.* in the second. Torrens arrived first at Meerut aged twenty-three and spent a longer period there, appointed Assistant to the Magistrate and Collector of Land Revenue in July 1829, and eventually promoted to Officiating Joint-Magistrate and Deputy Collector in June 1834. Elliot moved to Meerut aged twenty-two in July 1830 as Officiating Register and Assistant to the Magistrate of the Sudder Station, having previously been Assistant Political Resident and Commissioner at Delhi. Eighteen months later in January 1832 Elliot was posted to Moradabad, then Bareilly and Moradabad again, before returning to Meerut in April 1834 as Officiating Deputy Collector. Torrens was the first to leave the town permanently in March 1835 to become Officiating Deputy Secretary to Government in the General Department at Calcutta. Elliot moved from Meerut in November 1836 to Allahabad as Officiating Secretary to the Sudder Board of Revenue (Doss 1844: 111, 388). Although their career paths would not cross again, their fates played out in unison: they both died in their mid-forties within a year of each other, Torrens in 1852, still in service in India, and Elliot in 1853 en route to England.

Away from their administrative duties, both were leading lights in Meerut's expatriate society and also found time to develop serious academic interests in Indian history, economics and literature, as well as exercising their journalistic and literary talents. A double pen-portrait was published in the Agra newspaper *The Mofussilite* on 16 March 1854, shortly after their deaths, which extolled their virtues thus:

> They were both scholars; and men of great and varied information; they were both distinguished for their knowledge of Persian and Oordoo; they were both passionately fond of the stage, and, at Meerut, guided, in their day, all the theatrical arrangements; they were both high Masons, and endeared themselves to all with whom they came into contact; they were both addicted to writing for the press ... They were singularly alike in application ... They were alike, too, in their habits and their manners; courteous, gay, gentle, kind, humorous, firm, serious – just as the occasion demanded. It was this that made both men so popular – not only with 'society' but with *all* classes. (Hume 1854: cx)

Of the two, Elliot's written output was narrower in scope, stemming directly from his official involvement in the perennial problem of land-revenue collection. This was reflected in several contributions to *M.U.M.* such as 'On the Settlement of the North Western Provinces' (*The Meerut Universal Magazine*, 1837: 4, 333–94) and 'On the Resumption of Rent-free Tenures' (*The Meerut Universal Magazine*, 1835: 1, 339–75), which Joachim Hayward Stocqueler, the doughty editor of Calcutta's weekly *Englishman*, was reported as mockingly declaring 'we shall reserve for quiet perusal some Saturday afternoon during the rains' ('Well Water' 1836: 325).

Such interests led Elliot in 1845 to publish a 450-page masterly study of words used in agriculture and land ownership, *Supplement to the Glossary of Indian terms. A-J*. His principal sources were Persian and Arabic histories of Muslim rule in India, out of which grew his grand project to publish translated extracts from the more important works. This would, however, only appear posthumously, as *The History of India, as Told by its own Historians* (London, 1867–77), edited from his papers by John Dowson. In 1847 he was appointed Secretary in the Foreign Department to the Governor-General Lord Dalhousie, and two years later was entrusted with negotiating with the Sikh chiefs the treaty ending the Second Anglo-Sikh War.

Torrens was the more versatile writer, as skilled at producing academic papers as he was at creative literature. His contributions to *M.U.M.* included drinking songs and poems, translations from Italian and German literature, extracts from his novel *Madame de Malguet* (admired by Maria Edgeworth, no less), and literary criticism. He was the first to attempt an English translation directly from Arabic of the *Arabian Nights Entertainment*, with his renderings of the first fifty tales published as *The Book of the Thousand Nights and One Night* (Calcutta and London, 1838). Appointed Deputy Secretary to the Government of India and Bengal in the Secret and Political Department in 1838, Torrens became part of Governor-General Lord Auckland's inner circle of policy advisers, implicated therefore in the decision to prosecute the disastrous First Anglo-Afghan War. In Calcutta Torrens gradually shed his mofussil contempt for the metropolitan press, even resuming his journalistic career as co-editor of the weekly *Calcutta Star* in 1839, and as a regular contributor to the *Englishman*, for which Stocqueler paid him £500 per year (Stocqueler 1873: 110). Calcutta society adored him, as a contemporary recalled:

> He had read books of all kinds and in all tongues, and the airy grace with which he could throw off a French canzonet was something as perfect of its kind as the military genius with which he could sketch out the plan of a campaign, or the official pomp with which he could inflate a state paper. His gaiety and vivacity made him a welcome addition to the Governor-General's vice-regal court; and perhaps not the least of his recommendations as a travelling companion was that he could amuse the ladies of Lord Auckland's family with as much felicity as he could assist the labours of that nobleman himself. (Kaye 1851: I, 303)

Calcutta's Domination of Public Discourse

This metropolitan concentration of Europeans made Calcutta the epicentre of expatriate social, cultural and intellectual life and the exclusive crucible of public discourse. The dominant position of the Calcutta press in gathering news and providing an opinion space is demonstrated by the thirty-three titles in publication there by 1830, from dailies and weeklies to monthlies, quarterlies and annuals. They served a variety of purposes and catered for a wide range of audiences, meeting the information and entertainment needs of a very broad cross-section of the expatriate community. Their subscriber bases were well established not only in the metropolis itself but also via the postal system throughout the mofussil. The East India Company's Bengal administration had its own mouthpiece(s), principally the *Calcutta Government Gazette*.

Reflecting the views of different political parties in Britain, several newspapers such as the *Englishman* and the *Calcutta Courier* reported and commented on current affairs in India, Britain, continental Europe and America. Other titles catered specifically for the data needs and other interests of the mercantile sector, including the *Daily Advertiser* and *Commercial Price Current*. Those interested in literature could subscribe to the *Oriental Observer* or the *Calcutta Literary Gazette*. At least two magazines were aimed directly at the military, the *British Indian Military Repository* and the *East Indian United Service Journal*. Protestant missionaries had also entered journalism with titles such as the *Gospel Investigator* and the *Calcutta Christian Observer*. The predilection among the Company's civil and military officers for game-sports, from hunting tiger to shooting snipe, gave rise to the *Bengal Monthly Sporting Magazine*. The research outputs of members of the Asiatic Society of Bengal appeared in its journal. Finally, there were titles offering pure entertainment and amusement such as the *Trifler* and the *Spy* (Martin 1837: I, 165–6; Chanda 1987).

The most successful of the four Calcutta dailies was the *Bengal Hurkaru*, its financial security buoyed by a regular stream of advertising revenue, in addition to its healthy subscriber base. As a contemporary chronicler noted, 'It is as large as the London Morning Post, circulates now more than a thousand copies, has generally a page, if not more, of well paying advertisements' (Martin 1837: I, 167). The severe restrictions imposed on the press by previous administrations in Bengal, requiring proof copies of every issue to be vetted by government prior to publication, were rescinded by Sir Charles Metcalfe as Acting Governor-General under Act XI of 1835. The press in North India was apparently entering a golden age, 'unshackled by stamp duties, undepressed by taxes on paper or on advertisements, and unimpeded by penalty bonds and securities, devoid of all censorship, and practically free for every legitimate purpose which a good citizen can require' (Martin 1837: I, 164). However, in *M.U.M.*'s eyes, the Calcutta press was far from free. Being immediately under the ever-watchful eye of the Company's Bengal administration, editors imposed a degree of self-censorship for fear of incurring official sanctions:

> The Calcuttarians have boasted of their freedom, they danced with pretended joy, and forgot that the clank of the fetters must betray their condition; but we do not think they were deceived ... for the care with which they avoided all strictures on the existing Government, at the same time that they exposed to that Government the abuses of subordinates, clearly shews that they feared to come into collision with the uplifted scourge, or to do their duty either boldly or effectually. ('On the Press' 1835: 113)

Until the 1830 financial crash, some Calcutta titles were owned by the city's leading houses of agency, such as *John Bull* by Messrs Cruttenden, McKillop and Company, or the *India Gazette* by Mackintosh and Company. Through such means, merchant communities could exert a 'secret' influence over the metropolitan press, using their contacts and financial stakes in relevant titles, for instance, to insert material, leaders and opinion pieces condemning the Company's trading monopoly. Such overt manipulation was much commented on by contemporary observers. As a commentator in *The Asiatic Journal* concluded,

> A large portion of the Calcutta newspapers, which, to a certain extent, supply those of England and the rest of India with facts and notions concerning the subsidiary parts of the East-India question, have been under the direct influence and control of the mercantile interest at Calcutta . . . which tends to give security to dubious mercantile transactions, and to screen popular individuals from the scrutiny of public opinion. ('The East-India Question' 1833: 165)

Additionally, all newspapers were wary of offending those commercial interests upon whose financial support (through advertising) their viability depended (Barns 1940: 196–7). The vehement opposition of the Calcutta press to any competitor mofussil publication is explained partly by this financial precariousness.

Mofussil versus Metropolis: Challenging Calcutta

The Calcutta press represented formidable opposition to any challenge from outside the metropolis. Only subalterns possessing an innate opposition to authority, a fearless frankness and unquenchable optimism would have dared do so. Elliot and Torrens took on the challenge, flaunting their youthful idealism in their publishing manifesto, which proclaimed:

> The attempt to establish a periodical publication of this nature, in the Upper Provinces, may appear to many persons an absurd and presumptuous undertaking . . . The *Universal* is intended for the expression of private theories, and opinions on *every subject*, civil or military, Kings or Companies, medical or sporting . . . We are neither Whig nor Tory, Conservative nor Liberal, neither Ultra nor Republican; we are not exclusively scientific, wholly historical, altogether sentimental, or devotedly frivolous . . . We totally abjure all Calcutta-*ism*, all *If-and-it-ism*; and all kinds of *What-the-Devil-will-Government-say-to-me-ism*; we wish to point out as a peculiarity of M. U. M. that it will be *racy*, *lusty* and *spirited*; and of its conductors, that they are *all* Gentlemen, in the bloom of health, and thank God, under thirty years of age. ('Prospectus' 1835: iii–iv)

They never envisaged *M.U.M.* as a profit-making enterprise: they were embarking on a journalistic crusade. To ensure they maintained complete editorial independence and freedom of expression, they retained total ownership between themselves, rather than 'giving the copyright to a firm, for its sole benefit'. To limit their financial liability, they printed only as many copies as they had subscriptions, rather than loading 'shops and counters with unsold or unsaleable copies' ('Ourselves and Prospects' 1836a: 461), and set the price only to provide sufficient funding to cover production costs.

When *M.U.M.* first appeared, Torrens had already left Meerut several months earlier. The production of each issue was therefore a triangular operation between Elliot in Meerut, the printer in Agra, and Torrens in Calcutta. The editorial process –

exchanging and revising copy, finalising the mix of contents – involved material being posted back and forth between Meerut and Calcutta. Having Torrens in the metropolis allowed him to gather intelligence on current issues and concerns to feed into M.U.M.'s content. He even contributed commentaries such as 'Calcutta Society' (*The Meerut Universal Magazine*, 1835: 235–9) and 'Some Passages in the Life of a Maharatta Ditcher' (*The Meerut Universal Magazine*, 1836: 2, 396–411). With Elliot remaining in Meerut, it would have been his responsibility to liaise with the printer over proof-correction. The lack of any working press in the town itself reflected the limited, unreliable nature of mofussil printing infrastructure. The nearest available press was at Agra, a fact used repeatedly to explain M.U.M.'s irregular appearance, the original intention of issuing monthly never being achieved. In the concluding article of the opening issue, the problem was raised:

> Our press is 150 miles distant – the new type which has been some time expected has not yet arrived, and we have therefore not been able to correct the proofs; nor can they be sent to Meerut until a sufficiently large stock enables the printer to keep in type three or four sheets . . . Compositors are not to be picked up like stones on a high road, or satin glazed paper like the berries in a hedge, – as far as our copy is concerned, we could easily bring out a number of M. U. M. once a fortnight, *if* we could get it printed, for we have an overflowing stock of material. ('Ourselves and Prospects' 1835: 430)

And was reiterated in the final issue:

> We have often placed in his hands [i.e. the printer's] the whole copy of a second number, before the first was out. Indeed the delay that has sometimes happened may be attributed to a creaking ungreased printing press, to yawning compositors, to printer's devils, to the cholera, to Queen Victoria, or the Legislative Council, you are at liberty to choose a subject for yourselves. ('Ourselves and Retrospects' 1837: 589)

Financial viability was also a key factor. For periodicals (as opposed to newspapers), whether published at Calcutta or in the mofussil, revenue was confined to subscriptions since they held no appeal for advertisers. The paramount importance of subscribers featured in an imagined nightmare piece, in which M.U.M.'s creators were transported 'into the very centre of the enemy's camp' for a combative debate with Calcutta's editors on publication issues over a champagne-fuelled lunch. M.U.M.'s creators asserted that, if Stocqueler's *Bengal Monthly Sporting Magazine* or his *East Indian United Service Journal* were printed at Agra rather than Calcutta, they would lose 250 subscribers. By contrast, if M.U.M. were printed at Calcutta, it would gain 150. The Calcutta editors could not deny these assertions, but the exact ratio between metropolitan and provincial subscribers is impossible to judge (see 'Ourselves and Retrospects' 1837: 587–8).

Metropolitan periodicals enjoyed a further financial advantage over mofussil rivals. They could be cross-subsidised by a successful newspaper issuing from the same press, for instance, in the case of the two journals just mentioned, by the daily *Englishman*. Nevertheless, M.U.M.'s creators pointed out that their magazine brought in more revenue than the *Bengal Monthly Sporting Magazine*. Although *M.U.M.*'s subscribers numbered only 300, compared to 430 for Stocqueler's title, *M.U.M.*'s subscription rate was double. For the *Bengal Monthly Sporting Magazine* to match *M.U.M.*'s income, therefore, it would have needed 600 subscriptions (see 'Ourselves and Retrospects' 1837: 588).

Difficulties were intellectual as well as logistical and financial. The number of expatriates writing for the press, especially those producing creative literature, was limited but, as the quotation above emphasised, Elliot and Torrens were optimistic about receiving a steady flow of content. They relied largely on the goodwill and loyalty of authors offering pieces for free, an immediate disadvantage vis-à-vis Calcutta magazines, which paid contributors.

Publication at Calcutta also carried more kudos and enhanced reputations. It is remarkable that the Madras-based poet Robert Calder Campbell sent nine 'Lays of the Benighted' to *M.U.M.* while simultaneously contributing to paying Calcutta magazines such as the *Calcutta Literary Gazette* (Ní Fhlathúin 2011: I, 365–6). Even if pieces were originally published in *M.U.M.*, there was the ever-present danger of their being reprinted in Calcutta. This 'poaching' of content had serious potential to undermine *M.U.M.*'s subscriber base: why buy a mofussil magazine when its best pieces would reappear in a Calcutta title? Elliot and Torrens believed that the Calcutta press depended more on mofussil than metropolitan contributions as a result:

> If you see a clever paper in the Asiatic Journal, depend upon it the article comes from the Meerut division – open the Bengal Sporting Magazine, and Goorka, Pilgrim, Gunga [i.e. pseudonymous *M.U.M.* contributors] carry the day – hear of a new cover expected from England and rest assured the sketch went from Meerut. Look over the columns of the Englishman or the pages of the U. S. J. [*United Service Journal*] and Fiat Justitia [another pseudonym] bears everything before him, yet forsooth the Mofussil writer is scarcely deserving of a notice in Calcutta, unless when his articles appear in a Calcutta periodical, then as a matter of course the gentleman becomes possessed of all the cardinal virtues. ('Illustrations of the Law' 1836: 242)

In a later article in the same year, the editors asked, 'Do these people suppose we have no subscription list? Must we repeat – we prefer being read by our own subscribers' ('Ourselves and Prospects' 1836b: 451).

For Elliot and Torrens, *M.U.M.* was a 'declaration of independence' from Calcutta, a showcase for the latent literary talent and political awareness in the mofussil. As such it would demonstrate that 'seemingly isolated places were sites of cultural creativity and not simply settings characterised by the imitation of ideas and styles generated in metropolitan centres' (Collier and Connolly 2016: 7). With its own mouthpiece, the mofussil would no longer be a passive consumer of Calcutta's views and opinions, as they suggested:

> Our subscribers should remember, that they will not only be encouraging literature, in a part of the world where it is yet but in infancy; not only giving an impulse to the spirit which now pervades all classes, from the peer to the peasant; not only hailing with cheers the steady onward march of improvement, which is silently

and subtly undermining the stronghold of ignorance and barbarism; – but they are securing to themselves a periodical of *their own*, in which the bold and uncompromising expression of honourable and upright principles, will gain ready admittance. ('Prospectus' 1835: iv)

Subalterns versus Seniors: *M.U.M.*'s Contents and Concerns

M.U.M.'s mix of serious and light-hearted contents, in both prose and poetry, mimicked *The Universal Magazine of Knowledge and Pleasure*, published monthly in London from 1747 to 1814, after which it was perhaps named. It continually expressed the professional interests and political concerns of the military majority in the mofussil, with articles such as 'Curnin's Retiring Fund' (*The Meerut Universal Magazine*, 1835: 1, 46–51), a pension scheme opposed by the Company, 'Reminiscences of the First Anglo-Burmese War' (*The Meerut Universal Magazine*, 1835: 1, 60–7; 163–71), 'The Bengal Army Now' (*The Meerut Universal Magazine*, 1835: 1, 272–82) and 'Minutes of Military Evidence' (*The Meerut Universal Magazine*, 1836: 2, 3–24). *M.U.M.* also catered for the literary tastes of the classically educated officer cadre with, for instance, pieces on the life of Herostratus, arsonist of the Temple of Artemis at Ephesus, on Cicero as a philosopher, and translations of Sappho's poetry.

The most striking feature of the contents was the virulent condemnation of Company policies. That Elliot and Torrens focused their attacks on the Company's most powerful representative, the just-departed Governor-General, was remarkable in itself. To do so with impunity and without ruining their career prospects was astonishing. *M.U.M.*'s first number opened with an excoriating piece, 'What has Lord William Bentinck done for India?' (*The Meerut Universal Magazine*, 1835: 1, 1–12). The editors dubbed him 'the Devil Dutchman', alluding to his descent from a favourite of William, Prince of Orange. Elliot and Torrens implied that his appointment was nepotistic, Prime Minister George Canning's wife being the sister of Bentinck's sister-in-law. His prime qualities were 'cunning, avarice, ambition, obstinacy', contained in a 'contracted intellect, more suitable to direct the minutiae of private life, than the affairs of a great Empire'. Bentinck earned the military's enmity by reducing their allowances (*batta*) as a cost-cutting measure, with *M.U.M.* declaring 'a more unfit person for a Commander-in-Chief than Lord William Bentinck it would have been difficult for any Ministry to pitch upon' ('Lord William Bentinck' 1835: 289).

Elliot and Torrens were conservative in the sense of 'non-interventionist', respectful of Indian social, cultural and religious traditions and practices, belonging to the 'Orientalist' rather than the 'Anglicist' camp. Consequently they roundly condemned Bentinck's entire 'liberal' westernising agenda much influenced by Utilitarianism. For instance, he took credit for suttee's abolition, although planned before he held office. Under his stewardship India's imports and exports had both declined. Thousands of Indians had been 'hurled into the depths of poverty' by his despotic seizure of lands traditionally held rent-free. They concluded:

The varnish that has been so unsparingly laid by the hands of the liberals, on all the acts of His Lordship, hiding the defects and concealing the underdaubing, must be freely removed, ere anything approaching to a correct estimate, can be formed of the character or probable effects of His Lordship's administration . . . The Whig sinecurist of a Tory Government, deep taught in the arts of dissimulation, learned in the science of hypocrisy, hiding the extreme of heartlessness under the cloak of philanthropy. – A theorist without a system, a statesman without political knowledge, a general without the education of a soldier, or sympathy for his feelings. ('What has Lord William Bentinck' 1835: 2)

The second issue's lead, 'On the Press', mocked Bentinck's support for press freedom as political spin. He was 'an ardent admirer of theoretical liberty, a profound hater of practical freedom, permitting the press to linger on in a precarious existence, under a nominal *toleration* of free discussion' ('On the Press' 1835: 111). A later piece was supposedly Bentinck's advice to the next Governor-General on subverting the press:

The method I adopted was, always to compliment the Editors on the information they gave regarding the state of the country and the soundness of their views: – poor devils . . . You will soon discover the springs by which they are guided, and I found giving appointments of a few hundred rupees a month not so bad a reward for *independence*. ('William Bentinck' 1836: 436)

The third issue's opening article, 'Education' (*The Meerut Universal Magazine*, 1835: 1, 227–35), ridiculed the idea that the key to India's material progress was introducing western education to a minority of the population (Wahi 1990: 78–9) instead of tackling practical issues such as crime, law enforcement and improving infrastructure. The case for the latter was made a year later in 'Speculative Benevolence' (*The Meerut Universal Magazine*, 1836: 2, 229–62). In 1834, they had already published *Polyglot Baby's Own Book*, a ludicrous commentary on the nursery rhyme 'Hey Diddle Diddle, the Cat and the Fiddle', presented as written by Charles Edward Trevelyan, Deputy Secretary to the Bengal Government and brother-in-law of Thomas Babington Macaulay, a leading figure in the Company's switch to patronising English-medium instruction only.

For Elliot and Torrens their publication of these attacks demonstrated that it was the mofussil rather than the metropolis which was intellectually prepared and able successfully to exploit the greater press freedom introduced by Bentinck's successor Sir Charles Metcalfe:

The Mofussil press have spoken out boldly, they have exposed the Calcutta system, and consequently all persons concerned with up-country establishments are profligate, abusive libellers, in the eyes of the Calcuttarians. As the free towns of Germany were for a long series of years, the refuge of Continental liberty, the asylum where science and literature were necessitated to take up their abode, the place from whence impartial judges sent forth fearlessly their verdict, holding up to universal reprobation the imbecility or crime of the most powerful sovereigns; so has the press of Upper India unbiased and undeceived, ever stood forth the advocates of the oppressed, the champions of constitutional liberty. ('On the Press' 1835: 113)

M.U.M.'s Readership

A demographic analysis confirms *M.U.M.*'s success in channelling the concerns of subaltern civil and military officers in the mofussil. But did they read the *M.U.M.*?

Table 4.1 Military v. Civilian Readers of *The Meerut Universal Magazine* (*M.U.M.*)

Military		Civilian	
Individual officers	137	Individuals of Bengal Civil Service	48
Institutions (book-clubs, messes, etc.)	20	Institutions (book-clubs, libraries, etc.)	16
		Commercial companies	3
		Other civilians with identified occupations	3
Sub-total	157	Sub-total	70
		Occupation unidentified (either military or civilian)	23
	Total	**250**	

(The identified civilians comprised two Baptist missionaries and J. Ochterlony, editor of the *Madras Herald*; the unidentified included the only female subscriber, Mrs Turner at Simla.)

The answer to this question lies buried in a number of printed sources. The identification of individual subscribers can be established by combining brief details from the subscriber list in the first issue with information from contemporary sources such as *The Calcutta Annual Directory and Register*. The most striking feature is that roughly two-thirds of the 250 subscriptions came from the military, one-third from civilians (see Table 4.1).

As *M.U.M.*'s proprietors understood it, a military readership was essential for success, not only because of the numerical superiority of troops, but also because of their greater appetite for reading, being daily confined to barracks for long periods As they noted:

> A few years ago, the editor of a paper which could barely keep its head above water, made the discovery that the army was the body from which support must chiefly be expected. The army is so vastly the majority in India, and the other classes comparatively speaking so few in numbers, that no paper will succeed here, which has not a considerable share of the patronage of the army. ('Gosha Nusheen' 1836: 75)

And:

> Hundreds of educated individuals are scattered over the wilds of upper India, some of them distinguished for talents and acquirements, who, especially in the army, have plenty of leisure which they must often spend in idleness for want of indoor occupations. Field sports, fishing, and rackets, cannot be prosecuted with impunity in the long days of the hot winds nor, at any season, while the sun is high. ('Memos. for Magazines' 1836: 349)

Table 4.2 Breakdown of Military Readers of the *M.U.M.*

Brigadier-General	2	Medical staff	5
Major-General	1	Chaplain	1
Brigadier	3	Captain	44
Colonel	2	Lieutenant	42
Lieutenant-Colonel	8	Ensign	15
Major	11	Cornet	3
	Total	**137**	

(Medical staff: a surgeon, a doctor, two assistant surgeons and one apothecary)

M.U.M.'s individual military subscribers belonged to thirty-seven East India Company and three British Army regiments. Besides Meerut itself, these regiments were stationed at twenty-four other cantonments, including Agra, Benares, Delhi, Dum-Dum, Karnal and Mhow. The Company regiments were (with one exception) all Native Infantry, each with some twenty European officers. Three-quarters of the military subscribers (104) held subaltern ranks (ensign, cornet, lieutenant and captain). Apart from personal entertainment, some of the twenty-seven senior officers would have subscribed in order to take the pulse of their junior officers' opinions and concerns (see Table 4.2).

Of the civilian subscribers, the forty-eight East India Company officials resided in at least twenty-one different locations (Agra, Allahabad, Delhi, Etawah, Murshidabad, Saharanpur, etc.). The subaltern ranks are indicated by those post-titles beginning 'Officiating', 'Acting' or 'Assistant' (eighteen) (see Table 4.3).

Of the 211 individual subscribers both military and civilian, identified and unidentified, almost two-thirds (136) may be regarded as subalterns, while only one-fifth (forty-eight) belonged to the privileged inner circle of military and civilian seniors, i.e. military officers down to Major, and civil servants down to Magistrate and Collector.

Geographically, *M.U.M.*'s subscribers were widely spread in thirty-nine different locations: from Simla in the north to Madras in the south, and from Bombay in the west to Sylhet in the east. Few copies reached the metropolis itself, with only seven Calcutta subscribers listed, even though Thomas Ostell, proprietor of the British Library, was *M.U.M.*'s distributor there. Elliot and Torrens complained that rival magazine publishers in the city such as Samuel Smith, the 'very sulky' editor of the *Bengal Hurkaru*, 'never lets Calcutta know of our existence'. Nevertheless, a correspondent, 'Festus', at Calcutta claimed in March 1836 that Ostell and the bookseller Thacker 'had applications for about fifty copies of No. 4' ('Festus' 1836: 341). Earlier he had reported that twice the cover price was being offered for a copy but

> not one at the time was procurable, and Ostell was obliged to send to Agra. I trust you have some more copies left, for the demand is great, and likely to increase. Not that any man connected with Government House would acknowledge that he read your Magazine. There it is proscribed, but Government House you know is not Calcutta. ('Festus' 1835: 304)

Table 4.3 Breakdown of Civilian Readers of the *M.U.M.*

Governor-General	1	Officiating Additional Judge	1
Chief Justice	1	Officiating Agent to Lieutenant Governor	1
East India Company Resident, Kathmandu	1	Officiating Deputy Registrar of Courts	1
Civil and Sessions Judge	5	Officiating Magistrate and Collector	1
Principal Magistrate and Collector	1	Officiating Joint Magistrate and Deputy Collector	3
Collector of Government Customs and Town Duties	1	Officiating Deputy Collector	1
Secretary to Sudder Board of Revenue	1	Officiating Assistant to Collector of Government Customs	1
Commissioner of Revenue and Circuit	3	Acting Magistrate and Collector	1
Superintendent of the Baruipur Salt Chowkies	1	Assistant Judge and Sessions Judge	1
In-Charge of the Patrol Establishment	1	Assistant to Secretary to Sudder Board of Revenue	1
Magistrate and Collector	2	Assistant under Agent to the Governor General	2
Medical staff	9	Assistant under Commissioner of Revenue and Circuit	2
Deputy Collector of Customs	1	Assistant under Joint Magistrate and Deputy Collector	1
Officiating Civil and Sessions Judge	1	Position not identified	2
	Total	**48**	

(Medical staff: Presidency Surgeon, 6 doctors, 2 assistant surgeons)

M.U.M.'s total readership cannot be gauged precisely, but it may well have exceeded 1,000. Copies would have been informally circulated between soldiers in barracks, and literate men were known to read aloud to their illiterate comrades (Murphy 2009: 90). Likewise, copies would have been passed round in district administrative and judicial offices. Subscriptions were also shared between individuals owing to the relatively high costs of each issue (three rupees) and of postage (Barns 1940: 181). *M.U.M.*'s subscription list also testified to a more formal channel of circulation: the widespread establishment of book-club culture in the mofussil. Sixteen station book-clubs and libraries for civilians were listed (at Agra, Bhagalpur, Landour, Ludhiana, Tannah, etc.), along with twenty military book-clubs and mess libraries (at Almora, Bareilly, Dinapur, Nimach, Sitapur, etc.). At Meerut, both HM 11th Light Dragoons and HM 26th Regiment of Foot had their own libraries. Bizarrely, *M.U.M.*'s geographical reach even extended beyond the subcontinent. At St Petersburg, for instance, it was roundly condemned but eagerly read by Nicholas I, Emperor of All the Russias, as recorded by Major Davidson of the Bengal Engineers, who met a fellow officer desperate to read *M.U.M.* because he

> had been travelling in Russia where it was a proscribed book! The gloomy autocrat, although intensely curious of all important matters connected with the East, had publicly declared that the introduction of such a scandalous work, would ruin any government, *however paternal*, and that the punishment for a culprit detected in its perusal, should either be decapitation, or eternal banishment and degradation to himself and family in Siberia! . . . No sooner had the copy been furnished to the emperor, than he commenced its perusal, and strict orders were given that he should not be disturbed! (Davidson 1843: II, 32–3)

Conclusion

M.U.M.'s demise was not the familiar tale of declining revenue and rising debts. It was a calculated act by the editor-proprietors, due partly to the development of their careers away from Meerut, and especially Torrens's integration into Calcuttan society. It was also partly because they felt that this journalistic initiative had served its purpose, proving that, despite difficulties, it was possible for a mofussil periodical to flourish, as they noted in a relevant opinion leader:

> Time passes on and the very name of M. U. M. may be forgotten; yet from our grave must each step in Moffussil [*sic*] literature be taken, by our bones must the proportions of each aspirant be measured . . . Judge in all things for yourselves; but above all never hesitate to speak fearlessly and honestly from an apprehension of offending any portion of your readers. Be always what you have hitherto been – the honest – the fearless – the unbiassed Mofussil press. ('Bob Balaam' 1837: 572)

Albeit short-lived, *M.U.M.*'s success contributed to the emergence of a recognisably distinct mofussil identity. Public discourse was no longer to be conducted through the Calcutta press alone. A plurality of voices, views and opinions had been created, and *M.U.M.* played its part, leaving the editors to opine on the potential effects, for 'What must become of Calcutta and its press, when the Mofussil papers squeeze the curds of English journals and leave only the whey . . . when by the diabolical machinations of Mofussil writers people begin to think for themselves?' ('Posthumous Works' 1837: 59).

Bibliography

Barns, Margarita (1940), *The Indian Press: A History of the Growth of Public Opinion in India*, London: George Allen & Unwin.
'The Bengal Army Now' (1835), *The Meerut Universal Magazine*, 1, 272–82.
'Bob Balaam' (1837), 'Balaameana', *The Meerut Universal Magazine*, 4, 565–76.
'Calcutta Society' (1835), *The Meerut Universal Magazine*, 235–9.
Chanda, Mrinal Kanti (1987), *History of the English Press in Bengal 1780 to 1857*, Calcutta: K. P. Bagchi & Company.

Collier, Patrick, and James J. Connolly (2016), 'An introduction', in James J. Connolly et al. (eds), *Print Culture Histories Beyond the Metropolis*, Toronto: University of Toronto Press, 3–25.
'Curnin's Retiring Fund' (1835), *The Meerut Universal Magazine*, 1, 46–51.
Davidson, Charles James C. (1843), *Diary of Travels and Adventures in Upper India, from Bareilly, in Rohilcund, to Hurdwar, and Nahun, in the Himmalaya Mountains, with a Tour in Bundelcund, a Sporting Excursion in the Kingdom of Oude, and a Voyage down the Ganges*, London: Henry Colburn.
Doss, Ramchunder (1844), *A General Register of the Hon'ble East India Company Civil Servants of the Bengal Establishment from 1790 to 1842*, Calcutta: printed at the Baptist Mission Press.
'The East-India Question. The India Press' (1833), *The Asiatic Journal and Monthly Register for British and Foreign India, China and Australasia*, 9, New Series, May–August, 165–6.
Fane, Henry Edward (1842), *Five Years in India: Comprising a Narrative of Travels in the Presidency of Bengal; a Visit to the Court of Runjeet Sing, a Residence in the Himalayah Mountains, an Account of the Late Expedition to Cabul and Affghanistan, Voyage down the Indus, and Journey Overland to England*, London: Henry Colburn.
'Festus' (1835), 'Letter to the Editor of the *Meerut Universal Magazine*', *The Meerut Universal Magazine*, 1, 303–7.
—— (1836), 'Festus on the Cruci-fiction', *The Meerut Universal Magazine*, 2, 333–41.
'Gosha Nusheen' (1836), 'Thoughts on Humbug', *The Meerut Universal Magazine*, 3, 67–77.
Hume, James (1854), 'Memoir', in James Hume (ed.), *A Selection from the Writings, Prose and Poetical, of the Late Henry W. Torrens . . . With a biographical memoir*, Calcutta and London: R. C. Lepage and Co., i–cxiii.
'Illustrations of the Law' (1836), *The Meerut Universal Magazine*, 3, 240–2.
Joshi, Priti (2021), *Empire News: The Anglo-Indian Press Writes India*, Albany: State University of New York Press.
Kaye, John William (1851), *History of the War in Afghanistan*, London: Richard Bentley.
Kopf, David (1969), *British Orientalism and the Bengal Renaissance: The Dynamics of Indian Modernization, 1773–1835*, Berkeley and Los Angeles: University of California Press.
'Lord William Bentinck as Commander in Chief' (1835), *The Meerut Universal Magazine*, 1, 289–303.
Martin, Robert Montgomery (1837), *History of the Possessions of the Honorable East India Company*, London: Whittaker & Co.
'Memos. for Magazines' (1836), *The Meerut Universal Magazine*, 3, 349–55.
'Minutes of Military Evidence' (1836), *The Meerut Universal Magazine*, 2, 3–24.
Murphy, Sharon (2009), 'Imperial reading? The East India Company's lending libraries for soldiers, c. 1819–1834', *Book History*, 12, 74–99.
Ní Fhlathúin, Máire (2011), *The Poetry of British India, 1780–1905*, London: Pickering & Chatto.
'On the Press' (1835), *The Meerut Universal Magazine*, 1, 109–16.
'On the Resumption of Rent-free Tenures' (1835), *The Meerut Universal Magazine*, 1, 339–75.
'On the Settlement of the North Western Provinces' (1837), *The Meerut Universal Magazine*, 4, 333–94.
'Ourselves and Prospects' (1835), *The Meerut Universal Magazine*, 1, 430.
'Ourselves and Prospects' (1836a), *The Meerut Universal Magazine*, 2, 461–8.
'Ourselves and Prospects' (1836b), *The Meerut Universal Magazine*, 3, 449–51.
'Ourselves and Retrospects' (1837), *The Meerut Universal Magazine*, 4, 587–94.
'Posthumous Works of Mowenson Fitz Mowenson Esq. Ensign' (1837), *The Meerut Universal Magazine*, 4, 45–62.
'Prospectus' (1835), *The Meerut Universal Magazine*, 1, iii–v.

Ray, Indrajit (2011), *Bengal Industries and the British Industrial Revolution*, New York: Routledge.

'Reminiscences of the First Anglo-Burmese War' (1835), *The Meerut Universal Magazine*, 1, 60–7, 163–71.

'Some Passages in the Life of a Maharatta Ditcher' (1836), *The Meerut Universal Magazine*, 2, 396–411.

'Speculative Benevolence' (1836), *The Meerut Universal Magazine*, 2, 229–62.

Stocqueler, Joachim Hayward (1873), *The memoirs of a journalist . . . Enlarged, revised, and corrected by the author*, Bombay and London: Published at the offices of the Times of India.

Sykes, William Henry (1845), 'On the population and mortality of Calcutta', *Journal of the Statistical Society of London*, 8.1, 50–8.

Wahi, Tripta (1990), 'Henry Miers Elliot: A reappraisal', *The Journal of the Royal Asiatic Society of Great Britain and Ireland*, 1, 64–90.

'Well Water' (1836), *The Meerut Universal Magazine*, 2, 235.

'What has Lord William Bentinck done for India?' (1835), *The Meerut Universal Magazine*, 1, 1–12.

'William Bentinck' (1836), 'Billy's Budget', *The Meerut Universal Magazine*, 2, 432–8.

Yule, Henry, and Arthur Coke Burnell (1886), *Hobson-Jobson: Being a Glossary of Anglo-Indian Colloquial Words and Phrases, and of Kindred Terms; Etymological, Historical, Geographical, and Discursive*, London: John Murray.

5

Writing the 'Wooden World': Periodicals and Settler Environmental Knowledge in Colonial New Zealand

Philip Steer

Never before had I really seen the matchless New Zealand forest.

Hudson 1890: 337

A people settling in a forest country must destroy that forest or it will conquer them.

Best 1907: 200

Colonial New Zealand has been described as a 'wooden world' due to the thoroughgoing dependence of settlement's physical infrastructure on the exploitation of the forest (Wynn 2013: 127). This chapter extends that idea of a 'wooden world' to include the range of intersecting and often contradictory responses by settlers to the colony's trees and forests that began to emerge well before formal colonisation. At the point when Britain annexed New Zealand in 1840, forest covered an estimated two-thirds of the North Island and a quarter to a third of the South Island, and was known intimately by Māori as Te Waonui-a-Tāne – the great forest of Tāne (Royal 2010: 100). The Māori story of creation relates that the human world came into being when Tāne, the god of the forest, forcibly separated the embrace of Papatūānuku (Sky Mother) and Ranginui (Earth Father), and the forest was revered by Māori for 'its beauty, spiritual presence, and bountiful supply of food, medicines, and weaving and building materials' (Taonui 2010: 106). To settlers, by contrast, the forest was most often known simply as 'the bush', which many saw primarily as a source of timber, and many more regarded as merely an obstacle to be cleared so that agrarian capitalism might take root in its place. Some of my own ancestors participated in what has been described as the 'unrepentant, systematic destruction' that reduced those existing forests by roughly 50 per cent between 1840 and 1900 (Knight 2009: 325). At the same time, however, other views of the forest also circulated within the settler public sphere: a belief that its beauty was a cultural asset; nationalist associations with tree species such as kauri and the silver fern (ponga); alarm that its loss would cause erosion or climate change; and concerns its extirpation would cause economic and strategic harm. Periodicals provided one of the main venues for these ideas to be articulated, developed and challenged during the second half of the nineteenth century.

Critical accounts of New Zealand's colonial periodicals stress the proliferation of titles and the 'monotonous frequency' with which most of them failed in short order

(Tye 1996: 224). The hubs of periodical culture were the main population centres: Dunedin in the South Island, whose development had been supercharged by the gold rush in the 1860s, was the 'principal centre of serious periodical literature', alongside Auckland and Wellington in the North Island (Tye 1996: 229). However, given that the 1901 census registered a settler population of just over 770,000, and this was dispersed over a landmass larger than the United Kingdom, predominantly regional publications constantly struggled to attain sufficient subscribers. New Zealand's periodical market was also vulnerable to international competition: the proximity of the Australian colonies and the increasing regularity and speed of shipping connections to Britain provided settlers with ready access to competing overseas titles, and the 'mass transfer' of such writing helped bind the colony more tightly to metropolitan cultural production throughout the nineteenth century (Belich 2009: 120–3). Critics have consequently diagnosed an 'undistinguished and ... ephemeral' print culture, symptomatic of an inchoate sense of nationality that would only fully come into its own during the twentieth century (Stiles 1997: 139). I will argue, however, that this volatility might more usefully be seen as a cultural ferment that was actively defining the baseline of what would be deemed 'natural' by later generations of settler writers.

Considerable attention has been paid to the material facts of environmental change in colonial New Zealand, and to the legislative responses to it that were made from the 1870s onwards, but there is far less understanding of the range of ideas, attitudes and representations that collectively defined the possibilities and limitations of settler environmental knowledge. One survey of settler attitudes toward the forest at the turn of the twentieth century simply concludes that their destruction was 'for many individuals . . . accompanied by an increasing sense of sadness', while also noting that such sentiment 'cannot readily be quantified' (Lochhead and Star 2013: 156). Although there were no periodicals specifically focused on nature or the environment during this period – the first of these, the N. Z. Native Bird Protection Society's *Birds*, commenced in 1924 – writing about forests proliferated in publications spanning disparate domains of knowledge and social strata. Forest legislation was actively discussed in religious publications and professional magazines. Māori forest knowledge was remediated in literary magazines, while scientific journals published papers on forests suffused with literary references. The discussion that follows is divided chronologically into two parts: the 1860s–70s, which saw the first flourishing of settler periodical culture as British sovereignty was forcibly imposed across the breadth of the colony; and the period of the 1880s–1900s, when a nascent settler nationalism increasingly coloured the public sphere. The emphasis falls on identifying varieties of forest rhetoric that circulated in English amongst settlers, and it focuses on a representative range of periodicals that span disciplines and locations. At the broadest level, colonial periodicals reveal a 'wooden world' defined by multiple spheres of forest knowledge – aesthetic, scientific, economic and ethnographic – whose boundaries were often porous, whose claims and perspectives were often conflicting, and which collectively highlight the consequential choices that settler culture made at this time about how and why it would value the natural world.

1860s–70s

Historian James Belich argues that, 'as far as most Maori were concerned', imperial sovereignty was not yet 'real and substantial' in New Zealand prior to the 1860s (Belich

1996: 229). It was only following the 'long and bitter' colonial conflicts fought across the central North Island in the 1860s that 'real empire finally marched, flooded, or crept into even the innermost sanctums of independent Aotearoa' (Belich 1996: 246). Although the Māori and settler populations each numbered around 60,000 at the end of the 1850s, the spur to immigration provided by the discovery of gold in Otago in 1861 would see settlers outnumber Māori ten to one by 1878 (Pool 1991: 61). Even as government policy after 1870 accelerated 'the sawmillers' assault on the forest' (Wynn 2013: 128), the colony saw a 'false dawn of conservation' in the form of forest legislation (Young 2004: 80). The Forest Trees Planting Encouragement Act 1871 was followed by the New Zealand Forests Act 1874, which proclaimed it 'expedient to make provision for preserving the soil and climate by tree planting, for providing timber for future industrial purposes, [and] for subjecting some portion of the native forests to skilled management and proper control' (New Zealand Forests Act 1874: 121). Dennis McEldowney observes of settler print culture that the early 1860s saw 'the first signs of a sense of identity . . . or at least . . . a body of local knowledge' (McEldowney 1998: 633), and responses to the forest in periodicals during these decades reveal dominant themes of economic exploitation, scientific analysis and climatological anxiety.

In the extensively wooded Auckland province, articles at this time often discussed forests in the context of giving advice for settlers seeking to establish new farms (see Plate 1). *The Auckland Weekly Register, and Commercial and Shipping Gazette* (Auckland, 1857–62, ed. J. C. McDowell) confidently advised its entrepreneurial readership that 'the more desirable location for the newly arrived immigrant, more especially if his capital be small, is the forest or heavy bush of the Province of Auckland' ('The Soils of the Province of Auckland' 1860: 3). Similar views appeared in *The Southern Monthly Magazine* (Auckland, 1863–6, ed. H. H. Lusk), a journal that set out to 'please the taste of those who read for amusement, and stimulate the appetite of those who desire information' (Anon. 1863, *The Southern Monthly Magazine*: 1). An article in its second number stressed the forest's practical and economic value for new settlers:

> Putting aside altogether the ornamental aspect of the matter – which, however, the new settler ought not altogether to do – you will find that, whether for building purposes, or fencing, for firewood, or even for a shelter for cattle in bad weather, you cannot possess anything half so valuable upon your farm as a few acres of good and, if possible, flat forest land. ('Colonial Experience' 1863: 60)

Such advice was echoed further south, in the monthly *Saturday Review* (Dunedin, 1864–71, ed. J. G. S. Grant), even though perhaps as little as 20 per cent of the Otago province was forested at the point when formal colonisation began (Roche 1987: 33). An 'Address to the Farmers of Scotland', which nods to the region's predominantly Scottish settlers, stresses the ready availability of forest resources – 'of black, white, and red pine, of birch and totara, and manuka, covering tens of and even hundreds of square miles' – to sustain the new colonist: 'all ready at his hand, to be felled, sawn, split, planed, tongued, and grooved, and prepared for the purposes of building his house and farm steadings' ('Address to the Farmers of Scotland' 1864: 163). At other times, however, the same journal expresses concern at the 'nakedness' of the Otago landscape. 'The absence of forests is a very marked feature of this Province', one article argues: in contrast to the northern view of the forest as oppositional to settlement, a southern perspective sees the lack of trees as itself impeding colonisation, and 'requires greatly the labours of art to supplement the deficiencies of nature' ('Plantations' 1866: 470) (see Plate 2). In addition to remedying the immediate lack of timber and shelter for crops, tree planting is presented as achieving longer-term cultural benefits: 'Above all, let the public reserves for educational, religious, and municipal purposes, be adorned and protected with umbrageous orchards and groves and leafy circumvallations of plantations' ('Plantations' 1866: 471). In highlighting the circulation of metropolitan ideas of trees' civic value, such arguments also testify that New Zealand's dense, evergreen indigenous forests were not readily legible in such terms, providing an early insight into how efforts to conserve forests might be affected by those inherited values.

The colony's first Catholic periodical, *The New Zealand Tablet* (Dunedin, 1873–1996, ed. P. Moran), demonstrates the multiple perspectives that might also be taken toward forests within the religious public sphere. 'Whilst putting religious interests in the first place', as an early twentieth-century commentary put it, 'the "Tablet" does not neglect or overlook the interests of civil society, and, not being allied to any political party, it has at all times been free to discuss political principles and measures' (*The Cyclopedia of New Zealand* 1903: 232). This political interest is evident in editorial support for the preservationist ethos of the New Zealand Forests Act 1874: 'Not a moment should be lost in adopting efficacious measures to conserve the forests of the Colony, and to plant new ones' ('The Forests Bill' 1874: 5). Forests also feature in regular reporting on international scientific and economic news. One item marvelled at the finding that the leaves in an acre of forest are able to 'pump' some 800 barrels of water from the ground per day, 'turn[ing] the wheels that energize the machinery which gives employment to millions' ('Waifs and Strays' 1875: 15). By contrast, another lamented 'some of the ways in which the American forests are going', reporting on that nation's vast annual consumption of wood for consumer products, including '300,000 cubic feet of the best pine' to make matches, and '50,000 acres of forest consumed to bake bricks' ('General News' 1879: 15). Preservationist sentiments were not applied consistently to the New Zealand context, however, for *The Tablet* also offered affirmative coverage of the continuing expansion of settlement, as in a local report on the successful establishment of a church where 'but a few weeks previously [had] been a portion of the primeval forest' ('A Straight Tip' 1877: 7). These juxtapositions of sacred and secular insight accord with James Beattie and John Stenhouse's observation that 'Christian and environmental discourses interpenetrated in irreducibly diverse, complex and contingent ways' (Beattie and Stenhouse 2007: 415), even while affirming that such issues were viewed exclusively from a settler angle.

A surprising variety of evidence is also encompassed by the forest-related articles of the colony's first and most enduring scientific publication, *Transactions and Proceedings of the New Zealand Institute* (Wellington, 1868–, ed. J. Hector). Most of these were contributions to botanical science, either detailing the characteristics of existing regional flora – such as pastoralist David Monro's lengthy essay in the inaugural issue describing how 'the vegetation of Nelson, Canterbury, or Otago' diverges from 'the forest scenery of the Northern Island' (Monro 1868: 7) – or describing individual tree species, such as the article (one of seven in the same volume) by botanist Thomas Kirk, 'On the Habit of the Rata (*Metrosideros robusta*)' (Kirk 1871). Such accounts of discovery are often coloured by literary references, though few as extravagantly as missionary William Colenso's paper, 'On the Large Number of Species of Ferns Noticed in a Small Area in the New Zealand Forests' (1882). Colenso frames the identification of fern species with Romantic effusions on natural beauty, writing of 'one spot in particular, deeply secluded in the quiet recesses of the grand old forest, – (a spot very dear to me! one which I have almost invariably visited several times, and every time with increasing delight in each of my journeys inland)' (Colenso 1882: 312). As justification for this approach, he argues that the scientific observation of the forest must be conditioned by sensibility, maintaining, 'it is the *feeling* that teaches or evokes the *true seeing*; for, whoever possesses the heart to feel will also have the eye to see', and quotes in support the opening lines of William Cullen Bryant's poem 'Thanatopsis' (1817): 'To him who, in the love of Nature, holds / Communion with her visible forms, she speaks / A various language' (Colenso 1882: 314). The changing political status of the colony's forests is also visible in the *Transactions and Proceedings*. Just as the New Zealand Forests Act 1874 'mark[ed] the initial attempt to establish a scientific State forestry in New Zealand' (Roche 1987: 68), so the journal constituted the primary venue for initial attempts to conceive of the forest as a finite economic resource that ought to be managed scientifically. The nascent sense of scarcity is evident in pastoralist Josiah Clifton Firth's 'On Forest Culture' (1874), which argues that 'the almost total destruction of the forests of the North Island is but a question of time, unless stringent measures are taken to conserve them' (Firth 1874: 183). The *Transactions* also published two lengthy papers by Inches Campbell Walker, the colony's first Conservator of Forests: 'On State Forestry: Its Aim and Object' (1876) and 'The Climatic and Financial Aspect of Forest Conservancy as Applicable to New Zealand' (1876). The first of these outlined a goal of managing and 'improving' indigenous forests, according to European practice, in order to maximise their exploitation as a timber resource, and cited Alexander Pope's *An Essay on Criticism* (1711) as an argument against too-hasty deforestation:

> We must therefore note how Nature acts in the reproduction of forest trees, and follow in her footsteps. As Pope writes –
> 'First follow Nature and your judgement frame
> By her just standard, which remains the same,
> Unerring.' (Campbell Walker 1876b: 193)

Walker's second paper drew on George Perkins Marsh's *Man and Nature* (1864) to argue that the 'climatic influence of forests is a very important matter, which cannot be approached too early or with too much care and deliberation in the life of a nation or colony', and asserted that any financial gains from state forests 'should ever be subordinate' to this issue (Campbell Walker 1876a: xxvii, xl). In particular, he expressed concern about the impacts of mountain deforestation:

> [A]scending the narrow vallies of the Grey and Buller Rivers and their tributaries, walled in by steep forest-clad hills, a feeling almost of dread constantly presented itself to my mind as to what would be the result if these forests were ever to be cleared away without great discrimination and the retention of extensive reserves.... Once gone, farewell to the smiling fields in the vallies [*sic*] below and the abundant pasture on the lower slopes of the hills. (Campbell Walker 1876a: xxxviii–xxxix)

Such early scientific accounts published in the *Transactions* do not talk about the forests in ecosystem-like terms, but their alertness to hydrology and the water cycle enables them to articulate a sense of relation between the forests and the ongoing viability of the settler economy and society.

1880s–1900s

Between the 1880s and 1900s, a period that witnessed the 'first generation of cultural nationalism in New Zealand' (Stafford and Williams 2006: 14), the colony's remaining 'primeval' forests were increasingly valued by settlers as markers of local distinctiveness, even as forestry and agricultural expansion also remained fundamental to their sense of identity and economic future. The groundwork for such patriotic attachment was laid in part by the improving visual technology employed by publications such as the monthly *Illustrated New Zealand Herald for Home Readers* (Dunedin, 1868–83, ed. R. T. Wheeler) and its successor, *Illustrated New Zealand News* (Dunedin, 1883–7, ed. R. T. Wheeler), as well as *The Triad: A Monthly Magazine of Music, Science, and Art* (Dunedin, 1893–1915, ed. C. Baeyertz), whose full-page lithographs of the colony's beauty spots 'found their way onto the walls of humbler dwellings' (Tye 1996: 215) (see Figure 5.1). The growth of such aesthetic sentiment contributed to 'the most active [period] in New Zealand's conservation history' prior to the late 1960s

Figure 5.1 *Scene on Henderson's Creek, Auckland. Illustrated New Zealand News*, 13, 4 August 1884. Ref: S-L-1764.01. New Zealand periodicals' use of lithography assisted in disseminating ideas of local natural beauty. Courtesy of Alexander Turnbull Library, Wellington, New Zealand.

(Young 2004: 88): the State Forests Act 1885 created forest reserves; Arbor Day was established as a national observance in 1892; six national parks were created between 1887 and 1906; and the Scenery Preservation Act 1903 attempted 'a major effort to once and for all time preserve the remaining, threatened scenic areas of New Zealand' (Roche 2017: 175). Nevertheless, this was also the period when the rate of deforestation reached its maximum: 'The greatest losses occurred between 1882 and 1909', David Young points out, 'when the forests are estimated to have been diminished by almost 40 per cent from their original 11.4 million hectares' (Young 2004: 99). Such rapid change further intensified anxieties over the economic impact of the predicted extinction of many indigenous timber sources, leading to Royal Commission investigations into the timber supply (1909) and forestry (1913).

Among the literary periodicals of this period, *Zealandia: A Monthly Magazine of New Zealand Literature by New Zealand Writers* (Dunedin, 1889–90, ed. W. Freeman) notably encapsulates the increasingly nationalist tone of the public sphere and the licence this gave for such a publication to range widely in its forms of environmental engagement. As its editor announced in the first issue: 'ZEALANDIA has been established as a distinctively national literary magazine. Its contributors will all be New Zealanders, and no subject will be dwelt upon in its pages that is not of interest, directly or indirectly, primarily to New Zealanders' (Freeman 1889: 2). The first issue featured a column by the Presbyterian minister Rutherford Waddell, 'Some Social Responsibilities of a Young Community' (1889), which argued for the national importance of forests and other environments several years in advance of the Scenery Preservation Act 1903:

> Within a few hours' travel you may pass through all the wonders and wealths of the five zones, and yet fire and axe are busy by river and lake, and hill and city, reducing forests and ferns to ashes. Why should not Government step in and stop the Vandals and Huns who are turning our natural beauties into desolations? These also are trusts, and to allow them to be destroyed as we do is not only a disgrace to ourselves, but a crime against posterity. (Waddell 1889: 20)

The journal's engagements with the forest ranged across travel writing and poetry to a remarkable essay by the engineer William Newsham Blair, 'Artificial Earth Sculpture' (1890). Arguing that colonisation involves 'the physical moulding of the country', Blair maintained that 'the settlers of New Zealand are modifying the face of the country by cultivating the land and clearing the forests' (Blair 1890: 481, 477). The most significant alterations arise from the 'indirect result of their labours', however, notably the 'radical change in its effects' of rainfall upon hilly terrain (Blair 1890: 477). A later and more long-lived monthly literary periodical, the *New Zealand Illustrated Magazine* (Auckland, 1899–1905, ed. F. E. Baume), testifies to the increasing prominence of forest scenery – along with that of mountains, lakes and rivers – within settler culture. A two-part essay on the growing conservation movement by writer Edith Searle Grossmann, 'The People's Parks and Playgrounds in New Zealand' (1901), argued that the preservation of forest areas as scenic reserves was of a piece with the colony's progressiveness, 'one of the latest developments in modern democracy' (Grossmann 1901: 285). At the same time, settler conflict with the forest was also a staple of literary writing: Ned Reid's 'Bush-life' (1902) stressed the forest's 'appeal as a natural trade resource, and as a splendid field for enterprise', and offered a romanticised account of the 'life led by the stalwart bushman' (Reid 1902: 369).

A growing tension between two economic views of the forest – concern over its rapid diminishment as an exploitable resource, and frustration with its obstruction of ongoing agricultural growth – also played out in a diverse range of venues. *The North New Zealand Settler: And Land Buyers' Guide* (Auckland, 1882–4) was aimed at agriculturalists and pastoralists in the Auckland province and might have been expected to fully support the creation of farmland through deforestation (Pawson and Wood 2008: 347–8). Indeed, a discussion of 'bush farming' – that is, settling on 'a block of land, partly bush . . . and wholly unenclosed and unimproved' – gives a detailed account of the labour involved in 'bush clearing', culminating in the point where 'English grass seed is sown amongst the charred stumps and half-burnt logs that remain' ('G. L. P.' 1883: 262). Yet, an editorial in the same issue expressed forceful opposition to deforestation, due to the impact of possible climatic changes and the forest's value as a commodity:

> But the injury done to the climate is only one of the evils that will be brought about by the culpable neglect of our rulers to make some provision for protecting and renewing our splendid native forests. Saw-mills, bush fires, and bush settlers are doing their best towards making the kauri, the puriri and the totara a memory of the past. . . . Once exterminated in this country, and they are practically gone for ever; while if preserved, their timber may one day be worth as much per inch as it is now worth per foot. ('The Preservation of our Forests' 1883: 260)

These contradictions within the economic ethos of colonial modernity are also evident in a later monthly periodical aimed at urban readers, *Progress* (Wellington, 1905–23), which was dedicated to cataloguing and celebrating 'progress in engineering, processes, inventions, industrial work, and economics' ('Brief Foreword' 1905: 5). One article describes 'the upspringing of sheep on the ashes of the forest as one of the most remarkable things about the sheep industry' ('The Wool Industry' 1907: 213). Yet an article on the timber industry in the next issue begins by charting a shift from a past belief that 'the forests of these islands appeared to be destined to a permanence almost eternal', to a present-day concern that they appear 'within a distance of extermination which is but a small span in the history of a nation' ('Our Industries' 1907: 255–6).

The New Zealand Tablet demonstrates how a range of preservationist responses to the forest were articulated through reactions to the annual Arbor Day celebrations. An 1899 editorial had celebrated 'the progress of a young colony where the white man's hand and brain have been but little more than half a century at work turning forest and swamp into field, and dotting what had been a wilderness with . . . the busy hum of modern commercial life' ('New Zealand the Provider' 1899: 17). In the same year, however, a column castigated Arbor Day as an 'annual day of make-believe tree-culture' that paled into insignificance against 'the wilful and wholesale waste of our magnificent forest resources that is going on practically every day of the year's three hundred and sixty-five' ('The Ruin of our Forests' 1899: 17). Although environmental historian David Young has described early Arbor Day commemorations as expressions of 'contrition and atonement' (Young 2004: 96), *The Tablet*'s coverage of the subject veers more towards anger. An editorial in 1902 drew on recent literature from around the world to argue that a forestry science approach was imperative to avoid economic and climatic peril – 'Unless our legislators wake up . . . we shall see repeated in New Zealand the woful [sic] experiences which . . . have followed the wholesale and wasteful destruction of forests in other lands' ('Forest Destruction' 1902: 16) – while a front-page item the following year bluntly charged that 'while we are planting by the rood, we are destroying by the square mile' ('Arbor Day' 1903: 1). Despite the persistent expression of such concerns, their restriction to a single day of the year and broad support for the 'scientific' planting of introduced tree species are symptomatic of what Paul Star has called the 'fragile nature of the argument for native forest' associated with Arbor Day (Star 2002: 280).

There are few expressions in settler periodicals of an understanding of the forest as a space of ecological complexity, let alone that this might have intrinsic value. Indeed, a contribution to the *New Zealand Illustrated Magazine* by the historian and ethnographer James Cowan reveals how powerfully the idea of scenery preservation was able to mitigate settler concern for the wider environmental impacts their presence had wrought:

> I can almost share the cries of regret of the shy wood-birds for the vanished trees when I visit some locality where the well-remembered dense bush . . . has given place to blackened stumps and charred logs. Yet it is not reasonable to object to the wiping-out of the forest by the settler, for the heroic work of colonisation must go on[.] . . . The happy middle course seems to be in preserving, here and there, good-sized patches and clumps of the native bush[.] (Cowan 1902: 200)

The most sustained and nuanced expressions of ecological awareness are found in *Transactions and Proceedings of the New Zealand Institute*, which reprinted two lectures by artist and clergyman Philip Walsh, 'The Effect of Deer on the New Zealand Bush' (1892) and 'On the Disappearance of the New Zealand Bush' (1896). In the earlier article, Walsh asserts that he writes 'from the aesthetic rather than from the economic point of view' (Walsh 1892: 438–9), which allows him to consider the impact of introduced species in ecological terms:

> The forest has grown up through the course of ages undisturbed by any four-footed enemy whatever. . . . And, moreover, the constituent portions are so dependent on each other for nourishment and protection that, once the balance has been disturbed, the entire growth rapidly suffers. (Walsh 1892: 436)

Walsh's later paper similarly deploys emotive literary rhetoric to convey the complexity of a kauri forest ecosystem and its vulnerability to fire:

> The stately totaras, whose fibrous bark conducted the flames to the tops, when for a moment they became as so many blazing torches, now stand grim and black. . . . The fern-tree's feathery fronds and the glossy curving spikes of the neinei hang shrivelled and limp, while the netted ropes of the mange-mange are gone altogether – vanished in a puff of flame. All the ferns and mosses, the orchids and climbing plants, all the light and graceful undergrowth indigenous to the kauri bush, which made the place seem a fairy paradise, are charred and dead. (Walsh 1896: 494)

Even as Walsh's rhetoric expresses a demonstrably conservationist ethos, it also encapsulates the struggle to articulate a sense of ecological value that might be able to effectively counter the 'economic point of view' driving deforestation.

Māori environmental knowledge occupied a tenuous place within the settler public sphere at the end of the century, surprisingly visible yet typically framed by notions of romance and archaism. Literary venues such as the *New Zealand Illustrated Magazine* occasionally published ethnographic writing, such as James Cowan's 'Out in the Wilds' (1900), an account of his journey through the 'wild luxuriance of the forest primeval' of the Urewera region, homeland of the Ngāi Tūhoe *iwi* (people) (Cowan 1900: 262). Cowan contrasts the impersonal settler perception of the forest as 'a nameless, untravelled jungle' with the depth and relationality of Tūhoe knowledge: 'Even particular forest trees in various localities are distinguished by special names, given to them by the men of old from some peculiar circumstance or other, which is well known by oral traditions to every person in the tribe' (Cowan 1900: 266). The most substantial home for English-language accounts of such knowledge was the *Journal of the Polynesian Society* (Auckland, 1892–, ed. E. Tregear and S. Percy Smith), the official organ of its namesake society, 'formed to promote the study of the Anthropology, Ethnology, Philology, History and Antiquities of the Polynesian races' ('Polynesian Society' 1892: 3). Māori perspectives on the forest were related in lengthy ethnographic articles by Elsdon Best, a former sawmill owner, whose fascination was coloured by the belief that Māori were an irretrievably primitive people. In 'Notes on Maori Mythology' (1899), he highlights 'the respect in which the more valuable trees were held by the Maori' as the result of their sacred origin, quoting the 'aged and learned' Hāmiora Tumutara Pio (Ngāti Awa, Ngāti Tūwharetoa):

> No valuable tree may be felled without performing the strange rites of the *Ahi purakau* and the *Tumu-whenua*, and also repeating the sacred *karakia* (invocation) to Tane, that he may not resent (through his people, the forest elves) the destruction of one of his children. It is Tane that protects the forest and the birds thereof, and preserves the *mauri* (sacred life principle) of the forests. Should the mauri of a forest be desecrated by man, then assuredly that forest becomes *tamaoatia* – the sacred *mauri* is contaminated, and all bird denizens of such a forest will at once migrate to other lands. (Best 1899: 95)

Such writing brought to settler awareness the complex Māori view of interconnection between human and natural worlds even as it diminished it as the outmoded belief of a 'mythopœtic people' whose culture and identity was being rapidly and inevitably destroyed (Best 1899: 93). The memorialising tendency of Best's ethnography is paralleled by settler retellings of indigenous narratives, as in *Zealandia* magazine's publication of a poetic version of the Māori creation story by prominent writer Jessie Mackay. Adopting the perspectives of the separated Papatūānuku (Sky Mother) and Ranginui (Earth Father), the words given to Ranginui are inflected by the settler view that the kauri was the colony's most impressive and valuable tree species: 'Cursëd be Tane-Mehuta [sic], the God of the Forest, for he / With his strong sons the Kauris thrust me forth for ever to be / Here in the lone blue waste, and the stars for ever between!' ('Jessica' 1889: 331). The impulse to locate Māori forest knowledge in a 'mythopœtic' past exemplifies what Jane Stafford and Mark Williams describe as a defining 'contradiction' of late-century colonial culture, where 'archaism cohabits with and compensates for the colony's sense of its own modernity' (Stafford and Williams 2006: 11).

Periodicals from this time nevertheless also offer occasional glimpses that different settler valuations of indigenous forest knowledge were possible. While *Transactions and Proceedings of the New Zealand Institute* rarely published papers on literature, one notable exception was R. Coupland Harding's 'On Unwritten Literature' (1892), which sought to counter 'disparaging remarks' about the literary quality of Māori oral traditions (Harding 1892: 440). In concluding that settlers might yet 'find that there is something to admire in the uncivilised man, and even something to be learned from him', Harding highlights environmental knowledge in particular:

> As a typical example of the ghastly side of human progress and science, we have only to look at the desecrated Manawatu Gorge, where Nature is taking effective revenge for the outrages inflicted upon her. Primitive man lived nearer to Nature than we do to-day, and understood her better than we. Primitive man has left us from remote ages a legacy of literature that we cannot now surpass. (Harding 1892: 447)

Even though couched in the denigratory language of primitivism, such comments are nevertheless highly unusual in even allowing that Māori knowledge might be of ongoing relevance to settler society. An even more striking and atypical engagement with Māori literature is a short work of landscape writing, 'Mount Egmont' (1889), published anonymously by 'H. L. J.' in *Monthly Review* (Wellington, 1888–90, ed. J. R. Blair). The title refers to Taranaki Maunga, a dormant volcano on the west coast of the North Island that would become the centre of the Egmont National Park in 1900, and which provides the essay with a vantage point for observing a 'dun pall' covering the land ('H. L. J.' 1889: 576) (see Figure 5.2). This is revealed to be the smoke from forests being burned to establish pasture for dairy cattle – one branch of my family, farming in this area at the time, lit some of those fires – and 'H. L. J.' expresses passionate regret for this lost forest by describing its relationship with Tāne, god of the forest, in ongoing, familial terms:

> It is the smoke of burning forests, the smoke of the sacrifice of Nature's crown of glory, of Tane's beauteous children, – the wealth of the country stealing away in vapour. All day it has been driven seaward by the remorseless land-breeze: now, the gentle zephyrs of the evening bring it tenderly back – the spirit of Tane comes to wail over the ashy graves of his lost, his glorious children. ('H. L. J.' 1889: 576)

The sun is named as the god 'Ra' (Tama-nui-te-rā), whose 'fiery eyes' are 'red with weeping, weeping for the fate of Tane's sons', while the sea god Tangaroa's 'breast heaves slowly, as, with long-drawn sighs, he grieves in secret; grieves, silent, for the fate of Tane's sons!' ('H. L. J.' 1889: 576). The vignette finishes with the setting of the sun, when 'the darkness of night, the gloom of despair, settles down over land and sea' ('H. L. J.' 1889: 576). Even such unusual openness to Māori knowledge remains constrained, however, as the destruction of 'Tane's beauteous children' is not framed

Figure 5.2 Alexander Walker Reid, *Mountain with road and clearing farms of trees*, c. 1890–1900, gelatine half plate glass negative. The extent of deforestation in the vicinity of Taranaki Maunga by the end of the nineteenth century. Courtesy of Puke Ariki, New Plymouth, PHO2007-301.

as a loss for Māori, despite their dispossession going hand-in-hand with deforestation, while the agency of the settler population is concealed beneath the smoke of the fires they have lit.

Conclusion

This chapter has argued that settler periodicals constitute a missing link in past attempts to understand the cultural dimensions of settlement's 'wooden world'. If these publications reveal a more nuanced public sphere, which understood forests through the interpenetration of multiple domains of knowledge, they also reveal calamitous areas of blindness. Against the dominant economic and developmental arguments in favour of deforestation, settler writers drew primarily on two sources: climatological concerns about the colony's future derived from the work of George Perkins Marsh, and Romantic ideas of aesthetic beauty that stressed individual and collective identification with the environment. Those aesthetic claims were particularly important because they provided one of the only ways to imagine and value the forest in proto-ecological terms of species diversity, but their underlying logics of temporary visitation and external observation embedded a sense of distance that precluded ideas of interconnection with the human world. Settler periodicals do attest, however, that another powerful ecological framework was readily available – Māori environmental knowledge – but they also demonstrate how its insights were diminished and dismissed through its framing as the 'mythopœtic' expression of an earlier mode of society. Critics may once have disregarded many of these publications for their individual transience, but we are now challenged to recognise that they collectively flourished while the forests fell; as increasing numbers of these titles now gain renewed life through digitisation, their pages remain haunted by the ghosts of vanished landscapes and ecosystems.

Bibliography

'Address to the Farmers of Scotland. Otago versus Scotia' (1864), *The Saturday Review*, 23 July, 162–3.
Anon. (1863), *The Southern Monthly Magazine*, 1.1, March, 1–2.
'Arbor Day' (1903), *The New Zealand Tablet*, 31.29, 16 July, 1.
Beattie, James, and John Stenhouse (2007), 'Empire, environment and religion: God and the natural world in nineteenth-century New Zealand', *Environment and History*, 13.4, 413–46.
Belich, James (1996), *Making Peoples: A History of the New Zealanders, from Polynesian Settlement to the End of the Nineteenth Century*, Auckland: Penguin.
—— (2009), *Replenishing the Earth: The Settler Revolution and the Rise of the Anglo-World, 1783–1939*, Oxford: Oxford University Press.
Best, Elsdon (1899), 'Notes on Maori Mythology', *Journal of the Polynesian Society*, 8.2, 93–121.
—— (1907), 'Maori Forest Lore: Being Some Account of Native Forest Lore and Woodcraft, as also of Many Myths, Rites, Customs, and Superstitions Connected with the Flora and Fauna of the Tuhoe or Ure-wera District.—Part I', *Transactions and Proceedings of the New Zealand Institute*, 40, 185–254.
Blair, William Newsham (1890), 'Artificial Earth Sculpture', *Zealandia: A Monthly Magazine of New Zealand Literature by New Zealand Authors*, 1.8, February, 474–81.
'Brief Foreword' (1905), *Progress*, 1.1, November, 5.
Campbell Walker, Inches (1876a), 'The Climatic and Financial Aspect of Forest Conservancy as Applicable to New Zealand', *Transactions and Proceedings of the New Zealand Institute*, 9, xxvii–xlix.
—— (1876b), 'On State Forestry: Its Aim and Object', *Transactions and Proceedings of the New Zealand Institute*, 9, 187–203.
Colenso, William (1882), 'On the Large Number of Species of Ferns Noticed in a Small Area in the New Zealand Forests, in the Seventy-mile Bush, between Norsewood and Danneverke [*sic*], in the Provincial District of Hawke's Bay', *Transactions and Proceedings of the New Zealand Institute*, 15, 311–20.
'Colonial Experience' (1863), *The Southern Monthly Magazine*, 1.2, April, 58–61.
Cowan, James (1900), 'Out in the Wilds (The Land of the Urewera)', *New Zealand Illustrated Magazine*, 1.4, January, 262–8.
—— (1902), 'Te Wao-Nui-a-Tane', *New Zealand Illustrated Magazine*, 7.3, January, 200–9.
The Cyclopedia of New Zealand: Otago and Southland Districts (1903), Christchurch: The Cyclopedia Company.
Firth, Josiah Clifton (1874), 'On Forest Culture', *Transactions and Proceedings of the New Zealand Institute*, 7, 181–95.
'Forest Destruction' (1902), *The New Zealand Tablet*, 30.30, 24 July, 16–17.
'The Forests Bill' (1874), *The New Zealand Tablet*, 26.7, 8 August, 5.
Freeman, William (1889), 'To Our Readers', *Zealandia: A Monthly Magazine of New Zealand Literature by New Zealand Authors*, 1.1, July, 2.
'General News' (1879), *The New Zealand Tablet*, 7.319, 30 May, 15.

'G. L. P.' (1883), 'Some Aspects of Farming Life in the North Island of New Zealand', *The North New Zealand Settler: And Land Buyers' Guide*, 2.9, September, 262–3.

Grossmann, Edith Searle (1901), 'The People's Parks and Playgrounds in New Zealand', *New Zealand Illustrated Magazine*, 3.4, January, 285–91.

Harding, R. Coupland (1892), 'On Unwritten Literature', *Transactions and Proceedings of the New Zealand Institute*, 25, 439–48.

'H. L. J.' (1889), 'Mount Egmont', *Monthly Review*, 1.12, November, 576–7.

Hudson, W. B. (1890), 'A Holiday in the Highlands. I', *Monthly Review*, 2.6, June, 326–37.

'Jessica' [Jessie Mackay] (1889), 'Rangi and Papa', *Zealandia: A Monthly Magazine of New Zealand Literature by New Zealand Authors*, 1.6, December, 330–1.

Kirk, Thomas (1871), 'On the Habit of the Rata (*Metrosideros robusta*)', *Transactions and Proceedings of the New Zealand Institute*, 4, 267–70.

Knight, Catherine (2009), 'The paradox of discourse concerning deforestation in New Zealand: A historical survey', *Environment and History*, 15.3, 323–42.

Lochhead, Lynne, and Paul Star (2013), 'Children of the burnt bush: New Zealanders and the indigenous remnant, 1880–1930', in Eric Pawson and Tom Brooking (eds), *Making a New Land: Environmental Histories of New Zealand*, Dunedin: Otago University Press, 141–57.

McEldowney, Dennis (1998), 'Publishing, patronage, literary magazines', in Terry Sturm (ed.), *The Oxford History of New Zealand Literature in English*, Auckland: Oxford University Press, 631–94.

Monro, David (1868), 'On the Leading Features of the Geographical Botany of the Provinces of Nelson and Marlborough, New Zealand', *Transactions and Proceedings of the New Zealand Institute*, 1, 6–17.

New Zealand Forests Act (1874), 38 Victoriae No. 24, 121–4, enacted 31 August.

'New Zealand the Provider' (1899), *The New Zealand Tablet*, 27.20, 18 May, 17–18.

'Our Industries. No. XV. – The Timber Industry of New Zealand' (1907), *Progress*, 2.7, 1 May, 255–8.

Pawson, Eric, and Vaughan Wood (2008), 'Information exchange and the making of the colonial farm: Agricultural periodicals in late nineteenth-century New Zealand', *Agricultural History*, 82.3, 337–65.

'Plantations' (1866), *The Saturday Review*, 74, 9 June, 470–1.

'Polynesian Society' (1892), *Journal of the Polynesian Society*, 1.1, 3.

Pool, Ian (1991), *Te Iwi Maori: A New Zealand Population, Past, Present and Projected*, Auckland: Auckland University Press.

'The Preservation of our Forests' (1883), *The North New Zealand Settler: And Land Buyers' Guide*, 2.9, September, 260.

Reid, Ned (1902), 'Bush-life. With the Knight's Axe and Crosscut', *New Zealand Illustrated Magazine*, 5.5, February, 369–76.

Roche, Michael (1987), *Forest Policy in New Zealand: An Historical Geography, 1840–1919*, Palmerston North: Dunmore Press.

—— (2017), 'Seeing scenic New Zealand: W. W. Smith's eye and the Scenery Preservation Commission, 1904–06', *International Review of Environmental History*, 3.1, 175–95.

Royal, Te Ahukaramū Charles (2010), 'Te Waonui-a-Tāne | Forest Mythology', in Jennifer Garlick, Basil Keane and Tracey Borgfeldt (eds), *Te Taiao | Māori and the Natural World*, Auckland: David Bateman, 100–5.

'The Ruin of our Forests' (1899), *The New Zealand Tablet*, 27.30, 18 July, 17–18.

'The Soils of the Province of Auckland – Which to Choose, and Which to Avoid' (1860), *The Auckland Weekly Register, and Commercial and Shipping Gazette*, 4.200, 19 November, 3.

Stafford, Jane, and Mark Williams (2006), *Maoriland: New Zealand Literature, 1872–1914*, Wellington: Victoria University Press.

Star, Paul (2002), 'Native forest and the rise of preservation in New Zealand (1903–1913)', *Environment and History*, 8.3, 275–94.
Stiles, Clark (1997), 'Periodicals', in Penny Griffith, Ross Harvey and Keith Maslen (eds), *Book and Print in New Zealand: A Guide to Print Culture in Aotearoa*, Wellington: Victoria University Press, 138–40.
'A Straight Tip' (1877), 'Kumara', *The New Zealand Tablet*, 5.242, 21 December, 7.
Taonui, Rāwiri (2010), 'Te Ngahere | Forest Lore', in Jennifer Garlick, Basil Keane and Tracey Borgfeldt (eds), *Te Taiao | Māori and the Natural World*, Auckland: David Bateman, 106–15.
Tye, J. Reginald (1996), 'New Zealand', in J. Don Vann and Rosemary T. VanArsdel (eds), *Periodicals of Queen Victoria's Empire: An Exploration*, Toronto: University of Toronto Press, 203–40.
Waddell, Rutherford (1889), 'Some Social Responsibilities of a Young Community', *Zealandia: A Monthly Magazine of New Zealand Literature by New Zealand Authors*, 1.1, July, 17–21.
'Waifs and Strays' (1875), *The New Zealand Tablet*, 3.117, 23 July, 15–16.
Walsh, Philip (1892), 'The Effect of Deer on the New Zealand Bush: A Plea for the Protection of our Forest Reserves', *Transactions and Proceedings of the New Zealand Institute*, 25, 435–9.
——— (1896), 'On the Disappearance of the New Zealand Bush', *Transactions and Proceedings of the New Zealand Institute*, 29, 490–6.
'The Wool Industry of New Zealand' (1907), *Progress*, 2.6, 1 April, 213–17.
Wynn, Graeme (2013), 'Destruction under the guise of improvement? The forest, 1840–1920', in Eric Pawson and Tom Brooking (eds), *Making a New Land: Environmental Histories of New Zealand*, Dunedin: Otago University Press, 122–38.
Young, David (2004), *Our Islands, Our Selves: A History of Conservation in New Zealand*, Dunedin: University of Otago Press.

6

British Missionary Magazines at Home and Abroad: Southern Africa as Topic and Southern Africans as Readership

Lize Kriel, Annika Vosseler and Chantelle Finaughty

Introduction

By the time the last quarter of the nineteenth century opened its chapter in history, about 40 per cent of all periodicals in Britain were published under religious umbrellas, either by the various denominational publishing societies themselves or by commercial houses they were linked with. Leading cheap religious weeklies circulated up to 1,500,000 copies a week (Altick 1957: 361). The *Wesleyan Missionary Notices*, which will be discussed in some detail in this chapter, had a monthly circulation of about 54,000 copies (Barringer 2004: 72). Clearly, missionary periodicals were not a marginal phenomenon in nineteenth-century Britain.

However, by the early 2000s, they had become a 'neglected source' (Barringer 2004: 46) and their significance had to be explained by historians. In this chapter, we will argue that this was, at least in part, owing to the way in which the medium was gradually being overtaken by its own success. The missionary periodical was the bearer of a communication network which, over the span of the nineteenth century, became increasingly multi-directional as far as places of publication and intended audiences were concerned. As we will illustrate, by the first decade of the twentieth century, the offspring of nineteenth-century missionary periodicals in the British colonies had become so prominent in their own right that the concepts of 'home' and 'abroad' could be inverted.

For this overview chapter, we could select but a few titles from the richly diverse multitude of missionary and missionary-related periodicals dating from the nineteenth and the early twentieth centuries. We refer mostly to the *Wesleyan Missionary Notices*, *The Chronicle of the London Missionary Society*, *The Christian Express*, *Isigidimi Sama-Xosa*, *Mahoka a Becwana* and *Inkanyiso yase Natal* to demonstrate the changing dynamics of the home-abroad circuit and the resultant dislodging of these two notions.

When Terry Barringer appealed for more scholarly attention to missionary periodicals, the major argument was for their recognition as a source that could contribute to 'an understanding of how the Victorians perceived and portrayed the non-European world and how attitudes changed over time' (Barringer 2004: 46). But Barringer also made the argument that the serial nature of the source should be appreciated because it could yield a 'more nuanced understanding of the much-debated relationship between colonialism and Christianisation' (Barringer 2004: 46). A further milestone in the movement away from merely mining periodicals for factual information was Felicity Jensz and Hanna Acke's edited collection *Missions and Media: The Politics of Missionary Periodicals in the Long Nineteenth Century* (2013), which approached the missionary periodical as a genre, an object of study in its own right. This orientation also included a shift away from inquiring how Victorian views were imposed on the wider world; rather, the role of the periodical as medium was foregrounded, with a new focus on how periodicals could themselves shape interpretations of events in the mission field through their power to picture, frame and print observations in particular ways. An example of recent scholarship foregrounding the role of missionary periodicals as the key medium shaping the interpretation of events is Thoralf Klein's comparative discussion of missionary reportage on the Boxer War (1900–1) by five different missionary periodicals from different nations (Klein 2013: 399–404). Whereas the Anglican missionary periodical proclaimed the martyrdom of British missionaries, the German missionary periodical accused the Society for the Promotion of the Gospel (SPG) of promoting the 'spiritual expansion of the [British] empire' ('Imperialismus' 1901: 432).

Jensz and Acke emphasise the transnational character (Cox 2008: 5) of the Evangelical Revival and subsequent Protestant missionary endeavours, and Judith Becker and Katharina Stornig's edited collection on the role of pictures in missionary periodicals, *Menschen, Bilder, eine Welt: Ordnungen von Vielfalt in der religiösen Publizistik um 1900* (2018), proceeds in the same spirit. However, for the current investigation, by focusing specifically on British publishing and its networking with South Africa in particular, we wish to outline the long-term effect of the mission communication network through periodicals. By placing this selected sector of the expansive missionary network under the spotlight, we follow the network's changing shape and how this affected the direction of the flow of news: between missionaries and Britain; between missionaries and converts; between missionaries and settler societies; and eventually from converts to missionaries and settlers, and from black African Christians (no longer thinking of themselves as infants in the faith) to the imperial metropole.

An Open Communication System

The pervasive communication networks of missionary societies were built in a complex historical context. Protestantism may have been central to British national and imperial identity, but this could not dictate the role religion would play in the history of empire (Cox 2008: 9). The missionaries' inescapable involvement in Britain's worldwide expansion was 'both patchy and discontinuous while also highly competitive, decidedly negative as well as optimistically engaged. Attitudes ranged from total indifference or harsh criticism of empire, through discomfort and toleration, to enthusiastic support' (Porter 2004: 323–4).

Precisely because of this diversity of possibilities for missionary societies' operations 'abroad' (that is, in the colonies), it was extremely important that their public communication had to present their missionary strategies to their supporters and funders 'at home' (that is, in Britain) in an acceptable light. Paul Jenkins argued that one should think of missionary societies as 'open systems of communication' (1994: 441). At the core was the 'organisation', constituting the personnel at the headquarters as well as the ones sent overseas, and then there was also the 'movement', comprising the supporters of the missionary societies, initially thought of as 'home'-based, in the vicinity of the mission's headquarters. The 'movement', besides (or by) serving as a recruitment pool for missionaries (male and female) and providing a monetary basis for the work overseas, also cradled the 'conceptual framework' that grounded mission societies (Wendt 2012: 101).

This communication system was 'open' because, both 'at home' in Britain and 'abroad' in the mission field, 'further institutions and individuals attached themselves to the core, so that in both spheres of activity the mission societies had a diverse social foundation' (Wendt 2012: 101). The mission societies needed this open communication system to organise, finance, design, advertise, put into practice and defend their evangelising work. They needed a system through which they could both act and react. Once a mission society had constructed for itself 'an image of the cultures' it intended to target, this image was released into a system where everything was in flux: not only the 'movement', but also individuals and institutions the mission society engaged with, as well as missionaries' own perspectives on the non-European world. Subsequently, the views a mission society disseminated needed continual adjustment (Wendt 2012: 101).

This, in summary, was the tall order the missionary periodical had to deliver on, which also explains, at least in part, why there was such a proliferation of them, and why historians must accede that there is simply too much to read (Etherington 2005: 37). Barringer was able to list as many as 233 periodicals published in Britain between 1836 and 1901 (2004: 54–73).[1] When trying to make sense of this abundance, it helps to keep in mind the purpose of the missionary periodical: reports about faraway conversions were meant to strengthen religious devotion 'at home'. The study of religion in Britain and religious activities 'abroad' ought not to 'proceed in separate tracks' (Cox 2008: 7). In missionary periodicals, 'home' and 'abroad' simultaneously feature within a single view.

British Missionary Societies in Southern Africa in the Nineteenth Century

Much of the content of missionary periodicals was made up of letters from missionaries. These letters created a sense of close relationship with their readers – the supporters, or friends of the mission, which Jenkins had referred to as 'the movement'. Some letters were directly addressed to family members or the secretary of the society. The letters would often be edited and summarised by the editors back in Britain. Articles were also sometimes included from other publications. A form of argumentation used in missionary periodicals was the call for action to help those living in poverty. Amongst the many recurring topics of discourse in missionary periodicals were the biblical commission to spread the Gospel, conversion narratives, the spiritual state of the world, and the founding of mission stations. Metaphorical images that were used in missionary periodicals included darkness and light, war, sowing and reaping, journeys, and adventures (Acke 2013: 231–6). 'It is highly likely', writes Jeffrey Cox in his monograph on *The British Missionary Enterprise*, 'that the majority of people in nineteenth-century Britain who had any knowledge at all of one or more foreign cultures received their basic information about foreign peoples, and what is more important, their basic images of foreign peoples, from missionary literature' (Cox 2008: 114). It can therefore be argued that missionaries in the nineteenth century contributed to the globalisation of knowledge (Van der Heyden and Feldtkeller 2012).

Before zooming in on our case study of Methodist periodicals, we need an overview to understand where they fitted in as one of the larger British denominations that were represented by missionary societies in the Southern African 'field'. Considering the limited scope of this chapter, the Catholic print culture related to Southern Africa will not be included in this discussion. The process of knowledge exchange was bound up in a complex flow of capital and information. As Cox explains:

> The networks of support for missions created by the missionary societies, with their close links to parishes, chapels, local associations, and especially the largely working-class Sunday Schools, supported a flow of money in one direction, and a flow of literature in the other direction into the hands of a considerable portion of the people of Britain. (Cox 2008: 113–14)

The London Missionary Society (LMS), which started as a non-denominational organisation, and became increasingly associated with Congregationalism, launched its *Evangelical Magazine* as early as July 1793. Its early issues outlined the formation of the society, and missionary intelligence remained a significant part of its contents throughout its two-century run. The LMS published Annual Reports from 1795, and the *Missionary Magazine and Chronicle* from 1837 (Barringer 2004: 47). In 1869, it was renamed as *The Chronicle of the London Missionary Society* (Vosseler 2022: 337). In Southern Africa, the LMS developed its mission field in Bechuanaland (today Botswana) and the Cape Colony (today the southern provinces of South Africa) under the auspices of missionary legends such as John Philip, Robert Moffat and David Livingstone. By the end of the nineteenth century the missionary infrastructure in the Cape Colony was handed over to the Congregational Union of South Africa (Gerdener 1958: 51).

The fledgling, evangelical, Anglican Church Missionary Society (CMS), founded in 1799, sent out a missionary to South Africa in the 1830s, shortly after their dissenter status in England was lifted in 1828 (Elbourne and Ross 1997: 32). In 1853, the Anglican Church sent J. W. Colenso to South Africa as the Bishop of Natal (Gerdener 1958: 72), and in 1870, the Church of the Province of South Africa (CPSA) was established. The CPSA remained under the auspices of the Archbishopric of Canterbury and still represents the majority of Anglicans in South Africa, adjacent to the smaller and more evangelical Church of England of South Africa (CESA) (De Gruchy 1997). In the nineteenth century, the CMS was not as prominent in South Africa as the LMS, but because Congregationalist and Anglican clergy followed British settlers to South Africa throughout the nineteenth century, these denominations became well established, including amongst the indigenous population. The same applied to the Baptist, Methodist and Presbyterian Churches, which also arrived in South Africa at the beginning of the nineteenth century to serve British settlers. Each had missionary societies associated with the 'white' or 'European' churches. The mission congregations grew parallel to the settler ones, and news about their missionary activities continued to be reported to supporters in Britain via periodicals such as the CMS *Church Missionary Paper* (continued until 1917), the Anglican *Colonial Church Chronicle* (around until the 1870s) and the Baptist *Missionary Herald* (established in 1819) (Barringer 2004: 58, 47). In the twentieth century, the gradual merging of settler and mission churches (De Gruchy 1997: 155) produced parallel changes in the landscape of missionary periodical publication.

The Scottish Presbyterian missionaries of the Glasgow Missionary Society (later incorporated into the United Presbyterian Church of Scotland (UPCS)) became famous for the mission stations they established in the Eastern Cape from the 1820s, specialising in institutions of learning for African Christians (Hodgson 1997: 75). Educated at the most august of these, Lovedale, and then in Scotland, Tiyo Soga returned to his own Ngqika Xhosa community to establish the Mgwali mission for the UPCS in 1857 (Hodgson 1997: 83). Amongst the UPCS publications aimed at readerships in Britain were their *Missionary Record* (established in 1846) and a *Juvenile Missionary Magazine*, later continued as the *Children's Missionary Magazine* (Barringer 2004: 55, 71). Because Lovedale became such a prominent site for local publishing in South Africa, it will be featured in this chapter as a case study under the section dedicated to missionary publications not intended for the edification of supporters in Britain, but for the promotion of communication within local African Christian communities.

The Presbyterians and the London Missionary Society (LMS) may have been the dominant evangelical influence in the Southern Cape regions of South Africa in the nineteenth century, but further up north, it was the Wesleyan Methodist Missionary Society (WMMS) that predominated. The Wesleyan Missionary Society was founded in England in 1813. The first Wesleyan Methodist missionary to arrive in South Africa was Rev. John McKenny, who established a station at Namaqualand in the Cape Colony in 1814. Rev. William Shaw, the only paid clergyman to have accompanied the prominent group of 1820 British settlers to the Cape Colony, was also a Wesleyan Methodist, and had the conviction that settlers, soldiers and indigenous people should all be evangelised in the same manner (Hodgson 1997: 75). In 1820, Wesleyans began their work among the enslaved population in the Cape Colony. However, amongst the Methodists too, the general South African assumption that persisted throughout the nineteenth and well into the twentieth century was that missionaries converted black people and that pastors served white congregations. Wesleyan Methodist periodicals of the nineteenth century abound with reportage on missionary work among the black people of Southern Africa.

In 1822, a Methodist mission was founded in Bechuanaland, and in 1841 a missionary accompanied British troops to Natal (Finaughty 2016: 50). By mid-century, African Methodists could be found throughout South Africa as far east as Natal and as far north as the Transvaal (Davenport 1997: 54). The South African Conference was established in 1882 and covered the Cape Colony, Natal, Orange Free State, Tembuland, Pondoland and Griqualand. For the work north of the Vaal, a new mission for the Transvaal and Swaziland District was established, and for the remainder of the century this work continued to be carried out with funds provided by the Society from London (Telford 1906: 211). The Methodist stall of periodicals for 'home' supporters, Britons from various ranks and ages, will be discussed in the subsequent section.

Reportage on Southern Africa in British Missionary Magazines Intended for Readers 'at Home': A Methodist Example

Methodism, which began as a revival within the established Church of England in the eighteenth century, was a missionary movement from the start. It was aimed mainly at the growing working and middle classes, as John Wesley wanted to 'awaken the masses' discouraged by the effects of industrialisation (Comaroff and Comaroff 1991: 47). Wesleyan foreign missions date back to 1786, when the Rev. Thomas Coke, who had set out for Nova Scotia, ended up in British Antigua (Finaughty 2016: 48–9), where he built up a mission among both the enslaved and landowners. When the WMMS was officially formed in 1813, it was as the 'overseas' extension of a vibrant movement that had already been ministering to the most 'brutal and neglected portions of the population', now extending to 'unknown continents', 'jungles' and 'Africas' (Comaroff and Comaroff 1991: 47). The global expansion of Wesleyan Methodism continued apace: in 1811, Coke established a mission to Sierra Leone, with additional stations opening on the river Gambia in 1821 and the Gold Coast in 1834; in 1818 mission work began in Australia; in 1822 in New Zealand; in 1826 in the Friendly Islands, extending a few years later to Fiji; in 1854, an independent society was established in Canada; and a year later, the Australasian Methodist Missionary Society also became independent. Wesleyan Methodists were also active in mission work in China and India (Finaughty 2016: 48–9).

In 1815, the need for a mission publication was raised at the Methodist Conference in London. The primary need for the intended publication was to help raise funds to continue with the mission work started by Coke. Coke was a fervent fundraiser and after his death, as the need for resources increased, the society found it necessary to solicit support in a more systematic manner (Finaughty 2016: 132). The Missionary Committee deliberated on the best means of providing preachers and people with 'regular and early communication of missionary intelligence' (Telford 1906: 65). Thus, the *Wesleyan Missionary Notices* (*WMN*) was founded in London, the first issue published in January 1816.

A nineteenth-century missionary periodical's formal properties can be distinguished as periodicity, format and size, layout and fonts, use of a masthead, printed form, use of pictures, and types and lengths of articles (Acke 2013: 226). The *WMN* appeared monthly. In 1869 it cost one penny (1d), but it was distributed free of charge to subscribers who donated a minimum of one shilling (1s) per week (Barringer 2004: 72). The reportage it featured could have taken anything between two and six months to reach the London office from the 'field' (Kriel 2015: 260). Continuity in format and layout was important, as it created a sense of familiarity, recognition, reliability and emotional attachment (Acke 2013: 226). Periodicals generally retained much of their formatting, changing only to keep up with new technologies and the adjusting tastes of their audiences. A typical periodical, like the *WMN*, was the size of a small booklet. The number of pages for each issue could vary slightly from month to month, according to available content, but it mostly kept the same recognisable format. Any changes in format would normally be announced in the previous issue or in the editorial of the current issue to prepare readers for what was to come. The fact that the editors deemed it necessary to forewarn readers about change shows that stability with regard to format was highly cherished, the familiarity adding to the periodical's image as trustworthy (Acke 2013: 227–8).

For the same reason, the periodical's masthead or cover page was an important feature. The masthead helped create stability and familiarity and it helped in making the publication immediately recognisable and distinguishable from other periodicals. Even when the masthead or cover page changed, elements of continuity would be retained.

In 1887, in response to readers' 'increased demand for diagrams and curiosities' ('Editorial Notices' 1889: 1), illustrations were introduced into the *WMN*. This resulted in some changes to the cover page, and, as from 1889, the inclusion of a full-page advertisement on the back page which would previously have featured 'Contributions' or 'Announcements' at most. Drawings, engravings of photographs, and, as soon as technology started allowing it in the 1880s, more realistic reproductions of photographs vividly reified the stock rhetoric of the missionary periodical.

Alongside the *WMN*, niche periodicals were published for British children. The *Wesleyan Juvenile Offering* (1844–79) continued as *At Home and Abroad* (Barringer 2004: 72). From 1859 to 1932, the *Report of the Ladies' Auxiliary of the Wesleyan Methodist Missionary Society* was annually published in London (Barringer 2004: 70). These were common trends in most missionary societies. The phrase 'at home and abroad' was popular in titles for periodicals of different societies across the denominations (Barringer 2004: 54–73).

In 1893, a message appeared in the *WMN* urging British readers who wished to be informed month by month of the progress of the work carried out by the WMMS to read *Work and Workers in the Mission Field*. It was advertised as a new 'high-class missionary magazine', well illustrated, priced at 3d ('Announcements' 1893: 74). *Work and Workers* was the manifestation of a new quarto-size illustrated magazine made possible by new printing techniques. Running alongside this glossy new show dog from 1892 to 1904, the stalwart *WMN* appeared as quaint as an old workhorse. From 1899 to 1904, the WMMS also experimented with an annual called *Our Missionary Year: Being a popular report of the WMMS* (Barringer 2004: 68). In 1904, the *WMN* was finally discontinued and replaced by the *Foreign Field of the Wesleyan Methodist Church* (see Figures 6.1 and 6.2). The showy *Work and Workers* was also terminated and incorporated into the *Foreign Field*, which survived until 1932. Most striking in the early issues of this periodical are snapshots of British readers posing with their issue of the *Foreign Field*, affirming a self-awareness amongst British readers, often children, about their monitoring status – overseeing, and being educated and entertained by, the foreign missionary work from afar. These 'snapshots' are, however, also indicative of the conversation within and amongst different generations of the British community of Wesleyan readers (see Figure 6.3). Inherent in the British missionary enthusiasm for the world 'abroad' was an endeavour primarily aimed at the spiritual grooming of the self.

When 'Abroad' Becomes 'Home': British Missionary Publishing for White South Africans

Given the openness of the communication system, what had been designed as a flow of money in one direction in exchange for a flow of literature in the other (Cox 2008: 114) inadvertently also resulted in multiple circuits of communication at the local level – 'at home' as well as 'abroad'. In South Africa, the settler churches' strong involvement in missionary work, and the tendency amongst missionaries to settle in the colony themselves, resulted in a lively local periodical press in which strong missionary opinions were expressed on matters related to the rule, administration and education of the African population. One of the most prominent periodicals of this nature, *The Christian Express*, mutated from alternative intentions.

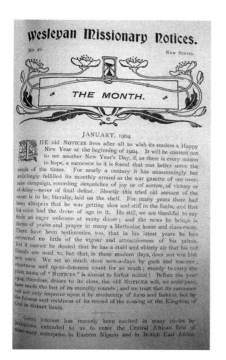

Figure 6.1 *Wesleyan Missionary Notices*, January 1904, p. 1. Courtesy of the author.

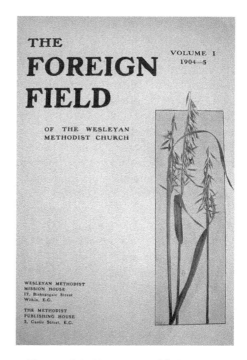

Figure 6.2 *Foreign Field*, 1, cover, 1904–5. Courtesy of the author.

Figure 6.3 A 'snap shot' of readers of the *Foreign Field* as seen in the *Foreign Field* ('The Business Side of the Magazine', 1907, p. 118). Courtesy of the author.

The early printing efforts of the LMS (in Setswana in the Northern Cape) and of the Glasgow Missionary Society (in isiXhosa in the Eastern Cape) were aimed at converting Africans. They started by producing spelling books and eventually translations of the Bible (Bradlow 1987: 9–11). The printing of newspapers for literate communities of African Christians followed somewhat later. The first edition of the *Kaffir Express*, printed at Lovedale in 1870, gives an overview of earlier attempts by British missionary societies to establish newspapers for black South African readers: *Umshumayeli Wendaba* [Publisher of News], *Isibuto Samavo* [Collection of Stories], *I-Kwezi* [Morning Star], *Isitunywa Senyanga* [Monthly Messenger], *Indaba* [News].[2] The editorial of the new paper born on 1 October 1870 exhorted prospective readers to take responsibility for its financial wellbeing, so that it might not happen that 'after a few numbers, its remains will be consigned to a quiet resting place among other similar curiosities . . . on the shelves of Sir George Grey's Library at Cape Town' ('To Our Readers' 1870: 1).

The *Kaffir Express* described itself as *An English-Kaffir Journal*, with the isiXhosa version appearing under the name *Isigidimi Sama-Xosa*. In 1876, after six years, the paper split into two separate periodicals. The *Isigidimi Sama-Xosa* became an independent paper: 'the first African newspaper edited by Africans in Southern Africa' (Switzer and Switzer 1979: 3). The last issue of the *Kaffir Express* announced that, as *The Christian Express*, the periodical would embrace that which its predecessor had in fact already mutated into: 'more generally a missionary newspaper for South Africa' ('The "*Kaffir Express*"' 1875: 1). In future the periodical would be a forum for 'Southern Africa's liberal, multi-racial Christian elite' (Switzer and Switzer 1979: 270) rather than a mouthpiece for African thought. The *Isigidimi*, which survived until December 1884, would embrace that role as an isiXhosa mouthpiece.

The mission statement for *The Christian Express* reveals the extent to which practices 'at home' in Britain were still considered the norm to be emulated in the colonies, while it also confirms that the open communication system facilitated parallel conversations about local dynamics in South Africa as it did in Britain:

> The change has arisen out of an expressed desire on the part of missionaries of various bodies in the [Cape] Colony, in Basotholand, and in Natal, to have some common means of communication. We are heartily willing to give effect to any such wish. It is not [*sic*] now necessary to issue a pro[s]pectus of what the *Christian Express* is intended to be. Its topics will be missionary work, interests, and information; Christian work in connection with the different churches in the [Cape] Colony; and education chiefly as connected with the progress of missions. The missionary information is not intended to be limited to South Africa, though its interest and even its freshness must depend a good deal on our being supplied with news of what is being done at our own doors. . . . It need hardly be said that the *Christian Express* will but very slightly resemble the weekly periodical known at home [in Britain] as *The Christian*, for the simple reason that there is not going on in South Africa such an amount of Christian work as to necessitate so full a record or make such a paper possible. ('The "*Kaffir Express*"' 1875: 1)

Nevertheless, the density and diversity of the local South African conversation in print culture, along with the exchange between so-called religious and secular discourse, is apparent from the list of publications thanked as supporters of and contributors to the content of the *Express*-soon-to-be-renamed-the-*Christian*: *Cape Argus, Bloemfontein Express, Queenstown Free Press, Queenstown Representative, Burghersdorp Gazette, Fort Beaufort Advocate, Cape Mercury, Penny Mail, Uitenhage Times, Somerset Courant, Richmond Era, Graaff-Reinet Advertiser, Empire, Northern Post, Grensburger* [Frontier Citizen], *Zuid-Afrikaan* [South-African], *Kerkbode* [Church Herald] and *Church News*.

The *Christian Express* appeared for the first time in January 1876. It was renamed again in 1922 as *The South African Outlook* and served as the official organ of the General Missionary Conference of South Africa and the Christian Council of South Africa (later South African Council of Churches) (Switzer and Switzer 1979: 270). *The Christian Express* offered a platform for white missionaries along with African Christian intellectuals to comment on: African customs ranging from puberty rites to 'witchcraft'; colonial racial politics ranging from the South African Native Affairs Commission Report (1905) to the passing of the Natives Land Act (1913); and, last but not least, more 'purely' religious issues such as the segregation between black and white Christian congregations and African movements towards independent black church formation (Elphick 2012: 65–70, 79, 83, 89–90, 99, 117, 143–4).[3]

Missionary-owned Periodicals for Black South African Readers

Around the time of the demise of *Isigidimi Sama-Xosa* another missionary-owned periodical aimed at African readers saw the light. The *Mahoka a Becwana*, published in Setswana by the LMS at Kuruman, would survive from 1883 to 1896. In 2006, the letters to the editor as they had appeared in the *Mahoka* were published in English. The translators demonstrated that the LMS ownership and editing of the paper did not prevent the Batswana writers from expressing themselves on topics ranging from education to theology, cultural change and colonisation. The letters were received from the whole Setswana-speaking region, from what was at the time either part of the British Cape Colony, the Bechuanaland Protectorate or the Boer republics of the Transvaal and the Orange Free State. Characteristic of an open communication system, writers acted writing about matters that came to their minds, and reacted responding to other letter writers or to missionary articles. As a result, several controversial issues were also debated (Mgadla and Volz 2006: xiii–xv). It is quite likely that missionary readers may have translated and relayed some of these Batswana words back to readers in Britain via periodicals serving that purpose, but it is only now that it is fully available in English translation that the intensity of the intellectual discourse in the paper, and the value it must have had for the community at the time, can also be grasped outside the Setswana-speaking world.

One striking difference between an LMS periodical like *Mahoka a Becwana* aimed at Batswana readers and *The Chronicle of the London Missionary Society* aimed at Congregationalists in Britain was that the latter was an illustrated periodical. In the *Mahoka* Batswana writers converted their oral art into text for sharing within the inner circle of fellow Batswana readers, but in *The Chronicle* British readers' imagination was being saturated with pictures. The interpretation of these pictures was informed by textual ekphrasis that schooled the readers in a particular visual literacy, a way of 'seeing' the faraway 'other' in a 'missionscape' which few of the British readers would actually ever set foot on. And those who might would be ready to frame their actual observations in accordance with their preconceived expectations.

Vosseler explains this process in her longitudinal visual analysis of series of pictures from *The Chronicle* and its predecessor, the *Missionary Magazine and Chronicle* (2022: 339, 343). The LMS had started including engravings in its publications as early as the 1830s – decades before a periodical like the *Wesleyan Missionary Notices*. Engravings provided a means through which the editors of missionary periodicals could codify the ways British readers would see the landscapes in Africa. The seemingly chaotic and unfamiliar environment as described in the missionary reports could be structured and organised for the reader's/viewer's eye. Mission stations and churches were the most frequent visual motif, showing the mission at the centre, surrounded by mountain ranges in the background and fields in the middle ground. The immediate area around the mission station was transformed by the impact of missionary landscaping – showing gardens and fields arranged in an orderly manner. The church or missionary house was generally huge and it basked in light compared to the houses of Africans which were tiny and sometimes darker (see 'Pacaltsdorp' 1838, and 'Mabotsa' 1846).

Black African Writing into the British World – 'To Give Expression to our Thoughts'

A periodical which started in a similar fashion to the *Mahoka a Becwana* was the CPSA's *Inkanyiso*, first published in May 1889. When it became a weekly publication in 1891, the name was changed to *Inkanyiso yase Natal*. Until 1894, the Editor-in-Chief was the Rev. F. J. Green, the headmaster of St Alban's College in Pietermaritzburg. It followed the example of many periodicals aimed at British readers 'at home' by funding itself through advertisements. By 1893, five other priests, some of African, some of settler descent, assisted Green in selling advertisements. On 4 January 1895, the publication went completely over into black ownership, with S. Kumalo and Company taking over as publishers. At the time, the only other South African newspaper owned by an African was John Tengo Jabavu's King Williamstown-based *Imvo Zabantsundu*.

Inkanyiso's participation in the open missionary communication system during the 1890s was remarkable (Saenger 2016: 141–6). In its lifespan of little under eight years, *Inkanyiso* referenced more than 100 periodicals from all over the world. Information from these newspapers and magazines was not just relayed, but also discussed and criticised. References to other Natal (secular and religious) papers are the most common, and then references to other Southern African papers, including *Imvo*, as well as white-owned missionary periodicals like *The Christian Express*, and other rising, often short-lived 'native papers' like the religious *Methodist Native Magazine* and *umHlobo waBantu*, or the more secular *Umsizi waBantu*.

However, *Inkanyiso*'s project of introducing its readers to periodicals from Britain, the United States, India and Australia most spectacularly illustrates the extent to which the initial intentional flow of missionary literature to the north had converted into multi-directional circuits by the end of the nineteenth century. This heralded the extent to which, in the twentieth century, the European missionary endeavour would increasingly recede in favour of a far more polycentric structure of world Christianity, with the majority of the adherents to the faith residing in the Global South (Koschorke and Hermann 2014: 17). The deliberate inclusion of an English rubric 'Native Thoughts' in *Inkanyiso* further emphasises that the periodical anticipated and targeted a diverse audience. Primarily, 'The newspaper wanted to give a voice to the Africans in the colony and to acquaint the white population of Natal with their thoughts. Thereby the paper wished to create a better understanding between the two groups' (Saenger 2016: 142).

There were also times when the writers in *Inkanyiso* went even further and engaged directly in commentary on international affairs with a clear confidence that they were participating in a global discourse. Saenger (2016: 144) points out the criticism raised on 5 January 1894 under 'Native Thoughts' against Britain's involvement in the opium trade in China. At times, the British Empire was addressed directly, as in an expression of condolences in 'Native Thoughts' of 4 February 1892. The death of Prince Albert Victor was elevated to an opportunity to make statements like the following:

> We, the Native races of Natal and South Africa generally . . . cannot refrain from sharing largely in that universal sympathy which is being shown towards the Royal Family . . . Under the benevolent reign of our gracious Queen, thousands of our people . . . and many millions more of our colour have been and are still being freed from the horrible bondage of slavery which, at the beginning of this reign, existed to so fearful an extent on this Continent. (Quoted in Saenger 2016: 141)

It thus makes sense that Klaus Koschorke used the phrase 'to give publicity to our thoughts' (Koschorke et al. 2016: 11–14) from the *Inkanyiso* as the motto for his entire project on independent Christian periodicals that arose in the southern hemisphere from the end of the nineteenth century: *Inkanyiso* in Natal (est. 1889); the *Sierra Leone Weekly News* (est. 1884), *The Gold Coast Leader* (est. 1902), *The Lagos Weekly Record* (est. 1891) and *The Lagos Standard* (est. 1895) in West Africa; *La Verdad* and *La Iglesia Filipina Independiente: Revista Católica* (both est. 1903) in the Philippines; and *The Christian Patriot* (est. 1890) in India. That so many of these periodicals were short-lived says much about the financial challenges they had to overcome to stay afloat. That they were continually replaced by new attempts is evidence that a vibrant, Christian discourse was flourishing amongst Africans and Asians at the time in reaction to the polyphony of other local and international periodicals they were accessing, whether these were 'intended' for them or not. The fervour with which these periodicals were kept alive, and the readiness with which new ones emerged as others disappeared, shows the heteroglossic assertiveness of Christianity beyond Europe, and its continual search for platforms of amplification.

Conclusion

By the beginning of the twentieth century, the missionary periodical that had started out as a medium to carry news from a foreign field 'home' to Britain showcasing the project 'abroad' was complemented with periodicals produced locally by South African Christians, initially ones of European descent, but soon also African Christians from the churches introduced by the British missionaries. From the start, the South Africa-based periodicals imagined an audience far more complex than the periodicals designed for British readers: fellow black African, white South African, fellow Christian readers in the Global South as well as British readers 'abroad' in the metropole were addressed and they responded.

A conspicuous difference between missionary periodicals published in Britain for British consumption and the ones published from the mission field is the absence of pictures – engravings and photographs – in the South African publications. Another obvious difference is the longevity of British publications compared to South African ones. While the British scene offers, as Etherington has remarked, more than one can read, the South African publications give evidence of the little that could be captured in print from the abundance that was thought and discussed.

Notes

1. Access to missionary periodicals is provided by the following publications and databases: the Currents on World Christianity research project's Missionary Periodicals Database (launched in 1999, and now hosted at the Yale Divinity Library's Missionary Periodicals Online); Robert A. Bickers and Rosemary Seton's edited collection *Missionary Encounter: Sources and Issues* (1996); the Cambridge Centre for Christianity Worldwide's library and archive; and the School for Oriental and African Studies at the University of London's website, Sources for Missionary and Church Archives.
2. Mgadla and Volz confirm that most early attempts were initiated by Wesleyan Methodist missionaries (Mgadla and Volz 2006: xix), although other mission societies also played a role, as in the case of the Paris Evangelical Missionary Society's Sesotho paper *Leselinyana la Lesotho* [Little Light of Lesotho] (est. 1863). In the 1850s, two short-lived periodicals in Setswana were published: *Mokaeri oa Becuana* [Instructor/Animator of the Batswana] by the LMS and *Molekoli oa Bechuana* [Visitor/Consoler of the Batswana] by the Wesleyans.
3. Extracts from *The Christian Express* and its successor, *The South African Outlook*, were published for the periodical's centenary (Wilson and Perrot 1973). Elphick's history of Protestant missionary thinking and racial politics, *The Equality of Believers: Protestant Missionaries and the Racial Politics of South Africa* (2012), draws extensively upon these two periodicals.

Bibliography

Acke, Hanna (2013), 'Missionary periodicals as a genre: Models of writing, horizons of expectation', in Felicity Jensz and Hanna Acke (eds), *Missions and Media: The Politics of Missionary Periodicals in the Long Nineteenth Century*, Stuttgart: Franz Steiner, 225–43.

Altick, Richard D. (1957), *The English Common Reader: A Social History of the Mass Reading Public 1800–1900*, Chicago: University of Chicago Press.

'Announcements' (1893), *Wesleyan Missionary Notices*, May, 74.

Barringer, Terry (2002), 'From beyond Alpine snow and homes of the East', *International Bulletin of Missionary Research*, 26.4, 169–73.

—— (2004), 'What Mrs Jellyby might have read in missionary periodicals: A neglected source', *Victorian Periodicals Review*, 37.4, 46–74.

Becker, Judith, and Katharina Stornig (eds) (2018), *Menschen, Bilder, eine Welt: Ordnungen von Vielfalt in der religiösen Publizistik um 1900*, Göttingen: Vandenhoeck & Ruprecht.

Bradlow, Frank R. (1987), *Printing for Africa: The Story of Robert Moffat and the Kuruman Press*, Kuruman: Kuruman Moffat Mission Trust.

'British South Africa' (1891), *Wesleyan Missionary Notices*, February, 58–9.

'The Business Side of the Magazine' (1907), *Foreign Field*, November, 118.
Comaroff, John, and Jean Comaroff (1991), *Of Revelation and Revolution: Christianity, Colonialism and Consciousness in South Africa*, vol. 1, Chicago: Chicago University Press.
Cox, Jeffrey (2008), *The British Missionary Enterprise since 1700*, New York: Routledge.
Davenport, Rodney (1997), 'Settlement, conquest and theological controversy: The churches of nineteenth-century European immigrants', in Richard Elphick and Rodney Davenport (eds), *Christianity in South Africa: A Political, Social and Cultural History*, Cape Town: David Philip, 51–67.
De Gruchy, John W. (1997), 'Grappling with a colonial heritage: The English-speaking churches under imperialism and apartheid', in Richard Elphick and Rodney Davenport (eds), *Christianity in South Africa: A Political, Social and Cultural History*, Cape Town: David Philip, 155–72.
'Editorial Notices' (1889), *Wesleyan Missionary Notices*, January, 1.
Elbourne, Elizabeth, and Robert Ross (1997), 'Combating spiritual and social bondage: Early missions in the Cape Colony', in Richard Elphick and Rodney Davenport (eds), *Christianity in South Africa: A Political, Social and Cultural History*, Cape Town: David Philip, 31–50.
Elphick, Richard (2012), *The Equality of Believers: Protestant Missionaries and the Racial Politics of South Africa*, Scottsville: University of KwaZulu-Natal Press.
Etherington, Norman (2005), 'The missionary writing machine in nineteenth-century KwaZulu-Natal', in Jamie S. Scott and Gareth Griffiths (eds), *Mixed Messages: Materiality, Textuality, Missions*, New York: Palgrave Macmillan, 37–50.
Finaughty, Chantelle L. (2016), 'Victorian design and visual culture in the *Wesleyan Missionary Notices*, ca. 1880–1902', MA diss., University of Pretoria.
Gerdener, Gustav B. A. (1958), *Recent Developments in the South African Mission Field*, Cape Town: N. G. Kerk-Uitgewers.
'Heathen and Christian Fingoes' (1891), *Wesleyan Missionary Notices*, December, 268–9.
Hodgson, Janet (1997), 'A battle for sacred power: Christian beginnings among the Xhosa', in Richard Elphick and Rodney Davenport (eds), *Christianity in South Africa: A Political, Social and Cultural History*, Cape Town: David Philip, 68–88.
'Imperialismus und Kirche in England' (1901), *Die evangelischen Missionen*, 432.
Jenkins, Paul (1994), 'Was ist eine Missionsgesellschaft?', in Wilfried Wagner (ed.), *Kolonien und Missionen: Referate des 3. Internationalen Kolonialgeschichtlichen Symposiums 1993 in Bremen*, Münster: Lit, 441–50.
Jensz, Felicity, and Hanna Acke (eds) (2013), *Missions and Media: The Politics of Missionary Periodicals in the Long Nineteenth Century*, Stuttgart: Franz Steiner.
'The "Kaffir Express"' (1875), *Isigidimi Sama-Xosa* (published as the *Kaffir Express*), 1 December, 1.
Klein, Thoralf (2013), 'Media events and missionary periodicals: The case of the Boxer War, 1900–1901', *Church History*, 82.2, 399–404.
Koschorke, Klaus, and Adrian Hermann (eds) (2014), *Polycentric Structures in the History of World Christianity*, Wiesbaden: Harrassowitz.
——, ——, E. Phuti Mogase and Ciprian Burlacioiu (eds) (2016), *Discourses of Indigenous Christian Elites in Colonial Societies in Asia and Africa around 1900: A Documentary Sourcebook from Selected Sources*, Wiesbaden: Harrassowitz.
Kriel, Lize (2015), 'A cultural production of fields? Missionary periodicals and their conflicting construction of colonial encounters, the *Berliner Missionsberichte* and the *Wesleyan Missionary Notices* on the Transvaal in the 1890s', in Michael Mann and Jürgen G. Nagel (eds), *Europa jenseits der Grenzen: Festschrift für Reinhard Wendt*, Heidelberg: Draupadi, 251–78.
'Mabotsa' (1846), *Missionary Magazine and Chronicle*, 120, May, 65.

Mgadla, Part T., and Stephen C. Volz (eds) (2006), *Words of Batswana: Letters to Mahoka a Becwana, 1833–1896*, Cape Town: Van Riebeeck Society.

Missionary Periodicals Online (2022), https://guides.library.yale.edu/missionperiodicals (accessed 31 August 2022).

'Pacaltsdorp' (1838), *Missionary Magazine and Chronicle*, 26, July, 98.

Porter, Andrew N. (2004), *Religion versus Empire? British Protestant Missionaries and Overseas Expansion, 1700–1914*, Manchester: Manchester University Press.

Saenger, André (2016), 'South Africa: Introduction', in Klaus Koschorke, Adrian Hermann, E. Phuti Mogase and Ciprian Burlacioiu (eds), *Discourses of Indigenous Christian Elites in Colonial Societies in Asia and Africa around 1900: A Documentary Sourcebook from Selected Sources*, Wiesbaden: Harrassowitz, 141–6.

Sources for Missionary and Church Archives (2022), https://www.soas.ac.uk/library/archives/links/missionary/ (accessed 31 August 2022).

Switzer, Les, and Donna Switzer (1979), *The Black Press in South Africa and Lesotho: A Descriptive and Biographic Guide to African, Coloured and Indian Newspapers, Newsletters and Magazines 1836–1976*, Boston: G. K. Hall & Co.

Telford, John (1906), *A Short History of Wesleyan Methodist Foreign Missions*, London: C. H. Kelly.

'To Our Readers' (1870), *Isigidimi Sama-Xosa* (published as the *Kaffir Express*), 1 October, 1.

Van der Heyden, Ulrich, and Andreas Feldtkeller (eds) (2012), *Missionsgeschichte als Geschichte der Globalisierung von Wissen: Transkulturelle Wissensaneignung und -vermittlung durch christliche Missionare in Afrika und Asien im 17., 18. und 19. Jahrhundert*, Stuttgart: Franz Steiner.

Vosseler, Annika (2022), 'The visual representation of South Africa in European missionary periodicals, 1836–1910', unpublished PhD thesis, University of Leipzig.

Wendt, Reinhard (2012), 'Southern Africa in Rhenish Mission Society outreach: "Images of Light and Shadow" depicting the "Improvement of Heathen Peoples" in the colonial era', in Hanns Lessing et al. (eds), *The German Protestant Church in Colonial Southern Africa: The Impact of Overseas Work from the Beginnings until the 1920s*, Pietermaritzburg: Cluster, 101–14.

Wilson, Francis, and Dominique Perrot (eds) (1973), *Outlook on a Century: 1870–1970*, Braamfontein: Lovedale and Spro-Cas.

7

The Sydney *Bulletin* and the Settler Colonial Subject

Tony Hughes-d'Aeth

The *Bulletin* is the most famous magazine in Australian history, commencing its weekly publication in Sydney in January 1880 and remaining in circulation until 2008. The magazine's influence peaked in the years either side of Federation in 1901, when the various Australian colonies of Britain constituted themselves as a federated nation. From its inception, the magazine strongly advocated the creation of an Australian nation centred on 'the working man'. Avowedly racist and masculinist, the *Bulletin* was nevertheless a crucial organ for the radical nationalist movement within Australia. It was also notable for its contribution to literary sensibility and style. The authors associated with the *Bulletin* (Henry Lawson, A. B. 'Banjo' Paterson, Barbara Baynton, 'Steele Rudd', Stella 'Miles' Franklin and Joseph Furphy) are amongst the most influential in Australia's literary tradition and are often referred to as the '*Bulletin* school' of writers. The magazine's influence waned after the First World War, but it has remained firmly in the cultural imagination.

The story of the *Bulletin* has been told many times, firstly in the memoirs of its writers, owners and other members of its coterie.[1] Key evaluations of its significance began to appear in the post-war period, notably Vance Palmer's *The Legend of the Nineties* (1954) and Russel Ward's *The Australian Legend* (1958). The most brilliant and penetrating account thus far is Sylvia Lawson's *The Archibald Paradox* (1983). Lawson's book focuses the journal through the lens of its co-founder and presiding genius, J. F. ('Jules François') Archibald (1856–1919). Born John Feltham Archibald to an Irish-Catholic family who had emigrated to Warnambool in Victoria, Archibald adopted his French moniker early in his journalistic life, also claiming fancifully that his mother was a French Jew. Archibald founded the *Bulletin* as a weekly magazine in Sydney with his friend and fellow journalist John Haynes (1850–1917) and the artist William Macleod (1850–1929). The first issue appeared on 31 January 1880, and consisted of eight printed pages, selling at four pennies. The first issue of 3,000 copies sold out quickly and the following week more copies were printed, and the price was dropped to three pennies. These sold just as swiftly. By the end of May, 10,000 copies were being printed each week. Thereafter, the circulation continued to rise, reaching something in the order of 100,000 by the turn of the century.

As a weekly, the *Bulletin* offered itself as a compact digest of the daily newspapers circulating in Sydney and New South Wales: 'The public eye rejects as uninteresting more than half of what is printed in the publications of the day. It is only the other half which will be found in *The Bulletin*' (Anon. 1880, *Bulletin*: 1). The tone of the *Bulletin* was broadly satirical, belonging to the tradition of the English *Punch* (1841–2002), and indeed it competed directly against the Sydney *Punch* (1864–88), styled on its English predecessor, eventually seeing it off. (The Melbourne *Punch* ran from 1855 to 1925, and the Adelaide *Punch* from 1878 to 1884.) Archibald and Haynes were also influenced by the American press, copies of which were by the 1880s arriving regularly by steamer from San Francisco only weeks after their publication. Papers like Charles Dana's New York *Sun* (1833–1950), with its mixture of invective and razor-sharp cartooning, offered a model for what might be possible in Australia. As Haynes recalled: 'It was pretty clear that we could do something on the same lines . . . Heaps of things wanted rectifying, and the cartoonist and a smart paper were to my mind the only remedy for the abuses of the hour' (S. Lawson 1983: 66). Sylvia Lawson notes that one of the defining features of the *Bulletin* was its own sparkling self-awareness. The magazine unfurls within an atmosphere of continual teasing irony, wherein the events reported were seemingly of the greatest possible moment and at the same time an overblown farce. One of the magazine's favourite sports was the merciless ridicule of its competitors: the *Daily Telegraph* (1879–) became the *Twaddlegraph*, and the *Town and Country Journal* (1870–1919) became the *Down and Gumtree Jernil*. For Lawson, the *Bulletin* 'would do much to awaken an unselfconscious audience to the nature and variety of printed communication itself, to show that newspapers did not appear from the clouds, but were human work, and for all their seeming authority, neither sacrosanct nor invulnerable' (S. Lawson 1983: 74).

Yet, beneath its quips, the magazine was also motivated by a serious politics, and often roused itself to passionate advocacy or, more often still, denunciation. Indeed, the *Bulletin* was the protest paper *par excellence*, channelling the pamphleteer's ethos of scathing indignation. One of the most persistent of its causes was its opposition to capital punishment. The very first issue carried a long article, written by Archibald himself, reporting on the execution of notorious bushrangers Captain Moonlight and Rogan (Andrew George Scott and Thomas Baker) at Darlinghurst Gaol on 20 January 1880, and including a scoop interview that Archibald had managed to obtain with the hangman prior to the executions. A more notorious feature of the *Bulletin* was its unremitting hostility to Chinese immigration. This was something close to an obsession for the magazine. The opposition was sometimes cast in material terms as undermining organised labour and 'white man's wages', and sometimes as a moral crusade to protect vulnerable women. However, it was the spectre of miscegenation that was at the root of its deepest fears. For a paper that purported to abhor moral cant, it had no problem climbing on its high horse when it came to race:

> There must be no compromise on the part of the people of this country. All the sophistry in the world will not remove these facts – that . . . the Chinese bring no women with them, and foster immorality wherever they settle; that the races should not be allowed to mix; that they are mixing to an appreciable extent in the lowest quarters of the large cities; and that the presence of the Chinaman must ever be a disturbing element in the at all times sufficiently strained relations between Capital and Labour. ('The Chinese Question', 1881, quoted in S. Lawson 1983: 87)

Although it did not pursue the matter with the same energy, the *Bulletin* also found time to vituperate the Aboriginal people of Australia: 'The wretched aboriginal who is now cast for death is . . . a worthless, drunken creature . . . It is high time that all dark men living under the British flag in New South Wales left the colony' ('Only a Nigger', 1880, quoted in S. Lawson 1983: 87). It was not exactly clear where the Indigenous people were supposed to go to, but a logic of expulsion and exclusion was at the heart of the *Bulletin*'s politics.

Another significant feature of the *Bulletin* was that, at an early point, it actively solicited contributions from its readership. From September 1880, the magazine carried the notice: 'The Editor of the *BULLETIN* will at all times be glad to receive information from correspondents living in town and country or the other colonies on subjects of general interest, more especially on matters connected with sport, the drama and fashion' (S. Lawson 1983: 83). The gesture was distinctive insofar as it embraced a pan-colonial readership – an audience it also in many ways brought into being. For Vance Palmer, the *Bulletin* was 'a paper that was largely to be written by its readers, reflecting their idiom, their ideals, and the substance of their lives' (Palmer 1954: 51). Indeed, the famous literary writers of the *Bulletin* school – Lawson, Paterson, Baynton, 'Rudd', Franklin, Furphy et al. – were, first of all, readers of the *Bulletin*. In the 1880s and 1890s, the Australian papers were located very firmly within their own colonies, and dominated by the metropolitan centres of Sydney and Melbourne. However, even though there does always remain a quintessential Sydney quality to the *Bulletin*, it was able to shake off this privilege in the name of an incipient and still nebulous 'Australian' subjectivity. That this now exists, with all of its attendant problematics, is not due solely to the *Bulletin*, but the magazine (and its coterie) played a significant role in the formulation of the genetic code of the Australian settler subject.

In terms of a critical evaluation of the *Bulletin*, it is worth signalling two main divergences. The first is around the particular mythology of the 'bush' and the 'bushman' that the *Bulletin* was so central in developing and placing at the centre of what was once called the 'Australian character', but what might more accurately be termed Australian settler subjectivity. Here, the main debate is whether the 'bush' existed as a material constellation or whether it was the romantic concoction of urban bohemians, with the *Bulletin* at the forefront of this exercise. The second divergence is narrower and more firmly situated on the nature of the *Bulletin* itself, although it does have wider implications for the study of periodicals. This concerns the question of whether the *Bulletin* is best conceived as the bearer of a unified ideology (with its very marked gendered, social and racial coordinates) or as a kind of Bakhtinian carnival in which vaunted positions were continually upended and undercut by irony, internal inconsistency, theatricality and absurdity.

Turning to the first of these debates, Vance Palmer cites Francis Adams's claim in *The Australians* (1893) that '[t]he one powerful and unique type yet produced in Australia is . . . the Bushman . . . the man of the nation' (Palmer 1954: 47). Whether this 'bushman' actually existed, that is, whether 'he' had some basis in historico-material reality, or whether he had been invented by poets and artists, became a major historiographical focus in Australia after the Second World War. Certainly, there was a class of what Russel Ward calls 'outback employees, semi-nomadic drovers, shepherds, shearers, bullock-drivers, stockmen, boundary-riders, station-hands and others of the pastoral industry' (Ward 1958: 2). But there was also, from early in the nineteenth century, an idealisation of this type into a proto-nationalist figure (Gelder and Weaver 2017: 91–116). Palmer and Ward conclude that this figure owed its existence both to material factors (the convict legacy, patterns of land settlement, the distribution of capital and labour, and the exigencies of climate and geography) and to cultural mediation – that is to say, the mediation of frontier life through poetry (notably the ballad tradition), art, drama and the periodical press. For Palmer, the existence of the 'bushman' as both a really existing social class and an already romanticised type was critical to the success of the *Bulletin*. Indeed, '[i]t was on them that J. F. Archibald counted when he founded the *Bulletin*' (Palmer 1954: 51). Ward, for his part, regards the *Bulletin* as a key component of the settler 'dreaming' of the 1890s, integral in sculpting the contours of national narratives and stock characters, and helping to shape these into a unifying (if far from coherent) mythology (Ward 1958: 227–8). Both Palmer and Ward saw that, while all of the key cultural ingredients were in place when the *Bulletin* commenced publication in 1880, the magazine played a decisive role in galvanising these elements into a discourse capable of interpellating a broader settler populace.

However, the credibility of this thesis – that the *Bulletin* galvanised and mobilised an actually existing social type (the rural worker and small selector) – was questioned in the 1970s, 1980s and 1990s. The key blow came with the publication of Graeme Davison's seminal 'Sydney and the bush' in 1978, which sought to expose the dubious and highly curated sense of the 'bush' by the *Bulletin* and its coterie. For Davison and the generation that followed, the 'bush' was primarily an urban 'construction' or 'projection', and its influence on Australian values and sensibilities was greatly overstated. With the 'bush' stripped of its material force, commentators instead saw the *Bulletin* as motivated by masculinism (Lake 1986) and racism (Broinowski 1992). There was no shortage of evidence for this critique in the pages of the *Bulletin*, which drip with wounded masculinity and the vilest racism. Under this critique, the 'bush' was not a place of radical possibility (forms of socialism), but a social imaginary confected to encrypt the reactionary positions (white supremacy, misogyny) of those who eulogised it.

The 'projection thesis' (Garner 2012: 453) became dominant in academic historiography, and the *Bulletin*, along with the Heidelberg school of painting, was regarded as among the key projectors. While a necessary corrective to the organicist views of culture that sat underneath the *Bulletin* and the more hagiographical accounts of its glory days, the critiques of the late 1970s and 1980s also tended to slightly misrepresent the positions of Palmer and Ward. Both had been at pains to emphasise that mediation was at the heart of the bush mythology; indeed, this was why the *Bulletin* was so important. The magazine was not, as it sometimes pretended to be, albeit usually with a gleam in its eye, the chthonic issuance of the 'Australian' (settler) spirit. But nor was it irremediably separate from rural material conditions (the settler situation), a mere parlour game for urban intellectuals and a largely urban readership. Instead, the key to the *Bulletin* was that it remediated, through the circuitry of its reader-correspondents, the material conditions of settler life (in cities, towns, stations, selections) into a structure of feeling. The purpose of this affective structure, and what powered it, was the need to belong – to weave a fabric of settler belonging (Curthoys 1999). Belong to what, though? To the greater British Empire? To the fraternity of white working men? To the nation that was to come? To a past that was stained with violence, suffering and injustice? The *Bulletin* created a structure of feeling that demanded a belonging to something it could not quite name. It is this structural uncertainty that electrifies the *Bulletin* and makes reading it today, in spite of its blatant bigotries, exciting.

The debate over whether the 'bush' was a material context or an ideological cipher in some ways takes us to the second critical divergence surrounding the *Bulletin*. The more strident critiques of the magazine leave the impression that its positions will always, in their limit, dissolve down to either its hatred of women or its hatred of racial others (most particularly, the Chinese). It is hard to deny the force of this criticism, and perverse to deny its substance. The *Bulletin* was undoubtedly racist and masculinist – indeed, it was overtly the magazine of the white working man. But it would be wrong to imagine that these positions originated in the corridors of the *Bulletin* and travelled outwards from there to infect an otherwise pristine and fair-minded Australia. Once again, the *Bulletin* was a mediator, which means it was neither the originary source of ideology, nor its neutral vehicle. Moreover, while some have sought to cast the *Bulletin* as a magazine that, for all its colourful stances and exuberant contrarianism, remained true to a particular ideological constellation, others have argued that the magazine remains harder to pin down. For Sylvia Lawson, the *Bulletin* cannot be tamed or made consistent, and its pages and positions remain stubbornly anarchic and contradictory. She characterises the paper as a kind of carnival – a 'print circus' – with Archibald as the histrionic ringmaster. John Docker, influenced by Lawson, also invokes the carnival, drawing on Bakhtin to model the *Bulletin*'s heteroglossia. And indeed, Archibald's original partner John Haynes expressed the *Bulletin*'s baroque gestures by invoking the circus: 'the circus was going real well, and we were playing to full houses all the time' (quoted in S. Lawson 1983: 82).

The *Bulletin*'s seemingly wanton eclecticism had the effect of making the daily news cycle look ridiculous, a bizarre cabinet of curiosities that defied easy schematisation. Its 'News in a Nutshell' column, for instance, was at one level just a compendium of headlines culled from the daily newspapers of the foregoing week. Yet, by streaming them together, stripped of any context, the *Bulletin* seemed to revel in the nonsensical collage that results:

> *Dunedin and Sydney aldermen are fraternising. The annual Masonic ball was a grand success. A pet monkey has severely bitten a Braidwood woman. Tramway motors should be fitted with cow-catchers. Melbourne larrikins have severely stabbed two Chinamen. General Grant has a good chance for a second re-election. 200 men are now employed at Peak Downs copper mine. The French man-of-war* Rhin *has left Sydney for Melbourne. Last month 250 signed the pledge at the Sydney Temperance Hall. More 'Chinkies' for Sydney per the ss.* Brisbane *– 151 of them. A swordfish measuring 13 ft. has been caught at Wollongong. A National Art Gallery will probably soon be established at Adelaide. Assaults upon females are of frequent occurrence in Auckland (N. Z.). Next British and Australian census is to be taken on 3rd April 1881. The railway to the summit of Vesuvius will be shortly opened for traffic.* ('News in a Nutshell' 1880: 2)

The effect replicated the practice of two people reading different newspapers to each other over breakfast, but by accelerating the process, and removing the murmurs of assent, outrage or bemusement, the *Bulletin* lent an absurdist edge to the conversation, as if we are in a play by Samuel Beckett. Indeed, by compounding the cacophony of the news feed, the *Bulletin* brought to the surface a defining feature of modernity itself, which is the fact that it (the symbolic order of contemporary modernity) maintains a stance of presumed knowledge over the facts it produces. Yet, because of the unprecedented and dizzying complexity of contemporary facticity, any totalising knowledge is manifestly impossible. This basic impasse, that the world is overwhelming but we must pretend to know it all the same, is the quotient of truth that the *Bulletin*'s pages yield up in a mixture of pantomime excess, sanctimonious pronouncement and cheap vaudeville.

While it seems a little perverse to be casting the *Bulletin* as a proto-modernist assemblage, it certainly did flirt ostentatiously with the absurdity of the incommensurate worlds that erupt in the pages of a newly globalised print media. This is a place, in other words, where one thinks nothing of a railway puffing its way to the top of Vesuvius meeting a 13 ft swordfish and a woman bitten by a pet monkey. The *Bulletin*'s 'News in a Nutshell' column was a form of free association that reads today like a transcript of the political unconscious of colonial Australia. And, like any free association, the chain of signifiers betray their hidden logic. Even a short sample like that above reveals the intrusion of recurrent thoughts, which interrupt the playful shuffling of cards. The modern eye will immediately feel the subtle change of tone that occurs when the matter of Chinese immigration is touched on – the deliberate insertion of racial slurs, the sense that this is a 'wave' that cannot be stopped, and the fact that of all the headlines, this one attracted a telling gloss ('151 of them'). The combination of obsessional thoughts on the one hand and an unruly chaotic dimension on the other is what has led to the critical divergence in relation to the *Bulletin*, in which it is both the virulent organ of foundational racism and misogyny, and a Bakhtinian carnival of inversions, grotesqueries and theatricality.

Another central element of the *Bulletin* was a radical recasting of Australian historicity. The orthodox position at the time was that Australia's separate colonies were all proceeding nicely in their whiggish trajectories. Agriculture, industry, science, arts and institutions of government were each advancing from their rudimentary beginnings to join the ranks of a modern western state. The key reference points were Britain, which provided the image of enlightened civility and responsible governance, and America, whose former collection of British colonies had risen to become a brash and mighty world power – a settler colonial continent that presented an enticing vision of what Australia could become. The *Bulletin*, however, was having none of this. Against the liberal story of progress, the *Bulletin* proposed a version of Australian history in which nothing had happened at all. For the *Bulletin*, though 100 years had passed since the arrival of the First Fleet, the settlers of Australia were still inside a prison camp perched absurdly on a continent in the middle of nowhere, trapped in a carceral colonial project presided over by bumbling sycophants and brutal overlords.

One can see a sharp picture of the magazine's historical sensibility in its treatment of Australia's 'Centenary'. The date 26 January 1888 marked one hundred years since Captain Arthur Phillip had landed at Sydney Cove with the First Fleet (consisting of eleven ships and 1,373 Marines, crew and convicts) and commenced the European settlement of the Australian continent. The looming event had prompted different proposals on how to celebrate this event – the opening of parks and memorials, yacht regattas and parades (Hughes-d'Aeth 2003: 220–2). The *Bulletin* found the much-anticipated celebration of this event utterly perverse. For them, 26 January was not the day that a future nation was born, but 'the day we were lagged'. The American centenary, which had in 1870 marked 100 years since its independence from Britain, provided a painful comparison with the Australian situation. While America had fought for its independence and seized its historical destiny, 'Australia . . . celebrates a century which began and ends alike in nothing. A hundred years have left her as they found her – a name but not a nation' ('The Day We Were Lagged' 1888: 4). For the *Bulletin*, the celebration of the Australian centenary was an empty masquerade, full of backslapping toadyism and cringing abasement to the British motherland:

> For some reason, not as yet very clearly defined, New South Wales hollers with an empty and artificial glee in honour of the hundredth anniversary of the day she was lagged . . . For months past the Parliament of New South Wales has been engaged in organising a feeble, fifth-rate drunk—a sort of combined scalp-dance and gin conversazione—in honour of the meanest event in her short history, and the nation which was built up on the triple foundation of cat and gallows and rum. ('The Day We Were Lagged' 1888: 4)

This neatly encapsulates the *Bulletin*'s stance. First, there is the emptiness of the years since colonisation; in front of this emptiness is a tawdry puppet show, and behind them both was the primal scene of Australian foundation – the convict 'system' that was the basis of settlement and persists in the fabric of colonial life. (No thought is given in all of this to the violent usurpation of the sovereign land of Aboriginal people, or the brutal frontier violence that was in full swing in the 1880s. The *Bulletin*'s victimhood drew its lines precisely.)

The *Bulletin* noted scornfully how the centenary celebrations airbrushed away the key fact of 26 January 1788; namely, that it created an open-air prison. It was true that this fact was carefully ignored in the official celebrations, with little mention of the waves of convict ships that transported some 164,000 convicts on 806 ships between 1788 and 1868, and which were hardly an incidental detail in Australia's settlement by Britain. As a satirical paper, the *Bulletin* sought to puncture the posturings of present-day politicians not willing to admit the bleeding obvious. Yet, the *Bulletin* went much further than this. It was not simply a matter of holding officialdom to account for the basic facts of its history, or of refusing to allow a facile sanitisation of the past. For the *Bulletin*, the 'system' was still in place. The brutalities of the contemporary moment – the continued usage of capital and corporal punishment, the exploitation of working people – were nothing other than the continuation of a pattern that was laid down with the arrival of a floating prison on the shores of the continent:

> One hundred years ago Governor Phillip landed in the little bight whereon now stands the city of Sydney. He named the cove after a viscount; the curse of official patronage began with the baptism of the settlement. He found 'a fine run of fresh water stealing silently through a thick wood.' The wood has vanished, the stream still flows, but polluted, subterranean and noxious. This is typical of our progress from the date of that eventful landing down to the present day. ('The Day We Celebrate' 1888: 5)

For the *Bulletin*, all the ills of the current Australian colonies were visible in the opening gestures of colonisation – the nepotism and the wanton despoliation, and the forcing of such things into a 'subterranean' netherworld that silently pollutes the purported advances of civil society. Indeed, for Archibald and the editors, the brutalities of the convict system constituted the only true inheritance for today's Australians:

> When the Australian colonist of to-day wakes up now and then, with a spasm of horrified disgust to find a creature of weak intelligence or otherwise mentally diseased, deliberately flogged in the police-stations at the corners of Australian streets, he is under no misapprehension as to where our flogging laws and customs come from. He knows they come down, with the people who make and administer them, in a kind of un-apostolic but strictly canonical succession, from the men and the manners of one hundred years ago at Botany Bay. ('History of Botany Bay' 1888: 6)

The magazine sponsored its writers, notably William Astley ('Price Warung', 1855–1911), to investigate the most baroque and hideous excesses of the convict era, to prove the 'pages' of Australia's history were 'stained with blood, with cruel, deliberate, but judicial murder. They smell of the gaol ... they are bruised and branded with the lash' ('The Day We Celebrate' 1888: 5). Quoting horrific eyewitness accounts of floggings from the convict days, the *Bulletin* reminded its readers of the reality of 'men who were cut to pieces from the neck to the knees' and with 'all semblance of humanity ... crushed out of the quivering jelly that represented the body' ('History of Botany Bay' 1888: 6). As the *Bulletin*'s reach grew, and its finances firmed, it began to publish books as the Bulletin Newspaper Company, and the very first book it published was Francis J. Donohue's ('Arthur Gayll') *History of Botany Bay* (1888), illustrated by its two leading cartoonists, Livingston Hopkin ('Hop') and Phil May. The book sold 20,000 copies in its first edition and ran into a second. In 1892, the Bulletin Newspaper Company published Price Warung's *Tales of the Convict System*, which also sold briskly and gained wide notoriety (Stewart 1977: 59–61).

What is interesting, then, is that the convict becomes, in the *Bulletin*'s version of history, the figure of the true settler. The image of the exiled, flogged, brutalised and executed convict stands in rather stark contrast to the positive image of the settler as the rugged individualist. It is not something one expects to find in a magazine credited with a central role in the definition of an authentic settler subjectivity. Theorists of settler colonialism have remarked on the way that settler polities will trumpet the emergence of revitalised settler subjects (that is, 'new men' and 'new women') that invert the supposition that colonists could only ever be pale imitations of those in their motherlands. James Belich and Lorenzo Veracini have noted how this discourse of the vitalising quality of settlement emerged in the nineteenth century to counteract 'the anxious perception of rebarbarised Europeans living at the edge of civilisation' (Veracini 2015: 13; Belich 2009).[2] As Veracini explains further:

> this was a momentous nineteenth-century transformation in the political imagination of emigration, a shift that radically altered the prospects of those who left the colonising cores for the settler peripheries of the 'Angloworld'. One result of this shift was that settler pioneers could be represented as inherently better humans – better than the peoples they had left behind and certainly better than the indigenous peoples they encountered. (Veracini 2015: 13)

The *Bulletin* was in many ways utterly consistent with this kind of project, both in its denigration of the Indigenous peoples of Australia and in its pillorying of the effete decadence of class-ridden Britain. Its Australians – white working men – were vital and no-nonsense souls, transvaluing values and overhauling the rotten substrate of their source culture. In openly hating the Chinese, they were fearlessly doing away with diplomatic niceties and daring to speak the truth of Britain's colonial actions, where might made right and there was never really a doubt as to who stood at the apex of God's tribes. This is what makes the *Bulletin*'s revivification of the convict figure and the convict period so intriguing. Remembering the convict origins of Australia seems to complicate unnecessarily the story of settler revitalisation. There was no pressure from the hegemony to deal with the humiliations of Australia's penal beginnings. As we have seen, they were all too ready to forget this. It was only the *Bulletin* that seemed hell bent on having the convict system at the centre of its history.

Some light is shed on this matter if we return to the figure of the bushman, which seems to be an exemplary instance of the revitalised settler subject, akin to the frontiersman in North America settler mythology. The bushman, like the American frontiersman, had been tempered on the settler frontier, hardened by hardship and surreptitiously indigenised. The bushman had an instinctive relationship to the land itself, and was in many ways its anthropomorphic extension. Yet, while they seem similar, there is a telling difference in tonality when one compares the Australian bushman and the American frontiersman. The key difference is that the Australian bushman has a life that is shadowed by failure and disappointment, and this is something that appears very distinctively in the *Bulletin*. The two most famous literary works to appear in its pages are 'Banjo' Paterson's ballad 'The Man from Snowy River' (1890) and Henry Lawson's short story 'The Drover's Wife' (1892). In both texts, we find – and at the same time do not find – the figure of the bushman. In Paterson's verse, the 'man' is a strangely diminutive and misshapen figure. He is shy and mute and rides a stumpy horse that seems his perfect equine mirror. What elevates the 'man' are his horsemanship and his courage, throwing himself down the mountainside to round up the wild horses that have made off with the station-owner's prize colt. He then disappears again and his triumph is only sustained in the elegiac account of the poet. In effect, what is being celebrated is the willingness the 'man' has to throw his life away to win back the master's horse; for the 'man', in other words, to sacrifice himself plaintively for the interests of the Man. In Lawson's story, 'The Drover's Wife' takes place under the condition that the drover is not there. There is just the mother and her children, and their pathetic impoverished selection of land. The fact that he is away droving sheep is the evidence that the land the drover owns cannot provide for the basic needs of his family. These figures are not quite what one expects as the image of the revitalised settler subject. Instead, they emerge as something rather more damaged and diminished.

In a pattern reminiscent of Kipling, Lawson's stories took place in a minor key and in the spirit of black humour, but his poems were more heavy handed and bombastic. Chris Lee has noted how Lawson 'used verse to respond to the critical forces directing him in unwelcome directions' (Lee 2004: 36). Lawson's poems have not aged well, but they reveal an effort to speak more assertively for a subjectivity that the characters in his stories could never seem to attain. His poem 'The Southern Scout; or, The Natives of the Land' channels the *Bulletin* ethos of a downtrodden periphery that was rising up – and chiding the hegemony to beware:

> Ye landlords of the cities that are builded by the sea—
> You toady 'Representative', you careless absentee—
> I come, a scout from Borderland, to warn you of a change,
> To tell you of the spirit that is roused beyond the range;
> I come from where on western plains the lonely homesteads stand,
> To tell you of the coming of the Natives of the Land!
> Of the land we're living in, The Natives of the Land.
> For Australian men are gath'ring—they are joining hand in hand!
> Don't you hear the battle cooey of the Natives of the Land? (Lawson 1892b: 20)

This messianic uprising is rather difficult to square with the pitiful figures of the 'man' from Snowy River, needlessly risking his life to save the squire's pet horse, or the 'drover' who keeps his family in poverty and terminal neglect. What it presages rather more poignantly are the Australians who died in their tens of thousands in the Great War, not in a heroic struggle for independence, but in defending the Empire's interests in Europe and the Middle East as part of the Australian Imperial Force.

While many of the political stances of the *Bulletin* have fallen into a rightful disrepute, one does not need to dig far to find that its views have not disappeared from Australian public life, let alone from its more intimate recesses. Indeed, the magazine offers up gestalt images of the anxieties that continue to define Australia's politics. The ardent xenophobia of the *Bulletin* is still a staple theme in the right-wing media, from Murdoch's daily papers, to talkback radio, to the televised hectoring of Fox News. Recent Australian elections have been heavily overdetermined by issues of migration and the spectre of foreign racial others 'flooding' the country. The impoliteness of the *Bulletin*, with its active disparagement of the settled positions of the mainstream media, makes it a progenitor of contemporary mediated alt-right populism. There is a certain fascist core to the *Bulletin* that is grounded in primordial abandonment (Curthoys 1999: 4–5); a kind of self-pity dressed up as truculence. Moreover, the distinctive discursive register of the *Bulletin* – its peculiar mixture of invective, wounded pride, ardent longing and acidic irony – provides the texture of its interpellations. In offering up the figure of the bushman, the *Bulletin* created something quite particular. Rather than a vitalistic settler *Übermensch*, the *Bulletin*'s bush 'battler' was a wounded martyr. This wound was given its historical correlative in the magazine's recovery of the traumata of convictism, such that we can clearly see that the suffering convict forms the obscene interior of the bushman.

When the *Bulletin*'s literary editor A. G. Stephens (1865–1933) compiled *The Bulletin Story Book* (1901), he reflected on the nature of the stories and sketches he had selected from those published in the *Bulletin* over the preceding twenty years. He noted how they were 'usually the literary dreams of men of action, or the literary realisation of things seen by wanderers' (Stephens 1901: i). These terms – 'dreams', 'action', 'realisation', 'wanderers' – are indicative of the particular political and libidinal dispensation that the *Bulletin* operated in. It was a world inflected by a crippling anxiety around what it meant for men to act. The assumption was that to be a man, one had to act – that is, to be a 'man of action' – but at the same time there was profound uncertainty about what constituted action, and whether this action man was not, after all, just some ghostly wanderer. When pushed, it seemed that the key action – the only thing that would suffice – was to give one's life for the system that hated you. The abject quality of this action was something that could never be quite 'realised' except in the fantasy structure of literature, until of course it could be acted out in the stony hills of Gallipoli and the grey mud of the Western Front. So, it is not for nothing that the *Bulletin* is most compellingly recalled today through the literature that it cathected. Stephens also noted that the stories in the *Bulletin* tended to be 'objective, episodic, detached – branches torn from the Tree of Life' (Stephens 1901: i). This visceral image of a limb torn from its tree suggests an underlying cause for the *Bulletin*'s literary style – at least the style that emerged in its prose sketches. The settler's plaintive detachment is preserved in the 'objective' and 'episodic' decontextualisation of its basic experience, a dislocation that the magazine's trademark grim humour does little, in the end, to mask. It was in recognising the constitutive displacement of the Australian settler that the *Bulletin* found its readership. The *Bulletin*'s achievement was to provide the Australian settler subject with a structure of feeling that reconciled its political contradictions.

Notes

1. See Macleod 1931; Jose 1933; Lindsay 1965; Stewart 1977.
2. This chapter draws its theoretical stance from the intervention in settler colonial studies precipitated by Patrick Wolfe's work, in particular *Settler Colonialism and the Transformation of Anthropology* (1999).

Bibliography

Adams, Francis (1893), *The Australians: A Social Sketch*, London: T. Fisher Unwin.
Anon. (1880), *Bulletin*, 1, 31 January, 1.
Belich, James (2009), *Replenishing the Earth: The Settler Revolution and the Rise of the Anglo-World, 1783–1930*, Oxford: Oxford University Press.
Broinowski, Alison (1992), *The Yellow Lady: Australian Impressions of Asia*, Melbourne: Oxford University Press.
Curthoys, Ann (1999), 'Expulsion, exodus and exile in white Australian historical mythology', *Journal of Australian Studies*, 23.61, 1–19.
Davison, Graeme (1978), 'Sydney and the bush: An urban context for the Australian legend', *Historical Studies*, 18.71, 191–209.
'The Day We Celebrate' (1888), *Bulletin*, 21 January, 5.
'The Day We Were Lagged' (1888), *Bulletin*, 21 January, 4.
Docker, John (1991), *The Nervous Nineties: Australian Cultural Life in the 1890s*, Oxford: Oxford University Press.
Garner, Bill (2012), 'Bushmen of the Bulletin: Re-examining Lawson's "bush credibility" in Graeme Davison's "Sydney and the bush"', *Australian Historical Studies*, 43.3, 452–65.
Gayll, Arthur (Francis J. Donohue) (1888), *The History of Botany Bay*, Sydney: Bulletin Newspaper Company.
Gelder, Ken, and Rachael Weaver (2017), *Colonial Australian Fiction: Character Types, Social Formations and the Colonial Economy*, Sydney: Sydney University Press.
'History of Botany Bay' (1888), *Bulletin*, 21 January, 6.
Hughes-d'Aeth, Tony (2003), 'History by installment: The Australian centenary and *The Picturesque Atlas of Australasia*, 1886–88', in Julie Codell (ed.), *Imperial Co-Histories:*

National Identities and the British and Colonial Press, Madison, NJ: Fairleigh Dickinson University Press, 219–41.

Jose, Arthur W. (1933), *The Romantic Nineties*, Sydney: Angus & Robertson.

Lake, Marilyn (1986), 'The politics of respectability: Identifying the masculinist context', *Australian Historical Studies*, 22.86, 116–31.

Lawson, Henry (1892a), 'The Drover's Wife', *Bulletin*, 23 July, 21–2.

—— (1892b), 'The Southern Scout; or, The Natives of the Land', *Bulletin*, 27 August, 20.

Lawson, Sylvia (1983), *The Archibald Paradox: A Strange Case of Authorship*, Ringwood, Victoria: Penguin.

Lee, Chris (2004), *City Bushmen: Henry Lawson and the Australian Imagination*, Fremantle, Western Australia: Fremantle Arts Centre Press.

Lindsay, Norman (1965), *Bohemians of the Bulletin*, Sydney: Angus & Robertson.

Macleod, Agnes Conor (1931), *Macleod of the Bulletin: The Life and Work of William Macleod, by his Wife*, Sydney: Snelling.

Magarey, Susan, Sue Rowley and Susan Sheridan (1993), *Debutante Nation: Feminism Contests the 1890s*, Sydney: Allen & Unwin.

'News in a Nutshell' (1880), *Bulletin*, 12 June, 2.

Palmer, Vance (1954), *The Legend of the Nineties*, Melbourne: Melbourne University Press.

Paterson, A. B. 'Banjo' (1890), 'The Man from Snowy River', *Bulletin*, 26 April, 13.

Stephens, A. G. (1901), *The Bulletin Story Book: A Selection of Stories and Literary Sketches from the Bulletin, 1881–1901*, Sydney: Bulletin Newspaper Company.

Stewart, Douglas (1977), *Writers of the Bulletin*, 1977 Boyer Lectures, Sydney: Australian Broadcasting Commission.

Veracini, Lorenzo (2015), *The Settler Colonial Present*, Basingstoke: Palgrave Macmillan.

Ward, Russel (1958), *The Australian Legend*, Melbourne: Oxford University Press.

Warung, Price (William Astley) (1892), *Tales of the Convict System*, Sydney: Bulletin Newspaper Company.

Wolfe, Patrick (1999), *Settler Colonialism and the Transformation of Anthropology*, London and New York: Cassell.

8

Periodicals and Australian Federation

Sam Hutchinson

Freeborn of nations, virgin white,
Not won by blood, nor ringed with steel
Thy Throne is on a loftier height,
Deep-rooted in the Commonweal!

George Essex Evans, 1901

Federation must rid Australia of the coloured alien

The Worker, 12 January 1901

Introduction

On 1 January 1901, six self-governing British colonies were, after a fractious decade-long process of conventions, conferences, debates and referendums, inaugurated as a federated government, the Commonwealth of Australia. Federation formally established a new polity spanning a continent – a milestone in British colonial history. But insofar as Federation was discussed at the time, it signalled more than a change to existing institutional arrangements; it spoke to a commitment to newly 'national' values and policies. This chapter looks at the response of prominent Australian periodicals to Federation in the weeks preceding and following it, and in light of settler Australians' beliefs about their Britishness and their assumed proclivity for historical progress.

The Colonial Press

By the time of Federation, Australian colonists could claim near-universal literacy, and had gained a justified reputation as readers. Locals and international visitors alike recognised the prominence of the press in Australian lives. Australia was, as local journalist Richard Twopenny put it in the 1880s, the 'land of newspapers' (Twopenny 1883: 221–2). Australians expressed pride in the quality of their papers, and overseas visitors echoed this (Cambridge 1903: 303; Wentworth Dilke 1890: 258, 312, 395). Contemporary statistics show the number of papers per capita in the colonies exceeding that of Britain, with distribution figures that commentators saw as 'remarkable' evidence of 'the social superiority of a civilized people' (Coghlan 1900: 359–60). Print media was, most importantly, also how many colonists encountered and imagined life outside their immediate circles. Accordingly, they perceived the meaning of Federation through the prism of the colonial press.

This chapter examines a number of prominent weekly and monthly publications to better comprehend the stories the nascent nation was telling itself, and the tensions internal to these. While the daily newspapers at the time had an unrivalled ubiquity in colonial life, they were complemented, and in some cases challenged, by periodicals more expansive in form and content. Elizabeth Webby has noted that by the end of the nineteenth century, weekly journals were by far the favoured form of periodical, with the most significant of these tied to prominent colonial daily newspapers (Webby 1996: 26, 46). They each competed for readers, and aimed to appeal to the sensibilities most likely to attract a loyal audience. These publications were commercial enterprises, often owned and managed by white colonial elites, and expressing the interests of various factions internal to that grouping.

The great majority of colonial publications therefore existed in a political band delimited by mainstream conservative and liberal views. Within this circumscribed space, perspectives were aired regarding the promotion of greater or lesser government intervention in the economy, or for varying gradations of support to British imperial causes. But these represented different denominations of a broader faith in the global market system, with their respective disciples and proselytisers. Either way, it was to be Australia's role to provide raw materials to the metropole, and to be a final market for goods produced in the major manufacturing centres, as well as a destination for the mother country's surplus population. And though mainstream journals offered shifts of emphasis, all insisted on the epochal significance of Federation. There were, however, publications offering countervailing views. They focused primarily on labour, women and other 'marginal' concerns, with an aim to expand the bounds of permissible thought in Australian society. Still other voices, particularly those of the Indigenous population, though spoken for from time to time, were rendered all but silent in the colonial press.

Federation and its Context

The Constitution that established the Commonwealth was drafted by colonial delegates in 1897–8 and approved through popular referendums around the country in 1899–1900. This major democratic achievement came after years of deliberations, setbacks and false starts (Irving 2013: 262–3). In early July 1900, after (most) colonial parliaments had adopted the Constitution, it was finally passed in an Act of the British Parliament to create a new jurisdiction in the following year. Only three weeks later did a recalcitrant Western Australia finally vote to join. On the first day of 1901, a date to symbolise a new beginning, the new Commonwealth was celebrated in Sydney, with great crowds treated to parades, pageantry, historical re-enactments, and speeches from august dignitaries and guests. Similar celebrations occurred throughout the continent.

Besides creating a political entity, the Constitution introduced a two-tier structure of federal and state-level (hitherto colonial) governments. The distinctive political model that eventuated borrowed from both the British system of responsible government and US federalism – an amalgam later neologised as 'Washminster'. And while certain defined powers were exclusive to the Commonwealth, the six states retained major responsibilities for matters affecting people's everyday lives.[1]

But why, besides sharing a continent (Tasmania excepted), did separate self-governing colonies desire formal union at all? In their various explanations, historians disagree over whether this was a top-down or bottom-up affair, and whether dry rationality or an ineffable idealism prevailed.[2] An obvious answer was the swelling sense of national identity at the time, though it is unclear whether this was more effect or cause. Certainly, the six states remained powerful political players in their own right, often in tension with one another and with the Commonwealth government. There were ongoing jealousies between the major eastern states of predominantly 'free-trade' New South Wales and 'protectionist' Victoria as to who would carry most political clout. Related reasons include changes in social understandings – an upswing in beliefs about liberal democratic rights – as well as demographic trends, including the fact the locally born population (or 'natives', as many colonists called themselves) were now a majority. A necessary, if insufficient, factor was the efficiency gained by integrating administration of matters suited to overarching governance. These included immigration and taxation policies, communications, transport, monetary and defence systems, and, not least, the imperative to address divergent economic and trade policies (Irving 2013: 244–7, 256, 260). The Colonial Office, for administrative ease and a desire to bolster the Empire, gladly obliged. Though rivalrous colonies weighed potential gains and losses of any new arrangement, on immigration there was agreement that Australia must be kept 'white'.

While all these motives hold to greater or lesser extents, some historians still sought an animating force. John Hirst found it in the impulse of a 'sentimental nation' with a passion for the 'sacred cause' of an enlightened union, one where colonists could transcend an ignoble past to embrace junior partnership in the Empire. This, for Hirst, trumped all cold political and economic manoeuvring (Hirst 2000). For Helen Irving, while 'there was not a single cause of Federation', it arose from 'a particularly Australian culture' which allowed the nation to be imagined before it was formalised (Irving 1999).

But these were arguments for later analysts. The pressing concern at the time was to ensure the moment's importance was recorded. The *Sydney Mail* (1860–1938), an illustrated weekly version of the *Sydney Morning Herald* – one of Australia's leading metropolitan dailies – assumed 'the occasion will be marked in the memories of all old enough to understand what they shall witness as an era in the individual and national life' (*Sydney Mail*, 15 December 1900: 1,395; *Sydney Mail*, 5 January 1901: 11). We now know that following a flutter of anticipation and excitement, Federation did not fully lodge in the public memory, at least not in the longer term (Holbrook 2020). Something was missing. But while the *Sydney Mail*'s prediction now seems quaint, the point was to assert that this moment should be understood as a major event.

Federation was a chance to display the nation's successes and its new standing, and it occurred in a moment brimming with historical import. Radical labour movements transformed the political scene. Unsatisfied with liberal reformism, they declared capitalism – and capitalists – the enemy and, audaciously, demanded parliamentary power through Australia's first political party. Labour and anti-labour blocs began to coalesce in relation to one another. Suffragettes tested the limits of politics and social convention with attempts to expand women's rights and the democratic franchise. These progressive movements occurred alongside, or were spurred by, a ruinous economic depression and a demoralising drought. The disconcerting sight of widespread poverty amid plenty, and a stubbornly indomitable earth, confounded the colonial faith in progress. All this called for a suitable interpretation of the nation's birth.

The Birth of the Nation

Coverage of Federation typically swung between high-flown rhetoric and the routine tasks accompanying the operational shift to federal government (*The Australasian*, 29 December 1900: 1,441; *The Worker*, 26 January 1901: 4; *The Queenslander*, 5 January 1901: 8; *The Australasian*, 12 January 1901: 89). Predictably, more grandiose language attended the celebrations themselves. Immediately after the festivities, *The Australasian*, an illustrated Melbourne-based weekly journal, suggested that

> Only one sentiment can prevail among those who witnessed and those who read of the stately inauguration of Australia's Commonwealth. Every fibre in the being of a true Australian must thrill with pride and joyfulness at recognising how nobly the birth of the nation was celebrated, with what lofty and splendid mien the country stepped across the threshold of its new existence. (*The Australasian*, 5 January 1901: 33)

The reader is given little guidance on what being a 'true Australian' entailed, besides describing all those who recognised the enormity of the occasion. In any case, the following week saw a steep descent from these heights, when the same paper, business-like, observed that, '[n]ow that the inauguration rejoicings are packed away in memory, public attention throughout the states is rapidly concentrating on the tariff issue' (*The Australasian*, 19 January 1901: 145; *Bulletin*, 5 January 1901: 6). As well it might. The question of whether 'free-traders' or 'protectionists' should dominate federal economic policy was a fiscal clash that pitched states against one another, and fomented sectional alliances within them (*Sydney Mail*, 12 January 1901: 73). Crucial as such practical issues were, however, the most prominent idea in the coverage was the emergence of a new community.

For most late nineteenth-century colonists, it seems their acquired designation as 'Australians' complemented rather than superseded their intuitive identification as 'Britons'. Occasionally in their more parochial moments, and depending on the interests in play, they took issue with decisions made by the British government – but they rarely questioned their innate Britishness. Formally and informally, Federation marked only a limited move toward national independence. The key theme was unity, and it appeared repeatedly. It was a political unification of individual colonies, of course, but only as the realisation of a preordained ideal. *The Queenslander* (1866–1939), the weekly and more literary version of the major Queensland daily the *Brisbane Courier*, put it simply: 'We are no longer colonies, though we are still part, and proud to be part, of the British Empire. We are a Nation' (*The Queenslander*, 5 January 1901: 8). Federation, and the sentiment that fortified it, was the culmination of certain ineluctable movements. For *The Queenslander*, 'Nothing could be more natural than the influences which led up to this event. They were irresistible in their naturalness' (*The Queenslander*, 5 January 1901: 8). 'It was' therefore 'monstrous that a people, one in blood, in language, in religion, in temperament, in all the traditions which make national unity . . . call themselves by separate names, and set up separate Governments, and mark themselves off from each other's industries by Customs walls'. It felt 'that nature was being outraged, and that we had common interests which could only be safeguarded by the preservation or the re-attainment of our unity' (*The Queenslander*, 5 January 1901: 8).

Likewise, for the *Sydney Mail*, the Commonwealth 'must aim at fostering union, and unity of sentiment directed towards the common national end' (*Sydney Mail*, 5 January 1901: 11). In an earlier editorial it stated: '[i]t is but natural that a population such as ours, one in race and blood, inspired by the same national aspirations, and informed by the same sentiment of imperial loyalty, should rejoice at the act which brings us together' (*Sydney Mail*, 22 December 1900: 1,483–4). Imperial feeling was here not contradicted by national feeling, but provided a basis for it. *The Australasian* pushed the metaphor into the familial realm. It spoke of

> the wholly undreamed of discovery that distant communities could grow into adolescence, take their rank as nations free and self governing, yet remain linked by the finest bonds with the motherland from which they sprang. . . . Australia remains an integral part of the empire, not because she is coerced into allegiance, but because she ardently prizes her place. (*The Australasian*, 5 January 1901: 33)

On its own terms, this natural unity of interests was an undisputed blessing for all. But as the frequent recourse to race-rhetoric implied, the terms of membership into the national family bore heavy costs. After all, though Federation in the discussion of major periodicals largely ignored the Indigenous population, Federation in practice further entrenched an imported legal and political order that assumed away Aboriginal counter-claims to settler sovereignty, which were simply unthinkable within a project to consolidate an indivisible nationhood.[3] The prevailing story was that Australia was the whole and healthy offspring of the mother country, retaining the unspoiled features inherited from a British lineage.

If bloodlines were one marker of national unity, bloodshed was another. For Federation took place during a major imperial war in South Africa (1899–1902), to which the Australian colonies had made a notable contribution. In the wake of Federation, *The Queenslander* observed that although the new Australian nation was not, like the United States, forged in war, 'we could not have chosen any course of events better fitted to cement the Commonwealth than that which has actually marked the year' (*The Queenslander*, 5 January 1901: 8). Invoking the egalitarian ethos that would feature in future wars involving Australians, the paper described '[o]ur common experiences in this Transvaal war, our unanimous recognition of the claims of the mother-country, our universal readiness to offer treasure and life in her defence, the standing together of our soldiers in the field of battle, the singling out of Australian troops for united praise'. Such things had 'given us a sense of oneness which alone would have forced Federation to the front' (*The Queenslander*, 5 January 1901: 8).

Some at the time felt the war was a rite of passage into a community of nations. In his 'Song of the Federation', the iconic Australian poet and *Bulletin* contributor A. B. (Banjo) Paterson intimated that Australia's involvement meant entry into national 'sisterhood' (Paterson 1993: 149). Evocations of sisters and mothers aside, coverage of martial exploits necessarily emphasised discussions of men by men, imbuing Federation with a stronger masculine tone than it already had. Louisa Lawson's famed early feminist magazine *The Dawn* (1888–1905) – suggestively for a publication by and for women – barely discussed Federation at all. Certainly not shy of political matters, *The Dawn*'s eloquent silence on the topic raised implicit questions about what the most important political questions and actions affecting people's lives really were.

The war's importance in defining the Commonwealth's imperial relationship was evident in a *Queenslander* editorial that described sending troops to South Africa as adding 'another rivet in the consolidation of the Empire' (*The Queenslander*, 20 January 1900: 104). It shut down 'loose talk indulged in not so long ago in some quarters of Australian independence'. The war had in a practical way 'ended the republican dream' as '[c]ommon action and common suffering have made Britain and Australia one, as they could not be made one by political theories, or even by the ties of origin and kindred'. Australian soldiers were sharing with the British a 'baptism of blood' such that Australians were connected to the mother country 'by our blood shed with hers in a common cause' (*The Queenslander*, 20 January 1900: 104; see also *The Queenslander*, 1 December 1900: 1,096). The longing for just such a cause was key. War, as with Federation, demonstrated a compulsion to prove the nation's fitness and a willingness to act as a mature nation presumably should act. It was also about embedding the national story in an appropriate historical setting – and one that skirted around the violent dispossession of Aboriginal land. The common appeal to blood ties also invoked an oath of loyalty, demonstrating that loosening the tethers to the mother country was as yet inconceivable. Or, to switch metaphors, if Federation was a celebratory ritual, war was its consummation.

Dissidents, meanwhile, expressed disdain for the martial mood sweeping the continent. The *Bulletin* (1880–2008), the infamous Sydney-based 'Bushman's Bible', was proudly iconoclastic and cultivated in its commentary and literary pages an antagonistic radical nationalism. And it struck a chord, with its circulation of between 80,000 and 100,000 by the time of Federation (see Chapter 7 in this volume, by Tony Hughes-d'Aeth). The *Bulletin* saw it as 'Australia's misfortune that its Commonwealth begins at a time of feverish Jingoism, when the public is not quite in its right mind' (*Bulletin*, 22 December 1900: 6). Similarly, *The Worker* (1890–1974), a monthly journal of the Queensland workers' federation and an organ of the nascent Queensland Labor Party, felt that a 'significant aspect of the Commonwealth celebrations is the striking manifestations of the spirit of militarism' which were 'sinister portents to the peaceful idealist' (*The Worker*, 5 January 1901: 2). For *The Worker*, this continued a process where elites inculcated 'the spirit of war into our peaceful Australian people' and where 'stupid Governments, for their own personal glorification, or for class purposes, are endeavouring to convert the continent into a recruiting ground for the British army' (*The Worker*, 5 January 1901: 2).

Striking as such statements were, those opposing the war remained a minority, outnumbered by those like the *Sydney Mail*, for whom the war and Federation coincided to mark a critical juncture. The year 1900 in this sense was the crucible from which Australia emerged fully formed. 'Warlike blasts from martial trumpets heralded its birth. The men of this budding nation were suddenly called upon to prove their loyalty and valour in support of a great Empire' (*Sydney Mail*, 29 December 1900: 1,543–4). The events that followed 'are matters of history. Australian blood was shed on South African soil', and Australia's 'claim to become a nation was universally acknowledged'. As such, 'it must be conceded that as a maker of history 1900 stands unrivalled' (*Sydney Mail*, 29 December 1900: 1,543–4). Events at Gallipoli in 1915 would soon surpass this announcement of historical uniqueness, though at least one rhetorical feature – warfare as the midwife of nationhood – would be repeated, more convincingly, in that year too. That later, greater war would, however, fundamentally challenge another defining idea of Federation commentary: History as progress.

Marked by Historical Progress

The historical weight Federation carried was clear to *The Queenslander*: 'Only the most superficial can fail to see that a far-reaching change is about to be made in the position and history of the Australian peoples' (*The Queenslander*, 22 December 1900: 1,248). This change was the next step in the grand march of Australian progress. Another long historically minded editorial a few days before Federation conceded that while temporal proximity prevented a proper assessment of the prior century, its main feature was the dazzling pace of advancement: 'The baldest chronicle of [the century's] many discoveries, its inventions, and general material progress, if such could have been written at the close of last century, would have appeared to the reader as the delirious ravings of an unsound mind.' And as if this was not heartening enough, it foresaw the same again for the new century (*The Queenslander*, 29 December 1900: 1,296). Recent history, in other words, was synonymous with forward momentum at an exponential rate, and Australia was to reap the benefits.

The *Australian Town and Country Journal* (1870–1919), an esteemed Sydney weekly connected to the *Sydney Evening News*, and featuring substantive essays alongside news reportage, claimed the nineteenth century was 'more remarkable than any of its predecessors'. It was characterised by 'the progress of scientific knowledge, by the revelation of the hidden forces of nature, and the taming of them to the service of man', and 'the great advance in the material welfare which mankind enjoys today'. This moment, moreover, holds 'particular significance' for Australia, which was itself a 'product of the nineteenth century'. Indeed, 'With the material progress which has marked it, the peaceful colonisation of this vast island continent . . . progressed, until to-day we are on the eve of consummating its maturity as a self-governing community, and', it concluded with a Kiplingesque flourish, 'the realisation of its fitness to share the burdens of the British Empire' (*Australian Town and Country Journal*, 15 December 1900: 20). The reference to 'peaceful colonisation' refers to a lack of violent revolution or warfare within the European population. Frontier violence was known at the time but the Aboriginal population, considered a vanishing remnant, did not rate a mention. In any case, such accounts were more about drafting a mythology than seriously chronicling the historical record. They acted as a kind of homily on what Australian history meant – and to incorporate this into the long arc of Britain's civilising mission.

The Australasian similarly presented a 'century of colonisation', recounting the growth of pastoralism and agriculture, the movement against convict transportation, the occupation and industrialisation of the continent, and the immense changes in wealth and demography (diluting the 'penal element') that followed the discovery of gold (*The Australasian*, 29 December 1900: 1,441–2). In a later editorial, *The Australasian* said Federation provoked 'a sense of the phenomenal progress' that had occurred since Arthur Phillip made landfall 112 years earlier on what was to become Sydney:

'The mere children who dwell on these shores to-day make a goodly population – the progenitors to be of a nation which will have grown to limits we can hardly guess at by the time another century dawns.' *The Australasian* claimed that 'New Year's Day, 1901, is a date for ever memorable in Australian history, and charged, too, with deep significance for the empire at large'. Indeed, 'Next to the foundation of the first settlement this celebration is the greatest day in Australia's calendar' (*The Australasian*, 5 January 1901: 33). There was, again, an insistent tone to such passages, the force of which rests less in a sober assessment of the present than in what Federation will come to symbolise in Australian memory and to the Empire.

The leading account of history at the time told not only of a maturing political actor, but of the physical conquering of a continent. *The Queenslander* could in this way claim that the century's 'pre-eminent distinction lay in the triumph of man over nature'. In this telling,

> The great laws of Nature have been determined, and its forces are each year being made more subservient to man's will. The lightning has been subdued and made to carry his messages to every corner of the globe; the sea is only the loom on which ply the shuttles of ocean steamers weaving a web of intercourse between the nations. (*The Queenslander*, 29 December 1900: 1,296)

Though an embarrassment of hubris to modern eyes, and barely credible then given the natural disasters, failed explorations and ecological spoliations already familiar to readers, it is true that communications technology had radically altered how 'unity' felt, making distance less tyrannical.

The 'triumph' over the natural world, moreover, could be claimed by fewer than *The Queenslander* seems to suggest, with 'man' here denoting a narrow range of white male settlers who were designated as History's makers, and 'nature' a category that subsumed within it the Aboriginal population. *The Queenslander* painted a classically settler colonial picture of development, moving from the 'struggling settler' camped on Sydney's shores, through the 'daring explorations through the interior, the settlement of the remote pastoral lands, the clearing away of the bush, the cultivation of the soil, the making of roads and railways'. And now, 'Australia thus equipped begins her nation's career under fairer auspices than those which have attended the birth of any other nation'. For *The Queenslander*, 'Our wealth, resources, and position give us the command of the greater portion of the Southern Hemisphere, and the worthy acceptance of the responsibilities thus laid upon our citizenship may crown our future history with a renown that shall be worthy of the lands from which we have sprung' (*The Queenslander*, 29 December 1900: 1,296). Or, to put all this another way, expropriating and subduing the land while acquiring and exploiting its treasures were foundational preconditions for the nation's prosperity and future development.

While these accounts focused on history, they were far from backward-looking. If history was an account of unyielding progress, this implied projection into the future. For the *Sydney Mail*, Federation meant the 'new nation enters history under auspices so promising and so benignant that its citizens may look with confidence to the future, and await its revelations without fear'. It foresaw a time of rapid change in international relations, and the necessity of great power alliances. A cautious optimism should thus prevail, with the only options being advancement or stasis: 'We must either progress or fall behind, for there is no such thing as immobility without stagnation. . . . Henceforth we are a factor to be reckoned with' (*Sydney Mail*, 5 January 1901: 11).

This was a comforting prediction, but if the future belonged to the new, it is unsurprising that the emergent workers' movement also saw promise in what was to come. In one of several pieces narrating labour's rise in the colonies, an author in *The Worker* hoped that the nation, 'inspired by the successes of the past', would 'enter the Commonwealth on the dawn of a new century feeling confident that the Labour Movement shall grow and prosper and be a mighty power for good in helping to build up a great Australian nation' (Democritus 1900: 3). Another piece announced that

> We are to take a part in founding the Australian Nation—a nation that in many respects will be unique in the world's history. It will have no tale to tell of domestic rapine and slaughter—of the blood of the weak ruthlessly shed for its baptism, for it comes together from the strong instincts of unity in the race. It will have no hereditary aristocracy for men to bow the knee to the title and not the individual; no racial feuds to embitter its existence and no differing languages to keep its peoples apart. (M'Donnell 1900: 4)

Leaving aside the historical veracity of a piece intended as political rhetoric, the point to note is, as the tenses employed make clear, this is a history foretold, describing a utopia that presumably follows the victorious struggle for the rights of labour. History was therefore important to *The Worker* largely because 'The question to be reiterated is "The Future"'. That is, how is the nation 'to be reckoned?' (*The Worker*, 5 January 1901: 2). *The Worker* saw the new Commonwealth's true distinction not in its vast acreage and 'material wealth' but in a genuine and non-plutocratic 'Democracy' (*The Worker*, 19 January 1901: 2). And yet if authentic democracy was the necessary goal, it could never be achieved without confronting the question of real political power, especially as it manifested in the great class divide.

Two Great Classes

The rise of socialism and organised labour as a serious political force in the late nineteenth century, if not entirely changing the political game, made clear the opposing sides. The loudest voices were the radical papers, who cautioned that material progress came at a cost to be borne by those who had done most to deliver it. In Western Australia, which for economic, political and geographical reasons hesitated to join the Commonwealth, the radical labourite weekly *Sunday Times* (1897–1902) had long been wary of Federation, and only one year on it offered a scorching rebuke of the high hopes initially held for it. Since Federation day 'we realised that the grandeur had been ostentatious extravagance, the greatness a vacuous display of national vanity, the sisterhood of states a political sham', while 'here in the West the anniversary of the proclamation of the Commonwealth will bring us not the free breakfast table so enthusiastically predicted, but will arrive with the burdens of the poor increased' (*Sunday Times*, 29 December 1901: 5).

For *The Worker*, which offered a strident declaration of a new class politics, the problem was simple: 'If the Federal Government is to work for the benefit of the masses, then the masses must dominate its Parliament.' Without a government representing working people there could be no democracy, by definition. Therefore, 'Labour Government *versus* Capitalistic Government is the straight Federal issue, and the toilers must have no other' (*The Worker*, 22 December 1900: 3 (original emphasis); see also the *Sunday Times*, 16 December 1900: 8). *The Worker* consequently had an entirely different understanding of unity – or solidarity – from mainstream periodicals that, in labour's view, only papered over social cracks with vague talk of nationhood. By contrast, *The Worker* asserted, 'The masters have learnt the value of unity from us, and we must not be beat at our own game' (*The Worker*, 29 December 1900: 3; see also Figure 8.1). It was blunter still in a later editorial that argued the population 'can be easily subdivided into two great classes': the one-third of the population who hold the land and the capital, and the remaining two-thirds who 'are the real wealth producers, extractors, or distributors, who by brain or hand, with the assistance of capital, are the makers of all the wealth produced from year to year'. Brooking no middle ground, *The Worker* concluded that the 'interests of these two great classes are diametrically opposed'. Therefore, 'no peace can be proclaimed until the division of the national wealth is equitable' (*The Worker*, 29 December 1900: 3).[4]

Labour's genius was to distil all social and political life into a binary contest between the winning few and the exploited many. The reality of the Australian experience, however, was never so simple. One complication of many for the basic class calculation was the 'Coloured Labour Question' (*The Worker*, 26 January 1901: 4). (See also Chapter 24 in this volume, by David Finkelstein, for more on this point from the typographical trade press point of view.) The rise of the labour movement coincided with, and facilitated, the push to limit legislatively both non-British immigration and Pacific Islander labour in Queensland's sugar industry. These laws had the double advantage of rousing popular sentiment, unified by a feeling of racial supremacy, while dampening fears that cut-price 'alien' labour would weaken the living standards of the white working classes (Irving 2013: 248). The desire for the unity of white labour was captured in a cartoon published on 2 February 1901 (see Figure 8.1).

By mid-century, increasing numbers of Chinese, Pacific Islander and Indian labourers, among others, were seen to be competing with white workers, undercutting the value of their labour power. This dynamic charged colonial society with an abiding racial animosity. The Pacific Island Labourers Act 1901 and the Immigration Restriction Act 1901 would repatriate Pacific Island labourers and prohibit non-British (particularly Chinese) immigrants, respectively. China in particular stirred dark forebodings in the settler imagination. Since the mid-century gold rushes in the eastern colonies, and later in the west, the increase in the Asian population represented the sum of all fears for certain colonists. Moreover, these fears went beyond the labour question to more existential nightmares. It entered some minds that leaving a land the size of theirs unfilled amounted to an open invitation to the 'teeming hordes' to their north (Hutchinson 2018: 171). Oxford historian Charles Pearson's influential *National Life and Character: A Forecast* thus warned his fellow white men near the end of the century of the danger of being swamped by a demographic deluge of 'black and yellow races' (Pearson 1893: 30). Future Australian Prime Ministers, including the very first, Edmund Barton, took the warning seriously and were hypervigilant to the idea. A ruthless logic now suggested itself. It was the relative lack of population and a perceived failure to use the land productively that had validated settlers' dispossession of the Aboriginal population – a rationale later termed 'terra nullius'. But if it turned

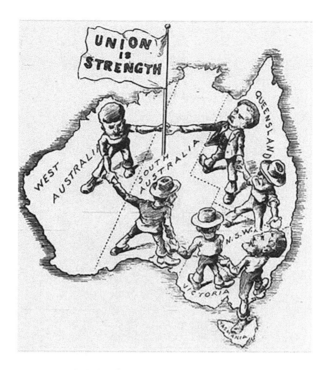

Figure 8.1 'Cartoon: What about trade unions federation?', *The Worker*, 2 February 1901, p. 1. Courtesy of the author.

out that white Australians too were not fulfilling their promise, did it not follow that they could be dispossessed in turn? Racial superiority alone was no match for sheer force of numbers. Further, if Australia could not be maintained as a paradise for the exclusive use of the white man, what exactly was its historical justification?

By pairing restriction with eviction, these immigration policies were envisioned as having a prophylactic effect on white settler jobs and wages, while simultaneously cleansing the body politic (see Figure 8.2). Marilyn Lake has argued that racial exclusion was inherent to the peculiarly Australian version of colonial liberalism that prevailed among key statesmen in the late nineteenth century, such that '[e]quality required exclusion; democracy demanded discrimination' (Lake 2008: 22). These principles undergirded Federation, as only the 'higher races' could be seen as capable of governing themselves and living up to the democratic ideals they praised (Lake 2009: 129–30). In this sense, both Indigenous and Asian populations represented a social threat – the first to legitimate claims to the land, the second to white wages. Both had to be excised; 'the Chinese to be legislatively excluded for being too many, and Aboriginal people to be imagined away as being too few' (Hutchinson 2018: 173).

Representing Queensland labour, *The Worker* had a particularly vested interest in seeing off the challenge presented by imported Pacific Island workers, a challenge that

Figure 8.2 'Cartoon: The Curse of Queensland', *The Worker*, 12 January 1901, p. 4. Courtesy of the author.

was biological as well as economic. *The Worker*'s attitude to imported labour was encapsulated in a cartoon published on 12 January 1901 (see Figure 8.2). *The Worker* was incensed that 'cheap-labour loving sugar planters' were again arguing that 'white men are unable to work in the northern canefields' (*The Worker*, 26 January 1901: 4). For, as *The Worker* saw it, the fact was 'the white race is far and away superior to the black and its power of adapting itself to new climates and conditions is greater immeasurably than that of the Pacific Island savage'. Accordingly, the 'rate of wages the planter offers the white man is governed by the wages he pays the black'. The problem was not that industry could not afford to pay white workers, but that with a surfeit of black labourers it did not need to. The coloured labour question could therefore be conclusively answered '[i]f every kanaka were to be taken away from it tomorrow' (*The Worker*, 26 January 1901: 4).

The *Bulletin*, which had no patience for the predicted pomp of Federation day, diagnosed still more profound problems with the health of the young nation. A cover article appearing in its renowned 'Red Page' foresaw 'the spectacle of soldiers marching, and the empty verbiage of temporary politicians' as merely gratifying 'sensual appetites' as a means to 'make intelligible to the crowd the supposed significance of the Commonwealth'. Though unopposed in principle, it was the *Bulletin* that asked of Federation the most profane question of all: so what?

Mercilessly cutting through the hype, the *Bulletin* saw 'no magical quality in this union: no millennium is to be reached by the declaration of a Federal Act in so many chapters, and so many clauses'. In other words, any positive consequences arising from Federation would need to be based on substantive actions rather than words and ceremony: 'The Commonwealth must justify itself' (*Bulletin*, 8 December 1900: inside cover). The article proposed three principles of 'statesmanship' to help it do so. The first was 'the development of natural resources, involving the settlement of the community on the land as self-supporting producers of the means of living'. This meant transferring 'non-productive' city-dwellers to the country and away from major urban centres – those 'huge cancers whose ramifications of disease spread far into national life' and which if 'not extirpated . . . may yet destroy the nation' (*Bulletin*, 8 December 1900: inside cover).

The second principle was 'the preservation of the race, the purification of the national blood'. This was because the 'mixed British breed on which we build our race is as good a breed, on the whole, as any to be found; and for all men who are fit to be merged in it the Commonwealth should have a welcome'. However, it warned that 'living as we do on the border of Asia, we are always exposed to the danger of Asiatic incursions, and it is certain that the establishment of Asiatic settlements, or of a Eurasian breed, will tend to degrade and destroy the white breed and the white Commonwealth'. For the *Bulletin*, 'Nothing at all – no question of local profit or temporary advantage – should be permitted to interfere with the vital and permanent necessity of preserving Australia for white Australians' (*Bulletin*, 8 December 1900: inside cover). Finally, there was 'the principle of the equalisation of fortunes. . . . the division between rich and poor tends to increase, and already we have a numerous class of paupers living from hand to mouth, and dependent on chance employment for subsistence. Good government can do much to level the disparity of classes' (*Bulletin*, 8 December 1900: inside cover).

For the mainstream papers, the unity of the Australian national body was naturally ordained, but this was more easily declared than demonstrated. The *Bulletin* showed how much work was needed to sustain its vitality: population transplants to prevent a social cancer from metastasising, purifying the blood supply of invasive impurities so as to prevent degradation, and suturing social wounds. As potential policy settings, the return to an organically agrarian community, a government willing to close the economic divide, and the primacy of reproducing an untainted white citizenry had the virtue of candour. But if the act of Federation by itself meant little, would this be the vision to generate enthusiasm toward it? The *Bulletin*, like its mainstream rivals, was betting on who Australians thought they were, and what they really wanted for their nation.

Conclusion

The Federation of Australia coincided with the beginning of a new year, and a new era. For major Australian periodicals, it was the culmination of an inexorable national progression rooted in a British imperial past. Federation allowed these publications to proclaim a particular interpretation of the moment, balancing inherited traditions with an imagined future. The dominant interpretation emphasised unity, progress and a teleology that confirmed Australia's role in the vanguard of history. The progress invoked was both quantitative (growth in material affluence and tangible advancements) and qualitative (the nation had arrived at a level of maturity sufficient to play its proper part in global affairs). But to other voices, Federation raised awkward questions about the history and future of the nation, and about what exactly was meant by the watchwords 'unity' and 'progress'. Was their so-called unity in fact a veil cast over fundamental exclusions and power struggles? If so, were the fault lines to be national, imperial, class-based, gendered or racial? Would progress, if it happened at all, endow all equally? The mainstream papers preferred to gloss over these questions, while radical papers supplied answers to test the social fabric. With a national mythology there for the making, these and other publications provided a sense of what the stakes were. The periodicals of the time were a key part of a media network that illuminated what the nation might be capable of, and why that mattered. Their responses helped to shape Australians' understanding of what they were embarking on as the Commonwealth braced itself for the mysteries of the twentieth century.

Notes

1. The Commonwealth would not be empowered to make special laws for Aboriginal people or include them in the national reckoning until 1967.
2. This paragraph is based on, among others, readings of Irving 1999; Irving 2013; Macintyre 2004: 120–44; de Garis 1993; and Souter 2000: chapters 1–3.
3. Who actually exercised authority on the ground could be another matter.
4. It was referring to Queensland Parliament, but the point had broader application.

Bibliography

The Australasian (1900), 29 December, 1,441–2.
The Australasian (1901), 5 January, 33.
The Australasian (1901), 12 January, 89.
The Australasian (1901), 19 January, 145.
Australian Town and Country Journal (1900), 15 December, 20.
Bulletin (1900), 8 December.
Bulletin (1900), 22 December, 6.
Bulletin (1901), 5 January, 6.
Cambridge, Ada (1903), *Thirty Years in Australia*, London: Methuen & Co.
Coghlan, Timothy Augustine (1900), *A Statistical Account of the Seven Colonies of Australasia, 1899–1900*, 8th issue, Sydney: William Applegate Gullick, Government Printer.
de Garis, Brian K. (1993), 'How popular was the popular federation movement?', *Papers on Parliament no. 21*, Canberra: Department of the Senate.
Democritus (1900), 'Australasian Labour Movement: Sketches of its Rise and Progress. Queensland', *The Worker*, 15 December, 3.
Essex Evans, George (1901), 'Ode for Commonwealth Day', *Australian Town and Country Journal*, 5 January, 18.
Hirst, John (2000), *The Sentimental Nation: The Making of the Australian Commonwealth*, Oxford: Oxford University Press.
Holbrook, Carolyn (2020), 'Federation and Australian nationalism: Early commemoration of the Commonwealth', *Australian Journal of Politics and History*, 66.4, 560–77.

Hutchinson, Sam (2018), *Settlers, War, and Empire in the Press: Unsettling News in Australia and Britain, 1863–1902*, Cham: Palgrave Macmillan.
Irving, Helen (1999), *To Constitute a Nation: A Cultural History of Australia's Constitution*, Cambridge: Cambridge University Press.
—— (2013), 'Making the federal Commonwealth, 1890–1901', in Alison Bashford and Stuart Macintyre (eds), *The Cambridge History of Australia, Volume 1: Indigenous and Colonial Australia*, Cambridge: Cambridge University Press, 242–66.
Lake, Marilyn (2008), 'Equality and exclusion: The racial constitution of colonial liberalism', *Thesis Eleven*, 95.1, 22.
—— (2009), 'White is wonderful: Emotional conversion and subjective formation', in Leigh Boucher, Jane Carey and Katherine Ellinghaus (eds), *Re-Orienting Whiteness*, New York: Palgrave Macmillan, 119–34.
Macintyre, Stuart (2004), *A Concise History of Australia*, 2nd edn, Cambridge: Cambridge University Press.
M'Donnell, Donald (1900), 'New South Wales', *The Worker*, 15 December, 4.
Paterson, Andrew Barton (1993), *The Works of Banjo Paterson*, Ware: Wordsworth.
Pearson, Charles H. (1893), *National Life and Character: A Forecast*, London: Macmillan & Co.
The Queenslander (1900), 20 January, 104.
The Queenslander (1900), 1 December, 1,096.
The Queenslander (1900), 22 December, 1,248.
The Queenslander (1900), 29 December, 1,296.
The Queenslander (1901), 5 January, 8.
Souter, Gavin (2000) [1976], *The Lion and the Kangaroo: The Initiation of Australia*, Melbourne: Text Publishing.
Sunday Times (1900), 16 December, 8.
Sunday Times (1901), 29 December, 5.
Sydney Mail (1900), 15 December, 1,395.
Sydney Mail (1900), 22 December, 1,483–4.
Sydney Mail (1900), 29 December, 1,543–4.
Sydney Mail (1901), 5 January, 11.
Sydney Mail (1901), 12 January, 73.
Twopenny, Richard (1883), *Town Life in Australia*, Harmondsworth: Penguin.
Webby, Elizabeth (1996), 'Australia', in J. Don Vann and Rosemary T. VanArsdel (eds), *Periodicals of Queen Victoria's Empire: An Exploration*, Toronto: University of Toronto Press, 19–59.
Wentworth Dilke, Charles (1890), *Problems of Greater Britain*, London: Macmillan & Co.
The Worker (1900), 15 December, 3–4.
The Worker (1900), 22 December, 3.
The Worker (1900), 29 December, 2–3.
The Worker (1901), 5 January, 2.
The Worker (1901), 12 January, 2.
The Worker (1901), 19 January, 2.
The Worker (1901), 26 January, 4.
The Worker (1901), 2 February, 1.

9

The *South African News* and the Anglo-Boer War of 1899–1902

Jonathan Derrick

On 2 May 1899, a few months before the outbreak of the Second Anglo-Boer War, the *South African News* began publication in Cape Town in daily and weekly editions (see Figure 9.1).[1] It was launched for a specific political purpose, as a response to growing division and tension among white South Africans. The prominent white personalities of the Cape Colony who started the newspaper had two related aims. One was to oppose the British policy which, under the direction of the High Commissioner of South Africa and Cape Colony Governor Sir Alfred Milner in Cape Town and the Colonial Secretary Joseph Chamberlain in London, was in confrontation with the Boer (Afrikaner) republics of Transvaal and Orange Free State. The other was to

Figure 9.1 The *South African News*, weekly edition, 12 December 1900. Courtesy of the British Library.

oppose the power of Cecil Rhodes, still immensely powerful in the Cape Colony but without formal political power since 1896.

Behind the new newspaper lay developments in the politics of the largely self-governing Cape Colony: politics of white supremacy but division between the English-speaking community and the Afrikaners, who outnumbered them considerably. Since responsible government in 1872 the English-speaking white people of the Cape Colony had predominated in successive governments. A loose but recognisable group of 'Cape liberals' emerged, and in the changed situation following Rhodes's attempt to overthrow the Afrikaner government of Transvaal and his subsequent resignation as Cape Premier in 1896, a number of these formed an alliance with the Cape Afrikaners' organisation, the Afrikaner Bond. This alliance, forming the South African Party (SAP), which was a parliamentary party only, narrowly won elections to the Cape House of Assembly in 1898. A leading liberal, William Philip Schreiner, then became Premier of the Cape Colony at the head of a ministry, dependent on Bond support, which opposed Milner's policy towards Transvaal and Orange Free State. To back this opposition, several of the liberal English-speaking group allied with the Bond pursued plans already started for a new newspaper, which came to fruition in May 1899.

The *South African News* was another paper started by white South Africans for white South Africans. Several such newspapers had been appearing in the Cape Colony since 1824, in English and Dutch, especially after the lifting of restrictions on the press by the British authorities in 1829. Notable among many serving the English-speaking white community were the *Cape Argus*, published from 1857, and the *Cape Times*, from 1876 (Cutten 1935: 13–33). There were also newspapers published by Africans from the 1860s, commonly using Xhosa and other African languages. They included *Imvo Zabantsundu*, founded in 1884 and edited by John Tengo Jabavu. Published in King William's Town, it sought to defend the interests of the Black majority and in particular served the more privileged section who had the vote under the Cape Colony's non-racial franchise in the constitution of 1854: Africans, but in Cape Town mainly of the Coloured community of part-Afrikaner, Khoi and Malay people. For some years Jabavu was the outstanding Black leader in the Cape Colony (Switzer 1997a: 59).

Switzer's study notes the gulf that existed from the nineteenth century onwards between the 'alternative press' and the 'established white press' of South Africa which 'has been owned and controlled by whites, aimed at or intended for whites, concerned almost exclusively with the political, economic and social life of the white population, and consumed mainly by whites for most of this two-hundred-year history' (Switzer 1997b: 2). The Cape Colony's white population reached half a million in the nineteenth century – it was 579,742 in the 1904 census, compared with 1,424,787 Blacks, 395,034 Coloureds and 10,242 Asians – and could support, through readership and advertising, many newspapers serving the white community in its fairly large bubble. They were published in many cities and towns; there was, for example, the *Cape Mercury* in King William's Town (1875), and in Kimberley the diamond boom led to the founding of the *Diamond Fields Advertiser* in 1875. Beyond the Cape Colony, with the gold rush in Transvaal – which already had the *Transvaal Advertiser* of Pretoria (1882) – many more were added (Cutten 1935: 56). In 1889 the Argus Printing and Publishing Co. was registered in Johannesburg, where it published *The Star*. In 1890 two papers already published in Johannesburg were merged to form *The Standard and Diggers News*; in 1899, as the war approached, the *Transvaal Leader* was started (Cutten 1935: 57–8).

Besides politics, the South African newspapers – including the *South African News* when it started in 1899 – covered all aspects of the life of the white communities: births, deaths and marriages, education, cricket, horse racing, the theatre, farming, business and much else. But always there was politics – the politics of the white communities. The Africans were one issue in the government and politics of the white settlers – the conflicts with African states that had retained independence for some time, such as Lesotho (Basutoland), and the role of the African and Coloured voters in the Cape Colony. Those voters were far outnumbered by white voters, but still had influence. None was ever elected to the Cape House of Assembly, the lower house of the Cape Legislative Assembly, after it was first inaugurated in 1854, but they were numerous enough to decide contests between rival white candidates in some constituencies; Jabavu sought to use this limited strength to good effect for his people. White supremacy was in no way threatened.

Cape Colony politics was without formal organised parties until the 1890s, but the Cape Boers had their organisations and their newspapers. The rise of Afrikaner nationalism was voiced by the 1870s in the newspapers *Zuid-Afrikaan*, *Het Volksblad* and *Die Afrikaanse Patriot*. They were in Dutch, and that was the language Afrikaners defended for decades, demanding its use in the Cape House of Assembly (accorded in 1882); the movement for recognition, with literary and official use, of the spoken *taal* or Afrikaans was growing, but was not a priority for Cape Boer leaders. In 1882–3, two existing Cape Boer organisations were amalgamated to form the Afrikaner Bond, which under its leader Jan Hofmeyr (1845–1909) was for over twenty years the main champion of the Cape Afrikaners (Davenport 1966: 28–69; McCracken 1967: 109–13). From 1892 its organ was the daily *Ons Land*, whose editor from 1895, François Stephanus Malan (1871–1941), was another leading defender of the 'Cape Dutch'.

Cape politicians of many stripes served under Rhodes or supported him after the tycoon who headed De Beers Consolidated Mines and the International Diamond Syndicate, and the British South Africa Company (BSAC) which was now occupying the territory to become Southern Rhodesia, became in addition Premier of the Cape Colony in 1890. Sir James Molteno, then a Cape MLA (Member of the Legislative Assembly), wrote much later that Rhodes had 'a private income so fabulous and staggering that he could not compute it himself' and also had the backing of the Cape parliament, the Bond and the British government, and was 'at that time the most powerful individual man in the British Empire, perhaps in the whole world' (Molteno 1923: 25). He fell spectacularly from political but not economic power when the Jameson Raid led by his right-hand man failed at the beginning of January 1896 and Rhodes's own responsibility was quickly exposed. After that several Cape liberals who had served under Rhodes opposed his policies and his still great influence in the Cape Colony, and opposed the government of the new Premier, Gordon Sprigg.

When news of the Jameson Raid became known, Sir James Molteno recalled, 'the devouring flames of race hatred rushed through this country' (Molteno 1923: 63). It was common at that time to talk of racial feeling and racist hatred in reference to British versus Boers, not White versus Black. Feelings had already been inflamed since the gold mining boom in Transvaal and the rapid growth of Johannesburg began in 1886, as the non-Afrikaner white migrants to the Rand, although many made good money, demanded equal rights with the ruling Boers and passed themselves off as victims of tyranny (while they and the Boer government worked together to exploit the real victims, the African mine labourers). They continued agitation after the defeat of the Raid which several of them had helped to plot, and won support from the new High Commissioner appointed in 1897, Sir Alfred Milner. He and his policies became the main target of an influential group of Cape liberals who, rejecting the increasing 'racial hatred', became allies of the Bond. Hofmeyr, who had not joined the Rhodes ministry but had supported it, was now a leader of the anti-Rhodes camp.

While allied to the Bond, most of the liberal group were of the English-speaking community, though Schreiner was half German. Besides Schreiner, who had been Attorney General under Rhodes, the group included notably John Xavier Merriman (1840–1926), a member of the Cape parliament for decades, who resigned as Treasurer General under Rhodes over corruption in the Logan Scandal in 1893, and broke with him altogether after the Raid. Other leading Cape liberals were the brothers James and Richard Rose Innes, and James Molteno and other children of the first Cape Premier, Sir John Molteno. A prominent leader of the group was an Afrikaner MLA, Jacobus Wilhelmus Sauer (1850–1913), who like Merriman left the Rhodes ministry over the Logan Scandal.

Another prominent member of the group behind the *South African News* was William Schreiner's famous sister, the novelist Olive Schreiner (1855–1920). Having first admired Cecil Rhodes greatly, she turned against him after the Jameson Raid, supported by her husband Samuel Cronwright-Schreiner, who added her surname to his after their marriage. She published in 1897 a novel set in the BSAC occupation of Southern Rhodesia, *Trooper Peter Halket of Mashonaland*, giving a grim picture of the treatment of Africans. She and other members of the liberal group allied to the Bond championed both Black people and Boers against Rhodes and the British regime.

By 1897 the group had recruited another person outside formal politics, the Manchester-born journalist Albert Cartwright (1868–1956).[2] Having gone to South Africa in 1889 and first worked for the *Cape Times*, he worked on the staff of *The Star* of Johannesburg from 1892 to 1896, when he left after the Jameson Raid. Then he became editor of the *Diamond Fields Advertiser* of Kimberley. Published in the town that was the Rhodes diamond empire's base, it was nonetheless critical of him, though not in a militant way, until it was taken over on 1 April 1898 by a company owned partly by the Rhodes empire; Cartwright was then replaced as editor by George A. L. Green, who supported Rhodes (Green 1947: 64–5).

By then Cartwright was in contact with the people planning a new newspaper. Olive Schreiner wrote in March 1898 that Cartwright 'is now to be the editor of the new paper in Cape Town, which is to represent, we hope, the true, liberal cause in South Africa, on the native question, taxation, and in opposition to the capitalist party including Rhodes' (Rive 1987: 314). In April Merriman wrote to the Afrikaner printer Frederick James Centlivres (mayor of Rondebosch) about the new newspaper, in which Centlivres was clearly a key player, welcoming the choice of Cartwright as editor and saying, 'At the present time almost every paper of any importance in the Colony is devoted to the interest of Mr. Rhodes, under the name of Imperialism, or the Progressive party, or some other alias; but to restore Mr. Rhodes to power in South Africa is what they really mean' (Lewsen 1963: 303–6).

The Progressive Party was the new political formation headed by Rhodes, which contested new elections to the Cape parliament following the Sprigg government's defeat on a no-confidence motion by Schreiner on 22 June 1898. For reasons unclear in the published correspondence of people involved, the new newspaper did not start publication before the elections. Instead, Cartwright became editor of the *Cape Mercury* at King William's Town, which was not under Rhodes's control. Rhodes's power over the press was certainly great: his group and the Eckstein mining group controlled the Argus newspaper chain; Rhodes's leading crony Rutherfoord Harris had half the shares of the *Cape Times* publishing company, though Edmund Garrett, the editor from 1895 to 1899, firmly opposed any interference in editorial policy by Rhodes or Harris. But Rhodes's power was not as overwhelming as Merriman suggested; the *Cape Mercury* and *Imvo Zabantsundu* (which shared the same printing press) were a centre of opposition. On the day after Sprigg's defeat in parliament Richard Rose Innes wrote to his brother James, 'Cartwright and Jabavu came rushing over to the office to discuss the situation' (Wright 1972: 237–8). In the new alignment of white political forces Africans had a part; Tengo Jabavu and his newspaper were allied with the Bond and the group of Bond allies including the Rose Innes brothers, Schreiner and Cartwright.

Although Cape Afrikaners fully shared the racism of the Boers of the independent republics, and directed it against the Coloureds (part Afrikaner, and speaking Afrikaans) among others, the Bond leadership felt it necessary to avoid all-out opposition to the Cape non-racial franchise. Hofmeyr proposed severe restriction of the numbers of Black and Coloured people entitled to vote, and this was carried out, under Rhodes's government and with his backing, by the Franchise and Ballot Act of 1892, with a big increase in the property value threshold; but many remained on the roll (see Davenport 1966: 118–23; McCracken 1967: 93–5). In 1898 Hofmeyr – who was to lead the Bond for ten years more – sought the support of the Black voters' champion Jabavu, who readily gave it.

On the other side Rhodes and the Progressives established a Dutch-language newspaper, *Dagblad*, to try to win over the Boers. They also subsidised the launch in November 1897 of a new African newspaper in East London in Xhosa, *Izwi Labantu*, started on the initiative of Walter Rubusana and A. K. Soga, who was its editor for ten years (Switzer 1997a: 63–5). *Izwi* encouraged black voters to support the Progressives. In these dealings both white politicians and black editors were – and each side surely knew that the other was – opportunistic. Rhodes was persuaded to change the wording of a statement supporting 'equal rights for every white man south of the Zambezi' to support equal rights for 'every civilized man' (Marais 1957: 277n). Generally Rhodes's racism was well known, but white politicians with racist ideas still accepted the non-racial franchise in the Cape Colony (also in force nominally in Natal, where few other than white people were able to register). The franchise was not an issue in the elections to the Cape House of Assembly held between 9 August and 5 September 1898.

The central issue there was Cecil Rhodes, and the result was a very narrow defeat for his attempt to return to political power. The Progressives won thirty-eight seats (Rhodes himself being elected at Barkly West), the Bond and its allies forty, and independents six. Thus the anti-Rhodes side was able to take over the Cape Colony government. After a no-confidence motion by William Schreiner was passed on 10 October 1898, he became Premier. The ministers included Merriman as Treasurer General and Sauer as Commissioner of Crown Lands. Hofmeyr was not in parliament or the government, but Schreiner's ministry depended on Bond support and was united with the

Bond in opposing Milner's policy. Thus, during the tense negotiations between the British government and Presidents Kruger of the South African Republic and Steyn of Orange Free State, Milner had the Cape government against him.

Besides opposing British policy towards the Boer republics, Merriman suggested another aim for the newspaper in a letter to Cartwright in October 1898: the newspaper 'would advocate a South African policy i.e. self-government on the lines of the Australian and Canadian colonies' (Lewsen 1963: 327–9). This would mean a regime of more solid white supremacy. However, clearly a constitutional change was a long-term aim, subordinated to the new paper's response to the immediate crisis. Merriman said the paper must advocate 'non-interference with the Republics', and in 1898–9 the group now in power in the Cape Colony, and the Bond, aimed at a peaceful settlement. The crisis was overtly about the position of the non-Boer immigrants (Uitlanders) in Transvaal, but basically about power. Milner adopted a confrontational approach; James Rose Innes wrote much later, 'Without Milner there would have been no war in 1899' (Innes 1949: 191). Milner was a major target for the *South African News* when it appeared on 2 May 1899.

From the published sources consulted by this author, the financial backing for the *South African News* is not clear. In a letter sent by Cartwright to a Mr Esselen, apparently in December 1898 (the letter, in the Cartwright papers, is illegible in parts), he said the aim was to raise £24,000 and a building had already been acquired for £3,000, but did not say who had bought shares. It later emerged that he himself had invested £300. William Schreiner's biographer, after describing the House of Assembly session of late 1898, comments that the Premier 'could agree that it had not been so bad; and it might be better now that he and Harry [Henry] Currey, sometime private secretary to Rhodes, had acquired the *South African News*, with Cartwright as editor, to put the ministerial policy to English-speaking South African readers who were beyond the reach of Malan's *Ons Land*' (Walker 1937: 121). But further details are lacking.

The *South African News* and the War

Schreiner went to Pretoria on his own peace initiative in June 1899, but it failed, as did his sister's proposals published in the *South African News* and the Transvaal *Standard and Diggers News* (Rive 1987: 353). When war began on 11 October 1899 the *South African News* and *Ons Land*, with other Afrikaner newspapers, opposed the British war effort totally. So did the Schreiner ministry, but its powers were limited. It was seen by enemies as an Afrikaner Bond ministry, and the *South African News* as a Bond newspaper. But the *News* and the Cape Boer papers continued to enjoy freedom of the press until this was suppressed in areas where martial law was imposed.

The *South African News*, published from its offices at 23 Church Street in Cape Town, carried plenty of ordinary news in its daily and weekly editions, and some advertising despite its political stance; the 9 January 1901 issue had just over three pages of advertisements out of thirty-two pages in all, for schools, booksellers, agricultural machinery, newsagents, tailors and so on. But it became known for its political stance, opposing the war, defending the Boers and calling for negotiations. On 22 February 1900, for example, it published a 'Special' entitled 'Twelve Plain Reasons Why We Are In the Wrong'.

The Schreiner government and the *South African News* were backed by many opponents of the war in South Africa and more in Britain (Davey 1978; Koss 1973). A South Africa Conciliation Committee (SACC) was established in London on 1 November 1899, with Leonard Courtney, a former Liberal Colonial Secretary, as President, and Frederick Mackarness, a barrister who had spent two years in South Africa and got to know Schreiner and Merriman, as Chairman of the Executive Committee. The SACC's manifesto on 15 January 1900 said it aimed to gather accurate information for the public, to advocate efforts to 're-establish goodwill between the British and Dutch races in South Africa by a full recognition of the just claims of both', and to urge a settlement based on those principles. Rejecting this moderate stance, W. T. Stead, editor of the *Review of Reviews*, was the moving force behind a more militant Stop the War Committee, which called the war 'a crime without justification or excuse' (Davey 1978: 76; Koss 1973: 82–3).

Prominent opponents of the British war effort included the *Manchester Guardian* editor C. P. Scott, whose correspondents covering the war included Leonard Hobhouse, J. A. Hobson and Albert Cartwright. A common theme of such critics was that the war was being fought for the interests of the mining capitalists, the diamond magnate Rhodes and the 'Randlords' of the Transvaal goldfields. From the Boer War Hobson developed his theory of imperialism as instigated by powerful financial interests; his book published during the war, *The War in South Africa* (1900), which had a chapter devoted to an interview with Olive Schreiner, was to be followed by his major work *Imperialism: A Study* in 1902. Regarding South Africa, he agreed with the views of Merriman, Cartwright and Olive Schreiner, who strongly denounced capitalism.

In March 1900 a South Africa Conciliation Committee was set up in Cape Town, with John Charles Molteno as Chairman and Cartwright as Secretary ('Conciliation Movement' 1900: 4). There were close ties between the opponents of the war in Britain and those in South Africa. Ernest Hargrove, an Englishman active in the Conciliation movement, went on a speaking tour in South Africa which culminated in a mass meeting at Graaff-Reinet on 31 May 1900, which opposed annexation of the independent Boer republics, now being steadily occupied; it was addressed by Cartwright, Malan, Hargrove and Olive Schreiner (Davenport 1966: 213–15; Davey 1978: 97–8).

The non-Boer critics were a small minority of non-Afrikaner white people of the Cape Colony, unpopular among the rest and infuriating to Milner. They included, besides those mentioned, James Butler, editor of the *Midland News* of Cradock (Hewison 1989), and Father Frederick Kolbe, a Catholic priest who had to resign as editor of the *South African Catholic Magazine* because the Catholic hierarchy in South Africa did not agree with his opposition to the war (Hale 1997: 100–1; Brown 1960: 189, 266–75, 319). The heart of the Cape Colony movement against the war was obviously the Cape Afrikaner community. Milner told Chamberlain that the Conciliation movement was an 'agitation got up by the most extreme section of the Bond party in the Colony to advocate the continued independence of the republic[s] and to threaten Great Britain with permanent disaffection of the Dutch of South Africa, if she does not adopt that policy' (quoted in Davenport 1966: 214). Milner was obsessed with fear of a general uprising among the Cape Boers, but this did not happen, though some Cape Boers joined the Boer republics' fight.

In the first months of the war the shaky alliance of Bondsmen and liberals fell apart, with William Schreiner increasingly at odds with some of his comrades, who saw him as weakening, while he saw them as too radical; these included his sister, as well as the editor of the *South African News*. Cartwright went too far for some; he was certainly outspoken – on 9 June 1900 the paper said, 'We only know there can be but one end to the policy of infamy inaugurated by the blind, conceited, narrow-minded, infatuated mediocrity that sits in Government House' (quoted in Hewison 1989: 94). Schreiner told him, 'Falsehood . . . is a mirage; sooner or later men distinguish it from water. Let us seek our truth in a well; or at any rate let me continue to do so' (Walker 1937: 221–2). The two had differing views when the question of how to deal with Cape Boers who joined in the fighting came before the House on 12 June; Schreiner, who accepted that there should be some punishment of those 'rebels', was opposed by some of his allies and voted down, and he resigned (Le May 1965: 69–71). A new ministry was headed by Sprigg, with James Rose Innes, who had been a leader of the liberal group, as Attorney General.

Now the government of the Colony was in agreement – within limits – with the imperial government, and the *South African News*, like the Bond, was able to oppose both. Merriman and Sauer did not join the new government and they and the South African Party remained strongly opposed to the war. On 24 July a meeting of the party was held at the *South African News* offices; it remained a parliamentary party only (Lewsen 1963: 227). Annexation of the South African Republic and Orange Free State (renamed the Orange River Colony), which the party opposed, was completed after British rule over the former was proclaimed on 25 October 1900. But the war was not over; in the latter part of 1900 it descended into fierce irregular operations, in which 450,000 British troops made only slow headway against skilful Boer guerrillas. On 24 November *Ons Land* reported that General French had ordered cannon fire on a house which had women and children in it; Malan was arrested and charged (Van Reenen 1984: 444–5).

The circulation of *Ons Land* and the *South African News* was banned in many districts, but for the moment their publication continued; according to Centlivres, managing director of the South African Newspaper Co. (testifying at Cartwright's trial, of which more shortly), the *News* sold about 1,300 copies daily ('The Press Libel Cases' 1901: 20). Organised anti-war protests also continued: on 6 December 1900 a 'People's Congress' was held at Worcester, with 7–12,000 people present according to the *South African News*'s estimate; Kolbe and Cronwright-Schreiner spoke, and resolutions were passed including one calling for Transvaal and Orange Free State to remain independent ('People's Congress' 1900: 21–6; Davenport 1966: 228–9). The Cape parliament was prorogued in October 1900, but the parliamentary South African Party remained; it held a meeting in Cape Town on 7 January 1901 which decided that Merriman and Sauer should go to Britain to defend the cause. They spent several months there, battling against the general belligerence of the British public which had led to the decisive victory of Lord Salisbury's Conservative government in the 'Khaki Election' of September–October 1900.

Following a Boer invasion of the Cape Colony in December, martial law was imposed on 17 January 1901 in all of the colony except the seaports, Wynberg and African tribal areas. In the martial law areas the *South African News* and *Ons Land* were banned, with the latter going out of circulation in early January. Also banned was *Imvo Zabantsundu*, which had been opposed to the war from the start, calling for a negotiated peace. It declared that the war was not being fought to give Africans of Transvaal the vote, and this was to prove quite correct, but Jabavu's stance went against the common view of Africans in South Africa, that British rule was relatively preferable to Boer rule; *Izwi Labantu* voiced this mainstream view, in a war of words with *Imvo*. In August *Imvo Zabantsundu* ceased publication (Ngcongco 1979: 142–55; Nasson 1991: 36–7). While Cartwright's political alliance with Jabavu was to continue, and the SAP was to remain committed to the non-racial Cape franchise, the *South African News*'s attitude to Black and Coloured South Africans – who were very much affected by the war, as willing or forced participants on either side and as victims – could be ambiguous. When the invading Boers in Calvinia executed the Coloured blacksmith Abraham Esau who had helped the British forces, the *News* published a brief comment seeming to palliate that crime ('The Esau Case' 1901: 20).[3] This illustrated the problems arising when Cartwright, like Olive Schreiner, saw both Boers and black people as victims of imperialism.

The *South African News* constantly returned to that theme, as when it attacked Sprigg, 'who throughout his political career, a career long and since 1876 utterly discreditable, has been the implacable enemy of Native rights and Native development' ('Mr. Solomon and Tembuland' 1901: 8), and when it accused Rhodes and other capitalists of the enslavement and oppression of Africans in South Africa and Rhodesia. This may seem like political opportunism, but the newspaper went further when the establishment of a new 'native location', with pass laws, was recommended for the city of Cape Town. The *South African News* argued, 'We do not like the clause empowering the removal of Natives by force to a location' ('The Native Location Question' 1901: 8) and went on to make a remarkable statement for the time: 'We should strongly protest against the idea that an artificial check should be put upon any man's development simply on the ground that he is black, just as we should protest if the same thing were proposed in regard to a man because he is Dutch or German or Irish or Jewish' ('The Location Question' 1901: 9). This was rejection of the entire basis of South Africa's racist legislation which had already begun and was to go much further. It was not a popular idea among the Afrikaners whose defence remained the main concern of the *South African News*.

The attack on Sprigg said that he now 'sits as the warming-pan of Mr. Rhodes, whose wish is to introduce slave-labour into South Africa' ('Mr. Solomon and Tembuland' 1901: 8). This suggests that Cartwright thought Rhodes might try to return to power in the Cape Colony. In fact, Rhodes's biographer who had been his close collaborator, Sir Lewis Michell, suggests that by the time of the war the ailing Rhodes was concentrating on Rhodesia, his business, and his scheme for the Cape to Cairo railway, rather than Cape politics. However, in late 1900 an English correspondent wrote to Michell, 'Lord Salisbury says, and I agree, that Rhodes should come out into the open and assume the Prime Ministership' (Michell 1910: 290). Thus a comeback may have seemed possible, for a time. But then Rhodes's condition worsened, and he died in Cape Town on 26 March 1902. Anyway, his critics always opposed his henchmen, like his political successor Leander Starr Jameson, his party, and capitalism in general, not just Cecil Rhodes himself.

Cartwright's Trial

On 6 February 1901 the weekly edition of the *South African News* carried a front-page story headed 'How We Are Waging War: A Dreadful Disclosure by a British Officer in Command', quoting a letter from an unnamed officer alleging an order from

Lord Kitchener, the new Commander-in-Chief in South Africa, to take no prisoners in operations against the Boer guerrillas under Christiaan de Wet.[4] Cartwright was arrested and charged with seditious libel. While on bail awaiting trial, Cartwright continued to edit the newspaper with undiminished defiance, despite hostile reactions including a raid on the *News*'s offices in March 1901 by some Australian soldiers angry at an alleged insult to them in the paper.

After a one-day trial on 18 April 1901, where the prosecution was led by his former political ally the Attorney General Rose Innes, Cartwright was sentenced to one year's imprisonment.[5] He told the court that he had taken the officer's statement from the British left-wing Christian weekly *New Age* of 17 January, and had published it to secure a denial; when a denial was issued he had published it. He mentioned that the substance of the anonymous officer's allegations had appeared in *The Times* of London, and also noted that after he was charged, the same report had appeared in the *Cape Daily Telegraph* of Port Elizabeth and nobody had been charged for that. This suggests that the authorities, angered by Cartwright's constant attacks on them, seized the opportunity to silence him, not caring much about others who made the same war crime allegation. Evidence was given that the editor had deleted a part of the officer's statement denouncing the army's 'policy of house-burning and women-hunting' and warning that the Cape Dutch would rise in revolt if they could. Having deleted this did not help Cartwright; neither did his acceptance in court that the report was totally false. He went to prison with François Stephanus Malan, editor of *Ons Land*, also given a one-year sentence, and two other Afrikaner editors sentenced to six months each – J. E. De Jong of the *Worcester Advertiser* and J. A. Vosloo of *Het Oosten* – for the separate war crime allegation against General French. A statement of Cartwright's case, not admitted in court, was published in the *News* of 1 May ('The Press Libel Cases' 1901: 20–1; Pugh 2009).

The officer who made the allegation against Kitchener was Maurice George Moore (1854–1939), brother of the Irish novelist George Moore. Much later, in 1924, he wrote from Dublin to Cartwright, then editor of *West Africa* in London, saying, 'I have never regretted writing the letter, which I am sure did great good. It saved the credit of the Army, and lives of many Boers and women and children' (Moore 1924). This was after Cartwright had felt guilty for many years about publishing a false allegation. According to George Moore's biographer the novelist had passed on a first article by his brother to W. T. Stead in October 1900, and in court Cartwright said he had been encouraged to publish the report by Stead, who vouched for its author (Frazier 2000: 296–7). The report appeared first in the *Freeman's Journal*, an Irish nationalist paper, on 15 January 1901, and then, in summary, in *The Times* of 16 January and, in full, in the *New Age* the next day. There was wide support for the Boers in Ireland and the Moore brothers had Irish nationalist sympathies, but Maurice Moore's testimony convinced not only Stead, a pro-Boer but a highly experienced editor, but also George Buckle of *The Times*. Most probably what Moore said was true, but the no-prisoners order was hastily countermanded.

There were many protests in Britain against the sentence given to Cartwright (Davey 1978: 174). In Britain strong criticisms of the conduct of the war continued, with Emily Hobhouse (Leonard's sister) campaigning against the imprisonment of civilians in concentration camps. The *South African News* continued after the gaoling of its editor, with no change in its attitude; Kolbe was its guest editor for a time (Hale 1997: 103–5).[6]

After a new Boer incursion into the Cape Colony in August 1901, commanded by Jan Smuts, martial law was imposed in the colony's seaports including Cape Town, though only after fierce discussions between the Sprigg government and Kitchener, who was persuaded to agree that some civil administration could continue. Martial law was proclaimed on 9 October and the *South African News*'s offices were raided by police. On 12 October the military authority warned that the paper would be banned if it published '"anything treasonable, seditious or of any value to the enemy [or] any articles ridiculing civil, military or naval officers of His Majesty the King"' (Hale 1997: 105). The directors of the company then decided to suspend publication rather than submit to such orders.

When he was released in April 1902 Cartwright wanted to go to Britain; when this was refused under the martial law regulations there were renewed protests. But the war ended with the Peace of Vereeniging on 31 May 1902 and Cartwright was able to go to England. Then, on 19 August 1902, the *South African News* resumed publication. *Ons Land* and *Imvo Zabantsundu* also came out again.

After the War

In the years following the war Cape Town had three daily newspapers: the *Cape Times* and *South African News* in the morning, and the *Cape Argus* in the afternoon. During the war and in the next few years several new newspapers appeared in South Africa. In the British-occupied Transvaal the *Rand Daily Mail* appeared from 1902. There were also new papers published by and for the Black, Coloured and Indian communities: from 1901 the Tswana-English weekly *Koranta ea Becoana*, edited from 1902 to 1905 by Sol Plaatje at Mafeking; *Ilanga lase Natal*, published in Durban, in Zulu and English, from 1903; the *South African Spectator*, founded in December 1900, the first Cape Town publication aimed at Black people, edited first by a West African (from modern-day Ghana) journalist, F. Z. Peregrino; and for the Asians, *Colonial Indian News*, founded in May 1901 in Pietermaritzburg, and then *Indian Opinion*, started by Mohandas Gandhi in Natal in 1903.

The resumed *South African News*, while always filled with ordinary news, remained a staunch political defender of the Boers, an ally of the SAP (operating in the reopened House of Assembly from August 1902) and its leader Merriman, of Hofmeyr and the Bond, and of Jabavu. Its enemies as before were the Progressives, now led by Jameson, and the mining 'capitalists'. The Progressives won the Cape elections in 1904, when many Boers were disfranchised, and Dr Jameson became Premier. The *News* called for the release of the remaining political prisoners ('Mr. Burger's Appeal' 1903: 10) and for equality of the English and Dutch languages ('Language and Loyalty' 1903: 10). It criticised the importation of Chinese workers for the Rand mines ('The Old Methods' 1903: 12), quoting in full a speech by Sauer against this proposal – widely condemned, but eventually implemented for a few years ('Mr. Sauer at Aliwal' 1903: 12).

When Milner urged that the franchise for local elections in the occupied former Boer republics should be non-racial, the *News* applauded him for repudiating exclusion of people from civil rights on the grounds of colour ('Across the Orange' 1903: 11); however, he felt unable to insist on that point, and when self-government returned to the Transvaal Colony and Orange River Colony at local and colony level, it was undiluted white supremacy ('Mr. Sauer at Aliwal' 1903: 12). A *South African*

News leader attacking Jameson on 18 March 1903 quoted from a publication exposing the treatment of Africans in Rhodesia, and on 22 April 1903 the paper published a long letter on 'The Labour Question' by Dr Abdullah Abdurahman, President of the African Political Organisation founded in 1902, the first important political pressure group of the Cape Coloureds, suggesting that the British government would tolerate the recruiting of forced labour for 'the mining magnates' ('The Labour Question' 1903: 10). Thus the newspaper continued to defend Black and Coloured South Africans. But its main political concern was to continue defending the Afrikaners in their defeat. When Emily Hobhouse returned to South Africa in 1903, it published a long and passionate letter from her on 16 August, talking of starvation among the Boer population and appealing for funds for their relief; she raised £5,000 plus donations in kind, but also aroused fierce hostility (Van Reenen 1984: 430–2).

In 1903 Professor Henry Fremantle, a graduate of Eton and Oxford who after research at the London School of Economics and lecturing at the University of Wales had taken up the chair of English and Philosophy at the South African College at Cape Town, was appointed joint editor of the *South African News* (De Kock 1968: 302–3). The following year, W. T. Stead visited South Africa and addressed a meeting in Cape Town in honour of Cartwright and Malan, paying tribute to the courage of the Boers and calling for a 'Golden Book' to commemorate heroism on both sides in the war. This was reprinted in the *South African News* of 14 March 1904 but condemned by Lord Milner (as he now was) and by Stead's friend Olive Schreiner, who accused him of reopening old wounds (Whyte 1925: II, 242–5).

Then, in mid-1905, Albert Cartwright left the *South African News* and went to work in London as head of the cable office of the *Rand Daily Mail*, now owned by the 'Randlord' Abe Bailey, who had inherited Rhodes's house at Muizenberg in Cape Town and been elected to his former seat in the House of Assembly. Fremantle remained editor of the *News* until 1908; it was said to have a circulation of 4,000 in 1907 (Shaw 1975: 237).

By 1908 the whole situation of South Africa was changing. The Transvaal and Orange Free State (as it was soon called again) obtained self-government under the rule of Afrikaner parties in 1907. Then, following new elections in 1908 in the Cape Colony won by the SAP, whose leader John Merriman became Premier, talks went ahead on union of the four territories of South Africa. Meanwhile the 'capitalists' with whom Cartwright had already come to terms himself came easily to terms with the Boer political leaders under Louis Botha and Jan Smuts, after years when the *South African News* and other campaigners had seen them and the Boers as mortal enemies. With the Union of South Africa created on 31 May 1910 came full independence, with complete white supremacy: Schreiner, Hofmeyr and others secured the Cape non-racial franchise in the Cape Colony, but not its extension to Transvaal and Orange Free State. The Boer vs Briton feud which lay behind the *South African News* was ended, largely on the Boers' terms; the newspaper, however, continued until 1915.

This was a newspaper which, while always conveying news in the usual way, had a particular, narrow political purpose, defending the Afrikaners and opposing the imperial government and the mining magnates. Its defence of Africans against them, which had cause, was subordinated to the main campaign which had an underlying contradiction in depicting both Boers and Blacks as victims. The denunciations of 'capitalism' by Cartwright, Merriman and their group were directed against Rhodes and the gold tycoons, and did not involve positive advocacy of socialism. Capitalism and the Afrikaners both won after a few years, and worked together for eighty years more.

Notes

1. The *South African News* is an example of how the distinction between periodicals and newspapers was blurred, with the weekly edition resembling a periodical, and the daily edition a newspaper. The references below refer to the daily edition unless the weekly edition is specified.
2. See Derrick's biography of Cartwright (2017).
3. On Esau's fate, see Nasson 1991: 36–7.
4. See 'How We Are Waging War' 1901: 3. The war crime allegation and Cartwright's trial and imprisonment are described in greater detail in Derrick 2017: 55–68.
5. There is a full account of the case in the unpublished thesis for a BA (Oxon) degree by Cartwright's great-granddaughter Sophie Pugh (2009).
6. Lead articles like 'Martial Law' (1901: 8) and 'Extermination' (1901: 8) continued to honour Cartwright's commitments.

Bibliography

'Across the Orange and the Vaal' (1903), *South African News*, weekly edition, 27 May, 11.
Brown, W. E. (1960), *The Catholic Church in South Africa*, ed. M. Derrick, London: Burns & Oates.
'Conciliation Movement' (1900), *South African News*, 28 March, 4.
Cutten, T. E. G. (1935), *A History of the Press in South Africa*, Cape Town: National Union of South African Students.
Davenport, T. R. H. (1966), *The Afrikaner Bond: The History of a South African Political Party, 1880–1911*, Cape Town: Oxford University Press.
Davey, A. (1978), *The British Pro-Boers 1877–1902*, Cape Town: Tafelberg.
De Kock, W. J. (ed.) (1968), *Dictionary of South African Biography*, vol. 1, Cape Town: Nasionale Boekhandel.
Derrick, Jonathan (2017), *Africa, Empire and Fleet Street: Albert Cartwright and 'West Africa' Magazine*, London: C. Hurst & Co.
'The Esau Case' (1901), *South African News*, weekly edition, 27 March, 20.
'Extermination' (1901), *South African News*, weekly edition, 18 September, 8.
Frazier, A. (2000), *George Moore, 1852–1933*, New Haven: Yale University Press.
Green, G. A. L. (1947), *An Editor Looks Back: South African and Other Memories, 1883–1946*, Cape Town and Johannesburg: Juta.
Hale, F. (1997), 'A Catholic voice against British imperialism: F. C. Kolbe's opposition to the Second Anglo-Boer War', *Religion and Theology*, 4.1–3, 94–108.
Hewison, H. H. (1989), *Hedge of Wild Almonds: South Africa, the Pro-Boers and the Quaker Conscience 1890–1910*, Portsmouth, NH: Heinemann; Cape Town: David Philip; London: James Currey.
'How We Are Waging War: A Dreadful Disclosure by a British Officer in Command' (1901), *South African News*, weekly edition, 6 February, 3.
Innes, James Rose (1949), *Autobiography*, Cape Town: Oxford University Press.
Koss, S. (ed.) (1973), *The Anatomy of an Antiwar Movement*, Chicago: University of Chicago Press.

'The Labour Question: Views of Dr. Abdurahman' (1903), *South African News*, 22 April, 10.
'Language and Loyalty' (1903), *South African News*, 18 February, 10.
Le May, G. H. L. (1965), *British Supremacy in South Africa 1899–1907*, Oxford: Clarendon Press.
Lewsen, Phyllis (ed.) (1963), *Selections from the Correspondence of John X. Merriman 1890–1898*, Cape Town: Van Riebeeck Society.
'The Location Question' (1901), *South African News*, weekly edition, 20 March, 9.
McCracken, J. L. (1967), *The Cape Parliament, 1854–1910*, Oxford: Clarendon Press.
Marais, J. S. (1957), *The Cape Coloured People*, Johannesburg: Witwatersrand University Press.
'Martial Law' (1901), *South African News*, weekly edition, 11 September, 8.
Michell, Sir Lewis (1910), *The Life of the Rt. Hon. Cecil John Rhodes, 1853–1902*, vol. 2, London: Edward Arnold.
Molteno, J. T. (1923), *The Dominion of Afrikanerdom: Recollections Pleasant and Otherwise*, London: Methuen.
Moore, Maurice (1924), Letter to Albert Cartwright, Dublin, 5 July 1924, Albert Cartwright Papers (private collection).
'Mr. Burger's Appeal' (1903), *South African News*, 7 January, 10.
'Mr. Sauer at Aliwal' (1903), *South African News*, weekly edition, 27 May, 12.
'Mr. Solomon and Tembuland' (1901), *South African News*, weekly edition, 6 February, 8.
Nasson, Bill (1991), *Abraham Esau's War: A Black South African War in the Cape, 1899–1902*, Cambridge: Cambridge University Press.
'The Native Location Question' (1901), *South African News*, weekly edition, 13 March, 8.
Ngcongco, L. D. (1979), 'John Tengo Jabavu 1859–1921', in Christopher Saunders (ed.), *Black Leaders in South African History*, London: Heinemann, 142–55.
'The Old Methods' (1903), *South African News*, 8 April, 12.
'People's Congress at Worcester' (1900), *South African News*, weekly edition, 12 December, 21–6.
'The Press Libel Cases' (1901), *South African News*, weekly edition, 1 May, 20–1.
Pugh, Sophie (2009), 'Freedom of the press and imperial war: The trial of Albert Cartwright in the Cape Supreme Court, 18th April 1901', BA thesis, University of Oxford.
Rive, R. (ed.) (1987), *Olive Schreiner Letters 1871–99*, Cape Town and Johannesburg: David Philip.
Shaw, G. (1975), *Some Beginnings: The Cape Times (1876–1910)*, London, Cape Town and New York: Oxford University Press.
Switzer, Les (1997a), 'The beginnings of African protest journalism at the Cape', in Les Switzer (ed.), *South Africa's Alternative Press: Voices of Protest and Resistance, 1880s–1960s*, Cambridge: Cambridge University Press, 57–82.
—— (1997b), 'Introduction: South Africa's alternative press in perspective', in Les Switzer (ed.), *South Africa's Alternative Press: Voices of Protest and Resistance, 1880s–1960s*, Cambridge: Cambridge University Press, 1–53.
Van Reenen, R. (ed.) (1984), *Emily Hobhouse: Boer War Letters*, Cape Town and Pretoria: Human & Rousseau.
Walker, E. A. (1937), *W. P. Schreiner: A South African*, London: Oxford University Press.
Whyte, F. (1925), *The Life of W. T. Stead*, 2 vols, London: Jonathan Cape.
Wright, H. M. (ed.) (1972), *Sir James Rose Innes: Selected Correspondence (1884–1902)*, Cape Town: Van Riebeeck Society.

10

THE WEEKLY *WEST AFRICA*: COMMERCE, EMPIRE AND DECOLONISATION

Jonathan Derrick

Introduction

THE WEEKLY *WEST AFRICA*, published in London from 1917 to 2003, was the principal regular publication in Britain which concentrated on the affairs of West Africa, especially the four former British territories now called Nigeria, Ghana, Sierra Leone and The Gambia. Started at the height of the colonial era by colonial business firms dealing with West Africa, for decades it dealt particularly with British relations with those West African countries. It followed a number of periodicals appearing at the turn of the century, when trade relations expanded greatly and colonial rule, mostly British and French, was established in the region. Among them, an earlier *West Africa and Traders Review Illustrated* appeared from 1900 as a monthly, then from January 1901 as a weekly, based in London and edited by Edwin Haigh Chalmers. These periodicals were business-oriented, though they covered a wide variety of topics. Those dealing with West Africa were backed by advertisements of the firms trading for decades past with the West Coast, such as John Holt and the African Association, and the Elder Dempster shipping empire which by the 1890s had been built up by Sir Alfred Jones to dominate (though it never had a complete monopoly) the shipping between West Africa and Britain. Despite the opportunities provided by expansion of trade, almost all those earlier Africa-oriented British periodicals closed within thirteen years (Derrick 2017: 91–130).

In the first *West Africa* there were many contributions by Edmund Dene Morel (1873–1924), whose exposure of the mass crimes of the Congo Free State government run by King Leopold II of Belgium began with articles there and in other publications (Cline 1980; Hochschild 1998). In 1903 Morel, who headed *West Africa*'s Liverpool office, broke with *West Africa* (which went on until 1906, possibly up to 1909) and founded the *West African Mail* in Liverpool. This was continued under a new name, the *African Mail*, from 1907. Still a weekly, it had monthly supplements which were the 'Official Organ of the Congo Reform Association'. Although that Association's campaign against Leopold II's Congo regime, based on the mass forced-labour collection of wild rubber, was Morel's main concern for years, the *African Mail* was filled with reports of other African developments, including the new British colonial administrations which Morel supported. He was always concerned to defend the established West African trading system, in which settlers were absent, capitalist plantations like those favoured by William Lever's oilseeds empire were strongly discouraged, and ordinary African villagers supplied the Liverpool trading firms with cocoa, palm oil, palm kernels, groundnuts and other agricultural and forest produce. For several years the *African Mail* was one of two major Africa-oriented periodicals published in Britain, the other being the *African World*, started in 1902, which was oriented towards Southern Africa.

After the outbreak of the First World War Morel founded with others, and vigorously organised, the Union of Democratic Control (UDC), opposing British policy and suggesting that Germany was not guilty alone, while in the *African Mail* he urged that Africa should be kept out of the war. Among the many prominent British people shocked by his views was Sir Frederick Lugard, Governor-General of Nigeria, whose government of that country Morel had much admired. Lugard wanted a periodical to replace the *African Mail*, and wrote on 13 October 1915 to Alexander Cowan of Miller Brothers, one of the major West Coast trading firms, suggesting that 'the Merchants of Liverpool' should start a new magazine in Britain and affiliated papers in West Africa. Cowan followed up the idea, while in November 1915 Morel severed his connection with the *African Mail*, as key advertisers – the Niger Company, and the firm founded by Morel's recently deceased friend John Holt – wanted to pull out because of the UDC.[1] The *Mail* was continued for the time being, but talks proceeded on a new magazine to be published in Britain. Lugard's idea of affiliated papers was not pursued.

The West Africa Publishing Company (WAPC) was registered in June 1916 with a nominal capital of £15,000. Allocation of 10,952 shares was listed on 1 September 1916, almost all going to leading companies involved in West Coast trade or shipping. Elder Dempster, John Holt & Co., Miller Brothers of Liverpool, the African Association and Paterson Zochonis of Manchester each had 1,000, and the Niger Company based in London (formerly the Royal Niger Co., which had occupied and ruled a good deal of Nigeria) had 800 ('Declaration of Compliance' (1916)). The chairman was Viscount (Alfred) Milner, formerly High Commissioner of South Africa and since 1910 the chairman of the Bank of British West Africa (BBWA). He chose as editor Albert Cartwright, who, as editor of the *South African News* of Cape Town during the South African War when Milner was High Commissioner, had been imprisoned for publishing a war crime allegation against Lord Kitchener. Milner resigned as chairman of the WAPC and of the BBWA on being appointed to the Lloyd George cabinet in December 1916. Two months later, on 3 February 1917, the weekly *West Africa* appeared, and, as promised, the *African Mail* then closed down. The first address of *West Africa* was 28 Fleet Street; its offices changed many times later but always remained in London.

West Africa, in its first editorial, promised to be 'an open forum for the discussions of every question involving the welfare of any of the peoples of West Africa' and 'a friend to every cause which holds out the prospect of advancing the position of West Africa as a prosperous and contented member of the Empire: a friend, using the equal language of a friend' ('The Toast' 1917: 12). The magazine covered the government and commerce of Britain and British West Africa extensively, but did not provide news on a regular basis. There were features of many sorts, many reproducing budget speeches and other speeches of governors, business leaders and others. *West Africa* was clearly aimed at European readers including colonial officials and business staff; it recorded officials' appointments and talked of their and their wives' lives in Africa and what they could do on home leave; there were some travel and wildlife articles. There was plenty of coverage of important events concerning government and business, and editorial comment on these. The editorials showed *West Africa* to be definitely an 'establishment' publication. There was never any government money in it, but Cartwright was always close to the governors and officials, and was fully committed to colonial rule which he, like most contemporaries, expected to last for a long time.

Hence criticism of colonial governments was rare and usually mild. On 24 August 1918, however, after a revolt among Nigerians at Abeokuta, the magazine blamed it on the 'practically autocratic government' under Lugard. The Governor-General had begun extending his Indirect Rule form of government – strengthening traditional authorities and ruling through them – from Northern Nigeria to other parts of the country. Cartwright believed that this policy, as it involved sheltering African culture from modern change, could not be maintained ('Government in Nigeria' 1918: 670–1). However, Indirect Rule remained British policy until the 1940s.

In its first year the magazine joined in the attacks from many quarters on the Empire Resources Development Committee (ERDC), formed by some politicians to promote greater exploitation of the colonies' raw materials in ways vaguely defined – and eventually not pursued – and potentially likely to lead to greater coercive European domination of export production in Africa. In denouncing the scheme Cartwright was allied with the West African colonial governments and the West Coast trading firms, all of whom were aware that the existing system of production of raw materials for export (except minerals) by ordinary African small-scale producers was both more efficient and less oppressive than production by capitalist estates or white settlers.[2] *West Africa* consistently maintained its support for the existing system and hence for the trading firms involved, which provided much of the magazine's plentiful advertising. This meant opposing Lord Leverhulme's (William Lever's) plans for palm oil plantations in West Africa, also opposed by the colonial governments which eventually allowed only a few, not adding much to production. The quarrel between Leverhulme and the British government of Nigeria came to a head in 1925 and was reported in detail in *West Africa* (which also devoted two pages of small type to his funeral soon afterwards).[3]

This controversy was mainly about palm oil, of which Nigeria was a leading exporter. *West Africa* covered extensively the trade in palm oil, palm kernels, cocoa, groundnuts and cotton. It defended Africans' control of production: an editorial on 2 May 1925 said, 'The prosperity of our shipping, mercantile, banking, and manufacturing interests is best served by the existence of millions of producers, independent in status, secure in title, throughout British West Africa' ('Land' 1925: 437). Similarly, the magazine criticised the Kenya white settler system when it was the object of controversy in the 1920s. But the magazine showed little awareness of the lives of ordinary Africans and of what very many of them had to endure from low prices paid for produce, colonial flat-rate taxation, and for some forced labour (as on the Nigerian tin mines). It reflected the complacency of the colonial rulers during the four decades when there was almost uninterrupted peace under their rule. Its full acceptance of colonialism was illustrated by its extensive coverage of the Empire Exhibition at Wembley in 1924–5 and the Prince of Wales's West African tour in 1925.

Common acceptance of colonialism in Britain in the interwar era did not exclude sharp arguments over colonial policy. These included arguments about Indirect Rule and about education for Africans. The two were related, because the British in the Muslim emirates of Northern Nigeria almost completely banned Western education, and in other areas also many British officials and many other British people did not readily agree with Africans receiving such education. But in fact Africans had received it from Christian missions since before colonial rule, and the colonial rulers added some government schools later. The growing numbers of Africans with modern education served the colonial rulers in many fields, but many voiced opposition to Indirect Rule. Arguments about this are visible in the pages of *West Africa* in the 1920s and 1930s. The editor was sceptical about Indirect Rule but was not polemical about that aspect of colonial rule, or about colonialism generally.

The Western-educated Africans were visible from the start in the pages of what was an essentially colonial magazine. In the first two years their opposition to the ERDC was recorded, and the Ghanaian nationalist writer Kobina Sekyi wrote a series of articles. Other contributions by Africans followed, especially in the correspondence columns. The magazine followed sympathetically the progress of the West African Students' Union (WASU) in Britain from its foundation in 1925.[4] It reported on the black and African organisations that arose in Britain after the First World War, such as the African Progress Union and the newspaper the *African Telegraph*, and showed some sympathy for their protests, against Indirect Rule for example; these did not call for early independence, but calls for more representation of Africans were spreading. *West Africa*'s response to this was cautious, suggesting it should be a long process confined for the time being to local government ('An Opportunity' 1918: 382).

After the National Congress of British West Africa (NCBWA) was founded in 1920 it sent a delegation to Britain; the delegates called on the editor of *West Africa*, which had reported on its founding conference in Accra. That conference called for more representation of Africans, including some elective representation, and an end to discrimination in government service, which was general but had aroused African resentment for decades already. Although the NCBWA declared loyalty to the British Empire, its claim to represent West Africans was contested by a leading Akan chief of the Gold Coast Colony, Nana Ofori Atta, and both the Governor of the Gold Coast, Sir Gordon Guggisberg, and the editor of *West Africa* backed him.[5]

British policy favoured governing through traditional rulers even where the full Indirect Rule system was not applied, as in the Gold Coast (where attempts were made to apply it fully later), and *West Africa* did not oppose this policy. In 1934 Cartwright, living in Bexhill-on-Sea, went with the visiting Ofori Atta to the grave of Guggisberg in that town. But earlier, in 1928, the magazine gave big publicity to Ofori Atta's visit to receive a knighthood but also agreed with his words, 'Education – that is where all our hopes lie' ('Sir Ofori's Visit' 1928: 817). And in 1927, when Prince of Wales College at Achimota in the Gold Coast was opened, teaching for University of London external degrees, the magazine condemned the notion that university education for Africans created 'an isolated and uncomfortable class' through 'English examinations altogether alien to Native life' and that these things should be avoided ('Two Landmarks' 1927: 77). Cartwright did agree with colonial officials – and some African intellectuals like Kobina Sekyi and James Kwegyir Aggrey – that education should be 'adapted' for African pupils, but Africans commonly insisted on Western education as it existed for others, and that was what colonial governments in fact allowed or even provided themselves, as at Achimota, though not on the scale Africans wanted.

In the 1920s Africans were given some elective representation in the Legislative Councils of Nigeria, the Gold Coast and Sierra Leone. Commenting on the elections of three Nigerian representatives from Lagos and one from Calabar in 1923, *West Africa* expressed hope that they would 'remember that the country is not, and cannot, for many years, be ready for self-government'; later it published a long interview with one of the new Legislative Council members, but added an editorial saying, 'It would be dishonest to pretend that self-government would not mean disaster' ('The Nigerian Elections' 1923: 1,137).[6] While the West African elite leaders commonly declared loyalty to the British rulers and did not call for their early departure, their newspapers' critical attitude was far removed from *West Africa*'s occasional mild criticisms.

The firms trading with *West Africa* and owning shares in the West Africa Publishing Company went through some changes in the 1920s, with mergers reducing their total number, notably the takeover of the Niger Company by Lever Brothers in 1920. There were minor changes in the companies' holdings in the WAPC, and in their representation on its board. In 1929 the merger of Lever Brothers and the African and Eastern Trade Corporation (AETC) created the giant United Africa Company (UAC).

The Great Depression caused additional hardship among Africans. It set in just when the colonial government of Nigeria started to implement Indirect Rule, with its accompanying flat-rate taxation, among the Igbo people who had no traditional tax-raising kingdoms like those in Northern Nigeria. The resulting protests by women in late 1929, suppressed with the shooting of many by troops, led to an inquiry and to a rare criticism by *West Africa* of the taxation decision – a brief mild comment ('The Nigerian Inquiry Report' 1930: 1,369; 'The S. E. Nigerian Disturbances' 1930: 1,374–81), like a brief comment on cotton growers' suffering in the Depression years: 'all of us connected with the country know that the producer's plight is desperate' ('Japan, Lancashire and West Africa' 1934: 493). The Depression hit government expenditure in the colonies, with many job losses resulting, and forced severe cuts on the firms, even the new giant UAC.

Although the WAPC had paid dividends over 10 per cent for about a dozen years, and the firms had derived other benefits from the magazine, they decided to sell their shares in 1931, presumably because of the slump. Then the staff of the magazine made an offer to buy it out, which was accepted. On 4 August 1931 Albert Cartwright, his wife Margaret Cartwright, and the advertisement manager John Nolan were appointed directors, and then the WAPC went into voluntary liquidation by a decision of an Extraordinary General Meeting on 11 August 1931 (Particulars of the Directors 1931). A new West Africa Publishing Company now ran the magazine. An editorial about the change on 15 August 1931 said that neither the outgoing chairman, the Earl of Scarbrough, nor other outgoing directors from the shareholding firms, 'nor any of the firms who were shareholders', had sought to interfere with the magazine's views ('Ourselves' 1931: 981). This clearly meant that the owners and the editor had the same ideas anyway, so that no interference would be thought necessary; and indeed the magazine's affinity with the West Coast trading companies remained.

Another magazine was started in 1922 by Elder Dempster in Liverpool, at first a quarterly house magazine called the *Elder Dempster Magazine* and then, in 1929, the *Elders Review of West African Affairs*. In 1930 it became a monthly. Then, in December 1930, Elder Dempster handed over ownership and control of the magazine to Newton-Griffiths Overseas Press Ltd. The facts about the change are not entirely clear, but it is known that the decisive role was played by Robert Benjamin Paul (1901–53), a senior employee of Elder Dempster (ED), who acquired (possibly with partners) the *Elders Review*, left ED and set up independently. The name of the journal was changed to the *Elders West African Review* in June 1931 and then to the *West African Review (incorporating Elders Review)* in September 1931. While it had offices in the same building as ED, Colonial House in Liverpool, until 1939, it was now legally separate from Elder Dempster. At this time ED lost 40 per cent of its trade because of the Depression and went through severe cutbacks – including disposing of the magazine – and then some reorganisation involving the creation of a new company, Elder Dempster Lines Ltd, which acquired the assets of the British and African Steam Navigation Company (BASNC) and the African Steam Ship Company (ASSC), becoming the full owner of their ships.

The *West African Review* was a well-presented, abundantly illustrated monthly, backed by plentiful advertising, and achieved a wide circulation. Even before its separation from ED it had become more than a house magazine. As a monthly it did not chronicle news, but published features, which were quite varied; many were paternalist-colonialist, but some contributions by Africans and others could touch on sensitive topics like taxation and the exercise of judicial functions by non-judicial colonial officials (a cause of many African protests, but ended in Nigeria in 1933). The *Review* seems to have been a more successful venture than *West Africa* for several years, but a weekly and a monthly were not competitors, and there was no political difference between them; both were at ease with colonial business and colonialism generally, but accessible and friendly to educated Africans. On 8 June 1935 *West Africa* announced that the companies publishing it and the *West African Review* had agreed to an exchange of shares and transfer of the ownership of both magazines to a new company, West African Newspapers Ltd ('Editorial Notice' 1935: 4). Some details of this transaction are obscure (Derrick 2017: 232–3), but it is clear that the publishers of the *Review* effectively took over *West Africa*, and Paul, its chairman, seems to have dominated the new company. Cartwright, who joined the new board of the *Review* while Paul joined that of *West Africa*, remained editor of the weekly. Both magazines had offices in London while the *West African Review* retained its Liverpool office.

In 1936 West African Newspapers Ltd acquired a majority holding in the Nigerian Printing and Publishing Company of Lagos, publishers of the *Nigerian Daily Times*, which had been founded ten years before ('Editorial Notice' 1936: 4). Because of these developments it has been suggested that Elder Dempster became owners of *West Africa* and the *Nigerian Daily Times*, but this is not strictly correct, however close Paul's relations with his former employers may have been. In any case both *West Africa* and the *West African Review* had been and would remain friendly to colonial big business, typified by ED. The *West African Review* had many business supplements and for some years an annual survey of West African shipping, commerce and finance.

The Early Evening of Empire

West Africa and the *West African Review* served a largely white readership, as was shown by advertisements aimed at the white 'Coaster'. However, in the 1930s both showed interest in the African students in Britain and their social activities such as those of WASU; the issue of racism faced by students was covered. A dispute between WASU and the Colonial Office over the hostels founded by each was settled after three years in 1936, with the government agreeing to provide funds for both; then the one originally founded by the government, Aggrey House, was placed under a trust, of which Cartwright was one of the four trustees.[7] Students were politically active and critical of the British government, as *West Africa*'s reports showed.

The magazine said relatively little about the growing political activity and protests in West Africa itself in the 1930s, including the formation of the West African Youth League (WAYL), active in the Gold Coast for some years from 1934 and widely popular in Sierra Leone in 1938–9 under the leadership of I. T. A. Wallace-Johnson. There were also strikes, and in 1937–8 a large-scale Cocoa Hold-Up in the Gold Coast, by farmers suspecting UAC and other firms of rigging prices downwards. The protests in Britain by the League of Coloured Peoples (LCP) and by other, more left-wing anti-colonial activists were covered to some extent in *West Africa*. Calls for African self-government were spreading in Africa and Britain, and within the Colonial Office there were moves towards more attention for African welfare issues. These developments were visible in the pages of *West Africa*, but the editorial policy accepted the status quo.

Government through chiefs remained official policy until the 1940s, but the question of which Africans better represented their people – chiefs or educated people – continued to be debated. In the Gold Coast both groups of African leaders agreed on opposing the government's 1934 Sedition Ordinance and on calls for restoration of the Asante (Ashanti) monarchy, eventually carried out in 1935. But the basic division remained and was reflected in *West Africa*. While he did not agree with many of their political demands, Cartwright was consistently on good terms with educated Africans. He accepted that they would be more numerous and more important in their countries' affairs, as many Europeans did not; in the magazine's regular photo spreads, Africans in the modern sphere – workers, sportspeople, students – were commonly shown as well as villagers.

On international issues which aroused feelings among Africans and the Diaspora, the two magazines gave them only limited support. *West Africa* did defend Liberia's independence when it seemed under threat, and condemned the Italian invasion of Ethiopia, but Cartwright's comments on Ethiopia showed a lack of real comprehension of Africans' outrage ('Signor Mussolini's War' 1935: 1,173–4). In the 1930s Albert Cartwright and Robert Paul both displayed, in their respective magazines, a major lapse of judgement in suggesting that the German demand for restoration of the former German colonies could be considered. After this and other forms of 'appeasement' failed, they fully backed the war effort from its beginning.

During the Second World War they covered the West African involvement – the military contribution in the Burma campaign being recorded in the *Review* in particular – and the wartime reorganisation of the colonies' export trade. They said very little about the extra burdens imposed on Africans by the war, but *West Africa* joined in the condemnation of racism displayed in Britain at that time, highlighting the notorious case involving Sir Learie Constantine ('But Will the Colonial Office Take Action?' 1943: 796). It also recorded something of the African political reaction to the war and the post-war prospects, highlighting the visit of a delegation of West African editors to Britain in 1943 (see Figure 10.1).[8] *West Africa* published a long feature over two issues, plus an editorial, on the Colonial Secretary's declaration of a pledge to 'guide our colonial peoples along the road to self-government within the framework of the British Empire' ('Colonial Affairs' 1943a: 637–9; 'Colonial Affairs' 1943b: 661–2).

Figure 10.1 'Arrival of West African Editors in Britain', *West Africa*, 14 August 1943, p. 704. Courtesy of the author.

But *West Africa*, while fully reporting it, showed little sympathy for the resolutions of the Fifth Pan-African Congress, held in Manchester in October 1945, which included a resolution calling for 'complete and absolute independence for the Peoples of West Africa' ('After-War Colonial Problems' 1945: 1,061–2).

By 1945 *West Africa* had declined in many ways since before the war, with the number of pages often reduced, down even to twenty pages compared with thirty-two pre-war. Only a few hundred copies were being sold by 1947. The *West African Review* by contrast flourished even in the war years, with over 100 pages at times.

Albert Cartwright retired as from the issue of 19 April 1947, succeeded by George H. Hunte. After negotiations during that year the Mirror Group acquired West African Newspapers on 18 December 1947 (Echeruo 1976; King 1969: 148, 158–9). Hunte returned to his native Barbados and David Morgan Williams (1913–93) became editor of *West Africa* from January 1949. After the takeover Cecil King took charge of the Mirror Group's African involvement, in which he took great interest as chairman of the group from 1951. Robert Paul died in 1953; the *West African Review* went on until 1962. The *Daily Times* of Lagos was included in the original takeover, and then the Mirror Group established the *Daily Graphic* in the Gold Coast and the *Daily Mail* in Sierra Leone. Eventually the latter two papers were transferred to local ownership after independence. The *Daily Times* remained, until well after Nigerian independence, in the hands of the International Publishing Corporation (IPC), which took over the Mirror Group in 1963; an IPC subsidiary, Overseas Newspapers, owned *West Africa* and the majority of the *Daily Times*. With close ties to *West Africa* and its editor, the

Daily Times expanded rapidly under the dynamic direction of Alhaji Babatunde Jose to become Nigeria's leading daily.

Decolonisation and *West Africa*

With David Williams as editor from January 1949, the *West Africa* magazine embarked on a new period of expansion and success, reflecting great changes in the British West African colonies. The 1950s saw the rapid expansion and development of education, trade and business, literature and the arts, accompanied by the growing African nationalist movements. Most spectacular was the growth of the Convention People's Party (CPP), founded in 1949 by Kwame Nkrumah in the Gold Coast. The process of British decolonisation in Africa was slow and uneven, carried out mainly under the Conservative governments in power from 1951 to 1964. *West Africa* agreed with those governments' cautious and gradual approach, rather than the more strongly anti-imperialist Labour Party opposition and some lobbyists further to the left.

Hence the magazine gained a reputation for political and economic conservatism. But it did not please British people who were unwilling to accept the end of Empire. When Nkrumah and other leaders were imprisoned for their campaign for self-government while plans proceeded for an election bringing greater African representation in government, *West Africa* declared, 'If logic points that way, the Gold Coast may have to find Ministers from gaol' ('Ministers from Prison?' 1950: 337), and some subscriptions were cancelled. In fact, the CPP won the election, its leaders were freed the following year by what *West Africa* called 'the Governor's act of statesmanship' ('Good Start' 1951: 121), and Nkrumah became head of the government serving under the Governor. When Nkrumah as Prime Minister put forward a 'Motion of Destiny' on 10 July 1953 calling for independence, *West Africa* called this 'a speech admirable in tone and weighty in argument' ('Patriots and Gentlemen' 1953: 673). Progress towards African rule continued through collaboration between Nkrumah and the Governor Sir Charles Arden-Clarke, despite serious violent unrest for a time led by the National Liberation Movement (NLM) in Asante, until the Gold Coast became independent as Ghana on 6 March 1957.

Political progress in Nigeria was more complicated because of the country's size and diversity, reflected to some extent in the division into three regions (Northern, Western and Eastern) in 1947. This led to the federal constitution of 1954, confirming the wide autonomy of the regions while Lagos became a separate federal territory. *West Africa* followed the progress closely, covering for example the several Constitutional Conferences held to discuss further steps towards self-government, two major ones being held in London in 1953 and 1957. As the three regions progressed towards self-government with powerful regional governments and regional parties and dominance by the major ethnic groups in the regions (Hausa-Fulani in the North, Yoruba in the West, Igbo in the East), there were fears among the numerous smaller tribes that they would lose out. *West Africa* examined this problem, to be a major one for Nigeria, in an editorial in 1957; it said, 'The fears of minorities in Nigeria's regions are natural' but advised against one solution proposed, the creation of new regions or states ('Secession or Safeguards?' 1957: 265–6). The British government took the same view, and probably missed an opportunity to avoid plentiful trouble to come. When the Federation of Nigeria became independent on 1 October 1960, an editorial in *West Africa*, recording the independence speech by the Prime Minister Sir Abubakar Tafawa Balewa, warned that 'in internal affairs the Federal Government must claim and assert leadership' – a seeming allusion, typical of the magazine's cautious wording, to the regional governments' very wide powers and, perhaps, to some Nigerians' perception of Tafawa Balewa as giving too much attention to foreign relations ('Policy for Independent Nigeria' 1960: 1,129–30).

There was an on-the-spot report of the Nigerian independence celebrations, some of it in 'Matchet's Diary', which was for decades a column written mostly by the editor himself, and there were 'Portraits' earlier in 1960 of Tafawa Balewa and the three regional premiers. Such profiles of prominent people were a regular feature of the magazine then and later; besides politicians they described chiefs, academics, businesspeople and others, African and European. There were many contributions by leading experts in the growing field of African studies, such as Daryll Forde, Anthony Kirk-Greene, Michael Crowder and Thomas Hodgkin, an expert on nationalist movements and on West Africa's earlier history. For African studies the magazine was for a long time a major source; by the 1960s each issue included regular news reports, which had not been the case in the first decades of *West Africa*. While useful to scholars the magazine was aimed at the general public, above all the West African public. The number of West African students expanded greatly in Britain and the USA in the 1950s, and they commonly valued the magazine and its coverage of politics, often writing for the correspondence columns.

The decolonisation of British West Africa was largely completed with the independence of Sierra Leone on 27 April 1961; there remained the small territory of The Gambia, which became independent on 18 February 1965. In 1960–1, in the run-up to Sierra Leone's independence, there was political division, with an Elections Before Independence Movement (EBIM) opposing the party that eventually led the country to independence, the Sierra Leone People's Party (SLPP); at one stage the EBIM's leader Siaka Stevens wrote a party statement in the offices of *West Africa* in London. Normally the magazine's editorial policy accepted the status quo, political and economic, after independence as before, with African rulers now benefiting from its established approach – sometimes mildly critical, almost never polemical. It did speak out against the political corruption which soon emerged; when this was exposed in the Gold Coast in 1954 an editorial suggested that the contractors paying bribes were 'far more blameworthy than the politicians who took their money, contemptible though these are' ('Corruption by Contract' 1954: 385). The normal non-confrontational policy of the magazine had an extra reason after independence, as the new national governments were more intolerant than the colonial governments of press criticism.

The business scene was still dominated by major West Coast trading firms, with the United Africa Company towering above others. There was considerable African resentment at the UAC's dominance, expressed by CPP politicians in the Gold Coast for example, but it proved adaptable – promoting Africans to senior management, establishing good relations with Nkrumah in Ghana, withdrawing from produce buying by the early 1960s, and setting up industries such as Nigerian Breweries. The role of the trading firms was altered by the creation from the late 1940s of marketing boards for the main crops grown for export or, on a small but increasing scale, for local processing: cocoa, groundnuts, palm oil and kernels, cotton and others; at first the established firms were buying agents for the boards, but these were non-commercial institutions supposed to guarantee farmers' prices. Whether they were the right answer for African agriculture and trade was often debated; in the columns of *West Africa* there were heated rival contributions by the economists Peter Bauer (opposed to such institutions) and Thomas Balogh. But the marketing boards continued until after independence.

Agricultural and forest products remained the main African exports for some time, but mineral production and exports grew in the 1950s. *West Africa* covered the rapid growth of diamond mining in Sierra Leone, which transformed the country's economy but in partly criminal ways. Mining companies like the diamond firm Sierra Leone Selection Trust joined the longer-established firms in providing advertising revenue for the magazine, and the magazine covered the firms' activities well as before, not only in the regular Commercial News pages.

The French colonial territories also became independent in 1960, except for Guinea, which had voted for independence against President de Gaulle's wishes in 1958. *West Africa* devoted plenty of attention to the French-speaking states and their political leaders such as Léopold Senghor of Senegal and Ahmed Sekou Touré of Guinea; also to the Belgian Congo (whose government, *West Africa* said in 1959, 'has joined all other governments with colonies in Africa in giving too little, too late' ('Accra and Congo' 1959: 49)), its independence in 1960, and the crisis that followed, and the UN peacekeeping operation, involving Ghana and Nigeria. *West Africa* gave some attention to Eastern and Southern African countries under British colonial or white settler rule, which the Conservative governments did not quickly or easily agree to end, in contrast to the policy followed in West Africa; the magazine backed Africans seeking independence in those territories and, in South Africa, condemning the apartheid policy now being rigidly applied. While Britain, at the UN, agreed at that time with the South African regime's insistence on non-interference in internal affairs, an editorial in *West Africa* commented that this was 'a very important principle' and 'it should be abandoned only in cases so flagrant that the country under criticism stands entirely alone. South Africa is such a country and her racial policies offer such a case' ('Cape Town' 1960: 169–70).

Besides politics and business, the magazine covered many other aspects of life in West Africa, such as education and the arts. In education as in other areas the 1950s was a time of great expansion, to continue later. There was for example the growth of the University College of the Gold Coast and the University College of Ibadan, founded in 1948, at first teaching for external (London) degrees. Similarly, there was the long-established Fourah Bay College in Sierra Leone (training for Durham degrees). Later these were all to become independent universities, and many more African universities were to be added. Developments in African literature and music were followed in the magazine, which publicised for example the writers Amos Tutuola of Nigeria and Camara Laye of Guinea and the eminent Ghanaian 'high-life' musician E. T. Mensah. With so much covered, every week's issue was filled with material, produced by a fairly small staff – whose names were, at that time, not displayed on the masthead – together with outside contributions of many sorts. For West Africans and people involved in their region's affairs, *West Africa* was something of an institution, and it did well as such for some decades more. By the 1960s its circulation was in five figures, and readership higher as each copy was commonly read by several people.

Notes

1. See Lugard 1915; Cowan 1915; Brabner 1915a; Brabner 1915b; 'Editorial Notice' 1915: 71.
2. See, for examples, the critical articles in *West Africa*: 'Lord Selborne and Empire Resources' 1917: 397–8; 'No Cause for Anxiety' 1917: 429–30; 'Naboth's Vineyard?' 1918: 17; 'The Empire Resources Development Committee and West Africa' 1918: 25–31.
3. See *West Africa*'s extensive coverage: 'Sir Hugh Clifford and Lord Leverhulme' 1925: 223–5; 'Lord Leverhulme and Nigeria' 1925: 309–10; 'Death of Viscount Leverhulme' 1925: 483–5; 'The Late Lord Leverhulme' 1925: 517–18.
4. See Olusanya 1982 and Adi 1994.
5. See the coverage in *West Africa*: Special Correspondent 1920: 668–72; 'Sir Hugh Clifford and a Movement' 1921: 1709; 'West African National Congress' 1921: 36; 'The Congress and After' 1921: 37; 'The West African Chiefs and the National Congress Delegates' 1921: 99–100; 'Chief Ofori Atta's Weighty Speech' 1921: 109. See too Kimble 1963: 381–5.
6. See also 'Two Interviews' 1924: 861 and 'Coast Affairs' 1924: 862–5.
7. See the coverage in *West Africa* in 'Opening of Africa House' 1938: 994–5; the letter by Ivor Cummings 1936; and Olusanya 1982: 26–35.
8. See 'West African Editors in Britain' 1943: 687; 'Arrival of West African Editors in Britain' 1943: 704; and 'An Appreciation by the West African Press Delegation' 1943: 778.

Bibliography

'Accra and Congo' (1959), *West Africa*, 17 January, 49.
Adi, H. (1994), 'West African students in Britain, 1900–1960: The politics of exile', in David Killingray (ed.), *Africans in Britain*, London: Frank Cass, 107–28.
'After-War Colonial Problems: A Week's Meetings in Manchester' (1945), *West Africa*, 3 November, 1,061–2.
'An Appreciation by the West African Press Delegation' (1943), *West Africa*, 4 September, 778.
'Arrival of West African Editors in Britain' (1943), *West Africa*, 14 August, 704.
Brabner, G. H. (1915a), Letter to E. D. Morel, 30 October 1915, Correspondence Files in E. D. Morel Papers, British Library of Political and Economic Science.
—— (1915b), Letter to E. D. Morel, 1 November 1915, Correspondence Files in E. D. Morel Papers, British Library of Political and Economic Science.
'But Will the Colonial Office Take Action?' (1943), *West Africa*, 11 September, 796.
'Cape Town and the Commonwealth' (1960), *West Africa*, 13 February, 169–70.
'Chief Ofori Atta's Weighty Speech' (1921), *West Africa*, 26 February, 109.
Cline, C. (1980), *E. D. Morel 1873–1924: The Strategies of Protest*, Belfast: Blackstaff Press.
'Coast Affairs: African Politicians Interviewed' (1924), *West Africa*, 23 August, 862–5.
'Colonial Affairs in the Commons' (1943a), *West Africa*, 24 July, 637–9.
'Colonial Affairs in the Commons' (1943b), *West Africa*, 31 July, 661–2.
'The Congress and After' (1921), *West Africa*, 12 February, 37.
'Corruption by Contract' (1954), *West Africa*, 1 May, 385–6.
Cowan, A. A. (1915), Letter to F. Lugard, 16 October 1915, MSS British Empire s. 76, 120–6, Lugard MSS, Weston Library, Oxford.
Cummings, Ivor (1936), Letter to the Trustees, 9 September, on meeting of Aggrey House Trustees, File CO 323/1398/8, National Archives, Kew.
Davies, P. N. (1973), *The Trade Makers: Elder Dempster in West Africa, 1852–1972*, London: Allen & Unwin.
'Death of Viscount Leverhulme' (1925), *West Africa*, 9 May, 483–5.
'Declaration of Compliance with the Requisitions of the Companies (Consolidation) Act 1908, on behalf of a Company proposed to be registered as West Africa Publishing Company'

(1916), 22 June; Statement of Nominal Capital 22 June 1916; Memorandum and Articles of Association; Copy of Register of Directors or Managers, registered 18 June 1916; Return of Allotments the 1st of September 1916; all in file BT31/23310/144163, National Archives, Kew.

Derrick, Jonathan (2017), *Africa, Empire and Fleet Street: Albert Cartwright and 'West Africa' Magazine*, London: C. Hurst & Co.

Echeruo, M. J. C. (1976), *The Story of the Daily Times*, Lagos: self-published.

'Editorial Notice' (1915), *African Mail*, 19 November, 71.

'Editorial Notice' (1935), *West African Review*, July, 4.

'Editorial Notice' (1936), *West African Review*, October, 4.

'The Empire Resources Development Committee and West Africa' (1918), *West Africa*, 9 February, 25–31.

'Good Start in the Gold Coast' (1951), *West Africa*, 17 February, 121.

'Government in Nigeria' (1918), *West Africa*, 2 November, 670–1.

Hochschild, Adam (1998), *King Leopold's Ghost*, Boston: Houghton Mifflin.

Irvine, W. H. (1953), 'A Pioneer of Publishing: Death of Mr R. B. Paul', *West African Review*, March, 269.

'Japan, Lancashire and West Africa' (1934), *West Africa*, 12 May, 493.

Jose, Babatunde (1987), *Walking a Tight Rope: Power Play in Daily Times*, Ibadan: Ibadan University Press.

Kimble, David (1963), *A Political History of Ghana*, Oxford: Clarendon Press.

King, Cecil (1969), *Strictly Personal*, London: Weidenfeld & Nicolson.

'Land and the Use of it' (1925), *West Africa*, 2 May, 437.

'The Late Lord Leverhulme' (1925), *West Africa*, 16 May, 517–18.

'Lord Leverhulme and Nigeria' (1925), *West Africa*, 4 April, 309–10.

'Lord Selborne and Empire Resources' (1917), *West Africa*, 14 July, 397–8.

Lugard, F. (1915), Letter to A. A. Cowan, 13 October 1915, MSS British Empire s. 76, 120–6, Lugard MSS, Weston Library, Oxford.

'Ministers from Prison?' (1950), *West Africa*, 22 April, 337–9.

Morel, E. D. (1915), Letter to J. Nolan, 3 November 1915, Correspondence Files in E. D. Morel Papers, British Library of Political and Economic Science.

'Naboth's Vineyard?' (1918), *West Africa*, 9 February, 17.

'The Nigerian Elections' (1923), *West Africa*, 29 September, 1,137.

'The Nigerian Inquiry Report' (1930), *West Africa*, 4 October, 1,369.

'No Cause for Anxiety' (1917), *West Africa*, 28 July, 429–30.

Olusanya, G. O. (1982), *The West African Students' Union and the Politics of Decolonisation, 1925–1958*, Ibadan: Daystar.

'Opening of Africa House' (1938), *West Africa*, 23 July, 994–5.

'An Opportunity' (1918), *West Africa*, 13 July, 382.

'Ourselves' (1931), *West Africa*, 15 August, 981.

Particulars of the Directors or Managers of West Africa Publishing Company Limited, and of any changes therein (1931), 4 August; Return of the Final Winding-up Meeting, 31 May 1932, and Related Documents in file BT31/23310/144163, National Archives, Kew.

'Patriots and Gentlemen' (1953), *West Africa*, 25 July, 673–4.

'Policy for Independent Nigeria' (1960), *West Africa*, 8 October, 1,129–30.

'Secession or Safeguards?' (1957), *West Africa*, 23 March, 265–6.

'The S. E. Nigerian Disturbances: The Special Commission Report: Reservations by Mr. Graham Paul and Mr. V. R. Osborne' (1930), *West Africa*, 4 October, 1,374–81.

'Signor Mussolini's War' (1935), *West Africa*, 12 October, 1,173–4.

'Sir Hugh Clifford and Lord Leverhulme' (1925), *West Africa*, 14 March, 223–5.

'Sir Hugh Clifford and a Movement' (1921), *West Africa*, 22 January, 1,709.

'Sir Ofori's Visit' (1928), *West Africa*, 30 June, 817.

Special Correspondent (1920), 'The British West African Conference', *West Africa*, 29 May, 668–72.
'The Toast is – "West Africa"' (1917), *West Africa*, 3 February, 12.
'Two Interviews' (1924), *West Africa*, 23 August, 861.
'Two Landmarks' (1927), *West Africa*, 5 February, 77.
'The West African Chiefs and the National Congress Delegates' (1921), *West Africa*, 19 February, 99–100.
'West African Editors in Britain' (1943), *West Africa*, 7 August, 687.
'West African National Congress' (1921), *West Africa*, 5 February, 36.

Part II

Women and Colonial Periodicals

11

Transnational Reprinting and the Colonial Women's Magazine: *The Montreal Museum*, 1832–4

Honor Rieley

The Montreal Museum was the first women's magazine to be published in a British colony, and the first colonial magazine to have a female editor. It launched in December 1832 and ceased publication after fifteen issues in March 1834 (see Figure 11.1). Its editor was Mary Graddon Gosselin, assisted for the first two issues by Elizabeth Tracey; both women largely vanish from the historical record once their involvement with the magazine is over.[1] *The Museum*'s brief life was typical of its time and place: an oft-cited statistic is that until *The Literary Garland* (as discussed by Cynthia Sugars and Paul Keen in Chapter 1 and by Fariha Shaikh in Chapter 2),

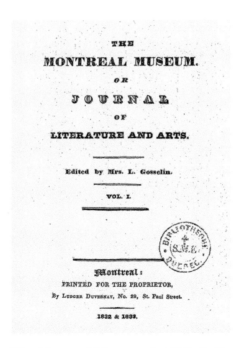

Figure 11.1 Title page, *The Montreal Museum*, 1, 1832–3. Courtesy of the Canadiana Collection of the Canadian Research Knowledge Network (*canadiana.ca*).

which ran from 1838 to 1851, no literary magazine in Upper or Lower Canada – present-day Ontario and Quebec – survived for more than three years (Vincent et al. 2004: 244–9; Rieley 2017: 130).

Mary Lu MacDonald, in the only previous article-length study of *The Museum*, notes that the magazine was positively reviewed in the local press; the support which Gosselin, in her final number, claims to have lacked was material rather than moral (MacDonald 1992: 139). The primary readership for a magazine like *The Museum* would have been Montreal's mostly anglophone merchant class, though according to Thomas Vincent, Sandra Alston and Eli MacLaren it was 'distributed at least as far as Hamilton' in neighbouring Upper Canada (Vincent et al. 2004: 247). This chimes with Gosselin's own statement in the second issue that 'The *Museum* [has] already obtained an extensive circulation in Upper and Lower Canada', and in the sixth number she makes further reference to 'Distant subscribers' who are asked to send six months' subscription up front (Gosselin 1833a: 128; Gosselin 1833e: 388). She also addresses herself here, slightly ominously, to 'Persons wishing to discontinue their Subscriptions' who wait too long to inform her of their decision and waste precious copies of the magazine (Gosselin 1833e: 388). Ultimately, the *Museum*, like many Canadian magazines before and after it, fell victim to the challenges of retaining and growing a subscriber base among the relatively small, highly dispersed educated English-speaking population. 'Most editors complained of a lack of material for their journals, and all lamented the scarcity of paying subscribers' (Vincent et al. 2004: 249). Neither Gosselin herself nor her reviewers attribute the failure of the *Museum* to its status as a magazine produced by and for women (MacDonald 1992: 140). The verdict was not that Gosselin had aimed at too narrow an audience in attempting a women's magazine, but that no viable audience was possible at that time.

That magazines like the *Museum* failed in material terms is an uncontroversial position. The question that has produced more critical debate is whether the make-up of early Canadian periodicals also represents an aesthetic failure; whether the large quantity of reprinted content that these publications include in response to the aforementioned 'lack of material' makes them derivative copies of metropolitan originals. Describing *The Montreal Museum* as '[d]oubtless modelled on the successful *Ladies' Museum* (London, 1798–1832)' is, on one level, a very fair assessment (Vincent et al. 2004: 247). It reprints work by many of the major female contributors to London periodicals, including Letitia Elizabeth Landon, Mary Shelley, Caroline Norton, Caroline Bowles, Catherine Gore and Maria Jane Jewsbury. Its original content, too, is largely typical of such metropolitan publications as the *Ladies' Museum* or *La Belle Assemblée*, mixing poetry and fiction with didactic pieces on female education and deportment, and snippets of writing on popular science, travel and nature. The first issue includes two engravings which seem to lend themselves well to a reading of the *Museum* as both imitative and belated. The first is an image of 'The Queen of the Belgians' which was printed in the *Court Magazine* in September 1832 (see Figure 11.2). The second, a plate illustrating 'Fashions for October 1832', accompanies a summary of the 'Newest London Fashions' (see Figure 11.3).

The *Museum* is providing its readers with images of clothes that were worn thousands of miles away, two or three months after they were 'new'. However, Gosselin is keen to 'direct the attention of our readers to the engravings in this number' less because of their content than because she is delighted to have had the magazine

Figure 11.2 'The Queen of the Belgians', *The Montreal Museum*, 1.1, December 1832. Courtesy of the Canadiana Collection of the Canadian Research Knowledge Network (*canadiana.ca*).

Figure 11.3 'Fashions for October 1832', *The Montreal Museum*, 1.1, December 1832. Courtesy of the Canadiana Collection of the Canadian Research Knowledge Network (*canadiana.ca*).

'embellished by the hand of a native artist', Adolphus Bourne (Gosselin 1832d: 64). The celebration of this most unoriginal of material as a sign of local cultural development is an early indication that binary divisions between 'borrowed' and 'original', or 'colonial' and 'metropolitan', might not tell the whole story. As if to emphasise this point, 'Fashions for October 1832' is in fact not a straightforward reproduction of a London original, but an adaptation: the figures are copied from two different plates in the October 1832 issue of the *World of Fashion*, and only appear side by side in the *Montreal Museum*, in a new composite image ('Newest Fashions' 1832).

In this chapter I argue that we should see this colonial women's magazine as equally closely entwined with the American periodical scene, where what is modelled is a practice of meaningful unoriginality, of fitting a reprinted text to a new context where it functions differently. Meredith McGill's groundbreaking work on the American 'culture of reprinting' grapples with the fact that 'the transnational status of reprinted texts makes it difficult for us to assimilate them into national literary narratives' (McGill 2003: 3), and Faye Hammill and Hannah McGregor make a similar point in relation to the Canadian context:

> [I]t can be tempting to cordon off Canadian print culture from its hulking American neighbor . . . This tendency, however, has the adverse effect of ignoring the transnationalism, as well as the regional formations, of print culture. It ignores in particular the way the Canadian periodical press has been in constant dialogue with that of the United States. (Hammill and McGregor 2018: 77–8)

Hammill and McGregor's focus is on the early twentieth century, but this insight holds equally true for the *Museum* in the 1830s. The *Museum*'s identity as a Canadian women's magazine is expressed partly in its vision for advancing polite literature in the Canadas, but also in its sense of itself as engaged in a transnational 'sphere' of women's periodical publishing. In order to understand this fully, it is necessary to look beyond the *Museum*'s original content and examine the material it takes from elsewhere. The *Museum*'s limited run allows for a close analysis of the twelve issues that comprise its first volume, and in what follows I trace routes of reprinting to London, Paris, the United States and the Anglo-Scottish border town of Berwick-upon-Tweed.

'Our Sphere, as Ladies'

Laying out her plan for the *Montreal Museum* in the introduction to its first issue, Gosselin strikes the same ambitious note as other Canadian editors of the 1820s and 1830s (Bowness 2012: 75–8; Rieley 2017: 134). Being 'deeply interested in the honour of our country', she aims to help cultivate a taste for literature in the Canadas and to provide a venue for the 'developement [*sic*] of native genius, and the increase of national respectability' (Gosselin 1832b: 1–2). She also joins her predecessors – and successors like *The Literary Garland* – in identifying certain obstacles to the realisation of her vision. The first of these is the 'supineness' of colonial society itself, but the real challenge, which Canadian readers, authors and publishers are failing to meet, is the 'extraordinary facility with which American Works may be obtained, and their multiplicity' (Gosselin 1832b: 1–2). The fact 'that in the Canadas there is not a single Literary Journal, whilst the neighbouring states abound with Periodical Publications, devoted to the general diffusion of knowledge' is for Gosselin a sign both of Canadian 'indifference' to the origin of their reading material, and of the threat posed by American imports to local literary production (Gosselin 1832b: 1; Bowness 2012: 102).

This assessment of the Canadian situation was, in 1832, already becoming conventional. Where the *Museum* differs from its contemporaries is in linking the cultural improvement it aims to promote to particular, gendered types of writing. Gosselin introduces the question of gender – of her magazine as women's magazine – in this way:

> The indulgent reception and ultimate success of one Work, will naturally lead to the establishment of others, perhaps of a more scientific and useful character. It is not within our sphere, as Ladies, to pretend to an acquaintance with those deep and abstruse studies necessary to the improvement and display of human ingenuity, in the great and important arts of life. Our views of utility are confined to the Domestic and social circle, and to those limits our capacities and inclinations alike restrict us. (Gosselin 1832b: 2)

At first glance this is a self-effacing statement of feminine incapacity, posing the light literature to be found in the *Museum*'s pages against the weightier, outward-looking, masculine publications for which it might one day pave the way. Mary Lu MacDonald argues, with justice, that 'words like "limit" and "restrict," and a denial of any acquaintance with what is "great" and "important," all indicate a narrow view of a lady's "sphere"' (MacDonald 1992: 144). In subsequent issues, though, statements about the proper sphere of female literary activity begin to take on a more assertive tone. In the second issue, Gosselin tries to encourage her subscribers to submit not just any writing about Canada, but writing in her preferred mode:

> Many of our Correspondents, more ready to furnish us with *matter of fact advice*, than with *fiction*, have recommended the topography of the country as worthy of our attention – we freely admit it . . . But mere geographical details – such as the circumference of a lake, the length and breadth of a river . . . would be dry and uninteresting, if imagination lent not its witching wand to enliven and animate the scenes. (Gosselin 1833a: 127–8)

Gosselin is soliciting imaginative literature, quite specifically: she is not at all interested in publishing the sort of topographical description that makes up a significant portion of the original content of other Canadian magazines in the 1820s and 1830s. A similar prescriptiveness is evident in an editor's note appended to a piece by a future regular contributor, 'Francis H', in the same issue. The 'fair writer' of 'Sketches of an Idle Moment' is advised 'to direct her descriptive talents to local society and manners . . . Sketches from her pen of fashionable life, as it is at home, would be more to the purpose, more piquant, than stories told of "gallant lords and ladies fair" who figure in a "far far land"' ([Francis H] 1833: 102). This instruction, which can be read as a desire to transplant polite literature from the metropole to the colony or as an independent-minded defence of the inherent literary interest of life 'at home', is probably the most obvious fusion of the *Museum*'s strictures on polite literature and its concern with the development of colonial society.

One way to read these editorial pronouncements is as an attempt to imagine, or shape, an ideal colonial woman reader. Margaret Beetham sees this as a key cultural function of the periodical press: magazines 'not only defined readers as "women", they sought to bring into being the women they addressed' (Beetham 1996: ix). MacDonald says something similar in evaluating the *Museum*'s literary-historical significance: 'It is for its perception of what women wanted to, or should, read that we find it most interesting today' (MacDonald 1992: 143). More recent scholarship on women's periodicals has cautioned against reading these texts as imposing a unitary conception of womanhood from the top down: for example, Jennie Batchelor has shown that we can have some scepticism about the *Lady's Magazine*'s claims to be '"supplied entirely by Female Pens" for the improvement of female minds' without this diminishing its claim to the title of 'women's magazine' (Batchelor 2011: 248). This kind of nuance is needed when considering Gosselin's position: while she makes overt appeals to ideals of feminine delicacy and refinement in establishing her magazine's editorial line and principles of selection, at no point does she suggest that she imagines her readership to be exclusively female – in such a small market this would hardly be tenable. JoEllen DeLucia's analysis of the way in which the *Lady's Magazine* adapts travel writing to 'the meridian of female reading' argues that it 'made the world a smaller and more delicate place' at the same time as 'extending the parameters of the feminine sphere well beyond domestic and even commercial concerns' (DeLucia 2018: 205–6). This offers a useful model for thinking through the *Museum*'s comparable definition of its 'sphere' of operation in simultaneously aesthetic and geographic terms.

All but one of the *Museum*'s local writers are unidentified, though there is a preference for female pseudonyms. The named contributor, of whose involvement much is made, is Diana Bayley, who was a published author in Britain before moving to Isle au Noix, Lower Canada. She supplies twelve original pieces to the *Museum*, where they are proudly attributed to 'the Author of "Tales of the Heath" – "Scenes at home and abroad" – "Employment, the true source of happiness", &c. &c.' (Bayley 1833: 201; MacDonald 1992: 148). Gosselin writes in the eleventh issue of the *Museum*:

> We have the more reason for grateful feeling toward Mrs Bayley knowing her to be almost constantly employed, either in completing a series of Moral Tales, she is about publishing in New York, or in writing in prose or verse for the London Literary Periodicals. (Gosselin 1833g: 706)

Bayley's triangular literary career is a concrete demonstration of the need to factor in to any reading of the Canadian literary scene 'the proximity and complexity of American print culture, in which women's bold and varied participation consistently offered inspiration for Canada's female writers' (Gerson 2010: xiii). Inspiration, but also a field of activity: Bayley is not confined to emulating American print culture but participates in it directly.

In the first number of the *Museum*, Gosselin introduces several pieces from Boston literary annual the *Token*, with an expression of anxiety about fluctuations in the American literary market:

> We notice with regret, a decrease in the number of American Annuals, but two have appeared for 1833 – the *Token*, and *Pearl* . . . The slightest deterioration is

more sensibly felt, than the most evident improvement, and any falling off in those works of taste, and refinement, give an unpleasant sensation, lest the public should become weary of the light and graceful productions of fancy. (Gosselin 1832c: 15)

Gosselin clearly views the *Token*'s 'public' as meaningfully similar to, or overlapping with, her own, the potential 'falling off' in demand for polite literature as something which would also negatively affect her. The female 'sphere' into which Gosselin attempts to write herself is a transnational one.

Routes of Reprinting

Maurice Lemire characterises the *Museum*'s content as 'distributed more or less equally between unpublished Canadian material and texts borrowed from other journals' (Lemire et al. 1992: 180, my translation).[2] However, reprints actually occupy far more space in the *Museum* than this estimate suggests: in the first volume of the magazine, there are forty-seven original contributions and 139 reprints. (The original contributions include Gosselin's editorials and addresses to correspondents; the reprints figure includes twenty-seven translated pieces, of which more below.) Original content is virtually always clearly labelled as such; it is the proof of Gosselin's success in promoting local literature. Attribution of reprinted material is far murkier, and digging beneath the surface of the partial, sometimes misleading information that the *Museum* provides about its sources reveals a more complex picture of where this content comes from and what that can tell us about the *Museum*'s priorities and perception of itself.

I have been able to trace all but five of the reprinted pieces to their original source. Of the 139 reprints, ninety-three are attributed to their author or original publication (or both), either in the relevant issue of the *Museum* or, failing that, in the first volume's table of contents. Forty-six pieces, almost a third of the total, are either unattributed or misattributed. I am defining misattribution in two ways: firstly, a handful of pieces are simply wrongly categorised in the table of contents – Letitia Elizabeth Landon's poem 'Changes' being listed as 'Original – By a Lady', for example (Gosselin 1832a). Secondly, and more interestingly, most are given an attribution which is not inaccurate – they really were originally published in the book or periodical in question – but which does not reflect where Gosselin actually sourced the text. On initial reading, the *Museum* appears to be drawing from an impressive, even dizzying range of works, but on further investigation this scope is narrowed and texts cluster together.

The tenth (September 1833) issue of the *Museum* offers a typical example. It includes an 'Account of an African Hunt' attributed to '*Owen's Travels*' (Owen 1833); excerpts from Lady Morgan's *Dramatic Scenes from Real Life* (1833); a review, with long extracts, of *Westward Ho!* (1832), a novel by American author James Kirke Paulding; and a sentimental poem entitled 'Are we almost there?' by 'Imogene'. The Morgan piece includes a brief attribution to '*Ath*', and Imogene's poem is also attributed to 'London Athenaeum' in the table of contents, though not in the issue itself. In fact, all four pieces are from the *Athenaeum*, where they appeared on 29 June (Owen), 13 July (Paulding and Morgan) and 20 July (Imogene). This date range tracks with the fact that the *Athenaeum*, a weekly periodical, was bundled in monthly instalments for the international market. Its title page throughout 1832–3 reads: 'For the convenience of persons residing in remote places, the weekly numbers are issued in Monthly Parts, stitched in a wrapper, and forwarded with the Magazines to all parts of the world.' While it is difficult to find much method in Gosselin's decisions about when and what to attribute, there is a general tendency for poetry and fiction which actually originates in a literary magazine to be attributed correctly. What is not consistently clearly signalled is the *Museum*'s reprinting of another periodical's excerpts from, or review of, a book-length work. Editorial practices which are inexact by modern standards are not at all unusual in this period: the real question is what a close examination of the magazine's sourcing – looking beyond the original content to the unoriginal, and beyond the attributed to the un- or misattributed – might be able to tell us about the *Museum*'s particular situation.

Ultimately, then, does the analysis of reprinting simply confirm that the *Museum* is more dependent on a relatively small number of metropolitan periodicals even than is evident from a surface reading? This would be taking a new route to an old insight: that Canadian magazines rely on their British counterparts for a large proportion of their content has, after all, been the prevailing view. The rest of this chapter will offer a few alternative ways of understanding what this information shows us, and will posit that the *Museum*'s reprinting practices actually open it out to multiple sites other than the British imperial centre.

One significant aspect of the *Museum*'s reprinting practice that is concealed by its attribution methods (or lack of them) is the full extent of its engagement with American literature. I have already suggested that the 'sphere' in which Gosselin understands herself to be operating extends to take in the neighbouring United States, and this is borne out by the patterns of reprinting. The eighth issue of the *Museum* features a set of short snippets which are all drawn from the same periodical: 'Catching Turtles on the Coast of Cuba', attributed to *The Penny Magazine*, 'Mode of Travelling in Kamtschatka', attributed to 'Goldsmith's Customs and Manners', and 'Filial Affection of the Moors'.[3] While Gosselin does draw from *The Penny Magazine* for other issues, 'Catching Turtles' is printed alongside 'Mode of Travelling in Kamtschatka' in the 20 April 1833 number of the *Family Magazine, or Monthly Abstract of General Knowledge*, which was published in New York from 1833 to 1834. 'Filial Affection of the Moors' appears in the same magazine on 4 May; again, this pattern suggests that Gosselin obtained a couple of months' worth of copies of the *Family Magazine* and mined it for content for the next issue of the *Museum*. While we might interpret such 'borrowing', when the source is the *Athenaeum*, through the lens of colonial dependency, it is difficult to view the American reprint economy in the same light, suggesting that it is more productive to see the process as a whole in horizontal rather than hierarchical terms.

In the sixth number of the *Museum*, Gosselin comments on the appearance of *Greenbank's Periodical Library*, a weekly subscription series from Philadelphia 'containing, in the cheapest possible form, a republication of new and standard works' (Greenbank 1833: i). 'We know not which to admire most, the individual spirit and enterprise of our neighbours in the States, in undertaking works of genius, or the liberality of the Republic in encouraging them' (Gosselin 1833d: 374). In spite of her earlier statements about 'American Works' threatening the development of literature in the Canadas, Gosselin comments here on the reprinting that was rife in the United States less as a problem than as something to be admired or emulated, an example of American get-up-and-go. This engagement with American reprint culture helps to explain one of the more incongruous items in the *Museum*, William Wordsworth's 'Harry Blake and Goody Gill', which appears (attributed to the poet) in the twelfth issue in December 1833. One of the 1798 *Lyrical Ballads*, the poem is an unusual choice for the magazine, which rarely reprints anything published before 1830. The reason for its inclusion is that it comes to the *Museum* not from *Lyrical Ballads* but from *Greenbank's Periodical Library*: the second volume of the series contains a 'Sketch of the Genius and Character of William Wordsworth, with Selections from his Lyrical Ballads' (Greenbank 1833: 181–202).[4] This thirty-five-year-old poem, which if its source was not known would appear to signal the *Museum*'s colonial belatedness, becomes current in the context of the cheap reprint-based American market.

'Translated for the *Museum*'

Although *The Montreal Museum* has always, and understandably, been read in the context of the early development of English-Canadian literature, Mary Graddon Gosselin's relationship to anglophone literary culture is not without complexity. Unlike the editors of earlier Montreal English-language magazines, Gosselin was not an emigrant from England or Scotland: she was born in Quebec City to an Irish Catholic merchant family and was convent educated.[5] In 1830 she married a French-Canadian lawyer and journalist, Léon Gosselin, and consequently was affiliated with Lower Canada's French-speaking majority by both marriage and religion. At the time of the *Museum*'s launch, Gosselin's husband was editor of the city's major French-language newspaper, *La Minerve*, and the two publications were issued by the same printer, Ludger Duvernay. Both Duvernay and Léon Gosselin were active in the radical Parti patriote, and according to Suzanne Bowness, Gosselin's erstwhile assistant editor Elizabeth Tracey was the sister of the reformist politician Daniel Tracey (Bowness 2012: 31n). The 1830s was a decade of increasing French-Canadian nationalism and agitation for greater political representation which would culminate in the rebellions of 1837–8, and while we have no explicit evidence of Gosselin's own political views, her associations are anything but conservative, and anything but pro-British. Mylène Bédard notes that in the French prospectus for the *Museum*, published in the *Canadien* newspaper on 23 November 1832, 'the founder, Mary Graddon Gosselin, attributes the absence in Canada of women of letters and publications like her own to "the introduction of political discussions"' (Bédard 2016: 77, my translation).[6] Her insistence that her magazine be 'confined to the Domestic and social circle' takes on a different shading when viewed in the context of the increasingly heated political atmosphere of the 1830s.

Gosselin seems initially to have conceived the *Museum* as being to some extent bilingual; she explicitly pitches the magazine to the francophone community in an address 'To Correspondents' in the first issue:

[A]ll communications worthy of a place in the *Museum* shall be inserted in the language in which they are written. This plan we are induced to adopt for the benefit of our French Subscribers and contributors, and as an inducement to those who write in that language to favour us with their productions. Such pieces as we may deem of sufficient interest to our English readers shall be translated. (Gosselin 1832d: 63–4)

No letters to the editor or other contributions in French ever appear, so the question of what it would take for a French composition to be 'of sufficient interest to our English readers' is left unanswered. There were precedents for this sort of linguistic outreach, as Jean Delisle notes: 'The periodical press in Quebec and Lower Canada was at first largely a product of translation, and even unilingual newspapers borrowed materials from other languages' (Delisle 2004: 295–6), and the bilingual *Quebec Magazine/ Magasin de Quebec* had been published as long ago as 1792–4. However, and perhaps due to the hardening political attitudes of the 1830s, 'the anglophone female reading public was more receptive than the francophone readership', and Gosselin's attempt to bridge the colony's linguistic divide was an abortive one (Lemire 1992: 181, my translation).[7]

The *Museum* turned out, whatever its editor's aspirations may have been, to be a monolingual magazine with no original content written by French Canadians. However, it does feature a large number of pieces – twenty-seven in total – translated from French. These include poetry, extracts from literary magazines including *Le Corsaire* and *Le Voleur*, and stories from two multi-volume miscellanies, *Paris; ou le Livre des Cent-et-Un* (1831–4) and *Le Salmigondis; Contes des toutes les couleurs* (1832). This is something which genuinely sets it apart from its local contemporaries: no other English-Canadian magazine shows any interest in keeping up with the French literary scene. The impact of Gosselin's identity as a cultural go-between with fluency in both languages is seen, then, not in any connections that she is able to forge between English- and French-Canadian literatures, but in her selection of non-original material; the orientation of her magazine towards Paris as well as London and the United States.

The *Livre des Cent-et-Un* was conceived as a project that would save its publisher, Ladvocat, from bankruptcy, and the 'hundred-and-one' of the title refers to the initial group of authors who signed on to contribute. These included famous or soon-to-be-famous figures like Chateaubriand, Hugo, Lamartine, Sue and Dumas. A selection of stories from the first eight volumes (of an eventual fifteen) were translated into English as *Paris; or, the Book of the Hundred-and-One* in 1833 (Parmentier 2014: 75). Relatively obscure in accounts of French Romanticism today, it was a publishing phenomenon in the early 1830s. As a series of sketches loosely tied together by the broad remit of representing contemporary Parisian life, it was particularly well suited to being extracted and recirculated in the periodical press (Cohen 1995: 229; Parmentier 2014: 80).

The *Museum* publishes translations of three stories from the *Cent-et-Un*, two in the fourth issue and one in the seventh: 'The Black Napoleon' ('Le Napoléon Noir') by Léon Gozlan, 'A Fashionable Milliner's Shop' ('Un Magasin de Modes') by Antoine Fontaney and 'The Commissary of Police' ('Le Commissaire de Police') by Antoine-Louis-Marie Hennequin. What is notable about these translations is that they are not all Gosselin's own: while 'A Fashionable Milliner's Shop' is headed 'From the book of the Hundred and one – Translated for the Museum' (Gosselin 1833b: 221), 'The Black Napoleon', published in the same issue, and 'The Commissary of Police' only have brief attributions to '*Livre des Cent-et-Un*'. This is because the latter two pieces are not original translations from the *Cent-et-Un* itself but reprints from Gosselin's perennial source, the *Athenaeum*, where they appeared on 8 December 1832 and 20 April 1833 ('Paris' 1832; '*Le Livre des Cent-et-Un*' 1833).

Gosselin's translation of Fontaney's 'Un Magasin de Modes: Histoire d'un Capote' differs substantially from the English book edition. In *Paris; or, the Book of the Hundred-And-One* the story's title is 'A Magasin de Modes: The History of a Hat', while Gosselin's is 'A Fashionable Milliner's Shop: The History of a Capote', with a footnote explaining that 'capote' is 'the name of a particular shaped bonnet' (*Paris* 1833: 109; Gosselin 1833b: 221). The book version opens with the line 'It was certainly the prettiest hat in the world', while Gosselin's begins 'Oh! It was the prettiest bonnet in the world', a translation closer in tone to Fontaney's 'Oh! C'était bien le plus joli chapeau du monde' (*Paris* 1833: 109; Gosselin 1833b: 221; Fontaney 1832: 327). It is clear that Gosselin is working here from the French original, and that some of her exposure to this text is mediated by English translations, but not all.

The case of the *Livre des Cent-et-Un* is typical of the complexity of Gosselin's approach to communicating French literature to her readers, and of the interconnectedness of her practices of reprinting and translation. She follows the same pattern with *Le Salmigondis*, a similar collection, reprinting the *Athenaeum*'s translated extracts of three stories, 'Pepita: A Mexican Anecdote', 'The Ring: Anecdote of the Polish War' and 'The Spectre Girl', and then serialising her own translation of a fourth, 'The Red Rose' by Alexandre Dumas. We might see in this the ingenuity of an editor maximising her relatively circumscribed range of sources. She selects French texts which have received notice in London, but also acquires them in the original language and provides her readers with access to additional material which could not be found in a London periodical. This tangling and doubling-back of the routes of reprinting – connecting to the Parisian literary scene through the London press, reading the same text in both direct and indirect translation – further breaks down the distinction between 'original' and 'borrowed' content.

'Grizel Cochrane': A Case Study

The ninth number of the *Museum* features a piece entitled 'Border Tales. Grizel Cochrane. A Tale of Tweedmouth Moor'. Grizel's father is a Scottish nobleman who is imprisoned and sentenced to death in 1685 for rebelling against James II. The death warrant is on its way, but a mysterious hooded figure robs the mail on Tweedmouth Moor just outside the border town of Berwick and steals the warrant. This ploy only serves to delay the sentence; a second warrant is issued, and once again this unknown person commits a daring robbery. This buys enough time for Sir John's friends to lobby for a pardon and save his life, whereupon his anonymous saviour is revealed to have been – his devoted daughter Grizel.

The story, which is unattributed in the *Museum*, is part of the series *Tales of the Borders* by Berwick author and journalist John Mackay Wilson. Wilson became the editor of the *Berwick Advertiser* newspaper in 1832, and beginning on 7 April published occasional 'Border Tales' in the paper's literary column. 'Grizel Cochrane', the seventh tale, appeared on 16 March 1833 (Wilson 1833a: 2). In November 1834, Wilson began to have the tales printed in broadsheet format and to issue them weekly, priced at a penny halfpenny. Detached from their original context in the local newspaper and repackaged into an accessible standalone text, the stories were able to gain an audience far beyond the parts of south-east Scotland and northern England covered by the *Berwick Advertiser*. Indeed, the series took off to such an extent that for most of its lifespan it was carried on by contributors other than Wilson himself, who died in 1835 aged only thirty-one. Broadsheet publication continued until 1840, and new, updated book editions appeared throughout the nineteenth century. This is only one of several ways in which 'Wilson's Tales' (as they are always known, even decades after his death) begin to break from the model of unitary authorship and from the initial place and time of their composition.

'Grizel Cochrane' has an additional route of circulation which separates it from its fellow 'Border Tales' and places it into a rather different literary context. It was included in the 1834 issue of the London literary annual *The Keepsake*, retitled 'Grizel Cochrane. A Historical Fragment' (Wilson 1833c: 224). Another story, 'The Soldier's Return', was published in the *Forget-Me-Not* annual for 1834. Placing selected tales in these bestselling annuals may have paved the way for Wilson's ambitious project of weekly serial publication, giving him confidence in its potential to appeal to a broad readership. Interestingly, when Wilson first introduces his tales to the readers of the *Advertiser* on 7 April 1832, he does invoke annual publication, of a kind, as the first step in his work's dissemination beyond the newspaper:

> [W]e intend giving from time to time a series of original Border Tales, embracing every subject 'from grave to gay, from lively to severe.' And our fair readers in particular, by preserving their papers, will thus have every Christmas an Annual, (the plates and the butterfly binding alone excepted,) we believe we may say without any great egotism, not much inferior in interest to the best of those publications. (Wilson 1832: 2)

The tongue-in-cheek nature of Wilson's remark notwithstanding, it is worth noting that he is imagining a reader for the 'Border Tales' who is also the target audience for annuals and giftbooks; a female reader, in short. And something of this scrapbooking approach does indeed seem to have informed the story's journey to the *Museum*, whose source is neither the annual nor the broadsheet. The story is printed in the *Museum* at a very early date – August 1833 – over a year before the first broadsheets, and probably shortly before the publication of *The Keepsake*, which would have been targeted at the Christmas market. As far as I have been able to determine, 'Grizel Cochrane' appears here before being reprinted anywhere else, and only the *Museum* takes the story directly from the original newspaper: the many later reprintings of the story in British, American, Canadian and Caribbean periodicals are all either from *The Keepsake* or from the broadsheet. 'Grizel Cochrane. A Historical Fragment' is excerpted in the *Morning Chronicle* on 28 December 1833, and this excerpt is later reprinted in the *Southern Patriot* of Charleston, South Carolina, on 22 March 1834. The full *Keepsake* story is reprinted in the Nashville *National Banner* on 1 April 1834 and the Halifax *Weekly Mirror* in September 1835. The *St George Chronicle* of St George's, Grenada, reprints the broadsheet version on 23 January 1836, as do the Quebec City *Literary Transcript* (23 June 1838) and Toronto *Cabinet of Literature* (November 1838). The *Baltimore Literary Monument* for June 1839 reprints the broadsheet version minus the final paragraph about Grizel's Berwickshire descendants, and this abridgement is reprinted in the *Connecticut Courant* on 13 July. A French translation is published in Quebec City's *Le Fantasque* on 4 August 1842. This also lacks the concluding paragraph, suggesting the translation was made from one of these recent American reprints.

How and why, then, does the story find its way to *The Montreal Museum* so early? In the table of contents to volume 1 of the *Museum* we find the following: 'Grizel Cochrane, a tale of Tweedmouth, Communicated' (Gosselin 1832a). The 'communicated' descriptor is applied to pieces that reached the editor through her personal networks (rather than from the periodical press) but were not direct author submissions. This means that a copy of the *Berwick Advertiser* was either sent to Gosselin by a correspondent living in the area of the paper's circulation, or was sent from that region to some other resident of Lower Canada who subsequently passed it on to Gosselin. We know that it was the newspaper itself – or at least, its literary column – that was 'communicated' and not just a manuscript copy of this particular story, because Gosselin also reprints the religious poem that appears directly above 'Grizel Cochrane' in the 16 March *Berwick Advertiser*, 'The Alpine Horn' by James Everett, a poet and bookseller from Alnwick in Northumberland (Everett 1833: 2). The poem is placed immediately after 'Grizel Cochrane' in the ninth issue of *The Montreal Museum*, but their common origin is obscured in the table of contents, where the entry for 'The Alpine Horn' does not inform the reader of its status as a 'communicated' item; it lists only the title with no further information about the poem's provenance (Gosselin 1832a).

Having disentangled the complicated lineage of 'Grizel Cochrane' as it makes it way from a newspaper on the Anglo-Scottish border to a colonial periodical, London literary annual and locally printed broadsheet, the question remains: what meaning, and what literary effect, is produced when it is transplanted from the Berwick newspaper to the Montreal women's magazine? The way in which Wilson concludes his story is interesting in this respect: 'Grizel Cochrane whose heroism and noble affection we have here hurriedly and imperfectly sketched, was the grandmother of the late Sir John Stuart of Allanbank, and great great grandmother of Mr Coutts, the celebrated banker' (Wilson 1833a: 2). (*The Montreal Museum* reads 'great grandmother' but this does not match any other version of the story and is presumably a simple transcription error.) The only significant alterations made to the story in the *Keepsake* version are to clarify for this new, less geographically circumscribed audience that Allanbank is 'in Berwickshire' and to change the spelling of 'Stuart' to the more anglicised 'Stewart' (Wilson 1833c: 230). The original newspaper version of Grizel Cochrane's story derives its interest largely from its local associations: it takes place in and around Berwick, and readers are expected to recognise the prominent people named as Grizel's descendants. When it moves into the London annual, its provinciality is to some degree smoothed away. These regional trappings are retained, however, in the *Museum*, for readers thousands of miles away from such Border scenes, living along some very different borders: the border with the United States, and also the linguistic and cultural divides between anglophone and francophone residents of Lower Canada.

So, does Gosselin's selection of 'Grizel Cochrane' for her magazine indicate an assumption that her colonial readers will assimilate such detail without being alienated; that they too feel interpellated by Berwickshire minutiae? One straightforward answer to this question would be that it has been chosen for its focus on exemplary feminine conduct, and its setting is secondary. It is certainly the case that this early reprinting comes at the beginning of a process of reframing Grizel Cochrane as a role model for young women rather than a figure from Borders history, which will culminate in retellings of the story for young readers at the end of the century, in works like Elia Wilkinson Peattie's 'Grizel Cochrane's Ride' (1887) and Evelyn Everett-Green's

True Stories of Girl Heroines (1901). But because the *Museum*'s version of the tale is not a reworking but a reprinting, these markers of Border locality remain, creating curious, disjunctive effects which demand interpretation. The textual connection between *The Montreal Museum* and the *Berwick Advertiser*, once excavated, brings certain parallels and affinities to the fore: it invites us to recognise the extent to which Gosselin's goals and challenges as a colonial editor in fact resemble those of an editor in the British provinces, who shares the experience of being at a distance (geographical but also cultural) from the metropolis, of watching hopefully for the signs of a 'growing taste for literature' in the neighbourhood (Gosselin 1833c: 255). The study of reprinting has the potential to uncover relationships which an exclusive focus on a periodical's original material cannot make visible, transnational and regional connections that greatly complicate the picture of a linear, unidirectional movement of literary influence and literary content from metropole to colony.

Notes

Thank you to Andrew Ayre of the Wilson's Tales Project for his help in tracing the publication history of 'Grizel Cochrane', and also to Linda Bankier, Carol Pringle and Beth Elliott from Northumberland Archives. Digitised copies of *The Montreal Museum* were accessed in the Canadian Research Knowledge Network's Canadiana collection.

1. In the tenth issue Gosselin 'considers it her duty to inform the public that she is the sole Editor and proprietor of this journal, Miss T. having had no connection with it since the publication of the second number' (Gosselin 1833f: 642). Gosselin's husband died in 1842 and she is mentioned in the *Montreal Transcript* as the proprietor of a Montreal boarding house in 1850 (MacDonald 1992: 148).
2. 'Le contenu, essentiellement littéraire, est reparti à peu près également entre les inédits canadiens et les textes empruntés à d'autres revues.'
3. 'Mode of Travelling in Kamtschatka' appears in two books by 'Rev. J. Goldsmith', the pseudonym of Richard Phillips: *A General View of the Manners, Customs and Curiosities of Nations* (1810) and *A Geographical View of the World: Embracing the Manners, Customs, and Pursuits of Every Nation* (1826). 'Filial Affection of the Moors' is extracted from a piece called 'A Ramble with the Travellers' in the *Monthly Magazine* ([W.] 1832). This paragraph-length anecdote circulated widely in the American press.
4. The 'Sketch' portion is reprinted from Hazlitt 1825.
5. *The Canadian Magazine and Literary Repository* (1823–5) was edited first by David Chisholme and then by A. J. Christie, both Scots; Chisholme left in 1824 to edit the rival *Canadian Review and Literary and Historical Journal* (1824–6). *The Scribbler* (1821–7) was helmed by the English-born Samuel Hull Wilcocke, whose wife, Ann Lewis, also played a major role in distributing and composing content for the magazine. The true extent and nature of her involvement is difficult to determine, as Wilcocke was the periodical's public face, but the *Dictionary of Canadian Biography* entry for her husband represents her as a shadowy yet vital creative collaborator (Klinck 2003). This raises the possibility that even the path-breaking Gosselin was not the very first woman to take a leading part in magazine publishing in the Canadas, though she remains the first female editor and proprietor in her own right.
6. '[L]a fondatrice, Mary Graddon Gosselin, attribue l'absence au Canada de femmes de lettres et de publications comme la sienne à "l'introduction de discussions politiques."'
7. '[L]e public lecteur féminin anglophone est plus réceptif que le lectorat francophone.'

Bibliography

Batchelor, Jennie (2011), '"Connections, which are of service . . . in a more advanced age": *The Lady's Magazine*, community, and women's literary histories', *Tulsa Studies in Women's Literature*, 30.2, 245–67.

Bayley, Diana (1833), 'The Young Soldier', *Montreal Museum*, 1.4, 201–11.

Bédard, Mylène (2016), *Écrire en temps d'insurrections: Pratiques épistolaires et usages de la presse chez les femmes patriotes (1830–1840)*, Montreal: Presses de l'Université de Montréal.

Beetham, Margaret (1996), *A Magazine of Her Own? Domesticity and Desire in the Woman's Magazine, 1800–1914*, London: Routledge.

Bowness, Suzanne (2012), 'In their own words: Prefaces and other sites of editorial interaction in nineteenth-century Canadian magazines', unpublished PhD thesis, University of Ottawa.

'Catching Turtles on the Coast of Cuba' (1832), *Penny Magazine of the Society for the Diffusion of Useful Knowledge*, 35, 20 October, 281–2.

Cohen, Margaret (1995), 'Panoramic literature and the invention of everyday genres', in Leo Charney and Vanessa R. Schwartz (eds), *Cinema and the Invention of Modern Life*, Berkeley: University of California Press, 227–52.

Delisle, Jean (2004), 'Translation', in Patricia Lockhart Fleming, Gilles Gallichan and Yvan Lamonde (eds), *History of the Book in Canada, Volume 1: Beginnings to 1840*, Toronto: University of Toronto Press, 292–6.

DeLucia, JoEllen (2018), 'Travel writing and mediation in the *Lady's Magazine*: Charting "the meridian of female reading"', in Jennie Batchelor and Manushag N. Powell (eds), *Women's Periodicals and Print Culture in Britain, 1690s–1820s*, Edinburgh: Edinburgh University Press, 205–16.

Everett, James (1833), 'The Alpine Horn', *Berwick Advertiser*, 16 March, 2.

Everett-Green, Evelyn (1901), 'Grizel Cochrane', *True Stories of Girl Heroines*, New York: E. P. Dutton & Co., 55–71.

Fontaney, Antoine (1832), 'Un Magasin de Modes: Histoire d'un Capote', *Paris; ou le Livre des Cent-et-Un*, vol. 7, 327–52.

Gerson, Carole (2010), *Canadian Women in Print, 1750–1918*, Waterloo, ON: Wilfrid Laurier University Press.

Goldsmith, Rev. J. (1810), *A General View of the Manners, Customs and Curiosities of Nations*, Philadelphia: Johnson & Warner.

——— (1826), *A Geographical View of the World: Embracing the Manners, Customs, and Pursuits of Every Nation*, New York: Hopkins & Reed.

Gosselin, Mary Graddon (1832a), 'Contents', *The Montreal Museum*, 1, n.p.

——— (1832b), 'Introduction', *The Montreal Museum*, 1.1, 1–3.

——— (1832c), '[We notice with regret. . .]', *The Montreal Museum*, 1.1, 15.

——— (1832d), 'To Correspondents', *The Montreal Museum*, 1.1, 63–4.

——— (1833a), 'To Readers, and Correspondents', *The Montreal Museum*, 1.2, 127–8.

——— (1833b), 'A Fashionable Milliner's Shop: The History of a Capote', *The Montreal Museum*, 1.4, 221–33.

——— (1833c), 'Montreal Museum', *The Montreal Museum*, 1.4, 255–6.

——— (1833d), 'Life &c. of Pestalozzi', *The Montreal Museum*, 1.6, 374–83.

——— (1833e), 'Montreal Museum', *The Montreal Museum*, 1.6, 388.

——— (1833f), 'Montreal Museum', *The Montreal Museum*, 1.10, 642.

——— (1833g), ['Since the last number. . .'], *The Montreal Museum*, 1.11, 705–6.

Greenbank, Thomas K. (1833), *Greenbank's Periodical Library*, vol. 2, Philadelphia: T. K. Greenbank.

[H, Francis] (1833), 'Sketches of an Idle Moment', *The Montreal Museum*, 1.2, 99–102.

Hammill, Faye, and Hannah McGregor (2018), 'Bundling, reprinting, and reframing: Serial practices across borders', *Journal of Modern Periodical Studies*, 9.1, 76–100.

Hazlitt, William (1825), *The Spirit of the Age; or, Contemporary Portraits*, London: Colburn.

Klinck, Carl (2003), 'Wilcocke, Samuel Hull', *Dictionary of Canadian Biography*, vol. 6, University of Toronto/Université Laval, http://www.biographi.ca/en/bio/wilcocke_samuel_hull_6E.html (accessed 25 July 2022).

Lemire, Maurice, et al. (1992), *La Vie Littéraire au Québec, Vol. 2, 1806–1839: Le projet national des Canadiens*, Sainte-Foy, QC: Presses de l'Université Laval.

'*Le Livre des Cent-et-Un*. Vol. X.' (1833), *Athenaeum*, 286, 245–7.

MacDonald, Mary Lu (1992), '*The Montreal Museum*, 1832–1834: The presence and absence of literary women', in Claudine Potvin and Janice Williamson (eds), *Women's Writing and the Literary Institution/L'écriture au féminin et l'institution littéraire*, Edmonton: Research Institute for Comparative Literature, 139–50.

McGill, Meredith (2003), *American Literature and the Culture of Reprinting, 1834–1853*, Philadelphia: University of Pennsylvania Press.

'Newest Fashions for October 1832: Evening Dresses' [illustration] (1832), *World of Fashion, and Continental Feuilletons*, 9.103, n.p.

'Newest Fashions for October 1832: Walking Dresses' [illustration] (1832), *World of Fashion, and Continental Feuilletons* 9.103, n.p.

Owen, Captain W. F. W. (1833), *Narrative of Voyages to explore the shores of Africa, Arabia, and Madagascar*, London: Bentley.

'Paris; or, The Book of the Hundred-and-One' (1832), *Athenaeum*, 267, 790–2.

Paris; or, the Book of the Hundred-and-One, in Three Volumes (1833), London: Whittaker, Treacher & Co.

Parmentier, Marie (2014), 'Commerce et littérature: Les processus de légitimation dans *Paris ou Le Livre des Cent-et-un*', *Romantisme*, 165, 75–86.

Peattie, Elia Wilkinson (1887), 'Grizel Cochrane's Ride', *St Nicholas Magazine*, 14, 271–8.

'The Queen of the Belgians in her Wedding Dress' [illustration] (1832), *Court Magazine and Belle Assemblée*, 1.3, n.p.

Rieley, Honor (2017), '"Every Heart North of the Tweed": Placing Canadian magazines of the 1820s and 1830s', *Studies in Canadian Literature*, 42.1, 130–53.

Vincent, Thomas Brewer, Sandra Alston and Eli MacLaren (2004), 'Magazines in English', in Patricia Lockhart Fleming, Gilles Gallichan and Yvan Lamonde (eds), *History of the Book in Canada, Volume 1: Beginnings to 1840*, Toronto: University of Toronto Press, 240–9.

[W.] (1832), 'A Ramble with the Travellers', *Monthly Magazine*, 13.74, 138–42.

Wilson, John Mackay (1832), 'Border Tales – By the Editor. No. 1', *Berwick Advertiser*, 7 April, 2.

—— (1833a), 'Border Tales – By the Editor. Grizel Cochrane; A Tale of Tweedmouth Moor', *Berwick Advertiser*, 16 March, 2.

—— (1833b), 'Border Tales. Grizel Cochrane. A Tale of Tweedmouth Moor', *The Montreal Museum*, 1.9, 547–53.

—— (1833c), 'Grizel Cochrane. A Historical Fragment', in Frederic Mansel Reynolds (ed.), *The Keepsake for 1834*, London: Longman, Rees, Orme, Brown, Green & Longman, 224–30.

—— (1834), 'Grizel Cochrane. A Tale of Tweedmouth Moor', *Wilson's Historical, Traditionary, and Imaginative Tales of the Borders*, No. 2, 15 November, 15–16.

Wordsworth, William (1833), 'Goody Blake and Harry Gill. A True Story', *The Montreal Museum*, 1.11, 643–6.

12

THE BIRTH OF THE AUSTRALIAN WOMEN'S MAGAZINE: THE *NEW IDEA*, 1902–11

Michelle J. Smith

THE *NEW IDEA: A Women's Home Journal for Australasia* was first published in Melbourne in 1902 by Thomas Shaw Fitchett as a monthly magazine. Remarkably, it is still published today, among a declining number of Australian print magazines, making it the longest-running women's magazine in the country. While there had been several magazines for women published in Australia since the 1880s, including the *Australian Woman's Magazine and Domestic Journal* (1882–4), *Woman's World: An Australian Magazine of Literature and Art* (1886–7), *The Dawn: A Journal for Australian Women* (1888–1905) and the *Parthenon* (1889–92), many were short-lived and had a limited circulation by comparison. Helena Studdert observes that many of these 'early attempts to address the social and political affairs of women . . . [w]ere soon challenged by the emerging general women's (or service) magazine' (Studdert 2001: 277). The feminist-oriented *Dawn*, edited by Louisa Lawson, for example, was sufficiently successful to enjoy a seventeen-year print run and attract 7,000 subscribers after two years of publication. In contrast, with its broader outlook, the *New Idea*, according to Fitchett, had reached a circulation of 40,000 after its first two years of publication, rising to 250,000 by 1908, meaning that at least one in ten Australian women bought the magazine at this time (Tucker 1974: 374, 376). Given the comparative popularity and long-standing appeal of the *New Idea*, it is surprising that it has not been the focus of any scholarly publications to date.[1] In this chapter, I consider the magazine's formative years, from its debut one year after Australia's Federation to its adoption of the title *Everylady's Journal* in 1911,[2] in order to examine how the *New Idea* inflected the typical contents of British and American women's magazines with a distinctive focus on Australian identity and femininity.

Maya V. Tucker suggests that Australian women's magazines published from the first decade of the twentieth century 'show an adherence to English tradition and made little attempt to define women's place in the now federated Australian nation' (Tucker 1974: 324). Serials and short stories, for instance, were rarely set in Australia, and Australian writers were eschewed for popular British and American authors (Tucker 1974: 324). The *New Idea* stands in marked contrast to other Australian women's magazines of the period for its deep interest in the place of women within the nation and regular publication of Australian women writers. In order to read the magazine's attempts to construct a sense of the life of Australian women in particular, I adopt the idea of the 'geographical imaginary'. This term has been applied by Victoria Kuttainen, Susann Liebach and Sarah Galletly in their study of Australian interwar magazines to describe how 'segments of culture come to form collective identities' (Kuttainen et al. 2018: 39), as distinct from the national 'imagined communities' described by Benedict Anderson. Derived from the work of geographer Michael John Watts, geographical imaginaries 'project fantasies of wish-fulfilment on the outer world in ways that both shape and reflect the self-images of the local population' (Kuttainen et al. 2018: 272). The concept of the 'wish image' invoked by Watts stems from Walter Benjamin's *Arcades Project* and refers to a collective dream or desire. In the case of the *New Idea*, a readership of middle-class women constitutes a segment of Australian culture, and the magazine seeks – often with the contribution of readers – to construct a shared, frequently idealised vision of what being an Australian woman entails, and to invite the reader to see herself in those terms. The key areas in which this shaping and reflection of the Australian woman is evident, and which I will discuss in this chapter, are the magazine's fiction and non-fiction by amateur and professional Australian writers, profiles and investigative pieces about the lives of Australian women of all classes, and the opportunities it provided for ordinary women and community leaders to mobilise in response to federal voting rights being extended to women aged over twenty-one via the Commonwealth Franchise Act in 1902.

The Birth of the *New Idea* and the Influence of the Anglo-American Women's Magazine

The *New Idea* was initially sold for three pence per issue, or three shillings for an annual subscription. Intriguingly, the magazine was also initially advertised as being available in a more expensive 'Drawing Room Edition' at six pence 'for the convenience of those women who attach special importance to paper with a surface like silk, and printing like photography' ('To Our Readers' 1902: 1). The magazine's original masthead depicted three women – who bear a resemblance to the modern Gibson Girl – sharing the experience of reading a giant, book-like issue of the *New Idea* (see Figure 12.1). The women, joined in their reading experience, symbolise the work of the magazine in uniting the women of Australia and New Zealand with information about home, the nation and the world. The masthead went through annual updates from 1908 to 1910, with the first change in 1908 broadening the emphasis from the reading of the magazine alone. The three women united by reading the same copy of the *New Idea* are replaced by two women on either side of the title, only one of whom reads the magazine, while the other three are engaged in sewing tasks. This masthead is soon replaced in 1909 by one that features only two women, one of whom is working with clothes, while the other reads a book (see Figure 12.2). The graphics surrounding the women include magazines, books and spools of thread, continuing the dual emphasis on reading and homemaking that had been introduced in 1908. The words 'home journal' and 'Australasia' are removed in 1909, with the more precise designation of 'Australian and New Zealand women' as comprising the magazine's readership. While there is one strand of scholarly thought that suggests that *The Dawn*'s subtitle change from 'A Journal for Australian Women' to 'A Journal for the Household' was intended to signal the inclusion of male readers, Fitchett devised an equivalent magazine to the *New Idea* for men in 1904, entitled *Life*, which meant that many households bought both magazines (Tucker 1974: 374).[3] By 1910, the *New Idea* masthead removes the woman readers, who are replaced by a

Figure 12.1 The *New Idea*, 1 August 1902, masthead. Courtesy of the author.

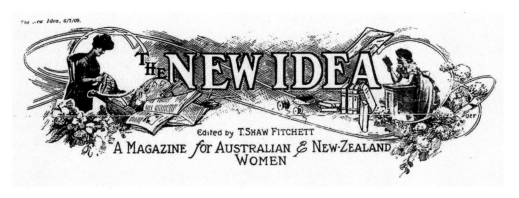

Figure 12.2 The *New Idea*, 6 July 1909, masthead. Courtesy of the author.

floral graphic, signalling the magazine's changing outlook, which would come to be less preoccupied with mapping the Australian geographical imaginary.

In its regular features, the *New Idea* resembled most Anglo-American women's magazines, with columns about society news, housekeeping, child rearing, health and beauty, dress, humour, short and serial fiction, and competitions. Like the earlier Australian magazine *The Dawn*, housework was understood as a central aspect of women's lives with importance for her and her family, as was evident in the 'Good Housekeeping' column in the *New Idea*'s first issue: 'Good housekeeping to-day is a science. It should be studied with as much care as any other profession. It should be neither despised, not looked upon as an incident, for upon it depend the health and well-being of the family' ('Good Housekeeping' 1902: 13). The two features that

Fitchett highlighted in an address to readers in the debut issue as being original were the paper patterns and prize competitions 'open to every woman and child' which held the possibility of financial reward ('To Our Readers' 1902: 1). He claimed to 'introduce . . . to Australasia, through the medium of "The New Idea," . . . the finest paper patterns in the world', which were sold to subscribers for nine pence ('To Our Readers' 1902: 1). Several major American women's magazines launched in the late nineteenth century, including the *Delineator* (1875), *McCall's* (1897) and *Pictorial Review* (1899), were developed to promote and sell paper clothing patterns (Zuckerman 1998: 12, 16). The *New Idea*, in contrast, was not intended as a promotional tool for pattern sales and had a lesser focus on fashions than these American titles. From 1903, the *New Idea*, like many British girls' and women's magazines, offered one free pattern per month, and from 1906 it included three free patterns, which contributed to its popularity among the many women who engaged in dressmaking at home (Tucker 1974: 372, 378).

Nevertheless, the influence of both American and British publications on the *New Idea* was critical to its success. As Studdert notes, 'successful marketing and viable publication' of an Australian women's magazine was difficult prior to the Second World War given that publishers were competing with these international titles (Studdert 2001: 276). Modelling the general Australian women's magazine 'on the successful format of its American equivalent' was crucial in their evolution from the small-scale productions that emerged in the 1880s and 1890s (Studdert 2001: 276). Fitchett was uniquely positioned to borrow not only ideas but specific content from American magazines. He was the Melbourne distributing agent for several American periodicals, such as *McClure's Magazine*, *Saturday Evening Post*, *Harper's Bazaar* and *McCall's*, which gave him the ability to reproduce their content first in Australia (Tucker 1974: 333). While, as a result, a significant proportion of the fiction published in the magazine was American, the *New Idea* was a surprisingly fertile ground for early Australian women writers, ensuring that the appeal of the imported format and content was heavily complemented by an emerging picture of Australian women's opinions, lives and creative outputs. Mary Gilmore, for example, published several series and poems between 1904 and 1908, and Katharine Susannah Prichard, who won the 'Love Story Competition' in 1903 with 'Bush Fires!', subsequently published a series about her time as a governess in the outback ('A City Girl in Central Australia' in 1906) and conducted interviews with Australian, English and European women resident in England (Tucker 1974: 337).[4] While the magazine did publish these significant women writers and engaged seriously with 'feminist issues', as Ken Gelder and Rachael Weaver point out in *The Colonial Journals and the Emergence of Australian Literary Culture*, the magazine was 'less radical' than the likes of *The Dawn*, and 'tied more to popular literary forms' such as the ghost story and the romance (Gelder and Weaver 2014: 315).

One of the most popular, if least respected, forms of fiction is children's literature, and the *New Idea*'s children's page published the work of several key figures in the genre, such as Ethel Turner, as well as a noteworthy number of Australian fairy tales that appeared first in the magazine. This was an especially important development given that there were effectively no colonial Australian children's periodicals owing to the small market and the importation of popular British titles such as the *Boys' Own Paper* and *Girls' Own Paper*. Ida Rentoul Outhwaite (publishing as Ida S. Rentoul) published her first illustrations as a sixteen-year-old to accompany 'The Fairies of Fern

Gully', a story written by her sister Anne Rattray Rentoul (under the pseudonym of 'Billabong') in the August 1903 issue. The next four issues of the magazine carried three more 'Australian fairy stories' by the Rentoul sisters, including 'The Wind-Maiden and the Bunny Boys', 'How Music Came to Australia' and 'Cinderella Retold for Australians' (in two parts).[5] While the latter story included little that made it distinctly Australian, the other stories made significant attempts to transport European fairy-tale models to bushland settings featuring native animals. A further three 'New Australian Fairy Tales' were published in 1905, marking an ongoing contribution to the shaping of localised fantasy fiction intended for the children of the *New Idea*'s readers.

Women writers and journalists were therefore central to the picture of Australian womanhood formulated within the magazine in its early years. In addition, Fitchett invited women to mould the *New Idea* through open requests for reader feedback, as well as consideration of their writing for publication. He described it as a 'wide-open magazine', in terms of being 'wide open to them [readers], their views, their perplexities, their questions, their criticism, their praise, their manuscripts' ('To Our Readers' 1902: 3–4). Prize and writing competitions were the primary way through which women readers contributed to the magazine and its vision of ideal femininity, and they often offered lucrative cash rewards. The first issue announced ten prize competitions. The first of these required the submission of suggestions for a future prize competition, signalling Fitchett's active attempts to obtain reader feedback and input into the direction of the magazine. The most prominent competition in the debut issue was the 'Good Taste' competition, which engaged fifteen Australian and New Zealand drapery firms to create dress designs that were displayed to readers in full-page photographs of women modelling the outfits. The first batch of designs were published along with the competition announcement, which explained that its object was 'testing the judgement of the women of Australasia on the absorbing question of perfection in dress' ('Good Taste' 1902: 32). Women readers were asked to rank the designs, and these responses would be collated to form a 'majority list', with the reader who came closest to matching the opinion of most readers being declared the winner ('Good Taste' 1902: 32). What is valued here is the collective judgement of the Australasian woman reader, and the woman who best reflects the predominant view of Australian women is rewarded. This competition was also significant because of the visibility it provided for Australian and New Zealand women's taste and for local fashion. Moreover, it signalled Fitchett's intent to actively involve, and appeal to, New Zealand readers, given that six New Zealand drapers were included in the competition out of the total of fifteen. Nevertheless, the content and coverage of the magazine was overwhelmingly Australian, particularly in its profiles of Australian women from all walks of life, from the factory worker to the international celebrity.

Catering to the 'Needs of the Australian Home and its Mistress'

Women's magazines oriented towards the subjects of home and fashion in this period tended to be reasonably consistent in their features and topical coverage, whether published in Britain, the United States, or in colonial contexts. While it was not unusual for British and American women's magazines to publish occasional articles on women's life in other countries, and thereby to include some reflection on nationality, in its early years of publication the *New Idea* was distinctively preoccupied with Australian identity and femininity. The *New Idea* was regularly praised in major and regional newspapers for this Australian focus. In response to the inaugural issue of the magazine, the *Canowindra Star and Woodstock Recorder* noted that the *New Idea* catered to a 'long felt want in Australia' for a women's magazine ('The New Idea' 1902: 2). The newspaper saw the magazine's locally produced content as striking the right balance in its provision of sensible leisure-time reading that did not transgress traditional feminine expectations:

> Its matter may not satisfy the blue stocking or the lady of the mannish tendencies; yet it is entirely free from the stupid sensationalism of the 'Lord-and-Milkmaid' order which permeates the flood of cheap English and American journals which pour, each week, into the Commonwealth and New Zealand. ('The New Idea' 1902: 2)

Through the first decade of the twentieth century, newspapers continued to laud the *New Idea* for its local content and literature. In 1904, *The Age* in Queanbeyan was 'glad to note that the Australasian tone in [*sic*] being maintained' ('The "New Idea"' 1904: 3). After the magazine expanded and increased its production values in the years that followed, one newspaper described it as becoming 'more thoroughly Australasian with each step of its progress', fostered by the quality writing and photography it published: 'In the enlarged issues before us are some of the finest little stories, sketches, pictures, and verses that any magazine has produced on this side of the world' ('The New Idea' 1908: 4). Indeed, as I noted earlier, the *New Idea* provided a space for the professional and paid publication of Australian women writers in a variety of genres when other opportunities were limited.

In the opening address to readers in the inaugural issue, Fitchett promised the magazine would be the first to be 'devoted exclusively to the needs of the Australian home and its mistress' ('To Our Readers' 1902: 1). This was evident on a small scale in the references made in articles to the distinct qualities of Australian girls and women, such as the description of 'nearly all Australian girls' as 'practical' in an article about 'Society Fads' ('Society Fads' 1902: 14). It was also visible in efforts to tailor advertisements for popular British products to the local audience, as in advertisements for Koko for the Hair. In an advertisement in the debut issue, celebrity endorsement is called upon, with English writer Eliza Lynn Linton's testimonial joined by the words of English stage performer Grace Palotta, whose words of praise for the hair tonic were obtained at Sydney's Theatre Royal in June of that year ('Advertisement: Koko' 1902: 55). There were also obvious practical differences between clothing the body and keeping a home in the Australian climate as compared with Britain, opening up room for a women's magazine that explicitly addressed these variations. An article on 'Christmas Cookery for Our Climate', for example, provided guidance on how to negotiate English expectations with the practicalities of Australian life, including high temperatures in summer. Those who remained 'in touch with the Old World' and who felt 'something of sentiment' would not welcome '[a] change that was too drastic' ('Christmas Cookery' 1902: 340). The suggestions for recipes therefore make minor adjustments to dishes that were old favourites, acknowledging that some British traditions, such as roast meat and hot plum puddings, would never be relinquished.

One of the most frequent and detailed ways in which the magazine helped to construct a sense of Australian identity was through portraits of Australian women, particularly notable figures in the community and celebrities. Occasional articles featured exceptional Australian sportswomen, such as swimming champion Annette Kellerman. Opera singer Nellie Melba was the subject of several articles, some of which included interviews at her home, a 'genre' that Margaret Beetham notes was used extensively in British 'ladies' papers' as 'a development of that well-established genre, the "illustrated life of a notable woman"' (Beetham 1996: 95). 'A Chat about Melba' briefly refers to the singer's appearances in Paris and London and the lucrative fees that she received, as well as the enthusiastic response of crowds in Melbourne on her return. The remainder of the article is concerned with describing Melba's elegant, urban femininity, both at home and abroad. In describing Melba's attendance at her school reunion at the Presbyterian Ladies' College, emphasis is placed on her bouquet, gown and hat, with the stylishness of her 'snuff-coloured voile' dress recounted in detail ('A Chat' 1902: 203). Though she spent her girlhood in small Australian towns, her 'luxurious tastes in the equipment of her beautiful residence in 30 Great Cumberland Place, London' link the local with the old world abroad, suggesting that beautiful and lavish objects – for both the home and the body – belong in Australia too. Melba's Grand Salon has reportedly been copied from the Grand Palace at Versailles, her bed belonged to the Dauphin of France, and the home exudes 'Oriental magnificence and richness' that awes the visitor ('A Chat' 1902: 203). The following month, in November 1902, 'Melba at Home and Abroad' promises to provide a perspective on Melba's life at her temporary Melbourne home 'Myoora', located in the wealthy suburb of Toorak. However, it proves to be an extended interview with her secretary Miss Ida Gill, who clarifies that Melba rarely grants interviews and has only personally spoken with two major Australian newspapers, the *Argus* and the *Age*. Gill nevertheless provides the reader with a vicarious glimpse inside Melba's temporary home, and the way in which her professional life is conducted both within Australia and overseas via her personal assistants. The article combines both photographs of Melba on stage – 'In Opera', 'In Evening Dress' and 'In Concert Attire' – and photographs of the buildings and grounds of 'Myoora', which cements the internationalised glamour of Melba's career within the wealthy Melbourne suburbs (Somerset 1902: 273).

The 'Noted Australasian Women at Home' series provided profiles of prominent, well-heeled women including Lady Audrey Tennyson (wife of Australia's second Governor-General) and author Ethel Turner, which provided an opportunity to explore the influence of notable women in the home and community. While the article on Turner clarifies that she 'is not, strictly speaking, an Australian. She is English', she becomes an 'Australasian woman' through the series title, and by virtue of her fiction and children. Her most popular and enduring novel *Seven Little Australians* (1899) cements Turner as the creator of recognisably Australian childhood in fiction, and its title is used to caption a full page of photographs of her children, Jean and Adrian, as 'Ethel Turner's Two Little Australians' (Hampshire 1903: 706, 707). While the exclusive photographs of Turner and her children at her suburban Sydney home 'Avenel' provide a glimpse into her domestic life, the profile largely concentrates on the history of her writing career from its humble beginnings. She talks candidly about Australia being a challenging environment for writers, and there being 'more room in England once you can get a hearing there', which is why she sends all her stories 'to the English magazines' (Hampshire 1903: 709). As the editor of the children's column in the *Australian Town and Country Journal*, Turner received many submissions from budding young Australian writers, and found 'a remarkable tendency among Australian girls to write' (Hampshire 1903: 709). However, she critiques them for writing about 'English baronial halls, lords, and earls', encouraging them to write 'with a distinctly Australian flavour' (Hampshire 1903: 709). This is, of course, the approach she adopted in her own fiction, and clearly Fitchett saw the value in seizing the opportunity to gain exclusive rights to the work of one of the country's most popular children's authors. By the August issue of the same year, her serial 'A White Roof Tree' (later published as a novel) commenced in the *New Idea*, which led Fitchett to describe the issue as the 'most Australian one yet printed' (Fitchett 1903: 153).

Profiles of upper-class and celebrity women offered readers wish-fulfilment and helped to formulate a vision of Australian women as sophisticated, refined, and capable of making contributions to national and international life. Nevertheless, the magazine made a point of documenting the lives of all classes of (white) Australian women. The working-class girl or woman is not presumed to be a reader of the *New Idea*, but the desire to define, understand and empathise with the working-class Australian woman was evident in the magazine's attempts to reflect Australian femininity as a collective, in all its manifestations. An ongoing investigative series published throughout 1903, 'The Women Who Toil. Our Australasian Factory Workers', included lengthy articles on workers at a tobacco factory, a clothing factory, a waterproof factory, and about the 'telephone girl'. The series was intended 'to give readers some true pictures of the life and work of thousands of their sisters' through the 'actual experiences of a woman-journalist who went into the factories, worked side by side with the girls, and came back with scarred hands, hardened muscles – and facts' (Davis 1903: 527). In the second article in the series, Helen Davis enters the areas where factory girls live and work, delivering extensive praise for the public benefit that they provide without recognition or appreciation. It was common for factory girls to be the subject of condemnation in British girls' and women's periodicals, particularly because of how they spent their unsupervised leisure time in public places. A *Girl's Own Paper* article from 1895, for example, notes that for many people the factory girl was 'something terrible; a rough, wild creature, scarcely to be considered human' (Canney 1895: 221).

In contrast, an egalitarian attitude towards the working-class girl is evident in the *New Idea*, as the series expressly attempts to value her contribution through her labour. Davis cautions the reader not to judge this entire class of girls on the basis of select individuals: 'The very fact that so many are battling in it with the hardest conditions that can be laid on them, of never-ceasing and sometimes ill-paid toil, should be sufficient evidence that the opprobrium so heedlessly meted out is not altogether deserved' (Davis 1903: 527). Davis mediates the usual class-based judgements of the factory girl by not only acknowledging that the work the girl performs is 'much to her profit and little to their own', but also asserting that she is not innately bad, but that any evil has 'grown up beside her' in the conditions in which she lives and works (Davis 1903: 527). She is also proud to make a distinction between the British history of workers living in misery and poverty, as depicted in Thomas Hood's poem 'Song of the Shirt' (1843), and the impossibility of 'such grinding of soul and body in the mills of commerce' occurring within Australia (Davis 1903: 527). While the factory girl may live from cradle to grave in the poorly paid world of industry, and may be discarded if she cannot maintain the standards required by her employer, the absolute worst of conditions found in Britain are avoided. While the voices of actual working-class girl and woman readers are scarce in the *New Idea*, not least because of the practical limitations on their leisure time and income, the geographical imaginary forged in the magazine is one that maps the working-class Australian woman within the urban environment, and which encourages the reader to understand her place in supporting their own comfortable existence and family life.

Defining the Australian Woman and her Social Role

Occasional short pieces on the nature of the Australian girl and woman formed a cumulative definition of their qualities and proposed areas in which they might 'improve' in order to fulfil an aspirational feminine ideal, as the process of defining and moulding the unique qualities of Australian femininity became more pronounced in the post-Federation years. A letter to the editor on 'The Australian Girl' in 1903 attempts to provide a balanced perspective on the 'southern transplanted Anglo-Saxon maid' (Wu-Wu 1903: 20). 'Wu-Wu' finds that 'capable and smart qualities' of the Australian girl become evident during the financial crisis of 1890 in which 'many of our girls who had hitherto led almost butterfly lives came boldly to the front, and helped to weather the storm; and in not a few cases it was the bright spirit and energy of these girls which succeeded in reinstating their parents in something like their former position' (Wu-Wu 1903: 20). While she may formerly have been preoccupied with her appearance and social events, Wu-Wu is impressed by the resourcefulness of the Australian girl when tested. The author also praises the Australian girl's devotion to education, which promises a future in which Australian women will 'be able to hold their own with those of other and older countries', aligning with the *New Idea*'s repeated emphasis on the ways in which they might contribute to the Commonwealth (Wu-Wu 1903: 20). We do not know the gender of Wu-Wu, but the letter writer associates the Australian girl with some tactless behaviours such as a lack of tenderness and empathy, as well as the use of 'hoydenish laugh' and 'slangy phrase' (Wu-Wu 1903: 20). Wu-Wu proposes a model to which Australian girls should aspire, which would combine their identifiable traits of '[p]luck, brightness, and good temper' with the '"sweet reasonableness" which is the special dower of the English girl' (Wu-Wu 1903: 20). The Australian girl, with her unique qualities, holds the potential to embody a superior model of femininity on the world stage, if she can only mediate it with the qualities most appreciated in the English girl, and which have seemingly been lost in colonial Australia.

The perspective of foreign visitors was another way to attempt to define the unique qualities of Australian girls and women. In the 'Informal Interviews and Casual Conversations' a pastor from a Chicago church and his wife are interviewed to provide their impressions of Australian women, which are overwhelmingly complimentary. Dr R. A. Torrey states that he has found 'Australian women very interesting and attractive', and his wife concurs, saying that she has never met 'so many bright, interesting, keen young girls—girls from seventeen to twenty—as I have since we came to Australia' ('Informal Interviews' 1902: 113). While the quantity of beautiful Australian women is mentioned repeatedly, so too is their 'independent and go-ahead' nature ('Informal Interviews' 1902: 113). However, the couple also signal areas in which Australian girls and women are not as progressive as their American counterparts, specifically in undertaking higher education and prominence in public works. The extension of the federal franchise to women in July of the same year opened up an aspirational area for enterprising Australian women to contribute to the public good.

Essay and fiction prize competitions were one way to incorporate within the magazine the perspectives of the *New Idea*'s readers on their lives and the changing role of women. The unnamed author of 'Woman and the Commonwealth' reflects the view that 'Woman's true sphere is her home' and that they are the 'mothers of the nation', defining a vital role that every woman could perform ('Woman' 1902: 329). This domestic focus, however, did not mean that the magazine ignored Australian women's new-found voting rights, with the Commonwealth Franchise Act passed in 1902 and extended to women in New South Wales in the same year. The author of the prize-winning essay noted that women can now 'weigh their influence with men in political life' ('Woman' 1902: 329). In addition to their direct influence on politics, the author proposes that women can contribute to the 'upbuilding of the Commonwealth' through their influence on their own children to instil a love of country; through their influence on other children by promoting Bible reading and the teaching of history in state schools; through encouraging other women to take an interest in politics; and by forming societies to advance these ideas ('Woman' 1902: 329). The franchise provided another opportunity to imagine the ideal Australian woman's self-image in a way that credited her with the power to impact upon the home, the community and the nation.

The magazine did not directly seek to influence women's power to exercise the vote. However, in 1903 it did publish 'The Australian Woman's Vote and How it Should Be Cast', which provided the perspectives of several male and female community and political leaders on the approaching federal election and how women's vote could best serve the Commonwealth. The majority of the women who offered voting advice were leaders within the Women's Christian Temperance Union (WCTU), with the exception of feminist Rose Scott, who founded the Women's Literary Society in 1889, whose members subsequently formed the Womanhood Suffrage League of New South Wales in 1891. Ellen Warne observes that Protestant women reformers in the WCTU, along with the Young Women's Christian Association, and the Mothers' Union, promoted social reform 'grounded in "family values"' within 'a distinctive political atmosphere where their early access to the suffrage nationally from 1902 added to the sense that Australia was a social laboratory with progressive legislation' (Warne 2017: n.p.).

Scott encouraged the *New Idea* readers to learn about the benefits of the franchise to women and children in New Zealand, four American states, and other states of Australia. She tells them they are now 'a free people' who have a voice in the care of vulnerable people, such as the poor, the elderly and children, as well as a voice in the country's laws and taxation system ('The Australian Woman's Vote' 1903: 235). Lady Holder (Julia Maria, who later became the Australasian President of the WCTU) was even clearer about the fact that the franchise meant the women could exert influence in 'matters which are peculiarly our own' ('The Australian Woman's Vote' 1903: 235). She encourages the woman reader and voter to 'not be a mere reflex of the manhood voter' and urges women to make their influence felt on '[q]uestions touching the home, the family, and child life' that are often neglected ('The Australian Woman's Vote' 1903: 235). President of the Victorian WCTU Mrs W. (Margaret) McLean likewise urged unity whereby the 'womanly heart, beating true to its divine instinct' would prompt voting for the best interests of the home and family ('The Australian Woman's

Vote' 1903: 235). The consistent vision provided suggests that women must unite in order to improve the nation, and that together they could enact a unique political influence that would improve the lives of all women within the home, and inflect issues beyond the home with the benefit of a women's perspective. Whether the result of a post-Federation focus on national identity, the granting of the federal franchise, the desire to define the *New Idea*'s readership in its early years of publication, or because of a combination of these factors, the magazine explained and promoted the ideal Australian woman and the role that she played – and could play in future – in shaping the home, the nation and the Commonwealth.

Conclusion

Periodicals commonly shift focus and direction throughout their print runs, especially after editorial changes and mergers with other publications.[6] The early years of the *New Idea* were distinctive for their attempts to chart the geography of Australian women's lives and the spheres they inhabited and to foster a sense of the collective contribution of women to home and the Commonwealth. However, the magazine's unique focus gradually transformed to place less importance upon national identity. The landscape of Australian women's periodicals changed during the first decade of the twentieth century, as other Australian women's magazines found ongoing success and provided choice for the woman reader who sought local publications, which, in addition, were also generally more affordable than imported titles. The *New Idea* and Sydney's *Australian Home Journal* (1894–1983) had become well established as the most popular monthly magazines, and a successful weekly magazine, the *Woman's Budget*, emerged in 1906 (incorporated into *Woman* in 1934), which was published by the established newspaper the *Town and Country Journal*. In June 1911, the *New Idea* became *Everylady's Journal*, a change which incontrovertibly signalled alterations that had already taken place in preceding years, and which Tucker describes as the loss of 'a sense of friendly intimacy, and the feeling that this was an *Australian* magazine for Australian women' (Tucker 1974: 380). The need to define the Australian woman and the Australian women's magazine against British and American imports was a passing one that the *New Idea* filled at a moment when Australian women writers were looking for spaces to publish in their own country and Australian women were exercising a new-found political voice. By 1911, the collective dream of white Australian womanhood had largely been realised, at least within the pages of women's periodicals.

Notes

1. Maya V. Tucker's 1974 unpublished doctoral thesis on Australian women's magazines includes a chapter on the *New Idea*.
2. The magazine reverted to the title the *New Idea* in 1928.
3. The debut issue of '"The New Idea's" Big Brother', *Life*, was published in February 1904, and sold 35,000 copies ('"The New Idea's" Big Brother', 5 March 1904: 801). A promotional article in the *New Idea* detailed the features that would be included in the second issue, which included an essay by Prime Minister Alfred Deakin on how he prepared his speeches, an article in which author Steele Rudd describes writing his popular story collection *On Our Selection* (1899), and an account from a Commonwealth Naval Commandant.

4. As Tucker notes '[m]ale writers and poets hardly featured at all' in the *New Idea* (1974: 343).
5. See 'Billabong's' 'The Wind-Maiden and the Bunny Boys', 3 September 1903, 237–9; 'How Music Came to Australia', 6 October 1903, 328–31; 'Cinderella Retold for Australians', 6 November 1903, 422–4.
6. The *New Idea* absorbed *Woman's News* in 1905, increased its size to folio and the number of free patterns to three, as well as improving its paper stock in 1906, and similarly increased its size and price in 1908. See Tucker for further details (1974: 376).

Bibliography

'Advertisement: Koko for the Hair' (1902), *New Idea*, 1 August, 55.
'The Australian Woman's Vote and How it Should Be Cast' (1903), *New Idea*, 5 September, 235.
Beetham, Margaret (1996), *A Magazine of Her Own? Domesticity and Desire in the Woman's Magazine, 1800–1914*, London: Routledge.
Canney, Mary (1895), 'The Story of a London Factory Girls' Club', *Girl's Own Paper*, 16, 221–2.
'A Chat about Melba' (1902), *New Idea*, 1 October, 203.
'Christmas Cookery for Our Climate' (1902), *New Idea*, 1 December, 340.
Davis, Helen (1903), 'The Women Who Toil. II. – Our Australasian Factory Workers', *New Idea*, 1.8, 527–33.
Fitchett, Thomas Shaw (1903), *New Idea*, 6 August, 153.
Gelder, Ken, and Rachael Weaver (2014), *The Colonial Journals and the Emergence of Australian Literary Culture*, Crawley, WA: UWA Publishing.
'Good Housekeeping' (1902), *New Idea*, 1 August, 13.
'Good Taste' (1902), *New Idea*, 1 August, 32.
Hampshire, J. A. (1903), 'Noted Australasian Women at Home. V. Ethel Turner, Authoress', *New Idea*, 1.10, 704–9.
'Informal Interviews and Casual Conversations' (1902), *New Idea*, 1 September, 113.
Kuttainen, Victoria, Susann Liebach and Sarah Galletly (2018), *The Transported Imagination: Australian Interwar Magazines and the Geographical Imaginaries of Colonial Modernity*, Amherst, NY: Cambria.
'The New Idea' (1902), *Canowindra Star and Woodstock Recorder*, 29 August, 2.
'The "New Idea"' (1904), *The Age* (Queanbeyan), 13 September, 3.
'The New Idea' (1908), *The Cumberland Argus and Fruitgrowers Advocate*, 20 May, 4.
'"The New Idea's" Big Brother' (1904), *Life*, 5 March, 801.
'Society Fads' (1902), *New Idea*, 1 August, 14.
Somerset, W. A. (1902), 'Melba at Home and Abroad', *New Idea*, 1.4, 273–7.
Studdert, Helena (2001), 'Case-study: Women's magazines', in Martin Lyons and John Arnold (eds), *A History of the Book in Australia, 1891–1945: A National Culture in a Colonised Market*, St Lucia, QLD: University of Queensland Press, 276–81.
'To Our Readers' (1902), *New Idea*, 1 August, 1–4.
Tucker, Maya V. (1974), 'The emergence and character of women's magazines in Australia', unpublished PhD thesis, University of Melbourne.
Warne, Ellen (2017), *Agitate, Educate, Organise, Legislate: Protestant Women's Social Action in Post-Suffrage Australia*, Carlton, VIC: Melbourne University Press.
'Woman and the Commonwealth' (1902), *New Idea*, 1 December, 329.
Wu-Wu (1903), 'Letter to the Editor: The Australian Girl', *New Idea*, 6 July, 20.
Zuckerman, Mary Ellen (1998), *A History of Popular Women's Magazines in the United States, 1792–1995*, Westport, CT: Greenwood Press.

13

WOMEN'S WRITING AND REPORTING ON WOMEN IN THE GHANAIAN AND NIGERIAN PRESS, C. 1880–1930S

Katharina A. Oke

ON 8 MARCH 1934, at the height of protest against the Criminal Code (Amendment) Ordinance (commonly known as the Sedition Bill) and the Waterworks Ordinance, the Women's Corner of the *Times of West Africa* newspaper published a letter to Bridget Thomas, the daughter of Gold Coast Colony Governor Sir Shenton Thomas. Signed under the pseudonym Yaa Amponsa, the letter conveyed, from the perspective of 'little African girls', the sorrows to be visited by the proposed bills upon fathers, mothers and 'wee little sisters and brothers yet unborn'. These proposals had become public the month before, and, amongst fears that they would be passed into law in the upcoming Legislative Council meeting the following week, they were met by heavy protest in the press and in meetings held across colonial Ghana.[1]

While the Waterworks Ordinance was set to introduce a levy for water from street taps, the Criminal Code (Amendment) Ordinance was seen as 'muzzling' the press: an expression of colonial anxieties over the effects of imported publications that sought to restrict the distribution of printed material and control what the press could publish. Underpinning this was colonial administrative fears that such outlets would become avenues for promoting 'Communist propaganda' (Newell 2013: 65–98). The simultaneous introduction of the two bills thus brought together two issues likely to incite protests in themselves, while seemingly affecting various sections of the community differently.

The Waterworks Ordinance was seen to particularly affect poorer sections of Ghanaian communities. The question of taxation levels led to several anti-tax protests in interwar West Africa, not least as additional taxation threatened already precarious modes of living (Byfield 2021: 20). On the other hand, key players from the so-called African educated elite, and in particular journalists, were especially concerned with the Criminal Code (Amendment) Ordinance, which threatened to sever ties to international anti-colonial networks and restrict freedom of expression, thus raising questions around how to challenge the colonial administration in the future.

The letter in the Women's Corner had been written by Mabel Dove Danquah, journalist, writer, feminist, and in the 1950s the first woman to be elected to the Gold Coast Legislative Assembly (see Newell and Gadzekpo 2004). This chapter situates Dove Danquah's letter in the broader context of women's publishing activity and publishing about women in 1930s Ghana and Nigeria. From 1931, Dove Danquah published successfully in newspapers in both contexts, commenting on a variety of issues, from advice to mothers to anti-colonial nationalism. As this chapter seeks to illustrate, in the 1920s and 1930s, women's powerful assertions in the West African press were becoming more frequent, and Dove Danquah's journalistic career is testament to this.

Dove Danquah had adopted the pseudonym 'Marjorie Mensah' for previous contributions to the *Times of West Africa*. With this letter, Dove Danquah seemingly experimented with a new position to speak from: she, a member of the African educated elite, sought to write from the perspective of one of 'hundreds of thousands of girls' in the Gold Coast and Asante. Her letter to the Governor's daughter thus also points to multifaceted ways in which women's contributions and voices made it into the press, and how their political activism was represented – another dynamic this chapter seeks to elucidate.

Judith Byfield has recently highlighted with reference to Abeokuta that the 1940s were a period of political experimentation in which various competing political narratives found expression in various forums (Byfield 2021). This seems to be relevant in this context too: this chapter closes by pointing to ways in which the press can be seen as one among other means of political expression women could turn to.

Women, Writing Women, and Women's Columns in the West African Press

Audrey Gadzekpo traces women's columns in Gold Coast periodicals back to the 1880s, roughly to the time when African-owned periodicals first began emerging. Featured sporadically and infrequently through to the early twentieth century, focused women's columns would not become regular features in Gold Coast newspapers until the 1910s (Gadzekpo 2001: 106). At this time, essay competitions for women, such as those hosted by Lady Clifford, the wife of Gold Coast and later Nigerian Governor Hugh Clifford, in 1914 and 1918, helped solidify the role of African women as reading and writing subjects in the colonial print-centred public sphere (see Gadzekpo 2001: 103; Newell 2013: 122–58; 'Prize Competition' 1914: 3–4). With regard to Nigeria, the weekly *African Sentinel*, the London iteration of *The Lagos Weekly Record*, briefly published a women's column in 1920 ('Entre Nous' 1920: 5).

Further substantial change came in the 1930s, with the rise of an innovative daily press, as well as generational changes that saw energetic new editors and proprietors entering into the journalistic sphere. Such developments contributed to the marginalisation of long-established weekly and bi-weekly West African publications. The launch of the daily *Times of West Africa* on the Gold Coast in 1931, for example, saw an important innovation with regard to gendered spaces in the press, with the paper becoming the first in the region to publish a daily women's column (Newell and Gadzekpo 2004: vii). The emergence of women's columns in Nigeria can be traced back to the *Nigerian Daily Times*, which introduced a weekly women's column in 1931, and the *Comet*, a weekly newsmagazine established by Duse Mohamed Ali in 1933 (Aderinto 2015a: 482–3; on Ali and the *Comet*, see Chapter 33 by Marina Bilbija).

Women's columns also emerged in British-owned periodicals focusing on West Africa – so-called Anglo-African periodicals – such as the monthly *West African Review* and the weekly *West Africa*, which were widely read on the West African coast.[2] It was during this period that Nigeria-born Ronke Ajayi became the first woman editor of a newspaper, the *Nigerian Daily Herald* (Omu 1978: 67, 254). However, in colonial Ghana, it was not until the 1950s that women became more prominent in editorial roles (Gadzekpo 2002: 9–10).

Well into the 1920s, Ghanaian and Nigerian periodicals and newspapers appeared to have constituted a largely male-orientated and elite-centred public forum (Gadzekpo 2001: 102; Newell and Gadzekpo 2004: xii; Gadzekpo 2005: 279). As Audrey Gadzekpo and LaRay Denzer point out, though, to what extent women contributed texts to the press is hard to discern, as their contributions were often obscured by the use of pseudonyms (see Denzer 2010: 258). In the 'economy of recognition' (Oke 2018: 111) that had characterised the print-centred public sphere until then, reporting on women had often focused on documenting and chronicling their place in the social and cultural life of the so-called African educated elite, that is a circle of highly trained and wealthy African professionals and businesspeople (Echeruo 1977). Gossip columns and society news generously covered elite women and their various social and organisational activities, and their lives were often commemorated and celebrated in newspaper obituaries (Denzer 1994: 38). Other female representations, such as early twentieth-century newspaper reporting on 'market women' (traders and women not considered part of the elite due to wealth or education) in Lagos, for example, were framed through issues of political concern to the elite or were written from the perspective of elite market customers.[3]

At times, elite women's speeches featured in the press, as did their participation in debates on pressing questions of the day pertaining to colonial rule (see 'News Items' 1885: 3–4). Women also contributed to the press in letters and as occasional columnists (Newell and Gadzekpo 2004: vii). Overall, women's voices and contributions to journalism appear as marginalised in the face of the dominant masculine voices in the Ghanaian and Nigerian press. Contextual factors certainly played their part in this imbalance: in colonial society, educational opportunities for women were limited, stereotypical views around what was appropriate women's reading shaped what women contributors were allowed to write, and press editors and proprietors were inhospitable to women contributors and journalists in general (Denzer 2010; Gadzekpo 2005: 280; Newell 2013: 134). At the same time, women contributed to the press behind the screen of print. Further work remains to be done on this for West Africa, but in the nineteenth century Emily Blaize's skills as compositor were considered essential for publishing the *Lagos Times*, as were those of a woman printer for the publication of *The Dawn* in the 1920s (see 'Obituary' 1895: 7; Omu 1978: 254).

A Female View and the Woman for New Africa

Women's writing and writing about women was situated at the intersection of various dynamics. Women negotiated gendered and other spaces in periodicals, and periodicals were one space in which women could participate in negotiating social, economic, political and cultural change. When women's columns emerged more prominently, they did so against a background of the public sphere becoming, from the 1920s, more accessible to the public beyond the African educated elite, and more open to textual experimentation (see Newell 2013: Introduction). As a greater proportion of the population began to access further educational opportunities, as Karin Barber shows for Nigeria, the African educated elite sought to reach down the social scale via press and periodical conduits, not least by using the Yoruba language to engage new readers (Barber 2005). The press was increasing in importance as a space for staging politics – not just vis-à-vis the colonial administration. The results were opportunities for people 'hovering on the outskirts' (Newell 2002: 8) of the African educated elite to contribute to the press and make their voices heard in their own right (Oke 2018: 121). Concomitantly, 'women' became more visible in the press – as authors of texts, but also as objects and means of negotiating and responding to colonial gender ideologies, codes, values and social change (Newell 2013: 122–58; Oyěwùmí 1997: 31–79). Editors, proprietors, contributors and letter writers were envisioning women as offering unique insights and making particular contributions to the print-centred public sphere, but still within areas seen as part of the female domain. When the *West African Times*, for example, solicited contributions for its women's corner, it asked for coverage of topics such as fashion, children, kitchen, sports and society, 'even literature, religion' – topics 'in which the cultured lady of fashion is interested'. The column was open to politics, but only from a female view, which 'must be moderately toned in harmony with the polite taste of women' (see Gadzekpo 2001: 104).

Women's columns available to readers on the West African coast in the 1930s were initially orientated towards white, British, upper-class notions of (colonial) femininity (Gadzekpo 2001: 112). The tone adopted by these columns suggests that their aim often was to provide (Gold Coast and Nigerian) women with knowledge and information for 'proper' moral living and self-edification. In this, women's columns in West African periodicals paralleled columns in the 'Anglo-African' press published in Britain, which directed white British women on how to support the West Coaster, meaning male colonial administrators and businessmen stationed in West Africa, in maintaining a British lifestyle and acceptable level of colonial sociability.[4] It could be argued that the content of such columns in parallel publications overlapped to the extent that 'Anglo-African' periodicals became concerned over copyright infringements, posting disclaimer notices next to their women's columns that 'reproduction in whole or part' was prohibited (see Goble 1934: 341).

West African women journalists and other writers who published texts enabled these spaces to be transformed and become more grounded in West African contexts, themes and experiences. In 1932, for example, one columnist for the *Lagos Daily News* wrote mockingly about the advice given in some of the women's columns, noting sarcastically that they had hoped but had failed to learn about a remedy 'for that never absent bugbear of housewives in Nigeria, viz: how to stop water pipes from freezing in frosty weather' ('Women and the "Nigerian Daily Times"' 1932: 2). Saheed Aderinto shows that in the 1930s and 1940s, commentaries, articles and editorials began offering more Nigerian-centred interpretations in the discussion of the politics of sex. Writers challenged British hegemony on the rhetoric of illicit sexuality amongst other things. Newell and Gadzekpo argue that Dove Danquah, for example, engaged with such material and applied it to Ghanaian society, not merely mirroring, but challenging, adapting and selectively deploying against Victorian and Edwardian colonial codes, values, dichotomies and ideologies (Aderinto 2015b: 14; Newell and Gadzekpo 2004: 15).

Although women's columns in the press could be viewed as restricting women's contributions to a designated space and a limited set of themes and perspectives, they also acted as a kind of 'nursery' for textual production in and beyond the press, as Audrey Gadzekpo argues in relation to colonial Ghana (Gadzekpo 2005: 284–5;

Newell and Gadzekpo 2004: xii). Aderinto observes that in Nigeria, such a connection existed between the women's column of the *West African Pilot* and the emerging Onitsha market literature (Aderinto 2015a: 483). For Dove Danquah, the press thus served as a means of publishing a variety of texts across a range of genres. While the above-mentioned letter was published in March of 1934, later in the year she published, in instalments, a novella and a play in the *Times of West Africa* (Newell and Gadzekpo 2004: 39–90). She would continue to challenge the boundaries of the women's column over the course of her journalistic career (Newell and Gadzekpo 2004: xiii; George 2014: 52).

Women's column spaces could at times feature contrasting texts, with some items that were seemingly removed from Ghanaian and Nigerian society (or the 'majority'), such as those advising women to visit a good chiropodist when 'on leave' (Eve 1936a: 5), or to seek ideas for the Nigerian home by touring large shopping centres in England (Eve 1936b: 5). Women's columns would also comment on local developments, such as the 'singing band movement' and frivolous behaviour in Accra ('Women's Corner' 1934a: 2; 'Women's Corner' 1934b: 2), while also discussing the work of Leonardo da Vinci or Mozart ('Women's Corner' 1934d: 2). On one page, the women's column could feature one piece on ideas for the perfect Christmas gifts alongside a piece discussing the merits of young adults taking over the political reins in reference to the formation of the Nigerian Youth Movement ('Youth and Age' 1936: 5).

With regard to the broader role and position of women in society, the press celebrated women's 'achievements'. These could be their entry into the higher echelons of institutions that emerged under and related to the colonial administration and popular politics after independence, such as the entrance into practice of newly graduate West African women doctors and lawyers.[5] This seemingly corresponded to Victorian conceptions of colonial femininity according to which education legitimised women playing a role in urban governance (George 2014: 39–40). At the same time, the press also criticised the lifestyle of elite women and their 'uppishness', and urged them to learn from the industriousness of 'traditional' women in their contribution to New Africa (Newell and Gadzekpo 2004: x; Mba 1982: 221; 'Female Industries' 1938: 6).

Similarly, Audrey Gadzekpo notes for Ghana that a range of competing views on women traders found expression in the press (Gadzekpo 2001: 171). Not least because of class difference, the majority of Lagos women were often presented in press spaces as the Other (George 2014: 43, 47, 52). When there were interactions between classes, Lagosian elite opinion framed these in paternalist fashion, viewing the 'lower classes' as in need of social transformation, or in the context of 'public health' issues, such as campaigns focused on the cleanliness of markets (George 2014: 42–50; Mba 1982: 198, 215–32). Under an operational mode of patronising self-involvement, the press reported on how African elite women intruded into people's homes seeking to implement colonial public policy in the course of home visits, and engaged in questions of 'quality of life' and social welfare in moralising ways (George 2014: 47; Mba 1982: 216). They did so for instance in reference to the question of girl hawkers, whom elite women associated with prostitution (Byfield 2021: 110; George 2014: 47, 53; Mba 1982: 218). At the same time, elite women and their associations also advocated vis-à-vis the colonial administration for poor and 'lower class' women. Press reporting reflected such calls for improvements in infrastructure and for education for girls and young women (Byfield 2021: 109–20; George 2014: 39–48).

There was much journalistic engagement in debates around gender roles. Examples included Ronke Ajayi, who published texts about marriage and women, education and empowerment in her *Nigerian Daily Herald*, and Oyinkan Abayomi, who addressed 'modern womanhood' in the *Daily Service* in 1935, criticising privileged women's uppishness (Aderinto 2015a: 482; Denzer 2010: 260; Mba 1982: 220). Dove Danquah contributed to these discussions as well, and turned to men and women (see Newell and Gadzekpo 2004: 4–5, 21–2, 95–6, 98–100).

In this context also relevant is what Stephanie Newell describes as 'gender crossing literary practices': men using feminine pseudonyms to articulate moralising and other positions pertaining to women and gender roles, which in this way might have been more readily accepted (Barber 2012: 11; Newell 2013: 126). In the late 1920s, a period which Saheed Aderinto describes as one of heightened public concern about sex and a sensationalisation of prostitution in the press, Isaac Babalola Thomas did so in his serialised publication of the fictional life story of Segilola, a former prostitute (Aderinto 2015b: 4–5, 18). Started as a 'letters to the editor' column for his weekly bilingual *Akede Eko*, it was later described as the first Yoruba novel, and was subsequently reissued in English in book form. Thomas drew on local knowledge, genres and texts, and by writing from the perspective of Segilola sought to enable his readers to draw moral lessons from her story (see Barber 2012: 11; Newell 2013: 126, 188; and also Chapter 21 in this volume, by Karin Barber).

When not appropriating women's voices in the press, men also acted as gatekeepers of women's writing, for instance in adjudicating the aforementioned Lady Clifford essay competition. Marjorie Mensah's work as women's columnist for the *West African Times*, for example, was moderated and co-written by male authors. As Newell and Gadzekpo have written on, male management and oversight of Mensah's work came to light in a court case over authorship and royalties associated with the column in 1934. During the course of judicial proceedings, it was revealed that Dove Danquah, who had carefully concealed her identity behind her pseudonym, also had a very substantial role contributing to the column (Newell and Gadzekpo 2004: x, 11).

Women became more visible as contributors to the press from the 1930s. This was also the time that political parties intensified their wooing of women, seeking to mobilise their support for political goals. Powerful assertions by women in the press became more frequent, and, as the following section shows, this period also saw multifaceted negotiations over how to represent the political activity of women in the press.

Reporting Women's Protest against Colonial Taxation

A significant area of women's political activities in late 1920s and 1930s Ghana and Nigeria were anti-tax protests (Byfield 2021: 20–30). Most prominent among those was Ogu Umunwanyi (also known as the Women's War): in 1929, the supposed taxation of women was considered one of the components that led to this resistance movement of women in Eastern Nigeria. They protested against the economic threat of and the undermining of their political power by colonial policies – sixty-nine women were killed (Byfield 2021: 111). During this period in Accra and Lagos, part of women's resistance centred on the aforementioned protest against the Criminal Code (Amendment) Ordinance and the Waterworks Ordinance in 1934 in Accra, and women's responses to the (rumoured) introduction of Income Tax in 1932 and 1940 in Lagos (see Mba 1982: 199).

The letter referred to at the beginning of this chapter is interesting in this context. In relation to protests in Ghana, Dove Danquah, a member of the African elite, seemingly sought to voice the concerns of someone of the 'majority' by assuming the pen name Yaa Amponsa. Her letter therefore points to dynamics among politically active women as well as undercurrents of representing women's agency in the press.

Critical reporting on the planned measures in Ghana began shortly after proposed measures were made public in February 1934. Initial press interest focused on the bill that directly affected publication activity, namely the so-called Seditious Offences Bill ('Monster Meeting' 1934: 18). It was the press's intention to channel popular feeling into opposition to this bill (see Shaloff 1972), and doing so led to sympathetic portrayals and reporting of popular demonstrations in support of this position. With reference to past press victories ('In Defence' 1934: 7), editors, proprietors and contributors advocated the role of the press as key space for self-expression and political accountability (see Newell 2013: 29–43), and produced material that drew explicit connections between the two issues: if the press was muzzled, then taxation in several forms would follow, with little public scrutiny and press-led accountability ('First an Attack' 1934: 1). The press argued that if readers were against one of the bills, they should be against the other. Such was the premise of a mass meeting convened by the Press Association at the Palladium, which subsequently galvanised protest in the Gold Coast (Shaloff 1972: 248; 'The Flame' 1934: 207).

The Seditious Offences Bill most immediately targeted the African educated elite, since it was most likely they who could be charged under it. Correspondingly, Dove Danquah and others robustly considered how the bill would affect their work as journalists.[6] The Waterworks Ordinance was judged to disproportionately affect the poorer sections of the community, who were already facing dire times. Bringing those two issues together thus also served as a way of demonstrating, vis-à-vis the colonial administration, that opposition to the Seditious Offences Bill was not merely a concern for the elite. This was a necessary strategy to take in the context of Indirect Rule and colonial reactions to the National Congress of British West Africa. Reactions to the latter had shown that colonial administrators were of the view that the African educated elite were merely interested in class privilege and that they were not representing 'the majority' of the people (see Bickford-Smith 2006: 194–227; Oke 2018: 110).

Against this background, a seemingly important feature of reporting on the protest against these ordinances was to illustrate that rallies and protest meetings were widespread across the Gold Coast, transcended class, culture and gender, and were robustly supported and led by various social institutions and associations ('Criminal Code' 1934: 1). This was the context in which the focus and the attention of the press turned to women after about two weeks of reporting (i.e. at the beginning of March). Columns featured news items that reported on a widespread women's presence at mass rallies and protests ('Mighty Booings' 1934: 1; 'Diary of a Man' 1934: 2). One item reported on how women had fought each other to gain seats at the front of a mass meeting with Ga Mantse ('Round About Accra' 1934a: 6). Another noted women's banging of tin cans and loud demonstrations to register their view at protest events ('Hundreds of Women' 1934: 1), and others featured Dove Danquah's letter to the Governor's daughter (Mensah 1934b: 2). Reporting on women's participation in protests thus helped to widen arguments that a broad sector of the wider Gold Coast community were uniting in their concerns over the proposed measures.

If the activities of 'market women' thus constituted a crucial facet of protest, in its reporting, the press more often privileged activities of African elite women when addressing the 'feminine' contribution to this mobilisation. Readers might have learnt in one piece on relevant rallies that '[t]he culmination of this feminine effort was the march to Christiansborg Castle by thousands of the women who interviewed his Excellency through their delegation' (a joint effort by elite and 'market women', which was preceded by a mass meeting) ('The Women of Accra Are Active' 1934: 1; 'The Women of Accra Get Astir' 1934: 1, 4). More frequent were pieces highlighting the role of elite women in 'educating' their sisters lower down the class scale ('Random Notes' 1934: 256). Elsewhere, 'market women' made brief appearances, as for example in items remarking on the history of the political mobilisation of 'market women' leading to their street protests in 1925 against the Corporations Ordinance, brief reports of female representatives meeting with key government officials, and notes of women abandoning their market stalls to take part in protests ('The Women of Accra Get Astir' 1934: 1, 4; 'Random Notes' 1934: 256; 'Round About Accra' 1934b: 6).

While the names of the various elite women participating in the protests were omnipresent in press reports of the time, less attention was given to identifying the 'market women' leaders who made the women's march possible ('The Women of Accra Are Active' 1934: 1; 'The Women of Accra Get Astir' 1934: 1, 4). Such omissions mirrored a broader mode of reporting on Ghanaian and Nigerian women in the press. Although the women's column of the *West African Times* occasionally referenced the protest, it did so in privileged fashion, highlighting examples of elite Gold Coast women activists through occasional pen portraits ('Women's Corner' 1934c: 2).

In the Gold Coast press, protests against the planned legislation served the press to construct a narrative of this being the moment when (elite) women became politically active. Examples for this include one contribution which contrasted the women's protest and their meeting the Governor with their 'usual indifference' ('Random Notes' 1934: 256). The contributor writing under the pen name 'Lizzie Sarbah' initially took an ambivalent stance: she noted in the *West African Times*'s women's column how 'it is now the correct thing for women to feign an interest in politics even when they have not the real love for it' (Sarbah 1934b: 2, 3). Such examples created the impression that most society women usually took a more reserved approach to politics – that they applauded the amount of energy and national zeal being exhibited, but they preferred to be left alone, avoiding the likelihood of encountering exhibitions of temper in public places (Mensah 1934a: 2, 4). But three days later Lizzie Sarbah called for the mobilisation of women to address the issue at hand, and recounted a brief history of women fighting for liberty and equality. She saw the role of women as supporting the small but no less important task of raising funds for the cause (Sarbah 1934b: 2, 3). This reference to women's mobilisation in terms of financial support was mirrored in other sections of the press. For example, an editorial in the *Times of West Africa* acknowledged women's contributions to the protest by thanking women – presumably both 'market' and 'elite' women – who were the first to make generous (monetary) contributions to the cause, and noted that their following the movement was testament to their patriotism ('Our Task' 1934: 2; see also 'Random Notes' 1934: 256).

Turning to 1932 Nigeria allows us to highlight a different concurrently operating local model of reporting on women's political activism. In 1932, only three years after Ogu Umunwanyi, a potential rumour about the proposed taxation of women alerted colonial officials. The government therefore called an open meeting with 'market women' to quell such rumours, and to assure women that no such measure was planned at present. The *Lagos Daily News* reported in detail on the event, on who was present, and thus seemingly put emphasis on giving its readers insight into what was happening 'on the spot' ('The Market Women', 1932: 3). Doing so might have in part reflected the fact that the paper's editor/proprietor, Herbert Macaulay, had been entertaining a close political alliance with the Lagos Market Women Association since the 1920s (see Adebanwi 2016).

Similar to other papers, the *Lagos Daily News* would report on women in domestic terms and from the point of view of the elite. It commented on the women's columns of other papers (see above), published its own take on the 'ideal woman', or published challenges to London papers that suggested there was no fine dressmaking in Lagos ('The Ideal Woman' 1932: 3; 'A Woman's Clothes' 1932: 1). In this case, however, the concerns of 'market women' were placed centre stage through a focus on issues relating to markets and business, such as discussing questions of infrastructure and stall rent.

More importantly, such reportage seemingly made visible to a wider audience 'market women' and their positions in their own right, without mediation by elite women. Later in 1932, the administration again called for a meeting with the 'market women' (i.e. the Lagos Market Women Association) to encourage them to move to the new Idumagbo market. A report of the meeting was published on the paper's front page, highlighting the positions brought forward by Aminatu Alaga Ereko, who criticised the lack of government consultation with them preceding the construction of the market, which was not needed, and emphasised that 'market women' were not prepared to pay for stalls at Idumagbo. The paper also reported on 'market women' demands that the Acting Administrator comply with custom and 'treat them' with something for coming to see him in his office on this occasion ('The Acting Administrator' 1932: 1). Besides encounters with the administration, the paper also highlighted 'market women' participation in anniversary celebrations commemorating the return of Eshugbayi Eleko to Lagos, part of wider celebrations of the one-year anniversary of a victory in a political battle with the colonial administration and more conservative Lagos politicians that had occupied Lagos in the 1920s ('First Anniversary' 1932: 1–2). The *Lagos Daily News* thus offered a portrait of 'market women' as initiators of political activity, and, moreover, as challengers of elite status quo representations of their alleged positions. This in turn tracks closely with Byfield's observation on women as important players in the political discourse of the period, particularly in the 1940s (Byfield 2021: 106). Moreover, this model of reporting reflects the importance of 'market women' for the political projects Herbert Macaulay was pursuing in and beyond the pages of the *Lagos Daily News*. The political positions of Macaulay's Nigerian National Democratic Party (NNDP) and those of the Lagos Market Women often overlapped, and Macaulay supported issues and themes raised by 'market women'. Furthermore, the support of 'market women' for Macaulay's NNDP bolstered his claim to political leadership. 'Market women' participated in large numbers at political rallies and demonstrations and supported the NNDP financially. In contrast to this, coalitions between elite and 'market women' were fragile in Lagos. Such a cooperation was particularly powerful in the course of protests against colonial food price controls in the course of the Second World War, but as press accounts clearly indicated, 'market women' also publicly disagreed with elite women, leading to a breakdown of such an alliance in the

1940s (Mba 1982: 231–3). By 1945, at the time of the Lagos General Strike, 'market women', and in particular Madam Alimotu Pelewura, their leader, were established political actors in their own right. At this time, Pelewura was hosting her own press conferences, and was courted by Nnamdi Azikiwe's political party, the National Council of Nigeria and the Cameroons.

Speaking for the 'Cloth Woman' – or the 'Cloth Woman' Speaks?

In discussing the political realm of the interwar period, Byfield concludes it was one marked by experimentation, which led to the emergence of new types of political organisations (Byfield 2021: 122). Aligning this with an assessment of periodicals as spaces for textual production, Dove Danquah's use of the pen name Yaa Amponsa can be viewed as part of her own experimentation with ways in which the various political positions of women could find expression in the press. Publishing and engaging with letters was a recurring feature of the women's column in the *Times of West Africa* (Newell and Gadzekpo 2004: ix–x, xviii). A week before the letter to the Governor's daughter was published, Marjorie Mensah's column responded to a letter sent to her and criticised 'all sorts of legislative outbursts' by the colonial administration. In issues following the publication of Yaa Amponsa's letter, Dove Danquah penned a tongue-in-cheek comment on the bills. In another installation, she sarcastically thanked the Governor for educating everyone on seditions and giving a refresher course in bonds and treaties (Newell and Gadzekpo 2004: 33–4, 36–8). The protest against the Seditious Offences Bill and the Waterworks Ordinance, however, was not a decisive moment kindling Dove Danquah's political activity. Her textual interventions in this arena dated back to women's columns she produced for the *Times of West Africa* in 1931 on topics addressing racism and feminism, themes which she continued to return to over the course of her journalistic career (see Newell and Gadzekpo 2004: 3–4, 7–8, 14, 32–3). Such involved activity has justifiably led Audrey Gadzekpo and Stephanie Newell to label Dove Danquah as a pioneer West African feminist.

Yaa Amponsa's letter also draws our attention to Dove Danquah's experiments with author personalities and modes of address, and thus also to potential experiments with positions to speak from. Over the course of her journalistic career, she employed various pseudonyms and created various alter egos. In the Gold Coast, she was also known as Dama Dumas (1935–40) and Akosua Dzatsui (1950s and 1960s). In Nigeria she published under the pseudonym Ebun Alakija (1936–7) (Newell and Gadzekpo 2004: 12).

But rather than creating a new character from the milieu of the African educated elite, it might be suggested that writing under the pen name Yaa Amponsa, Danquah sought to speak from a position of someone who was at best 'hovering on the outskirts' of this group. In the letter, it is 'learned lawyers and laymen' that explain the Ordinances to Yaa Amponsa's father, and the father refers to the family's poverty. Danquah nevertheless constructs Amponsa as someone who goes to school, while reiterating that she is one of many, that there are hundreds of thousands like her in the Gold Coast and Ashanti. It might be argued that she was assuming the position of someone who might, from an elite perspective, be considered as being part of the 'masses' and therefore put on a similar footing to 'market' women (Newell and Gadzekpo 2004: 13). As far as this author knows, Dove Danquah did not revive this character in subsequent contributions to the press.[7] Thus, this might be considered as merely intimating a change of address by introducing a 'new' speaker to the print-centred public sphere (Barber 2007). It might be likened to Lagos elite women changing the name of one of their associations from Lagos Ladies' League to Lagos Women's League in 1923 – a rebranding without structural changes to their membership (Mba 1982: 214ff). As outlined above, such identification also served to illustrate the wider point of support for the elite-driven protest against the bills finding resonance in broader sections of the community. Therefore, Danquah's singular use of Yaa Amponsa might also be interpreted as mirroring the fragility of alliances between various groups of women, as illustrated with reference to Lagos.

While Dove Danquah did not reuse Yaa Amponsa as a pseudonym, she later picked other non-anglicised names in the Gold Coast and Nigerian press for contributions which more resembled those by Marjorie Mensah. Newell and Gadzekpo suggest that Dove Danquah was particularly addressing young women, and, also in her other writing, was contributing to the creation of a modern black girl. Although she declared that she preferred cloth over frock – i.e. the social marker of 'illiterate women' (cloth) over that of educated women (frock) – she was not invested in a 'usable African past' that was rooted in a revival of marriage patterns, or an engagement with African heroes and histories, positioning her thus in relation to the nationalist discourse (Newell and Gadzekpo 2004: vii–viii, xv, xvi). Nevertheless, she could admire the business acumen of women traders, and insist that things that are beautiful should not be indiscriminately mimicked, but she seemingly does so again in relation to her project of modern girl and womanhood, and it can be read together with her calling on young women to read more (Newell and Gadzekpo 2004: x, xiii, 18–9, 28–9, 31–2, 38).

Women's Engagement with the Ghanaian and Nigerian Press

It is daunting to generalise too broadly about the ways in which women registered their presence in the public sphere of 1930s Gold Coast and Nigerian societies in and beyond print. Especially when viewed against the background of Byfield's work, which highlights that this was a period of political experimentation. She turns our attention to competing political discourses in various gendered forums of expression. Nevertheless, what this chapter highlights is how, over the first half of the twentieth century, powerful assertions by women in the press, as well as reporting on representations of women's political activities, became more frequent.

In the press, different models of how women's political engagement was represented are discernible in 1930s Ghana and Nigeria. This chapter has highlighted, in reference to Ghana, a model which clearly focused on the African educated elite woman, her supposed political awakening, her mobilising 'market women', and her financial support to protests. When turning to press reporting in Nigeria, this chapter has at the same time elucidated a model which seemingly presented 'market women' as political actors in their own right.

It can be suggested that it was particular and shifting configurations of issues, personalities and other contextual factors that informed the relationship between women's writing, the representation of gendered identities, and reporting on women's activities in the press. Although women's contributions were largely marginalised in the press, Audrey Gadzekpo and LaRay Denzer convincingly highlight how their published contributions should not be minimised, not least as female authorship was often obscured by the use of pseudonyms. Men appropriated women's voices to make points when discussing and negotiating social change. At the same time, Mabel Dove Danquah and other women made critical interventions in such discussions. Local configurations as well as perceived (momentary) political needs could, at the same time, result in a focus on non-elite women and an engagement with their positions: turning to them was part of the way in which the support by the general 'masses' for political positions was expressed in the press. Dove Danquah's letter to the Governor's daughter in this context points to how the press represented elite women as speaking for 'market women', and frictions between these groups of women.

In this context, Byfield's point about political experimentation reminds us: it can be too simplistic to subscribe solely to a notion that there was a progressively intensifying engagement with the press, and a press that successively became more accessible to a broader group of women. Although the print-centred public sphere became more permeable from the 1920s, it was not always an attractive means through which to communicate political positions and various subjectivities. Denzer shows that working for Nnamdi Azikiwe's *West African Pilot* meant for Millicent Douglass being exposed to abuse and insults from business and works managers (Denzer 2010: 262). Nina Emma Mba notes how Funmilayo Ransome-Kuti's Abeokuta Women's Union faced opposition from Lagos newspapers, whose editors supported their political opponents, and how Elizabeth Adekogbe's Women's Movement faced opposition by newspapers she had previously written for (Mba 1982: 153, 181, 186). At the same time, women could and did embrace the increasing opportunities the press offered – from the 1940s other women besides Madam Pelewura of the Lagos Market Women gave press conferences and sought out the press to communicate political positions (Mba 1982: 229, 249). But it also seems important to emphasise that the press, with its close connection to political parties, was only one institution for mediating and engaging in 'politics' and the expression of various subjectivities. Pauline Baker emphasises the importance of the office of the Oba of Lagos for large sections of the Lagos community up to 1950, not least for arbitration proceedings. She also argues that it was only in the 1930s that the colonial administration started to intervene in the running of markets more directly (Baker 1974: 209, 232). Jimah Korieh and Mutiat Oladejo moreover emphasise the importance of petitions as a means of political activity, to voice protest and to seek remedy for grievances (Korieh 2010; Oladejo 2018).

While political parties (and the press) were, at the latest from the 1930s onwards, seemingly seeking to recruit women (Gadzekpo 2001: 106), both Byfield's and Mba's work illustrate clearly how women's organisations could keep their distance from such anti-colonial projects, rejecting the terms under which parties sought to incorporate them (see Byfield 2021: 2–3). Mba also highlights that no member of the Lagos Market Women Association assumed an official position in Herbert Macaulay's NNDP, despite their close links. Perhaps the press can thus be perceived as a 'political' means that, although it was generally increasing in importance, was selectively sought out by women – particularly in the context of other political means and avenues for self-expression. Against this background, an approach which reflects and contextualises moments and circumstances in which women turned to the press promises to contribute to the writing of multifaceted political histories.

Notes

1. Meetings were held in Accra, Axim District, Cape Coast, Koforidua, Kumasi, Saltpond, Sekondi and Winnebah ('The Flame' 1934: 207; 'Around the Town' 1934: 230).
2. There were various instances in which the West African press referred to these so-called Anglo-African periodicals. See, for example, 'Speculation' 1934: 2 and 'Do We Live' 1934: 3. On the periodical *West Africa*, see Chapter 10 of this volume, by Jonathan Derrick.
3. See for instance 'Forced Labour' 1907: 4; 'Weekly Notes' 1911: 3; and 'Lagos Food Supply' 1918: 10.
4. A regular column in the *West African Review* in 1932 was 'Making a Home in West Africa'. In 1934, the column 'Woman and the Home by Micky Goble' was transformed and published as 'A Woman's West African Pocket Book' (Goble 1934).
5. As Denzer shows, the press for instance reported on Agnes Yewande Savage and Dahlia Whitbourne, who had qualified as doctors in 1928 and 1929 respectively, and Stella Jane Thomas (later Marke), who was called to the bar in 1933.
6. 'Lizzie Sarbah' highlights in the women's column that her editor told her to be careful should the Sedition Bill become law. Also, Dove Danquah – as 'Marjorie Mensah' – suggests that the Governor could 'shut me up one way or the other' (Sarbah 1934a: 2; Mensah 1934b: 2).
7. This is based on research in the *Nigerian Daily Times* and the *Accra Morning Post* conducted by this author, as well as on the collection of writings compiled by Newell and Gadzekpo.

Bibliography

'The Acting Administrator of The Colony and The Lagos Market Women' (1932), *Lagos Daily News*, 13 July, 1.

Adebanwi, Wale (2016), 'Colonial modernity and tradition: Herbert Macaulay, the newspaper press, and the (re)production of engaged publics in colonial Lagos', in Derek R. Peterson, Emma Hunter and Stephanie Newell (eds), *African Print Cultures: Newspapers and their Publics in the Twentieth Century*, Ann Arbor: University of Michigan Press, 125–48.

Aderinto, Saheed (2015a), 'Modernizing love: Gender, romantic passion and youth literary culture in colonial Nigeria', *Africa*, 85.3, 478–500.

——— (2015b), *When Sex Threatened the State: Illicit Sexuality, Nationalism, and Politics in Colonial Nigeria, 1900–1958*, Urbana: University of Illinois Press.

'Around the Town and other Matters' (1934), *Gold Coast Independent*, 10 March, 230.

Baker, Pauline H. (1974), *Urbanization and Political Change: The Politics of Lagos, 1917–1967*, Berkeley and London: University of California Press.

Barber, Karin (2005), 'Translation, publics, and the vernacular press in 1920s Lagos', in Toyin Falola (ed.), *Christianity and Social Change in Africa: Essays in Honor of J. D. Y. Peel*, Durham, NC: Carolina Academic Press, 187–208.

——— (2007), *The Anthropology of Texts, Persons and Publics*, Cambridge: Cambridge University Press.

——— (2012), *Print Culture and the First Yoruba Novel: I. B. Thomas's 'Life Story of Me, Segilola' and Other Texts*, Leiden: Brill.

Bickford-Smith, Vivian (2006), 'The betrayal of creole elites, 1880–1920', in Philip D. Morgan and Sean Hawkins (eds), *Black Experience and the Empire*, Oxford: Oxford University Press, 194–227.

Byfield, Judith A. (2021), *The Great Upheaval: Women and Nation in Postwar Nigeria*, Athens: Ohio University Press.

———, LaRay Denzer and Anthea Morrison (eds) (2010), *Gendering the African Diaspora: Women, Culture, and Historical Change in the Caribbean and Nigerian Hinterland*, Bloomington: Indiana University Press.

'Criminal Code Amendment. Big Protest Meeting' (1934), *Times of West Africa*, 15 February, 1.
Denzer, LaRay (1994), 'Yoruba women: A historiographical study', *The International Journal of African Historical Studies*, 27.1, 1–39.
—— (2010), 'Intersections: Nigerian episodes in the careers of three West Indian women', in Judith A. Byfield, LaRay Denzer and Anthea Morrison (eds), *Gendering the African Diaspora: Women, Culture, and Historical Change in the Caribbean and Nigerian Hinterland*, Bloomington: Indiana University Press, 245–84.
'Diary of a Man About Town' (1934), *Times of West Africa*, 9 March, 2.
'Do We Live under Dictatorship?' (1934), *Times of West Africa*, 22 March, 3.
Echeruo, Michael J. C. (1977), *Victorian Lagos: Aspects of Nineteenth Century Lagos Life*, London: Macmillan.
'Entre Nous. "Nefertari"' (1920), *African Sentinel*, 17 January, 5.
Eve (1936a), 'The Care of Feet', *Nigerian Daily Times*, 1 August, 5.
—— (1936b), 'Gadgets and Ideas for the Home', *Nigerian Daily Times*, 5 September, 5.
Falola, Toyin (ed.) (2005), *Christianity and Social Change in Africa: Essays in Honor of J. D. Y. Peel*, Durham, NC: Carolina Academic Press.
'Female Industries' (1938), *West African Pilot*, 13 March, 6.
'First an Attack on Liberty, then Taxation' (1934), *Times of West Africa*, 15 February, 1.
'First Anniversary of the Return of Prince Eshugbayi Eleko to Lagos' (1932), *Lagos Daily News*, 6 July, 1–2.
'The Flame of Protests Spreads' (1934), *Gold Coast Independent*, 3 March, 207.
'Forced Labour at Ikorodu' (1907), *The Lagos Weekly Record*, 7 September, 4.
Gadzekpo, Audrey S. (2001), 'Women's engagement with Gold Coast print culture from 1857 to 1957', unpublished PhD thesis, University of Birmingham.
—— (2002), *The Hidden History of Gender in Ghanaian Print Culture* (Legon), https://link.springer.com/chapter/10.1007/978-1-137-09009-6_15 (accessed 2 January 2024).
—— (2005), 'The hidden history of women in Ghanaian print culture', in Oyeronke Oyěwùmí (ed.), *African Gender Studies: A Reader*, New York: Palgrave Macmillan, 279–95.
George, Abosede (2014), *Making Modern Girls: A History of Girlhood, Labor, and Social Development in Colonial Lagos*, Athens: Ohio University Press.
Goble, Micky (1934), 'Woman and the Home. A Woman's West African Pocket Book', *West Africa*, 31 March, 341.
'Hundreds of Women March out in Protest' (1934), *Times of West Africa*, 8 March, 1.
'The Ideal Woman' (1932), *Lagos Daily News*, 3 February, 3.
'In Defence of Our Rights and Liberties!' (1934), *Times of West Africa*, 17 February, 7.
Korieh, Chima J. (2010), '"May It Pleas Your Honor": Letters of petition as historical evidence in an African colonial context', *History in Africa*, 37, 83–106.
'Lagos Food Supply' (1918), *Nigerian Pioneer*, 5 April, 10.
'Lagos Markets and Street Hawking Committee' (1932), *Lagos Daily News*, 18 July, 1.
'Making a Home in West Africa' (1932), *West African Review*.
'The Market Women of Lagos' (1932), *Lagos Daily News*, 29 January, 3.
Mba, Nina Emma (1982), *Nigerian Women Mobilized*, Berkeley: University of California Press.
Mensah, Marjorie (1934a), 'Women's Corner', *Times of West Africa*, 27 February, 2, 4.
—— (1934b), 'Women's Corner', *Times of West Africa*, 8 March, 2.
—— (1934c), 'Women's Corner', *Times of West Africa*, 9 March, 2.
'Mighty Booings By the Women of Accra' (1934), *Times of West Africa*, 7 March, 1.
'Monster Meeting of Protest at Palladium' (1934), *Gold Coast Independent*, 24 February, 18.
Morgan, Philip D., and Sean Hawkins (eds) (2006), *Black Experience and the Empire*, Oxford: Oxford University Press.
Newell, Stephanie (2002), *Literary Culture in Colonial Ghana: 'How to Play the Game of Life'*, Bloomington: Indiana University Press.

—— (2013), *The Power to Name: A History of Anonymity in Colonial West Africa*, Athens: Ohio University Press.
—— and Audrey Gadzekpo (eds) (2004), *Mabel Dove: Selected Writings of a Pioneer West African Feminist*, Nottingham: Trent Editions.
'News Items' (1885), *Lagos Observer*, 19 February, 3–4.
'Obituary for Emily Blaize' (1895), *The Lagos Weekly Record*, 24 August, 7.
Oke, Katharina Adewoyin (2018), 'The politics of the public sphere: English-language and Yoruba-language print culture in colonial Lagos, 1880s–1940s', unpublished PhD thesis, University of Oxford.
Oladejo, Mutiat Titilope (2018), *The Women Went Radical: Petition Writing and Colonial State in Southwestern Nigeria, 1900–1953*, Ibadan: Book Builders.
Omu, Fred I. A. (1978), *Press and Politics in Nigeria, 1880–1937*, Atlantic Highlands, NJ: Humanities Press.
'Our Task' (1934), *Times of West Africa*, 5 July, 2.
Oyěwùmí, Oyeronke (1997), *The Invention of Women: Making an African Sense of Western Gender Discourses*, Minneapolis: University of Minnesota Press.
—— (ed.) (2005), *African Gender Studies: A Reader*, New York: Palgrave Macmillan.
Peterson, Derek R., Emma Hunter and Stephanie Newell (eds) (2016), *African Print Cultures: Newspapers and their Publics in the Twentieth Century*, Ann Arbor: University of Michigan Press.
'Prize Competition. House Keeping on the Gold Coast' (1914), *Times of Nigeria*, 3–4.
'Random Notes' (1934), *Gold Coast Independent*, 17 March, 256.
'Round About Accra' (1934a), *Times of West Africa*, 8 March, 6.
'Round About Accra' (1934b), *Times of West Africa*, 13 March, 6.
Sarbah, Lizzie (1934a), 'Women's Corner', *Times of West Africa*, 24 March, 2.
—— (1934b), 'Women's Corner', *Times of West Africa*, 27 March, 2, 3.
Shaloff, Stanley (1972), 'Press controls and sedition proceedings in the Gold Coast, 1933–39', *African Affairs*, 71.284, 241–63.
'Speculation' (1934), *Times of West Africa*, 9 February, 2.
'Weekly Notes' (1911), *The Lagos Weekly Record*, 12 August, 3.
'A Woman's Clothes Cannot Be Bought in Lagos' (1932), *Lagos Daily News*, 20 July, 1.
'Women and the "Nigerian Daily Times"' (1932), *Lagos Daily News*, 13 July, 2.
'The Women of Accra Are Active' (1934), *Times of West Africa*, 14 March, 1.
'The Women of Accra Get Astir' (1934), *Times of West Africa*, 16 March, 1, 4.
'Women's Corner' (1934a), *Times of West Africa*, 3 February, 2.
'Women's Corner' (1934b), *Times of West Africa*, 5 February, 2.
'Women's Corner' (1934c), *Times of West Africa*, 17 March, 2.
'Women's Corner' (1934d), *Times of West Africa*, 22 March, 2.
'Youth and Age' (1936), *Nigerian Daily Times*, 24 October, 5.

14

Indian Women's Pre-Independence Periodicals in English: *The Indian Ladies' Magazine*, *Stri-Dharma* and the Indian New Woman

Deborah Anna Logan

Two significant women's publications originated in Madras (Chennai) during the British Raj and pre-independence period: *The Indian Ladies' Magazine* (1901–18, 1927–38) and *Stri-Dharma* (1918–36). Both were English-language publications, established, written and edited by women, for women; both addressed Indian women while welcoming British and Anglo-Indian readers, ideas and contributions; and both embraced a perspective aimed at social unification, religious tolerance, cultural collaboration and identity politics. That said, reflecting the unique spirit of the age that distinguishes the World War I era (Victorian, Edwardian) from the pre-Second World War era (Modern), these two publications diverged regarding the appropriate means for defining modern Indian womanhood – initially, within the context of the Raj, and subsequently, in terms of separatist national identity politics.

The Indian Ladies' Magazine, edited by Kamala Satthianadhan, synthesised traditional Indian and British Victorian literature, promoting the Angel in the House as a suitable model for modernising Indian womanhood while retaining its signature qualities of purity and self-effacing gentleness. *ILM* advocated universal education and community service, ladies' philanthropy and international 'social intercourse', and celebrated the accomplishments of women throughout the world, while maintaining conventional separate-spheres gender ideology. *Stri-Dharma*, edited by Dorothy Jinarajadasa, was affiliated with the Theosophists. As the organ of the Women's Indian Association (WIA), it enjoyed more vigorous bi-cultural support through such outreach activities as women's classes and reading rooms sponsored by chapters established throughout the country. It was comparatively feminist and political in its emphasis on women's visible participation in the nationalist movement, from political conferences to marches to street protests. Together, these two publications reflect the decline of the Raj, the rise of Indian nationalism, and women's increased influence through education, the professions and the franchise. They also reflect a time when women's activism – East and West – was welcomed less as a permanent fixture than as the temporary means to a political end, after which women were expected to return to subservience, conformity and domesticity. With the second war-to-end-all-wars looming, neither publication could withstand the global economic impact of the Great Depression: *Stri-Dharma* ceased publication in 1936 and *ILM* in 1938.

Francesca Orsini identified three distinct stages shaping the history of Indian women's periodicals: those aimed at reforming women and their role through modernising traditional practices (second half of the nineteenth century); the radical-critical, political phase marking the first half of the twentieth century; and the post-independence return to a focus on conventional domestic divisions of labour (Orsini 1999: 137). The focus of this discussion is the period leading up to independence (1947), a time when the 'other' half of India's population came to represent a valuable resource, rather than a liability, to the freedom movement. The 'upliftment' of Indian womanhood was reflected in the proliferation of woman-centred periodicals in English and the vernaculars, offering a safe platform for women to express themselves, to educate themselves in the absence of formal schooling, and to access news of female activities, achievements and accomplishments, in India and throughout the world. This international focus emphasised that gender issues are universal, transcending geopolitical, socio-cultural and religious boundaries, and that women's progress depended on global gender solidarity. But events shaping 1920s–30s India sharpened the nationalist project, which – in order to achieve its aim of independence – chose to step back from involvement in world events to unify, create and defend the incipient Republic of India.

The influence of Victorian literature and culture on Indian women's 'upliftment' discourse surfaced in 'contemporary literature, official documents, [and] the growth of publishing', indicating 'a diffusion and absorption of Romantic and Victorian sentimental discourse and forms . . . [E]ducational projects . . . were promulgated on the terrain of colonial discourse', primarily Victorian (Bannerji 1991: 59). Against the backdrop of Indian Woman Question debates, both *ILM* and *SD* display ambivalence toward 'the wisdom of the patriarchal Victorian worldview', even as they were shaped by and advocated it. Thus, Indian women writers and activists are revealed to be 'both active agents and colonised interpreters'. Perceived boundaries distinguishing the Victorian Angel in the House from Bharat Mata/Mother India proved to be remarkably porous, resulting in 'both a continuity and a break with the past' (Sreenivas 2003: 60), and it is this factor that shapes the Indian Woman Question.

Given women's traditional domestic confinement, whether or not in purdah, Indian women's periodicals culture 'did not represent an already existing women's community but shaped a female reading public according to the demands of ideology, politics, and the market for print' (Sreenivas 2003: 61). This community was by definition elite, privileged by education, leisure and liberal attitudes, rarefied in terms of literacy, since few males and far fewer females had access to formal education at that time. Both publications addressed the literacy disparity in several ways: the relatively apolitical *ILM*, in both creative and non-fiction features, prioritised such controversial issues as the civil and human rights of 'Untouchable' castes, of widows and child brides, of devadasis (temple prostitutes) and the poor, and of all religious faiths. More pragmatically, *Stri-Dharma*'s national network of WIA branches provided women with reading rooms, lectures, courses and practical training conducted in regional languages. Both *ILM* and *SD* disseminated these new women's communities by contributing copies to schools, libraries, reading rooms and institutions, and both featured articles translated into regional languages.

British Victorians' formulation of the Woman Question represented an attempt to address women's changing role at the very time that it was being hardened, in legal, political, social, economic, professional and cultural terms, into separate-spheres divisions of labour. The contested complacency of the Angel in the House, who, as submissive wife and mother, had no need for education or external interests and activities (compare with India's purdah system), evolved into the late-century New Woman. This iteration of gender ideology resisted – or at least delayed – compulsory marriage and motherhood in favour of formal education and professions, economic autonomy and women's suffrage. The New Woman challenged entrenched claims that good women were passive and docile, uneducated and unopinionated, and home-bound.

The West's gender revolution paralleled India's formal absorption into the Empire (1858), the rise of Indian nationalism, the post-Macaulay spread of English literacy, and the increased socio-cultural interactions between Indians and Anglo-Indian settlers. Such interactions involved education, through government-sponsored and Christian-mission schools, accounting in part for the prominence of British Victorian literature and ideology in Indian gender-reform discourse. The Indian Woman Question, dating from the *fin de siècle* and reflected in a proliferation of woman-centred periodical publications, grew into one of the most pressing issues shaping nationalist debates. How can ancient India achieve unification and defeat the British Empire? What role, if any, should women play? How can gender reforms find a viable balance between western progressiveness and the preservation of indigenous cultural values?

The two English-language periodicals considered here are unusual Indian vernacular press examples for the way they aimed to establish productive links between English speakers throughout the world and Indians newly literate in English language and literature. By the *fin de siècle*, the British Empire's reach had made English the world's lingua franca, with significant implications for colonised and colonisers. Shared language strengthens community between East and West, ancient and modern, spiritual and material, empire and colony. Alternatively, the language question fuelled nationalist resistance, given that native languages are fundamental to cultural identity. While those at the forefront of the independence endeavour were 'England-returned' graduates (Nehru, Gandhi, Jinnah, Naidu, Chattopadhyaya), calls for instituting Hindi as the nation's official language surfaced early in the process, directly challenging Macaulay's 1835 Minute making English language acquisition mandatory.

Initially, *ILM* accepted the British Raj and promoted accord between empire and colony, encouraging 'social intercourse' linking men and women, East and West. Editor Satthianadhan was a devout Christian, and this opened certain avenues for the magazine, in terms of global reach through Christian-mission networks. But Christianity was the religion of the imperialists, and this presented a complicating factor, despite *ILM*'s many features highlighting world and indigenous religions. Alternatively, the politically radical *Stri-Dharma* contested imperialism, emphasising gender reform and cultural preservation (two ideas considered by some to pose a contradiction in terms). Despite *SD*'s earnest advocacy of India's cause, Theosophists were, like Christians, outsiders with an alien spiritualist-philosophical agenda. Initially distinguished by their varied efforts to facilitate cross-cultural communal networks, both *ILM* and *SD* found themselves marginalised by the exclusivity of the socio-political climate that characterised the final years of the Raj.

The Indian Ladies' Magazine: 1901–18, 1927–38

ILM launched in July 1901, shortly after the death of Queen Empress Victoria (see Figure 14.1). Edited by Kamala Satthianadhan (1880–1950), its first run was 1901–18; its second (1927–38) featured daughter and biographer Padmini Satthianadhan Sengupta (1905–88) as assistant editor. It was published monthly in Madras by the Methodist Publishing House, with subscriptions sold in the East (4 Rs), England (6 shillings) and America ($1.50). Selected articles were translated into Telugu, Tamil, Urdu and Malayam. Initially without external revenue, the magazine, like many of its kind, found a welcome funding resource through advertising Indian-made and woman-centred products. Early drawings and engravings later shifted to photographs illustrating women's accomplishments and scenes depicting rural communities, people and activities.

ILM stressed national and international, gender and religious, social and cultural cooperation by favouring common ground and shared concerns over political divisiveness. Presented within the context of the Raj, *ILM*'s promotion of intercultural understanding foregrounded India's ancient literary history and myriad socio-cultural influences for the edification of non-Indian readers. Various features highlighted Indian concerns: Women's Work in India, Things Seen (regional interests, with photographs),

Figure 14.1 *The Indian Ladies' Magazine*, July 1901, front cover.
Courtesy of the author.

Indian Cookery, Indian Classical Dance, Our Special Indian Lady Contributors' Column, and What is Being Done for India's Daughters. Also predominant was literature in the forms of original creative writing – poems, plays, short stories, serial fiction and writing contests – and literary and socio-literary criticism. The journal frequently featured comparative analyses examining literary, religious and mythological heroines of the East and West.

Instructive features included needlework (patterns and instructions for knitting, embroidery, sewing), cooking (Indian and western recipes), modern domestic science, childhood ailments and home health remedies. Regular columns focused on Reviews, Editorial Notes, News and Notes, Home Talks, Friendly Chats (moral, ethical topics), Fashion Suggestions (how to make a tennis sari that preserves one's dignity) and Household Hints. Religious ideologies were explored through features on Christian missions, missionaries and saints; on Muslim, Parsi, Buddhist and Jain customs; on Hindu heroes and heroines; and on holidays, pilgrimages and places of worship (shrines, temples, churches). While expressing concern that domestic integrity and womanly grace risked being compromised by public activism, *ILM* did present transcripts of women's conference proceedings and congress speeches, such as the National Indian Association, Women's Indian Association and All India Women's conferences. *ILM*'s range of offerings was impressive, reflecting a wide array of contributors' perspectives and expertise and encouraging readers' broad engagement in the world beyond their homes.

ILM's primary 'aims and objects' were to 'advance the cause of the women of India', a cause long neglected by privileging the status of men. As its lead introduction noted,

> The new influences that are at work in this land, owing to its connection with Great Britain, have not appreciably affected the women of the land; the men having been benefited more largely than the women in matters of education and social development. But a nation of educated and enlightened men alone is an impossibility; and, if the people of India are to advance, and take their right place among civilized nations, they should realize that 'the woman's cause is man's: they rise or sink together'. ('Introduction' 1901: 1)

The quote from Tennyson's *The Princess* – a line destined to serve as the unofficial motto of Indian Woman Question discourse – reveals *ILM*'s founding principles. While the union between Great Britain and India was unquestioned, Satthianadhan's critique is clear: that union has done little to improve the condition of Indian women – a national and imperial Woman Question needing resolution. That literacy and education – whether in English or the vernaculars – was a key factor in realising nationhood is today a matter of historical record.

Editorial topics emphasise the amelioration, through education and social reforms, of 'social and other evils which the daughters of India have been labouring under for centuries' ('Introduction' 1901: 1). Socio-cultural values, such as 'Indian ideals of womanhood', surface in studies of ancient literature and in fiction 'delineating different phases of Indian life ... [including] the customs and manners of Indian women ... interpretative of their inner life'. The future of India depends on its educated women – who, 'without losing what is distinctly Indian, have come under the best influences of the West' through interactions with Anglo-Indian women who are 'spending their very lives for the emancipation of their Indian sisters'. Satthianadhan emphasised women's 'inner life', her reform philosophy starting with the individual and expanding outward to family and community, nation and world. This centre-to-circumference perspective was predicated on civil rights and responsibilities earned through personal self-development. *ILM* continued advocating these principles even as they were rendered old-fashioned by the radical activism represented by such publications as *Stri-Dharma*. Defending *ILM*'s editorial platform, Satthianadhan wrote:

> I am sometimes blamed for not concentrating more on the [political] activities of Indian women: but ... since there are other papers to do that, my journal can enlarge upon the general aspect, and upon the inward advance of Indian women and their preparation for increased responsibilities ... mere intensification is not enough without extending [influence] ... both are needed ... Indian womanhood ... should be based, not only on our ancient ideals, but also on some of the forward movements of Western nations. ('Ourselves' 1930: 275–6)

Whereas in 1918 Satthianadhan had asserted that *ILM* 'scarcely touches on political questions' ('Viceroy' 1918: 252), national circumstances had changed so drastically by its second run that such a claim was no longer true.

Given the signature parallels linking these two English-language women's journals, both published in Madras, 'other papers' refers pointedly to *Stri-Dharma*, with its self-defined politicisation of the Indian Woman Question. But from 1930 onward, *ILM* shifted to a comparatively political tone by addressing current events as they affected Indian women. For example, *ILM* does not mention the Dandi Salt March until two months after the fact, in an article focused not on Gandhi's activism or imprisonment, but on his wife, Kasturba Gandhi, who was forced to travel without her incarcerated husband. Kasturba's message to Indian women activists stresses that the Salt March is over and 'Swaraj was won', therefore women should return home and take up their 'spinning and weaving', now that they have proven themselves ('Kasturba Gandhi' 1930: 556). Aside from being premature, the assertion is telling in that Kasturba Gandhi here serves as her husband's mouthpiece, an authority not to be questioned. That said, printed right next to 'Kasturba Gandhi' is the article 'Purdah Picketers', which praises a group of purdah-women who 'picketed the gates of the civil and criminal courts' to protest Gandhi's incarceration, a gathering the police were 'helpless' to control, 'the roads being blocked against them' ('Purdah Picketers' 1930: 557).

ILM's earlier features on Sarojini Naidu, revered as 'the nation's poetess', now emphasise her primary role in the freedom movement: marching alongside Gandhi, representing India at congresses and Round Tables debating India's sovereignty, arrested and jailed for her activism, and serving as Gandhi's unofficial ambassador in America. To readers throughout the world shocked by the arrests of Naidu and Gandhi, 'few events have given so much cause to ponder over the happenings in India' ('Sarojini' 1930: 558). The article 'Women's War' revealed that Indian women's groups had submitted resolutions to the London Round Table 'demanding that all political prisoners ... be unconditionally released; ... participation [in LRT] while Mr. Gandhi and others were in prison, would be regarded as a betrayal' ('Women's War' 1930: 612). Indeed, Indian women's public participation in nationalist activism, and the brutal beatings and arrests of unarmed, non-violent activists, 'makes the Indian question worldwide in its interest' ('Women's War' 1930: 611).

ILM continued reporting on related events throughout the 1930s, revealing a distinct shift from its earlier ameliorative tone linking imperial with national interests to exposing injustices that served to thwart the freedom movement. Examples included articles entitled 'Women's Congress', which provided evidence that prominent Indian women activists were targeted for arrest by British authorities, and 'Vienna', which argued that the notion of international sisterhood had given way to national self-interest in countries who were reluctant to alienate Great Britain by siding with Indian nationalists, seen in the rejection of Indian women's petitions supporting independence by the Vienna's International Union of Women conference that year.

Satthianadhan was outspoken about the rise of the Nazis, fascists and dictators propelling the world into the Second World War. The editorial piece 'Hitler', for example, critiqued Hitler, Hess and Mussolini by exposing the misogyny underpinning their insistence, worthy of Victorian Old Men, that women stay home. On the contrary, New Women of every nation were responsible for putting their intellect and talent to work in 'service to the world' ('Place of Women' 1933: 207). Such service meant neither confining women to the home nor forcing German girls to undertake military training or 'martial games of a purely masculine nature' ('Military Training' 1936: 70).

While *ILM* avoided radical female militancy as unwomanly, whether German military girls or Irish home-rulers, English suffragists or Indian freedom fighters, it was committed to gender reforms facilitating women's service to the world beyond their own family. Rabindranath Tagore's observation, 'females being needful, and males barely necessary, nature indulges male creatures in their fighting propensity to kill one another' ('Glimpse' 1932: 265–6), casts women as peacemakers. The international women's peace movement was an encouraging sign in this dark interwar period, but incidents of radical female violence, including assassination attempts and shootings, bombings and arsenal raids, was the behaviour of unsexed 'man-women':

> It is with feelings of regret and of shame that we read of the Comilla shooting outrage by two women of India. This wanton act is a serious 'blot on the womanhood of India' . . . where women, among all women, are so celebrated for tender-heartedness and generous mercy. ('Comilla Shooting' 1931: 257)

ILM continued to essentialise women through its final number, emphasising domestic interests and ideology and promoting female education as beneficial to family, community and nation. But its editorial perspectives did change with the times: if Satthianadhan did not condemn outright what the Raj was doing to her country, she did use her unique platform to promote and celebrate the unprecedented 'upliftment' of her countrywomen, an accomplishment in which she and *ILM* played a direct part.

Stri-Dharma: 1918–36

Stri-Dharma, or 'The Sphere of Women', was published in Madras by the Theosophical Society's Women's Indian Association from January 1918 through to August 1936. Its originating board featured editor Dorothy Graham Jinarajadasa (English), Irish activists Annie Besant (1847–1933) and Margaret Cousins (1878–1954), and Indian activists Mahadeva Sastri (1861–1926), Srimati Patwardhan and Muthulakshmi Reddy (1886–1968). While *SD* was a joint venture shared by Anglo and Indian women activists, as the organ of the WIA, it represented the values of Theosophy: religio-philosophical and occult, Gnosticism and Neoplatonism. Its broad emphasis on the existential human condition led to its establishment in India during the 'de-colonising' period, as activists welcomed outsiders' support against the British Empire. Surviving copies of *Stri-Dharma* are available in university collections throughout the United States, and at the British and Bodleian Libraries.

Following two years of irregular publication, *SD* stabilised into a monthly magazine featuring select articles translated into Tamil, Kannada, Hindi and Telugu. True of many women's magazines, it aimed less at profit than at recovering production costs while reaching a wide audience of women readers. Thus, it sold cheaply (2 annas) and was widely available in educational institutions and reading rooms. As it initially appeared without advertisements, that revenue became a necessity (for a time, at least), as did experiments with paper quality, size and frequency (monthly, bi-monthly, quarterly).

Like *ILM*, *SD*'s history was punctuated by repeated appeals for subscriptions in order to continue its work. That *SD* ceased publication in 1936 can be read less as a financial failure, perhaps, than as the successful realisation of its aims. When newly 'awakened' Indian women publicly asserted that 'leadership of the Indian feminist movement should rest in the hands of the women whom it claimed to serve' (Tusan 2003: 631) – not in those of foreign activists, however empathic – *SD*'s purpose had, in effect, been accomplished.

SD's striking cover image featured a standing woman dressed in a sari, arms outstretched, superimposed on a map of India, her feet grounded in Madras (place of publication), her heart in Benares (Varanasi, sacred to Hinduism), her head at the Himalayas ('clear and cool'). Evoking Victorian domestic ideology, she represents 'the ideal influence of woman . . . in every detail of daily life in every part of India' ('Dedication' 1918: 1). Reflecting the international scope of gender issues, her outstretched arms welcome sisters and brothers, East and West, to be united in the spirit of 'love for humanity, the fire of patriotism, the fire of zeal for reform . . . offered freely to Mother India'. The enterprise is dedicated 'To the women of India today, and to the memory of the Indian women of all past ages who have set an example of Courage, Wisdom, and Devotion to Truth'.

SD's fusing of internationalism with the 'upliftment' of Indian women posits the sisterhood of 'a great family, bound together . . . for the welfare of humanity' ('Dedication' 1918: 1). Individually and communally, family and home values are uppermost, aligning woman's role in its unblemished functioning with religious renunciation, her every act sacred and 'consecrated by Him' – suggesting a Christian allusion not linked with Theosophy ('Ourselves and Our Purpose' 1918: 2). Traditional Dharma, Women's Sphere, must be preserved fully intact in order for India to 'take her place among the great Nations'. In a striking parallel with *ILM*'s self-fashioning, *SD*'s opening statement moves from God to Dharma to Tennyson's *The Princess* – 'Woman's cause is man's, they rise or sink together . . . if she be small, slight natured, miserable, how shall man grow?' – thus cementing the Angel in the House as divinely ordained, for the benefit of man, for the patriotic cause, for the nation's independence. Here, British imperialism and Victorian domesticity are absorbed into Indian nationalism, blurring distinctions between Dharma and Angel ideology, purporting to represent reform while actually reifying tradition. Like *ILM*, *SD* confronted the Indian Woman

Question by condemning harmful traditions (suttee, widow abuse, child brides and mothers, devadasis) while advocating the domestic and maternal ideology compellingly illustrated by the iconic Bharat Mata.

SD differed from its counterpart in its emphasis on women's political activism. Indian New Women must do it all: be exemplary wives and mothers, educate themselves, and be political activists. Domestic ideology finds expression through community social work. But whereas *ILM* discouraged more visible modes of activism as potentially compromising to sexual honour, *SD* urged women not only to weave and wear khaddar but also to picket liquor stores, to attend political conferences, to submit to arrest and imprisonment for civil disobedience. The examples of Kamaladevi Chattopadhyaya and Sarojini Naidu, both incarcerated under brutal conditions for their association with Gandhi, dramatised the sacrifices every Indian woman must be prepared to make to redeem Bharat Mata. The emphasis on public activism was facilitated by the WIA's network of branch offices throughout India, where women could study together and read transcripts of conference lectures and proceedings in their own language ('Ourselves and Our Purpose' 1918: 2). In this version of Indian New Women, patriotism required the Angel in the House to take her purifying presence out into the streets, for the benefit of community and nation.

SD's regular features include reports of WIA and All India Women's Conference (AIWC), All-Asian Women's Conference, Women's International League and London's Round Table meetings (discussions between Indian National Congress and imperial officials regarding terms for independence), and transcriptions of speeches. Other columns include Suggestions for Conducting Branch Meetings, Editorial Notes, Association News, Study Notes (science lessons for branch meetings), Women the World Over, Ideal of Indian Womanhood, Woman's Movement in India, and Notes and Comments. Feature articles explored political debates and proposed policies impacting women, such as child and infant mortality, cultural prejudice against girl babies, hygiene and sanitary reform, suffrage, the Girl Guide Association, the exploitation of women and children, dowries, infanticide and bride-murder, women convicts, slum-reformation work, the Sarda Act and age of consent, Hindu marriage and divorce-law reform, home economics in college and university programmes, women's public activism, and women in relation to India's constitution.

From its inception, *SD*'s orientation was political, committed to a conventional domestic ideology brought into the service of patriotism. It offered a wealth of resources during this time of women's unprecedented participation in meetings and conferences, congresses and lectures, marches and picketing. Later, it offered occasional poems, typically dedicated to Gandhi, Cousins, Besant or Mother India, but generally avoided the arts or features for children or entertainment. In this, *SD* adheres strictly to substantive content, compared with *ILM*'s mixture of serious debates, instructive articles, and a variety of literary and artistic features.

SD's originating radical-feminist, international-sisterhood emphasis, focused on Indian womanhood in the context of nationalist activism, shifted markedly around 1930, when Dr Muthulakshmi Reddy took over as editor. Her editorship marked a general political and cultural shift away from a prevalence of outsiders in the freedom movement towards Indian activists' participation in civil disobedience. Reddy was a brilliant activist with an impressive list of accomplishments in education, medicine and social reforms aimed at such reviled categories as devadasis and brothel workers, trafficking in women and children, and – in a telling sign of the times – incorporating women into the police force to manage the arrests and incarceration of women while preserving their sexual honour and reputation. An eloquent speaker, she represented India at conferences and congresses throughout America and Europe, serving as one of the most effective and influential ambassadors for India in the western world.

Reddy's editorship of *SD* thus coincided with a number of key events. On 26 January 1930, the Indian National Congress formally declared independence from Britain. From March through to May, Gandhi's high-profile Dandi Salt March openly defied British authority, with Indian activists submitting to beatings and imprisonment, endured without resistance or retaliation. The world looked on in wonder at the unravelling of the British Empire's 'civilising mission' when faced with this radical form of assertive, yet non-violent, warfare. *SD*'s features by and about Gandhi in this period include pieces with titles such as 'The Women who Follow Gandhi' (exploring the international range of his support base), 'Feminism and Gandhi', 'Gandhiji's Message from Yerawada' on Harijans, and the 'Curse of Child Marriage'.

The Dandi Salt March represented a significant turning point in terms of Indian women's public activism. Gandhi had earlier rejected women's participation, claiming that the British would see their inclusion as a sign of cowardice, of Indian men hiding behind their women; women's presence would only 'complicate things'. But as women activists were quick to point out, their participation in fact exemplified Gandhi's 'appeal to a new method of warfare, soul-force, self-sacrifice without bloodshed or violence ... a supreme gesture of individual disarmament and national ahimsa [non-violence], while refusing to submit to subjection' ('Gandhiji and Women' 1930: 247). The author condemns women's exclusion as 'unnatural, and against all the awakened consciousness of modern womanhood'. Indeed, there should be no activism or meetings, congresses or marches, picketing or public events without women's participation, a pronouncement Gandhi himself subsequently seconded. The piece concludes with this encouraging note: 'As we go to Press news comes that women are now invited to share all phases of the campaign' ('Gandhiji and Women' 1930: 247).

Gandhi's appeal 'To the Women of India' clarifies shifts in his perspective on women's unique contributions to nationalist activism. Here, he praises 'the impatience of some sisters to join the good fight' as a 'healthy sign'; while men are associated with 'brute strength', woman's attribute is 'moral power' ('To the Women of India' 1930: 302). Regarding the brand of 'non-violent warfare' he advocates, woman is 'immeasurably man's superior' in terms of intuition, self-sacrifice, endurance and courage: 'Without her man could not be. If non-violence is the law of our being, the future is with woman.' The battle for India must be peaceful in order to educate people – a matter of 'conversion, moral suasion' rather than coercion, force or violence. By representing a moral centre in the midst of international conflict, it is those women who are willing to sacrifice the safety of home for the uncertainty of the streets that will ensure India's success. This renders women activists and prisoners a far more palpable threat than men, their signature modesty and gentleness not degraded but elevated by these events.

Three aspects of nationalist activism had particular impact on women's domestic roles. First, salt was a commodity traditionally harvested for free by Indians and used in cooking; Britain's salt tax disadvantaged many Indians who were already enduring extreme poverty. Second, the prevalence of liquor stores impacted women married to men who drank, spending wages and brutalising wife and children through domestic violence. The third factor involves textiles, a traditional Indian craft nearly decimated by Britain's mills and factories and imported fabric. Thus, women had a practical interest in offering packets of self-harvested salt for sale in public, for picketing liquor stores, for boycotting imported fabric (Gandhi famously ignited public bonfires fuelled by British fabric), and in weaving khaddar (homespun cotton) to clothe their families. Khaddar weaving and wearing, participated in by men, women and children, became a potent symbol of the independence movement, fashioning a sort of uniform symbolising nationalist solidarity. 'As a war measure', noted Gandhi, khaddar 'is not to be beaten' ('To the Women of India' 1930: 302).

Gandhi's emphasis on 'educating the people concerned' – those in power who knew and cared nothing about India, interested only in its profitability – found expression in the overarching endeavours represented by *ILM* and *SD*. Emphasising the centre-to-circumference dynamic, it is education and literacy that will uplift India and propel it on to the world stage. By association, it is certainly inescapable that the 'England-returned' core of the independence movement was so well schooled in European Enlightenment principles as to metaphorically defeat the imperialists at their own game. It was those very imperialists who needed to learn that India was more than a collection of natural resources there for the exploitation, hence the special significance of English-language Indian periodicals. The question of literacy applies in various ways to women's political activism. In Gandhi's words, 'in this agitation thousands of women literate and illiterate can take part' ('To the Women of India' 1930: 303). While one need not be literate in any language to march, picket or weave, 'highly educated women' activists have a special 'opportunity of actively identifying themselves with the masses and helping them both morally and materially'. The reminder that literacy was enjoyed by precious few emphasised that it was the educated and literate who had the greatest patriotic responsibility to put their talents to use for the national cause.

SD's review of Romain Rolland's book *Mahatma Gandhi* clarifies key points of Gandhian ideology. India's biggest social problem, along with untouchability, is 'the sexual problem . . . an all-pervading, oppressive and badly directed sensuality' ('Feminism of Gandhi' 1933: 278), seen in such customs as child marriage and motherhood, widow abuse and prostitution. Defence of such practices underpins some Hindu nationalists' 'degrading attitude' toward women. Child marriage was an issue Gandhi pronounced on – no girl under eighteen should be married; he 'takes the women's side' while also expecting 'more from the oppressed than from the oppressors'. He 'calls upon women to demand and inspire respect by ceasing to think of themselves as the objects of masculine desire'. Let them forget their bodies, forget luxuries, dowry jewels and foreign goods, and emulate the 'many distinguished women [who] have faced arrest and imprisonment in Calcutta. This shows proper spirit.' Indeed, he concludes, 'one who knows how to die need never fear.' Encouragingly, he posits that as a result of picketing, boycotting and weaving, 'they might even find themselves in prison. It is not improbable that they may be insulted and even injured bodily. To suffer such insult and injury would be their pride.'

Indian women activists' loyalty to Gandhi surfaces in 'Mothers of India', written in a forthright and aggressive tone: 'Gandhiji has been arrested. The truth is that Mother India, who has been in fetters for centuries, is going to be free; and the arrest of Gandhiji is its guarantee . . . the spirit of Gandhi can never be jailed, it broods over myriads of men, women and children of this country' – including the as-yet unborn ('Mothers of India' 1930: 409). 'Truly we are living in marvellous times . . . the mothers of India have joined the standard of revolt. . . . Let the Britisher make peace with Gandhiji. . . . the generation that is coming will . . . tolerate the Britisher no longer.' Interestingly, reports of Gandhi's arrest in *ILM* and *SD* convey an indomitable spirit, a relentless optimism that detects in India's darkest hour the signs of triumph. Why else would 'the Britisher' be so troubled by Gandhi, his pacifism and his global celebrity status, however unsought?

In January 1936, toward the end of its run, *SD* asserted 'we have successfully fought against the communal and provincial outlook, which has been a disquieting feature of public life in India' ('AIWC' 1936: 4), that persistent 'degrading attitude' toward women. But the true independence or 'upliftment' of women, despite international gains in their 'legal emancipation', is still far from being realised:

> the full recognition and the securing of the individual position of women in domestic relations are yet insecure because of the survival of the old doctrine of tutelage . . . It is a commonplace that woman's cause is man's and that men and women sink or swim together, but experience has taught us that self-help and organisations are the only methods to secure success as distinguished from mere reliance on generosity or patronage. ('AIWC' 1936: 5)

After nearly a century of reformists, East and West, quoting Tennyson's *The Princess* as the ultimate pronouncement on gender cooperation, this assertion clarifies an aspect of that ubiquitous statement long overlooked and ignored. Woman's cause is man's, but this is not reciprocated. Men continue to be in charge, occasionally and grudgingly conceding certain rights and privileges to women, insofar as that suits their own agenda. Indian New Women must work and prepare and agitate on their own behalf to break free from the 'old doctrine of tutelage' defining patriarchal privilege: for the sake of themselves, for the sake of their children and the yet-unborn, for the sake of Bharat Mata.

Ominously, the same number revealed that 'the affairs of *Stri-Dharma* are at a crisis', voicing appeals to readers for contributions 'literary and financial' in order to keep going ('Announcement' 1936: 131). An invitation to AIWC to assume responsibility for *SD* was declined. Reflecting its fraught beginning in 1918, the May 1936 number apologises for ongoing 'delays and irregularities' in publication. The August 1936 number marked the final issue of *Stri-Dharma*.

The Indian New Woman

The period 1901 to 1938 featured an unbroken line of English-language, woman-centred periodicals, published in Madras and distributed nationally and internationally. By catering specifically to the Indian Woman Question, *ILM* and *SD* were unique among vernacular women's publications (accessible only to regional speakers) and male-edited periodicals (not woman-centred). Macaulay's 1835 Minute on Education rendered English-language literacy a prerequisite for Indian men with ambitions to work in government and public positions, providing a strong motivation for acquiring the Empire's language. With rare exceptions, Indian women – expected to work only in the home – were consistently left behind, in English or in any other language.

The striking rise in woman-centred publications from the *fin de siècle* forward attested to women's determination to confront the literacy gap: formal schooling being inaccessible to most, resources for home-schooling – such as those provided by inexpensive, instructive periodicals – served to ameliorate the situation. While it is true that many vernacular magazines offered a similar service, English-language magazines provided dual instruction – first, to newly educated Indian women, and second, to the British, who were instructed in Indian ways and customs, culture and ideology. By design, the cultural exchange worked both ways. In turn, what began as attempts to forge intercultural solidarity evolved into a unique historical account of the 'upliftment' of Indian womanhood up to the Quit India period. Women's unprecedented shifts from purdah to street protests, and from mental purdah to leading roles in nationalist organisations, are eloquently recorded in *ILM* and *SD*.

Between 1901 and 1918, *ILM*'s content represents neo-Victorian values, always seeking ways to highlight the similarities and common ground linking British and Indian society and culture. Empire and colony were joined; therefore, facilitating harmonious relations was a central concern. But the stronger concern was Indian womanhood: advancing women through modernisation; encouraging them through news, resources and opportunities; and promoting their full participation in world events – all while preserving their signature self-effacing, gentle demeanour. For *ILM*, this was the real challenge: bringing women forward, out of physical and mental purdah, to participate in the modern world, without losing their culturally defining purity.

Between 1918 and 1936, *SD*'s content navigated a similar challenge in its advocacy of radical-feminist, political activism while also preserving Indian women's 'special' qualities. *SD* was anti-imperialist, interested not in finding common ground but in advancing Indian culture for its own sake. Initially, the Anglo-Indian influence was a strong driving force in support of Indian independence, but ultimately, newly empowered Indian women assumed this role for themselves. While the defiant activism and notorious arrests of Annie Besant (1917) and Margaret Cousins (1932) provided suggestive models for women's activism, it was the shocking arrests of such privileged Indian women as Sarojini Naidu (1930) and Kamaladevi Chattopadhyaya (1930) that signalled a turning point, one leading inevitably to Quit India. Once Gandhi re-examined his attitudes against women's public activism, the Indian New Woman came forward in public life, her very presence now representing that signature purity, incapable of being tarnished in the service of Bharat Mata. This New Woman, who publicly protested and willingly presented herself for arrest, manifested the very definition of a good woman, a pure woman, a modern woman.

The two publications, then, shared the goal of advancing womanhood and Indian nationalism, although by alternative means. Both relied on an essentialist view of gender roles, using that ideology as the fulcrum from which to promote change. Aside from the neo-Victorianism of *ILM* and the radical-feminist politicising of *SD*, a comparative survey reveals little differentiation between the two. Responding to the unique circumstances unfolding in the 1930s, both reported on the activities and arrests of nationalist activists, directly defying Britain's Indian Press Emergency Powers Act that was designed to suppress just such news. *ILM* and *SD* managed to escape censors' notice, perhaps considered inconsequential as woman-centred publications. But it was economic stress, not imperial censors, that ended the lives of both periodicals.

As the timeline of *ILM* and *SD* aptly demonstrates, first-generation Indian women activists found their voice through literacy, while the second generation directly engaged in the public realm (Logan 2017: 244). The impact and significance of *The Indian Ladies' Magazine* and *Stri-Dharma* represent a chapter in modern Indian history that witnessed the transformation, in just a few decades, of illiterate purdah-women into soldiers serving at the frontlines of the war of 'national ahimsa'. In 1942, Gandhi demanded that Britain 'Quit India'; in 1947, it did.

Bibliography

'AIWC' (1936), *Stri-Dharma*, 19.1, January, 4–5.
'Announcement' (1936), *Stri-Dharma*, 19.4, May, 131.
Bannerji, Himani (1991), 'Fashioning a self: Educational proposals for and by women in popular magazines in colonial Bengal', *Economic and Political Weekly*, 26.43, 26 October, 50–62.
'Comilla Shooting' (1931), *Indian Ladies' Magazine*, 5.5, 257.
'Dedication' (1918), *Stri-Dharma*, 1.1, January, 1.
'Feminism of Gandhi' (1933), *Stri-Dharma*, 16.6, April, 278.
'Gandhiji and Women' (1930), *Stri-Dharma*, 13.6, May, 247.
'Glimpse of Tagore's Ideal Womanhood' (1932), *Indian Ladies' Magazine*, 5.6, 265–6.
'Hitler . . . Hess' (1936), *Indian Ladies' Magazine*, 9.4, 148–55.
'Introduction' (1901), *Indian Ladies' Magazine*, 1.1, 1–2.
'Kasturba Gandhi' (1930), *Indian Ladies' Magazine*, 3.11, 556–7.
Logan, Deborah Anna (2017), *The Indian Ladies' Magazine, 1901–1938: From Raj to Swaraj*, Bethlehem, PA: Lehigh University Press.
'Military Training for German Girls' (1936), *Indian Ladies' Magazine*, 9.21, 70–1.
'Mothers of India' (1930), *Stri-Dharma*, 13.9, 409.
Orsini, Francesca (1999), 'Domesticity and beyond: Hindi women's journals in the early twentieth century', *South Asia Research*, 19, 137–60.
'Ourselves' (1930), *Indian Ladies' Magazine*, 3.6, 275–6.
'Ourselves and Our Purpose' (1918), *Stri-Dharma*, 1.1, January, 2.
'Place of Women' (1933), *Indian Ladies' Magazine*, 6.5, 207–10.
'Purdah Picketers' (1930), *Indian Ladies' Magazine*, 3.11, 557.
'Sarojini' (1930), *Indian Ladies' Magazine*, 3.11, 557–8.
Sreenivas, Mytheli (2003), 'Emotion, identity, and the female subject: Tamil women's magazines in Colonial India, 1890–1940', *Journal of Women's History*, 14.4, 59–82.
'To the Women of India' by Gandhi (1930), *Stri-Dharma*, 7.13, June, 302–4.
Tusan, Michelle (2003), 'Writing *Stri Dharma*: International feminism, nationalist politics, and women's press advocacy in late colonial India', *Women's History Review*, 12.4, 623–48.
'Viceroy' (1918), *Indian Ladies' Magazine*, 18, 252–3.
'Vienna Women's Conference' (1930), *Indian Ladies' Magazine*, 4.2, 110.
'Women's Congress' (1930), *Indian Ladies' Magazine*, 4.2, 109.
'Women's War' (1930), *Indian Ladies' Magazine*, 3.12, 611–12.

15

MARRIAGE HYGIENE AND THE INTERNATIONALISATION OF EUGENICAL SEXOLOGY IN THE 1930S

Tanya Agathocleous, Ruwanthi Edirisinghe, Jessica Lu, Jaïra Placide and Sarah Schwartz

MARRIAGE HYGIENE WAS a sexology journal published in India from 1934 to 1937. In its early years, its articles predominantly focused on sex education, birth control and sterilisation, issues that were also of central concern to eugenicists. Further demonstrating the substantial overlap between sexology and eugenics in this period, the journal was edited by a prominent doctor named A. J. Pillay, who was involved with a number of influential eugenics initiatives in India. He founded the Bombay-based Society for Study and Promotion of Family Hygiene and strove, successfully, to forge links with eugenics activists abroad, setting up Margaret Sanger as Vice-President of the Society and introducing her to local birth control advocates during her Indian tour. He also worked tirelessly, at his own expense, to win his journal a global audience. By giving them an international platform at a time when both sexology and eugenics were controversial subjects in their own countries, Pillay secured interest and contributions from high-profile western thinkers such as renowned British sexologist Havelock Ellis and the American sociologist Norman Himes; they, in turn, championed the journal among audiences in Britain and America. After *Marriage Hygiene* ran into financial problems in 1937 and had to temporarily cease publication, Pillay travelled around the world to raise funding and managed to launch a second run from 1947 to 1955 that had even more international visibility; in 1948, the title was changed to the *International Journal of Sexology*, reflecting the increased acceptance of sexology that the journal had itself helped to instantiate. As a 1947 editorial noted, 'in 1934, the word "sexology" was thoroughly disreputable', so the editors had made a calculated decision, in using the compound term 'Marriage Hygiene', to 'find a name which should connote what the Journal actually deals with, and at the same time *sound* innocuous to the ear of the public and "non-obscene" to the ear of customs authorities' (Dickinson 1947: 1). The switch from *Marriage Hygiene* to the *International Journal of Sexology* may have also reflected the growing public distrust of eugenics that followed the defeat of Nazi Germany, as the word 'hygiene' was often used in eugenics discourse: Alfred Ploetz, the prominent German eugenicist, coined the term 'racial hygiene' in 1895 to describe the set of eugenics ideas that would eventually underpin Nazism (Turda 2010: 64).

This chapter will focus on *Marriage Hygiene*'s first run which started in 1934, when it was still a colonial journal, to demonstrate the importance of the imperial

Figure 15.1 *Marriage Hygiene*, 1.2, November 1934, cover. Courtesy of the authors.

context to its subject matter and to its influential role in international sexology and eugenics debates (see Figure 15.1). Though largely unknown to contemporary scholars, the story of *Marriage Hygiene* and its internationalism is a significant one, for it helps us to understand how the eugenics focus on birth control in the first half of the twentieth century got transformed into one on population control in the second half. If '[t]he strong continuities between colonial eugenics agendas and postcolonial population control efforts are striking elements in the history of eugenics in South Asia' (Hodges 2010: 228), they also demonstrate the transition from British to American global influence in the postcolonial world order, and the ways 'modern' views of race and gender were used in the service of that influence.

Marriage Hygiene's editorial advisory board at first consisted entirely of Indian male medical practitioners, with Pillay at the helm. Early issues featured Indian issues prominently, such as 'The Problem of Sterilisation in India' by Bhaskar Namdeo Adarkar; 'Difficulties Regarding Marriage Reforms in Hindu Society' by S. K. Chaudhuri; 'Some Aspects of Contraception for Indian Women' by Marie C. Stopes; and 'Indian Outlook on Sex Relations' by R. C. Rakshit. But from its first issue, *Marriage Hygiene* also boasted a transnational, comparative outlook, showcasing a large number of prominent western writers, including Ellis, Stopes, Julian Huxley and C. P. Blacker, all of whom were, or would become, renowned members of the British Eugenics Society. As part of its international profile, the journal would maintain close ties with the Eugenics Society throughout its first run, not only publishing its members but reprinting many articles from the Society's publication the *Eugenics Review*, and publishing adverts for it; correspondingly, the *Eugenics Review* included notices and reviews of *Marriage Hygiene* and listed it as one of the journals with which it regularly exchanged copies.

In its August 1935 issue, *Marriage Hygiene* added a 'World News' section that profiled Dutch birth control clinics alongside developments in India and the United States, and with each subsequent issue it put more and more pins on the world map: by the August 1936 issue, the front matter listed editors for America (Norman E. Himes), the Continent (Felix Tietze), England (Edward F. Griffith), Far East Countries (Amos Wong) and Soviet Russia (Max Hodann), and its 'World News' section included coverage of birth control in China and South Africa, as well as abortion policy changes in Russia. By the end of its second year, it had been noticed and favourably reviewed in the American scientific journals *Human Biology* and *Nature* as well as the *Eugenics Review*, and 'H.G. Wells [had] acclaimed it as the leading journal in English' (Ramusack 1989: 45). By the time it became the *International Journal of Sexology*, it was far more international than Indian in outlook, boasting contributors and editors from twenty-three countries, including Australia, China, Norway, Japan, Israel, Switzerland and South Africa.

The journal's objectives, listed on the inside cover of each issue, were expressed in international terms from the start. In its first run, these included some combination of the following:

1. To publish contributions which are believed to be necessary for scientific same sex teaching, with an outlook on physiology rather than pathology, on normal functions of life rather than on the abnormal.
2. To bind its readers together into a brotherhood of clean thinkers and bold fighters against prejudice, evasion, and meaningless taboos.
3. To interpret marriage as a social and biological institution, to rid it of all meaningless taboos, evasion and prejudice by focusing on it the light of modern science and to secure for the science of conjugal hygiene a proper place in preventive medicine by persistently setting forth the importance of this subject and its interactions, on the personal, domestic, and social life and happiness *of nations* (our emphasis).
4. To promote, coordinate and unite the interests of contraceptive clinics and marriage hygiene consultation centres in *various parts of the globe* (our emphasis).

These objectives underscored the journal's attempt to intertwine the goals of sexology (as outlined in points 1 and 2) and eugenics (points 3 and 4) while positioning itself, like these discourses did, as forward-thinking, scientific, educational and international in outlook. As the italicised language above suggests, *Marriage Hygiene* imagined itself as an activist as well as an intellectual force, one that would advance the interests of individual nations around the world by putting them in conversation, League of Nations-style.

The first issue, published in August 1934, accentuated the journal's international purview by reprinting an essay by Ellis (first published in *Twentieth Century*) entitled 'The Problem of Sterilisation'. Ellis was part of 'a second generation of sexual scientists, who self-consciously and explicitly broadened the disciplinary scope of sexual science' (Fisher and Funke 2015: 97). Alongside his influential and progressive work on human sexuality, women's rights and sex education, he played a pivotal role in British debates about eugenics that came to prominence after the devastation of World War I and its effects on the population's so-called 'good stock'. In the first two decades of the twentieth century, his writings on eugenics were particularly concerned with the various methods of sterilisation used in eugenic practices, as well as the question of how to encourage people to choose sterilisation voluntarily, since the notion of involuntary sterilisation had encountered widespread public opposition in Britain.

Being granted permission to republish a pioneer like Havelock Ellis in its premiere issue would have been a coup for *Marriage Hygiene*, but also for Ellis himself, as well as the British and American eugenicists with whom he was in conversation. Not only did it gain their work wider circulation, but it gave them an inroad into one of the regions – South Asia – that epitomised to many western eugenicists the problem of overpopulation. It is not surprising, then, that according to the editorial notes in the very first issue, it was Norman Himes who encouraged Pillay to 'expand the journal into an international publication with a Board of Editors [that included] representatives from the major countries', even as Pillay initially expresses scepticism about the 'difficulty of working this up from a city like Bombay' ('Editorial Notes' 1934: 2). Similarly, Ellis felt that 'this Journal should form the literary organ of all societies and organisations in the English-speaking countries working on marriage and sex' ('Notes and Comments' 1935: 117). Concerned about 'intercontinental, interregional, and often interracial movement' during the interwar period, reformist thinkers like Himes and members of the British Eugenics Society believed that eugenics had to take a planetary perspective, because it 'involved consideration of apparently universal principles of evolution and the inheritance for humanity as a whole [while] somewhere in between lay close consideration of the role of eugenics in regulating and monitoring international human movement' (Bashford 2010: 158).

If *Marriage Hygiene*'s internationalism seemed a boon to Himes and Ellis, it was also advantageous to Pillay, for different but related reasons: it gave the journal's eugenics outlook additional scientific credibility and helped to establish not only that India was capable of progressive approaches to sexuality and birth control, but that it was helping to shape a global conversation and movement that tackled both head on. This was politically significant because both sexuality and birth control – issues concerned with individual self-determination – were also subjects at the heart of questions of national self-determination in this period:

> Eugenicists asserted that Indians could manage their own reproduction and in so doing breed a better India. Some connected individual reproductive self-governance to demonstrating fitness for political autonomy. Elected Indian officials in provincial ministries repeatedly called on the government to fund contraceptive advice as part of material and infant welfare initiatives. (Hodges 2010: 230)

Thus, while the movement for Indian independence was never an overt subject of the journal, by putting itself at the forefront of an international conversation about sexology, *Marriage Hygiene* was implicitly aligning itself with the anti-colonial, nationalist impulses of the period, with its focus on birth control and family planning serving, in effect, as a large-scale counter-argument to colonial sexological discourses that fed into racist narratives about Indian sexual depravity and civilisational backwardness that in turn served as an apologia for colonialism. While these discourses had encouraged anti-British sentiment, direct imperial interventions around marital and sexual issues – seen as insulting attacks on Indian identity – had actively fanned the flames of anti-colonial nationalism: incidents included early attempts by the British government to combat sati (1829) and to introduce an Age of Consent Law (1891) and, more immediately, US journalist Katherine Mayo's notorious travelogue about the depravity of Indian marriage and child-bearing customs, *Mother India* (1927).

In her study of the controversy around Mayo's publication, Mrinalini Sinha describes it as a historic event that transformed India's political trajectory, during both its anti-colonial struggle and its subsequent attempts to establish itself as a modern nation state following its independence in 1947 (Sinha 2006). *Mother India* positioned itself as a humanitarian intervention that chronicled the social and sexual degeneracy of native populations, with a particular focus on child marriage and infant mortality, in order to advocate Britain's continued rule in India. The book gleaned a huge international audience, outraged Indians, and lit a fire under feminist-nationalist reform movements. Mayo's critics countered her arguments by suggesting that the problems she outlined were a result not of Indian cultural norms but of colonial rule, and backed support for a law against child marriage in India – the Child Marriage Act of 1929 – as 'the most fitting nationalist riposte to *Mother India* . . . the colonial state, far from being absolved of responsibility for the social backwardness of India, was shown up for its timid and obstructionist response to modernizing social reform' (Sinha 2006: 11).

Some of the way the assumptions of *Mother India* were countered in *Marriage Hygiene* can be seen in articles such as the 1934 essay titled 'Indian Outlook on Sex Relations' published in the journal's first series, in which author Romeschandra Rakshit implicitly counters Mayo's criticism of Hinduism as the root cause of Indian degeneracy by undertaking a close reading of how ancient Hindu philosophy advocates 'the enjoyment of the pleasures of the flesh for the full and complete development of all [human] functions'; '[l]ong before the advent of the Christian era our ancestors could recognize the fact that the exercise of the normal sex impulses was a paramount necessity and imperative for the preservation of health' (Rakshit 1934: 147). The author situates the Victorian frameworks of sexual morality that were imported to colonised spaces as a gross impediment to Indian sexual and social reform, thereby reversing the conceptual framework of *Mother India* while simultaneously denouncing and correcting western assumptions about pre-colonial Indian sexuality (Rakshit 1934: 149).

But the journal's overall emphasis on women's reproductive capacities, with its articles on and advertisements for birth control, sex education and marital mores, also demonstrates how profoundly the nationalist imagination of this period was shaped by what Asha Nadkarni calls 'eugenic feminism' (Nadkarni 2014: 1) (see Figure 15.2). The kind of eugenics-focused sexology showcased by *Marriage Hygiene* reshaped the synonymity of woman with the nation that underwrote both the idealised figure of 'Mother India' in early anti-colonial discourses and the abject figure of Mayo's book, by transforming her from traditional and passive to modern and progressive: a subject whose growing autonomy was crucial to the liberal imagination of the postcolonial state.

Women went from being regarded as biological reproducers and idealised symbols of traditional community to signifiers of India's modernity via their participation in 'positive' eugenics, for their growing ability to take charge of reproduction via birth

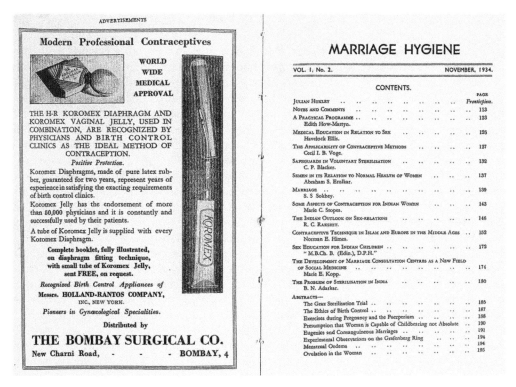

Figure 15.2 *Marriage Hygiene*, 1.2, November 1934, advertisement for contraceptives and table of contents. Courtesy of the authors.

control made them active rather than passive participants in family planning, and thus a key part of the eugenic endeavour to harness the power of evolution to the ends of national regeneration by encouraging the fittest to breed. Examining Margaret Sanger's eugenic feminist impulse and the manner in which nineteenth- and twentieth-century feminisms across the globe sought to bolster their authority within nationalist discourses by finding 'common cause between feminism and eugenics', Alexandra Minna Stern maintains that Sanger's 'tireless advocacy of contraception was tied always to a desire to lower birthrates among the labouring classes, immigrants and racial minorities, whom she deemed to be biologically inferior', thus paving the way for fellow educated, middle-class women in colonised spaces to 'discourag[e] rural and urban poor women from reproduction' (Stern 2010: 178).

In many ways the new agency, invested in women on behalf of their 'race' or 'nation' (the two terms often used interchangeably in the journal and in eugenics discourse more broadly), opened the door on to ostensibly progressive ideas about gender and sexuality. For example, 'The Erotic Rights of Women' by Lieutenant Colonel Owen Berkeley-Hill argued that women must be liberated from the myths about their sexuality created when 'her natural impulses towards pleasure were first banned and then sealed with a satisfying fiction that sexual pleasure is dangerous or even degrading to women' (Berkeley-Hill 1937: 30).

But despite essays such as this – and its ongoing advocacy for contraceptives and abortion – *Marriage Hygiene*'s potential allegiance with feminism was compromised by its failure to represent the voices of Indian women who were identified with the movement and who were agitating for reproductive rights in other forums during this period, such as the All India Women's Conference, whose first meeting in 1927 pre-dated the journal (Ramusack 1989: 41). While it did publish occasional articles by prominent western female birth control advocates such as Sanger and Marie Stopes, the journal's Indian writers were almost exclusively male and the journal as a whole presented women as objects of study rather than subjects of their own political struggle.[1]

It was also compromised by the fact that potentially feminist topics such as woman's sexual satisfaction were consistently framed within the context of marriage, for, according to eugenics discourse, the goal of sexual pleasure was to increase marital harmony and longevity, thereby ensuring a healthy environment for raising children.[2] Berkeley-Hill's article ultimately asserted that 'Every woman is entitled to consummate her biological destiny, that is to give birth to a child. What, on the other hand, she is not entitled to is to give birth to a child whose prospects are very poor through bad inheritance of becoming a worthy member of society' (Berkeley-Hill 1937: 33). As Jeffrey Weeks explains in relation to the British context, because eugenics was born out of conversations around the development of a national population policy, there was 'a partial shift in the dominant discourses, away from the nineteenth-century stress on woman as wife towards an accentuated (though not of course new) emphasis on woman as mother' (Weeks 2017: 126).[3] Woman's role as mother, in other words, was modernised by sexology but remained as ideologically central to twentieth-century ideas about the family as it had been to nineteenth-century ones.

A contribution to the journal by zoologist and fellow of the Indian National Academy of Science P. R. Awati provides a salient example of the way women's biological and social function were linked, underscoring Weeks's point that the shift in focus on motherhood correlated with the rise of concerns about national populations globally. 'Evolution of Mother's Love', the first part of Awati's serial contribution 'Mother's Love and Constitution of the Family', described 'successive stages and different types among the animal world, of the parental care which has ultimately blossomed into Mother's Love among human beings' (Awati 1935: 241). The work traces the shifts in parental care from amoeba and protozoa to birds, worms and other small creatures, then to mammals, and finally to humans. In humans, 'social education' turns 'mammalian physiological maternal care into the psychological mother's love'. 'Mother's love' then 'constitutes a new psychological development by which an individual mind is linked up with others to form a new organisation and that is the human family' (Awati 1935: 244). This logic not only naturalises the role of mother within the human family using evolutionary theory, but it also centres her role in holding the family together. The article both represents a pervasive logic in the journal whereby the figure of woman is tied to her biological function – motherhood – and also accentuates the central role motherhood has to play in the eugenical project of human improvement by locating maternal love at the vanguard of the evolutionary process.

An even more extreme version of women's reproductive bind and its relation to eugenic nationalism can be seen in 'The Problem of Sterilisation in India', Bhaskar Namdeo Adarkar's implicit defence of the logic underlying Nazi Germany's sterilisation campaign, which he reads as a pro-nationalist move carried out 'for the purity and happiness of [the German] race' (Adarkar 1934: 180). Citing Germany and other western countries such as England, Switzerland and Denmark as examples, the author calls for the legalisation of sterilisation in India. By making the cultural and biological currency of women's bodies the crux of his argument, the author argues that women, especially those 'who have reached the point of exhaustion as a result of repeated pregnancy and who are incapable of exercising continuous self-discipline, either in the way of abstinence or birth control', should be made privy to the possibility of sterilisation, and maintains that eugenic sterilisation is especially needed among 'feebleminded' and lower-class women, given their general poverty, lack of education and judgement, limited access to contraception and other 'practical difficulties', such as hunger and life-threatening illnesses, that confront them daily (Adarkar 1934: 183). That eugenic sterilisation is figured as emblematic of the modern nation-building project is further reinforced by the author's insistence that India should diverge from Germany in its sterilisation policies by making the process voluntary: the focus on consent in the ongoing sterilisation debates in the US and Britain, as well as India, was crucial to differentiating the liberal national project from more authoritarian ones, such as Germany's.

Though its scientific and modern approach to sexology attempted to counter the racist and pro-imperial arguments of works such as *Mother India*, then, the journal seemed not to recognise the degree to which it was contributing to the scientising of colonial racial paradigms. For example, an article entitled 'Race-Crossing and Glands', extracted from the *Eugenics Review*, noted that an experiment in 'blood-mixing' found disharmonies in the 'hybrids' of Nordic and Indigenous populations and that this was supported by 'observations made on animal crossings' (Anon. 1934b, *Marriage Hygiene*: 95). Along with Adarkar's article, with its sympathy for Nazi Germany, the 'Race-Crossing' piece suggests that *Marriage Hygiene* – like much eugenics discourse of this period – was playing with fire in terms of racial politics and in terms of the potential effect of its advocacy on women who, as we have seen, were imagined as the beneficiaries of the journal's liberation, but were in effect marginalised as contributors to its discourse and essentialised by its focus on motherhood and the biological determination of gender.

Two different legacies of the journal give a sense of the lasting and varied effects of the fraught 1930s moment of eugenics internationalism of which it was a part. The first was its impact on the global circulation of birth control information. Even as attention to Indian topics became more attenuated in the journal as it internationalised over time, the fact that *Marriage Hygiene* was published in one of the few English-speaking countries in which birth control information could legally circulate, and that it had international visibility, made the journal crucial to the eugenical mission of globally expanding the availability and acceptance of contraception.

Marriage Hygiene, and eventually the *International Journal of Sexology*, readily supplied information on family planning resources through its copious adverts, and targeted both women and men. For example, in the journal's second issue, an oral contraceptive named Contrafant was advertised at the end of Adarkar's 'The Problem of Sterilisation in India'. Contrafant tablets were sold by a Bombay-based pharmaceutical company known as the 'Anglo-German Drug Co.' and touted as 'the new German oxygen contraceptive [that] affords the best possible means of preventing contraception safely, quickly, and reliably' (Anon. 1934a, *Marriage Hygiene*: 184).

Aimed specifically at men, the advert centred men's obligations to women and the national benefits of fulfilling them: 'The necessity of preserving the health and beauty of women and the increasing economic depression requires every man to adopt methods of birth control.' The third issue of the journal, published in February 1935, featured an entire section of birth control and sanitary advertisements, including an antibacterial contraceptive disinfectant foam called Semori, spermicidal vaginal suppositories (Pantatex and Controid), and a birth control method that combined a diaphragm and 'vaginal jelly'.

Along with these adverts, there were also advertisements for products that treated male impotence and venereal disease. One of the adverts published in the journal's first issue featured medicines named 'Gonoral' and 'Chromolan': oral tablets designed to treat gonorrhoea and syphilis respectively. The diseases were dubbed by the advertisements – which were strategically located at the end of C. P. Blacker's essay 'Eugenics in Relation to the Maintenance of Health and Avoidance of Disease' – 'the enemies to a happy marriage!' (Blacker 1934: 75). Collectively, these advertisements reminded readers that eugenical sexology sought not to curb sex but to control it, by drawing it into the sanctity of medicine, scientific study and, above all, marriage.

But even as the journal as a whole sidelined the voices of Indian women and represented them chiefly as a problem to be managed, its adverts partially countered these representations, along with the image of the helpless and uneducated Indian mother that populated works such as Mayo's *Mother India*, by constructing women as savvy consumers taking charge of family planning and of their own sexuality. In suggesting that birth control was freely advertised and readily available in India, if not elsewhere, the journal's advertisements – in the global context in which they circulated – emphasised Indian eugenical vanguardism. Not only did the journal provide information about birth control, but it also included information about sex, reproduction and sexuality in general that was hard to find elsewhere.

One of the most notable effects of the journal's progressivism in this regard was on the dissemination of birth control information in the US. After its first few issues made it to American shores and began to circulate, *Marriage Hygiene* was increasingly confiscated and banned by US customs for violating the 1875 Comstock Act, which made it illegal to circulate information about birth control. In 1937, however, with the support of Margaret Sanger and American Civil Liberties Union lawyer Morris Ernst, the journal took the government to court for censorship and won; as a result, birth control information was no longer prohibited in the US (as long as it was disseminated to and by approved individuals, such as physicians). As Norman Himes put it in a victorious letter to the editor of the *Eugenics Review*, thanks to *Marriage Hygiene*, 'the Comstock Act has been notably amended, if not all but wiped out' (Himes 1938: 227).

The second, far less salubrious long-term effect of *Marriage Hygiene* and the international eugenics discourse of which it was a part was the adoption by the postcolonial Indian state of a eugenics agenda that would have lasting pernicious consequences. In 1938, a year after the journal's first run ended, the Indian National Congress passed a resolution stating that 'The state should follow a eugenic programme to make the race physically and mentally healthy. This would discourage marriages of unfit persons and provide for the sterilization of persons suffering from transmissible diseases of a serious nature such as insanity or epilepsy' (Klausen and Bashford 2010: 105). After independence, Jawaharlal Nehru followed up on this recommendation by proactively adopting a eugenics platform: he 'chaired the National Planning Commission, and its 1951 report called for free sterilisation and contraception on medical, social, and economic grounds, as well as birth control research' (Klausen and Bashford 2010: 105).

This left the door open to US influence on the region via developmental aid tied to birth control. Neo-Malthusians such as Sanger were particularly concerned about overpopulation in large countries such as India and China, in part because of the large waves of Asian immigration to the Global North in the 1920s and 1930s: overpopulation in these countries was seen as both a racial threat in global eugenics terms, and a security threat in geopolitical terms. The kind of ties that *Marriage Hygiene* had forged with western birth control advocates such as Sanger had laid the groundwork for national birth control schemes, initially focused on changing the behaviour of individuals, to global population control agendas, focused on changing the behaviour of states (often via the work of NGOs): 'the earlier connections forged among eugenics associations in Britain, the United States, and independent South Asian nations endured and, in some cases, intensified as voluntary family planning associations administered population control development aid on behalf of state agencies' (Hodges 2010: 234).

Marriage Hygiene was not directly responsible for these state positions, of course. But the complex place the journal occupied at the intersection of scientific racism, anti-colonialism, eugenics and feminism made it a volatile agent of history, whose role in the international circulation of eugenics discourse in the lead-up to the Second World War has had indubitably lasting consequences still to be fully recognised or reckoned with.

Notes

1. Although it had some anonymous articles which may have been authored by Indian women, and although it did regularly report on the activities of the All India Women's Conference, the journal seems to have published few, if any, Indian women authors in either its first or second series.
2. As Susanne Klausen and Alison Bashford argue, eugenicists were often 'intensely anti-feminist'. See Klausen and Bashford 2010: 109. Nonetheless, as Alexandra Minna Stern notes, 'Eugenicists broke barriers, especially when it came to discussing female bodies and sexuality' (Stern 2010: 183).
3. Weeks examines the regulation of sexuality in the nineteenth and twentieth centuries in the British Isles, but the trend he identifies tracks with international trends in thinking (Weeks 2017: 122–40).

Bibliography

Adarkar, Bhaskar Namdeo (1934), 'The Problem of Sterilisation in India', *Marriage Hygiene*, 1.2, November, 180–4.
Anon. (1934a), *Marriage Hygiene*, 1.2, November, 184.
—— (1934b), 'Race-Crossing and Glands', *Marriage Hygiene*, 1.1, August, 95; reprinted from *Eugenics Review*, April 1933.
Awati, P. R. (1935), 'Mother's Love and Constitution of the Family', *Marriage Hygiene*, 1.3, February, 241–4.
Bashford, Alison (2010), 'Internationalism, cosmopolitanism, and eugenics', in Alison Bashford and Philippa Levine (eds), *The Oxford Handbook of the History of Eugenics*, New York: Oxford University Press, 154–72.

Berkeley-Hill, Owen (1937), 'The Erotic Rights of Women', *Marriage Hygiene*, 4.1, August, 30–3.
Blacker, C. P. (1934), 'Eugenics in Relation to the Maintenance of Health and Avoidance of Disease', *Marriage Hygiene*, 1.1, August, 75.
Dickinson, Robert L. (1947), 'Editorial Notes', *Marriage Hygiene*, 1.1, August, 1.
'Editorial Notes' (1934), *Marriage Hygiene*, 1.1, August, 2.
Fisher, Kate, and Jana Funke (2015), 'British sexual science beyond the medical: Cross-disciplinary, cross-historical, and cross-cultural translations', in Heike Bauer (ed.), *Sexology and Translation: Cultural and Scientific Encounters across the Modern World*, Philadelphia: Temple University Press, 95–114.
Himes, Norman (1938), 'Birth Control Laws in the U.S.', *Eugenics Review*, 30.3, October, 227.
Hodges, Sarah (2010), 'South Asia's eugenic past', in Alison Bashford and Philippa Levine (eds), *The Oxford Handbook of the History of Eugenics*, New York: Oxford University Press, 228–42.
Klausen, Susanne, and Alison Bashford (2010), 'Fertility control: Eugenics, neo-Malthusianism, and feminism', in Alison Bashford and Philippa Levine (eds), *The Oxford Handbook of the History of Eugenics*, New York: Oxford University Press, 98–115.
Nadkarni, Asha (2014), *Eugenic Feminism: Reproductive Nationalism in the United States and India*, Minneapolis: University of Minnesota Press.
'Notes and Comments' (1935), *Marriage Hygiene*, 2.2, November, 117.
Rakshit, Romeschandra (1934), 'Indian Outlook on Sex Relations', *Marriage Hygiene*, 1.2, November, 147–9.
Ramusack, Barbara N. (1989), 'Embattled advocates: The debate over birth control in India, 1920–1940', *Journal of Women's History*, 1.2, Fall, 34–64.
Sinha, Mrinalini (2006), *Specters of Mother India: The Global Restructuring of an Empire*, Durham, NC, and London: Duke University Press.
Stern, Alexandra Minna (2010), 'Gender and sexuality: A global tour and compass', in Alison Bashford and Philippa Levine (eds), *The Oxford Handbook of the History of Eugenics*, New York: Oxford University Press, 173–91.
Turda, Marius (2010), 'Race, science and eugenics', in Alison Bashford and Philippa Levine (eds), *The Oxford Handbook of the History of Eugenics*, New York: Oxford University Press, 62–79.
Weeks, Jeffrey (2017), *Sex, Politics, and Society*, New York: Routledge.

Part III

Language and Colonial Periodicals

16

MAKING MĀORI CITIZENS IN COLONIAL NEW ZEALAND: THE ROLE OF GOVERNMENT *NIUPEPA*

Lachy Paterson

Introduction

WHEN MĀORI CHIEFS signed the Treaty of Waitangi in 1840 which incorporated New Zealand into the British Empire, they and their people gained 'all the Rights and Privileges of British Subjects'. Despite significant translation differences between the English-language treaty and the Māori-language *tiriti* around the actual cession of sovereignty and what specific native rights Māori retained, its third article establishing the principle of legal equality between indigenous Māori and Pākehā (British settlers) is reasonably consistent between the two versions. That Māori gained a status not conferred on many other indigenous peoples in the Empire, such as Australian Aborigines, can be put down to European ideas on racial hierarchies and to the ascendancy of the British humanitarian movement at that time, who insisted that the settlement of New Zealand should be less detrimental to the indigenous people than previous colonisations (Mutu 2010: 26–7, 34). Although the Māori experience ended up being not too dissimilar to that of other indigenous peoples in settler colonies, with economic marginalisation, demographic swamping, state violence and loss of land, it nevertheless occurred within an environment of nominal legal equality.

Citizenship of course entails both rights and duties. The 'Crown' *in situ* to which Māori were now subject underwent three phases during the period covered in this chapter. The London-appointed governor initially wielded full authority under crown colony status, but when a settler parliament was established from 1854, able to form 'responsible' ministries two years later, the governor retained responsibility over Native Affairs and defence (Ballantyne 2009: 105, 111–12). This system of dual government continued until 1865 when, facing costly wars against their Māori subjects, the British government passed on its last responsibilities to a now 'self-reliant' New Zealand state (Ward 1995: 177). Although, under their treaty rights, Māori men might vote or stand for parliament from 1854, almost all were effectively excluded as their communal native-title lands did not legally meet the required property qualifications. To enable their participation, the New Zealand parliament conferred on Māori men the right to vote for their own representatives in four special seats from 1867 (Ballantyne 2009: 115–17).

The government used *niupepa* (periodicals) to communicate with Māori, and draw them closer to the state. This case study seeks to interrogate the role of the government periodicals in developing the notion of 'citizenship' for Māori during the thirty-five years it published newspapers to 'elevate and enlighten the native understanding, and to render the Maori a fit and civilised associate of his English fellow subject' (Anon. 1849, *Te Karere Maori*: 1). These government newspapers form two distinct sets. Auckland-based officials produced the *Karere* series from 1842 to 1863, to promulgate the benefits of British rule, and the need to engage with the law, government and colonial development. The *Waka Maori* series was first published in Napier for local Māori by the Hawkes Bay Provincial Council from 1863 to 1871, then as a national Māori paper from Wellington until 1877.

The Use of Print and Newspapers

Practical reasons drove the official use of *te reo Māori* (Māori language), including for government newspapers directed at Māori. Missionaries preceded British annexation by twenty-six years. That Māori possessed a common language (notwithstanding differences in dialects) enabled a single indigenous literacy which by 1840 was already well established. The new state therefore operated in two languages, addressing Māori or Pākehā in *te reo* and English respectively. Notwithstanding the 1840 Treaty, the government's *mana* was nominal at best and it was in its interests to encourage Māori to tolerate, and hopefully cooperate with, the new regime, something best achieved through their own language. Less than two years after the Treaty signing, New Zealand's first Māori-language newspaper, *Te Karere o Nui Tireni*, appeared from the Auckland office of the Chief Protector of Aborigines (see Figure 16.1).

Determining the reach of these publications is difficult. Print runs were small, with the government initially printing only 250 copies, later 500, of each *Karere* issue, which were sent free to prominent chiefs. In contrast Māori were expected to subscribe to *Te Waka Maori*, at '10s. per year, payable in advance' (Anon. 1877, *Te Waka Maori o Niu Tirani*: 168). In 1877 the government accounts suggest subscriptions (paid and due) of £544/10/-, equating to 1,089 copies, although more copies may still have been circulated gratis ('Cost of Publication of "Waka Maori" (Return Showing the)' 1877: 1). Issues often appeared fortnightly or monthly, and only occasionally weekly (Parkinson and Griffith 2004: S1, S3, S5, S11–12, S16, S18), and news might be weeks or months old. However, the impact of *niupepa* was far greater than the circulation and frequency might suggest. Newspapers were often shared, and literacy practices generally complemented a wider oral culture, with groups gathering to listen to *niupepa* being read aloud and to discuss their contents (Paterson 2020: 92–3). Moreover, despite widespread Māori literacy, few other secular or non-educational publications were available to Māori, so newspapers form a far more important part of Māori reading material than in societies where a wider range of literature was produced.

Niupepa encompassed a wide variety of forms. Some resembled the settler broadsheets, others were more like journals. The government's newspapers were not physically large, ranging in their various iterations from 231 x 170mm to 460 x 300mm, most often with four to sixteen pages. In a period of over 100 years, numerous titles appeared, as the government, church groups, Māori political movements (including some critical of the government) and wealthy Māori chiefs promulgated various social, religious and political messages (Curnow 2002: 17–41), none of which made any money. A few flopped after one or two issues.

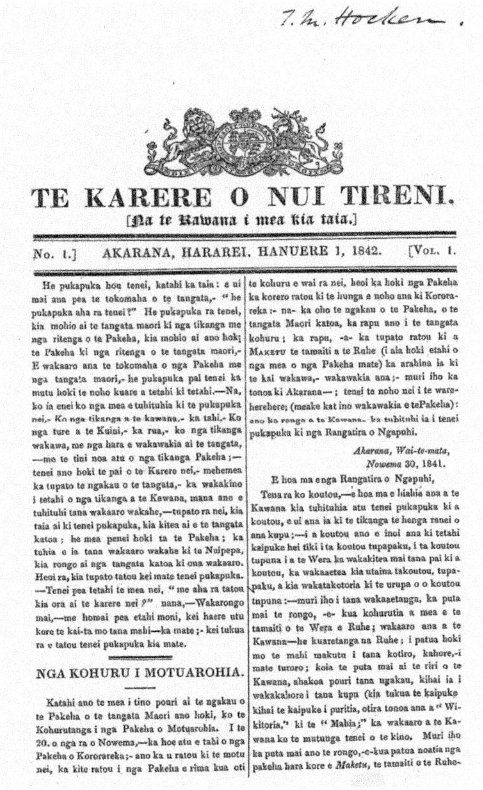

T. M. Hocken.

TE KARERE O NUI TIRENI.

[Na te Kawana i mea kia taia.]

No. 1.] AKARANA, HARAREI. HANUERE 1, 1842. [Vol. 1.

He pukapuka hou tenei, katahi ka taia: e ui mai ana pea te tokomaha o te tangata,- "he pukapuka aha ra tenei?" He pukapuka ra tenei, kia mohio ai te tangata maori ki nga tikanga me nga ritenga o te Pakeha, kia mohio ai ano hoki te Pakeha ki nga ritenga o te tangata maori,- E wakaaro ana te tokomaha o nga Pakeha me nga tangata maori,- he pukapuka pai tenei ka mutu hoki te noho kuare a tetahi ki tetahi.—Na, ko ia enei ko nga mea e tuhituhia ki te pukapuka nei,- Ko nga tikanga a te kawana,- ka tahi.- Ko nga ture a te Kuini,- ka rua,- ko nga tikanga wakawa, me nga hara e wakawakia ai te tangata, —me te tini noa atu o nga tikanga Pakeha;— tenei ano hoki te pai o te Karere nei,- mehemea ka tupato te ngakau o te tangata,- ka wakakino i tetahi o nga tikanga a te Kawana, mana ano e tuhituhi tana wakaaro wakahe,—tupato ra nei, kia taia ai ki tenei pukapuka, kia kitea ai e te tangata katoa; he mea penei hoki ta te Pakeha; ka tuhia e ia tana wakaaro wakahe ki te Nuipepa, kia rongo ai nga tangata katoa ki ona wakaaro. Heoi ra, kia tupato tatou kei mate tenei pukapuka. —Tenei pea tetahi te mea nei, "me aha ra tatou kia ora ai te karere nei?" nana,—Wakarongo mai,—me homai pea etahi moni, kei haere utu kore te kai-ta mo tana mahi—ka mate;- kei tukua ra e tatou tenei pukapuka kia mate.

NGA KOHURU I MOTUAROHIA.

Katahi ano te mea i tino pouri ai te ngakau o te Pakeha o te tangata Maori ano hoki, ko te Kohurutanga i nga Pakeha o Motuarohia. I te 20. o nga ra o Nowema,—ka hoe atu e tahi o nga Pakeha o Kororareka;- ano ka u ratou ki te motu nei, ka kite ratou i nga Pakeha e rima kua oti te kohuru e wai ra nei, heoi ka hoki nga Pakeha ka korero ratou ki te hunga e noho ana ki Kororareka:- na- ka oho te ngakau o te Pakeha, o te tangata Maori katoa, ka rapu ano i te tangata kohuru; ka rapu, -a- ka tupato ratou ki a Maketu te tamaiti a te Ruhe (i aia hoki etahi o nga mea o nga Pakeha mate) ka arahina ia ki te kai wakawa,- wakawakia ana;- muri iho ka tonoa ki Akarana—; tenei te noho nei i te wareherehere; (meake kat ino wakawakia e tePakeha): ano ka rongo a te Kawana,- ka tuhituhi ia i tenei pukapuka ki nga Rangatira o Ngapuhi.

Akarana, Wai-te-mata,
Nowema 30, 1841.

E hoa ma enga Rangatira o Ngapuhi,

Tena ra ko koutou,—e hoa ma e hiahia ana a te Kawana kia tuhituhia atu tenei pukapuka ki a koutou, e ui ana ia ki te tikanga te henga ranei o ana kupu;—i a koutou ano e inoi ana ki tetahi kaipuke hei tiki i ta koutou tupapaku, i ta koutou tupuna i a te Wera ka wakakitea mai tana pai ki a koutou, ka wakaaetea kia utaina takoutou, tupapaku, a kia wakatakotoria ki te urupa o o koutou tupuna:—muri iho i tana wakaaetanga, ka puta mai te rongo, -e- kua kohurutia a mea e te tamaiti o te Wera e Ruhe; wakaaro ana a te Kawana—he kuaretanga na Ruhe; i patua hoki mo te mahi makutu i tana kotiro, kahore,-i mate turoro; koia te puta mai ai te riri o te Kawana, ahakoa pouri tana ngakau, kihai ia i wakakahore i tana kupu (kia tukua te kaipuke kihai te kaipuke i puritia, otira tonoa ana a "Wikitoria," ki te "Mahia;" ka wakaaro a te Kawana ko te mutunga tenei o te kino. Muri iho ka puta mai ano te rongo,-e-kua patua noatia nga pakeha hara kore e *Maketu*, te tamaiti o te Ruhe-

Figure 16.1 *Te Karere o Nui Tireni* (The Messenger of New Zealand), 1 January 1842, p. 1. This was the first issue of a Māori-language newspaper. The nameplate sports the crown's coat of arms, and the statement 'Na te Kawana i mea kia taia' (Printed under authority of the Governor). The first article explains the purpose of the paper, such as providing information on law and government procedures. The rest of the page relates to the capture and imminent trial of Maketū, a Māori who murdered a Pākehā settler family. Courtesy of Hocken Collections – Uare Taoka o Hākena, University of Otago.

The relative longevity of the government's own *niupepa* reflects the financial and official support they received. *Te Karere o Nui Tireni*, a fully Māori-language periodical, ceased in 1846 when George Grey, the new governor, laid off the Chief Protector and his staff. The Native Secretary's office resurrected the publication in 1849 as the bilingual *Maori Messenger: Te Karere Maori*. This survived in several formats until 1863, although it was temporarily rebranded as *Te Manuhiri Tuarangi and Maori Intelligencer* during 1860. Three months prior to its demise in September 1863, Donald McLean, the former Native Secretary and now Superintendent of the Hawkes Bay province, initiated his own local paper, *Te Waka Maori o Ahuriri*, solely in *te reo Māori*. This was transformed into a national *niupepa*, *Te Waka Maori o Niu Tirani*, in 1871, becoming bilingual two years later. A combination of McLean's resignation, accusations of *Te Waka*'s partisan editorialising, and an expensive libel case saw the government withdraw from *niupepa* publication in 1877 (Paterson 2016; Paterson 2017).

The government's Māori-language newspapers are historically significant not just because they provide a window onto Māori engagement with the state as the nature of that state was transforming, but because, as official publications, they sought to shape Māori understandings and behaviours. This study first discusses Māori periodicals of this time more generally, but the main focus is on the government's attempts to align Māori with the new colonial order through its *niupepa*. The discussion on the *Karere* papers centres on its discourses of law and order, and an attempt at Māori local government. It then moves to the *Waka* newspapers from which Māori involvement in parliamentary politics is explored.

The *Te Karere* Series: Advancing Colonisation

The function of *niupepa* was to effect change in Māori attitude and behaviour. Colonialism confronted Māori first with Christianity and literacy, then with a colonial regime and mass immigration within a few short decades. Missionaries and officials, and their *niupepa*, championed *nga tikanga pai o te pakeha* (the good customs of the white man) as the path to modernity. Along with cultural, social and religious changes, Māori were expected to accept the government administration and English law. We might interpret this (through modern, western understandings) as becoming a 'citizen'. Certainly the discourse was implicit; in the hundreds of bilingual pages in the two government *niupepa*, the term 'citizen' only appears once in the English texts, in a 1856 *Te Karere* article on drunkenness (with the same article reprinted seventeen years later in *Te Waka*) (Anon. 1856c, *Te Karere Maori*: 17; Anon. 1873c, *Te Waka Maori o Niu Tirani*: 146). But by obeying the law, advancing the colony's development through engaging in the market, and selling land to the government for Pākehā settlement, Māori could, according to the newspaper message, expect their material lives to improve, and to share in the benefits of progress (Paterson 2006: 69–135).

As a means of gaining Māori acceptance, *Te Karere* portrayed a loving and altruistic Queen Victoria acting through her agent, the governor: 'The Governor and our Queen want you to advance together, and not live as workers and servants for the Pākehā, but cultivate your own land to sell potatoes, corn and other things' (Anon. 1842c, *Te Karere o Nui Tireni*: 24). The Crown supposedly sat impartially above both races, whose relationship was to be based on the notion of improvement through racial fraternity: 'The Queen says the people of New Zealand [Māori] will be as younger brethren to the Pākehā, so they can also acquire the customs to be the same as Pākehā. What does she want in return? Nothing!' (Anon. 1844b, *Te Karere o Nui Tireni*: 51). Tapping into religious conversions that many had experienced, Governor Fitzroy informed Māori in the paper in 1844, 'You have the good government of the Queen, and the reason it is right for you is that its source is from the heart of Christianity. My friends, I am striving for your good, and I am happy to be as a father to you' (Anon. 1844a, *Te Karere o Nui Tireni*: 3).

Māori acceptance of English law (expressed as *ture*, a term also used for God's laws) was central to the government's plans. Despite the mass conversions and advent of British government, Māori *iwi* (independent kin-based groups) still occasionally warred against each other. Tensions between Māori and settlers could also be fraught, and in rare cases turn violent. As the government initially did not have sufficient troops available to impose its will, it used the newspaper to promote peaceful relations between settlers and Māori, and between tribal groups. First Māori needed to eschew their former ways. 'So, the Māori are still holding onto the things of their childhood. Before, they were children of darkness; now they are children of knowledge, and that is why it is right to abandon old customs' (Anon. 1843, *Te Karere o Nui Tireni*: 47).

It was important that Māori could see the law in action. When Maketū, a young Ngāpuhi man, was tried for murdering a Pākehā family in 1842, *Te Karere* used it to enlighten Māori on the legal process. The governor's letter to the *iwi*, printed in the *niupepa*, extolled them for handing Maketū over, 'And now all the Pākehā will see that you don't insist on holding murderers back [from justice]' (Anon. 1842a, *Te Karere o Nui Tireni*: 2), although, given one of the victims was also the granddaughter of a prominent chief, their motivation was more likely to avoid internal warfare. The paper subsequently provided its Māori readers with an extensive account of the trial and sentencing (Anon. 1842a, *Te Karere o Nui Tireni*: 1–2; Anon. 1842b: *Te Karere o Nui Tireni*: 13–17; Oliver 1990: 262). When a Pākehā, Charles Marsden, murdered a Ngāti Whakaue woman in 1855, many of her *iwi* travelled to Auckland to attend the trial. This no doubt perturbed the authorities, who feared that an acquittal might lead to bloodshed. One issue of the *niupepa* covered the matter in depth. It published an account of the chiefs' meeting with the acting governor, where they had informed him 'if [Marsden's] life is spared their hearts will be very dark' (Anon. 1856a, *Te Karere Maori*: 12–14). The paper was at pains to portray a dispassionate and impartial justice system, explaining first how the coroner's court worked, printing the judge's address to the chiefs about how the trial would proceed, and generally discussing the advantages of the English legal system (Anon. 1856a, *Te Karere Maori*: 1–7). The following issue provided a report of the trial (translated from a settler paper) and an account of the execution, concluding with a letter from a grateful governor to the chiefs. Justice was blind, so 'let no man ask whether he is a Maori or an [*sic*] European, a Chief or a poor man' (Anon. 1856b, *Te Karere Maori*: 4–16).

The British parliament passed the New Zealand Constitution Act in 1852 to establish a parliament (an elected House of Representatives and appointed Legislative Council) and provincial councils. These bodies perhaps mark a transition from 'subject' to 'citizen', although the latter term first appeared in a settler newspaper in 1840 (Anon. 1840, *New Zealand Gazette and Wellington Spectator*: 4). For Māori, the distinction was less clear. The government acknowledged in 1856 that Māori were not excluded from participating, but due to native-title land not being recognised under the act, there were only a 'limited number of Natives who possess an Electoral qualification'. These few individuals might enjoy 'an intelligent exercise of the privilege' nevertheless ('Correspondence relative to the Registration of Native Voters' 1858: 2, 3). Although *Te Karere* might assert that 'the country must advance when the aboriginal inhabitants go hand in hand with their civilised and educated brethren' (Anon. 1855a, *Te Karere Maori*: 8), and Māori, in theory, possessed political equality with Pākehā, the assumption was that most were not yet capable of fully engaging in the political system.

With provincial elections looming in Auckland in 1855, *Te Karere* presented an explanation in the form of a dialogue between hypothetical characters, 'Pakeha' and 'Maori'. The latter states, 'The white people seemed very much excited, constantly cheering one another and running to and fro. This is a new thing to us Maories, and we do not understand it.' Without irony, the Pākehā states that Queen Victoria 'has graciously given her consent that the inhabitants of these islands should govern themselves' (Anon. 1855a, *Te Karere Maori*: 28). It is clear, however, that the new bodies were primarily Pākehā affairs. The following month the *niupepa* declared, 'We think that the native population should not interfere in politics, nor be concerned as regards the issue of elections; they may be rest assured that whatever changes take place in the Government, their interests will be carefully guarded', that is, by the governor (Anon. 1855b, *Te Karere Maori*: 3). Henceforth, although it occasionally provided information on laws affecting Māori, *Te Karere* avoided discussion of parliamentary business.

The Kohimarama Conference

By 1860, the government was under pressure from two fronts. Two years earlier, *iwi* of the central North Island formally installed the aged chief, Pōtatau Te Wherowhero, as the first Māori king in an attempt to retain the remaining Māori land, bolster Māori authority, and restrain the inter- and intra-tribal violence stirred up by government land agents. In March 1860, a botched purchase of Te Āti Awa land precipitated the year-long First Taranaki War, a conflict that drew in neighbouring tribes and warriors of the Kīngitanga (Māori King Movement) in opposition to the British troops. In an effort to contain the warfare, which was then going badly for the government, and to discourage further Māori support for Te Āti Awa, in July 1860 Governor Browne called a conference of chiefs to Kohimarama near Auckland, who gathered and discussed the political situation for about a month. Almost immediately, *Te Karere Maori* eschewed its normal fare and began publishing the chiefs' 'speeches', likely précis of notes taken by an official. In addition, it printed the governor's speeches in opening and closing the conference, and those of Donald McLean, the Native Secretary, who was attempting to stage manage the event. Six issues (and almost 300 pages) were devoted to the conference; the last, in which the chiefs' written replies to the governor's initial speech were printed, appeared on 30 November.

It is clear that, although few of the chiefs present had much time for the Kīngitanga, many sympathised with Wiremu Kīngi Te Rangitāke, the Te Āti Awa chief then battling the British Army, because his predicament could easily have been their own. Even after the governor's opening speech that threatened destruction and land confiscation on *iwi* that did not accept the queen's sovereignty, many chiefs initially proffered a solution to the bodged land deal that reflected the rhetoric of peace and civility normally espoused by missionaries, officials and the government's own newspaper. Part way through the conference, McLean took one of the days to deliver a long speech outlining the government's case, which effectively quietened the opposition, even if it changed few minds. In the end, the conference passed a number of resolutions; it condemned the Kīngitanga and, despite some misgivings, blamed Te Rangitāke. The conference had been a government attempt to garner support from uncommitted *iwi* for its cause. Even if it was not completely successful in this, its newspaper certainly suggested that chiefs were now solidly loyal to the queen and her government.

The Kohimarama Conference is significant because it appeared, on the surface, to be a genuine attempt to consult with Māori, and to bring their opinions to the highest levels of government. As the Ngāti Toa chief, Mātene Te Whīwhī, stated, only now was the government fulfilling the intent of the Treaty of Waitangi. 'This pleases me. I am glad because of this Conference. Let our work be carried on every year. Let the Governor, on each succeeding year, invite us to a Conference' (Anon. 1860a, *Te Karere Maori*: 4). Arama Karaka, of Te Uriohau, advocated a union of the races. 'Let these words be printed in the newspapers and sent to the Queen, and let the Queen send an answer to us, that it might be a firmly established covenant for us and our children, so that we may be as the Pakehas' (Anon. 1860c, *Te Karere Maori*: 15). Māori were also able to discuss their own land concerns, mixed-race juries, their desire for modernity, and many other issues in their 371 recorded speeches and written submissions published in *Te Karere*. Browne was conciliatory in his closing address, reassuring Māori of the guarantees of the Treaty, and promising another conference in a year's time (Anon. 1860b, *Te Karere Maori*: 11–13).

Ngā Tikanga Hou: The New Institutions

The second conference was not to happen. Browne's officials advised against it; although some chiefs were keen, others from more unsettled areas were reluctant to appear to be in the government's pocket. Grey's return as governor in 1861 settled the matter. He questioned 'whether it would be wise to call a number of semi-barbarous Natives together to frame a Constitution for themselves', instead suggesting he himself draw up some kind of system for Māori to engage in the machinery of government ('Grey to Duke of Newcastle' 1862: 34). From 1861 the *niupepa* instead focused on the government's new scheme of Māori local councils known as Tikanga Hou, or New Institutions. Although *Te Karere* had printed the Native Districts Regulations Act when passed in 1858, the deteriorating political situation, with a new Māori King and tensions over land in Taranaki and elsewhere, had put its implementation on hold (Anon. 1858b, *Te Karere Maori*: 2–3; Anon. 1858c, *Te Karere Maori*: 3–4; Anon. 1858d, *Te Karere Maori*: 2–3; Anon. 1858e, *Te Karere Maori*: 2–3). Grey's Tikanga Hou revived the concept, and aimed to draw 'friendly' and wavering chiefs more closely to his embrace, while also undermining the Kīngitanga's resistance to the Crown's claims of sovereignty.

The boundaries of various Native Districts were duly printed in *Te Karere* in late 1861 (Anon. 1861, *Te Karere Maori*: 1–4; Anon. 1862a, *Te Karere Maori*: 1–6; Anon. 1862b, *Te Karere Maori*: 19–22; Anon. 1862c, *Te Karere Maori*: 25–32). An explanation of the new system began with the usual discourse of the queen's desire for Pākehā and Māori to work together, that the latter 'may be a happy people, rich, wise, well instructed, and every year advancing in prosperity' (Anon. 1861, *Te Karere Maori*: 5). Villages would choose assessors (generally chiefs) to superintend policemen and assist Pākehā magistrates, and form a district *rūnanga* (council) 'to propose the laws for that district' under a Pākehā civil commissioner. Their potential powers were wide-ranging, overseeing trespassing cattle, weeds, roading, education, health, registering land, and 'putting down bad customs of the old Maori law' (Anon. 1861, *Te Karere Maori*: 5–8). Loyalty was bought with official salaries, but the new system was of course meant to be transitional. In a speech at Mangonui, the civil commissioner stated he hoped 'to live to see the day when, through the working of these Runangas, the New Zealanders will send their representatives to the General Assembly of the country, and take their places side by side with the Europeans in framing the laws for the whole country' (Anon. 1862i, *Te Karere Maori*: 13).

Te Karere devoted much of its precious space to reporting on and promoting the Tikanga Hou. It detailed the visits and speeches of the governor and premier to encourage Māori participation (Anon. 1862b, *Te Karere Maori*: 7–10; Anon. 1862c, *Te Karere Maori*: 20–4; Anon. 1862e, *Te Karere Maori*: 1–2; Anon. 1862g, *Te Karere Maori*: 3–8). In the case of his visit to Northland, the governor arrived by warship, and rode into Kerikeri with a cavalry-like escort and flags streaming (Anon. 1862b, *Te Karere Maori*: 1–3). The paper occasionally published reports on elections, such as in Whāingaroa where the people now 'know they have the good wishes of the Europeans [and] will therefore be stimulated to proceed in the work of law and order' (Anon. 1862d, *Te Karere Maori*: 7). It printed reports from the local Pākehā officials on how well the system was working (Anon. 1862e, *Te Karere Maori*: 9–11; Anon. 1862h, *Te Karere Maori*: 3), such as that the Māori police at Ōtaki were able to execute arrest warrants, 'where European police would probably have failed' (Anon. 1863, *Te Karere Maori*: 21). On several occasions, the paper reproduced extensive accounts of *rūnanga* proceedings (Anon. 1862f, *Te Karere Maori*: 4–16; Anon. 1862i, *Te Karere Maori*: 4–12). But as the tabulated returns of office holders show, some *iwi* entered enthusiastically in the Tikanga Hou, while others engaged passively or totally rejected the system (Anon. 1862i, *Te Karere Maori*: 12–16). However, the experiment proved short-lived and was largely abandoned in mid-1863 after war resumed at Taranaki and the British Army invaded Waikato, the centre of Kīngitanga opposition. The time for soft diplomacy was over, with the increasingly belligerent *Te Karere Maori* printing its final issue two months later.

The *Te Waka* Series: Engaging with Parliamentary Politics

Te Waka Maori o Ahuriri's birth preceded *Te Karere*'s demise by three months. Donald McLean's *niupepa* did not start as a national newspaper but as an effort (although ultimately in vain) to keep war from spreading into the Hawkes Bay province. McLean served in the provincial council from 1859 to 1871, and as its superintendent from 1863. Elected to parliament in 1866, he resigned his superintendency in 1869 to take up the position of Native Minister. Parliamentary politics at this time was unstable and fluid; eight different ministries, based around personality and local interests, formed between 1869 and the newspaper's demise in 1877. But such was McLean's reputation as the most capable politician to deal with 'native affairs', he served in every ministry except one that lasted a bare month (Scholefield 1950: 34–6, 124, 198, 201). He shifted the newspaper, now *Te Waka Maori o Niu Tirani*, to the new capital, Wellington, in 1871, and as Native Minister retained control of it until his resignation in December 1876 due to ill health.

Partly in response to British disquiet at the military and political situation, in 1867 McLean ushered the Maori Representation Act through parliament, to create four separate Māori seats.[1] The Native Land Court, introduced in 1862, had been expected to help Māori gain voting rights through the conversion of Māori land from native title, held collectively by tribal groups, into more easily adjudged (and saleable) crown title. With their land ownership now officially recognised, it was expected Māori would soon satisfy the property qualifications required of electors. However, the disruption of the ongoing wars and Māori antipathy or resistance to the 'land-grabbing' court meant that many did not become enfranchised (Sorrenson 2014: 65–6). Under McLean's new law, Māori voted through a separate system based on universal male suffrage rather than property qualification, and although four representatives left them severely under-represented, the state now recognised them more formally as participating citizens. Although some settler newspapers were opposed to 'special' representation, or believed Māori insufficiently 'intellectually fit' to sit as members (Anon. 1867, *Nelson Examiner*: 2; Anon. 1867, *Hawkes Bay Herald*: 2; Anon. 1867, *Wellington Independent*: 7), the act passed with minimal opposition in both houses ('New Zealand Parliamentary Debates' 1867: 655, 816).

Te Waka, then based in Napier, saw a role in educating Māori and encouraging involvement, at least in the Eastern Māori Electoral District. On the law's passing, it enthusiastically told its Māori readers that 'in this move could be seen the good heart-edness of the Pākehā to his Māori friends of this country. There is no greater action than this by which peace may settle on the peoples of New Zealand. . . . for the Pākehā is taking Māori as colleagues to work together on business concerning everyone. This is the very heart of [racial] unity' (Anon. 1867a, *Te Waka Maori o Ahuriri*: 69; Anon. 1868b, *Te Waka Maori o Ahuriri*: 15). Because the four electorates covered a multi-tude of *iwi*, some with traditional enmities, the paper also stressed the need to elect a member who could represent all: 'In each of the districts there are many *iwi*; people of one *iwi* will perhaps object because the person they desire, from within their own *iwi*, is not selected' but the role was 'to be able to peacefully pursue in the Great Council the things desired by everyone' (Anon. 1867b, *Te Waka Maori o Ahuriri*: 100). As the first election approached, the paper gave instructions on how to nominate a candidate, and how the voting would take place (Anon. 1868a, *Te Waka Maori o Ahuriri*: 9) (see Figure 16.2). It also suggested that people look past the candidates' chiefly genealogy, and to 'his knowledge and honesty—whether a chief or an ordinary person' (Anon. 1868a, *Te Waka Maori o Ahuriri*: 10). The *niupepa* was unrealistic, however, to think that Māori would vote for anyone but a chief; besides, the £1 allowance per sitting day meant only chiefs with additional income could afford to participate in parliamentary business (Scholefield 1950: 91).

The *Hawkes Bay Herald* published an account of the 'election', prepared for *Te Waka* but seemingly not published.[2] On 15 April 1868, Māori assembled in the Napier courthouse. The name of Karaitiana Takamoana, an important Ngāti Kahungunu chief, was called, with several chiefs giving speeches in his favour. The returning officer stated he would wait five minutes: if no other names were given, Karaitiana would be elected. With seconds remaining, another chief stood and nominated Tāreha Te Moananui, another senior chief of the *iwi*, followed by more speeches. A show of hands resulted in a thirty-four to thirty-three win for Tāreha, although the report notes, 'A large number of Karaitiana's men, it was said, were absent in the stores about town.' Karaitiana, it seems, was also missing and as no poll was called for, 'Tareha was duly elected' (Anon. 1868, *Hawkes Bay Herald*: 2). Thus, the Māori population residing in an area about a fifth of the whole country, comprising many *iwi*, gained their first elected representative.

Needless to say, queries and complaints soon followed. *Te Waka* published a letter from one group of Ngāti Porou, an *iwi* in the north of the electorate, who met fifteen days after nomination day to discuss their candidate. The paper informed them that they were too late, and not to carry on (Anon. 1868c, *Te Waka Maori o Ahuriri*: 28).

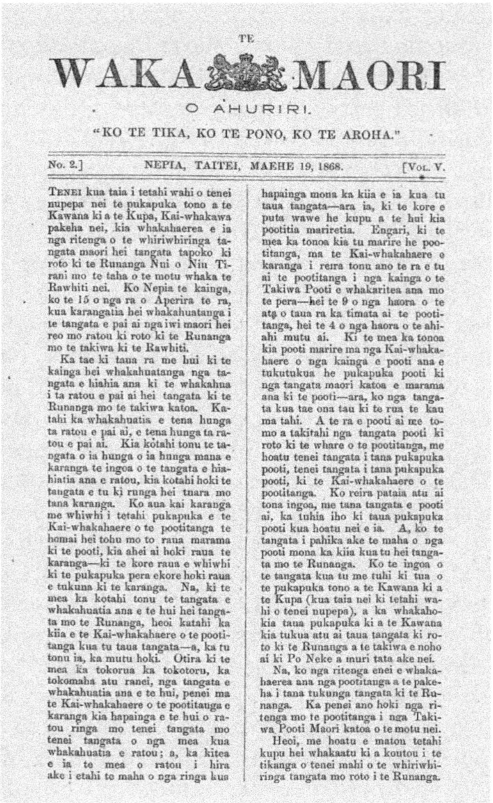

TE

WAKA MAORI

O AHURIRI.

"KO TE TIKA, KO TE PONO, KO TE AROHA."

No. 2.] NEPIA, TAITEI, MAEHE 19, 1868. [Vol. V.

Tenei kua taia i tetahi wahi o tenei nupepa nei te pukapuka tono a te Kawana ki a te Kupa, Kai-whakawa pakeha nei, kia whakahaerea e ia nga ritenga o te whiriwhiringa tangata maori hei tangata tapoko ki roto ki te Runanga Nui o Niu Tirani mo te taha o te motu whaka te Rawhiti nei. Ko Nepia te kainga, ko te 15 o nga ra o Aperira te ra, kua karangatia hei whakahuatanga i te tangata e pai ai nga iwi maori hei reo mo ratou ki roto ki te Runanga mo te takiwa ki te Rawhiti.

Ka tae ki taua ra me hui ki te kainga hei whakahuatanga nga tangata e hiahia ana ki te whakahua i ta ratou e pai ai hei tangata ki te Runanga mo te takiwa katoa. Katahi ka whakahuatia e tena hunga ta ratou e pai ai, e tena hunga ta ratou e pai ai. Kia kotahi tonu te tangata o ia hunga o ia hunga mana e karanga te ingoa o te tangata e hiahiatia ana e ratou, kia kotahi hoki te tangata e tu ki runga hei tuara mo tana karanga. Ko aua kai karanga me whiwhi i tetahi pukapuka e te Kai-whakahaere o te pootitanga te homai hei tohu mo to raua marama ki te pooti, kia ahei ai hoki raua te karanga—ki te kore raua e whiwhi ki te pukapuka pera ekore hoki raua e tukuna ki te karanga. Na, ki te mea ka kotahi tonu te tangata e whakahuatia ana e te hui hei tangata mo te Runanga, heoi katahi ka kiia e te Kai-whakahaere o te pootitanga kua tu taua tangata—a, ka tu tonu ia, ka mutu hoki. Otira ki te mea ka tokorua ka tokotoru, ka tokomaha atu ranei, nga tangata e whakahuatia ana e te hui, penei ma te Kai-whakahaere o te pootitauga e karanga kia hapainga e te hui o ratou ringa mo tenei tangata mo tenei tangata o nga mea kua whakahuatia e ratou; a, ka kitea e ia te mea o ratou i hira ake i etahi te maha o nga ringa kua hapainga mona ka kiia e ia kua tu taua tangata—ara ia, ki te kore e puta wawe he kupu a te hui kia pootitia mariretia. Engari, ki te mea ka tonoa kia tu marire he pootitanga, ma te Kai-whakahaere e karanga i reira tonu ano te ra e tu ai te pootitanga i nga kainga o te Takiwa Pooti e whakaritea ana mo te pera—hei te 9 o nga haora o te atą o taua ra ka timata ai te pootitanga, hei te 4 o nga haora o te ahiahi mutu ai. Ki te mea ka tonoa kia pooti marire ma nga Kai-whakahaere o nga kainga e pooti ana e tukutukua he pukapuka pooti ki nga tangata maori katoa e marama ana ki te pooti—ara, ko nga tangata kua tae ona tau ki te rua te kau ma tahi. A te ra e pooti ai me tomo a takitahi nga tangata pooti ki roto ki te whare o te pootitanga, me hoatu tenei tangata i tana pukapuka pooti, tenei tangata i tana pukapuka pooti, ki te Kai-whakahaere o te pootitanga. Ko reira pataia atu ai tona ingoa, me tana tangata e pooti ai, ka tuhia iho ki taua pukapuka pooti kua hoatu nei e ia. A, ko te tangata i pahika ake te maha o nga pooti mona ka kiia kua tu hei tangata mo te Runanga. Ko te ingoa o te tangata kua tu me tuhi ki tua o te pukapuka tono a te Kawana ki a te Kupa (kua taia nei ki tetahi wahi o tenei nupepa), a ka whakahokia taua pukapuka ki a te Kawana kia tukua atu ai taua tangata ki roto ki te Runanga a te takiwa e noho ai ki Po Neke a muri tata ake nei.

Na, ko nga ritenga enei e whakahaerea ana nga pootitanga a te pakeha i tana tukunga tangata ki te Runanga. Ka penei ano hoki nga ritenga mo te pootitanga i nga Takiwa Pooti Maori katoa o te motu nei.

Heoi, me hoatu e matou tetahi kupu hei whakaatu ki a koutou i te tikanga o tenei mahi o te whiriwhiringa tangata mo roto i te Runanga.

Figure 16.2 Instructions to Māori voters and potential candidates on how the first election for the Eastern Māori seat will proceed. *Te Waka Maori o Ahuriri*, 19 March 1868, p. 9. Courtesy of Hocken Collections – Uare Taoka o Hākena, University of Otago.

Another group of Ngāti Porou chiefs asserted they had held a number of meetings, including with other *iwi*. Having selected their candidate, they posted in their nomination along with the names of all who wanted him in February. Their lack of a candidate was not through want of interest, but because their letter had arrived too late (Anon. 1868d, *Te Waka Maori o Ahuriri*: 40). Expecting one chief to represent such a huge area was unrealistic. A year after the election, chiefs from a number of Bay of Plenty *iwi* met at Whakatāne to discuss political matters, and agreed 'That Tareha should cease to represent them in the Parliament, because his way of acting is not clear, but that another person be put in his place' ('Correspondence between the Government and Maori Chiefs' 1870: 5). The first four Māori members seldom spoke, and due to language difficulties generally could not follow debates or read the documentation. In addition, neither house followed their own standing orders that bills affecting Māori be translated and printed (Parkinson 2001: 10–11, 14, 17). It is therefore of little surprise they were ineffective.

Elections and Parliamentary Business

When the second election rolled around in early 1871, all four Māori seats were contested with three going to a full poll (Anon. 1871, *Taranaki Herald*: 3; 'Further Reports from Officers in Native Districts' 1871: 2). *Te Waka*, still based in Napier, covered the Eastern Maori contest, with two Ngāti Kahungunu chiefs, Hēnare Matua and Karaitiana Takamoana, opposing each other. The latter won through a show of hands at the nomination, and as no poll was called was declared the winner (Anon. 1871a, *Te Waka Maori o Ahuriri*: 8). The paper was happy he had been elected: 'We think he's a thoughtful man. He will see in Parliament what the Government thinks about the Māori tribes of the country, and he will see the fervent desire of the Pākehā that goodness, justice and prosperity are put forward through their laws and practices' (Anon. 1871a, *Te Waka Maori o Ahuriri*: 8).

Certainly the new members were more active than their predecessors. Karaitiana declared at a meeting after his election that 'he wasn't going there to be a statue, he will speak his mind', which *Te Waka* interpreted as a dig at Tāreha (Anon. 1871b, *Te Waka Maori o Ahuriri*: 8). Language difficulties still remained. The four chiefs shared just one interpreter, but from 1872 some bills affecting Māori were translated and printed for them. *Te Waka*'s move to Wellington meant a national rather than regional focus. The *niupepa* covered all four Māori members and provided significantly more Māori-language coverage of parliamentary debates relating to Māori issues, particularly those of the Māori members. They were neither silent nor submissive, discussing a variety of issues, in particular land claims and the Native Land Court, but also repeatedly calling for more Māori representatives.[3] For example, the four members proposed in December 1871 that Māori be appointed to the Legislative Council, that a Māori be appointed to cabinet to sit with the Native Minister, and that parliament triple the number of Māori seats (Anon. 1871, *Te Waka Maori o Niu Tirani*: 133). Although the number of Māori seats remained at four, the government appointed two Māori chiefs to the Legislative Council the following year (see Anon. 1872c, *Te Waka Maori o Niu Tirani*: 133). Their speeches too were broadcast in the *niupepa*'s pages.[4]

However, despite their engagement in parliamentary politics, the Māori members were well aware of their limited influence. In 1875 Karaitiana Takamoana, in a speech to the House, compared their position to that of *kākā mōkai*, or tame parrots (Anon. 1875, *Te Wananga*: 225). At this time he also threw his *mana* and wealth behind the Repudiation Movement, a tribal organisation that attempted to overturn a number of questionable land deals in the Hawkes Bay province. For four years the movement also ran its own newspaper, *Te Wananga*, in an attempt to counteract the official *Te Waka Maori* (Waymouth 2002). Many Māori also remained disaffected from the government and its institutions. In particular, the Māori King and the Tainui *iwi* had retreated south into the 'King Country' in 1864, where they remained apart from any governmental control until the early 1880s (Belgrave 2017: 1–158), with no engagement with parliamentary politics at this time.

Te Waka's reporting shows that Māori started thinking very early about the 1876 election. In October 1874 Ngāti Porou met at Wharekāhika to discuss various issues, including the 'election of Henare Potae to represent Ngatiporou in Parliament' (Anon. 1874e, *Te Waka Maori o Niu Tirani*: 297). At a meeting in the Western Māori electorate in January 1875, 'the Natives held a meeting in Matahiwi for the purposes of

NGA POOTITANGA.	THE ELECTIONS.
Ko nga ingoa enei o nga tangata i whakahuatia i te 4 of Hanuere nei kia pootitia hei Mema mo te Runanga Nui o te motu mo nga Takiwa Pooti Maori katoa, ara :—	THE following are the names of the candidates who were nominated on the 4th instant for election as Members of the House of Representatives for the various Maori Electoral Districts :—
TAKIWA POOTI MAORI WHAKA-TE-RAKI.	NORTHERN MAORI ELECTORAL DISTRICT.
Wiremu Katene, o Waimate; Mitai Pene Taui, o Ohaeawai; Hirini Taiwhanga, o Kaikohe; Hori Karaka Tawiti, o Hokianga; Timoti Poihipi, o Kaitara.	Wiremu Katene, of Waimate; Mitai Pene Taui, of Ohaeawai; Hirini Taiwhanga, of Kaikohe; Hori Karaka Tawiti, of Hokianga; Timoti Poihipi, of Kaitara.
TAKIWA POOTI MAORI WHAKA-TE-RAWHITI.	EASTERN MAORI ELECTORAL DISTRICT.
Karaitiana Takamoana, o Pakowhai, Nepia; Hotene Porourangi, o te Tai Rawhiti; Mita Hikairo, o Ngatirangiwewehi; Kepa Rangipuawhe, o Tuhourangi.	Karaitiana Takamoana, of Pakowhai, Napier, Hotene Porourangi, of East Coast; Mita Hikairo, of the Ngatirangiwewehi tribe; Kepa Rangipuawhe, of the Tuhourangi tribe.
TAKIWA POOTI MAORI WHAKA-TE-RATO.	WESTERN MAORI ELECTORAL DISTRICT.
Wi Parata, o Waikanae; Meiha Keepa, o Whanganui; Hoani Nahe, o Hauraki.	Wi Parata, of Waikanae; Major Kemp, of Whanganui; Hoani Nahe, of Hauraki.
Ko te pootitanga ka tu i te 15 o nga ra o Hanuere nei, i nga wahi pootitanga kua oti ke te panui.	The polling will take place on the 15th of January instant at the several polling places as published.
Ko TAIAROA kua tu mo te Takiwa ki te Tonga. I tu ia i runga i te hapaingatanga ringa anake, kaore he pootitanga, no te mea kaore he tangata i tauwhaawhai ki a ia.	TAIAROA was elected without opposition for the Southern District—that is, by a show of hands only.

Figure 16.3 Notification of candidates for upcoming election. *Te Waka Maori o Niu Tirani*, 11 January 1876, p. 5. Courtesy of Hocken Collections – Uare Taoka o Hākena, University of Otago.

choosing a "fit and proper person" to be put forward as a candidate . . . The voice of the meeting was in favour of Major Kemp, Te Rangihiwinui.' His supporters then canvassed the district, collecting names. This, the paper suggested, 'is a very proper thing to do, and an example which might be followed by other districts' (Anon. 1875a, *Te Waka Maori o Niu Tirani*: 61). *Te Waka* printed the usual information on polling stations, returning officers and voting instructions for its Māori readers, although now covering all four Māori electoral districts (Anon. 1875e, *Te Waka Maori o Niu Tirani*: 299–308). In Southern Māori, Hōri Kerei Taiaroa was elected unopposed but multiple candidates contested the remaining electorates, including four for Eastern Māori (Anon. 1876a, *Te Waka Maori o Niu Tirani*: 5) (see Figure 16.3).

Unfortunately, severe flooding prevented returning officers reaching several areas, causing the Ngāti Porou *iwi* to dispute the result (Anon. 1876b, *Te Waka Maori o Niu Tirani*: 36). *Te Waka* provided its Māori readers with a full account of the parliamentary investigation. Initially a select committee recommended a fresh election, despite protestations from the other Māori members. The House finally agreed the missing votes were not pivotal to the result (Anon. 1876d, *Te Waka Maori o Niu Tirani*: 177, 178–81), and Karaitiana was declared elected seven months after polling day (Anon. 1876e, *Te Waka Maori o Niu Tirani*: 198).

It is difficult to get a sense of why some chiefs put themselves forward as candidates, exposing themselves to rejection, for the opportunity to enter a very foreign environment. After the election, *Te Waka* published a letter from Hoani Nahe, the new member for Western Māori, thanking voters. He expressed his 'dread of this great responsibility put upon me'. He had suggested another man, but 'the old men of my own tribes here in Hauraki . . . insisted that I should stand'. He also explained that 'some of my friends telegraphed me to make known my (political) opinions before the election, in the same way as the Pakehas do', but had felt unable to do so. But, 'if I am to represent this district, I shall always endeavour to carry out any measures which may be committed to my charge by the people—that is to say, measures which I consider would be for the good of the whole Native population inhabiting these islands' (Anon. 1876c, *Te Waka Maori o Niu Tirani*: 43). He would not get involved in Pākehā issues, or join any factions. He would evaluate 'the schemes of the Pakehas who are struggling each to secure place and money for their own exaltation and advantage', and support 'whichever party can honestly show me that prosperity for the Maori lies with them' (Anon. 1876c, *Te Waka Maori o Niu Tirani*: 44). The Māori members were becoming more acquainted with parliamentary functioning, and more strategic in trying to use their limited power to safeguard Māori interests.

Conclusion

In 1840 the Treaty of Waitangi promised Māori the same social and political rights as Pākehā, a principle to which successive governments have paid lip service. But the new state was barely embryonic in 1840 and Māori, although engaging with Christianity and literacy, still lived largely according to their own rules and customs. Between 1842 and 1877 the new colonial state employed *niupepa* in an attempt to persuade Māori to accept its government and laws, in effect to become a citizen.

While the new country was no *tabula rasa*, it nevertheless transformed fundamentally over the thirty-five years of the state's newspaper publication, and the nature of the government's *niupepa* discourses adjusted as the nature of its administration changed. New Zealand's initial crown colony status meant the governor and his officials constituted the government, and the newspaper message was designed to persuade Māori political compliance on the one hand, and active participation in the economy, education, modernity and other facets of 'civilisation' on the other. The creation of representative bodies from the mid-1850s, stocked with Pākehā settlers, changed the country's political landscape, but Māori were little affected. Most did not qualify to vote, and the governor retained control over Native Affairs. Rather than cover the business of the new parliament and provincial councils, the *niupepa* ignored it, and at times even sought to discourage Māori interest.

Although the New Zealand state began with a tenet of racial equality, and the government initially used its newspapers to draw Māori into greater engagement, it also sought to moderate such aspirations when they conflicted with the more powerful colonial enterprise of Pākehā settlement. While some Māori embraced the opportunity for involvement, by the late 1850s many had become increasingly disillusioned with the colonial vision. Government land agents were disrupting Māori communities through increasing pressure to sell land for the swelling Pākehā population, which in 1860 sparked all-out war in Taranaki. Some *iwi* also came together to select a king who would protect their land and mana, and control the violence. At a time of crisis, Governor Browne sought to bring *iwi* to his side through a large and lengthy conference at Kohimarama, and his officials employed *Te Karere* to both threaten and cajole potentially 'friendly' Māori, and to portray to a wider audience that the chiefly attendees had indeed supported the government's cause. Browne's successor, Grey, introduced a system of local Māori government, the Tikanga Hou, as a means of bolstering Māori support, and isolating the Māori king, allowing participants to engage as citizens, at least within their own districts. Despite the patchy uptake, the government's *niupepa* was the mechanism to promote the new system, and to demonstrate Māori engagement. Ultimately *Te Karere Maori* folded once war in the Waikato exposed the newspaper's failure to convince enough Māori to cleave to the government's side.

By 1867 the political environment changed again, when the settler parliament gained responsibility for Native Affairs and waging war on Māori 'rebels'. It was now deemed time to allow Māori representation within parliament, albeit through a different electoral system to Pākehā. Donald McLean, first as Superintendent of the Hawkes Bay province, then as Native Minister in parliament, utilised his *Te Waka* series of newspapers to provide information on elections and to circulate parliamentary news, including the speeches of the four new Māori members in the House of Representatives. Just as with the Kohimarama Conference, and the Tikanga Hou, some *iwi* chose to engage with the new system as one of the few political means of improving the position of their people, and embracing modernity. Māori had few illusions, however, about how parliamentary politics might advance their standing as citizens, or how *niupepa* discourses of engagement and inclusion aligned with the government's own colonial needs and aspirations.

Notes

1. Two earlier attempts, in 1862 and 1865, had failed. See Parkinson 2001: 5–7.
2. Both digital and hard copies of the 23 April 1868 issue have missing pages.
3. For examples, see Anon. 1872a, *Te Waka Maori o Niu Tirani*: 31; Anon. 1872b, *Te Waka Maori o Niu Tirani*: 120; Anon. 1872c, *Te Waka Maori o Niu Tirani*: 134; Anon. 1873a, *Te Waka Maori o Niu Tirani*: 90; Anon. 1873b, *Te Waka Maori o Niu Tirani*: 107; Anon. 1874b, *Te Waka Maori o Niu Tirani*: 208; Anon. 1874c, *Te Waka Maori o Niu Tirani*: 234.
4. For examples, see Anon. 1874d, *Te Waka Maori o Niu Tirani*: 246; Anon. 1874a, *Te Waka Maori o Niu Tirani*: 194; Anon. 1875b, *Te Waka Maori o Niu Tirani*: 223; Anon. 1875c, *Te Waka Maori o Niu Tirani*: 311; Anon. 1875d, *Te Waka Maori o Niu Tirani*: 255.

Bibliography

Anon. (1867), *Hawkes Bay Herald*, 29 August, 2.
—— (1868), *Hawkes Bay Herald*, 18 April, 2.
—— (1867), *Nelson Examiner*, 13 August, 2.
—— (1840), *New Zealand Gazette and Wellington Spectator*, 18 July, 4.
—— (1871), *Taranaki Herald*, 8 February, 3.
—— (1849), *Te Karere Maori*, 4 January, 1.
—— (1855a), *Te Karere Maori*, 1 January, 8, 28.
—— (1855b), *Te Karere Maori*, 1 February, 3.
—— (1856a), *Te Karere Maori*, 31 January, 1–7, 12–14.
—— (1856b), *Te Karere Maori*, 29 February, 4–16.
—— (1856c), *Te Karere Maori*, 29 February, 17.

────── (1858a), *Te Karere Maori*, 9 November, 3–4.
────── (1858b), *Te Karere Maori*, 22 November, 2–3.
────── (1858c), *Te Karere Maori*, 29 November, 3–4.
────── (1858d), *Te Karere Maori*, 20 December, 2–3.
────── (1858e), *Te Karere Maori*, 27 December, 2–3.
────── (1860a), *Te Karere Maori*, 3 August, 4.
────── (1860b), *Te Karere Maori*, 15 August, 11–13.
────── (1860c), *Te Karere Maori*, 1 September, 15.
────── (1861), *Te Karere Maori*, 16 December, 1–8.
────── (1862a), *Te Karere Maori*, 3 January, 1–6.
────── (1862b), *Te Karere Maori*, 15 January, 1–3, 7–10, 19–22.
────── (1862c), *Te Karere Maori*, 5 February, 20–32.
────── (1862d), *Te Karere Maori*, 25 February, 7.
────── (1862e), *Te Karere Maori*, 14 April, 1–2, 9–11.
────── (1862f), *Te Karere Maori*, 23 May, 4–16.
────── (1862g), *Te Karere Maori*, 1 July, 3–8.
────── (1862h), *Te Karere Maori*, 20 July, 3.
────── (1862i), *Te Karere Maori*, 20 September, 4–16.
────── (1863), *Te Karere Maori*, 30 March, 21.
────── (1842a), *Te Karere o Nui Tireni*, 1 January, 1–2.
────── (1842b), *Te Karere o Nui Tireni*, 1 April, 13–17.
────── (1842c), *Te Karere o Nui Tireni*, 1 June, 24.
────── (1843), *Te Karere o Nui Tireni*, 1 December, 47.
────── (1844a), *Te Karere o Nui Tireni*, 1 January, 3.
────── (1844b), *Te Karere o Nui Tireni*, 1 October, 51.
────── (1867a), *Te Waka Maori o Ahuriri*, 26 September, 69.
────── (1867b), *Te Waka Maori o Ahuriri*, 19 December, 100.
────── (1868a), *Te Waka Maori o Ahuriri*, 19 March, 9–10.
────── (1868b), *Te Waka Maori o Ahuriri*, 9 April, 15.
────── (1868c), *Te Waka Maori o Ahuriri*, 14 May, 28.
────── (1868d), *Te Waka Maori o Ahuriri*, 13 August, 40.
────── (1871a), *Te Waka Maori o Ahuriri*, 9 February, 8.
────── (1871b), *Te Waka Maori o Ahuriri*, 21 June, 8.
────── (1871), *Te Waka Maori o Niu Tirani*, 2 December, 133.
────── (1872a), *Te Waka Maori o Niu Tirani*, 5 January, 31.
────── (1872b), *Te Waka Maori o Niu Tirani*, 18 September, 120.
────── (1872c), *Te Waka Maori o Niu Tirani*, 16 October, 133–4.
────── (1873a), *Te Waka Maori o Niu Tirani*, 13 August, 90.
────── (1873b), *Te Waka Maori o Niu Tirani*, 17 September, 107.
────── (1873c), *Te Waka Maori o Niu Tirani*, 29 October, 146.
────── (1874a), *Te Waka Maori o Niu Tirani*, 11 August, 194.
────── (1874b), *Te Waka Maori o Niu Tirani*, 25 August, 208.
────── (1874c), *Te Waka Maori o Niu Tirani*, 22 September, 234.
────── (1874d), *Te Waka Maori o Niu Tirani*, 6 October, 246.
────── (1874e), *Te Waka Maori o Niu Tirani*, 1 December, 297.
────── (1875a), *Te Waka Maori o Niu Tirani*, 23 March, 61.
────── (1875b), *Te Waka Maori o Niu Tirani*, 5 October, 223.
────── (1875c), *Te Waka Maori o Niu Tirani*, 5 November, 311.
────── (1875d), *Te Waka Maori o Niu Tirani*, 2 December, 255.
────── (1875e), *Te Waka Maori o Niu Tirani*, 14 December, 299–308.
────── (1876a), *Te Waka Maori o Niu Tirani*, 11 January, 5.

――― (1876b), *Te Waka Maori o Niu Tirani*, 8 February, 36.
――― (1876c), *Te Waka Maori o Niu Tirani*, 22 February, 43–4.
――― (1876d), *Te Waka Maori o Niu Tirani*, 25 July, 177, 178–81.
――― (1876e), *Te Waka Maori o Niu Tirani*, 22 August, 198.
――― (1877), *Te Waka Maori o Niu Tirani*, 17 July, 168.
――― (1875), *Te Wananga*, 18 September, 225.
――― (1867), *Wellington Independent*, 7 September, 7.
Ballantyne, Tony (2009), 'The state, politics and power, 1769–1893', in Giselle Byrnes (ed.), *The New Oxford History of New Zealand*, Melbourne: Oxford University Press, 88–124.
Belgrave, Michael (2017), *Dancing with the King: The Rise and Fall of the King Country, 1864–1885*, Auckland: Auckland University Press.
'Correspondence between the Government and Maori Chiefs' (1870), *Appendix to the Journals of the House of Representatives*, A-21, 5.
'Correspondence relative to the Registration of Native Voters' (1858), *Appendix to the Journals of the House of Representatives*, E-02, 2, 3.
'Cost of Publication of "Waka Maori" (Return Showing the)' (1877), *Appendix to the Journals of the House of Representatives*, G-01, 1.
Curnow, Jenifer (2002), 'A brief history of Maori-language newspapers', in Jenifer Curnow, Ngapare Hopa and Jane McRae (eds), *Rere Atu, Taku Manu! Discovering History, Language and Politics in the Maori-language Newspapers*, Auckland: Auckland University Press, 17–41.
'Further Reports from Officers in Native Districts' (1871), *Appendix to the Journals of the House of Representatives*, F-06A, 11; *Press*, 2 February, 1871, 2.
'Grey to Duke of Newcastle' (1862), *Appendix to the Journals of the House of Representatives*, E-01, Section II, 34.
Mutu, Margaret (2010), 'Constitutional intentions: The Treaty of Waitangi texts', in Malcolm Mulholland and Veronica Tawhai (eds), *Weeping Waters: The Treaty of Waitangi and Constitutional Change*, Wellington: Huia Publishers, 13–40.
――― (2020), 'Niupepa Māori', *New Zealand Digital Library*, University of Waikato, https://www.nzdl.org/cgi-bin/library.cgi?a=p&p=about&c=niupepa (accessed 2 January 2024).
'New Zealand Parliamentary Debates' (1867), Vol. 1, Part 2, 655, 816.
Oliver, Steven (1990), 'Maketū, Wiremu Kīngi', *Dictionary of New Zealand Biography, Volume 1: 1769–1869*, Wellington: Allen & Unwin/Department of Internal Affairs.
Papers Past, National Library of New Zealand, https://paperspast.natlib.govt.nz/ (accessed 21 August 2020).
Parkinson, Phil (2001), *The Māori Language and its Expression in New Zealand Law: Two Essays on the Use of Te Reo Māori in Government and in Parliament*, Wellington: Victoria University of Wellington Law Review.
――― and Penny Griffith (2004), *Books in Māori 1815–1900: Ngā Tānga Reo Māori: An Annotated Bibliography: Ngā Kohikohinga me Ōna Whakamārama*, Auckland: Reed Books.
Paterson, Lachy (2006), *Colonial Discourses: Niupepa Māori 1855–1863*, Dunedin: Otago University Press.
――― (2016), 'The New Zealand Government's niupepa and their demise', *New Zealand Journal of History*, 50.2, 44–67.
――― (2017), 'The *Te Waka Maori* libel case of 1877', *law&history*, 4.1, 88–112.
――― (2020), 'Māori literary practices in colonial New Zealand', in Tony Ballantyne, Lachy Paterson and Angela Wanhalla (eds), *Indigenous Textual Cultures: Reading and Writing in the Age of Global Empire*, Durham, NC: Duke University Press, 80–98.
Scholefield, Guy H. (1950), *New Zealand Parliamentary Record 1840–1949*, Wellington: Government Printer.
Sorrenson, M. P. K. (2014), *Ko te Whenua te Utu: Land Is the Price: Essays on Maori History, Land and Politics*, Auckland: Auckland University Press.

Ward, Alan (1995), *A Show of Justice: Racial 'Amalgamation' in Nineteenth Century New Zealand*, Auckland: Auckland University Press.

Waymouth, Lyn (2002), 'Debate and ideology in *Te Wananga* and *Te Waka Maori o Niu Tirani*, 1874–8', in Jenifer Curnow, Ngapare Hopa and Jane McRae (eds), *Rere Atu, Taku Manu! Discovering History, Language and Politics in the Maori-language Newspapers*, Auckland: Auckland University Press, 153–73.

17

Language and the Making of the Colonial Modern: Periodicals from Late Nineteenth-Century Kerala, India

G. Arunima

Both Malayalam, the language mainly spoken in the south-western Indian state of Kerala, and its script have a long history. Yet its modern, and presently recognisable, form would not be much more than two centuries old. The start of the process of standardising Malayalam, like in other parts of India or the world, can be traced back to the emergence of print technology. By the mid-nineteenth century, printing presses had been set up in different parts of Kerala, and new forms of publications, and genres of writing, were becoming more readily available. The early newspapers and periodicals were responsible for the creation of a print culture and a literary public sphere. The debates and views aired in the pages of these new artefacts created the conditions for shaping public opinion – at least among those who could read or had access to these.

In this chapter I focus on two of the most significant early Malayalam periodicals – *Bhashaposhini* (Language Advancement) and *Vidyavinodini* (Knowledge as Pleasure). The vibrant discussions in both these periodicals, from the 1890s onwards, were central to framing questions about language, writing, the region, and the more vexed problem of cultural identity. This is perhaps the earliest attempt to address what it meant to be a 'Malayali' – an identity rooted in, structured by, and repetitively invoking linguistic origin. In other words, this is the time when there is an attempt to forge a link between language (Malayalam), region (Kerala) and ethnic identity (Malayali). In a multilingual country like India, not only was this relevant in shaping early nationalism by emphasising regional distinctiveness, but it continues to have significance even today, when the pushback against the attempts to impose Hindi as India's national/official language comes from its multilingual history, and immense cultural pluralism.

The work on early periodicals in different parts of the world demonstrates how this newly arrived form opened up a new world of reading materials that, along with books and pamphlets, offered its readers different types of information. While many of these focused on what could be characterised as 'light' reading, usually comprising stories, sketches, satire and other titbits, this was not the only form of information that was disseminated by periodicals. Many focused on 'contents which related to the notion of national identity and which distinctly stated a national political agenda during a vibrant period of formation and transformation of nations' (Martin 2006: 8).

What is however interesting to note is that there was a marked similarity in the anxieties expressed by early writers and publishers worldwide. At the end of its life,

Plate 1 Frederick Stack, *View from the Ranges, overlooking the entrance to the Manukau Harbour, Auckland*, 1862, hand-coloured lithograph, 203 × 405 mm. The forested landscape of the Auckland province was generally seen as an encumbrance to settler agriculture. Courtesy of Auckland Art Gallery Toi o Tāmaki, purchased 1989.

Plate 2 George O'Brien (1821–88), *View of Otago Heads and Port Chalmers from Signal Hill near Dunedin*, c. 1866, watercolour with pencil & opaque white on paper, 288 x 634 mm. The relative absence of forest in the landscape of the Otago province. Courtesy of Hocken Collections Uare Taoka o Hākena, University of Otago, 7,302.

Plate 3 *Eastern Horizon*, December 1967, cover. Courtesy of the authors.

Plate 4 *Busara*, 3.4, 1971, cover. Courtesy of the author.

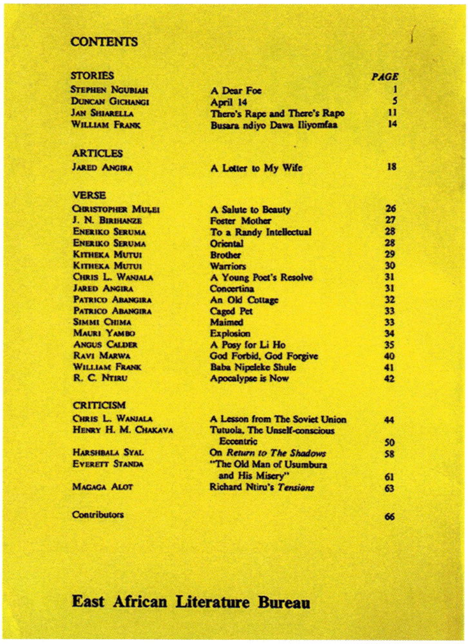

Plate 5 *Busara*, 3.4, 1971, table of contents. Courtesy of the author.

after having run for eight years, the *New York Magazine* said, 'Shall every attempt of this nature desist in these States? Shall our country be stigmatized, odiously stigmatized, with want of taste for literature?' (Mott 1966: 13–14). Even though this was being written almost a century before analogous worries were expressed in late nineteenth-century Kerala, the concerns about the need for good literature, and the creation of a literary sensibility, are very similar, issues that I shall open up later in this chapter.

Histories of print media in Kerala often include long lists of newspapers and periodicals that were printed in the nineteenth century. The problem faced by the researcher when confronted with such lists is trying to verify the scanty information accompanying these. To begin with, it is unclear how these were generated. Most nineteenth-century sources pertaining to print histories or cultures in Kerala, with the exception of what was referred to as the Native Newspaper Reports (discussed by Sukeshi Kamra in Chapter 31), give one insufficient detail about presses, papers or periodicals. Nor does the scanty information available permit one to piece together a reliable story about such early print histories.

We do know that by 1905 there were twenty-eight functional presses in Travancore, and many others are mentioned as operating throughout the latter half of the nineteenth century. But excepting their names and locations, most sources offer little further supporting information.[1] The Native Newspaper Reports, while not chronicling such histories, offered summary notes culled from such sources for mostly anglophone colonial officials who wished to get a sense of what they considered to be significant news from different regions in India.

Undoubtedly what was reported in such sources was by no means comprehensive, yet they do provide us with names of publications and dates of relevant news items that were published. Moreover, they provide an insight into what aspects of news, or discussions, the state thought relevant and worthy of translation and reportage.

A. D. Harisharma, journalist, writer and scholar of Malayalam, was amongst the earliest to address head on the unreliability of the many lists that have been anthologised in media histories (Harisharma 1959). Through a close reading of some of the early periodicals, he demonstrates that many of the 'facts' about print histories are erroneous, and he shows how these have been simply reproduced by different authors without adequate cross-checking. However, despite the errors and lacunae in these early print histories, it would be safe to assume that by the end of the first decade of the twentieth century, these publications could well have been read by not only a small section of the educated elite, but a wider cross section of the public, especially in the princely states of Travancore and Cochin. Both these places benefited from the reform activities of benevolent monarchs, who wished to encourage education and offered government employment as a reward for those who opted for the opportunities presented by the new vernacular schooling system. This meant that by 1911, literacy rates in Travancore and Cochin were thrice that of the Indian average (Jeffrey 1992: 57).

Keeping this in mind, it would be safe to say that the earliest surviving periodicals in Kerala that were published in the latter half of the nineteenth century, notably *Bhashaposhini* and *Vidyavinodini*, might have been read in different parts of the region and by a readership that was not restricted to a tiny elite. Their pages carried some of the most important debates of the period on Malayalam, and the region. *Bhashaposhini* was started in 1892 by Kandathil Varghese Mappilla, and was printed by the Manorama Press that he started as a joint stock company. *Vidyavinodini* was started a few years before in 1889 by C. P. Achyutha Menon, and was published until 1903 by the Vidyavinodini Press, located in Trichur.

Prior to the development of these and other periodicals in the latter stage of the century, there was a scattering of one-off newspapers published in the 1840s and 1850s, mostly in the form of a few cyclostyled sheets bound together, launched by Protestant missionaries as part of their proselytising efforts. Many of these newspapers did not last beyond two or three years.

By the late nineteenth century, a newer genre of publication emerged – the Malayalam periodical, of which *Vidyavinodini* was a good example (see Figure 17.1). These periodicals were different from previous publications in the sense that the subject matter was more 'secular' in nature, and combined literature (poetry, essays and in time the short story) with interventions by contributors on a variety of themes that could be broadly defined as social, cultural and sometimes scientific. An interesting minor detail about *Vidyavinodini* was that it was named after the press at which it was printed. A well-known bookseller in Trichur, V. Sundarayyar, started a press there in 1887 and named it Vidyavinodini. His son and the founder editor of the periodical, C. P. Achyutha Menon, happened to be friends. The story goes that the periodical was named after the press as a sign of the friendship between the two men. That aside, Sundarayyar and Sons didn't just print the periodical; they also took on the responsibility of managing it (Priyadarshanan 1971: 8).

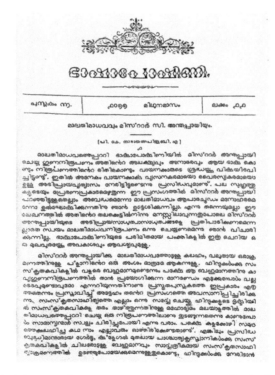

Figure 17.1 Nineteenth-century Malayalam periodical *Bhashaposhini*.
Courtesy of Sree Chithirai Thirunal Library, Trivandrum, Kerala.

The first issue of *Vidyavinodini* stated the reason for its own existence in the following way:

> As books providing knowledge are almost negligible in Malayalam, readers who value knowledge go to great pains to study Sanskrit and English. Needless to say, there are very few who can afford to spend time and money on studying other languages in order to enhance their education. As long as our language remains in its present condition, it will be impossible for the people of Malayalam[2] to gain knowledge, or reap the benefits of modernization that accrue from it. Everyone who has benefitted from an education must strive hard to generate easily understandable books, both prose and poetry, that will help increase people's knowledge, and aid in modernization. (Priyadarshanan 1971: 8–9)

The Malayalam periodicals of this period were characterised by a self-reflexive strain, and many pieces spoke of the role they thought literary associations and periodicals had in creating a literary sensibility. Well-known littérateurs of the period, including Kunjikuttan Thampuran, Appan Thampuran, C. S. Gopala Panikkar and others, were part of a group, also called Vidyavinodini, that attempted to create a taste, and discernment, for Malayalam literature. C. P. Achyutha Menon, the founder editor, remained one of its main contributors during the journal's lifetime, and one can find innumerable articles written by him in its pages, many of which were on non-literary topics ranging from wealth, capital and wages to rent and profit (Priyadarshanan 1971: 11). Yet this periodical remained best known for its literary engagements, and for providing space for generating one of the liveliest debates on the Malayalam language itself.

Many noteworthy literary works first saw the light of day in the pages of *Vidyavinodini* (they were either serialised or reviewed in it), and Priyadarshanan suggests that of these perhaps the most significant were the plays of the period. Kandoor's *Malavikaagnimitram*, Kocchunni Thampuran's *Phalgunaviryam* and C. Govindan Ilayadath's *Sunandasarasaveeram* were amongst these (Priyadarshanan 1971: 14–15). Book reviewing was also a prominent feature of the journal, and many of the early novelists in Malayalam gained a readership because of the exposure they acquired through this form of literary engagement. In 1896, when *Vidyavinodini* had managed a steady print run for about seven years, the then editor wrote, '[T]here is just the one monthly magazine like *Vidyavinodini* in Malayalam. It would be shameful if Malayalis allow it to die out' (Priyadarshanan 1971: 18). By the time it had reached its twelfth year, editor P. Gopala Menon, who had been responsible for changing the character of the periodical somewhat, wrote, '*Vidyavinodini* isn't simply about knowledge or pleasure, it is also matters relating to statecraft. This can be considered as one of the chief issues of interest here' (Priyadarshanan 1971: 18).

Bhashaposhini too saw itself as a periodical dedicated to the furthering of Malayalam language and literature, and in part this was linked to its origins (see Figure 17.2). Its distinctive feature was that it was a periodical named after a literary association of the same name. Poets and poetry enthusiasts set up the Bhashaposhini Sabha, the association, in 1892 after they first met in Kottayam, as a means to get together occasionally and share their recent creations (Priyadarshanan 1971: 22–3). After a few meetings, they decided to bring out a periodical four times a year, and the surviving print copies

Figure 17.2 Nineteenth-century Malayalam periodical *Vidyavinodini*. Courtesy of Sree Chithirai Thirunal Library, Trivandrum, Kerala.

of the early editions suggest that the periodical itself may have included, at least in part, the proceedings of the association's meetings (Anon. 1893a, *Vidyavinodini*: 23).

The early years of *Bhashaposhini* were riddled with controversies, which appear to have been engineered by certain vested interests that wanted the periodical's publication to shift away from Kottayam, and the Manorama Press, to Kochi (Harisharma 1987: 81). This meant that for a short while *Vidyavinodini* took over the publication of *Bhashaposhini*, a move that invoked the ire of many, and led to a protracted battle of words in the pages of the leading newspapers of the day. Eventually in 1897 the two periodicals were separated again, with the responsibility for *Bhashaposhini*'s publication being restored to Varghese Mappilla (Priyadarshanan 1971: 23). The presidential address of the association's fifth meeting, in 1898, placed Valiakoyi Thampuran's appreciation of Varghese Mappilla on record.

There is no doubt that the excellent meeting held three years back in Thiruvananthapuram marked the culmination of this association's growing maturity. The fate of the association since then has been such that it felt as though the association had lost the rewards gained by its good actions, making all those faithful to it deeply pained. Therefore, its [*Bhashaposhini*'s] rebirth is due only to the fact that Mr. Varughese Mappilla has resumed charge of his post as secretary of the association, after having previously stepped down from this post. I wasn't at all surprised that [this association] became incomplete when the person who had been its life and soul since its beginning stepped down, and that it came back to life with renewed vigour when he rejoined it. In the one year that the periodical [*Bhashaposhini*] was merged with *Vidyavinodini*, even its name was obliterated by the *Vidyavinodini* office bearers . . . The secretary needs to be congratulated for the work he has done, and continues to do, for the association. (Quoted in Priyadarshanan 1971: 23)

At this point *Bhashaposhini* became a monthly publication, and went on to create a place for itself in the Malayalam literary public sphere. Even though it was discontinued in the early twentieth century after Varghese Mappilla's death, it was later revived (in 1977) and continues to be an influential literary magazine even today.

From the surviving copies of both periodicals, one can see that the layout is similar, with the name of the periodical placed at the centre of the page in an arc, and the specificities of the year and month of publication and the volume and issue numbers printed just below that. Significantly, the dates mentioned followed the Malayalam calendar, which is a 'solar and sidereal Hindu calendar', and its origin dated to 825 CE, which was when, according to the historian Shungoonny Menon's conjecture, the then king of the region, Udaya Marthanda Varma, decided to launch a new era associated with his reign (Sarma 1996: 93–9). The months in the Malayalam calendar correspond to astral configurations, and have different names from the now almost standardised, and universalised, Roman calendar. Even the numerals used in the text of the periodicals follow the Malayalam numbering system that was created using a notation system that uses the letters of the Sanskrit alphabet to represent the nine digits and zero (Menon 1985: 65–6; Sarma 1996: 96–7). While such periodicals could be viewed as a colonial import of literary stylistics, some of their formal properties, including the layout, showed signs of indigenised reclamation. The few surviving copies of the early decades of these periodicals (1892–1930) do not mention their cost. However, we do know from later scholars that not only were these priced, they may also have been distributed on the basis of prior subscriptions, though this is hard to correlate on the basis of current information. By the 1920s, in the face of competition from newer periodical arrivals, the layout of *Bhashaposhini* changed, for instance by noting on its cover both Malayalam and English dates, in both Malayalam and Arabic numerals.

Despite the changing content of the periodicals, the formal structure continued to have certain other common features in the early decades. Of these the most notable was a short quatrain of praise (*mangalam, deivasthuthi*), usually, though not always, to a god, at the beginning of each issue of the periodical. One of the early issues of *Bhashaposhini*, for instance, features a quatrain written by the well-known poet Keralavarma welcoming 'new fellow travellers', or younger poets, into the literary world (Priyadarshanan 1971: 24). It also added a motto in Sanskrit, *vidyadhanam sarvadhanena pradhanam* [knowledge is the greatest wealth] to its cover page.

In time, these periodicals became the site of energetic debates on many issues related to interests of the Malayalam reading public, enough to sustain publication over a number of years. Even though precise information on important questions related to the histories of presses like readership, forms of circulation and profitability are sadly under-researched for the Kerala material, it is perhaps likely, looking at the continuing success of the *Manorama* newspaper and larger groups of companies, that their early journalistic venture was, on the whole, fairly successful.

Periodicals and the Making of the Malayalam Literary Public Sphere

In the rest of this chapter, I shall look at the debate on Malayalam language that raged in the pages of some of these periodicals, especially *Bhashaposhini* and *Vidyavinodini*. Central to this debate was the growth and sustenance of modern Malayalam (the writing of new grammars, lexicons and histories of language and literature accompanied this), even as there was a preoccupation with its linguistic origins. The different elements of this debate – including the writers involved in it and their differing positions, the links drawn between language and identity – and the conditions considered necessary for developing modern Malayalam are all significant as they were integral to reimagining Kerala residents as a linguistic community.

The 'Malayali' – or the one who speaks Malayalam – could belong to any caste, religious community or region of Kerala, but was linked to others through a linguistic kinship. These periodicals, and others that were to come after them, played a central role in such a self-fashioning. Over time, the periodical became central to Kerala's literary and artistic imagination, with prominent poets, writers and cartoonists using this space to engage a wide readership. The periodical produced its own form, particularly in prose writing, and I would suggest that the Malayalam essay came into being because of this literary form. These could be polemical, didactic, literary, scientific or philosophical. The essays that defined the contours of the language debate were polemical and political in nature, and emerged in a context where the newly popularised printing press, and a new print culture, had enabled mass publication of a wide range of genres and styles of writing.

Nineteenth-century Kerala, like other parts of the subcontinent, and indeed the world, saw an explosion in writing and publishing. The new books and early periodicals spanned a variety of themes – religious, literary, scientific, and what could be considered as early studies of society, be it on history, geography, ethnography or culture. These were accompanied by literary experiments of other kinds, namely the novel and the short story. The modernity of these literary experiments gave form to many early colonial periodicals. So, for instance, the earliest of these in Kerala, the *Sathyanatha Kahalam*, was but a few pages, didactic in nature and born out of the needs of the missionary publicists. By the 1890s, however, new periodicals such as *Bhashaposhini* and *Vidyavinodini* were more diverse in content, with essays devoted to different themes – from poetry and literary reviews to over time even sections dedicated to 'scientific' issues, especially agriculture – and less involved in presenting products of any kind of a religious nature. Such new periodical forms enabled a parallel emergence of subject experts in Kerala, such as cultural commentators, and political interlocutors. Many of the writers of this period were to remain significant figures in Malayalam literature and journalism. Others, despite their sharp and significant interventions, seem to have disappeared without a trace.

Researching, understanding, categorising and evolving early theories of language was central to the nineteenth-century colonial preoccupation in India. In seeking to classify and identify the varieties of Indian language-related activities that were a response to the colonial encounter, one needs also to account for the emergence of new educational systems, pedagogies and modes of examination that were being standardised during this period.

Recent research in this area, specifically north Indian literary cultures, shows that while the nineteenth century produced 'textual communities' and 'cultural identities' centred round language and social identity, these were not necessarily co-constitutive, nor could cultural identitarian predilections be taken to be the bases for the production of modern writing or the establishment of a relatively recent print public sphere (Orisini 2018). In other words, the attempt to cement the supposed divisions of Hindi and Urdu by the mid-twentieth century belied the long history of multilingualism and shared cultural traditions of the periods leading up to this time. The discussions about modern Malayalam in the early periodicals of the latter half of the nineteenth century, while combining different issues, people and aspirations, were quite different from the trajectory of language politics in north India. One part of it was concerned with the need to modernise the language, and how to go about doing this. At the same time there was no clear consensus on how to conceptualise this modern Malayalam, particularly in relation to some of the chief preoccupations of that period – what the roots of Malayalam were (Tamil or Sanskrit), and whether it should follow an English or a Sanskrit model for its future development. Yet where the north Indian language battles were mapped on to religious differences, with Hindi being portrayed as a Hindu and Urdu a Muslim language, in Kerala the linguistic community of Malayalam speakers was imagined as one that brought different castes and communities within the same fold. This did not mean that such differences disappeared; it was simply that despite differences, all Malayalam speakers were meant to have an overriding linguistic, and cultural, kinship that made them Malayali.

Another element in the discussion on Malayalam's modernity in the pages of *Vidyavinodini* and *Bhashaposhini* centred on questions about style, taste and related literary matters. The writers involved in this were language scholars, writers and journalists, and at least some wrote about such matters in the pages of Malayalam newspapers and other periodicals of the period. Terms like 'growth' and 'development' (of Malayalam) proliferated in these pieces and were a reflection of the growing need felt in the literary public sphere for a standardised Malayalam. This meant that many writers emphasised the need for developing tools, like an adequate grammar and lexicon, that would help in the growth of the language. Most people involved in the discussions in these two journals agreed that the reform in language needed to be linked to changes in the systems of education, examination and employment, without which no tangible change could take place. To enable these, they wrote and argued strenuously about the urgent need for changes in the printing and publishing industry that would help in creating a new culture of reading.

These were some of the themes that dominated the pages of the two main literary journals of this period, *Vidyavinodini* and *Bhashaposhini*, throughout the decade of the 1890s. In the rest of this brief chapter, I shall look at the themes of language 'origin', 'modernisation', and the ongoing reflections in this period on the need for a new literature. As was to be expected, these were not restricted to some pure and abstracted sphere of thinking about linguistic modernity, but also revealed deep societal fissures. What appeared to be a discussion on language could well be read also as a discussion on caste, differences in religious community or intra-regional variations. It also gestured to an increasing discomfort with those who considered themselves to be the custodians of language, literature and culture in Kerala, the Brahmins, and a desire to break with their hegemony on culture and the print public sphere. Arguments about ridding Malayalam of excessive Sanskritic usages were located in the discomfort with the over-representation of Brahmins in the Malayalam literary world. That said, there was no clear consensus on how this was to be achieved, and nor did many who wished to give modern Malayalam a different direction agree that the model to be emulated was the one often referred to in these essays as 'the English model'.

One of the arguments of this period that was repeated forcefully in the two journals under review was that language 'improvement' was the consequence of identifying, and studying, its origins and organisation. Malayalam, these writers noted, despite being a union of Sanskrit and Tamil, was actually a *dravida*[3] language. In their view, most Malayalam phrases, as well as its grammar, were *dravida* in origin, and the excessive use of Sanskrit and the 'aryanisation' of the language actually spoilt it (Anon. 1893b, *Vidyavinodini*: 26–8). Additionally, the anonymous author of this essay, entitled 'Bhashaparishkaram' [Language modernisation], emphasised the need to be tolerant towards dialect difference whilst searching for an 'ideal' language. This was possibly one of the earliest articulations of the link between language, its history and regional spread that we find for the Malayalam language, where despite the urge for change in its written form, there is a tolerance for the spoken tongue. Significantly, it linked the modernising of the language with achieving a sort of original state of purity, both in structure and in content. Language therefore comes to be seen as an organic, living entity, whose modernising was understood in developmental terms of evolution, growth and change. Intrinsic to such a metamorphosis was also its 'purification', which interestingly did not involve a Sanskritic but, on the contrary, a *dravida* affinity. The move away from a Sanskritised Malayalam was clearly influenced by such a concern, and writers like O. Chandu Menon were strong votaries of such a shift.

This position was most sharply stated by the versatile and acerbic critic and littérateur Murkoth Kumaran in 1900 (Kumaran 1900a: 17–21; Kumaran 1900b: 73–6). In a set of essays examining the ongoing debate on the Malayalam language, its roots and its subsequent transformation, he had both a practical and a more contextual understanding of the question. Regarding the standardisation of the language, he felt that the more people from Trivandrum published in papers from Calicut and the other way round, the more likely it was that differences in Malayalam usage would disappear.

Regarding the use of Sanskrit words, however, and what form Malayalam literature should take, Murkoth Kumaran had a more complex view. He criticised what he saw as the indiscriminate use of Sanskrit (this was in the context of a discussion on Malayalam poetry, challenging the then current Brahmanical scholarship) and by quoting examples from *manipravala slokas* argued that these had both Sanskrit and *dravida* words. Yet he did not feel that the 'English' model should be followed, as was apparently suggested by Raja Raja Varma Thampuran, as it would make Malayalam dependent on a European language, besides being called '*pathiri* Malayalam' (missionary Malayalam). This was despite Kumaran's immense regard for the German missionary Hermann Gundert's contributions to the Malayalam language, including producing one of its earliest grammars which, as he pointed out, had been ignored in the ongoing discussions. As he noted quite rightly, with the focus having shifted to A. R. Raja Raja Varma's *Keralapaniniyam*, Gundert was no longer given his due in the histories of Malayalam being produced at that time. Apart from these factors that contributed to the development of the language, he also maintained that it was journals like *Vidyavinodini* and *Bhashaposhini*, newspapers like *Malayala Manorama*, and individuals like Kandathil Varghese Mappilla who had significantly helped grow the use of the Malayalam language.

From the 1890s onwards, the two issues, one about *bhashaparishkaram* or modernising the language, and the more fundamental underlying issue of who the participants of such a 'modernisation' were, were addressed in all manner of ways in the pages of these journals. As early as 1892, C. D. David, a regular columnist in *Vidyavinodini*, wrote that 'Malayalam language is the equal right of everyone in the Malayala *rajyam* [region] ... and must be treated as a community wealth (*samudaya swathu*)' (David 1892a: 219). In this piece, David urged people to engage in what he saw as an urgent task – that of reviving Malayalam, which he described as a 'flickering wick' – and wrote continuously about its 'revival'. Amongst the many reasons that he saw for its decline were the absence of a rich and diverse literature and a lack of pride in the language. The problem was that 'those who have studied Sanskrit, and the Malayalam Brahmins, have scorned Malayalam ... those who have learnt English ... many do not even speak Malayalam ... [and] others mix it with English' (David 1892b: 268).

In an attempt to imbue the spirit of reviving the language, he exhorted the readers to rise to the occasion by asking, 'is there anyone who does not love their land and their language?' (David 1892a: 219). C. D. David was not alone in speaking about language as 'common property'; Joseph Muliyil, author of the novel *Sukumari*, was another who spoke of Malayalam in a similar vein. In fact, his position was sharper and addressed the problem head on. He wrote that 'educated and illiterate alike have equal rights to language and need not fear expressing themselves ... Malayalam language differed from *jillah* to *jillah* and from caste to caste' (Muliyil 1902: 65–8).

Regarding the 'reforms' in language that were currently extant, he said that they could be divided into two kinds: *shuddhikarikyuka*, or to 'cleanse' it by removing the 'lacunae or accretions in it', and to develop it (*bhashaposhanam*) by making knowledge, for instance of new prose and poetry forms, in other languages like English available in Malayalam as well (Muliyil 1902: 65–8).

While the idea of the 'development' of Malayalam (or its relationship with English) remained fraught, there was a much greater consensus amongst most people writing in this period that '*shuddhi*', or 'cleansing', Malayalam meant ridding it of an excess of Sanskrit. Writers like O. Chandu Menon in their creative and polemical writing urged for the growth of a new Malayalam that did not have an excessive overlay of Sanskrit words and usages. In his review of Chathukutty Mannadiar's translation of *Uttararamacharitam* he wrote, 'One of the specialties of your work is that you have tried as far as possible to use Malayalam words and phrases. Sanskrit words have been used only where it is absolutely necessary' (Menon 1891: 228).

Striking in this discussion on modernising Malayalam is the fact that the 'progress' of the language is not conflated with the language of progress. This is particularly significant in a period when the language of nature, evolution and progress was familiar, and used in more predictable ways in discussing reforms in society, especially in relation to the matrilineal community (Arunima 2003: chapter 5). Whereas in the context of matrilineal reform, the language of 'progress' and evolutionary developmentalism implied abolishing matrilineal kinship, in the language debate, invoking terms like 'progress' and 'cleansing' (*shuddhikarikyuka*) implied the creation of a more inclusive, non-Sankritic, language. 'Progress' here referred to growth, and going beyond Malayalam's dependence on Sanskrit. By extension, this also implied a revaluation of those who were considered to be 'language experts'. This becomes evident if one examines the community and caste origins of many of the vocal participants in this debate. The presence of lower castes, Christians and even Nayars should also be read as a way by which these groups were laying claims to such 'expertise' and to being 'knowledge producers'.

Such a claim displaced the supposed natural authority that the Brahmins and members of the royalty claimed within the domains of language and literature. It included figures like Kandathil Varghese Mappilla, long-time editor of *Bhashaposhini* and *Malayala Manorama*, who wrote extensively on the growth and development of Malayalam, claiming that the heart of modernisation lay in the language. 'The English want to modernize India. And if a place must modernize it has to happen through its language' (Mappilla 1897: 25).

Mappilla analysed what he perceived to be the extant changes as a result of a variety of different impulses. For him, both the growth of newspapers and 'authors of books like Indulekha' contributed to pruning Malayalam of its Sanskritised excess, even as they played a critical role in the creation of a new language, and literature. Unlike Murkoth Kumaran, however, he saw the proximity to the English, and 'English education', as something that benefited the development of Malayalam. 'It is the European missionaries who highlighted the fact that Malayalam could stand on its own without Sanskrit. Now the Travancore state's efforts of starting Malayalam medium schools has spread through the region'; this, along with the Madras University making Malayalam a language of examination, in his view, had helped the language, as proficiency was no longer measured by the ability to learn by rote, but by being able to make creative use of it (Mappilla 1897: 27–8). Modern Malayalam, as it had emerged in the nineteenth century, in his view, was clearly a product of a curious blend of missionary enterprise and the modern state apparatus.

However, the importance of new literature for early language reform was also recognised because of its ability to popularise a new idiomatic usage. Mappilla wrote that, 'while initially Malayalam was highly Sanskritised, later this declined as a result of newspapers and journalism. The authors of books like *Indulekha* too are responsible for the creation of a new Malayalam and the making of a new literature' (Mappilla 1897: 27). While many contemporary critics had several reservations about *Indulekha* and its literary merits, all agreed that its novelty really lay in the form and language use. The need for novels was something that many critics and writers continually pressed for. But even as developing a modern literature comparable to a western corpus was considered important by some, others wrote about the importance of printing, or the need for a new educational and examination system that would help to provide the language with a more formal status.

The absence of a 'wide and vast literature' on different topics was clearly felt by many writers in the 1890s. In a trenchant critique of the prevailing conditions, C. D. David wrote that the reason that Malayalam did not have as high a status as English was that it had no literature worth the name of its own, and people took no pride in their language. There were no readers, buyers or publishers for Malayalam books, because it was not a profitable business (David 1892b: 265–71). Even the recent translation of *Indulekha*, he lamented, was done by an Englishman. 'We should be as aware as they are' (David 1892b: 269). Even though English was often cited as the model language, whose example in having developed a vast literary oeuvre was to be emulated in every respect, none of the writers in this period endorsed abandoning Malayalam. On the contrary, their exposure to English via the new educational system fired them up with enthusiasm to reform the language and to gain respect for it in the same way as the English had gained for theirs. Respect for the English literary traditions did not mean a desire for anglicisation; on the contrary, most critics argued strenuously against this kind of tendency, which they feared was becoming rampant in Kerala. As the author of 'Bhashaparishkaram' wrote in *Vidyavinodini* in 1893:

> We have very few books in Malayalam that are read and enjoyed. In English, new books sell up to twenty or thirty thousand within a couple of months of their publication. Here if three hundred copies were sold in three months the author would be grateful. While education is necessary for the creation of such a reading public, it would be helpful if there were entertaining books that could aid such a process. And these, we believe, would be of greater use than scientific or religious texts. So while writing scientific books is very difficult, we still would praise the authors of plays, *Bhasha Shakuntalam*, and novels, like *Indulekha*, more. However, translations from English are avoidable, as neither the language nor the content relates to Malayalam. (Anon. 1893c, *Vidyavinodini*: 5)

The worries of the nineteenth-century writers notwithstanding, Kerala was to go on to develop a high rate of literacy by the 1930s, alongside a thriving publishing industry and a reading public. Even today, magazines and periodicals are central to Kerala's literary public sphere, with important debates first finding a voice in their pages. That aside, before the introduction of digital media and sound-based technologies, magazines were one of the preferred spaces for public reflection. Many of the significant Malayali publicists, like writers, poets and critics, of the late nineteenth and twentieth centuries emerged within such a literary culture.

The centrality of the periodical can be seen as an integral part of the growth of Kerala's political culture. The 'literary public sphere' continues to perform a critical political function in Kerala, thereby underwriting the importance of both the relationship between ideas, politics and public presence, and the ways in which such a public is produced. The continued life of the 'colonial periodicals' in the postcolonial world is not merely about a form that survived over a hundred years or more, but is more about the kinds of spaces these opened up, for established writers and novices alike. The extraordinary range of written and visual forms contained in these periodicals bear testimony to their importance in literary and political contexts.

Notes

1. See, for example, http://www.keralaculture.org/printing-press-kerala/293 (accessed 21 November 2020).
2. In the late nineteenth century, the region that was designated as the linguistic state of Kerala in 1956 was variously referred to as Malayalam, Malanad or other similar terms.

At this time this region was subdivided into three parts, of which Malabar was under direct British rule from 1792 onwards, and the 'native states' of Thiruvthamkoor (anglicised to Travancore) and Kochi (anglicised to Cochin) were ruled by kings and maintained their distinct political identity.
3. The term *dravida* here is meant to possess two kinds of properties: first, that it was non-Sanskritic, and hence, by association, non-Brahmin; second, that it was aligned with Tamil, which was often represented as the 'original' language of the south Indian region. Therefore, representing Malayalam as '*dravida*' was also to suggest that its linguistic origins lay in the Tamil language.

Bibliography

Anon. (1893a), 'Bhashaparishkaram' [Language modernisation], *Vidyavinodini*, 4.1, 23.
—— (1893b), 'Bhashaparishkaram' [Languge modernisation], *Vidyavinodini*, 4.2, 26–8.
—— (1893c), *Vidyavinodini*, 4.1, 5.
Arunima, G. (2003), *'There Comes Papa': Colonialism and the Transformation of Matriliny in Kerala, Malabar, c. 1850–1940*, Hyderabad: Orient Longman.
David, C. D. (1892a), 'Kerala Bhashaposhini Sabha' [Kerala Bhashaposhini Society], *Vidyavinodini*, 3.10, 219.
—— (1892b), 'Malayalabhasha' [Malayalam language], *Vidyavinodini*, 2.12, 265–71.
Harisharma, A. D. (1959), *Keralathile Adyakala Patramasikakal* [Early periodicals in Kerala], *Mathrubhoomi Azhchapathippu* [Mathrubhoomi Weekly], 24 May, 19–20.
—— (1987), *Kandathil Varughese Mappilla*, Kottayam: Malayala Manorama Press.
Jeffrey, Robin (1992), *Politics, Women and Well-Being: How Kerala Became 'A Model'*, New Delhi: Oxford University Press.
Kumaran, Murkoth (1900a), 'Bhashaparishkaram' [Language modernisation], *Vidyavinodini*, 11.1, 17–21.
—— (1900b), 'Bhashaparishkaram' [Language modernisation], *Vidyavinodini*, 11.2, 73–6.
Mappilla, Kandathil Varghese (1897), 'English Cherna Malayalam' [Malayalam mixed with English], *Bhashaposhini*, 1.2, 25–8.
Martin, Michèle (2006), *Images at War: Illustrated Periodicals and Constructed Nations*, Toronto: University of Toronto Press.
Menon, O. Chandu (1891), 'Uttararamacharitam', *Vidyavinodini*, 3.2, 228.
Menon, Shungoonny (1985), *History of Travancore*, Trivandrum: Kerala Gazetteers.
Mott, Frank Luther (1966), *A History of American Magazines: 1741–1850*, Cambridge, MA: Harvard University Press.
Muliyil, Joseph (1902), 'Bhashaparishkaram' [Language modernisation], *Bhashaposhini*, 6.3, 65–8.
Orisini, Francesca (ed.) (2018), *Before the Divide: Hindi and Urdu Literary Culture*, Hyderabad: Orient Blackswan, e-publication.
Printing Presses of the Nineteenth Century (n.d.), website at http://www.keralaculture.org/printing-press-kerala/293 (accessed 21 November 2020).
Priyadarshanan, G. (1971), *Manmaranja Masikakal* [Forgotten magazines], Kottayam: National Book Stall.
Sarma, K. V. (1996), 'Kollam Era', *Indian Journal of History of Science*, 31.1, 93–9.

18

Simple Letters? British and Pacific Literacies in the Victorian Missionary Periodical

Michelle Elleray

In late 1844 Joseph John Freeman received a letter from Aperaamo.[1] As the Joint Foreign Secretary for the primarily Congregationalist London Missionary Society (LMS), Freeman had met Aperaamo, a Samoan whose conversion to Christianity is apparent in his name (a transliteration of 'Abraham'), during the latter's visit to England from July 1843 to June 1844. Aperaamo had sailed to England with Leota, a fellow Samoan and a matai (chief), as well as Thomas Heath, a British LMS missionary working in Sāmoa. Together the three had travelled to places such as Norwich and Bath to promote the LMS's South Seas Mission and met with the LMS Directors in London; Aperaamo's letter indicates that he also had social engagements with Freeman's family. While Aperaamo's letter to Freeman seeks to maintain this English connection, Freeman's publication of it positions the letter as an encapsulation of the interwoven dynamics of empire, evangelicalism and alphabetic literacy that are evident in and disseminated by the mid-Victorian children's missionary periodical.

Freeman was the founding editor of the LMS's *Juvenile Missionary Magazine* (1844–87), which by 1871 could claim a monthly circulation of 50–60,000 and, as its editors regularly declared, was passed from child to child, thereby expanding these numbers (see Figure 18.1). Even accounting for possible exaggeration, this periodical's circulation underlines the importance of attending to the cultural messages it disseminates. When Freeman published Aperaamo's letter in the *Juvenile Missionary Magazine*, he introduced it as a 'simple letter [that] has just come to hand from Abraham' (Aperaamo 1845: 6) (see Figure 18.2). 'Simple' here might designate a desired simplicity, in the sense of an innocence or purity of spirit that was assigned value in Christian culture of the time – certainly Aperaamo's profession in the letter of good will to Freeman and personal faith in God fits this rubric. But the letter is also understood as 'simple' in the sense of displaying only a basic command of English, as evident in grammatical errors and infelicities of expression. As such, Freeman's introduction designates the Pacific Islander as newly incorporated into the potential of alphabetic literacy as well as Christianity. I use the term 'alphabetic literacy' deliberately to signal the specific skill of deriving meaning from sequentially organised letters, since it conveys that there are other forms of literacy required for other semiotic systems. In Aperaamo's home community of Tutuila, Sāmoa, for example, different patterns on siapo (patterned barkcloth) or the lines of the malofie or malu (forms of tattoo)

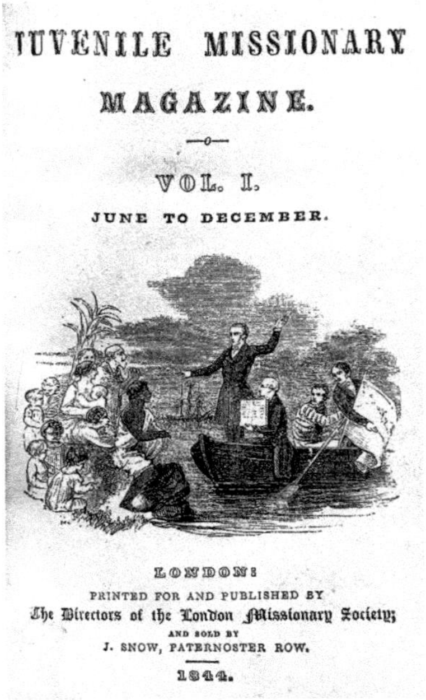
JUVENILE MISSIONARY
MAGAZINE.

VOL. I.

JUNE TO DECEMBER.

LONDON:
PRINTED FOR AND PUBLISHED BY
The Directors of the London Missionary Society;
AND SOLD BY
J. SNOW, PATERNOSTER ROW.

1844.

Figure 18.1 Title page, volume 1, the *Juvenile Missionary Magazine*, 1844. Courtesy of the author.

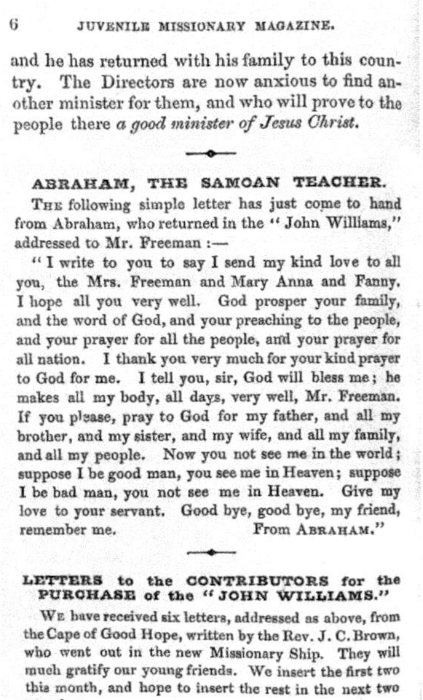
6 JUVENILE MISSIONARY MAGAZINE.

and he has returned with his family to this country. The Directors are now anxious to find another minister for them, and who will prove to the people there *a good minister of Jesus Christ.*

ABRAHAM, THE SAMOAN TEACHER.

The following simple letter has just come to hand from Abraham, who returned in the "John Williams," addressed to Mr. Freeman :—

"I write to you to say I send my kind love to all you, the Mrs. Freeman and Mary Anna and Fanny. I hope all you very well. God prosper your family, and the word of God, and your preaching to the people, and your prayer for all the people, and your prayer for all nation. I thank you very much for your kind prayer to God for me. I tell you, sir, God will bless me; he makes all my body, all days, very well, Mr. Freeman. If you please, pray to God for my father, and all my brother, and my sister, and my wife, and all my family, and all my people. Now you not see me in the world; suppose I be good man, you see me in Heaven; suppose I be bad man, you not see me in Heaven. Give my love to your servant. Good bye, good bye, my friend, remember me. From Abraham."

LETTERS to the CONTRIBUTORS for the PURCHASE of the "JOHN WILLIAMS."

We have received six letters, addressed as above, from the Cape of Good Hope, written by the Rev. J. C. Brown, who went out in the new Missionary Ship. They will much gratify our young friends. We insert the first two this month, and hope to insert the rest in the next two months :—

Figure 18.2 Aperaamo's letter, the *Juvenile Missionary Magazine*. Courtesy of the author.

Figure 18.3 Cover page, *O le Sulu Samoa*, 1839. Image reproduced with kind permission of Special Collections, State Library of New South Wales.

would convey information to the Samoan that would not be legible to the uninitiated European, and thus require a non-alphabetic form of literacy. In this chapter I use a specific scene of British children's alphabetic literacy acquisition – Aperaamo's letter in the January 1845 issue of the *Juvenile Missionary Magazine* – to attend to the reading processes that are normalised through the Victorian children's missionary periodical, and the attendant erasure of Indigenous literacies. Aperaamo's letter provides the occasion to consider more broadly how we might read examples of Indigenous writing in the Victorian missionary periodical, and to this end I reposition his letter from the sole context of the *Juvenile Missionary Magazine* to the Samoan-language missionary periodical produced and read by Aperaamo's home community, *O le Sulu Samoa* (1839–present), and the literacies to which *le Sulu* bears witness (see Figure 18.3). Drawing on the work of Indigenous Oceanian scholars I convey how these scholars' reading practices, aligned with their communities' cultural priorities, offer an alternative model of the knowledge to be gleaned from nineteenth-century letters and periodicals emerging from the missionary movement in Oceania.[2] To put it another way, how simple is Aperaamo's letter really?

Alphabetic Literacy: Simple Letters

The long nineteenth century, as David Vincent notes, saw England transition to an alphabetically literate society, with approximately half the population able to write in the mid-eighteenth century, whereas 99 per cent of people were able to sign the marriage register by 1914 (Vincent 2019: 507). Within Protestant evangelicalism the central role of reading the Bible for oneself saw evangelicals invest in improving the literacy rates of the British working class in the first half of the nineteenth century, deploying Sunday schools as an important institutional mechanism for enabling the skills of reading and, to a lesser extent, writing to be taught to working-class children specifically (Laqueur 1976: 113); thus 'three-quarters of working-class children . . . attend[ed] Sunday schools by 1851, receiving instruction from teachers drawn largely from their own community' (Vincent 1993: 69). Victorian children's missionary periodicals supported these efforts by providing what were understood as appropriate and affordable reading materials for the emerging class of alphabetically literate children. Reading matter such as magazines, pamphlets and giftbooks, all of which grew cheaper to produce in this period, rewarded British children for desired behaviours and skills, and in the decade before the *Juvenile Missionary Magazine* began publication libraries increasingly appeared in Sunday schools (Laqueur 1976: 117–18). Thus, the evangelical Sunday school, sympathetic to and entwined with the missionary project, was a key site for working-class children's acquisition of alphabetic literacy and provided the means for these students to access missionary periodicals. Additionally, children's missionary magazines were seen as a mechanism to corral the new skills of alphabetic literacy to evangelically approved ends, since as J. S. Bratton notes in her analysis of the Victorian child reader, literacy was viewed by the evangelical community as 'an edged tool in irresponsible hands' (Bratton 1981: 31).

In the early to mid-nineteenth century Oceania also saw alphabetic literacy rates increase exponentially as people recognised its potential capacities.[3] As with the working class in Britain, evangelical institutions were a key source of instruction such that alphabetic literacy and Christianity were deeply intertwined. Notably, alphabetic literacy skills became an occasion for, and not just the means of, engagement between different communities as one group of Islanders taught these skills to another. For example, a version of the monitorial system saw more advanced Islander converts teach others to read and write; as converted Islanders from the Cook Islands, Sāmoa and Hawai'i became foreign missionaries in the western Pacific, they brought to their new congregations the Protestant emphasis on alphabetic literacy; and as David A. Chang notes, Mā'ohi converts from Tahiti were central to Kānaka 'Ōiwi's keenness to acquire alphabetic literacy skills in Hawai'i. Although alphabetic literacy was catalysed by the European- and American-centred missionary movements, Indigenous Oceanian use and redeployment of alphabetic literacy practices exceeded the narrow expectations of non-Indigenous ministers.

Samoans' widespread attention to reading and writing began with the 1830 arrival of LMS Pacific Islander missionaries from the Society Islands and what were then known as the Hervey Islands (now part of the Cook Islands).[4] Permanent British missionaries arrived six years later. The context within which Aperaamo would have learned to read and write can be gleaned from A. W. Murray, the British LMS missionary working in Aperaamo's home district, who describes the Tutuila mission in 1836:

> School was held once a day, five days in the week, for about an hour and a half, but, at intervals of leisure throughout the day, the book was the constant companion of the more eager and zealous, hence their rapid progress. In about three months some had learned to read tolerably, and those who were in advance of their fellows were soon set to work to assist in teaching them. (Murray 1876: 41–2)

In 1843 Heath conveys that 'About 27,000 (nearly one-half the population) of Samoa have learned to read. Many of them read portions of the Scriptures which we have translated, and others elementary books. Some thousands can write upon slates' ('London Missionary Society' 1843: 522). Through these accounts we see that Aperaamo was a participant in a major cultural shift resulting from the Oceanic embrace of alphabetic literacy.

British children in LMS circles were made aware of the Pacific Islanders' pursuit of alphabetic literacy, whether through missionary accounts of Islander children at local Sunday schools or missionary requests for paper, slates and writing implements, all of which regularly appeared in the *Juvenile Missionary Magazine*. In this way the periodical benefited the LMS by introducing British children to missionary work and encouraging the child's engagement in missionary philanthropy. Distributed through the extensive network of British Sunday schools – primarily, though not solely, Congregationalist – the *Juvenile Missionary Magazine* included short factual articles, imagined scenes narrated as factual, letters from missionaries or converts, a song or poem, and a significant number of woodcut images, as well as donation pages recording the progress of major fundraising ventures. Monthly issues sold for a halfpenny, or in some cases were given away free by Sunday schools, with the pricing consciously chosen to make the magazine accessible for British families at the lower end of the socio-economic scale. This strategy is made explicit in the opening issue when the title character of 'Little Emma's Corner' wishes the magazine were published more often; her mother explains this would make the periodical less affordable for those who could buy a monthly, but not a weekly. The interaction conveys the intended class range of the periodical's readership, with Emma's family depicted as financially comfortable but committed to extending readership to those who were not. We witness another financial consideration when the opening editorial for the *Juvenile Missionary Magazine* signals the LMS's recognition of the challenge inherent in launching a new missionary periodical without diminishing demand for already existing publications (Freeman 1844: 3–6). Freeman recommends that while buying the *Juvenile Missionary Magazine* his readers should also purchase titles such as the *Missionary Repository for Youth* (1839–[1850?]), the *Children's Monthly Missionary Newspaper* (1843–61), the *Children's Missionary Magazine* (1838–59) and the *Church Missionary Juvenile Instructor* (1842–90), thereby conveying to us the increasingly crowded print culture space of missionary periodicals directed specifically at British children. The *Juvenile Missionary Magazine* nevertheless carved out its own niche, with 200,000 issues sold in the first seven months.

Freeman, the periodical's editor until 1849 and a former missionary to Madagascar, drew on official correspondence to the LMS for the *Juvenile Missionary Magazine*'s content.[5] In the case of Aperaamo's letter Freeman exploits a personal communication, but British missionaries in the Pacific regularly sent letters addressed directly to the child reader for publication in the *Juvenile Missionary Magazine*, reflecting an ongoing arrangement between foreign-located missionaries and periodical content. Since the *Juvenile Missionary Magazine* began as a means to secure British children's continued interest in the LMS's missionary ship to the Pacific Islands, the arrangement was mutually beneficial: British missionaries in the Pacific sent content for the children's periodical, and the child reader financially supported the ship necessary to maintain and expand missionary work in the region. In fact, Aperaamo, Leota and Heath's journey to Britain was undertaken to convince the LMS Directors of the South

Seas Mission's need for a bigger ship, resulting in the eventual purchase of the *John Williams*.[6] Aperaamo and Heath subsequently returned on the *John Williams*'s first voyage to the Pacific, and Heath writes to the *Juvenile Missionary Magazine* reader that crowds came to see the new ship, including 1,400 people in Apia, Sāmoa, who listened to Aperaamo and Heath's account of their time in England (Heath 1845: 254).

Scenes of Reading

'Little Emma's Corner', mentioned above as discussing the ideal pricing of the *Juvenile Missionary Magazine*, presents Emma parsing the periodical's title in a manner that alerts us not only to ties between missionary work and alphabetic literacy, but also to the complexities of language and interpretation. Young Emma's effort to decipher the word 'juvenile' relies on her brother's explanation that words have histories, since the term's Latin etymology derives from the past presence of Romans in Britain. The word 'missionary', however, Emma is able to discern easily and explains it to the reader as 'a good man that goes abroad to tell people about the Saviour and the way to go to Heaven' ('Little Emma's Corner' 1844: 17). The alignment of 'good' with the activity of intervention in (primarily) non-European cultures is thereby normalised as both positive and unidirectional. Yet the apparent obviousness of the missionary as 'a good man' is destabilised by Emma's exposition of the word 'magazine', which she knows as a site for storing explosives rather than, as her mother explains, 'a collection of different pieces to please, and to inform, and to instruct the readers' ('Little Emma's Corner' 1844: 18). Emma now sees that the multivalent potential of words requires an attention to context. Insofar as the British child reader learns alongside Emma that words are shaped by history and context, but that missionary work is unquestionably good, the piece displays an attention to the semiotic complexity of language that is not extended to the intercultural dynamics of missionary evangelicalism.[7]

'Little Emma's Corner' demonstrates reading to be a complex process, but this awareness is not apparent in the framing of Aperaamo's letter, published in a later issue of the *Juvenile Missionary Magazine*. The LMS regularly sought to maintain a connection between British children and Pacific Islanders, including converts who had travelled to Britain where they visited Sunday schools and juvenile missionary meetings. The hope was that such connections might facilitate further donations to the missionary cause, or a future career choice to be a missionary. To this end Pacific Islanders' letters occasionally appear in the *Juvenile Missionary Magazine*. Such is the case with Aperaamo, whose letter I present in full:

> I write to you to say I send my kind love to all you, the Mrs. Freeman and Mary Anna and Fanny. I hope all you very well. God prosper your family, and the word of God, and your preaching to the people, and your prayer for all the people, and your prayer for all nation. I thank you very much for your kind prayer to God for me. I tell you, sir, God will bless me; he makes all my body, all days, very well, Mr. Freeman. If you please, pray to God for my father, and all my brother, and my sister, and my wife, and all my family, and all my people. Now you not see me in the world; suppose I be good man, you see me in Heaven; suppose I be bad man, you not see me in Heaven. Give my love to your servant. Good bye, good bye, my friend, remember me. From Abraham (Aperaamo 1845: 6)

We can see several forms of literacy on display here: the writer understands the genre conventions of the letter, displays knowledge of Christian phrasing and precepts, and demonstrates the social expectations (both British and Samoan) of recognising Freeman's familial relationships. In his faith, generosity and the alphabetic literacy to write this letter, Aperaamo is presented as a suitable recipient of British missionary philanthropy and acts as evidence that British children's donations to the missionary cause are well directed. At the same time, the letter displays some alphabetic illiteracy, with grammatical infelicities such as unnecessary repetition, misuse of 'the', and the singular used for plural nouns. The letter and letter writer are thus easily co-opted into a hierarchy of civilisational attainments in which some peoples – through class, nationality or race – show promise but are yet to attain the alphabetic fluency of the British middle class.

A moment of reflection, however, should make us question the apparent alphabetic illiteracy of Aperaamo's letter. Aperaamo wrote in Samoan, not English, and what we might read as errors or clumsy phrasing appear to be literal translations of Samoan grammar. Take, for example, Aperaamo's request for 'your prayer for all nation' – Samoan nouns do not have a plural form, and so in translating from Samoan to English the plural form needs to be inserted. The translator has not done this. A similar lack of fluency is apparent in the statement 'Now you not see me in the world; suppose I be good man, you see me in Heaven; suppose I be bad man, you not see me in Heaven'; here the awkward English phrasing results from mistranslation, specifically the need to recognise that one is translating phrases, not simply words. The alphabetic illiteracy, then, resides not with Aperaamo but with the unknown British translator, who has taken what we can assume to be fluent Samoan and rendered it as stilted English. Meanwhile the editor, whose task it is to oversee the quality of the work he prints in the periodical, takes for granted that the illiteracy resides with Aperaamo, not the British translator. Thus Aperaamo's letter performs the convert's alphabetic literacy as a sign of the capacity to read the Bible and engage in the LMS's print culture networks; at the same time, the stilted or ungrammatical phrasing reinforces extant assumptions that Samoan society is less complex and knowledgeable than British society. In reading this periodical, the Victorian child is interpellated into an imperial framework that positions the British as more fluent in writing and associated skills, yet the letter is in fact evidence of the limits of British literacy: the translator can translate words from Samoan to English but lacks the facility to render fluent Samoan as fluent English, while the editor is unable to read the translation and see that what is simple, in the sense of operating at a basic level, is the translation rather than the letter.

In British missionary and imperial texts, however, literacy is repeatedly presented as something Britain bestows on the Islanders, rather than something the British reader might lack. By designating Aperaamo's published communication a 'simple letter' Freeman positions himself and his ilk as the central actors in the scene of alphabetic literacy, with the skills and responsibility to assess the literacy capabilities of others. British child readers, insofar as they agree with Freeman's assessment and are able to recognise the grammatical and stylistic infelicities of the published letter that designate it as simple in Freeman's eyes, align themselves with a hierarchy of alphabetic literacy mapped on to assumptions about civility and Christianity, with themselves positioned above Aperaamo, though closer to him than Freeman given their age. For the British child reader still learning to write, Aperaamo is presented as a peer in the effort to meet the requirements of sentence structure, grammar and the genre of the letter, while Freeman embodies the promise of one day being the adjudicator of the alphabetic literacy of those understood as spiritually within, but racially on the margins of, the Christian community. Positioning Aperaamo's letter as 'simple' therefore does significant work in justifying ongoing British missionary presence and intervention in Samoan society: the existence of the letter is displayed as evidence of what has been accomplished through British missionary teaching, but its apparent simplicity points to the need for ongoing supervision of these newer Christians.

Teu le vā: Sustaining Harmonious Relationships

What happens if we read Aperaamo's writing through a lens other than that of British evangelicalism? I turn now to the work of Indigenous Oceanian scholars working with nineteenth-century letters and periodicals as sites for engaging with Indigenous values, protocols and knowledge. In '"I do still have a letter": Our sea of archives' Māori scholar Alice Te Punga Somerville discusses her great-grandfather's letter alongside a photo of him taken at Concordia Lutheran seminary in Illinois, where he was training to be a pastor. The letter is written in Māori and describes his efforts to learn Latin, which was being taught to him in German. Te Punga Somerville draws on this material to show how the Indigenous letter is not a solitary artefact of relevance primarily for its content, but also a creator and reflection of community through the connections the letter enables, the histories it traces, the places through which it moves: 'The 1906 letter can be read by itself, on its own terms, but it is richer – and indeed it is only visible – when considered within the world of the photo, the other letters, the telegram, the Lutheran archive and the great-granddaughter who only has the ability to write in English' (Te Punga Somerville 2016: 127). To read the letter simply for information on the task of gaining literacy in Latin, fascinating though this is, stops short of the contexts that shape how the letter is read, and the places, people and histories connected through the letter's travels. Te Punga Somerville is not simply undertaking a material history of the letter as object though; her title invokes a foundational article in Oceanian scholarship – 'Our Sea of Islands' by Tongan intellectual Epeli Hau'ofa – which replaces the western view of Pacific islands as isolated dots against a vast oceanic background, with an attention to the ocean as a connecting presence that enables the interrelationships of its inhabitants; hence the move to refer to the region as 'Oceania'. Similarly, Te Punga Somerville investigates how the letter reflects and enables connections within and across communities.

The attention to relationships in Te Punga Somerville's article reproduces a value common across Indigenous Oceania that in Sāmoa is embodied in the word 'vā'. While vā might be translated as 'relationship' or 'space (between two places, things or people)' (Milner 2001: 307), the translation requires further attention to the social and spatial cultural work of such relationships and spaces, which is where the concept's value resides. Non-Indigenous literary scholars who have come across the term often know it through Samoan author Maualaivao Albert Wendt's definition of the vā as 'the space between, the betweenness, not empty space, not space that separates but space that relates' (Wendt 1996: 19).[8] The definition emphasises what enables the relationship between things and what is produced through those relationships, rather than a western sense of negative space as background, something that recedes. The value accorded to the vā is apparent though the Samoan saying 'teu le vā', which Samoan scholar and Presbyterian minister Uili Feleterika Nokise translates as to 'order the space or relationship' (Nokise 1983: 19), that is, to consciously attend to sustaining the relationship in a manner that is productive and harmonious for all concerned. In his scholarship on the LMS, Nokise uses the saying to pinpoint the difference between Samoan and western conceptions of the self within society: for him, teu le vā

> suggests the socio-centric orientation in the Samoan idea of proper behaviour. The *va* (space/between) is as crucial to the Samoan theory of action as is the 'self' in its Western counterpart . . . the Samoan (and Polynesian) stress is on relation, on things in their context . . . a Samoan looks after his culture by taking special care of the social relationships. (Nokise 1983: 19)

The Samoan value of teu le vā centres the social relationships that, Nokise argues, enabled the local understanding of Christianity to become 'Samoanise[d]' despite its origins in British evangelicalism (Nokise 1983: 60).

Recognising the importance of the vā within Samoan society, how might we refocus our reading of Aperaamo's letter on to the relationships it embodies and enables? Aperaamo's letter is a textual means to sustain a relationship between the writer, Freeman, and Freeman's family. But if the letter is a means for Aperaamo to maintain interpersonal relationships with those in England, Freeman reframes this intent when he publishes the letter in the *Juvenile Missionary Magazine*. The letter is instead positioned hierarchically as an example of an initial step on the Anglocentric ladder of spiritual and alphabetic literacy advancement. The issue is not Freeman's publication of the letter – Aperaamo was no doubt aware of this potential given it was common practice within the LMS – but rather the lack of reciprocal generosity when Freeman uses the letter as the occasion for paternalistic judgement, since in Freeman's assessment of the 'simple' nature of Aperaamo's letter, the letter serves an evidentiary function that reinforces racial hierarchies. At the same time the letter's publication enables further solicitation of the child reader for donations, and so the relationships the letter enables are subordinated to the instrumentalisation of that connection into financial support for the missionary cause. In the *Juvenile Missionary Magazine* Aperaamo's letter is used to leverage relationships rather than maintain them.

The Indigenous-language Periodical: *O le Sulu Samoa*

Aperaamo's letter exists within a Samoan-language context as well as an English-language one, and as such our attention to how we might read his letter and the periodical in which it is found can benefit from the arguments of Kānaka 'Ōiwi scholars about typography and the translation of Hawaiian-language periodicals, and the work of Samoan scholars on *O le Sulu Samoa*, a Samoan-language missionary periodical. As described above, Aperaamo's conversion to Christianity was accompanied by a communal interest in acquiring alphabetic literacy skills. This was further consolidated with the arrival of a printing press in May 1839, which was used to print Samoan-language texts for the mission. Samoans quickly become central to the work of the press: J. B. Stair writes that by late 1845 'there were fourteen Samoans, young men and lads, engaged in the [printing] office, as compositors, press-men, and binders; also several girls employed in stitching and folding', who together helped produce 7,721,000 printed pages of text (Stair 1847: 210). Among the first of these publications was *le Sulu* which, over 180 years later, is still being published by the LMS's successor, the Congregational Christian Church of Sāmoa.

The nineteenth-century prevalence of the LMS over other denominations in Sāmoa would have seen *le Sulu* distributed widely through local mission stations, while the demand for printed texts to reinforce the newly acquired skills of alphabetic literacy, as well as interest in reading about local and international matters, would have ensured an interest in the periodical extending beyond religious affiliation. In LMS publications *le Sulu* was discussed in terms of the printers rather than editors: in the mid-nineteenth century these were J. B. Stair (1839–45), James P. Sunderland (1845–8) and Samuel Ella (1848–c. 1862). In the catalogue of the George Grey Collection, the earliest issues are described as duodecimos of mostly '12 pages each . . . ornamented with woodcuts', and with content that would have ensured Samoan familiarity with happenings elsewhere in Oceania, including British accounts of Samoan missionaries (Bleek and Grey 1859: 111). Samoan scholar and minister Latu Latai writes that while initially *le Sulu* published articles written and edited by the British missionaries, from the 1880s it increasingly published Samoan-authored material (Latai 2016: 19–21). Although British missionaries controlled the contents of *le Sulu* in the period before and immediately after Aperaamo's journey to Britain, its existence suggests Aperaamo's knowledge of the format and genre of the periodical, and therefore the context in which his letters might circulate in Britain. In other words, we can presume a level of familiarity with print culture formats that belies Freeman's assumption of Aperaamo's simplicity.

In 1890 George Cousins described *le Sulu* as an eight-page quarto edited by S. J. Whitmee, though by 1891 Arthur Edward Claxton was editor, and later James Edward Newell. Cousins lists the contents as including 'African Slavery', 'A Jewish Rabbi', 'Spurgeon' and 'Saaga's Visit to England', the latter about a young Samoan (Cousins 1892: 204). This is also when Robert Louis Stevenson first serialised 'The Bottle Imp' in *le Sulu*, which at this point cost sixpence. In her work on twentieth-century volumes of *le Sulu*, Samoan scholar Wanda Ieremia-Allan describes content ranging from missionary information and local Samoan events, to translations of 'literature from Persia, Greece, America, Canada, Russia and Europe' (Ieremia-Allan 2019: 5). *Le Sulu* thereby bears witness not only to Samoan geographic mobility propelled by foreign missionary work, but also to Samoans' engagement with international texts.

Le Sulu presents us with Samoans' eventual appropriation of the missionary periodical genre to record their own histories, concerns and efforts within the mission field, and to extend into textual form the Samoan valuing of relationships and forms of intertextual reference. Ieremia-Allan speaks of the 'philosophical underpinnings of Tofāmanino (ancient Sāmoa philosophy) which predated Christianity' in the Samoan contributions, thereby positioning them as enabling a relationship between pre-Christian and Christian values, rather than the British missionaries' view of the latter supplanting the former; instead the writing is 'carefully constructed along Va tapuia – sacred relationships that are bound by cultural covenants of seniority, gender and familial affiliations' (Ieremia-Allan 2019: 2, 3). As with Te Punga Somerville's account of her great-grandfather's letter, the periodical provides a site of connection between ancestors and the present generation, thereby enabling a textual instantiation of the genealogical ties fundamental to Samoan culture.

Ieremia-Allan shows that in adapting alphabetic literacy to Samoan needs the ancestors writing in *le Sulu* incorporated a traditionally Samoan organisation of the world, interwoven with the new religion. Reading these texts therefore requires the knowledge to recognise when the text exceeds imported Protestant conventions and the literal translation of words, allowing what Ieremia-Allan describes as 'the lafi a taga usi – the delightful and unexpected reveal of a concealed malofie [man's tattoo]' (Ieremia-Allan 2019: 3). The proverbial saying 'e lafi a taga usi' uses the momentary glimpse of a tattoo usually covered by clothing to indicate 'secrets that have been divulged' (Schultz and Herman 1949: 177), or in Ieremia-Allan's deployment of the phrase, the interplay of different layers of signification. Her analysis indicates that the Samoan missionary periodical is more than a Samoan-language version of a British genre; instead the 'writing merges Christian faith and Indigenous philosophies; combining local vernacular and local metaphors, parables, alagaupu [proverbs] . . . muagagana fa'aSāmoa [Samoan idioms] and Biblical scripture to reinforce genealogical ties to the new Atua [God]' (Ieremia-Allan 2019: 5).

In her work on the missionary periodical Ieremia-Allan enacts a form of scholarship advocated by Noelani Arista, who uses Hawaiian periodicals to argue for the necessity of Indigenous-language scholarship that recognises the multi-layered resonances of Oceanian languages – in Arista's case 'ōlelo Hawai'i (Hawaiian language) – and the cultural contexts and knowledges specific to those languages. Alphabetic literacy in Arista's model therefore requires one to read for the ways in which the language use integrates culturally specific references for the listener's or reader's amusement, to demonstrate skill, or in some cases to convey meaning to the initiated that the uninitiated will not perceive. Discussing the artistic and politic use of kaona, or veiled meaning, as methodology, Arista declares the necessity of 'us[ing] *kaona* to think . . . in a way that reflects Hawaiian systems of thought and connection and their tolerance and preference for multiplicity in the relation between not only words but also *worlds*' (Arista 2010: 666). In Noenoe K. Silva's work on nineteenth-century Hawaiian-language newspapers that were published before macrons and 'okina[9] were used to signal pronunciation, Silva notes that 'writing and print allowed for more kaona even than speech and spoken poetry, as words that may have been easily distinguishable to the ear became homographs in print' (Silva 2017: 12). Thus, to use one of Silva's examples, the nineteenth-century printed word 'pua' might now be rendered 'pua', 'pu'a' or 'pū'ā', and since each of these separate words in turn has multiple definitions, a skilled writer could play on the interrelationships between their diverse meanings (Silva 2017: 12). To translate 'pua' by a single English word would arrest the interwoven web of potential interpretations catalysed in the original.

Ieremia-Allan, Arista and Silva point to translation as more than the equating of words, instead positioning Indigenous-language texts as access points to complex cultural formations. Their scholarship indicates the wealth of opportunity embedded in the nineteenth-century Indigenous-language periodical, which is as much a context for Aperaamo's letter as the *Juvenile Missionary Magazine*. Insofar as they direct us to the capacities of Oceanian languages, their work pushes us to wonder about the register, allusions and import of Aperaamo's choice of specific Samoan words and phrases in his letter, and the extent to which these were erased by its translation into English.

Reading the Missionary Periodical Archives

While 'teu le vā' articulates the importance of attending to and maintaining relationships, not all texts are institutionally valued and stored to maintain or enable ongoing relationships: sometimes a space is a gap, an absence, an erasure. Such a gap, and the question of the extent to which it represents a Victorian imperial erasure (or at least classificatory choice), is visible through institutional holdings of the LMS's periodicals. The official LMS archive, now held at the School of Oriental and African Studies, UK, contains full runs of the *Juvenile Missionary Magazine* and its sequel, the *Juvenile*, from 1844 to 1894, and the *Evangelical Magazine and Missionary Chronicle* from 1793 to 1865, whereas only issues of *le Sulu* from 1890 are available as the holdings are incomplete.[10] An incomplete collection of volumes 1 and 2 of *le Sulu* were available to the Victorian reader, but as we learn from the 1885 catalogue of the British Museum Library's periodical publications, they were not housed in the LMS's archive, and are now in the British Library (Miller and Garnett 1885: 30). Physical holdings of the English-language and early Samoan-language LMS periodicals are therefore divided across institutions. Notably the LMS archives contain a full run of the English-language companion to *le Sulu*, the half-yearly *Samoan Reporter* (1845–62, new series 1870), initially edited by Heath (1845–8) and then by George Turner (1848–[62?]), in which the British missionaries recorded their mission work and ethnological observations. The nineteenth-century institutional allocation of the *Samoan Reporter* to the LMS's archive holdings and *le Sulu* to the British Museum Library positions the latter as of anthropological interest (or, with Sir George Grey's collection of *le Sulu* in mind, philological interest), whereas the English-language periodical is situated through location as central to missionary history. Present-day research within the official LMS archives therefore requires navigation of nineteenth-century institutional decisions about where historical items should be located; such classificatory choices skew today's scholar of LMS publications toward English-language sources, while obscuring the Samoan-language periodical production that preceded and existed during the time Aperaamo was in Britain, indeed preceded the first issue of the *Juvenile Missionary Magazine*.

What appears to be the singularity of Aperaamo's engagement with alphabetic literacy through the published letter in the *Juvenile Missionary Magazine* can be read instead as official LMS underestimation of Samoan print culture and its place within the institutional archive. The LMS's nineteenth-century decisions about what to preserve and archive, and in what institutional location, reflect a presumption that Oceanian converts were the subject matter for missionary periodicals rather than themselves producers and readers of periodicals, and that missionary history is centred in London even if its work is conducted in Oceania (among other regions); in this respect the absence of early issues of *le Sulu* from the official LMS archive has not traditionally been recognised as a loss. Periodical studies has of course been aware of and attentive to gaps; as James Mussell writes of the genre, 'each attempt to exert bibliographical control exposes how much more there is to know and how much can never be known . . . Page after page offers references and allusions to people, texts, commodities, and publications of which there is little trace' (Mussell 2015: 344). My point here, however, is to call attention to gaps we may have overlooked as gaps. When settler scholars such as myself read the Indigenous letter in the British missionary periodical, what don't we see that we don't see, and what might we therefore misread?

As we encounter Aperaamo through the *Juvenile Missionary Magazine*, the markings of the printed letter are legible to those of us working in English, but our glimpse of the Samoan is partial, a momentary glimpse in a much wider and more complex story; or, to redeploy Wanda Ieremia-Allan, we have 'the lafi a taga usi – the delightful and unexpected reveal of a concealed malofie [men's tattoo]', only in the case of the non-Indigenous reader the tattoo is not so much revealed (in the sense of known) as shown to exist (Ieremia-Allan 2019: 3). Rather than a simple letter, Aperaamo's textual presence in the child's missionary periodical is an aperture that directs us to the historical presence of Indigenous-language texts, readers and writers, and the Indigenous scholars whose linguistic and cultural knowledge presents the opportunity of productive relationships for periodical scholarship in Victorian studies. For those of us who are settler readers of the Victorian missionary periodical, our task is to not re-enact the British child reader of Aperaamo's 'simple' letter who, persuaded by the editor's authoritative assessment of Aperaamo's status, takes for granted the Samoan's illiteracy rather than acknowledging the limits of their own.

Notes

Faʻafetai to Wanda Ieremia-Allan for generously sharing her doctoral work in progress and to Alice Te Punga Somerville for connecting us.

1. While my chapter attends only to this first letter, a second was published in the *Juvenile Missionary Magazine* (Aperaamo 1847: 138–9), and the *Evangelical Magazine and Missionary Chronicle* transcribed his speech to LMS officials at Finsbury Chapel ('London Missionary Society' 1843: 520).
2. A term reinvigorated by Epeli Hauʻofa's essay 'Our Sea of Islands' (1994), Oceania encompasses the islands of the Pacific Ocean basin, as well as Australia and Aotearoa New Zealand; in Hauʻofa's sense the term prioritises the interconnections of the Indigenous peoples of this region. The term 'Pacific Islander' refers to those for whom the Pacific Islands are home through residence or genealogy; it does not usually refer to the Indigenous peoples of Australia or Aotearoa unless there is an additional genealogical connection.
3. For work in this field see Van Toorn 2006, and Ballantyne, Paterson and Wanhalla 2020.
4. Pacific Islander missionaries were known at the time as 'teachers'. I use 'missionaries' to reflect their work as consistent with that of British missionaries.
5. Freeman was followed by Ebenezer Prout (1850–65) and Robert Robinson (1866–84). During Edward Henry Jones's editorship (1885–92) the periodical became the *Juvenile* (1888–94), with Jones succeeded by Arthur Newton Johnston (1893–4). In 1895 it was replaced by *News from Afar: A Magazine for Young People* (1895–1967).
6. For details of British children's fundraising for the *John Williams*, which reached an apex of almost £12,000 in 1865, see Elleray 2020: 31–6.
7. A similar dynamic is apparent in an accompanying article in the same issue, directed at the older child reader ('Hints About China' 1844: 20–3).
8. For a further discussion of the vā, see Kaʻili 2017.
9. A macron is the line above a vowel, signalling a longer sound, while the ʻokina (a diacritical mark seen at the beginning of the word ʻokina) indicates the glottal stop.
10. As well as the British Library's incomplete holdings of *le Sulu* from 1839 to 1843, various issues from 1839 to 1847 are held in the Grey Collection, National Library of South Africa (see the description of these, including some indication of content, in Bleek and Grey 1859:

111–12), while within Oceania various issues from 1839 to 1912 are held in the Mitchell Library, State Library of New South Wales, and the Auckland Turnbull Library, National Library of New Zealand.

Bibliography

Aperaamo (1845), 'Abraham, the Samoan Teacher', *Juvenile Missionary Magazine*, 2, January, 6.

―――― (1847), 'Letter from Aperaamo – Samoan Teacher', *Juvenile Missionary Magazine*, 4, June, 138–9.

Arista, Noelani (2010), 'Navigating uncharted oceans of meaning: Kaona as historical and interpretive method', *PMLA*, 125.3, May, 663–9.

Ballantyne, Tony, Lachy Paterson and Angela Wanhalla (eds) (2020), *Indigenous Textual Cultures: Reading and Writing in the Age of Global Empire*, Durham, NC: Duke University Press.

Bleek, Wilhelm H. I., and George Grey (1859), *The Library of His Excellency Sir George Grey, K.C.B.: Philology, Vol. 2.4 Continued: Polynesia to Borneo*, London: Trübner.

Bratton, J. S. (1981), *The Impact of Victorian Children's Fiction*, Totowa, NJ: Barnes & Noble.

Chang, David A. (2018), 'The good written word of life: The native Hawaiian appropriation of textuality', *The William and Mary Quarterly*, 75.2, April, n.p.

Cousins, George (1892), 'From the Editorial Secretary', *The Chronicle of the London Missionary Society*, 1.9, September, 204.

Elleray, Michelle (2020), *Victorian Coral Islands of Empire, Mission and the Boys' Adventure Novel*, New York: Routledge.

Freeman, Joseph John (1844), 'Editor's Salam', *Juvenile Missionary Magazine*, 1, June, 3–6.

Hauʻofa, Epeli (1994), 'Our Sea of Islands', *The Contemporary Pacific*, 6.1, Spring, 148–61.

Heath, Thomas (1844), 'A Brief Memoir of the Native Chief, Leota', *Missionary Register*, 32, August, 338–9.

―――― (1845), 'Letters to the Contributors for the Purchase of the *John Williams*', *Juvenile Missionary Magazine*, 2, November, 251–4.

'Hints About China' (1844), *Juvenile Missionary Magazine*, 1, June, 20–3.

Ieremia-Allan, Wanda (2019), '"O le lotonuʻu moni": *Le Sulu* and histories of Samoan transnationalism', paper given at the New Zealand Historical Association conference, Victoria University, Wellington, 29 November.

Kaʻili, Tēvita O. (2017), *The Tongan Art of Sociospatial Relations*, Tucson: University of Arizona Press.

Laqueur, Thomas (1976), *Religion and Respectability: Sunday Schools and Working-Class Culture, 1780–1850*, New Haven: Yale University Press.

Latai, Latu (2016), 'Covenant keepers: A history of Samoan (LMS) missionary wives in the western Pacific from 1839 to 1979', unpublished PhD thesis, Australian National University.

'Little Emma's Corner' (1844), *Juvenile Missionary Magazine*, 1, June, 17–18.

'London Missionary Society' (1843), *Evangelical Magazine and Missionary Chronicle*, 21, October, 519–25.

Miller, Arthur William Kaye, and Richard Garnett (eds) (1885), *British Museum Catalogue of Printed Books: Periodical Publications*, Part 1 Aarau–Dusseldorf, London: William Clowes.

Milner, G. B. (2001) [1966], *Samoan Dictionary*, Auckland: Pasifika Press.

Murray, A. W. (1876), *Forty Years' Mission Work in Polynesia and New Guinea, from 1835 to 1875*, London: James Nisbet.

Mussell, James (2015), 'Repetition: or, "In Our Last"', *Victorian Periodicals Review*, 48.3, 343–58.

Nokise, Uili Feleterika (1983), 'The role of London Missionary Society Samoan missionaries in the evangelisation of the South West Pacific 1839–1930', unpublished PhD thesis, Australian National University.

Schultz, E., and Brother Herman (1949), 'Proverbial Expressions of the Samoans', *Journal of the Polynesian Society*, 58.4, December, 139–84.

Silva, Noenoe K. (2017), *The Power of the Steel-Tipped Pen: Reconstructing Native Hawaiian Intellectual History*, Durham, NC: Duke University Press.

Stair, J[ohn] B[etteridge] (1847), 'Samoan Printing Establishment', *Evangelical Magazine and Missionary Chronicle*, 25.292, April, 210.

Te Punga Somerville, Alice (2016), '"I do still have a letter": Our sea of archives', in Chris Andersen and Jean M. O'Brien (eds), *Sources and Methods in Indigenous Studies*, New York: Routledge, 121–7.

Van Toorn, Penny (2006), *Writing Never Appears Naked: Early Aboriginal Cultures of Writing in Australia*, Canberra: Aboriginal Studies Press.

Vincent, David (1993), *Literacy and Popular Culture: England 1750–1914*, Cambridge: Cambridge University Press.

—— (2019), 'The modern history of literacy', in John L. Rury and Eileen H. Tamura (eds), *The Oxford Handbook of the History of Education*, Oxford: Oxford University Press, 507–22.

Wendt, Albert (1996), 'Tatauing the Post-Colonial Body', *SPAN*, 42/43, April and October, 15–29.

19

Interrogating the Imperial Factor and Convoking Black South Africa: The Cape African Newspaper *Izwi Labantu*, 1897–1909

Janet Remmington

'IZWI LABANTU'
A [Xhosa]-Sesutho-English Weekly[1]
The authority PAR EXCELLENCE on intelligent Native thought and feeling.
The largest Circulation through out the Colony, Basutoland, Transvaal, O. R. C. [Orange River Colony], and Rhodesia.

'*Izwi Labantu*' 1903

Introduction

THIS CHAPTER ADDRESSES the boldly conceived and audaciously executed African-owned newspaper *Izwi Labantu* [The Voice of the People] (1897–1909) of the late Cape colonial period, which has to date received less attention than its longer-lived arch-rival *Imvo Zabantsundu* [Native Opinion] (1884–1997). I explore how *Izwi*, publishing weekly with some interruptions over a momentous twelve-year period, shaped itself in dramatic fashion as a forum for both targeted contestation and cooperation, when so much was at stake for the region's black majority at the turn of the twentieth century. It emerged as a response to rising tensions across the region, with black resources and rights coming under increasing pressure from colonial impositions, African leaders and groupings jostling for influence, and British- and Boer-ruled polities fighting for control over what was already being called South Africa.

Izwi was launched in the closing years of the nineteenth century, surviving and even gaining some ground during the epoch-making South African War (1899–1902). In relation to the post-war settlement, which advanced white conciliation and power, *Izwi* fought to convene an engaged trans-ethnic black public across the region, while making ardent claims to an idealised superstructure of imperial belonging with attendant rights of citizenship.[2] The newspaper's imperial leanings increasingly came under strain, however, as Britain and the former Boer republics moved towards political union, informed by a vision of a white South African state closing out the twentieth century's first decade.

Since the early nineteenth-century beginnings of press print culture in Southern Africa, there has been 'a revolving door around journalism, politics and activism', Anton Harber writes, as newspaper men and women carried 'their politics into journalism, and their journalism into the fight for rights' (Harber 2019: xiv). While black editors, compositors and writers took active roles in mission periodicals, and black contributors published in white newspapers in the hard-won free media environment of the Cape, key black figures increasingly sought to develop independent 'native press' outlets (Cutten 1935: 4–29, 79–82). Funding, however, was always in short supply. The relatively small black paying reading public, competition for advertisers, and strains of the broader economic climate especially during and after the war were all factors in determining the fate of such publications, which operated 'on the edges of the world of print capitalism' (Hofmeyr and Peterson 2019: 7). Precarity characterised the black press, especially so, arguably, for outspoken, autonomous outlets such as *Izwi*. While it was taken seriously in the press world, entering into exchanges with, and cited by, other newspapers in the region and across the seas, it was considered provocative, even troublesome, in some quarters, including by Lovedale Missionary Institution, around various issues ('A Mischievous Delusion' 1901: 145–6). In sum, *Izwi* choreographed a complicated dance between invoking imperial belonging, signalling Christian values, critiquing colonial practices, negotiating African factionalism, and promoting black activist efforts across the South African stage.

In what follows, I situate the establishment and life cycle of *Izwi* within broader historical and socio-political contexts, drawing on print culture scholarship to explore the newspaper's staging for audiences near and far. Opening with the story of the newspaper's founding in the high-stakes *fin de siècle* political theatre of the Cape Colony, and with imperial Britain's sights set on the broader reaches and riches of the South African region, I move on to discuss *Izwi*'s progression through the South African War, and its heightened advocacy efforts in the war's aftermath. To explore *Izwi*'s make-up, motivations, range and vicissitudes across its lifespan, I examine its contents (at least what has been preserved), while delving into available archival records concerning its operations. I close with reflections on the newspaper's liquidation in 1909. In bidding farewell to its readers, *Izwi* signalled its role in mobilising multilateral protest efforts against the draft South Africa Act, challenging the consolidation of white power under the aegis of empire.

'For Political Guidance and Social Education': Establishing *Izwi*

Thirteen years to the month after *Imvo* was founded in King Williamstown, *Izwi* was set up in nearby East London. Both African independent periodicals arose from the Eastern Cape with its long history of missionary education, the qualified African franchise since 1853, and growing socio-political organisation and assertion among the black educated classes interacting in various ways with traditional chiefdoms. *Imvo* had powerfully paved the way for independent black journalism in Southern Africa, with young teacher and journalist John Tengo Jabavu launching this newspaper of 'native opinion' in order 'to see us as we see ourselves' (J. T. Jabavu 1884: 3; Mkhize 2018; D. D. T. Jabavu 1922). In 1884, Jabavu had resigned as editor of Lovedale's Xhosa-language newspaper *Isigidimi sama Xosa* to publish content more political in nature and more directly informed by African concerns and interests.

Imvo, free of mission ties, did, however, have the financial backing of white supporters, who recognised the periodical's prospective commercial and electoral reach, though it was led editorially by Jabavu. If *Imvo* was the clear forerunner of the independent African press in Southern Africa, *Izwi* arrived as the challenger more than a decade later as political cleavages came to a head in the Cape.

By the mid to late 1880s, the numbers of educated or 'school' Africans in the Eastern Cape – though far from a homogeneous group (Mills 1990) – had grown to such an extent that their voting impacts could be felt, causing sectors of the white political classes to feel threatened. It was in this constraining environment where African rights and opportunities were being curbed that broader-based black political organisations beyond immediate town or district took shape, with affiliated publications.

The Cape government tightened the franchise qualification criteria in 1887, affecting some 20,000 men, largely members of the black elite; about one in three lost the vote. It was described as 'about the severest blow that has ever been aimed at Native rights since representative institutions were introduced in this country' (Anon. 1887b, *Imvo Zabantsundu*). The law was dubbed *u Tung' umlomo*' in isiXhosa (Mouthshutter), which Cape Africans were determined to defy through a variety of means, not least through print activism (Switzer 1997: 62). The franchise qualification criteria were toughened in 1892, 1894 and 1899. Out of these developments and pressures, two main political camps emerged in the Eastern Cape of the late 1880s–90s, although there were many social interconnections. The first became formalised as the Imbumba Eliliso Lomzi Yabatsundu or the Union of Native Vigilance Associations (hereafter Imbumba or Union) centring on the dominant persona of Jabavu, supported by a largely, but by no means exclusively, older-generation Mfengu constituency with deep missionary ties, with its widely read *Imvo* lending significant coordination and influence. The second assumed an organisational form as the Ingqungqutela or the South African Native Congress (hereafter Congress or SANC), which arose as an alternative centre of socio-political focus and mobilisation, led by mainly Xhosa and Thembu figures, including Nathaniel Umhalla, James Pelem, Jonathan Tunyiswa and Walter Rubusana, with a more radical agenda to contest the erosion of African rights, the desire for greater organisational formalisation, and a vision for wider black political coordination, including African-led bodies such as the independent 'Ethiopian' churches, both in the Cape and ultimately beyond (Odendaal 2012: 139–46). *Izwi* emerged out of SANC activism and organisation, labelling itself boldly as 'The Voice of the People'. It countered both the 'mouth-shutter' of settler colonial constraints and what it considered to be *Imvo*'s singularity of black perspective.

Even before the SANC's inaugural conference on 30 to 31 December 1891, rumours circulated about the inauguration of a Congress periodical to contest Jabavu's 'national newspaper'. The new press outlet with its distinctive voice and trilingual content offered a vital channel to magnetise and mobilise scattered publics.[3] *Izwi* was intent on convening an imagined community of engaged readers across the Cape, and increasingly across the broader South African arena to stir the region-wide coordination of the struggle for black rights, which included claims for imperial inclusion. It set itself up in contradistinction to *Imvo*, if at times downplaying this oppositional aspect.

Letters in IsiXhosa to Jabavu, the editor of *Imvo*, accompanied by his responses, give us a sharp insight into the disruptive effect that even the idea of a rival African newspaper had on *Imvo*'s executive and a significant sector of the isiXhosa reading public. In November 1891, *Imvo* published Robert Mantsayi's isiXhosa letter, which urged Imbumba networks to 'wait a bit and not just paint [the prospective Congress newspaper] dirty [ahead of reading it]' (Mantsayi 1891; trans. Majola). An even harder hitting letter to the editor in isiXhosa was published in *Imvo* by the pseudonymous 'Mdengentonga', a confrontational name referring to an adept stick fighter who was, in essence, 'declaring war' (Majola, personal communication, 24 April 2022):

> Let us attend [the inaugural SANC conference], son of Jabavu, and the whole of your cabal, especially with the supporters of *Imvo*. . . . [T]here are rumours that there is an urgent conspiracy to destroy *Imvo* – let us all go so that we could be a sufficient force to announce and report on anything that may show up related to the conspiracy. (Mdengentonga 1891; trans. Majola)

Jabavu's rejoinder dismissed the provocation. As he wrote back to 'Mdengentonga': 'A whole lot of people – you know that – choose to follow leaders and go attend an event they know nothing about, some will ask you hard questions, and another handful will choose to stay home' (Editor *Imvo* 1891; trans. Majola). Neither *Imvo* nor *Izwi* held back in publishing critical letters to the editor, though they combined these with editorial ripostes. Such were the practices and standards of the early black newspapers in surfacing and performing debate in line with free press protocols (Cowling and Mwale 2020), while connecting with and rousing their readerships.

Irrespective of all the commotion around a SANC-oriented newspaper emerging in the same public sphere as *Imvo*, it took some six yeas for *Izwi* to appear after the Congress was inaugurated. Publishing in English, isiXhosa, and to an under-recognised extent also in Sesotho,[4] thus representing major language groupings of the South Africa region, though by no means all, it conjured the imagined formulation of a 'black South Africa', which needed to recognise itself and work across boundaries in the face of white colonial consolidation of power.

The new newspaper's first year of publication, 1897–8, coincided with a major realignment in Cape electoral politics, which heightened the articulation around its differences with *Imvo* and galvanised the work of the SANC. After the disastrous Jameson Raid on the Transvaal, Cecil John Rhodes resigned as Prime Minister of the Cape, and the alliance between Rhodes and the Afrikaner Bond dissolved. To distance themselves from Rhodes, two leading liberals, so-called 'friends of the Natives' John X. Merriman and J. W. Sauer, became associates of the Bond, which would later develop into the South African Party (SAP). To the shock of many African readers and anti-Bond white newspapers like the *Cape Argus* and *Cape Mercury*, Jabavu followed Merriman and Sauer, despite his stated principle in *Imvo*'s inaugural issue that 'measures' were more important than the individuals who articulated them (in Ngcongco 1970: 6–7).

Having long been pro-British in its electoral politics, *Imvo* conveyed a change of tone in the closing years of the nineteenth century through its open support for a number of Bond candidates. Opposition to Jabavu's Afrikaner alliance links mounted as the majority of the region's black inhabitants had British loyalties, and indeed aspirations of further freedoms stemming from the logic of the Cape African franchise and the legacy of Victorian liberalism (Saunders 2000; Thompson 2003).

In reality, black voters and organisations had no easy choices in terms of political party alliances. As Odendaal observes, Jabavu and *Imvo*'s association with the

Bond in this realignment 'complicated African politics', though it was 'perfectly logical and consistent', given that Rhodes and Gordon Sprigg of the pro-imperial South African League (later to become the Progressive Party) had a record of backing policies that undermined African rights (Odendaal 2012: 149–50; Wehner and de Kadt 2023). However, *Imvo*'s Bond links came in for censure from many quarters, on which *Izwi* capitalised. A group of Congress officials thus appealed to the African community to contribute to a fund of £500 to set up a new oppositional SANC newspaper (Anon. 1906, *Izwi Labantu*), with additional capital provided by Rhodes. As early as 1895, James Pelem, a Congress leader, had written to Rhodes, then Prime Minister, to seek financial support for launching the envisioned SANC newspaper to publish perspectives beyond Jabavu's sphere of influence (Odendaal 2012: 146–7). This proposal came to align with Rhodes's interests in currying electoral favour among enfranchised black voters for the League. In November 1899, the Eagle Printing Press Company Ltd was registered to take on the publishing of *Izwi*. All listed shareholders and directors were black ('Memorandum of Association' [1899]).

Walter Mpilo Rubusana, a leading Xhosa missionary, educationist and political figure, who served as Eagle Printing Company's Managing Director, wrote to Rhodes in May 1900, thanking him for his support for *Izwi*, while firmly setting the operational boundaries. In addressing the paper's financial performance 'wholly managed' by Rhodes's associate Mr C. P. Crewe, Rubusana called out Crewe's lack of transparency and cooperation. He also accused Crewe of editorial interference, overreach and disdain for staff members. '[T]he direction of the paper itself as well as the staff [should be left] in the hands of the Directors,' Rubusana concluded. He took the opportunity to rehearse and amplify the remit and reach of the newspaper, with its ambitions for 'political guidance and social education' of the people (Anon. 1900, *Izwi Labantu*; Luzipho n.d.: 18–19).

Rubusana, who would go on to assume an increasingly influential political role in South African affairs, was not afraid to push back the parameters of white oversight in business, the press, the mission field and electoral politics, regularly striking a radical, Africanist note. Over the next decade and beyond, he would jostle with his great rival Jabavu for prominence at home and abroad. In 1910, Rubusana would be elected to the Cape Provincial Council, the first African to assume this position, but in 1914 he lost his Thembuland seat owing to Jabavu standing against him, diluting the African vote.

Izwi had a number of contributing editors in its early years, starting with Nathaniel Umhalla and George Tyamzashe. Within a year, Alan Kirkland Soga had taken over from Umhalla, steering the newspaper editorially overall; he assumed a leading commentating role over the next decade and more until the newspaper's closure. He had studied in Glasgow like his pioneering father, Tiyo Soga, the first overseas-educated African minister from the South Africa region. The *Colored American Magazine* carried a sketch of Soga, discussing his editorship of *Izwi* which 'supported the British ideal', his presidency of the newly inaugurated Native Press Association, and his aspirations to 'hasten a Conference of black men from the four worlds to discuss the black man's future' (Allen 1904: 115–16). Among other issues, Soga highlighted black worker conditions and carried items from British and American socialist newspapers, but urged action through representative bodies, not direct means (Limb 2000: 86–7). Replacing Tyamzashe in 1900 was Richard Tainton Kawa, followed by J. N. J. Tulwana, and then S. E. K. Mqhayi, who became the foremost Xhosa 'Poet of the Nation' (Odendaal 2012: 147–8; Switzer 1997: 57–66). Rubusana was a frequent contributor and significant shaping force behind *Izwi*, among his numerous other responsibilities. *Izwi* also received coverage in the white press, with the *Cape Argus* publishing an article and a photograph of its staff ('Directors and Staff' 1903: 17). In addition to its leading editorial figures, *Izwi* was developed and curated by a number of editors, sub-editors, correspondents, columnists and adjuncts over time.

Two major missionary newspapers in African languages had recently closed – *Isigidimi* in 1888 and *Inyankaniso lase Natal* in 1896 – so *Izwi* offered a welcome forum for indigenous language contributions, literary items and engagement with readers (Odendaal 2012: 147). It also helped to stimulate the development of other black independent newspapers in a range of languages across the Southern African region in the years to come, including *South African Spectator* (1900), *Koranta ea Becoana* (1901), *Ilanga lase Natal* (1903), *Indian Opinion* (1903) and *Naledi ea Lesotho* (1904). The twentieth century saw a spurt of black newspapers coming into being as leading figures of diverse communities recognised the importance of having a voice in the public arena, convening audiences in the South African region and building connections across the world, especially as white South Africa was inaugurated into the global halls of power and configured through various cultural means. Newspapers were integral to democratic expression here, there and everywhere, especially where direct representation for the majority was largely barred.

'For the Dissemination of Useful Information amongst the Natives': The Shaping of *Izwi* and the South African War

The South African War of 1899–1902 caused shockwaves across the region, the empire and the globe. It had manifold impacts on all sectors of society across Southern Africa. In his 1900 letter to Rhodes, Rubusana lamented the economic impacts of the 'deplorable' war on the financial success of *Izwi*. In the same breath, as if to counter a focus on the negative, Rubusana also painted a picture of the newspaper's impressive advance and positive reception across the increasingly connected region. '[E]vinced by many pleasing communications to the Editor, and by [a] growing increase in the list of subscribers', *Izwi*'s 'value' was recognised by 'the Native Public of all sections and backed by many Europeans' (Luzipho n.d.: 18–19). Appealing to advertisers and the wider public, *Izwi* lauded its 'enormous and constantly increasing circulation among the Native Races of the whole of South Africa' ('Advertise' 1901: 4). Recurring notices in *Izwi* over the years presented the newspaper as a significant media force.

We cannot pin down *Izwi*'s circulation figures, but can speculate that they may have been in the region of *Imvo*'s, reaching approximately 4,000 (Switzer 1997: 27), although newspaper copies were often shared among multiple readers. Publicly affirming and amplifying the newspaper's reach and influence was vital for continued support on all fronts. *Izwi*'s bold self-styling is suggestive of what Karin Barber calls the 'presumptive quality' of the modern 'emergence and multiplication of publics' (Barber 2007: 138). It is a register of its ambition to invoke black South Africa across the expanses of the region, as well as readers well beyond, imagining and conveying seemingly boundless readerly connection.

Other in-text filler notices echoed the advertising calls and reinforced this self-fashioning. '*Izwi Labantu* is the only medium in the Eastern Province for the dissemination of useful information amongst the natives' was one such advertising example from 27 August 1901 (see Figure 19.1). *Izwi*'s claim about being the sole forum for 'useful information' for African readers in the Eastern Cape was double-edged. Factually, it was true that *Izwi* was the only available isiXhosa newspaper at the time, as *Imvo* had been suspended under court martial from August 1901 through to October 1902. *Imvo*, with Jabavu at its helm, had officially adopted a neutral, if notably critical, pacificist position to the war, referring, for example, to the British 'war party' of Alfred Milner and Joseph Chamberlain, though it articulated imperial fealty overall (Saunders 2000: 143). However, even if *Imvo* had been operational at the time, *Izwi*'s rhetoric was geared to vilify, even nullify, its rival. In the same 27 August 1901 issue under the spotlight here, *Izwi*'s isiXhosa editorial was vituperatively headlined: '*Imvo* R I P':

> NEMESIS – which punishes the arrogant and tyrannical abuse of prosperity, has found out our native contemporary at last. . . . It is surprising the Military authorities are now only convinced of the necessity of this [court martialling] step. Frankly, we have consistently opposed the pro-Boer policy of *Imvo* and its unfriendly attitude towards those friends of progress and Good Governance. . . . Speaking from a native point of view, we feel deeply the humiliation cast upon the native press just entering on the threshold of life, with all its possibilities for good. . . . The first principle to justify the existence of any paper, white or black, is loyalty to the Imperial factor. ('*Imvo* R I P' 1901: 3)

A month after *Imvo*'s suspension, Mqhayi published an isiXhosa poem in *Izwi* articulating disillusionment with Jabavu and his newspaper: 'With self-promotion becoming the king . . . / Our unity is now over . . . / Our people are deeply hurt' (Mqhayi 1901, trans. Phyllis Ntantala, in Masilela 2010: 253). Jabavu and his business venture took a heavy financial and reputational blow from the court martialling, though he did win a defamation case. Bill Nasson observes that 'apart from facing white hostilities, any pro-peace black paper stood little chance against the strongly British identity and imperialist temper which coursed through the veins of Cape black political culture'. Nasson goes on to argue that the black educated and political class 'was not pacific': after all, the future of Cape Africans and black peoples across the South Africa region was at stake (Nasson 2003: 38).

There was thus a strong logic to *Izwi*'s outspoken, partisan approach at the turn of the century. The principle of non-racial citizenship and claims to belonging were in the balance. It was therefore 'polarisation, disruption, and struggle between settler factions, not white conciliation', underlines Nasson, 'which provided orientation and identity for the core values of citizenship and an ideology of rights' (Nasson 2003: 38). Strategically, *Izwi*'s '*Imvo* R I P' editorial magnified the newspaper's imperial credentials and valorised the idealised association with, and potential for, racial equality and shared rights within a British constitutional framework: 'United we stand, divided we fall, and God help the native races should the British Empire lose its influence in South Africa' ('*Imvo* R I P' 1901: 3).

While *Izwi* focused on its political agenda of advancing black rights and representation, not least through magnifying its lens of imperial loyalty during and in the immediate aftermath of the war, the newspaper also catered for a diverse range of content, appealing to multi-sited audiences near and far. In addition to politically oriented editorials,

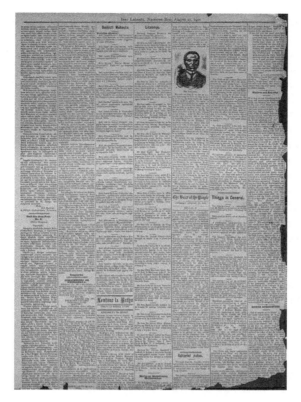

Figure 19.1 *Izwi Labantu*, 27 August 1901, p. 2. Courtesy of the National Library of South Africa, Cape Town.

opinion pieces and commentary, it assembled, spliced and shared general news from the Cape, the South African region and the world, via correspondents' reports, exchanges and cuttings. It brought into conversation happenings at home and abroad, forging solidarities and reflecting on differences. Letters to the editor from the likes of Nigerian journalist and medical doctor-in-training Moses Da Rocha, based in Edinburgh, showed the reach of the newspaper (Da Rocha 1908: 2). Furthermore, it highlighted features and developments of social and literary-cultural life, including news of notable black figures, schools, churches and organisations, and it published book reviews, news of competitions, and poetry, including written forms of isiXhosa praise poems or *izibongo*. Fundamental to *Izwi*'s viability were the income-generating advertisements, amounting to about half the page allocation – front, back and throughout – in addition to the inclusion of official government notices for which it received payment.

With a few exceptions, *Izwi*'s issues comprised four broadsheet pages, the front emblazoned with visually striking advertisements in English of major consumer brands, such as Bovril and Royal Baking Powder, still with us today, as well as those in isiXhosa for general and specialist dealers, for example. The back page was dominated by a mosaic of smaller adverts, notices and announcements, mostly in isiXhosa. These ranged from promoting African hotels to colonial post office services, from advertising jobs in the coal and gold mines to featuring magistrates' communications, subscription notices and SANC activities. In the war years, *Izwi*'s masthead was bold, presented in a large typeface approximating cursive script. This could be said to conjure both a sense of readerly accessibility and a certain formality with its subtle flourishes. Subscription and advertising prices were displayed in isiXhosa and English in the left and right top corners respectively.

At the turn of the century, at the heart of the newspaper, each of *Izwi*'s three languages had its own dedicated editorial header that drew attention to its commissioned, sourced and reader-generated content for the distinctive, yet overlapping, reader constituencies. The isiXhosa section was up front, covering the entirety of page two, with page three divided between Sesotho and English. The African-language content assumed prime position in serving *Izwi*'s key readerships, reinforcing the Africanist impetus of the SANC networks behind the periodical. To offer wide-ranging content coverage, value for subscribers, and tailored material for specific communities, there appears to have been little content reproduced in direct translation across the three language sections, at least not obviously mirrored in the same format. A significant intersection of African readers, and some white readers such as those in missionary, business, farming and government spheres, would have been conversant potentially in all three, and certainly in two, of the languages.

A closer look at the structure of a typical *Izwi* issue brings home the textured variety of its coverage. The editorial headers of 27 August 1901, for example, displayed three distinctive headlines in isiXhosa, Sesotho and English. They introduce different stories and developments, yet on some level address, and nuance, each other. Complementing *Izwi*'s English editorial '*Imvo* R I P', which luxuriated in its rival's demise and magnified 'loyalty to the Imperial factor', the isiXhosa article under the headline 'Ihambo Endlamafa' gave an account of the Duke and Duchess of Cornwall and York's visit to reward colonial efforts in fighting the war and to instil a sense of imperial South African identity. It featured the Duke and Duchess's meeting in Cape Town with the 'Black Royalties', regal and chiefly representatives of isiXhosa- and Sesotho-speaking nations, ending with a written rendition of the praise singer's account. If the article, in essence, valorised the meeting of the white and black royal delegations, emphasising equivalence and a sense of shared values and endeavours, the praise poem, typical of *izibongo* (Opland 1998: 100), captured tension and discursive layering in commemorating the notable occasion. If the British royal ('the visiting Beast') was lauded, he was also treated as a foreign peculiarity to be evaluated. At the same time that the praise poem critically assessed the Duke, the future king, it weighed up the British Crown's convening power over the heads of the black nations and groupings, resonating with the newspaper's imperial leanings and leverage:

> And I saw the giants together
> Oh please, on my behalf, ask Dalindyebo [the Thembu king]
> How the eyes of the visiting Beast look
> On my behalf, ask Makaula [king of the Ngqika and Gcaleka]
> What the smell of the Beast from another land feels like
> I once said the white man can cause people to fight amongst each other
> . . .
> Here I am retreating like that erstwhile star with a tail! ('Ihambo Endlamafa' 1901: 3; trans. Majola)

The Sesotho headline focused on a different development, with an Africanist self-help orientation and message of uniting for mutual support. This piece, 'Empowerment Strategy for Black People', reported on the business entrepreneur (and *Izwi*'s sports editor) Paul Xiniwe's 'smart partnership initiatives', which he promoted at public meetings ('Kopano ea Ba Batso' 1901: 3; trans Buti and Buti). The piece ended on a note of mission-inflected criticism around African pasts, as well as an implied exhortation to pull together for the sake of black people's futures. Such was *Izwi*'s impetus to convoke black community across the region. 'We never had a say in national matters', the editorial contended, 'because our ancestors were primitive and scattered all over, not being able to unite and strategise' (trans. Buti and Buti).

Across its variegated content, then, *Izwi* conveyed stories and sentiments of convening black solidarity and campaigns, not relying on white support. At the same time, it signalled allegiance to the imperial Crown. These two positions and inclinations were not mutually exclusive, but operated in a complex negotiation. Dubow highlights how colonised subject-citizens 'challenged the unstated assumption that the British Empire refers to territories and peoples which were somehow owned or collectively possessed by [Britain]', activating instead a Britishness of 'a more capacious category capable of including elective, hyphenated forms of belonging' (Dubow 2009: 2). Clear targets of *Izwi*'s approbation, on the other hand, were the Afrikaner states with their principle of 'no [racial] equality in church or state' and the Cape settler colonialists' failure to uphold idealised and invoked imperial justice for all.

Izwi did, however, at various points hold the imperial government itself to account, increasingly so as the momentum increased towards white state unification. Shortly after the Treaty of Vereeniging, the SANC drew up a clear-eyed petition addressing London, delivered to the Governor of the Cape, which it printed in full in *Izwi*, excerpted below:

> [Y]our petitioners fear that the Eighth Clause of the Peace Articles ... indicates a desire on the part of the British Government to withhold its decision as to the extension of similar privileges [the qualified non-racial franchise] to our Native and Coloured friends in the Orange River Colony and Transvaal for the decision of the Federated States. (Mqanda et al. 1902a: 3)

A letter by the SANC executive accompanying the petition appealed to the imperial powers to take a stand lest black inhabitants are 'deprive[d] of their just rights as citizens of the Great British Empire'. It concluded that 'His Majesty's subjects ... had a right to look for better results' (Mqanda et al. 1902b: 3).

'For the Cause That Lacks Assistance': *Izwi*'s Post-War Mobilisation

If *Izwi* gained ground during the war years by amplifying its imperial loyalties (especially with the court martialling of its rival *Imvo*), it faced bigger challenges as a white pact between British and Afrikaner leaders gathered force to keep the black majority in check. 'South Africa was born in war,' Simpson observes, encapsulating the violent origins of the nation state (Simpson 2021: xi).

While there was combat on the battlefield, there was high-stakes manoeuvring in the court of public opinion, as socio-political actors and periodicals, black and white, fought for attention, influence and resources in trying to precipitate their version of a future South Africa. With Britain winning the war, it sought to consolidate its control over swathes of Southern Africa with its significant mineral wealth. It was a costly, cruel, drawn-out conflict against a far less-militarised Afrikaner opponent fighting against imperial annexation, leaving Britain battered reputationally and with a hole in the national purse. A number of events laid the groundwork for regional unification, including the 1903–5 South African Native Affairs Commission (SANAC), approving the principle of racialised territorial segregation, and the 1906 granting of responsible government to the Transvaal and Orange River Colony, codifying the principle of imperial non-interference (Loveland 1999: 66, 121). The 1907 Selborne Memorandum triggered the envisaged unification, originally conceived of as a federation. *Izwi* thus mobilised its reading publics, boosting efforts to appeal to its predominantly black readers in the Cape and well beyond to collaborate with other black newspapers and organisations across the South Africa region, and to evoke solidarities with other 'race' causes around the world.

In these heightened post-war years, *Izwi* developed a new bold masthead in upright, upper-case lettering, and inserted a rousing motto at the head of each editorial, a gloss on journalist and Methodist George Linnaeus Banks's 'What I Live For' poem, proclaiming the newspaper's higher purpose. It was in no doubt about its campaigning orientation: 'For the cause that lacks assistance, / Gainst the wrong that needs resistance, / For the good that we can do'. This verse-motto in translation headed up the isiXhosa section as well. The cause was ultimately about promulgating the rights, opportunities and cultures of black South Africans, refuting demeaning constructs of the 'native question' or the 'native problem', and in particular fighting for full citizenship under the imperial banner.

Izwi continued to publish its four-page span, but some way into the twentieth century it dropped its Sesotho section. Already in 1901, it was apologising in its 'Editorial Notes' for fluctuations in its Sesotho coverage. Its 27 August 1901 issue notes that it was trying to secure a correspondent 'to take charge of these columns' ('Editorial Notes' 1901: 3). It also shifted its English coverage to its second page, a more prominent position, arguably to reach a more variegated, primarily black, readership across the South African arena, and to reinforce its strategic, though increasingly not uncritical, British allegiance. The isiXhosa coverage remained extensive and dominated the other pages.

Over the years, *Izwi* and *Imvo* continued to spar in the public arena, as black socio-political life faced increasing pressures and uncertainty in the broader conflicted landscape of the South Africa region. Overall, however, *Izwi* projected a strong message about being the discerning 'voice of the people', casting itself, for instance in a letterhead of the post-war period, as 'the authority PAR EXCELLENCE on intelligent Native thought and feeling' (*'Izwi Labantu'* 1903). Though *Imvo* is unmentioned, it is evoked by implication.

The two newspapers were not only at odds with respect to electoral politics, but also on a number of other matters, including the development of native higher education, independent African churches, and reaction to the white unification movement. In the years after the war, *Imvo* regained its momentum, continuing its support for the

SAP, not least in the 1904 elections, and it received a new avenue for profile-raising in the form of the Inter-State Native College Scheme in collaboration with Lovedale.

The Inter-State Scheme was set up in 1905 shortly after publication of the SANAC Report, which recommended that 'a central Native college or similar institution be established, and aided by the various States, for training Native teachers and in order to afford opportunities for higher education to Native students' (SANAC 1905: 72). *Izwi* was particularly outspoken about the SANAC Report, with its politics of reconstruction focused on exclusionary white rule, including its native college recommendation, which the Congress considered a direct appropriation of its imperially oriented Queen Victoria Memorial Scheme already five years in existence ('The Victoria Memorial' 1902: 3). *Izwi* leveraged its SANC networks and links with independent churches, featuring the Memorial Scheme prominently in its pages, but a number of factors meant it could not compete with the resources from the government- and mission-supported Inter-State Scheme promoted by *Imvo* (Odendaal 2012: 327). The Memorial Scheme, like its parent organisation, the SANC, and organ, *Izwi*, negotiated the interface between imperial invocations and black self-determination with greater South Africa in its sights.

Unsurprisingly, *Izwi* was vocal in its censure of the exclusionary politics of the Selborne Memorandum around envisaged federation or unification, which led to the SANC issuing a call to conference in 1907. It signalled a landmark gathering of African and Coloured representatives from across the Cape and beyond, including some of the Protectorates, although Imbumba with its *Imvo* mouthpiece abstained. This event foreshadowed the even more regionally representative, trans-ethnic assembly of the South African Native Convention in March 1909, which the SANC, mobilising *Izwi*, convened to counter the whites-only Convention determining the future of South Africa.

A recurring theme in *Izwi* of this period centred on black unity across the South African region to counter the gathering white forces across the land (see Figure 19.2). A 1908 *Izwi* editorial, for example, seized upon the language of a march to mobilise the constellated black reading public across different constituencies to 'close up [their] ranks'. In cooperation with a number of other black newspapers, it called for black peoples to journey together under the same vision, and to strive for coordinated civic and political action. 'There [was] but one road to travel and no other, and that is Upward, Onward, Forward' towards the ultimate goal of securing greater rights and opportunities in the face of plans for white unification of industrialising South Africa at the expense of the black majority (Anon. 1908a, *Izwi Labantu*). This call amounted to evoking and convening a black 'nation' for the new century, the nationalist stirrings of an imagined community.

Izwi's focus on black self-determination became amplified in this period, with more critical editorial comments referring, for example, to the history of 'white civilisation' leaving 'a trail of blood and savagery' (Anon. 1908b, *Izwi Labantu*). Mqhayi, similarly, articulated the deadening impact of British imperialism in his praise poem, even if he balanced it out in other parts: 'You will leave this land like a stillborn / As always we will still say we are British' (Mqhayi 1908; trans. in Saunders 2000: 143). Much is bound up, yet too little recognised, in African-language newspapers, speeches, poems and interactions, as Peter Limb underlines, regarding black communities' multivalent commentary on and critique of empire (Limb 2015: 600).

Figure 19.2 *Izwi Labantu*, 18 February 1908, p. 1. Courtesy of the National Library of South Africa, Cape Town.

Ahead of the delegation and the Union Bill being signed into law, *Izwi*'s editorial for 16 February 1909 defiantly likened the new South African state-in-formation to a ship in the dockyard about to be released into the shared oceans of the world:

> 'Equal rights for all South of the Zambesi' is the motto that will yet float at the masthead of this new ship of state which has been launched under the Union, and no other will be permanently substituted while there is one black or coloured man of any consequence or self-respect in the country, or any white man who respects the traditions of free Government – so help us God. (Anon. 1909, *Izwi Labantu*)

Izwi insisted upon a national motto that accentuated equal rights across the colour line to encompass South Africa's democratic duty to all its inhabitants. It evoked Rhodes's words from his electioneering a decade earlier for their stated, if far-from-realised, principle of 'equal rights for all'. Though Rhodes deployed this phrase in strategic and slippery fashion to appeal to Cape liberal sentiments for voting support (Beinart 2022: 584), *Izwi* in turn used it to its advantage, highlighting the insistent notes of inclusive imperial citizenship for the 'cause that lacks assistance'.

Conclusion: *Izwi*'s Departure without 'Surrender'

Izwi published regularly until the newspaper announced immediate closure on 16 April 1909 owing to the 'unsatisfactory financial position' of the company ('Liquidation' 1909: 2). While the editorial gave some context for *Izwi*'s cessation, including pointing to shortfalls of support for the 'Native and Coloured press', it highlighted in the same breath the potential for broader collective action in the emerging political structures it had helped to engender. It suggested new horizons of coordinated activism under the South African Native Convention, headed by Rubusana with Soga as Secretary, along with key representatives from Natal and elsewhere across the region, in the form of a planned delegation to the 'Imperial Authorities'. Though the political headwinds were strong, *Izwi* struck a final note of defiance and hope:

> We have sailed this ship for a decade and while we strike our flag meantime under compulsion it is not to surrender, and we trust, in fact are sure, that the principles of freedom and human liberty for which we have battled will yet be established and our flag will float from the masthead once more over a United South Africa in the not distant future. ('Liquidation' 1909: 2)

Although the 'new ship of state' was setting sail without the guiding motto of a racially inclusive South Africa, and despite *Izwi*'s 'flag' of an activist Cape African and black South African community being lowered, the newspaper was insistent that this was not the end of the journey ('Liquidation' 1909: 2). Black South Africa had been evoked as a configuration while representatives of the regionally inclusive Native Convention (to develop into the South African Native National Congress) would insist on a national horizon where 'the King and the Empire owe good and just government to every class of their subjects' ('Special Convention' 1909: 2). Right to the end, *Izwi* issued its distinctive clarion call for unified action among the black peoples of South Africa to resist political exclusion, while insisting on justice for all British subjects.

Though *Izwi* was not in existence to report on the delegation to London in July 1909, one of its prime movers, Rubusana, found himself alongside rival newspaperman and political figure Jabavu, who appeared at the eleventh hour, in the diverse group that was unified at that moment in London to represent the black cause (Plaut 2013). The South African Act with its entrenched Colour Bar, other than for the qualified franchise exceptions of the Cape, could not be overturned in the twentieth century's first decade, but the dream of democratic representation could not be quashed. *Izwi*'s provocative 1897–1909 contribution to the public arena, claiming to speak for engaged black people of the Cape and indeed for a broader progressive black South African constituency, in conversation with other kindred press organs, left an indelible mark and indeed strains of a strident Africanist voice.

Notes

My thanks to Fundile Majola and to Mokheseng Buti and Mabuti Buti for the accomplished translations from isiXhosa and Sesotho respectively. I am indebted to Peter Limb for the generous sharing of items from the South African National Archives during Covid lockdown, to Peter Coates for alerting me to the *Izwi Labantu* staff photographs in the *Cape Argus*, and to

Mike Kenyon for making available the Eagle Press Printing Company records. I am grateful to the National Library of South Africa for providing the images of *Izwi Labantu* and for Melanie Geustyn's attentive assistance.

1. In place of 'Kafir', which appears in the original source, the term 'Xhosa' has been inserted. The term 'Kafir' was commonly, but erroneously, used in the nineteenth- and early twentieth-century contexts to refer specifically to isiXhosa-speaking peoples and the language itself. It fell out of use as an ethnic/linguistic referent for Xhosa and came to be used more generally as a pejorative term. It is considered highly offensive today.
2. 'Black' is used in this chapter primarily as an inclusive political category, taking into account African communities and other peoples of colour historically disadvantaged by colonialism. Referring to mixed-race peoples, the term 'Coloured' has long been used in the South African context with ongoing negotiation as to its deployment.
3. In discussing the convening power of newspapers, I draw on the work of Anderson 2006; Mokoena 2009; Barber 2012; Peterson et al. 2016; and Hofmeyr and Peterson 2019.
4. Sesotho speakers were integrated into largely isiXhosa-speaking Eastern Cape mission school and print networks. Sesotho correspondents and editors are not named in *Izwi*, but we can speculate on the involvement of figures like Shad B. Mama, a SANC supporter with experience of working on *Isigidimi*, and Simon Phamotse, who launched *Naledi ea Lesotho* (Odendaal 2012: 174). Motaung, a reader from Basotholand, believed that *Imvo* would get more subscribers if it were to publish articles in Sesotho (Anon. 1887a, *Imvo Zabantsundu*; Moropa 2010: 137).

Bibliography

'Advertise in *Izwi Labantu*' (1901), *Izwi Labantu*, 10 December, 4.
Allen, S. (1904), 'Mr Alan Kirkland Soga', *Colored American Magazine*, February, 114–16.
Anderson, Benedict (2006), *Imagined Communities: Reflections on the Origin and Spread of Nationalism*, London: Verso.
Anon. (1887a), *Imvo Zabantsundu*, 23 February.
—— (1887b), *Imvo Zabantsundu*, 23 March.
—— (1900), *Izwi Labantu*, 12 May.
—— (1906), *Izwi Labantu*, 21 August.
—— (1908a), *Izwi Labantu*, 14 April.
—— (1908b), *Izwi Labantu*, 27 October.
—— (1909), *Izwi Labantu*, 16 February.
Barber, Karin (2007), *The Anthropology of Texts, Persons and Publics: Oral and Written Culture in Africa and Beyond*, Cambridge: Cambridge University Press.
—— (2012), *Print Culture and the First Yoruba Novel: I. B. Thomas's 'Life Story of Me, Ṣẹgilọla' and Other Texts*, Leiden: Brill.
Beinart, William (2022), 'Cecil Rhodes: Racial segregation in the Cape Colony and violence in Zimbabwe', *Journal of Southern African Studies*, 48.3, 581–603.
Cowling, Lesley, and Pascal Newbourne Mwale (2020), 'Media orchestration in the production of public debate', in Lesley Cowling and Carolyn Hamilton (eds), *Babel Unbound: Rage, Reason and Rethinking Public Life*, Johannesburg: Wits University Press, 64–87.
Cutten, Theodore Edward Gurney (1935), *History of the Press in South Africa*, Cape Town: National Union of Students.
Da Rocha, Moses (1908), 'Appreciation', *Izwi Labantu*, 15 December, 2.
'Directors and Staff of Izwi Labantu' (1903), *Cape Argus Weekly Edition*, 18 March, 17.

Dubow, Saul (2009), 'How British was the British world? The case of South Africa', *The Journal of Imperial and Commonwealth History*, 37.1, 1–27.
Editor *Imvo* (1891), *Imvo Zabantsundu*, 24 November.
'Editorial Notes' (1901), *Izwi Labantu*, 27 August, 3.
Harber, Anton (ed.) (2019), *Southern African Muckraking: 300 Years of Investigative Journalism That Shaped the Region*, Johannesburg: Jacana.
Hofmeyr, Isabel, and Derek R. Peterson (2019), 'The politics of the page: Cutting and pasting in South African and African-American newspapers', *Social Dynamics*, 45.1, 1–25.
'Ihambo Endlamafa' (1901), *Izwi Labantu*, 27 August, 3.
'*Imvo* R I P' (1901), *Izwi Labantu*, 27 August, 3.
'*Izwi Labantu*: Offer to Publish Government Notices' (1903), *Izwi Labantu* letterhead, CO 192 5243/03, South African National Archives.
Jabavu, D. D. T. (1922), *The Life of John Tengo Jabavu, Editor of Imvo Zabantsundu, 1884–1921*, Alice: Lovedale Press.
Jabavu, John Tengo (1884), 'The Launch', *Imvo Zabantsundu*, 3 November, 3.
'Kopano ea Ba Batso' (1901), *Izwi Labantu*, 27 August, 3.
Limb, Peter (2000), '"Representing the labouring classes": African workers in the African nationalist press, 1900–60', in Les Switzer and Mohamed Adhikari (eds), *South Africa's Resistance Press: Alternative Voices in the Last Generation under Apartheid*, Athens: Ohio University Center for International Studies, 79–127.
—— (2015), 'The empire writes back: African challenges to the brutish (South African) empire in the early twentieth century', *Journal of Southern African Studies*, 41.3, 599–616.
'Liquidation' (1909), *Izwi Labantu*, 16 April, 2.
Loveland, Ian (1999), *By Due Process of Law? Racial Discrimination and the Right to Vote in South Africa, 1855–1960*, London: Bloomsbury.
Luzipho, S. W. T. (n.d.), 'U-Boni Buka Dr. Walter Benson Rubusana', unpublished biography, Rubusana Papers, GB 102 MS 380263, School of Oriental and African Studies Special Collections.
Mantsayi, Robert (1891), 'Ingqungqutela nepepa elitsha', letter of 26 September in *Imvo Zabantsundu*, 5 November.
Masilela, Ntongela (2010), 'African intellectual and literary responses to colonial modernity in South Africa', in Peter Limb, Norman Etherington and Peter Midgley (eds), *Grappling with the Beast: Indigenous Southern African Responses to Colonialism, 1840–1930*, Leiden: Brill, 245–75.
Mdengentonga (1891), 'Ingqungqutela', letter of 18 September in *Imvo Zabantsundu*, 24 November.
'Memorandum of Association' (1899). Eagle Printing Press Company Ltd. 15.11.1899, CA:LC228/14A/C298, Western Cape Archives and Records Service.
Mills, Wallace G. (1990), 'The rift within the lute: Conflict and factionalism in the school community in the Cape Colony, 1890–1915', Collected Seminar Papers, Institute of Commonwealth Studies, 38, 29–39.
'A Mischievous Delusion' (1901), *The Christian Express*, 1 October, 145–6.
Mkhize, Khwezi (2018), '"To see us as we see ourselves": John Tengo Jabavu and the politics of the black periodical', *Journal of Southern African Studies*, 44.3, 413–30.
Mokoena, Hlhonipa (2009), 'An assembly of readers: Magema Fuze and his *Ilanga lase Natal* readers', *Journal of Southern African Studies*, 35.3, 595–607.
Moropa, Koliswa (2010), 'African voices in *Imvo Zabantsundu*: Literary pieces from the past', *South African Journal of African Languages*, 30.2, 135–44.
Mqanda, Thomas, Jonathan Tunyiswa and W. B. Rubusana (1902a), 'Petition', *Izwi Labantu*, 19 August, 3.
——, —— and —— (1902b), 'To His Excellency', *Izwi Labantu*, 19 August, 3.

Mqhayi, S. E. K. (1901), 'Wolokohlo Kwelimnyama', *Izwi Labantu*, 17 September.
—— (1908), 'Sise kwelidala! Sigama Britani', *Izwi Labantu*, 7 January.
Nasson, Bill (2003), *Abraham Esau's War: A Black South African War in the Cape, 1899–1902*, Cambridge: Cambridge University Press.
Ngcongco, L. D. (1970), 'Jabavu and the Anglo-Boer War', *African Historical Review*, 2.2, 6–18.
Odendaal, André (2012), *The Founders: The Origins of the ANC and the Struggle for Democracy in South Africa*, Johannesburg: Jacana.
Opland, Jeff (1998), *Xhosa Poets and Poetry*, Cape Town: New Africa Books.
Peterson, Derek R., Emma Hunter and Stephanie Newell (eds) (2016), *African Print Cultures: Newspapers and their Publics in the Twentieth Century*, Ann Arbor: University of Michigan Press.
Plaut, Martin (2013), 'A menu for change – the South African deputation to London, 1909', *Quarterly Bulletin of the National Library*, 67.2, 64–8.
Saunders, Chris (2000), 'African attitudes to Britain and the Empire before and after the South African War', in Donal Lowry (ed.), *The South African War Reappraised*, Manchester: Manchester University Press, 140–9.
Simpson, Thula (2021), *History of South Africa: From 1902 to the Present*, Cape Town: Penguin Random House South Africa.
SANAC (1905), *Report of the South African Native Affairs Commission, 1903–1905*, London: HM Stationery Office.
'Special Convention Number' (1909), *Izwi Labantu*, 16 April, 2.
Switzer, Les (ed.) (1997), *South Africa's Alternative Press: Voices of Protest and Resistance, 1880s–1960s*, Cambridge: Cambridge University Press.
Thompson, Andrew (2003), 'The languages of loyalism in Southern Africa, c. 1879–1939', *English Historical Review*, 118, 477, 617–50.
'The Victoria Memorial' (1902), *Izwi Labantu*, 7 October, 3.
Wehner, Joachim, and Daniel de Kadt (2023), 'The tools of voter suppression: Racial disenfranchisement in the Cape of Good Hope', *SocArXiv Papers*, 3 October, https://doi.org/10.31235/osf.io/by82s (accessed 15 November 2023).

20

COLONIAL GOVERNMENT PERIODICALS IN 1920S EAST AFRICA: *MAMBO LEO* AND *HABARI*

Emma Hunter

Introduction

IN JULY 1922, the Kenya Government began publishing a periodical in Swahili and English called *Habari* or *News*. A few months later, the Tanganyika Government launched *Mambo Leo* or *Current Affairs*. The two publications had much in common in terms of the context in which they were founded, the audiences they sought to reach, their content and the aims of the governments in publishing them. Yet they had very different trajectories. In Tanganyika, *Mambo Leo* survived for forty years, adapting itself to changing conditions over that long period. In Kenya, in contrast, *Habari* survived only a few years in its first iteration, pausing publication in the middle of the 1920s, then closing for good in 1931.

Why did the two periodicals follow such different paths? At one level, the answer seems obvious. The Kenya Government invested little in *Habari* in the early years when it was run directly from the office of the Commissioner for Native Affairs, and the Kenya Government's own commentary suggested its failure was overdetermined. The potential readership, the government maintained at the time of its first closure in 1926, was tiny, few understood the Swahili and English in its pages, and Kenyans would be better served by a collection of locally produced mission newspapers, along the lines of the Catholic Mission in Mombasa's *Rafiki Yetu*, which had recently been launched.

Nevertheless, in this chapter I seek to show that examining the different trajectories of these two East African newspapers contributes to the broader project of this volume of thinking through the place of periodicals in the British colonial world and their varied histories. While *Mambo Leo* is well studied, *Habari* has attracted less attention from historians (see Figure 20.1). In this chapter, I argue that exploring these two publications alongside each other brings into focus aspects of the history of government newspapers in twentieth-century East Africa that might otherwise be missed, and in turn sheds light on the colonial government projects of these two territories, their contrasting approaches to language policy, and the relationship between language and governance.

Government Newspapers

By the time *Mambo Leo* and *Habari* were launched there was a long history reaching back into the nineteenth century of European colonial governments publishing newspapers in vernacular languages to reach colonised subjects (for example, Paterson

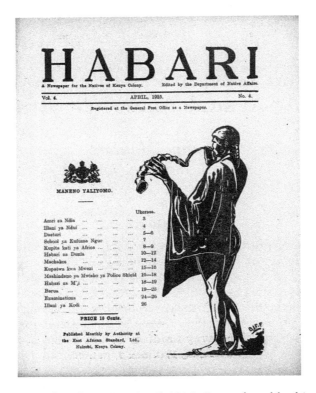

Figure 20.1 Cover of *Habari*, 4.4, April 1925. Reproduced by kind permission of the Syndics of Cambridge University Library.

2020: 367). Publishing such periodicals was part of a wider colonial project to create new kinds of political society and new kinds of political subjects (Hunter and James 2020: 237).

Within East Africa, the German colonial government in German East Africa, modern-day mainland Tanzania, supported the newspaper *Kiongozi* [The Leader]. By the time the First World War began in 1914, *Kiongozi* had a substantial readership (Krautwald 2021: 6; Lemke 1929: 20). In the 1920s, government newspapers very similar to *Habari* and *Mambo Leo* existed across the continent and across different colonial regimes. For example, the Cameroonian *La Gazette du Cameroun* [The Cameroon Gazette] had many similarities to *Habari* and *Mambo Leo* in terms of both imagined readership and content (Hunter 2012: 283–6). This is not surprising, as not only were colonial powers subject to shared routines of international supervision in the 1920s, but they also shared a set of ideas in which newspapers were a key didactic tool, and they saw the existence of newspapers as part of a modernising project.

Government periodicals of this sort, like other similar periodicals such as those run by missions, were once neglected in histories of the press in twentieth-century Africa in favour of a focus on the independent African press. The historiography tended to focus on what such periodicals, linked in various ways to the colonial state, did not do, rather than what they did do. What they certainly did not do was provide a space for public and explicit criticism of colonial regimes. As the South African periodical *Umteteli wa Bantu*, itself a product of the organ of the Native Recruitment Corporation of the South African Chamber of Mines, noted in an article offering a 'cordial but belated welcome' to *Habari* in 1927, '[w]e do not expect much in the way of political news or views in a Government paper' ('Government Control' 1927: 2; Erlank 2019: 78). It continued:

> For the dissemination of technical instruction in such subjects as agriculture or education a Government paper is useful if there are no independent Native papers available or willing to do this work; but for the setting up of sound policies or for the free expression of views and criticisms, a Government paper has little value. When 'Habari' is released from the control of the Government it may become the real voice of the Native people of Kenya. ('Government Control' 1927: 2)

But in recent years historians have increasingly come to pay more attention to such newspapers, building on earlier studies (for example, Scotton 1978: 7–8). Those government newspapers that were successful attracted a readership because they were not simply vehicles for colonial government ideologies, but succeeded in building a community of readers who in turn shaped the contents of the pages. This process is particularly clear in the case of the Tanganyikan newspaper *Mambo Leo*.

Historians of Tanganyika have written extensively about *Mambo Leo*, showing, for example, that while on one level it was a production of the colonial state, it was also shaped by its East African readers and writers. It was a space of intellectual production, in which East African intellectuals, such as the poet Shaaban Robert, translated literary works and published poetry (Mulokozi 2002: 7). It functioned as a space of public deliberation where, for example, the meaning of 'civilisation' and changing gender relations were debated.[1] Its readers and writers were often employed by the colonial state and wrote in Latin-script 'standard' Swahili, in contrast to the Arabic script. In this way *Mambo Leo* built on earlier communities of newspaper and magazine readers and writers who had read, and written for, titles like the Anglican Universities' Mission to Central Africa (UMCA)'s *Msimulizi*, the German Government School's *Kiongozi* or *Pwani na Bara* [Coast and Hinterland] (Robinson 2022: 115).

Mambo Leo's importance stemmed in part from its relative lack of competitors within Tanganyika. This was due to the Tanganyikan colonial government's strict regulation of publishing in the territory. A hefty bond was levied by the colonial government which made it very difficult for independent vernacular newspapers aimed at African readers to be published (Sturmer 1998: 73; Westcott 1981: 93). In contrast, Kenya and Uganda both saw the emergence in the 1920s of a vibrant newspaper publishing scene, particularly in the Kikuyu and Luganda languages (Scotton 1971: 101; Scotton 1978: 1). *Habari* has been described as the Kenya Government's response to this emerging anti-colonial independent press in Kenya, notably Harry Thuku's Swahili-language *Tangazo*. In his history of the vernacular press in East Africa, James Scotton wrote that *Habari* was published as 'an effort to counter the propaganda published by Thuku and Desai and to keep "anti-government, anti-European, and anti-Christian" papers from gaining a readership' (Scotton 1971: 177).

Compared to the scholarship focusing on *Mambo Leo*, historians have paid much less attention to the content of *Habari* or its development between its first run in the early 1920s and its trajectory in the late 1920s and early 1930s. This reflects its relative marginality and small circulation. Whereas *Mambo Leo*'s circulation quickly climbed to 9,000 after its launch in 1923, and demand always outstripped supply, *Habari*, in contrast, had a smaller circulation. It averaged around 3,000 in the early years. By late 1927 it was close to 4,000, prompting a push to increase circulation to 5,000 for January 1928 (Bagnall 1927).

Mambo Leo and *Habari*

In this section, I will briefly set out the path that led to these two newspapers being published and their divergent histories. *Mambo Leo* was published from 1923, replacing the German colonial-era newspaper *Kiongozi*. *Mambo Leo*'s roots lay in the changed geopolitical context of the aftermath of the First World War. In 1922, the former colony of German East Africa formally became a League of Nations mandate under British administration. In this context, *Mambo Leo*, produced from within the Tanganyikan Education Department, was an important tool of education and propaganda, a means of binding Tanganyikans into the British Empire, even if their precise constitutional status, given Tanganyika's formal status as a League of Nations mandate, put them at one remove from the British Empire. It had much in common in this regard with government newspapers elsewhere in the British colonial world. The editor was always unnamed, although we can reconstruct the editor's identity to some degree from other sources. It was published entirely in Swahili, and in Latin-script Swahili more specifically (Hunter 2012: 299).

The Kenyan context was different. The First World War had not led to occupation and the transfer from one European colonial regime to another, as in Tanganyika. However, the war years did galvanise anti-colonial activity. The intellectual and political activist Harry Thuku recounted in his autobiography how in the 1910s he became increasingly conscious of the injustices to which he and other Kenyans were subjected through working on the newspaper *The Leader*, which was published for a white settler readership. He recalled how when he travelled to look for work '[s]everal of my friends, including Josiah Njonjo, were at that time working on the newspaper, the *Leader of British East Africa*'. He went to work for the newspaper too, and 'was given the job of composing type. Later I was taught to print, and I spent my time between those two jobs of compositor and machine man. Of course some people did not think it a very honourable position, but looking back I can see I was rather lucky to be there. All my further education, or self-education, I gained from there' (Thuku 1979: 15). In his work at the newspaper, he continued, 'I read many of the articles that the settlers wrote to the *Leader* (the paper was strongly in favour of the white settlers), and when I saw something there about the treatment of Africans, it entered into my head and lay quiet until later on' (Thuku 1979: 14–15). It was, he wrote, 'at the *Leader*, from about 1915, that I first began to think seriously about some of our troubles as Africans – especially this question of forced labour' (Thuku 1979: 16). Later, following his deportation and exile, he continued his correspondence with his close ally the newspaperman Desai, publisher of the *East African Chronicle*, and received copies of the Garveyite newspaper *Negro World* (Gasirye 1925).

The context in which *Habari* began to be published in 1922 was therefore one in which political argument was taking place in the pages of newspapers, and, as we have seen, one way of understanding why the colonial government launched *Habari* is as a response to this environment and particularly to Harry Thuku's *Tangazo*. But as Phoebe Musandu emphasises in her recent book, *Habari* should also be understood as the project of a particular colonial official, Oscar Ferris Watkins (Musandu 2018: 230).

In her biography of her father, Elizabeth Watkins suggests that in fact Oscar Watkins had initially launched it as a newssheet during the First World War. She writes: '[I]n 1916 Oscar had started the monthly newspaper, *Habari*. It was the first newspaper ever to be published in Swahili printed in the Latin script, a light, cheerful news sheet full of jokes and puns. Oscar had found it invaluable to explain wartime events. Carrier officers had arranged for it to be read to their men and it had become extremely popular' (Watkins 1995: 173). For Elizabeth Watkins, there was a direct line to peacetime editions of the newspaper when, she writes, 'it became even more popular as each year more literates left school' (Watkins 1995: 173).

But the path to publishing *Habari* in the post-war world was not as smooth as this account suggests. Watkins was passionately committed to the importance of the newspaper and drove it forward in the face of considerable opposition. Yet he regularly complained that it lacked proper support from the colonial government, including the Chief Commissioner for Native Affairs, Gerald Maxwell, who had been appointed above Watkins in 1921. As Elizabeth Watkins writes, 'The fact that it came out under Maxwell's name although Maxwell could not read Swahili did not worry him. What hurt him more than any other snub or disappointment was Maxwell refusing to continue the subsidy to keep it published. It cost £700 a year, the salary of a senior district commissioner' (Watkins 1995: 173).

Annual reports point to the challenges the newspaper faced. The 1923 report of the Native Affairs Department made grim reading for those who hoped the newspaper would succeed. 'During the year 1923, Habari was contending with many difficulties,' the report began. 'The cost of printing more than swallowed up all the profits, and the unpunctuality in delivery made it difficult to sell the paper. Up to the end of the year every month showed a loss' (Native Affairs 1923: 19). While the report expressed the view that '[t]he circulation of the paper is very much greater than its figures would appear to show, since every copy circulates through many hands or is read to a group of illiterate natives by those who can read', nevertheless its financial state was distinctly shaky and, the report suggested, it was 'doubtful ... whether it can ever be made a paying proposition on the present lines. Without illustrations, and with few advertisements, it is unlikely that the circulation alone can ever meet the cost' (Native Affairs 1923: 19). In this context, its survival depended on government support.

Responsibility for *Habari* was passed from the Native Affairs Department to the Education Department when its first editor, Watkins, went on leave in 1926, and then after a year's pause it reappeared in April 1927, edited initially by James W. C. Dougall, the first headmaster of the new Government Jeanes School in Kabete which was responsible for training teachers to play a supervisory role in rural education, then by Dougall's successor T. G. Benson, and finally by W. H. Taylor. It was printed by the *East African Standard*. But it lasted only a few more years before closing again at the end of 1931, this time for good.

Turning to the content of the two newspapers reveals differences as well as similarities and connections, alongside hints as to the ways in which their histories were shaped by the political contexts of which they were a part. As with other government periodicals published across colonial Africa in the 1920s, in both *Mambo Leo* and *Habari* the tone was didactic. A key priority for colonial governments in publishing newspapers was to convey information on agricultural practice and health advice. These topics took up substantial space and could also be republished as complete volumes. In September 1928, for example, an announcement in *Habari* invited readers to write in to request a book entitled 'Lectures in Elementary Agricultures' which was 'a complete collection of articles which have been published in "Habari" this year and [which] will be finished in the month of December' (Anon. 1928, *Habari*: 29).

The primary imagined readership of both papers was a relatively small group of literate men. Articles stressed the benefits of British rule and attempted to engage readers in emerging systems of local government. They encouraged the publication of folk stories and discussion about a circumscribed range of cultural topics. The editors of both stressed their secular nature. Editors of *Mambo Leo* were adamant that the periodical would not become a forum for religious debate, despite attempts by some of its readers to make it so. A monthly column, which published responses to readers' questions, as well as the 'Postbox' section, explained why some contributions would not be published, and often their religious content was the reason for non-publication. For example, a poet was told that his poem included too much religious material and so would not be published (Anon. 1932, *Mambo Leo*: 246). In a 1923 editorial, the editor of *Habari* emphasised that this was not a missionary paper: 'We want it to be read by and to be useful to Mohamedans and Heathans [sic] as well as Christians. Consequently we do not publish long letters about Christian teaching' (Editorial 1923, *Habari*: 4).

Both periodicals invited readers to think of themselves as citizens of a British Empire. An editorial in *Habari* in September 1924 entitled 'Dola' or 'Empire' was typical in this regard, with the call to readers: 'Consider these things, men of Kenya. Remember that you are not only Swahili or Kikuyu or other tribes, but are part of a great empire' (Editorial 1924b, *Habari*: 3–4). The book *Uraia*, or 'Citizenship', which conveyed a similar message of imperial citizenship and was first published in *Mambo Leo*, then issued as a book for use in schools in Tanganyika, was reviewed in *Habari* in 1928, and extracts were published in the issues which followed (Hunter 2013: 263; 'Books/Vitabu: Citizenship/*Uraia*' 1928: 17).

Both periodicals published news from across the world, and the news they published reflected editorial worldviews. In the early issues of *Habari*, the editor at times made his view of the news very clear, in his own distinctive style. For example, in May 1925 news of Hindenburg's election in Germany included the reflection that Hindenburg 'has always been an ardent supporter of the Prussian methods of Government, that is to say, a king supported by a highly trained army with officers chosen from the Nobles. It remains to be seen how far he will carry out republican ideals', while in commenting on the death of Sun Yat Sen in China the editor wrote: 'It is not thought that his death will make much difference' (Anon. 1925, *Habari*: 22). In *Mambo Leo*, the commentary was less personal, but the choice of news presented a distinctive view of the world. For example, news of Turkey's modernising ruler Kemal Ataturk was a regular feature.

The two were connected through their content too. In 1925, a speech by the Ghanaian Pan-Africanist James Aggrey was reprinted from *Mambo Leo* in the pages of *Habari*.[2] Following *Habari*'s relaunch in the later 1920s, and as it increasingly presented itself as part of a regional project to develop Swahili-language publishing, the reprinting of material from *Mambo Leo* increased.

Government newspapers, like their independent counterparts, also travelled further afield. For example, if we return to the announcement in the South African newspaper *Umteteli wa Bantu*, we find reference to the 'useful purpose' served by *Habari*, for '[f]rom the first number we have been privileged to see we perceive that Natives in Kenya are just as sensitive about land matters as are Natives in the Union'. This in turn invited comparative thinking and an invitation to the Union of South Africa to follow the Kenya Government's lead: 'It is clear, also, that when the Kenya Government proposes to set up a Research Board it takes pains to explain to the Native population what it is all about. We commend this system of full explanation to the Union authorities' ('Government Control' 1927: 2). In this way, government newspapers served as a way of exchanging knowledge and information across borders.

But there were also differences. One difference related to language. *Mambo Leo* was published entirely in Swahili, and requests to publish in English and Swahili were rejected. While the readership included colonial officials and European settlers, they were expected to read the text in Swahili (Hunter 2020: 187). In contrast, when *Habari* was launched in 1922 there were two columns, one in English, the other in Swahili. The two columns were not identical. Some articles were published only in Swahili, though in the early years this was the case with relatively few. At times the Swahili column had an extra address to readers. For example, in launching a debate on the question of whether bridewealth payments should be made in livestock or money, the content between the Swahili and English columns was broadly the same until the end, when the Swahili column included an extra sentence with an explicit invitation to readers to send their views (Anon. 1923, *Habari*: 11).

The relaunched *Habari* of the late 1920s took on a more active role as an agent to develop the Swahili language, explicitly drawing on *Mambo Leo* as a model. A significant shift took place in January 1930, when the editor alerted readers to 'the first editorial ever written for Habari which is not a translation of the words written in the Maongezi ya Mtengenezaj' (Editorial 1930, *Habari*: 3). The newspaper was split into two parts, one in English and one in Swahili, 'so that each may be complete in its own way'. As the editor at that time, T. G. Benson, explained, 'as the majority of the 3500 or more readers of this paper understand and read Swahili much more easily than English the largest portion is naturally printed in Swahili' (Editorial 1930, *Habari*: 3). But as we shall see, this was in a context of deep scepticism as to the potential for Swahili to become a widely used language in Kenya.

The second contrast lay in the issue of naming and pseudonymity. *Mambo Leo* never named its editor, despite repeated appeals from readers that it should do so. In contrast, the early issues of *Habari* named its editorial committee, and when the move was made from editorship by a committee to having a single editor, this was announced in its pages (Editorial 1924a, *Habari*: 3). Following *Habari*'s relaunch in 1927 the editor's name, initially James W. C. Dougall, appeared prominently on the editorial page.

A third contrast was that of the relationship between readers and writers. Karin Barber has referred to the 'porous and hospitable' nature of periodicals, in which readers become writers. In these terms, *Mambo Leo* was far more porous and hospitable than *Habari*. In *Mambo Leo* considerable space was given to contributors who were in no sense formally employed by the newspaper, particularly in the section 'Habari za Miji' or 'news of the towns', in the poetry section, in the letters' pages, and in the section where the editor gave his response to readers who had submitted material which for one reason or another would not be published. Many poets and writers initially published their work in *Mambo Leo* and developed reputations as respected writers on the basis of these contributions. When there was discussion in the early 1930s about having one Swahili-language newspaper for all of East Africa, Tanganyika strongly resisted this, emphasising that it was the local news that sold the paper, though it always attracted readers from outside Tanganyika, notably in Kenya. In Tanganyika, government-published periodicals – both nationally and at the local level – remained a very important part of the publishing landscape into the 1950s, while the later history of government periodical publishing in Swahili in Kenya was quite different.

Early issues of *Habari* sought to invite contributions from readers in a similar way. Announcing the publication's shift from having an editorial committee to becoming the responsibility of one editor, and an accompanying reduction in price from 30 shillings to 10 shillings, *Habari*'s editorial stated: 'Remember that this paper is your friend and your spokesman. If you are in any difficulty write to us, and we will bring the matter to notice. If you want advice or information we will give it to you. In all things we are here to help you and to represent you' (Editorial 1923, *Habari*: 4). Yet the published contributions from readers were always marginal to the overall volume of content in the paper.

Political Subjects and the Role of a Lingua Franca

We have already seen hints of the ways in which the contrasting histories of *Habari* and *Mambo Leo* owe something to the governmental contexts in which they were produced and their respective political contexts, and we turn now to explore this theme in more detail. Reading the *Habari* of the early 1920s, when it was edited by Oscar Watkins, in the context of other British colonial periodicals published by colonial governments, either directly, as was the case with *Mambo Leo*, or at one remove from them, the similarities with those other periodicals are striking.

The annual report of the Native Affairs Department for 1923 referred to the success of *Habari*'s new 'debate' pages, noting that 'a discussion on marriage customs has been productive of considerable correspondence'. And the report took the growing body of correspondence and apparent interest in the newspaper as evidence that 'the natives are beginning to show an increasing interest in the Government of their own country'. *Habari* deserved support, it was argued, 'in spite of its financial loss'. The reason given was:

> In this Colony there is a distinct danger that an irresponsible newspaper might be used by Anti-Government, Anti-European or Anti-Christian Agencies as a medium for the dissemination of their propaganda. So long as 'Habari' is in existence it is unlikely that any other paper could be started and maintained without a very large financial expenditure. If 'Habari' were to be abolished, while at the same time the number of literate natives is rapidly on the increase, an opening would be provided for other enterprise. (Native Affairs 1923: 19)

The *East African Standard*, Kenya's leading daily newspaper aimed at the white settler readership, agreed. For the *East African Standard*, *Habari* had a crucial role to play in the life of the colony:

> There are many outside influences which are intruding into Africa to-day, influences from the East and from Moscow. There are many internal causes of trouble, too, and those dangers are largely encouraged by the absence of knowledge. The African is thirsting for knowledge: it is part of the duty of Government to see that the knowledge imparted to him is not only accurate but can be usefully applied in improving his life and his surroundings. We cannot plead too strongly for a continued and improved 'Habari'. (Editorial 1926, *East African Standard*: 16C)

A letter from Watkins to the Senior Provincial Commissioner in Mombasa in 1924 set out the role he saw for *Habari*:

> What I want to aim at is one subscriber in every group of villages. In every village in England there is a village 'oracle' (that is to say, a gentleman who reads the papers and gives his version of what he has read, with his comments, in the public house each evening). This is the sort of thing we want here. Discussions on happenings in the world, or on letters sent in by correspondents to Habari, must have an educational value and must help to arouse interest in what is going on in the world. (Watkins 1924)

For this to happen, Watkins believed, engagement was required from district officers on the ground: 'If some of your Officers would only try to get things going on these lines I am certain the sale of the paper would rapidly spread' (Watkins 1924).

When considered in the context of similar enterprises elsewhere, it is the lack of traction that these arguments had in Kenya's colonial government which is striking. In a strongly worded editorial in January 1926, the *East African Standard* criticised the government's lack of support for *Habari*, leaving the work to be done 'during the leisure hours of an enthusiastic officer'. The *East African Standard*'s view was clear: 'We cannot plead too strongly for a continued and improved "Habari"' (Editorial 1926, *East African Standard*: 16C). This sustained support was not forthcoming, either from district officers or from the Kenya administration in Nairobi. In response to appeals to provide material for the paper, district officers responded by pointing to the lack of time to do this and called for a proper staff.

There were similar complaints about district officers not doing more to promote *Mambo Leo* in Tanganyika. Letters from the Secretariat in Dar es Salaam to district officers in Lindi in southern Tanganyika in the late 1920s and early 1930s shared complaints they received from readers not able to get copies of *Mambo Leo*, and criticised district officers for insufficient efforts in this regard. 'It is regrettable', the Chief Secretary wrote in 1932, 'to have to record that District Officers do not always display that interest in "Mambo Leo" without which an improvement in the present circulation cannot be expected to take place' (Chief Secretary 1932). Distribution networks developed, with district officers making use of missions and asking local clerks to take copies to sell, and then over time there were moves to pay local shopkeepers to act as agents.

Yet the case of *Habari* seems to indicate something more than lack of time in the schedules of busy district officers, and to be suggestive of contrasting visions of Kenya's future within its government. In its early years as a publication of the Native Affairs Department, *Habari* can be seen as a vehicle for government policies and in particular for Oscar Watkins's vision of a future Kenya built around a middle-class elite of 'imperial citizens'. For example, an article in October 1924 on the subject of 'Native Industries' referred to government spending 'on the encouragement of native industries, to help develop such additional means of earning money which are offered to natives by the manufacture of baskets, mats, carved figures, and other such work, and also to encourage native trading', and directly linked this to the newspaper in stating that '[o]ur Editor, Colonel Watkins, is now organising these useful branches of work' ('Native Industries' 1924: 10). This focus on encouraging the production and consumption of goods fed through into Watkins's idea of how the newspaper could become sustainable. The 1923 Native Affairs Commission Report which pointed to the newspaper's financial insecurity also suggested that a way forward lay in increasing the number of advertisements, and concerted efforts were made to do this. An announcement in Swahili in 1922 was circulated encouraging businesses to advertise in *Habari*, encouraging them to do so on the grounds that this would be good for their business. To colleagues in the Kenya administration, Watkins argued that in this way *Habari* would serve as a way of stimulating trade and the purchase of consumer goods by those living in rural areas (Musandu 2018: 233).

But in a colonial setting marked by tense relations between European officials, settlers and missionaries, others in the Kenya Government privileged a different approach. We can see these divisions in particular in relation to the question of publishing translations of government laws and other key documents in Swahili, and using *Habari* to do so. This was an old debate which went back to the 1910s. In 1914 the administrator John Ainsworth, later Chief Native Commissioner, argued against the wishes of the then Governor in favour of there being a newspaper published 'in an African language with a prime aim of the announcement of laws, regulations, and policy' (Spencer 1975: 47). In the early 1920s, Harry Thuku had called for the publishing of laws, and this became the focus of a long-running campaign throughout the 1920s by the Anglican Archdeacon W. E. Owen (Spencer 1975: 47). Owen undertook some publishing along these lines in the Church Missionary Society's newspaper *Lenga Juu*, and Oscar Watkins published translations of key government documents in *Habari*, notably a Translation of Crown Land Ordinance 1915 (see, for example, Anon. 1924, *Habari*: 4–6).

With the restarting of *Habari* in 1927, it was proposed to publish Swahili translations of laws. But the Governor's response was a firm no. The objection was two-fold: first, a belief that laws should not be printed in Swahili, but should be explained orally in *barazas* or public meetings; and second, a conviction that the Swahili used in *Habari* was not now a lingua franca in Kenya, and should not be promoted to become one (Native Affairs 1927; Spencer 1975: 52). In their argument against publishing translated laws in *Habari*, the government echoed those who critiqued the Swahili used in *Habari* as an artificial Swahili which, in its drive to reach readers for whom Swahili was a second language, had changed its nature so far as to be unrecognisable. An editorial in August 1928 referred to 'a discussion in the paper of the Mombasa Catholic Mission, "Rafiki Yetu" of July 1928 to the effect that the Ki-Swahili of Habari is not good, that is to say it is not current Kiswahili, but is modelled on the English way of saying things' (Editorial 1928, *Habari*: 3–4). *Habari*'s editor's response was that '[t]hese remarks are certainly true, but let us remember that "Habari" is not published for Swahili only, but for all natives of Kenya Colony, for schools in town and country also' (Editorial 1928, *Habari*: 3–4), and this explained the type of Swahili they used. But this view remained marginal and the Kenya Government's language policy in the interwar years instead focused on vernaculars such as Kikuyu and Luo on the one hand, and English on the other (Peterson 2006: 191). There are hints in these arguments of a wider tension between a conception of colonial governance based on reified ideas of culture and custom and an alternative rooted in conceptions of imperial citizenship.

In contrast, *Mambo Leo* was adopted both as a space in which to articulate Tanganyika Government policy, and in which to build on earlier developments in the late nineteenth and early twentieth centuries which had already seen a 'standard' Swahili develop in Tanganyika, as Morgan Robinson has recently shown, and to further develop Swahili as a lingua franca for the territory.[3]

Afterlives and Conclusion

The end of *Habari* did not entirely signal the end of government-sponsored Swahili-language newspaper publishing in Kenya. During the Second World War, the Kenya Government agreed to pay a small subsidy to the *East African Standard* to publish a new Swahili-language newspaper, *Baraza*, as a way of bringing war propaganda to a wider audience (Musandu 2018: 240). The first issues of *Baraza* saw its editor-in-chief once again in conflict with the colonial government as he insisted on publishing the complaints of readers. That editor-in-chief was Oscar Watkins, working closely with the Kenyan journalist and later politician Francis Khamisi. While Watkins died shortly after its launch in 1943, *Baraza* went on to become the most widely read Swahili-language newspaper in East Africa, and had a life after independence under the editorship of Francis Khamisi, who returned to edit *Baraza* in 1961. The letters pages of *Baraza* continued to be filled with letters debating the question of what role Swahili might or might not have as a lingua franca for Kenya and for East Africa more broadly. In this way, we can trace *Habari*'s afterlives in a longer history of Swahili-language publishing in Kenya and its limits.

Putting these two newspapers together also contributes to further developing our understanding of the world of Swahili-language periodical publishing in the 1920s as a transnational one across East Africa's territorial borders. Texts crossed borders directly, through reprinting, but editors also situated their newspapers within a wider East African newspaper ecosystem. Government newspapers were an important part of this wider ecosystem. At the same time, this case study reminds us that while the similarities and parallels between the government periodicals published across British colonial settings are striking, their trajectories were also embedded in and shaped by very local political, linguistic and economic contexts.

Notes

1. On *Mambo Leo*, see Bromber 2006: 68–9; Suriano 2011: 41–3; Brennan 2006: 417; and Wenzek 2022: 53–4.
2. See 'Hotuba ya Dr Aggrey (Speech)' 1925: 27; and 'Hotuba ya Dr Aggrey (from *Mambo Leo*)' 1925: 21–2.
3. See Robinson 2022; Brumfit 1980: 278; Whiteley 1993: 79–94; and Anon. 1925, *Mambo Leo*: 1.

Bibliography

Anon. (1923), *Habari*, July, 11.
—— (1924), *Habari*, November, 4–6.
—— (1925), *Habari*, May, 22.
—— (1928), *Habari*, September, 29.
—— (1925), *Mambo Leo*, December, 1.
—— (1932), *Mambo Leo*, October, 246.
Bagnall, Thos. (1927), Letter from Business Manager to 'All subscribers to Habari', 1 December, KNA PC Coast 1/20/61, f. 88.
'Books/Vitabu: Citizenship/*Uraia*' (1928), *Habari*, June, 17.
Brennan, James (2006), 'Realizing civilization through patrilineal descent: The intellectual making of an African racial nationalism in Tanzania, 1920–50', *Social Identities*, 12.4, 405–23.
Bromber, Katrin (2006), 'Ustaarabu: A conceptual change in Tanganyika newspaper discourse in the 1920s', in Roman Loimeier and Rüdiger Seesemann (eds), *The Global Worlds of the Swahili*, Berlin: Lit Verlag, 67–81.
Brumfit, Ann (1980), 'Rise and development of a language policy in German East Africa', *Sprache und Geschichte in Afrika*, 2, 219–331.
Chief Secretary (1932), Tanzania National Archives 16/32/1.
'Debating Society' (1923), *Habari*, July, 11.
Editorial (1926), *East African Standard*, 16 January, 16C.
—— (1923), *Habari*, December, 4.
—— (1924a), *Habari*, January, 3.
—— (1924b), *Habari*, September, 3–4.
—— (1928), *Habari*, August, 3–4.
—— (1930), *Habari*, January, 3.
Erlank, Natasha (2019), '*Umteteli wa Bantu* and the constitution of social publics in the 1920s and 1930s', *Social Dynamics*, 45.1, 75–102.
Gasirye, J. J. (1925), Copy of letter from J. J. Gasirye to Harry Thuku, 7 July, UK National Archives FCO 141/6440, f. 3a.
'Government Control of Native Newspapers' (1927), *Umteteli wa Bantu*, 18 June, 2.
'Habari' (1926), *East African Standard*, 16 January, 16C.
'Hotuba ya Dr Aggrey (Speech by Dr Aggrey)' (1925), *Mambo Leo*, February, 27.
'Hotuba ya Dr Aggrey (from *Mambo Leo*)' (1925), *Habari*, May, 21–2.
Hunter, Emma (2012), '"Our common humanity": Print, power and the colonial press in interwar Tanganyika and French Cameroun', *Journal of Global History*, 7.2, 279–301.
—— (2013), 'Dutiful subjects, patriotic citizens and the concept of "good citizenship" in twentieth-century Tanzania', *Historical Journal*, 56.1, 257–77.
—— (2020), 'Print media, the Swahili language and textual cultures in twentieth-century Tanzania, ca. 1923–1939', in Tony Ballantyne, Lachy Paterson and Angela Wanhalla (eds), *Indigenous Textual Cultures: Reading and Writing in the Age of Global Empires*, Durham, NC: Duke University Press, 175–94.
—— and Leslie James (2020), 'Introduction: Colonial public spheres and the worlds of print', *Itinerario*, 44.2, 227–42.
Krautwald, Fabian (2021), 'The bearers of news: Print and power in German East Africa', *Journal of African History*, 62.1, 5–28.
'Kutengeneza namna moja ya kuandika Kiswahili katika nchi hii' (1925), *Mambo Leo*, 1.
'Lectures in Elementary Agricultures' (1928), *Habari*, September, 29.
Lemke, Hilda (1929), 'Suaheli-Zeitungen und Zeitschriften in Deutsch-Ostafrika', unpublished PhD thesis, University of Leipzig.

Mulokozi, M. M. (ed.) (2002), *Barua za Shaaban Robert 1931–1958, zilikusanywa na kuhifadhiwa na Yusuf Ulenge*, Taasisi ya Uchunguzi wa Kiswahili, Chuo Kikuu cha Dar es Salaam.
Musandu, Phoebe (2018), *Pressing Interests: The Agenda and Interests of a Colonial East African Newspaper Sector*, Montreal: McGill-Queen's University Press.
Native Affairs (1923), Department Annual Report for 1923, Kenya.
Native Affairs (1927), Department Circular No. 35 G. V. Maxwell to all Provincial Commissioners (27 October), 'Publication of Laws in Ki-Swahili', KNA PC Coast 1/20/61, no. f.
'Native Industries' (1924), *Habari*, October, 10.
'News of the World' (1925), *Habari*, May, 12.
Paterson, Lachy (2020), 'Te Karere o Poneke: Creating an indigenous discursive space?', *Itinerario*, 44.2, 365–90.
Peterson, Derek R. (2006), 'Language work and colonial politics in Eastern Africa: The making of standard Swahili and "school Kikuyu"', in David L. Hoyt and Karen Oslund (eds), *The Study of Language and the Politics of Community in Global Context*, Lanham, MD: Lexington Books, 185–214.
Robinson, Morgan (2022), *A Language for the World: The Standardization of Swahili*, Athens: Ohio University Press.
Scotton, James Francis (1971), 'Growth of the vernacular press in colonial East Africa: Patterns of government control', unpublished PhD thesis, University of Wisconsin.
——— (1978), 'Tanganyika's African press, 1937–1960: A nearly forgotten pre-independence forum', *African Studies Review*, 21, 1–18.
Spencer, Leon P. (1975), 'Towards Africans as defenders of their own interests: The translation of laws into Swahili in Kenya, 1920–1927', *Kenya Historical Review*, 3, 47–54.
Sturmer, Martin (1998), *The Media History of Tanzania*, Mtwara: Ndanda Mission Press.
Suriano, Maria (2011), 'Letters to the editor and poems: *Mambo Leo* and readers' debates on *Dansi, Ustaarabu*, respectability, and modernity in Tanganyika, 1940s–1950s', *Africa Today*, 57.3, 39–55.
Thuku, Harry (1979), *Harry Thuku: An Autobiography, with Assistance from Kenneth King*, Nairobi: Oxford University Press.
Watkins, Elizabeth (1995), *Oscar from Africa: The Biography of Oscar Ferris Watkins, 1877–1943*, London: Radcliffe.
Watkins, O. F. (1924), Letter from O. F. Watkins to MacLean, 11 August 1924, KNA PC Coast 1/20/61.
Wenzek, Florence (2022), 'La fabrique genrée de la nation tanzanienne: Éduquer et former les filles et les femmes (1939–1976)', unpublished PhD thesis, University of Paris.
Westcott, Nicholas J. (1981), 'An East African radical: The life of Erica Fiah', *Journal of African History*, 22.1, 85–101.
Whiteley, William (1993), *Swahili: The Rise of a National Language*, Aldershot: Gregg Revivals.

21

Print Networks and Linguistic Interaction in the Early Yoruba Press

Karin Barber

The Lagos Press

EARLY PRINT CULTURE in the crown colony of Lagos was pervasively bilingual. English and Yoruba coexisted and interacted at every level: between publications, within publications, within single texts and often within single sentences. Writers in each language were acutely conscious of the other, viewing it with a mixture of pride, pleasure, emulation and competition. This coexistence and interaction stimulated a form of linguistic creativity to which the format of the weekly local newspapers, and the print networks which sustained them and formed a continuous discursive field, were particularly hospitable. Subsequent scholarship has tended to separate out the strands, with social historians drawing on the English-language press as a source, and Yoruba literary historians identifying early Yoruba-language texts as the starting point of what grew into a major African-language written literature. But I will suggest that this is to miss the properties and potentials of a distinctive generative phase in Nigeria's print history, in particular during the feverish newspaper activity of the 1920s.

The local press of Lagos began almost immediately after the city state's colonisation in 1861, and expanded into a lively print culture two decades later. It was dominated by English-language newspapers produced mainly by the small, highly acculturated 'Saro' elite who were – or were descended from – receptives from the slave trade, who had been deposited by the British Naval Squadron in Sierra Leone and who from the mid-nineteenth century onwards made their way back to their putative homelands in the Yoruba-speaking region of what is now Nigeria. The economic pinnacles of this elite were successful merchants who profited from the position of Lagos as a port and administrative centre. But the cultural pinnacles were those who had received tertiary education, either in Sierra Leone's Fourah Bay College or in British universities, Inns of Court, medical schools and theological colleges, qualifying for one of the white-collar professions – medicine, law, the church, the civil service or civil engineering. Their status depended on their cultural proximity to the tiny British official presence and their mastery of the English language. Though they often sought to re-establish ties with their 'home' communities inland, they were not closely linked to the mass of the Lagos indigenous population. The Lagos majority were predominantly non-literate Yoruba speakers, Muslims or propitiators of indigenous deities, and often resistant to changes introduced by colonial rule. However, towards the end of the nineteenth century the Lagos commercial elite had begun to be squeezed by European trading monopolies and the professional elite were increasingly racially excluded from administrative and professional roles they had previously been able to occupy. Some sections of the elite began to make common cause with the Lagos 'natives' in a succession of conflicts with the colonial authorities, over water rates, land expropriation and above all the status of the traditional ruler of the city, the Eleko, whom the colonial government suspended three times and finally, in 1925, deposed and exiled. Throughout the 1920s the Eleko case was the centre of political debate and contestation, splitting the elite between radical and conservative sections and attracting mass popular support for the radicals led by the great proto-nationalist populist Herbert Macaulay.

This was the context for a huge expansion of press activity in the 1920s and the emergence, for the first time, of a sizeable cohort of Yoruba-language papers. At the beginning of the decade there were three English-language weekly papers (one of which had already ceased publication by the end of January 1920) and none in Yoruba. By the end of the decade, eight new English-language papers had been launched – including four dailies – and five Yoruba weeklies, as well as another Yoruba-language paper based in Ibadan (Omu 1978: 252–4). Some were short-lived, but others flourished well into the 1950s. Though Yoruba-language print culture was long established – the Church Missionary Society's paper *Iwe Irohin* (1859–67), based in Abẹokuta, was the first periodical to be published in what is now Nigeria, and there had been a Yoruba-language newspaper in Lagos which survived for four years (1888–92), as well as books in Yoruba (collections of proverbs and riddles, town histories, works on religion, and missionary translations of the Bible, hymn books and *The Pilgrim's Progress*) – it had not given rise to a flourishing Yoruba-language newspaper culture until the 1920s. In the political furore over the Eleko, it became desirable for the cultural elite to demonstrate, simultaneously, their mastery of the colonial discourse and their ability to speak for, and to, the wider population. The Yoruba newspapers, edited by men in the outer circles of the Lagosian elite, pulled out every stop in an effort to forge a relationship with the large potential public who could read – or be read to – in Yoruba but not in English.[1]

The Lagos press of the 1920s was not only conducted in two languages lying alongside each other – the rolling Victorian prose of the highly educated English speakers, the supple colloquialisms of those experimenting with Yoruba oral genres and popular speech (Barber 2016). It was also constructed as a network of texts in which English and Yoruba constantly interacted, competing, emulating, evaluating and translating one another. Indeed, the papers referred to as 'Yoruba' were actually bilingual. The most important sections, including the all-important editorial, were always in Yoruba, but there were always a few pieces in English. When the political ferment intensified in the early 1920s, some of the English-language papers followed suit and began to include columns in Yoruba, though they never became as consistently bilingual as the Yoruba papers. There was thus interaction between the two languages within the pages of a single paper, as well as between the predominantly English and predominantly Yoruba papers.

The Newspaper Networks

Linguistic interaction was heightened by the networks that newspaper editors depended on. These locally published newspapers were small-scale operations, usually managed, edited and to varying degrees authored by a single editor-proprietor, often financially precarious and with print runs of a few thousand copies at most. But the more successful ones were popular, were carried by rail, road and coastal steamer to subscribers in many other towns, and were read by far more people than bought them. The editor-proprietors relied on personal networks of contacts, friends and associates to provide material for publication, as few of them had the resources to employ professional reporters. Over the course of the 1920s, the Yoruba papers increasingly incorporated pieces of news from inland towns, mostly about social and personal events in the lives of their subscribers. This was supplied by personal contacts forged by the editors, in some cases by making long trips into the hinterland on editorial journeys to promote the paper and gather material for serialised travelogues (see Jones 2016). They also cultivated a nearer constellation of regular contributors that mirrored the social networks on which they constantly reported in their notes and news. Their papers were hospitable to letters from readers writing from different social and geographical locations. Editors did not stipulate that such submissions should be exclusively in Yoruba. They were published as they stood, in English of different levels or in Yoruba, sometimes in non-Lagosian dialects or using orthography different from the style the Lagosian editors had adopted. The papers, as hosts to a diversity of contributions, inevitably juxtaposed different languages and language styles.

Networks among the editors themselves also fostered textual exchanges and bilingual cross-fertilisation. E. M. Awobiyi, the editor of the short-lived *Eko Igbẹhin* (1926–7), had previously worked at the Samadu Press, which published both the English-language *Lagos Weekly Record* and the Yoruba-language *Iwe Irohin Ọsọsẹ*, both of which were edited by Thomas Horatio Jackson. After Awobiyi's sudden death in 1927, I. B. Thomas, who had written in both English and Yoruba for several papers in the mid-1920s, took over *Eko Igbẹhin*, before going on to found his own highly successful paper, *Akede Eko*, in 1928. In 1929 Thomas also started an English-language daily, the *Nigerian Evening News*, though this only lasted six months. Adeoye Deniga, after his own paper *Eko Akete* closed in 1929, did a brief stint as editor of the English-language *Nigerian Daily Telegraph*, preceded by its founder H. Antus Williams and followed by a rapid succession of other well-known editors including Duse Ali (who soon afterwards founded the popular *Comet*) and Ernest Ikoli (who had previously edited the *African Messenger*, and subsequently the *Nigerian Daily Mail*), before Antus Williams took back the reins. Most editors, then, had experience of working on more than one paper; most of the Yoruba papers' editors had also contributed to, or edited, an English-language paper; and most had a flair for the English language as well as Yoruba. Adeoye Deniga, the most brilliant and versatile of the Yoruba stylists, also had long experience of giving public lectures in English on a range of topics, and then publishing them as pamphlets. He continued to publish an annual *Who's Who in Nigeria* in English, and he used English in *Eko Akete* from time to time. When indignant, he could resort to a high-flown style spiced with archaisms and Latin tags: 'Impertinent newsmonger', he thundered when a newly launched paper, *The Nigerian Advocate*, dared to criticise longer-established publications, 'Is your organ A Foeman worthy of the Steel? *Ne Sutor Ultra Crepidam*!' ('Eko Akete' [Adeoye Deniga] 1923b: 3; see Figure 21.1). E. A. Akintan, the editor of *Eleti Ọfẹ*, was a schoolmaster who went on to co-found and head the Lagos Public School and to write schoolbooks on English and Yoruba languages alike.[2] I. B. Thomas was also a schoolmaster early on in his career. A flamboyant and innovative stylist, he developed a speech-like, emotional, chatty style in Yoruba and a resonant rhetoric in English.

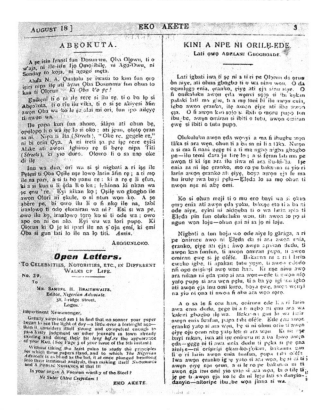

Figure 21.1 'Impertinent newsmonger!' Adeoye Deniga's open letter to the *Nigerian Advocate*. *Eko Akete*, 18 August 1923, p. 3. Courtesy of the author.

These conditions made it possible for the Lagos newspapers themselves to be constituted as a network – a textual interchange. Drawing on each other for materials was so pervasive as to constitute the press as a shared field of indefinitely wide extent though with a definite local core. This was typical of colonial print culture: as Isabel Hofmeyr observes, the periodical and the pamphlet were 'the forms of empire par excellence. A cut-and-paste assemblage of publications from elsewhere, the periodical on every page convened a miniature empire' (Hofmeyr 2013: 13).[3] The Lagos newspapers hosted materials from a wide range of named and unnamed sources. Their interaction took the form of reporting or commenting on what another paper had said; quoting, excerpting or reprinting in full pieces published in other papers; and addressing themselves to the editors of other papers.

In the 1920s the Yoruba papers were particularly attached to their short-lived Lagosian forerunner *Iwe Irohin Eko* (1888–92) and frequently republished entire articles from it. The editors also read the Gold Coast and Sierra Leone papers and republished pieces from them as well as a variety of British publications, especially weekly periodicals. For example, in its second-ever issue, on 22 July 1922 (the first issue is not in the Nigerian National Archive), *Eko Akete* reprinted an article from *Iwe Irohin Eko*, dated 16 March 1889, on the origins of the ethnonym 'Nago', and an article titled 'Are we a nation?' from *The Gold Coast Leader*, dated 6 March 1922. Two weeks later it carried the striking headline 'THIRTY-SEVEN YEARS AGO!!!' above a reprinted item from the *Lagos Observer* about proposals to raise money to erect a statue, or a hall, in honour of the first British Governor of Lagos, John Hawley Glover. It went on, over the first eighteen months of its existence, to carry extracts or reprint whole articles from the London-based *West Africa* magazine more than a dozen times, and to draw on the British *Daily Mail*, *John Bull* magazine, *Reynolds's Newspaper*, *Times* (weekly edition), *Sunday Times* and *News of the World*. It used *The Gold Coast Leader*, the *Gold Coast Independent* and the *Sierra Leone Weekly News*, and Marcus Garvey's paper *Negro World*. At the other end of the decade, the latest new Yoruba paper *Akede Eko* was equally lavish in its excerpting and cross-referencing, though the focus had now shifted from the Gold Coast and Sierra Leone to fellow Nigerian papers: it was in constant dialogue with the *Nigerian Daily Times* (numerous references, usually hostile, most savagely so when that paper trashed the editor I. B. Thomas's pioneering serialised work of fiction, *Itan Igbesi-Aiye Emi Ṣẹgilọla*) and also drew from Herbert Macaulay's paper the *Lagos Daily News*, the conservative *Nigerian Pioneer*, the long-running radical *Lagos Weekly Record*, the new *Nigerian Daily Telegraph* and the Yoruba paper *Eleti Ọfẹ*. Though *Akede Eko* showed a shift in orientation from the West African coastal culture zone to the Nigerian national entity, the connections out to England and the British press were retained. Thomas drew on *West Africa* magazine for information or for whole articles; he also read and made use of *The Overseas Daily Mail*, the *Journal of the West African Students' Union*, *News of the World* and *Pearson's Weekly*.

The British papers were available to anyone with the means to buy them through subscription services like the one advertised in the *Nigerian Pioneer* by a company based in Plymouth:

> Send 13/- and we mail you regularly every week for 52 weeks a copy of any British Weekly Newspaper, such as: Lloyd's, People, Tit Bits, Pearson's, etc., etc., etc. Hundreds of papers on our Big List mailed free. A different paper sent weekly, or the same publication for 52 weeks . . . Most unique and up-to-date service, greatly appreciated by members throughout the Empire. (Anon. 1922c, *Nigerian Pioneer*: 11)

It was not only newspaper editors who read the British weeklies: sometimes readers wrote in to the Lagos papers with comments on things they had read in *Tit Bits* or *West Africa* magazine.

It is clear from the editors' observations that they not only eagerly awaited and keenly scanned the imported British papers, but felt themselves to be in dialogue with them. Though the British press, predictably, did not show anything like a reciprocal interest in the West African press, the traffic was not entirely one way. Soon after its inception in 1922, *Eko Akete* was proud to report that *West Africa* magazine had welcomed its arrival:

> Saara rẹ ni yi, Iwọ Iwe-Irohin 'West Africa'
> A ṣọpẹ lọwọ Ọrẹ wa ni Ilu Oyinbo, ti a npe ni Iwe-irohin West Africa, fun ọrọ yinyin ati iṣiri to sọ fun wa, ninu Iwe-irohin rẹ ti ọjọ kejila oṣu to kọja, to ba ọkọ 'Ekari' de, ni lọlọ, nigbati o ri Iwe-irohin wa, 'Eko Akete' gba ni ilu ọba lọhun. (Anon. 1922a, *Eko Akete*: 2).[4]

We appreciate it, you 'West Africa' newspaper!
We thank our Friend in Britain called *West Africa* magazine, for the praise and encouragement it gave us in the issue of the twelfth of last month, which has just arrived by the steamship *Ekari*, when it received our own paper *Eko Akete* in England yonder.

Interaction was not always so friendly. *Eko Akete*'s editor, Adeoye Deniga, did not hesitate to lambast British publications and journalists when they disparaged West Africans. When *John Bull* magazine reported that 'The Gold Coast niggers are still at their old game of writing to strangers asking for miscellaneous goods in return for which they promise to send African curios – which, of course, never arrive . . .' (Anon. 1923, *John Bull*: 7), Deniga was incensed: 'Old Negrophobist', he expostulated in an open letter to the editor, Charles Pilley, 'Really, you have no idea of the low depth into which your rag – John Bull is rapidly sinking mainly by your idiotic sneer, cheap jibe, and *Un-British* manner in which you undertake to edit its pages' ('Eko Akete' [Adeoye Deniga] 1923a: 8).

Nigerian voices sometimes appeared within the British press itself, most often through interviews given by prominent Lagosians during their visits to Britain. Some of the most furious debates in the 1920s Lagos press revolved around statements made in such interviews. Herbert Macaulay, when he accompanied Chief Oluwa to a hearing of the Apapa Land Case at the Privy Council in 1920, allegedly told the *Daily Mail* that the Eleko ruled over the whole seventeen million population of Nigeria rather than just the city of Lagos. The Governor of Nigeria, Sir Hugh Clifford, was furious and demanded that the Eleko publicly repudiate this claim by sending his bell-ringer around town denouncing it, which the Eleko refused to do. This precipitated his third suspension and eventually his deposition. The conservative Dr John Randle gave an interview to *West Africa* magazine criticising Herbert Macaulay. This was reprinted, closely scrutinised and commented upon by the Lagos press over several weeks. And when the founder of the Lagos branch of the Ahmadiyya, the Indian Maulvi Abdur Rahim Nayyar, left Lagos for London, he spoke to a British newspaper about Lagos's problems in terms that the Yoruba papers found outrageously disparaging, and spent weeks rebutting. Lagosians were thus to be found within the pages of the publications of the imperial centre, as well as being assiduous readers of their content at home.

If interactions with the British press consisted mainly of excerpting and commenting, within the Lagos press there was more dialogue, often of a triangular nature. No newspaper was intended to provide a self-sufficient compendium of everything its public might want to read; rather, it was assumed that readers would read across a range of publications and engage in debates and disputes between them. And readers did often write letters to the editor of one paper taking issue with something published in another. 'Majek', for example, wrote to *Eleti Ofẹ* praising an article by Herbert Macaulay published in *The Lagos Weekly Record*; this was taken up by 'Otitọ Koro', who wrote to the *Nigerian Pioneer* commenting on Majek's letter, and Majek wrote again to *Eleti Ofẹ* replying to Otitọ Koro (Majek 1923: 6). In the editors' view, the press was the locus of 'public opinion'; debates in the press were where public deliberation happened; and Lagos papers had been known to lament that public opinion in Lagos was not sufficiently well developed, or not as advanced and enlightened as the public opinion of the Gold Coast, their most frequent point of comparison. The editors saw themselves as public benefactors fostering civic consciousness through their exchanges, even though these were often acrimonious.

These networks of press interaction involved not only juxtaposition of English and Yoruba texts but also selective translation in both directions, though often in an incomplete and temporally displaced manner. In the Yoruba papers, it was fairly unusual for the same item to appear in both languages. The editors did not translate most of their own original Yoruba-language material. Editorials, most of the local news snippets, many of the topical commentaries, and poetry and songs were not translated from Yoruba into English. Conversely, English-language items were often not accompanied by a Yoruba version. *Eleti Ọfẹ*, for example, had a much-appreciated column of witty topical commentary in English by 'Scrutator' which was not translated into Yoruba. Each piece occupied its own space and found its own readers in the relevant language. Though the editors' professed objective was to reach the large number of potential Yoruba-language readers, some readers particularly valued the English sections. One 'Pane' wrote a letter to the editor of *Eleti Ọfẹ* soon after its launch, commending the whole paper and pointing out the value of the small English sections:

> Nigbati mo ka iwe na lati ibẹrẹ titi de ipari rẹ, emi ko ri ọrọ aṣanu ninu rẹ tabi ọrọ ti ko mu iṣiri wa, mo si wa dupẹ lọwọ rẹ fun aye diẹ ti ẹ fi silẹ fun ede Gẹsi nitori awọn ti ko le ka ede Yoruba daradara. (Pane 1923: 5)

> When I read the paper from beginning to end, I found nothing I didn't like or that wasn't inspiring, and I also thank you for making a little space for the English language for the sake of those who cannot read Yoruba very well.

Usually, it was only texts presented as being of great importance or urgency that would appear in both English and Yoruba in the same publication: official government notices, for example on voter registration, and highly significant items such as Governor Clifford's negative response to the 'Monster Petition', signed by thousands of Lagosians to ask for the reinstatement of the Eleko. Or when regular contributors were especially anxious that their message should be heard by all, they might write a version in each language. On one occasion 'Awọlujẹ' wrote in Yoruba in *Eleti Ọfẹ* to praise and thank an ultra-rich member of the Saro elite, S. H. Pearse, for his sponsorship of two boys to attend the CMS Grammar School, and on a different page of the same issue of the paper I. B. Thomas did the same in English. One of the two boys was Thomas's younger brother, and 'Awọlujẹ' was Thomas's Yoruba pseudonym (Awọlujẹ 1924: 5; Thomas 1924: 8).

More often, however, the Yoruba papers, in accordance with their undertaking to 'explain' the politics of Lagos to their non-English-reading readers, would publish Yoruba translations or summaries of English-language articles that had been published in other periodicals, such as the Randle and Macaulay interviews mentioned above. They also liked to bring anglophone literature to the table, in the form of translations of popular poems such as Walter Scott's 'Breathes there the man with soul so dead' and Ella Wheeler Wilcox's 'Settle the question right', along with well-known passages from Shakespeare. *Eko Akete* even undertook a translation of a whole book, Samuel Smiles's *Character*, which was serialised (irregularly, and in short excerpts) for more than a year and a half, from August 1927 until the paper's last issue in April 1929.

The reverse process, from Yoruba to English, was less frequent, but it did occur. The most significant instance was I. B. Thomas's *Itan Igbesi-Aiye Emi Ṣẹgilọla*, a serialised epistolary narrative purporting to be written by an ageing and repentant former goodtime girl, which with its combination of the salacious and the pious, the cadences of the Bible and the slang of the street, caused a sensation in Lagos. After the end of Ṣẹgilọla's story, which had run in *Akede Eko* for nine months in 1929 and 1930, Thomas republished the episodes as a book which immediately sold out (Anon. [Thomas] 1930). The following year, he began a serialised English translation, prompted, as he said, by many requests from people who were not proficient at reading Yoruba (Barber 2012).

Language Ideology

Linguistic competence was keenly appraised and the value of both English and Yoruba was frequently discussed in the Yoruba press. In their editorial overviews and in public meetings called to rouse support for their publications, Yoruba-language editors emphasised above all their mission to inform and enlighten the members of the public who could not read English (the majority); but they also affirmed that the Yoruba language was valuable in itself, as a distillation or repository of indigenous cultural knowledge. They urged the elite, some of whom were more fluent in English and Sierra Leonean pidgin than in Yoruba, to make more effort to improve their command of the language by reading the Yoruba press. They lambasted those who pretended not to know a word of the language in the mistaken belief that this would make them seem more distinguished. Failing to learn one's own native language is more shameful than stealing, says 'Asalu', a frequent contributor to *Eleti Ọfẹ*, but 'what is even more despicable is when a Yoruba person deliberately speaks their own language like a European or a Kurumọ who has just arrived. Or when a Yoruba with a face as black as a civet-cat's, like mine, wants to talk to a group of Yoruba people and asks for an interpreter.'[5]

Some of their contributors and correspondents apologised for having to write in English because of their inability to write good Yoruba.[6] Some modestly confessed that they had hesitated to take up the editor's invitation to contribute in Yoruba, fearing that they were not sufficiently good, but then proceeded to write eloquently and extensively in the language: one such was 'Balogun Dodondawa', one of I. B. Thomas's most prolific contributors to *Akede Eko* (for examples of his contributions, with English translation, see Barber 2012: 262–71, 298–319, 326–39). Several readers also wrote in to thank the newspaper for helping them become competent at reading the language.

The value of the Yoruba language as repository of cultural heritage and identity was brought out in *Eko Akete*'s first competition for readers; they were to write an essay on the benefits of one's own mother tongue. The winning entry, by E. A. Akintan – who soon afterwards started his own newspaper, *Eleti Ọfẹ* – went so far as to suggest that some things could not be said except in Yoruba:

Ogunlọgọ ọrọ ati orukọ ati ọfọ ati ogede ati egbogi ti ilẹ wa, ti o njẹ bi idan, ni a ko le fi ede-elede kọ bikoṣe ni ede wa, anfani wo l'o to eyi? Ọpọlọpọ itan ilẹ wa ati aṣa ilẹ wa ti a ko le fi ede elede kọ bikoṣe ni ede wa, ati awọn Orin Ile wa, bi orin Danmọle, bi orin Bẹgbaji, ati Biṣi ati ti awọn Ẹgbado ti a npe ni Ẹfẹ, ko si anfani ti o to eyi nigbati a nkọ ede ilu wa sinu Iwe-Irohin ti a le gbọ ohun ti o ṣe l'arin wa ati ni ilu okere ninu ọṣẹ kan. (Akintan 1922: 6–7)

> Countless words and names and incantations and spells and herbal medicines of our land, which are instantly efficacious, cannot be written in any language but our own, and what greater benefit is there than that? The many histories of our land and our culture which cannot be written down in any language but our own, and our native Songs, like the songs of Danmọle, like the songs of Bẹgbaji, and Biṣi and those of the Ẹgbado that are called Ẹfẹ, there is no benefit to compare when we write our language and can hear what's happening amongst us here and far afield within a week.

Akintan here affirms a general perception that the 'deep' elements of Yoruba culture, including its esoteric knowledge and its history and oral poetry, were literally untranslatable. Precious cultural knowledge inhered in language and was inseparable from it. When he went on to publish his own paper, Akintan made a point of inviting readers to retrieve, write down and send in the poems of the popular local poets mentioned in this essay – Danmọle, Bẹgbaji and Biṣi – who had sung topical and philosophical commentaries on local affairs a few decades earlier.

But the Yoruba readers and writers who contributed to the Yoruba papers also expressed admiration for splendid feats of English rhetoric. They seemed especially admiring when the speakers were chiefs or schoolmasters in the hinterland rather than members of the high Lagos elite. Thus Adegboyega Ẹdun, the noted chief, political actor and cultural intermediary of Abẹokuta, is praised for his impressive English speech at the Alake's fiftieth birthday party: he almost 'finished' the whole language single-handed, and used up all the resplendent English contained in the dictionary (Bright 1922: 5). At another occasion in Abẹokuta, the opening of the new Baptist School for Boys, one speaker was singled out for special praise: the Ogbomọṣọ teacher and historian-to-be N. D. Oyerinde, whose eloquence in English was 'unparalleled in the experience of us youngsters, both boys and girls . . . if one has splendid robes one will always find space in which to display them. Throughout his speech, he was rolling out "knock-out" English by the yard . . . He continued to bring out ever-varied pronouncements for about forty minutes, without getting tired, and without us getting tired either.'[7] However, bombastic English could also raise hackles. *Eko Igbẹhin*, which most consistently among the Yoruba papers presented a 'view from below', published a vehement denunciation of the language used in a recent public meeting:

> If there is too much 'I know book, I know book' within an association, such that when the Chairman tosses out one piece of Grammar, the members of the Association throw back six, without caring about respecting seniority, the result for the kind of Association that does not make one's mother tongue predominant in its speech, the Association where the members don't respect the Chairman, just Grammar! Grammar! right and left, everyone speaking, [is,] it's sad to say publicly, that too much Grammar breaks up an association, it does not unite it . . .[8]

Eko Igbẹhin's polemic takes the point of view of a Yoruba speaker who resents the better-educated showing off in high-flown English (which is what is meant by 'Grammar'). This, it seems, is mainly because it is associated with loss of proper manners and deference between seniors and juniors – speaking 'Grammar' to one's seniors is a form of disrespect. Such views, however, only surfaced occasionally even in *Eko Igbẹhin*, whose editor, though less highly educated than his fellow editors, was also capable of writing well-worded commentaries in English when his purpose required it.

The Creativity of Linguistic Interaction

The creativity of the juxtaposition and interaction of English and Yoruba is most clearly visible when a text in one language resorts to a quotation in the other – for these quotations usually involved a repurposing and a reflection on the potentials of language to yield new meanings. In 'News and Comments', one of the English-language sections of *Eleti Ọfẹ*, there was a piece about Grindell-Matthews, 'a great English inventor', who had found a way to add realistic sound to movies:

> What a new world we live in! Formerly, we had a Yoruba adage saying Ẹsin inu iwe ki ta, i.e. a horse in the Picture never kicks, but in these days the advent of Cinematograph makes this adage a dead letter. Nowadays Yoruba people are prepared not only to accept that the horse in the picture kicks but also that the noise of the kicking can be heard! (Light 1923: 5)

The Yoruba saying was itself a shrewd observation on what had once been a novelty when introduced into a predominantly oral culture – printed drawings or photographs (the word translated as 'Picture' is *iwe*, a more general word for paper, book, letter or document); but here it has become the old common sense by contrast with which the amazing effect of the talkie can be highlighted. In another item, headed 'Africans and staff appointments', the columnist Scrutator condemns the 'race prejudice' that has blocked 'our Countrymen' from appointments to the higher grades of the Civil Service: 'Good men have been pushed out by affronts and indignities. Though an effort has now begun to create higher posts for Africans, this will be of no value unless the appointees are given a free hand, because "Ẹni a nṣọ ki mọ'wa hu"' (Scrutator 1923: 7). The person under surveillance – the person who is constantly monitored – does not learn good behaviour. This Yoruba saying, which Scrutator does not translate, encapsulates, more eloquently than the preceding discussion, a whole philosophy of the path to independence as the 1920s Lagosian elite saw it. The suggestion is that it is only through freedom that one can learn self-discipline and responsible action.

Conversely, quotations of English sayings or lines of poetry embedded in a Yoruba text are often repurposed to yield a new meaning, while retaining an ironical shadow of their original one. A moralising piece in *Eko Akete* is headed 'O ntọ wọn lẹhin' (It follows after them), with a very slightly misquoted epigraph from Mark Antony's speech over the dead body of Caesar in *Julius Caesar*: 'The evils that men do lives after them / The good is often interred with their bones' (Anon. 1922b, *Eko Akete*: 3). The writer (probably Adeoye Deniga himself) does not take up an obvious possible implication of Mark Antony's statement – that the conspirators are trying to justify the murder of Caesar by remembering his excessive ambition while forgetting all the good he has done for Rome. Instead, he picks up the more veiled suggestion that they, the conspirators, will find that their evil deed – the assassination – is not forgotten but brings its own retribution. This choice of emphasis is underlined by the writer's translation of the Shakespeare quote: 'Gbogbo iwa buburu ti enia nhu mba wọn lọ / Iwa rere wọn si ntọ wọn lẹhin' (All the bad deeds that people do go with them / And their good deeds follow after them); in other words, neither good nor bad behaviour is forgotten – both have their consequences. The writer goes on to say that bad and good come into the world together and their coexistence is inescapable, but when the bad exceeds the good, that's when we see 'oniruru iwa aitọ, ati iwa ti ko yẹ, rikiṣi, tẹmbẹlẹkun, iyapa, ija, ọtẹ, asọ, at ohun bawọnni' (all kinds of wrong actions, and improper behaviour, cheating, conspiracy, deviance, fighting, dissension, quarrelling and things like that). 'Owe ilẹ wa kan ni "Tika tore ki igbe"' (One of our indigenous proverbs is 'Neither wickedness nor goodness will ever fade away'). The writer goes on to apply these observations to the current machinations of certain people in Lagos who are jeopardising the peace or well-being of the town in their efforts to curry favour – they should remember that they will reap the consequences of their deeds which will 'follow after them'. Thus this writer has ended up erasing the distinction made by Mark Antony between the good and evil that men do: neither is interred with their bones, both live on and both have their inescapable consequences in this world or the next. In developing this short disquisition, the writer inflects the Shakespeare text to align it with a well-established Yoruba view, expressed in many genres, about the inevitable co-presence of good and evil, friends and enemies, in the world – and their inescapable consequences.

Conclusion

Though English was the language of authority, of the higher levels of education and the professions, and of the imperial power, the linguistic cohabitation of 1920s Lagos was not a scene of glottophagia, of the colonial language killing or rendering useless the native tongue. Rather, the coexistence and interaction of the two languages, which permeated everyday life in Lagos and was fashioned into a conscious art in the pages of the local press, seems to have acted as a stimulant to creativity. The sense that Yoruba was being sidelined by those who foolishly only valued English gave rise to vigorous counter-attacks and exhilarating displays of Yoruba linguistic virtuosity. The Yoruba weeklies were a place of experimentation where new genres such as I. B. Thomas's epistolary novel were pioneered and new forms of address to new reading publics were forged. This moment of potentiality needs to be restored to narratives of literary, cultural and political history in Nigeria.

Notes

1. The 1921 census showed that there were about 30,000 people in Lagos who could read, though only about 10,000 who could write, out of a population of about 100,000 (see Baker 1974: 76). Those who could read but not write were unlikely to have learnt enough English to read the elevated prose of the English-language press.
2. His textbooks included *Training in English* (1933), *Iwe Itumọ Awọn Ede ati Owe Gẹsi (Yoruba Translation of English Phrases and Proverbs)* (1936) and its mirror image, *English Translations of Yoruba Phrases and Proverbs* (1945), *First Steps in Yoruba Composition* (1947), *Second Step in Yoruba Composition* (1947), as well as at least two fictional works in Yoruba.
3. Hofmeyr makes a thought-provoking distinction between newspapers and periodicals, the latter being published with longer intervals between issues – fortnightly, monthly or

quarterly rather than daily – and therefore lending themselves better to slow, ship-borne transmission between far-flung parts of the English-speaking world: pieces in imported periodicals were more likely to be still relevant than topical items in newspapers which quickly became dated. However, the Lagos press in the 1920s consisted mainly of weeklies – a periodicity that seems to combine the two temporalities evoked by Hofmeyr; on this, see Barber 2023: 75–87.
4. All quotations from newspapers are reproduced here with the original orthography and spelling. All translations are my own, except where I refer to items which the newspapers themselves translated.
5. 'Ṣugbọn ohun ti o ma nri ni l'ara lati ri i ni wipe ki ọmọ Yoruba ma sọ ede ilu rẹ bi igbati Oyinbo tabi Kurumọ ti o ṣeṣe de ilẹ yi iba ma ni on nsọ ede Yoruba. Tabi ki o dẹ jẹ wipe ti ọmọ Yoruba (ti oju rẹ dudu bi oju akata, bi ti emi nibi) ba fẹ lati ba agbajọ enia (Yoruba) sọrọ ki a ni lati ma gbufọ fun u' (Asalu 1924: 5).
6. For an example, see Otitọ Koro 1922: 4.
7. 'Ko n'araru ni gbogbo ọrọ rẹ jẹ fun gbogbo awa ọdọmọde, lọkunrin at lobinrin, l'ori ẹkọ aye, ti o si ye koro ti ko di pẹta rara. Nitoripe ko si igbati a d'aṣọ ti a ko ri ilẹ fi wọ. Gbogbo ọrọ rẹ, gba-kan-nṣubu ede Gẹsi lo nyi silẹ rabata-rabata, pẹlu itumọ ti o ye koro. Eyiti o fi sọrọ ikan ko jọkan, o to bi iwọn ogoji iṣẹju, sibẹ, ko su u, ko su wa' (F. O. 1923: 5).
8. 'Bi mo mọ iwe, mo mọ iwe ba ṣe npọju ninu ẹgbẹ kan bi Alaga (Chairman) ba ju girama kan, ti ọmọ Ẹgbẹ ba nju girama mẹfa, ti ko bikita ti ko mọ agba l'ẹgbọn, ohun ti o nilati gbẹhin irufẹ Ẹgbẹ ti ko jẹki ede ilu ti a bi on si pọju ninu ọrọ sisọ, Ẹgbẹ ti ọmọ ẹgbẹ ko ntẹriba fun Alaga (Chairman) ẹgbẹ, Girama ṣa! Girama ṣa! lọtun losi, olohunyọhun, anu ṣe ni lati sọ fun aiye gbọ wipe Girama pupọ ma nfọ ẹgbẹ ni, ki tun ẹgbẹ ṣe . . .' (Alade'gbo 1926: 4).

Bibliography

Akintan, E. A. (1922), 'Anfani ti o wa ninu ede ilu ẹni', *Eko Akete*, 7 October, 6–7.
Alade'gbo (1926), 'Ga sa! Pa ga! Wọn fẹ fi Girama (Grammar) fọ ẹgbẹ na jalẹ kọ bayi?', *Eko Igbẹhin*, 25 June, 4.
Anon. (1922a), 'Saara rẹ ni yi, iwọ Iwe-Irohin "West Africa"', *Eko Akete*, 9 September, 2.
——— (1922b), 'O ntọ wọn lẹhin', *Eko Akete*, 7 October, 3.
——— (1922c), 'News from the Old Country', *Nigerian Pioneer*, 1 December, 11.
——— (1923), *John Bull*, 3 February, 7.
——— [I. B. Thomas] (1930), *Itan igbesi aiye emi 'Ṣegilọla, ẹlẹyinju ẹgẹ', ẹlẹgbẹrun ọkọ l'aiye*, Lagos: no publisher.
Asalu (1924), 'Ohun ti o yẹ ki o ti ni l'oju ju ole lọ wa tabi ko si?', *Eleti Ọfẹ*, 5 March, 4–5.
Awọlujẹ [I. B. Thomas] (1924), 'Honourable S. H. Pearse (ọmọ igba-lẹ'rọ), tani nfi ẹ ṣere?', *Eleti Ọfẹ*, 16 January, 5.
Baker, Pauline H. (1974), *Urbanization and Political Change: The Politics of Lagos, 1917–1967*, Berkeley, Los Angeles and London: University of California Press.
Barber, Karin (2012), *Print Culture and the First Yoruba Novel: I. B. Thomas's 'Life Story of Me, Ṣegilọla' and Other Texts*, Leiden: Brill.
——— (2016), 'Experiments with genre in Yoruba newspapers of the 1920s', in Derek R. Peterson, Emma Hunter and Stephanie Newell (eds), *African Print Cultures: Newspapers and their Publics in the Twentieth Century*, Ann Arbor: Michigan University Press, 151–78.
——— (2023), 'Oral genres and homegrown print culture', in Charne Lavery and Sarah Nuttall (eds), *Reading from the South: African Print Cultures and Oceanic Turns in Isabel Hofmeyr's Work*, Johannesburg: Wits University Press, 75–87.
Bright, E. A. Oluyẹle (1922), 'Kabiyesi! Alake Ọba Ẹgba, ẹ ku agba. Ẹ ku inawo ọjọ', *Eko Akete*, 21 October, 5–6.

'Eko Akete' [Adeoye Deniga] (1923a), 'Open Letters. To Celebrities, Notorities, etc., in different walks of life: no. 19', *Eko Akete*, 24 February, 8.

—— (1923b), 'Open Letters. To Celebrities, Notorities, etc., in different walks of life: no. 29', *Eko Akete*, 18 August, 3.

F. O. (1923), 'Ṣiṣi ile ẹkọ giga ti ijọ Baptist fun awọn ọdọmọkunrin', *Eko Akete*, 24 February, 4–6.

Hofmeyr, Isabel (2013), *Gandhi's Printing Press: Experiments in Slow Reading*, Cambridge, MA: Harvard University Press.

Jones, Rebecca (2016), 'The sociability of print: 1920s and 1930s Lagos newspaper travel writing', in Derek R. Peterson, Emma Hunter and Stephanie Newell (eds), *African Print Cultures: Newspapers and their Publics in the Twentieth Century*, Ann Arbor: Michigan University Press, 102–24.

Light (1923), 'News and Comments. Making Picture Speak', *Eleti Ọfẹ*, 21 March, 5.

Majek (1923), *Eleti Ọfẹ*, 28 February, 6.

Omu, Fred I. A. (1978), *Press and Politics in Nigeria, 1880–1937*, Atlantic Highlands, NJ: Humanities Press.

Otitọ Koro (1922), *Eko Akete*, 26 August, 4.

Pane (1923), *Eleti Ọfẹ*, 21 February, 5.

Scrutator (1923), 'Africans and staff appointments', *Eleti Ọfẹ*, 7 March, 6–7.

Thomas, Isaac B. (1924), 'A faithful stewardship or the noblest help to the country', *Eleti Ọfẹ*, 16 January, 8.

22

Colonial Entanglements: Black South African Periodicals and the Colonial Printsphere, 1920s–30s

Corinne Sandwith and Athambile Masola

Introduction

SCHOLARSHIP ON THE African periodical press tends towards a loose division between pro-government and missionary publications, on the one hand, and anti-colonial periodicals on the other.[1] The greater priority given to the modes of the anti-colonial – and the corresponding weight given to editorial independence – has led to a relative neglect of more moderate publications.[2] This schematic division, however useful, diminishes the space for engagement with those colonial publications which had more ambiguous alignments – in particular, those periodicals which enjoyed the financial support of white backers but which were edited by black journalists. The privilege given to anti-colonial resistance also tends to obscure the historical possibility of black conservatism, thus occluding an important dimension of colonial experience. In this chapter, we draw new attention to the genre of the white-supervised periodical – and the unequal power nexus that this arrangement implied – as a commonplace genre of the colonial public sphere and consider the implications of this entangled material configuration for political articulation, newspaper form, modes of address, rhetorical style and patterns of use.

The black-edited/white-funded periodical was a particular feature of dominion colonial contexts: semi-colonial spaces that were nominally part of the British Empire but were dominated economically and politically by a white settler minority. Focusing on the early years of two such examples, namely *Umteteli wa Bantu* (launched May 1920) and *Bantu World* (launched April 1932), this chapter foregrounds these newspapers' explicit self-positioning in the colonial public sphere as a form of moral pedagogy and highlights the ways in which this conspicuous didacticism played out in newspaper form. The focus on various genres of the editorial paratext such as glossing, footnoting and 'Notes to Correspondents',[3] all of which signal an overt editorial presence, represents a departure from conventional engagements with the editor as historical-political agent, thus highlighting a reading of the editor as textual performance and verbal trace.

Against this view of the colonial periodical as pedagogic performance, the chapter foregrounds the ways in which the insistent editorial invitation was also routinely ignored or undercut, thus exploring the genre's propensity for both didactic design and irreverent disruption. This has everything to do with the form of the newspaper itself: its typical structural features of multi-modality, assemblage, juxtaposition and repetition, in particular the ways in which the compositional organisation of disparate elements into a surface conformity invites tension, polyvocality and unanticipated meanings. In this way, the chapter extends existing attention to 'newspaper form' – layout, typography, headlining and font styles (Barnhurst and Nerone 2001: 3) – by engaging with the politics of form more generally. Central to this are the newspapers' multilingual formats, where front pages dominated by English are followed by isiZulu, isiXhosa, Sesotho and Setswana sections (in varying configurations but often including up to four or five languages). Given the close alignment of the editorial commandment with the English language itself, the question of the newspapers' multilingualism will also be foregrounded: what kinds of possibilities for editorial disruption, reconfiguration or heterogeneity, we ask, are opened on the African-language pages? The predominance of English is of course a statement in itself, potentially marking a particular form of alignment. In the case of *Abantu-Batho*, *Umteteli*'s closest rival, for instance, the English pages tended to be 'relegated to the middle pages' with isiZulu and Sesotho taking centre stage (Limb 2012: 30).

Revisiting the 'Captive' Press

An influential strand in the study of the South African printsphere introduces the rubric of the 'captive press' as a way of naming the form of the white-supervised/black-edited periodical as distinct from those with more editorial independence (Switzer 1988: 351–3; Switzer 1997: 189–212). The rubric of capture, implying behind-the-scenes control, invites attention to the ways in which black editors and contributors might have negotiated or evaded regulation through a range of tactics such as avoidance of controversial issues, 'trivial' content or intermittent risk-taking. In short, the idea of capture provokes interest both in the specific interpellative practices and formulas these periodicals employed – the forms they took and the legitimacy they were able to secure – as well as in the multiple ways in which the official transcript may have been destabilised or revoked.

Against the idea of capture, we propose a reading of these periodicals as a form of colonial entanglement, a genre which merges voices and interests which may have appeared to be at odds with each other but were able to collaborate in the process of creating the black public sphere. The unequal power nexus inscribed in this form is best understood in terms of partial or strategic alignments and significant common ground. The evidence suggests that power was constantly negotiated rather than flowing in one direction, thus questioning assumptions about the docile black editor and the dominant white funder. This is especially seen in the papers' polyvocality and multilingualism: many interests were represented in these papers. A close reading of the early years of *Umteteli wa Bantu* and *Bantu World* thus leads us to a more nuanced understanding of the colonial periodical as comprising complex, contradictory allegiances and unexpected performative effects.

These tensions in the twentieth-century newspaper world were set in motion in the nineteenth century with the arrival of the printing press, which established written material which was used for the purpose of Christian missionary work. This resulted in the emergence of a variety of missionary periodicals in the mid-nineteenth century. Figures such as Reverend Tiyo Soga became one of the leading contributors to *Indaba*

(Jordan 1973: 39). Amongst his contemporaries were figures such as William Gqoba, Elijah Makiwane and John Tengo Jabavu in the Eastern Cape region. Other newspapers which emerged during this early period include the Morija-based *Leselinyana la Lesotho*. This burgeoning press in the latter half of the nineteenth century is directly linked to the networks which were being established through letter-writing and travel by missionary-educated Africans who were first- and second-generation Christians.[4] By the time *Umteteli wa Bantu* and *Bantu World* are established, they are part of a tradition of the black press and a growing public sphere.

As suggested, the wider colonial printsphere in early twentieth-century South Africa – sectarian, unequal and racialised – comprised a diverse assortment of publications including various examples of the white capitalist press, popular magazines and a number of mission-linked periodicals. Alternative perspectives were voiced in a range of publications associated with the Communist Party, the Industrial and Commercial Workers' Union (ICU) and the African National Congress. In short, black newspapers of various political perspectives operated on the margins of an inhospitable, even hostile, settler-dominated public sphere, one in which even moderate black publications like *Umteteli* and *Bantu World* were regarded with suspicion and subject to routine state scrutiny.[5]

Umteteli wa Bantu

Umteteli wa Bantu, a weekly newspaper funded by the Johannesburg Chamber of Mines – in particular its recruiting arm, the Native Recruiting Corporation (NRC) – was launched in the aftermath of a mineworkers' strike as a counter to the growing influence of radical ideas (Switzer and Switzer 1979: 7, 110). Also pertinent to the story of the newspaper's founding is that, early in 1919, the Acting Chairman of the NRC Finance Committee Mr F. G. A. Roberts had been approached by 'certain prominent natives' with regard to the necessity of establishing a moderate black paper and requesting financial assistance (Chamber of Mines 1919). Recognising the potential of such a paper – although not acceding to the request for a loan, or the independence that this implied – the Chamber of Mines approved the formation of a 'native newspaper' in February 1919. This was to be managed by NRC assistant secretary Harold Mayer.[6] An account of the newspaper's origins which appeared in *Umteteli* also gives prominence to the role of African agents, suggesting that it 'was due to their urgent representations that this paper was launched' (Editorial 1924a, *Umteteli*: 2). On this basis, it is plausible to conclude that *Umteteli* represented a strategic alignment with, rather than conflict of interests between, a group of black political leaders and white agents of the mining industry, both of whom were anxious to mitigate an emergent black radicalism. The question of oversight in *Umteteli* was also complicated by a division of labour between the white managing director and the black editor which would appear to have granted a measure of editorial independence (Erlank 2019: 84). In the first year, however, as the archive suggests, 'nearly all leading articles' were written by Mayer himself, a fact which was obscured by the appearance of the names John Langalibalele Dube and Sol Plaatje on the newspaper's masthead from May to August 1920 (Chamber of Mines 1921).[7]

In the first ten years of the newspaper's existence, this alignment of interests is evident in a strong antipathy for radical politics and 'mere citations of grievance' (Anon. 1921a, *Umteteli*: 2) including Marcus Garvey's 'Back to Africa' movement, the Communist

Party, the ICU (and its various splinter groups), and the Transvaal branch of the African National Congress (TNC) and its newssheet, *Abantu-Batho*. Also subject to sustained editorial harassment, across the English- and African-language pages, are various movements of radical prophecy and their leaders. Further points of convergence between white capital and the editorial line are to be found in *Umteteli*'s support of moderate, constitutional opposition and the ideology of race reconciliation as well as in its open hostility for the black labouring class, frequently characterised as indolent and irrational (Editorial 1920c, *Umteteli*: 2; Editorial 1924b, *Umteteli*: 2). A year after the launch of the paper, the NRC Finance Committee reported on the excellent work the paper had done to counteract radical thought: as the Chairman reported, 'the propaganda work carried on in the *Umteteli wa Bantu* had practically given the death blow to the [TNC]' (Chamber of Mines 1920b).[8]

Umteteli's offensive against political radicalism was pursued within a primary understanding of the colonial periodical as the repetitive induction of potentially wayward readers into decorous politics and appropriate affect. As such it promoted the value of social responsibility and race cooperation against race hatred and 'vituperous and inflammatory speeches' (Anon. 1920c, *Umteteli*: 2). *Umteteli* lists as its aims 'the development of the mind [of the 'Native'] and the direction of his thought' and asserts its commitment 'to demonstrate the respective duties and obligations of workers and bosses' (Anon. 1920b, *Umteteli*: 6). Central to this project was the larger-than-life editor, Abner Mapanya, whose public decisions on proper content are a conspicuous element of the newspaper page from the early 1920s until his retirement at the end of the decade.[9] Attention to the formal arrangements of the periodical itself — a broadsheet format favouring dense print and the long vertical line over sectioned layout — reveals the extent to which this personality-driven pedagogy was imprinted in newspaper form. It is also evident in the predominance of comment and opinion rather than news reportage, the melding of news and commentary, as well as the rhetorical positioning of the editor as visible channel of news.

Also important were the ubiquitous editorial genres of footnoting, prefacing, glossing and 'Notes to Correspondents'. In these paratextual genres, the editor calls readers' attention to particular items, admonishes readers for their illogical arguments and ungrammatical speech, and rationalises his decisions to censor their letters. These heavy-handed editorial interventions — directed as much at grammatical lapses as at radical politics — speak to one version of the colonial periodical as intolerant pedagogic project designed to show its readers the error of their ways. In *Umteteli*, the editorial paratext is an explicit performance of authority: working against the democratic potential of newspaper form, the editor sought to impose a singular, dominant perspective as a way of controlling and curating an unpredictable public debate. Against assumptions of editorial docility, Mapanya emerges as an active, authoritative, even powerful, agent who used the opportunity provided by the paper to advance his moderate, law-abiding politics.

Further complicating the idea of the 'captive' press is the surprisingly direct and authoritative tone of the English-language editorials. Despite what might be described as a moderate, even conformist, pro-capitalist stance, the editor is strikingly outspoken, non-deferential and dismissive of white officialdom. The newspaper includes frequent attacks on South African politicians, colonial officials, respected clerics and adjacent white newspapers, particularly *The Star* and the *Rand Daily Mail*. Under

Mapanya's direction, white speech is deployed not as authoritative treatise but rather as sounding board, point of departure and opportunity for vigorous rebuttal. By placing white speech under scrutiny, the newspaper extends its pedagogical oversight to white authorities and the colonial order they represent. This paradoxical editorial stance may be an example of what Stephanie Newell describes as the 'contradictions of existing "after Empire"' (Newell 2013: 53); what is also indicated is that a strategic alignment with white capital did not preclude an aptitude for irreverence and critique.

Further, despite its persistent efforts to school its readers into decorous politics, the periodical also gave extensive space to radical voices themselves, this through lengthy, often extravagant, quotation and republication of articles. Thus Marcus Garvey's provocative call for white expulsion, for example, appears in bold italic font on the prominent editorial page: 'We shall not ask England, France, Italy and Belgium "why are you here?" We shall only command them to get out' (Editorial 1920b, *Umteteli*: 2). Similarly, Clements Kadalie's speech calling for the building 'of an African national labour organisation' to 'break the wall of white autocracy and capitalism' is quoted at length (Anon. 1925a, *Umteteli*: 2), as is Communist Party of South Africa member Sidney Bunting's call to boycott the visit of Prince George (Anon. 1925b, *Umteteli*: 4).[10]

The faithful reproduction of radical speech may have been understood as an attempt to expose the dangers of irrational hyperbole. Nevertheless, by quoting radical commentators, the paper also opened an unexpected space for the dissemination of alternative views, many of which were given editorial-page prominence. One possible reading of this paradox is that the obligation of the periodical form to broadcast contemporary news – to 'make public' – also tended to work against its censorious pedagogy. Thus the pressures exerted by the genre itself – particularly its composite arrangements and the inclusion of accessed voices, reported speeches and republished articles – pushed the paper to include political perspectives which it was also at pains to reject.

Despite all these efforts to direct the discussion along the lines of political moderation, the English sections of the paper were immediately seized by a number of intellectual-activist figures, including Henry Tyamzashe, Allison Champion and Kadalie, who used the publicity the periodical afforded to develop a much more radical critique of South African racial capitalism, specifically questioning colonial falsehoods such as the 'dignity of labour', the 'happy Native' and British 'justice and fairplay', while also highlighting racial discrimination, worker exploitation and everyday state violence. In this way, a mine-owned periodical played host to a range of anti-capitalist, pro-worker arguments, while also developing an important incipient critique of both white liberal intervention and colonial rule. The most prominent space for this kind of engagement was the popular genre of the Letter to the Editor. In this space, readers frequently broke conventional readerly codes of conduct – such as respectful salutation ('Dear Sir', 'Mhleli') and ritualised permission-seeking – to express anger, despair and bitterness, and to call the editor to account.

What is suggested by the degree of radical interjection in this paper is the way in which the colonial periodical was also shaped by readers themselves, thus also undoing conventional distinctions between editorial production and reader consumption (Newell 2013: 46) and further complicating distinctions between the moderate and 'anti-colonial' press. In particular, the problem of the censorious editor was frequently taken up and resisted by readers themselves. In open defiance of the editorial commandment, the paper was subject to persistent and often hostile scrutiny of its 'compromised' allegiances and its role as a tool of white capital (Kadalie 1926: 3; Anon. 1921c, *Umteteli*: 4). The evidence, throughout the 1920s, of robust public debate suggests that readers exerted pressure on the original design of the paper as pedagogic containment, thus also rejecting their interpellation as docile recipients of authoritative instruction.

A close reading of the Nguni sections of the paper suggest that there were similar complexities in the African-language sections. While there are similarities in content with the English sections, there are also new genres which appear in the African languages which stretch the possibilities of the paper. As in Maria Suriano and Portia Sifelani's work on *Bantu World* (2021), we focus on the Nguni languages rather than Sotho and Tswana, which also need attention. The first editorial in *Umteteli* on 1 May 1920 is worthy of analysis as it is an introduction to readers and an invitation to be part of the community of readers being created. The title of the editorial is simple: 'Siyanibulisa' ('We Greet You'; see Figure 22.1). The isiXhosa editorial describes the paper as the birth of a new baby, something which is already part of an important conversation. It also includes a list stating the intentions of the paper:

Abantu bafundiswe imisebenzi,	People will be taught about work,
Kupakanyiswe ingqondo yabo, ingcinga zabo zikokelwe ngemfanelo.	To elevate their thinking so their thoughts may be directed accordingly.
Banikwe indaba zalemihla ngendlela elula enomkita.	People will be given daily news in a way that is easy and of interest.
Benekelwe indaba zelizwe zingadityaniswa nobukwele namabango amaqela ngamaqela.	To be given national news without jealousy and claims about other groups (organisations).
Kubekwe pambi kwaba Ntsundu ezozinto ezijonge ubulungisa nokupapamela inqubela pambili.	To place before black people issues that look towards goodness and encourage success.
Bafundiswe, banikwe amabakala kowazi ukungcina impilo yabo.	People will be taught and given advice about their health.
Bacazelwe imfanelo epakati kosebenzayo nosetyenzelwayo.	People will be shown their responsibilities as employees and employers.
Kuziswe umoya wokuvana pakati komlungu noNtsundu.	This paper will foster a spirit of harmony between white and black people.
Ngokufupi, ipepa lincokela umzi indaba, babone abantu okokuba lingumhlobo wabo.	In short, this paper will share news with the people so that people can see that the paper is their friend. (Editorial 1920a, *Umteteli*: 3)

This introduction positions not only the newspaper but also the imagined reader. Interestingly, the newspaper does not include an editorial in English and on page seven there appears an editorial in seTswana. However, on 15 May, an English editorial appears with similar ideas. The use of African languages to introduce the newspaper points towards an understanding of African languages as reaching the readers in a way English cannot. The paper becomes an undoubtedly African paper speaking to Africans in their languages. This is the case throughout many editions of the newspaper where there is at times a translation of the English news into African languages, and at times there is

Figure 22.1 *Umteteli wa Bantu*, 1 May 1920, p. 3. Courtesy of the National Library of South Africa, Cape Town.

content only in African languages which is not available in English. This further raises questions about the kind of reader imagined: are they multilingual? Can they read all the languages represented in the paper? What are the consequences of these distinctions for how information is curated? While the African-language sections offer international news, the bulk of the content is directed towards local issues, mainly through the genres of the essay and social gossip. International news in African languages is often a translation from the English rather than a divergence. While the advertisements for remedies and chemists are in both English and African languages, the advice on health – 'Health Notes' – appears only in English. Given the power dynamics of English and what it represents, the advice on hygiene and the body thus acquires a different status to the advertisements for the remedies and chemists. This can also be read as an unresolved tension in the newspaper in relation to what is translated and what is not. Translation patterns in the newspaper are also connected to power and the ways in which African languages are being used to employ a discourse suitable for the newspaper.

It is important to note that this editorial follows a full front-page advertisement in isiXhosa and English for health remedies and financial services – which fall under the heading 'Gcina Imali Yako' ('Save Your Money') – along with an advert for a clothing shop. One could read these items as forming the elements of a modern, urbanised black subject: ensuring a healthy body which can contribute to the labour market, and providing the clothes which will distinguish these workers from their 'uncivilised life' in the rural areas. The paper therefore becomes the representation of urban consumer culture, one in which the newspaper takes central place. The use of African languages in advertising creates a different register which reinforces the construction of black urban modernity.

The front and back cover of the first edition of *Umteteli* (and subsequent editions) positions readers in relation to the growing consumer culture which, as Hlonipha Mokoena has shown, was being established in urban centres. These genres are part of what create, recreate and imagine the black urban reader. Mokoena characterises this as textual density and argues that multilingual newspapers should be read as 'an almanac of African letters' (Mokoena 2020: 456). The number of products present in the paper give a sense of the kind of consumption which was being made available to the readers in order for them to participate in the life of the city. This act of translation and creating new products, which will be familiar to the African-language readers, expands the work of the paper beyond simply delivering news.

This expansive discourse is not only in advertising but also in the genres available in the paper. Starting in the second week of the paper, there is a serialised essay by Saul Msane. This is acknowledged as a posthumous account of his work and introduced as a way to commemorate his involvement as one of the people involved in initiating the paper. Entitled 'Intlalo yaba Ntsundu eSouth Africa' ('The Life of a Black Person in South Africa'), the essays offer a lyrical account of South African political and social history. The essays are described as 'yinyaniso yonk le, kwaye kungekho mathandabuzo ukuti ayinakupikwa' ('this is all truth and there's no doubt or disagreement') (Anon. 1920a, *Umteteli*: 3), thus giving them authority as accounts of black life. This is an unusual genre which does not appear in the same way in the English pages. The essays are written in isiXhosa and offer reflections on the conditions of black people in relation to the political changes and the new, discriminatory laws introduced. The essays also speak to black leaders as those in power, and suggest ideas about how to navigate the new power structures.

A further example of the heterogeneity of the African-language pages can be found in how praise poetry emerges in the paper in ways that it does not appear in English. Nontsizi Mgqwetho's poetry, which also appeared in *Abantu-Batho*, is a genre that dominates the pages in the 1920s and could also be seen as 'intlalo yaba Ntsundu eSouth Africa' in poetic form. It is significant not only because of how prolific she was but also because of the ways in which she reconfigured the genre of traditional praise poetry for the new periodical format. The inclusion of these genres in African languages offers not only a range of content but also a textured newspaper that is not as homogeneous as it is in English. The rest of the African-language pages are divided into sections such as 'Izinto ngezinto' ('News Tit-Bits'), essays, reader letters to the editor, gossip sections, advice columns and serialised literature which echoes the English pages.

Bantu World

Launched in 1932, the weekly *Bantu World* represented an informal coalition between commercial-advertising interests and several Johannesburg liberals who hoped to enhance race relations and encourage a more moderate politics through a range of activities and institutions. R. V. Selope Thema, a graduate of Lovedale College in the Eastern Cape, took on the editorship of the paper from its inception, having switched allegiance from *Abantu-Batho*. A member of the more radical Transvaal National Congress (TNC), he fell under the influence of the ideas of James Aggrey and the welfare work of Johannesburg liberals, becoming more and more convinced of the 'possibility of different races and cultures working together' in the interests of gradual political change (Thema 2016: 83). Working in this vein, *Bantu World* set an ameliorative political agenda through an explicit pedagogy of restraint, alongside the repetitive articulation of liberal race reconciliation and welfarist paradigms.

The newspaper's moderate politics, based on the importance of 'making the most of opportunities' rather than 'nursing grievances' (Anon. 1934a, *Bantu*: 8), was explicitly framed within Booker T. Washington's self-help ideology and the discourse of race reconciliation. In the English sections of the paper, these aims were summarised as follows: 'to humanise and harmonise the relations between White and Black in a manner that will be beneficial to both' (Anon. 1933, *Bantu*: 1), thus establishing the periodical as part of a web of liberal-paternalist institutions including the Joint Council movement, the Bantu Men's Social Centre and the Institute for Race Relations, all of which were focused on arousing favourable white opinion through the demonstration of African goodwill.

In *Bantu World*, the newspaper's pedagogic performance is elaborated through striking headlines, multiple subheadings and banner headings along with various kinds of editorial framing, glossing and prefacing. Headlines in bold upper-case font and straplines on each page isolate and highlight particularly important stories while also co-opting potentially wayward stories into the dominant developmentalist frame. Like *Umteteli*, the paper overrides distinctions between news reporting and opinion, with various genres of moral commentary (editorial, opinion piece, sermon, stories and 'moral talks') taking precedence over conventional news. Further examples of didactic form are to be found in the dominance of the genres of moral exhortation, feel-good stories of exemplary blackness, stories of white beneficence and sacrifice, and the genre of moral-diplomatic political appeal. Making up the bulk of the newspaper content – and working in tandem with the ubiquitous genre of middle-class portraiture – these discourses do important work in prescribing appropriate emotional registers and political behaviour while also confirming contemporary understandings of the colonial periodical as moral signpost or guide, a paper which points 'the way of salvation' (Anon. 1932c, *Bantu*: 1).

The practice of editorial glossing, while not as prominent as in *Umteteli*, formed an important part of *Bantu World*'s didactic project. Operating in a threshold zone between newspaper print and reader, the editorial paratext attempts to cue readers into a privileged interpretation, thus also highlighting the processes of editorial curatorship that usually remain hidden. While this genre is a relatively consistent feature of the black colonial periodical in this period, it could take a more or less insistent form: where Mapanya's approach was openly censorious, confrontational and commanding, Thema's approach was more circumspect. As in *Umteteli*, editorial glossing was usually seized as an opportunity to script appropriate politics and affect as part of a respectable race performance. In a preface to a letter from J. G. Coka on violence in black townships, for example, readers are advised to 'give grievances a holiday, forget the white man' and concentrate on problems in the black community. An editorial preface to a poem by S. H. Maloy, 'Toil on Ye Africans', asserts, 'In the following poem, Mr Maloy urges Africans to "toil on" in spite of the many disabilities under which they labour ... "No nation" the poet says, has become great without passing through the same crucible' (Anon. 1934b, *Bantu*: 9). In this way, Maloy's poem is aligned with the general Christian truism of the value of endurance; it is also explicitly linked to a prominent editorial perspective on colonial conquest as a necessary trauma on the route to black modernity (Thema 2016: 32). At the same time, aspects of the poem – such as the image of 'devouring foes', the idea of Africa as 'cursed', and references to the ICU – are more in keeping with contemporary traditions of radical resistance and therefore slightly at odds with the editorial gloss (Maloy 1934: 9). This example of the editorial paratext as a mode of attempted containment also points to one of the particular affordances of the print medium – that the juxtaposition of opposing views opens up greater space for reader negotiation and agency.

Editorial injunctions against despair are closely aligned with the periodical's emphasis on individual self-help and the virtues of hard work and resilience as part of a developmentalist teleology. In the English-language sections, what is striking is the way in which the orthodoxy of cheerful endurance in the face of adversity is also destabilised by various genres of lament, including an emergent tradition of melancholy poetry. Several contributions by Durban poet E. C. Jali in the early 1930s offer a reading of black experience as a condition of unremitting suffering and hopelessness:

> I've lost all hope, all faith and cling to Fate;
> Let good or ill come nigh and not too late,
> Make all your laws and hang me by the rope
> Or lead me to a stony mountain slope. (Jali 1932a: 4)[11]

Other contributions, drawing on the biblical book of Lamentations, reimagine black history in terms of the narrative of Jewish dispossession, suffering, wandering and exile (Dhlomo 1933a: 6; Nhlapo 1935: 8). These genres of lament form a visible contrapuntal narrative on the moderate newspaper page.

A focus on newspaper form reveals the preponderance of quotation in the English portions of the paper, the preference for 'talking genres' of various kinds (political speeches, addresses and government pronouncements), as well as a ubiquitous white presence (photographs, opinion pieces and letters). The practice of ventriloquising white speech, in particular, in keeping with the periodical's close alignment with its liberal funders, also serves to instrumentalise white authority and to stamp its presence in the paper. White citation in *Bantu World* is not just an attempt to fill up space in constrained editorial conditions but, as Leslie James writes, is also 'a kind of opportunity' presented by the genre itself (James 2016: 66). As in *Umteteli*, the harnessing of white speech provides an opportunity – in the absence of political visibility or parliamentary representation – to engage in public debate by placing critical views in the mouths of others. While providing a rare legitimacy for black political claims, this practice also guards the paper's reputation as moderate, reasoned interlocutor. *Bantu World* took a very pragmatic approach to citation: any speech was seized, no matter what the provenance, as long as it could be made to serve the editorial line. The newspaper frequently employed this device in order to speak the words of government back to itself.

Thus, white speech, rather than being offset or rivalled by other kinds of commentary, was consciously worked into and absorbed by the newspaper text.

Also at issue are the many ways in which the pedagogical project was undermined. This has to do in part with the continually evolving character of the periodical form itself, particularly the need to experiment with different genres in response to a competitive commercial climate, to establish influence and to attract new readers (Barber 2016: 151–7). As in *Umteteli*, the genre of the Letter to the Editor remained a potentially volatile and uncontrollable part of the paper. Although not as marked as in *Umteteli*, dissonant voices are always in play despite the conservative template, with several contributors such as Aug Swartz and Stanley Silwana taking aim at the paper's promotion of race-relations discourse (Silwana 1932: 4) and the consolations of Christian suffering (Swartz 1933: 8). In the English pages, these are met with irate responses, mostly from white readers, who resorted to the tactics of shaming and deflection (Brookes 1932: 6). Unlike Mapanya, Thema could usually rely on the outrage of white privilege to carry out the work of political containment.

As suggested, newspaper form encourages stylistic and generic experimentation and is inherently elastic and transformable. Aside from its attempts to increase readership through various forms of interactivity such as beauty contests and essay-writing competitions, *Bantu World* also encouraged the emergence of several new genres. Chief amongst these was the form of the personal anecdote, a provisional and tangential form in which an observer-walker figure narrates the particulars of personal encounters and urban scenes. A pioneer in this genre is R. R. R. Dhlomo, writing under the pen name 'Roamer', whose anecdotal travels in English begin in the letters page (Dhlomo 1933a: 6), and subsequently migrate to the form of the satirical column, 'R. Roamer'. The anecdotal genre, which breaks many of the newspaper's rules of expressive decorum, is also taken up by 'Scrutator' (Thema) as well as a number of readers; this meandering, non-teleological and frequently irreverent form represents a further antidote to the newspaper's dominant pedagogy.

Bantu World's approach to including African languages is apparent in the first edition in 1932 (see Figure 22.2). The front page has a column listing how the paper is organised according to languages, where English and Afrikaans are reserved for the front-page feature, special articles and the editorial page. SeSotho and SeTswana (Suto-Chuana) have the opinion and correspondence page. IsiXhosa (Xosa) and isiZulu also have opinion and correspondence pages, and the rest of the paper has farming, labour and trade news, beginner's supplement, social notes, entertainment, music and the sports page.

In the opinion and correspondence page – 'Izimvo Zetu Nezababhaleli' – there are a variety of genres which enhance multivocality. The editorial appears to be an abridged translation of the English editorial. It is titled 'Into Esiyimeleyo' ('What We Stand For') and introduces the paper's framework by stating that 'ipepa eli lona lenzelwe isizwe esintsundu' ('this paper is for black people'). Like *Umteteli*, *Bantu World* also states its position in relation to collaboration between races as it stands for 'imvisiswano noxolo pakati kwabantsundu nabamhlophe' ('harmony and peace between black and white people') (Anon. 1932a, *Bantu*: 5). The editorial also refers to the promotion of literacy which is part of the upward mobility for the readership. The mixture of genres in this page (it includes articles about political meetings within other organisations, a report on court cases and a book review) which

Figure 22.2 *Bantu World*, 9 April 1932, p. 5. Courtesy of the National Library of South Africa, Cape Town.

lie side by side disrupts the contemporary understanding of a newspaper. Given the use of columns as a way to delineate articles, this mixture might be a design feature from the period, but the effect of it makes for interesting editorial work and leads to speculation about the editor's decision to align opinion and news together and what this reveals about the editor's choices.[12] This continues into the 'Farming, Labour and Trade News', where there is a combination of language and genres (opinion and news). This changes in subtle ways over time: while the English sections become more separated, the African-language sections continue to mix genres on one page. This is a form of hybridity in the newspaper which can be seen as an example of code-switching between language and genre. Suriano and Sifelani point to the ways in which the isiZulu sections were a vibrant space of debate which 'facilitated the creation of an expansive imagined community and played a pivotal role in the formation of a "sub-community" of Zulu-speaking writers who discussed progress-related issues' (Suriano and Sifelani 2021: 304), while also opening up the space for more open and unrestrained political critique.

Conclusion

This chapter reads the black-edited/white-funded periodical as a distinctive and commonplace genre of the colonial public sphere, and as an entangled form in which a range of interests both coalesced and diverged. In the South African context, this typical colonial genre tended to take shape as an explicitly didactic project in which the bounds of legitimate behaviour, habitus and sensibility were marked out and performed. This anxious moral pedagogy, accompanied by a conspicuous editorial hand, suggests that the work of political containment and moral pedagogy was as important for black newspapermen as projects of anti-racist or anti-colonial resistance. Central to this argument are the ways in which these pedagogic practices are elaborated in newspaper form through various modes of the editorial paratext; of equal importance are the ways in which newspaper form also incites destabilisation and resistance. This textual ambiguity is particularly evident in the papers' multilingual and multigeneric formats: the presence of African languages not only affirms the centrality of the African language but also opens up even greater opportunities for textual experimentation and rhetorical and generic diversity. The translation process as well as the inclusion of new genres such as poetry stretches the possibilities of the paper as it becomes a multivocal text. The heteroglossic, multi-modal form of the newspaper encourages the inclusion of incompatible registers and a proliferation of genres leading to a dissonant, non-consensual and heterogeneous discourse, one which makes it difficult to locate even the nominally moderate newspaper within a clear political frame.

Notes

1. This chapter works with the loose conception of the periodical form and avoids hard-and-fast distinctions between the newspaper and the periodical. See King et al. 2016: 4–5; Vann and VanArsdel 1996: 8.
2. For a similar point, see Hunter 2016: 283–4.
3. See Newell 2013: 51–3 on the genre of 'Notes to Correspondents' in West African newspapers.
4. See Chapter 6 by Lize Kriel, Annika Vosseler and Chantelle Finaughty.
5. *Umteteli* made several appearances in parliamentary debates (Anon. 1924, *Umteteli*: 3; Editorial 1924a, *Umteteli*: 2; Editorial 1925, *Umteteli*: 2).
6. Harold Mayer was appointed Managing Director in April 1920 (Chamber of Mines 1920b). According to Mweli Skota, it was John Dube, Saul Msane, Isaiah Bud M'Belle and Marshall Maxeke who made the initial approach to the Chamber of Mines (cited in Limb 2012: 320). See also Willan 2018: 371–3.
7. See also Chamber of Mines 1920a.
8. See also the Chamber of Mines Minutes of 6 June 1920 and 24 June 1920.
9. Mapanya was never formally acknowledged as editor; he is referred to as such in several newspaper inserts.
10. For examples of hostile reporting on the ICU in *Umteteli*, see Johnson and Dee 2022: 84–6, 131–3, 141–2, 146–8, 155–8.
11. See also Jali 1932b: 2 and Jali 1933: 9.
12. For similar practices in *Umteteli*, see Erlank 2019: 77, 94.

Bibliography

Anon. (1932a), *Bantu World*, 9 April, 5.
—— (1932b), *Bantu World*, 18 June, 9.
—— (1932c), *Bantu World*, 22 October, 1.

—— (1933), *Bantu World*, 11 March, 1.
—— (1934a), *Bantu World*, 24 March, 8.
—— (1934b), *Bantu World*, 27 October, 9.
—— (1920a), *Umteteli wa Bantu*, 8 May, 3.
—— (1920b), *Umteteli wa Bantu*, 15 May, 6.
—— (1920c), *Umteteli wa Bantu*, 5 June, 2.
—— (1921a), *Umteteli wa Bantu*, 18 June, 2.
—— (1921b), *Umteteli wa Bantu*, 14 August, 2.
—— (1921c), *Umteteli wa Bantu*, 31 December, 4.
—— (1924), *Umteteli wa Bantu*, 23 August, 3.
—— (1925a), *Umteteli wa Bantu*, 18 April, 2.
—— (1925b), *Umteteli wa Bantu*, 2 May, 4.
Barber, Karin (2016), 'Experiments with genre in Yoruba newspapers of the 1920s', in Derek R. Peterson, Emma Hunter and Stephanie Newell (eds), *African Print Cultures: Newspapers and their Publics in the Twentieth Century*, Ann Arbor: Michigan University Press, 151–78.
Barnhurst, Kevin. G., and John Nerone (2001), *The Form of News: A History*, New York: Guilford Press.
Brookes, Edgar (1932), 'Letter to the Editor', *Bantu World*, 24 September, 6.
Chamber of Mines (1919), Finance Committee Minutes, 20 February, University of Johannesburg Special Collections, The Employment Bureau of Africa Ltd (TEBA) NRC File, File 64A.
—— (1920a), Finance Committee Minutes, 12 January, University of Johannesburg Special Collections, TEBA NRC File, File 64A.
—— (1920b), Finance Committee Minutes, 19 April, University of Johannesburg Special Collections, TEBA NRC File, File 64A.
—— (1921), Finance Committee Minutes, 24 June, University of Johannesburg Special Collections, TEBA NRC File, File 64A.
Couzens, Tim (1976), 'The black press and black literature in South Africa, 1900–1950', *English Studies in Africa*, 19.2, 93–9.
Dhlomo, R. R. R. [R. Roamer] (1933a), 'Letter', *Bantu World*, 14 January, 6.
—— (1933b), 'What Roamer Sees About Town', *Bantu World*, 1 July, 8.
Editorial (1920a), *Umteteli wa Bantu*, 1 May, 2.
—— (1920b), *Umteteli wa Bantu*, 14 August, 2.
—— (1920c), *Umteteli wa Bantu*, 4 September, 2.
—— (1924a), *Umteteli wa Bantu*, 30 August, 2.
—— (1924b), *Umteteli wa Bantu*, 18 October, 2.
—— (1925), *Umteteli wa Bantu*, 4 April, 2.
Erlank, Natasha (2019), '*Umteteli wa Bantu* and the constitution of social publics in the 1920s and 1930s', *Social Dynamics*, 45.1, 75–102.
Hunter, Emma (2016), 'Komkya and the convening of a Chagga public, 1953–1961', in Derek R. Peterson, Emma Hunter and Stephanie Newell (eds), *African Print Cultures: Newspapers and their Publics in the Twentieth Century*, Ann Arbor: Michigan University Press, 283–305.
Jali, E. C. (1932a), 'Despair', *Bantu World*, 21 May, 4.
—— (1932b), 'The Poet Looks Back', *Bantu World*, 17 September, 2.
—— (1933), 'The Poet's Defiance', *Bantu World*, 4 February, 9.
James, Leslie (2016), 'Transatlantic passages: Black identity construction in West African and West Indian newspapers, 1935–1950', in Derek R. Peterson, Emma Hunter and Stephanie Newell (eds), *African Print Cultures: Newspapers and their Publics in the Twentieth Century*, Ann Arbor: Michigan University Press, 49–74.
Johnson, David, and Henry Dee (eds) (2022), *'I See You': The Industrial and Commercial Workers' Union of South Africa, 1919–1930*, Cape Town: HiPSA.

Jordan, A. C. (1973), *Towards an African Literature: The Emergence of Literary Form in Xhosa*, Oakland: University of California Press.
Kadalie, Clements (1926), 'Letter to the Editor', *Umteteli wa Bantu*, 18 September, 3.
King, Andrew, Alexis Easley and John Morton (2016), 'Introduction', in Andrew King, Alexis Easley and John Morton (eds), *The Routledge Handbook to Nineteenth-Century British Periodicals and Newspapers*, London: Routledge, 1–14.
Limb, Peter (ed.) (2012), *The People's Paper: A Centenary History and Anthology of Abantu-Batho*, Johannesburg: Wits University Press.
Maloy, S. H. (1934), 'Toil on Ye Africans', *Bantu World*, 27 October, 9.
Mokoena, Hlonipha (2020), '"The hardness of the times and the dearness of all the necessaries of life": Class and consumption in bilingual nineteenth-century newspapers', *Social History*, 45.4, 453–75.
Newell, Stephanie (2013), *The Power to Name: A History of Anonymity in Colonial West Africa*, Athens: Ohio University Press.
—— (2016), 'Paradoxes of press freedom in colonial West Africa', *Media History*, 22.1, 101–22.
Nhlapo, Walter (1935), 'Letter to the Editor', *Bantu World*, 17 August, 8.
Peterson, Derek R., Emma Hunter and Stephanie Newell (eds) (2016), *African Print Cultures: Newspapers and their Publics in the Twentieth Century*, Ann Arbor: University of Michigan Press.
Silwana, Stanley (1932), 'Letter to Editor', *Bantu World*, 10 September, 4.
Suriano, Maria, and Portia Sifelani (2021), 'Unsettling the ranks: 1930s Zulu-language writings on African progress and unity in *The Bantu World*', *African Studies*, 80.3–4, 287–309.
Swartz, Aug (1933), 'Letter to Editor', *Bantu World*, 15 July, 8.
Switzer, Les (1988), '*Bantu World* and the origins of a captive African commercial press in South Africa', *Journal of Southern African Studies*, 14.3, 351–70.
—— (1997), '*Bantu World* and the origins of a captive commercial press', in Les Switzer (ed.), *South Africa's Alternative Press: Voices of Protest and Resistance, 1880–1960*, Cambridge: Cambridge University Press, 189–212.
—— and Donna Switzer (1979), *The Black Press in South Africa and Lesotho: A Descriptive Bibliographic Guide to African, Coloured and Indian Newspapers, Newsletters and Magazines, 1836–1976*, Boston: G. K. Hall.
Thema, Richard Victor Selope (2016), *From Cattle-Herding to Editor's Chair: The Unfinished Autobiography and Writings of Richard Victor Selope Thema*, ed. Alan Cobley, Cape Town: Van Riebeeck Society.
Vann, J. Don, and Rosemary VanArsdel (1996), 'Introduction', in J. Don Vann and Rosemary VanArsdel (eds), *Periodicals of Queen Victoria's Empire: An Exploration*, Toronto: University of Toronto Press, 3–18.
Willan, Brian (2018), *Sol Plaatje: A Life of Solomon Tshekiso Plaatje 1876–1932*, Johannesburg: Jacana.

Part IV

Trans-Colonial Connections in Colonial Periodicals

23

Samuel Revans and Company: Colonial Commercial Trade Newspapers in the Age of Responsible Government

Melodee H. Wood

Introduction

In 1833, Samuel Revans and Henry Chapman, boyhood friends from Lambeth who had both been clerks and merchants in Canada, founded the first daily publication in Montreal, the *Daily Advertiser*. After eighteen months of publication in an environment of rising political tensions, Chapman returned to England, followed later by Revans, where both were actively involved in colonial and parliamentary reform. In 1839, the New Zealand Company's ships set sail to establish their first colonial settlement; Samuel Revans and his new Columbia press were on board. For the next four years, Revans published the *New Zealand Gazette and Wellington Spectator*, the first newspaper in the colony, until disposing of his ownership in 1844 to return to full-time mercantile pursuits. The *Daily Advertiser* has been labelled as a radical newspaper in the service of Papineau, leader of the Patriotes Rebellion in Lower Canada. The *New Zealand Gazette* has been dismissed as a blunt instrument of Wakefield's New Zealand Company. Previous scholarship has mischaracterised the nature of both publications – and failed to understand their similar practical focus on economic development – through flawed extrapolations from their editors' biographies and personal beliefs.

This chapter re-examines the content of these two newspapers to reassess their historical role within the colonial newspaper press. It will begin with a discussion of the current discourse around these publications and the reasons for their mischaracterisation. It will examine their structures and editorial styles to demonstrate how both their stated remits and their content have been misunderstood. Finally, it will analyse the way these two men – particularly Revans – were able to produce two consistently commercial rather than political newspapers, aimed at promoting the economic development of their respective colonies.

Assuming Newspaper Content from an Editor's Reputation

Discussions of the *Advertiser* and the *Gazette* appear most often in semi-biographical works on Chapman and Revans. The *Advertiser* is featured most prominently in discussions of Henry Chapman and the most frequent depiction originates in the 1972 work of R. S. Neale, who hoped to 'rescue Chapman from oblivion' through his case studies of nineteenth-century radicalism (Neale 2016: 76). His brief description of the *Advertiser* drew from a small number of newspaper articles, published writings and family papers, but his citations are undetailed and often glib (Neale 2016: 180, n. 3). Neale characterises Chapman as a young man whose conflicting aspirations and economic status led to dissatisfaction and a complete commitment to ultra-Radicalism (Neale 2016: 81). Twenty years later, Peter Spiller's biography, *The Chapman Legal Family*, expands this portrayal with additional reflective and political writings from Chapman himself, though his description of the *Advertiser* remains that it was used to 'expose and criticise abuses of economic and political power and to promote the politico-economic principles of philosophical radicalism' (Spiller 1992: 21). To support these claims, he draws from Neale and retrospective details from Chapman's later writings. Almost all other mentions of the *Advertiser* are brief notices of its existence, with the radical label firmly attached, in discussions that cite Neale and Spiller (Woollacott 2011: 83; Spiller and Woollacott 2015: 109). Even in biographies of Revans, descriptions of the newspaper are brief and do not deviate from the narrative laid out by Neale. The radical nature of the newspaper is taken as common knowledge.

A similar fate has befallen the *Gazette*. Its role as the first newspaper in New Zealand has ensured its mention in the history of early settlement. However, discussions of the precise details of its foundation and management have been scarce, one notable exception is Patrick Day, who speaks of both Revans and the *Gazette* in a tightly woven narrative about the political framework of the New Zealand press and its rocky relationship with the colonial government and the New Zealand Company (Day 1985: 43–50). As with discussions of the *Advertiser* itself, Revans's personal beliefs, and their influence on the newspaper, are inferred from biographical details, complaints from rival publications, and the fact of the *Gazette*'s debt to the New Zealand Company.[1] In contrast to these press histories, commemorative biographies of Revans are more nuanced in their discussion of his opinions but provide little to no support for their characterisations of the *Gazette* itself (Fyfe and Fyfe 1985; Robertson 1989). In general, these portray a man of limited means, but of solid education and significant ambition, who took an interest in the 'philosophy of a number of young radicals' as a response to the general economic depression of his youth, and who, from an inferred apprenticeship, learned the printing trade and was called upon by his like-minded childhood friend to found a radical newspaper (Fyfe 1993: 5; Robertson 1989: 6–7).

The standard characterisation of the *Advertiser* as a vehicle for radical political agitation and of the *Gazette* as the opposite, a pro-establishment newspaper in support of the New Zealand Company, are both derived from a narrow selection of editorials on political issues and an overstatement of the complaints of their rivals. That both Revans and Chapman were political agitators is not contested; however, the relationship between their political agitation and their newspapers is problematic given alternative interpretations of, and inconsistencies within, the content when taken as a whole.

It is well documented that both Revans and Chapman personally supported Henry Arthur Roebuck in his work with the Parti patriote in Lower Canada as well as with parliamentary reform in Great Britain; their most cited publication is explicitly dedicated to him (Chapman and Revans 1834). However, the claim that Revans and Chapman 'made the pages of the *Daily Advertiser* open to Papineau and his Radical supporters' and penned 'powerful and bitter' editorials in his favour appears tenuous, relying on its final issue rather than its overall character.[2]

Moreover, these biographers interpret the motivations behind the same editorials very differently. Neale ascribes commentaries on the mistreatment of immigrants and the value of systematic colonisation to Chapman and his personal 'belief that it would destroy the economic basis of aristocratic privilege' with careful truncation and paraphrasing of the material to create this interpretation. Robertson attributes the same piece to Revans and his 'enthusiastic' support of Wakefield's system of colonisation.[3] Inferences such as these are understandable, given that Neale believed that only the final six months of the *Advertiser* still existed in hard copy at the time of his writing and that both Neale and Robertson ascribed its editorship to solely either Chapman or Revans (Neale 2016: 180, n. 7). Nonetheless, these inferences are unsustainable in light of the wider publication, wherein commentaries on immigration and colonisation tend to be commercially focused.

As for the *Gazette*, the indivisibility of Revans's reputation as a 'controversial journalist' in Montreal with the aims of his Wellington newspaper is often taken as read (Tye 1996: 209–10; Coleridge 1990: 89). In various essays on the early New Zealand press, Kathleen Coleridge provides a catalogue of biographical sketches, including several of Revans, his editors and printers, and their presumed radical tendencies, family connections and future behaviour, using these as evidence of the radical atmosphere of the *Gazette*'s office (Coleridge 1986: 66–7, 70–1; Coleridge 1990: 89–94). She focuses explicitly on the character of the men behind the presses, rather than the newspapers themselves, and from this extrapolates the nature of the publications without any detailed engagement in their content. In contrast, both Patrick Day and Struan Robertson do examine the printed editorials, and both suggest Revans used the *Gazette* to discuss his personal opinions on the state of the Wellington settlement, though they frame the nature of these opinions differently. Day concludes that Revans provided a 'one-sided and exaggeratedly pro-New Zealand Company understanding of affairs in Wellington' (Day 1985: 45–6). Although he concedes that this was a willing obsequiousness, he also argues that Revans's view was unrepresentative of the growing discontent of the settlers and that the *Gazette* was immediately punished by the officers of the Company when its new owner took a more critical stance, suggesting that the control of the Company over the *Gazette* was real and powerful (Day 1990: 30–2). On the other hand, Robertson concludes that Revans held and promoted a consistent and directed stance against Governor Hobson, rather than a pro-Company one (Robertson 1989: 26). The two views are not contradictory, but both depict the *Gazette* as a fundamentally political rather than commercial publication and one in which the content directly reflects Revans's personal ideology and adherence to the Company line.

While the above characterisations of the *Advertiser* and the *Gazette* are relatively consistent within their own discourses, the two newspapers are portrayed as almost opposites, despite all authors agreeing that the editors shared the same beliefs, that they were consistent in these beliefs, and that their personal opinions and political connections dictated the content of the newspapers. This obvious contradiction can be seen most clearly in Robertson's biography, wherein he first describes the *Advertiser* as a commercial publication catering to the 'Montreal business community' who needed 'up-to-date information on all aspects of economic life', then immediately recasts it, without further explanation, as a vehicle for 'political comment on the English parliamentary scene from radical correspondents', and a platform of support for the local Reform Party (Robertson 1989: 9). This momentary characterisation as 'commercial' is very rare for either newspaper. In *Periodicals of Queen Victoria's Empire*, for example, N. Merrill Distad uniquely situates the *Advertiser* as part of the rise of a daily press aimed at serving commercial business. Nonetheless, he concludes that the *Advertiser* was before its time and a financial failure (Distad 1996: 69).

Meanwhile, J. Reginald Tye notes a connection between the two newspapers but, like Robertson, offers no explanation for Revans's presumed ideological *volte-face* (Tye 1996: 209). Day, for his part, concedes that newspapers such as the *Advertiser* and *Gazette* were motivated by an 'economic rationality' rather than an ideological one, but dismisses the idea that any newspaper, especially an isolated colonial publication, could afford to be apolitical, suggesting instead that profitability was a secondary consideration, a claim directly rebutted by Revans in his personal correspondence (Day 1985: 7, 11; Revans 1841f). It is this implicit and contested characterisation of both newspapers as commercial trade publications, and of Revans's aims for them, that this chapter will clarify.

Inferring an Editor's Intentions from Newspaper Content

Over the course of forty years, the biographers of Revans and Chapman, as well as a growing number of colonial press histories, have cemented an unambiguous image of both publications as the political mouthpieces of ultra-Radical and anti-government ideologues. This simplistic characterisation prevents a proper examination of their influence on the commercial development of their respective colonies and obscures how their commercial remit – rather than their editors' personal ideologies – shaped the structure, governance and legacy of these publications.

The *Advertiser*, in structure, content and periodicity, was holistically focused on engaging with the mercantile community of Montreal. The newspaper was published daily at 8 a.m. Included were advertisements from as late as 4 p.m. the previous afternoon, allowing for rapid dissemination and correction of commercially sensitive information (Anon. 1833a, *Daily Advertiser*: 2; Anon. 1833x, *Daily Advertiser*: 2). Like many provincial newspapers, it relied on advertising but did so to such an extent that it explicitly postponed news content in favour of inserting additional adverts, and its dissolution was ultimately blamed on loss of advertising revenue, not a lack of subscribers to its journalistic content (Anon. 1833q, *Daily Advertiser*: 3; Neale 2016: 79–80).

Moreover, the character of the advertising suggested the paper targeted a specialised audience. Rather than one to two pages of short-term advertising for consumer and wholesale products, as was typical in anglophone provincial press, the *Advertiser* typically published nearly three full pages of standing advertisements, most of which were for commodities, wholesale implements or business services, with space purchased on an annual basis. These were supplemented by extensive shipping lists, price tables and market commentaries as well as a regular 'Strangers' List' of recent arrivals, and their hotel lodgings, providing leads for sales and other business opportunities (Anon. 1833b, *Daily Advertiser*: 3).

Moreover, by its third month of publication, the *Advertiser* had become a clearing house for statistical information on immigration to North America and the American northeast. The newspaper included regular discussions of this important source of labour with several issues a week providing detailed information on immigrant shipping and the character and employability of those arriving (Anon. 1833v, *Daily Advertiser*: 2–3).

Three months into their run, the company also began publishing a *Weekly Abstract*, a digest of the *Advertiser* and 'a faithful record of facts, illustrative of the growing character of the Colony', targeting a European audience and raising their awareness of opportunities for investment, particularly in land, along the St Lawrence River (Anon. 1833n, *Daily Advertiser*: 2). Although the discussions of immigration that were featured were largely reprints from other publications, or derivative summaries, the general tenor of these was supportive, providing practical advice for both labourers and those wishing to purchase land, as well as information on conveyances – reprinting letters of praise, condemnation and rebuttals on various shipping concerns.[4] This combination of a concern for consumer rights and a supply of appropriate labour is likely why Revans submitted evidence to the House of Commons regarding emigration and the Poor Laws in 1834 (Great Britain Parliament, House of Lords 1834: 303–26). The interpretation of Neale and Spiller that Chapman's commentaries on immigration were part of his wider radical ideology fails to recognise the commercial context, and the remarkable evenhandedness, with which these issues were generally discussed in the *Advertiser*'s pages.

The news content of the newspaper ranged widely, although it was united by a common thread of the impact of the political upon the commercial, namely parliamentary and assembly debates on the lowering of tariffs, changes to banking regulations and the budget.[5] Reprints and editorials beyond commercial news still had commercial implications: discussions of emancipation and race relations in the West Indies and United States were explicitly contextualised in terms of the West Indian trade, the colonisation of Liberia – commercial rival to Britain's Sierra Leone – and the welcome influx of emancipated and runaway slaves from the United States as conscientious immigrant labour.[6]

The general thrust of these articles implied a pro-emancipatory stance from the editors, but sceptical reprints likewise appeared without commentary, offering readers a wider view of the reaction to and impact of emancipation, insofar as it would explicitly affect Atlantic trade. Pieces directly on radical or reform causes were relatively rare in 1833; those cited by Neale almost exclusively appeared in the final weeks of publication. Those that did appear largely consisted of reprinted pieces on the Coldbath Fields Riot and meetings of the Birmingham Political Union, both heavily covered in the British press.[7] Original commentary on these points was limited, with one item musing on the uncharacteristic response of certain London newspapers and providing a light-hearted note, under the heading 'Editorial Misery', that there could not have been a riot in Birmingham as an acquaintance had been able to purchase an inexpensive knife there – an item that would be dear if violence were erupting (Anon. 1833k, *Daily Advertiser*: 2; Anon. 1833i, *Daily Advertiser*: 2).

These events were ripe for radical commentary. That it did not appear suggests that it was not in the interest of the newspaper to produce it. Perhaps it would have alienated subscribers and advertisers, or perhaps it did not bear immediate relevance as commercial intelligence. In either case, it reduces the likelihood that the *Advertiser* can be characterised as a radical newspaper. Instead, original content in 1833 dealt principally with market conditions, gleaned from exchange copies, with original analysis. Alongside this we find conversational commentaries on the frequency and quality of newspaper exchange copies, as well as on the trials and tribulations of journalism, the printing business, and prospectuses for new periodicals in the colony. These ranged from musings on the 'Franklinian Fraternity' and the 'Politeness of Printers', to reprinted commentaries on press neutrality, to direct sparring with rival publications over misrepresentations of their explicitly neutral political stance, declaring that 'we are wholly unconnected with any party'.[8] These comments echo points from the first issue, where it was stated that 'we recognise no party', and the newspaper's characterisation in the 1834 *History of the British Colonies*, which listed the *Advertiser* as the only neutral newspaper in Montreal excepting the *Sun*, which contained only advertisements (Anon. 1833a, *Daily Advertiser*: 2; Montgomery 1834: 179).

Friendly banter with readers, such as notices on the installation of a new stove in the newsroom and the promise of a full review in due course, suggests an attempt to create a sense of community between local commercial traders and the commercial trade press. This was a consistent tack by Revans, even if he later suggested that he disliked filling his columns with '"chit chat"' rather than proper intelligence (Anon. 1833x, *Daily Advertiser*: 2; Revans 1841e). Neale's assertion that the content was radical is taken primarily from an editorial appearing in the final issue, which stated that the newspaper's advertisers had pulled out because

> we did not sign the petition against the Resolutions [for political reforms]; we did not denounce the [Whig newspapers] *Vindicator* and *Minerve* when they expressed their detestation of [the Governor] Lord Aylmer; we never called the Canadians all sorts of names, we never denounced the Assembly as seditious and treasonable . . . All our articles had a Radical tendency. (Neale 2016: 80)

The final line, truncated by Neale, is probably sarcastic, given the list of supposed grievances, and their previous bouts with rival publications, or exaggerated in a fit of pique following the newspaper's collapse.

Contextualising Newspaper Content with Community Concerns

Despite the newspaper's ultimate commercial failure, Revans prided himself on the skill with which it catered to the needs of the mercantile community, noting that, despite their personal political differences, '[w]e had no disputes about commerce; the merchants will do me the justice to say they never had such a commercial newspaper in the country before, nor have they since replaced it' (Great Britain Parliament, House of Commons 1835: 186). That he explicitly referred to the *Advertiser* as a commercial newspaper is not acknowledged by Neale, Spiller or the historians who cited them. The ability of Revans and Chapman to maintain this commercial enterprise for eighteen months was probably owing to both being active members of the community that they served. Despite protestations by Neale that Chapman was not a merchant in Canada, Spiller and others concede his earlier forays into trade, and he regularly advertised the sale of wholesale goods during the run of the *Advertiser*.[9] Likewise, Revans, after his original employment as a clerk in Quebec, had taken up the potash trade before concentrating his full efforts on the newspaper in 1833 (Great Britain Parliament, House of Commons 1835: 186). Chapman certainly considered Revans commercially minded, introducing him as being 'known for the extent and accuracy of his knowledge of mercantile statistics' in his pamphlet on the corn trade ('Canada Corn Trade' 1832: 365). Revans furthermore secured short-term employment with the Board of Trade before returning to Lower Canada and, in 1835, gave testimony before the House of Commons Select Committee on Timber Duties, suggesting he had built up a reputation for his ability to gather and provide analysis on commercial matters (Great Britain Parliament, House of Commons 1835: 186). There is, therefore, no reason to believe that these men were incapable of creating a commercial rather than a political publication or seeing the profitability of doing so.

Whether it was for his printing experience, or his long-standing admiration for systematic colonisation, or his personal friendships with its stakeholders, in 1839, the New Zealand Company provided Revans with partial financial support for the creation of the *New Zealand Gazette* ('The Press' 1843: 351; Robertson 1989: 11, 14). Although in service of a different community, in different developmental circumstances, the *Gazette* largely continued the style of the *Advertiser*, a four-page newspaper supported by advertising with a particular focus on commercial intelligence, immigrant labour and political news directly relevant to trade and economic development. Chapman, meanwhile, edited the contemporaneous *New Zealand Journal*, a twelve-page, fortnightly periodical in London, comprising lengthy essays, reprinted correspondence and articles, and advertising focused on emigrant services. The immediate discontinuity of style and content of the *Journal*, compared with the *Gazette*, strongly suggests that the *Advertiser* was laid out by Revans and that the motivations behind both his newspapers were the same.

The *Gazette* was published weekly for the first eighteen months of its run (see Figure 23.1). Its advertising was initially aimed at a new settlement rather than an established trading port, with most advertisements relating to land sales, labour needs and basic sundry goods. Yet, over the course of 1840, as the settlement grew, the range of advertising began to emulate the *Advertiser*, including formal notices of partnership, calls for investment in new commercial ventures, and banking services, with the proportion of advertising growing from fewer than two pages to occasionally three. In late 1841, Revans made the newspaper semi-weekly, explaining that this would make it 'more useful to the advertising public' (Anon. 1841b, *New Zealand Gazette*: 2). Conversely, the proportion of directly reprinted news articles, rather than brief summaries, was initially greater than in the *Advertiser*. These served local subscribers by providing them with regular information about other parts of the empire, including local elections and economic conditions. Much of this content originally came from Chapman, through either forwarded exchange papers or his *Journal*, but Revans's needs soon outstripped his friend's ability to provide. In 1841, he wrote that '[y]our journal does not give me any shipping news nor prices of oil, and bone—flax, wood, wool and hides—we shall want to know all about these matters. *The Australian Record* has a good shipping list[,] the plan of which it would be well for you to adopt' (Revans 1841a). Exchanging newspapers also offered opportunities for Revans to explicitly applaud or rebut depictions of the settlement appearing abroad. In January 1841, he chided newspapers in Hobart Town for describing them as in desperate want of basic foodstuffs – though he politely thanked Sydney for their unneeded concern six months later (Anon. 1840b, *New Zealand Gazette*: 3; Anon. 1841a, *New Zealand Gazette*: 2). Indeed, from the very start of the venture, he attempted to put his newspaper into the hands of as many English editors as possible, though he worried that he could not afford to send more than fifty 'at my own expense' as exchange newspapers – hoping instead that they would purchase subscriptions (Revans 1839).

Figure 23.1 The first issue of the *New Zealand Gazette*, printed in Wellington on 18 April 1840. Courtesy of the National Library of New Zealand.

That Revans saw the *Gazette* as the primary means by which the settlers could make their true situation known to the rest of the world can be seen in smaller acts as well, such as allowing free insertion of birth, death and marriage notices, which he felt highlighted the colony's progress and brought joy to families back home (Anon. 1840b, *New Zealand Gazette*: 3). As time and development progressed, there was an increasing stream of local reportage, ranging from the policing of petty vandalism to the ostentatious, but respectable, celebrations of St Andrew's Day by local Scots.[10] Taken together, this combination of material suggests a newspaper whose primary aim is commercial, not political: to facilitate interest and development in the fledgling settlement.

The final vein of content for the *Gazette* was related to the ongoing struggle between the New Zealand Company and the first Governor of New Zealand, Captain William Hobson. That these struggles made up a significant proportion of the newspaper's content, and that Revans consistently favoured the actions and rights of the Company over the proclamations and demands of Hobson, is true, but to label the newspaper as the mouthpiece of the Company, enthusiastic or not, fails to understand the specific arguments presented in these articles. Early on in its run, many of these were advertisements or notices regarding land allotments or minutes from council meetings, both of which were easily reusable content for Revans as principal printer and secretary for the Company during these first few months; they were also important notices for the settlers as subscribers or employees of the Company (Revans 1840a). As in the *Advertiser*, original commentaries focused on the benefits of systematic colonisation continued to appear, as well as details of how these would promote economic prosperity for the Wellington settlement. Alongside this were specific complaints about Hobson, whose actions endangered this prosperity by casting doubt on land titles already paid for by the settlers and dismissing the sovereignty of the Company Council, which Revans considered an example of the responsible government he had personally advocated for in Canada and continued to praise in South Australia (Anon. 1841c, *New Zealand Gazette*: 2). Similarly contentious was indecision about establishing the colonial seat of government. If they were to lose their local sovereignty and be transformed into a crown colony, it was only right to place the seat in Wellington, which would support its economic development as well as reward hard-working settlers who had already made significant progress without governmental subsidy. The conflict outlived both Hobson and the *Gazette* and was a fundamental feature of its content across its run, but always with the prosperity of the colonists, and not the Company, at its heart.

Although colonial press histories characterise Revans and his newspaper as subservient to the New Zealand Company, and there would have been personal benefits to having been so, Revans made it clear in his testimony to the House of Commons and his private letters to Chapman that his ultimate aims were never public office, a lifetime behind the editor's desk or even outlandish wealth (Revans 1840b; Revans 1841d). Instead, he considered himself a careful student of commercial trends, content to make a respectable income from various trading ventures, and to spend his remaining time and energy in the promotion and development of the communities where he resided. During his time in Canada, Revans promoted the idea that interference in the economy of the colonies, whether through tariffs, subsidies, banking regulations or immigration policies, hampered economic development and the prosperity and wellbeing of the colonists. This led him to consistently support local, responsible government, in one form or another, throughout his adult life.

His practical relationship with governing bodies, however, was complicated by his preference to correct or inform those in power in a face-saving manner, rather than engage in direct, hostile confrontation (Revans 1841f). Although the Company claimed to embody the ideals of responsible government, Revans privately worried that their ability to implement sound economic policy was tenuous and relative. During his journey out, he had come into conflict with other Company officials but had always avoided public confrontations and attempted to mend fences amongst the crew and passengers (Revans 1840c). He likewise made clear distinctions between his opinion of Colonel William Wakefield (E. G. Wakefield's brother) as a person, whom he liked sufficiently well, and as a director of the company, attempting to discreetly inform the directors in London that he was not fully competent in the role. Even when discussing how they might remove Hobson, whom he considered corrupt rather than simply incompetent, he was careful that they should not 'brag' about any successes (Revans 1841d). When the Company officials deviated from systematic colonisation, such as the bringing out of too many labourers in proportion to those with capital to employ them, he urged Chapman to explain these points to their colleagues in person in the hope of discreetly correcting their ill effects. He felt that the Company, however poorly they were implementing economic policies, still provided relatively better governance than the colonial government.

These private concerns for his community contextualise Revans's supposed fawning in the *Gazette*. He confided to Chapman that 'I have not thought it well to speak of our excess of labourers in the paper, as it would suit the purpose of our Auckland enemies' (Revans 1841c). He knew something must be said about the mismanagement of Company affairs, but

> [h]ow was it to be done. If I complained thro the paper I must support my complaint by reasons, or it would not operate on the public. If I did this, then would the purpose of the Auckland people be served. They would maintain that if I complained things must indeed be bad – and would hasten to charge the Company with breach of faith, while I only attacked the inefficiency of their servants. (Revans 1841b)

In the end, he feared that remaining silent would destroy the Company and the settlement. Instead, he hatched a plan, 'by conversation[,] to make our office holders uneasy. Numbers address their complaints to me of late.' It was devised in May 1841, and its implementation later that year seems to have created much of the evidence used by Day and others to mistakenly paint Revans as a Company messenger.

Although Revans's editorials consistently attempted to show the settlement in the best possible light, and to encourage investment and growth, in December 1841 he printed, in full, a letter condemning Company management of land distribution and complaining of the hardships facing new immigrants. Although he had refused an earlier draft of the letter, he provided a full rebuttal in response and, upon receiving a second version, inserted it with minimal comment. When, a few weeks later, another settler orally accused the *Gazette* of being the 'organ of the New Zealand Company', he declared himself to be no 'mere mouth-piece', but rather under the independent impression that the hardships faced by the colonists were caused by the Auckland government, not the Company (Anon. 1841d, *New Zealand Gazette*: 2). Revans then printed a further complaint, which he explicitly left without commentary in the spirit of 'fair play'. The complainant conceded that Revans was probably acting for the well-being of the settlement, even if the perceived lack of dissenting opinion in his newspaper undermined that aim (Anon. 1842, *New Zealand Gazette*: 2). It is these specific complaints, tolerated and disseminated by Revans himself, that Day points to when describing the *Gazette*'s bias.

In the wake of this debate, and as the settlement became increasingly established and the settlers more directly harmed by government actions, the newspaper moved to an explicitly anti-Hobson rather than pro-Company stance. When, in 1842, his newly hired editor veered into blatant flattery of a Company official, Revans became irate, accusing his new editor of unscrupulously using the newspaper to secure a lucrative post in the Company and harming the paper's reputation for independence in the process (Revans 1842a; Revans 1842b). By the end of its run under Revans, the editorials made a clear distinction between systematic colonisation, which he continued to support to the same degree he had in the first issue of the *Advertiser*, and its current implementers (Anon. 1844, *New Zealand Gazette*: 2). In this light, the

Gazette, though founded in different economic and demographic circumstances from its predecessor, follows the same purpose and structure.

Looking carefully at the shift towards a more consistently anti-Auckland rather than pro-Company stance, his disagreements with his editor over flattering pieces on Colonel Wakefield in 1842, and his attempts to dispose of his ownership of the newspaper altogether as his concerns about Company management grew, it is difficult to conclude that either Revans or the *Gazette* were ever mere servants of the Company. Instead, Revans aimed to inform readers locally and abroad of the opportunities for trade and development in the colony and to advocate policies that he felt would best aid in the prosperity of the settlement. When his efforts to correct and direct the actions of policymakers through his newspaper failed, he sold his interest in it and proceeded to support the economic development of the colony directly through various commercial ventures, noting that 'I should not mind making a moderate loss to set the trade a-going', and that he felt 'pledged to lend my aid to the progress of Port Nich. [Wellington]' (Revans 1841d). In contrast to arguments by Neale and Day that Chapman and Revans used their newspapers to further contradictory political ideologies and ambitions, the content of both newspapers suggests they served the consistent purpose of providing extensive and accurate commercial intelligence to colonial regions experiencing similar circumstances in trade, immigration and calls for responsible government.

Conclusion

Revans's writings and personal correspondence show that his political beliefs did influence the content of both the *Advertiser* and the *Gazette*, though in different ways than has been assumed by a cursory examination of his biography; it was Wakefield's programme of systematic colonisation, rather than specific parties, politicians or organisations, that best unified his various economic and political preferences. His explicit support of this system, and its implementers, appeared in the first issue of the *Advertiser* and throughout its run (Anon. 1833a, *Daily Advertiser*: 2; Revans 1839). In 1834, he likewise explained to the House of Commons that emigration 'must be adopted upon a system in which selection as regards age, and concentration as regards settlement, are kept constantly and steadily in view' (Great Britain Parliament, House of Commons 1834: 326). On his journey to New Zealand, he put these views into practice, sizing up his fellow passengers and hoping that 'henceforward the Emigration Department will be very particular' (Revans 1839); he qualified these criticisms, as always, by stating that they were 'made in the best spirit'. Finally, it was through the lens of this system that Revans and his later editors at the *Gazette* explained policy mistakes by the British and Auckland governments, hoping to buoy the confidence of the settlers and present a united and optimistic vision of the settlement to those abroad.

The clear contradiction between the current discourse's characterisation of Revans and the *Advertiser* as ultra-Radical and the characterisation of his *Gazette* as a direct mouthpiece of the New Zealand Company establishment is due to a persistent mischaracterisation of the man and both newspapers. Revans acted as an independent and active editor for both publications, and, in practice, he largely delivered what he claimed – not Reform Party politics, or establishment propaganda, but the curation of commercial information and analysis of economic policy, independent of party influence.

Extrapolating from generalised biographical data created unexplained inconsistencies in Revans's character and between him and his newspapers; in contrast, holistic examination of the publications, contextualised with reference to Revans's beliefs about governance and economic development, reveals a consistent set of beliefs reflected in his body of work, encouraging renewed study of these early commercial newspapers.

While the *Advertiser* and *Gazette* were published in distinct environments, Revans provided a consistent service relative to each community's level of development. In both, accurate and complete information regarding the markets for labour, natural resources and manufactured goods was provided through a wide selection of reprints and summaries and contextualised with analyses of economic policies that might affect them. In sharp contrast to depictions by Neale and Day of the *Advertiser* and *Gazette* as blinkered in their perspectives, Revans did not practise direct censorship over what he printed. He sometimes argued in detail against what he felt was faulty data or shaky analysis, but nevertheless published dissenting or contradictory opinions without ad hominem disparagement – all of which is in keeping with his consistent interest in obtaining actionable data and his general principle of informing and correcting rather than making personal attacks. Considered as a whole, the newspapers of Samuel Revans consistently supported the development of colonial markets, the engagement of colonists in global trade, and the improvement of government to better support free enterprise and reward hard work and good character. The individuals involved, and the level of development in Montreal and Wellington, were different, but Revans's purpose remained consistent in both cultural spaces.

Notes

1. See Fyfe 1993: 7; Tye 1996: 209–10; Day 1985: 43.
2. See Neale 2016: 80; Fyfe 1993: 5–6; Robertson 1989: 9.
3. Cited in Neale 2016: 80 and Robertson 1989: 11.
4. For examples, see Anon. 1833e, *Daily Advertiser*: 2; Anon. 1833t, *Daily Advertiser*: 2; Anon. 1833w, *Daily Advertiser*: 2.
5. For examples of such reports, see Anon. 1833f, *Daily Advertiser*: 2; Anon. 1833c, *Daily Advertiser*: 2; Anon. 1833o, *Daily Advertiser*: 2.
6. See Anon. 1833d, *Daily Advertiser*: 1; Anon. 1833l, *Daily Advertiser*: 2; Anon. 1833r, *Daily Advertiser*: 1–2.
7. See Anon. 1833f, *Daily Advertiser*: 2; Anon. 1833j, *Daily Advertiser*: 2; Anon. 1833h, *Daily Advertiser*: 2; Anon. 1833p, *Daily Advertiser*: 2.
8. See Anon. 1833v, *Daily Advertiser*: 2; Anon. 1833m, *Daily Advertiser*: 2; Anon. 1833s, *Daily Advertiser*: 2.
9. See Neale 2016: 180, n. 3.
10. For examples of such reports, see Anon. 1840a, *New Zealand Gazette*: 2; Anon. 1840b, *New Zealand Gazette*: 2; Anon. 1840c, *New Zealand Gazette*: 3.

Bibliography

Anon. (1833a), *Daily Advertiser*, 14 May, 2.
—— (1833b), *Daily Advertiser*, 15 May, 3.
—— (1833c), *Daily Advertiser*, 7 June, 2.
—— (1833d), *Daily Advertiser*, 8 June, 1.

—— (1833e), *Daily Advertiser*, 2 July, 2.
—— (1833f), *Daily Advertiser*, 3 July, 2.
—— (1833g), *Daily Advertiser*, 3 July, 4.
—— (1833h), *Daily Advertiser*, 6 July, 2.
—— (1833i), *Daily Advertiser*, 8 July, 2.
—— (1833j), *Daily Advertiser*, 9 July, 2.
—— (1833k), *Daily Advertiser*, 12 July, 2.
—— (1833l), *Daily Advertiser*, 1 August, 2.
—— (1833m), *Daily Advertiser*, 9 August, 2.
—— (1833n), *Daily Advertiser*, 13 August, 2.
—— (1833o), *Daily Advertiser*, 14 August, 2.
—— (1833p), *Daily Advertiser*, 16 August, 2.
—— (1833q), *Daily Advertiser*, 9 September, 3.
—— (1833r), *Daily Advertiser*, 10 September, 1–2.
—— (1833s), *Daily Advertiser*, 13 September, 2.
—— (1833t), *Daily Advertiser*, 7 October, 2.
—— (1833u), *Daily Advertiser*, 10 October, 2.
—— (1833v), *Daily Advertiser*, 28 October, 2–3.
—— (1833w), *Daily Advertiser*, 29 October, 2.
—— (1833x), *Daily Advertiser*, 30 October, 2.
—— (1840a), *New Zealand Gazette*, 2 May, 2.
—— (1840b), *New Zealand Gazette*, 6 June, 2–3.
—— (1840c), *New Zealand Gazette*, 5 December, 3.
—— (1841a), *New Zealand Gazette*, 16 January, 2.
—— (1841b), *New Zealand Gazette*, 2 October, 2.
—— (1841c), *New Zealand Gazette*, 1 December, 2.
—— (1841d), *New Zealand Gazette*, 29 December, 2.
—— (1842), *New Zealand Gazette*, 25 January, 2.
—— (1844), *New Zealand Gazette*, 28 August, 2.
'Canada Corn Trade' (1832), *Fraser's Magazine for Town and Country*, 6.13, 362–5.
Chapman, Henry S., and Samuel Revans (1834), *What Is the Result of the Canadian Elections? Fully Answered, from the Daily Advertiser*, Montreal: [Printed at the Daily Advertiser Office].
Coleridge, Kathleen (1986), 'Printing and publishing in Wellington, New Zealand in the 1840s and 1850s', *Bulletin (Bibliographical Society of Australia and New Zealand)*, 10, 61–81.
—— (1990), 'Thriving on impressions: The pioneer years of Wellington printing', in David Allan Hamer (ed.), *The Making of Wellington, 1800–1914*, Wellington: Victoria University Press, 89–105.
Day, Patrick Adam (1985), *New Zealand Newspapers, 1840–1880: A Sociological Analysis of the Political and Organisational Concerns*, Hamilton: University of Waikato.
—— (1990), *The Making of the New Zealand Press: A Study of the Organizational and Political Concerns of New Zealand Newspaper Controllers, 1840–1880*, Wellington: Victoria University Press.
Distad, N. Merrill (1996), 'Canada', in J. Don Vann and Rosemary T. VanArsdel (eds), *Periodicals of Queen Victoria's Empire: An Exploration*, Toronto: University of Toronto Press, 61–174.
Fyfe, Adam, and Frank Fyfe (1985), *Revans: Father of the Press*, Greytown: Broadoak Press.
Fyfe, Frank (1993), *Gullible Sam: The Story of Wairarapa's First Member of Parliament and the Sad Fate of New Zealand's First Newspaper Printing Press*, Greytown: Wakelin House.
Great Britain Parliament, House of Commons (1834), *Report from His Majesty's Commissioners for Inquiring into the Administration and Practical Operation of the Poor Laws: Appendix C, Communications* [London: s.n].

—— (1835), *Report from the Select Committee on Timber Duties: Together with the Minutes of Evidence, an Appendix, and Index*, [London: s.n.].
Great Britain Parliament, House of Lords (1834), *Report from His Majesty's Commissioners for Inquiring into the Administration and Practical Operation of the Poor Laws*, London: B. Fellowes.
Montgomery, Martin (1834), *History of the British Colonies*, vol. 3, London: James Cochrane and Company.
Neale, R. S. (2016) [1972], *Class and Ideology in the Nineteenth Century*, London: Routledge.
'The Press' (1843), *Colonial Magazine and Commercial-Maritime Journal*, 4, 342–53.
Revans, Samuel (1839), Letter to Henry Chapman, 13 October, Copies of letters from Samuel Revans vol. 1, Copies of letters from Samuel Revans, principally to H. S. Chapman dated at sea and at Wellington qMS-1687, Alexander Turnbull Library, Wellington, NZ [hereafter labelled SRL1].
—— (1840a), Letter to Henry Chapman, 15 May, SRL1.
—— (1840b), Letter to Henry Chapman, 12 June, SRL1.
—— (1840c), Letter to Henry Chapman, 25 October, SRL1.
—— (1841a), Letter to Henry Chapman, 29 April, SRL1.
—— (1841b), Letter to Henry Chapman, 26 May, Copies of letters from Samuel Revans vol. 2, Copies of letters from Samuel Revans, principally to H. S. Chapman dated at sea and at Wellington qMS-1688, Alexander Turnbull Library, Wellington, NZ [hereafter labelled SRL2].
—— (1841c), Letter to Henry Chapman, 13 June, SRL2.
—— (1841d), Letter to Henry Chapman, 7 July, SRL2.
—— (1841e), Letter to Henry Chapman, 17 August, SRL2.
—— (1841f), Letter to Henry Chapman, 24 October, SRL2.
—— (1842a), Letter to Henry Chapman, 10 February, SRL2.
—— (1842b), Letter to Henry Chapman, 16 September, SRL2.
Robertson, Struan (1989), *The Life and Times of Samuel Revans, 1808–1888: 'Father of the New Zealand Press': Pioneer, Politician, Publisher*, Tauranga: S. Robertson.
Spiller, Peter (1992), *The Chapman Legal Family*, Wellington: Victoria University Press.
—— and Angela Woollacott (2015), *Settler Society in the Australian Colonies: Self-Government and Imperial Culture*, Oxford: Oxford University Press.
Tye, J. Reginald (1996), 'New Zealand', in J. Don Vann and Rosemary T. VanArsdel (eds), *Periodicals of Queen Victoria's Empire: An Exploration*, Toronto: University of Toronto Press, 203–42.
Woollacott, Angela (2011), 'Political manhood, non-white labour and white-settler colonialism on the 1830s–1840s Australian frontier', in Barbara Brookes and Alison Holland (eds), *Rethinking the Racial Moment: Essays on the Colonial Encounter*, Cambridge: Cambridge Scholars Publishing, 75–96.

24

COLONIAL TRADE IDENTITY AND LABOUR INFORMATION EXCHANGE IN THE INTERNATIONAL TYPOGRAPHICAL TRADE PRESS, 1840–1910

David Finkelstein

Introduction

THE TRADE AND professional press is a subject for which no major general history has been written to date. There are examples of studies of specific professional titles in areas related to medical, legal, business and scientific journals.[1] There are surprisingly few examples taking the same approach for the general trade press, and in particular the colonial trade press (Finkelstein 2018a; King 2020). Yet throughout the second part of the nineteenth century, and well into the twentieth, there was an abundance of journals dedicated to multifarious trades and professions. By 1900, *Mitchell's Newspaper Press Directory* listed a hefty 1,947 newspapers and 2,328 periodicals specifically focused on these areas in the United Kingdom (*Mitchell's Newspaper Press Directory* 1846–1900; King 2020: 572). What can be said about trade periodicals circulating in British colonial spaces? This chapter looks at one such genre example, the print trade press, to explore the dynamic means by which a transnational network of trade-specific journals, produced by a literate labouring class elite, reflected trade information and news to its readers as means of fomenting and maintaining a distinctive trade identity. Backed often by trade unions, produced and written by active community-based print trade personnel, such journals circulated across colonial spaces as means by which to inform and reaffirm particular trade values. These values, though emerging from a common shared skilled worker identity, were often bent and refracted to fit colonial geopolitical labour stances prevalent at the turn of the twentieth century.

Anglophone print trade unions had their origins in the early 1800s. Print unions emerged from the Western European trade guild systems that had governed the trade since the start of commercial printing in the mid-fifteenth century. Beginning in the 1840s, emerging print trade unions and trade pioneers began launching typographical trade journals in the UK and overseas. Many were short-lived, or underwent multiple transformations of title, frequency and format throughout their appearance. They included London-based titles such as the *Compositors' Chronicle* (1840–3), the *Typographical Gazette* (1846–7), the *Typographical Protection Gazette* (1846–7) and the *Typographical Circular* (1854–8).

In the US, trade-focused journals were started later, and included titles such as the New York-based *The Printer* (1858–75), the *Printer's Circular* (1880–9) and the *Typographical Journal* (1889 onwards). From 1866, when Canadian union branches began joining the International Typographical Union, such US journals added Canadian reports to general branch activity news, thus linking English-speaking printers across North American borders. A more Canadian-focused non-union example, the *Printer's Miscellany* (1876–82), was edited for six years from St. John's, Nova Scotia, by the printer Hugh Finlay, launched with the aim of placing 'before our readers the latest and most reliable news in relation to the craft, together with such articles and items of interest and useful information as we may from time to time have at our disposal', as well as offering space for employers and print employees to advertise 'their wants' (Finlay 1876: 2).

Linked print trade journals joining Edinburgh, London and Melbourne included the *Scottish Typographical Circular* (1857–1909), renamed the *Scottish Typographical Journal* in 1909, the London-based *Typographical Circular* (1854–8) and *The Australian Typographical Circular* (1858–60). UK regional titles included the Manchester-based *Typographical Societies' Monthly Circular* (1852–74), transformed into the *Typographical Circular* in 1877, and the *Leeds Typographical Circular*, begun in 1888. Between 1870 and 1912, colonial print trade journals would be launched in Australia (*Australasian Typographical Journal*), South Africa (*South African Typographical Journal*) and India (*Indian Printers' Journal*).

Ambitious Aims

As I've noted elsewhere, the aim of these journals was to inform, to entertain, to support the development of a cooperative, shared professional trade identity, and to shape industrial relations locally, regionally and internationally (Finkelstein 2018a). In addition to featuring trade news, mid-century print trade journals encouraged readers to submit contributions of both practical and creative form. Several journals also featured resident compositor poets, often called upon to compose items for performance at public trade events and celebrations, the results of which were then reprinted in subsequent issues (Finkelstein 2018b).

The written word was seen as a powerful tool for engaging with fellow print trade members. As the *Compositors' Chronicle* announced in its launch issue of 7 September 1840, 'our principal object is to promote a better understanding in regard to the general interests of the trade, and to ensure a more perfect and sincere co-operation on the part of its members, whether in town or country, or whether connected or disconnected with societies' ('Address' 1840: 1). The *Typographical Circular* welcomed contributions from its readers, 'because it is the epitome of such men – thoughtful, studious, and well-informed – which generally sway the decisions of the Trade Delegates in chapel, and are of more importance than the windy speeches of empty orators' ('Address' 1854: 1).

An early Antipodean example, *The Australian Typographical Circular*, launched in January 1858 by the Victoria Typographical Association, saw its mission similarly in providing a trade resource for everyone involved in Australian printing. 'It will be sufficient to say, here,' noted the editor, 'that in its design it is intended to be the receptacle of information forwarded by the authorised contributors of the various districts,

Figure 24.1 *The Australian Typographical Circular*, 1, January 1858, p. 1. Courtesy of the print collection of the British Library.

and not at all with the view to enforce the individuality or editorial eccentricities of its conductor upon the members of the profession' (Anon. 1858, *The Australian Typographical Circular*: 1). The goal, as the initial editorial made clear, was to be as comprehensive as possible, and to extend knowledge beyond the regional boundaries of the trade in Victoria. 'We disclaim any desire on our part to limit its sphere of usefulness to this colony,' it noted, though its comprehensiveness had then to rely on the willingness of regional correspondents to supply the journal with supporting material (Anon. 1858, *The Australian Typographical Circular*: 1) (see Figure 24.1). Its combination of creative material and trade information was greeted positively by many in the trade, including the editor of the *Scottish Typographical Circular*, who declared, 'We wish to our contemporary a useful and a successful career' ('Book Notices' 1858). Long lasting it was not to be, ceasing publication two years later, having failed to attract sufficient paid subscriptions to fully cover printing costs.

Australian print trade journal interest resurfaced in November 1870, when the *Australasian Typographical Journal* was launched, backed by Melbourne print union members, and covering trade news focused on Australia and New Zealand. Like its earlier counterpart, the journal served as a labour organising outlet, educating colonial print journeymen on Australasian trade policies, industrial regulations and labour issues, while also preparing the ground for wider national organisation (Fitzgerald 1967: 54).

When the newly formed South African Typographical Union launched an accompanying monthly journal, the *South African Typographical Journal*, in March 1898, it also declared a mission to represent the print trade and provide South African-related news. Its lead editorial noted:

> One great complaint hitherto existing has been that no definite information was to be readily obtained as to the state of the printing trade and other details in the towns of South Africa. The Conference felt that the time was ripe for the issue of a thoroughly representative Trade Journal, and decided to issue the same monthly. Today therefore sees our first issue. ('The New Union' 1898: 1)

Indian-based titles were less prevalent, hampered by the lack of organised print trade unions capable of financially backing such operations. An Indian Printers' Union would only haltingly emerge in Calcutta in 1905, aimed at supporting its members with social benefit schemes, night schools, educational stipends and bereavement funds (Finkelstein 2018a: 10; see also Sharma 1998). Two monthly journals, both entitled the *Indian Printers' Journal*, flourished briefly in 1895–6 (published out of Rajkot) and 1912–13 (issued from Bombay). Both held dear the need to inform fellow Indian print colleagues of trade news and innovations, with the 1895 version also committed to raising standards of Indian printing through encouraging best practice and featuring exemplars in its pages. As the lead editorial opined,

> The time has arrived when something may be said to enlighten and assist Native compositors in the production of a superior class of work than has hitherto been attempted. To encourage this we shall offer prizes to be competed for, and their work will be reproduced as specimens on a special inset in this Journal. ('Our First Issue' 1895: 5)

Subscriptions and Reader Base

Key factors often brought up in managing such journals was the lack of a consistent subscription base and funding to cover publication costs. Those outside India often relied on union subsidies to survive. Those that did not have such support had to find relevant ways of reducing costs and extending their circulation to remain solvent, often failing within the first few years of production. This was a particular side effect of many such trade journals focused on trade information provision, rather than serving as advertising-based, independent press publications. In key examples, union subsidies were required to make up for the lack of paying subscribers. Such was the case with the *Australasian Typographical Journal*, launched in 1870, which was forced to pause publication in 1901 due to lack of paid subscriptions. At the union's annual convention in December 1901, delegates agreed it was absolutely necessary to restart the journal to represent their interests, and a motion was passed agreeing to fully subsidise the *Typographical Journal*'s production costs, sharing the financial burden across union branches.

The Australian journal was not the only trade publication to suffer from an inconsistent subscription base. Union members might have enjoyed catching up on local trade activity news and debates, but as one US branch reporter humorously reprimanded fellow Baltimorean unionists in 1901, North Americans didn't seem prepared either to cough up the monthly dues needed to pay for their union-focused *Typographical Journal*. 'Every two weeks we have a nice, clean little journal placed before us, with the latest news and gossip from national and local circles, and many questions discussed and things suggested that should interest and ought to be read by all members of the craft,' our craft correspondent observed. 'Yet they remain in their comatose state and seem to think the Journal can exist on moral support.' Reminding members of the journal's existence required drastic action. 'I'm going to lambast you all,' he warned, 'so you had better send in your subscriptions at once and see what I have to say about you' (Rastus 1901: 245).

Information Conduits

Trade journals were information conduits for the so-called 'tramping system', which trade guilds and print unions across the colonial world utilised throughout the nineteenth and early twentieth centuries as a means of organising and controlling labour activity. Unions financially supported movement of members across local and regional trade circuits during moments of strike action or when economic and trade conditions dictated, and from the mid-nineteenth century onwards also provided emigration grants to part cover travel costs of members ranging overseas. Typographical journals tracked such membership movement by publishing monthly lists logging arrivals of emigrant artisans registered with international union branches. They also provided information on printers who had 'cleared' their membership and taken up bona fide union cards and passes, allowing travel and work further along national and international print trade networks.

Likewise, such journals featured lists of 'rats', or scab union members who had crossed lines to take up roles in non-unionised workplaces, and were thus to be named, shamed and barred from membership until they had repented appropriately of their errant ways. As an example, when the owner of the New Zealand-based *West Coast Times* decided in June 1871 to sack several workers and replace them with boy apprentices, local printers blackballed the paper, closing it to 'all fair journeymen printers', and widely publicised the names of the five employees who had chosen to remain and work in the non-unionised space. Reports of the incident and a list of relevant scab workers were sent to Melbourne to be featured in the July and August 1871 issues of the *Australasian Typographical Circular*.[2]

Union journals were also used to track errant members as they made their way across print centres. 'The following is a list of the "free-traders", who are again at large,' warned a typical notice in the *Scottish Typographical Circular* of 1864, going on to list eight Scottish and Irish blacklisted members then roving regional print centres in search of work (Anon. 1864, *Scottish Typographical Circular*: 32). A later Canadian example involved a scab worker brought in during a strike in June 1900 at the Halifax offices of the *Herald and Mail*. The strikebreaker, a machine tender by the name of Hartley, was subject to numerous notices in the International Typographical Union's mouthpiece the *Typographical Circular*, tracking his movements across the

Canadian dominions before and after the strike. Originally employed at the government printing bureau in Ottawa, Hartley broke ranks while on leave in Halifax to cross the picket line and work for the *Herald and Mail*. In noting this, the *Circular* gleefully commented, 'As soon as the Ottawa authorities learned of his unfair action in Halifax he lost his position in the bureau. He is now out in the cold, looking for sympathy' (Anon. 1900a, *Typographical Circular*: 26). A few weeks later, Hartley was on the move again, as the *Circular* announced: 'Hartley, the machinist who left the printing bureau for Halifax, to rat, is back on the *Montreal Herald*.' Members were warned in strong terms to blacklist this unrepentant ex-member who had betrayed class solidarity: 'Montreal card-holders should shun the fellow in remembrance of the badly used Halifax contingent' (Anon. 1900b, *Typographical Circular*: 69).

Such details were part and parcel of journals acting as labour information exchanges, participating in an international circulation of news and material through the printing of trade letters and notices, the issuing of news items from locally based sources, and the reprinting of official lists and communiqués from union representatives and secretaries. The international recirculation of news and trade items was often done through 'scissors-and-paste' journalism methods, whereby cuttings gleaned through exchanges of journal issues between editors were reprinted verbatim. Thus common threads of news, speeches and announcements could be found moving across time and space, reported and repeated from one international journal to the next.

A good example of such news recirculation was the reporting of Charles William Bowerman's activities and commentary as part of the Mosely Commission on Industry in 1902. The Commission (misspelled as 'Moseley' in some reports) was one of several fact-finding missions funded by British businessman, philanthropist and entrepreneur Alfred Mosely in the early 1900s to examine US industry and education. Mosely had made his fortune working alongside Cecil Rhodes in the South African diamond mining industry, and used his wealth to sponsor a range of philanthropic endeavours, such as the 1902–3 trade and educational surveys. The first mission, covering US industrial practices, sent twenty-five UK trade representatives on a fact-finding tour of US cities and industrial workplaces between September and December 1902. Among the delegates was 'Courteous Charlie' Bowerman, popular trade union leader, one-time secretary of the London Society for Compositors, and later a Labour MP for Deptford (Martin 2020). Bowerman's report on US print operations featured as a section in the Mosely Commission on Industry report issued in April 1903. His positive conclusions on US trade working conditions were widely reported across the UK and the colonial print trade industry, as well as bundled into news reports circulated in US, Australian, British and South African press outlets.[3]

Typographical journals were conscientious in noting advancements and individual successes of trade members, recording the taking up of newspaper ownership and journalistic and editorial roles by printing colleagues, as well as departures for new postings. Celebrations and announcements of such aspirational successes were publicised in relevant trade news sections, often in terms of reports on farewell suppers, presentations and summary notes. Typical was the example of Mr John Imrie, who left Glasgow to take up an overseas post in 1871. Shortly before his departure, the *Scottish Typographical Circular* included news of a presentation by his ex-colleagues in Bell & Bain's case chapel of 'two very handsome volumes of poetry, on his occasion of his leaving here for the Canadian dominion' ('News from Glasgow' 1871: 524). Information received on overseas achievements was also celebrated. 'We learn with pleasure that two old friends and fellow-comps, – Mr D Stark and Mr Henry Mackintosh,' ran one example in the *Scottish Typographical Circular* in June 1869, 'both of Edinburgh, and at one time of the *North British Advertiser* – have started a newspaper in Otago, New Zealand under the title of the *Independent*' ('News' 1869: 94).

A common feature of print trade journals was trade news provided by overseas correspondents, many of whom were cultural mediators active in union organisation. South Africa and Australia in particular were strongly linked through a two-way flow of skilled print labourers, many of whom frequently crossed borders to hone printing and union organising skills in both countries. One such cultural intermediary was Jack Farrell, itinerant compositor of Australian background, known variously as 'Australian Jack', 'Johannesburg Jack' and 'Transvaal Jack', but not to be confused with his contemporary namesake 'Capetown Jack' (see Figure 24.2). Farrell, born in Ireland, raised in a small town outside of Melbourne, trained as a compositor in Victoria, then in the early 1890s tramped across international trade circuits in search of work, taking in Sydney, New Zealand and a number of US states, before returning to Sydney for further employment ('J. Farrell' 1902: 13–14). Not content to stay put, he shifted to

Figure 24.2 'J. Farrell: First President of S.A.T.U.', *South African Typographical Journal*, 4.39, January 1902, p. 13. Courtesy of the print collection of St Bride's Library, London.

Cape Town and then Johannesburg in 1896, where he was heavily involved in South African union spaces for the next decade. At a gathering of print labour organisers in Johannesburg in January 1898 to create a national South African Typographical Union, Farrell was elected by acclamation as its first president. He played a decisive role in launching the *South African Typographical Journal* just months later in March 1898 ('J. Farrell' 1902: 13–14; Downes 1952: 811–13).

Farrell was among a dozen union members (dubbed the 'Twelve Apostles') sent on request by the British authorities in July 1900 to occupy the Transvaal-run printing offices in Pretoria (captured by British forces from the Boers earlier that year). They subsequently relaunched it as the official Government Printing Office. News of this rebranding was greeted with enthusiasm by the US *Typographic Journal*, which congratulated the union on its role in restoring the printing works, and declared to its readers, 'It speaks well for the vitality and influence of the South African Typographical Union that the decision to continue the Pretoria printing office as a state department was arrived at on the strong representation of that body' ('Notes of Interest' 1900: 283).

Despite such onerous work commitments, Farrell took time to contribute book reviews and commentary to the *South African Typographical Journal*, and acted as correspondent for the *Australasian Typographical Journal*, offering updates on South African print industry news, commentating on trade politics, and issuing occasional warning on trade challenges and strikes. In his despatches, particularly after the conclusion of the Boer War in 1902 and subsequent period of industrial reconstruction, he offered welcoming notes to South African print entrants, mindful of union protectionist moves to prevent industry oversaturation. 'At present it may be said of South Africa generally,' he reported in the October 1902 issue of the *Australasian Typographical Journal*,

> that the country is in a very satisfactory condition, considering the fact that, viewed from the industrial standpoint, it is like a big sick giant stumbling around after being on a sick-bed for two years and a half – the duration of the war. There's a heap of all kinds of work –developing and other – to be done throughout this sub-continent, and it's going to take quite a while to do it. In the meantime, whether the various floatations are 'wild cats' or real pie, the printer is a primary requisite in the land, for without his innocent aid the wild cat prospectuses . . . would be things of 'innocuous desuetude,' as Grover Cleveland so poetically put it. (Farrell 1902: 4)

In the same issue, however, recirculated *South African Typographical Journal* clippings gave short shrift to scab workers then entering Durban to take up strike-breaking roles. Such newcomers had made their way originally in hopes of striking it rich in African gold mines, but had found more sustenance through plying their printing skills in non-unionised spaces. They were seen not just as betraying union ideals, but also as lacking the enterprise and commitment to unionism that had been present in earlier emigrant white print labourers. 'Durban seems to be the "haven of rest" latterly for many gentlemen which Australia has no use for,' the report fumed.

> There is no room or excuse on the part of these 'new chums'; they lack in many cases any sort of credential, have not in any way assisted in maintaining a living wage standard in Australia, and come here and expect the hand of friendship. Durban, also, has no use for them, under the circumstances. ('General News' 1902: 8)

Restricted Moral Communities

Such trade journals saw themselves as chroniclers of contemporary print labour discourse and concerns. The rhetoric in their pages espoused a moral community of labour brotherhood bound by shared trade heritage, artisanal skill and craft history (Finkelstein 2018a). They offered aspiring contributors and readers a vision of craft identity that extended beyond the compositor space, and complicated notions of rigid class and professional identity through extolling and celebrating cross-class movement and success.

Printing personnel and print trade union organisers were global figures with international reach, traversing freely across imperial spaces, intent on building up connected print trade outlets and communication centres. However, when it came to colonial spaces, not all printers were created equal. As Isabel Hofmeyr has noted, 'These laboring men were less print capitalists than what we might call "print laborists" – men who attempted to define printing as part of white racial privilege. The print capitalists, proprietors, and master printers for whom they worked shared their racial ideologies if not their laborist proclivities' (Hofmeyr 2013: 34).

Print unions in colonial spaces invariably emphasised colonial divisions of race, identity and trade skills. Official labour union rhetoric, particularly in South Africa and Australia, emphasised a trade identity that was overwhelmingly white, male and colonialist in intention. Typographical union journals in Australia and South Africa represented such dominant voices and opinions in editorials and trade columns, supporting consensus trade union views in favour of white labour dominance in a white-dominated country (Hyslop 1999, 2010; Katz 1976; Markus 1979; Ngai 2021; Visser 2004). Some critics have noted, though, that not all labouring classes in South Africa and Australia subscribed to such restricted views on race and class privilege (Kenefick 2010).

South African and Australian typographical trade texts in those spaces steered firmly in favour of majority labour opinion, having little positive to say about Indian, African and other non-white workers labouring as outsiders on the margins of white colonial trade spaces. When such print trade artisans appeared in the pages of such colonial trade journals and union records, they made their entrance surreptitiously, used to exemplify existential threats to white artisanal livelihoods, offered as examples of inferior masters of the art of printing (requiring time and effort to oversee, manage and shape), or seen quietly requesting and being denied equal opportunities for representation in the wider 'brotherhood of printing' espoused in the slogans, banners, training and rituals marking craft uniqueness.

Ethnically Marginalised Labourers and Print Artisans

A general labour issue wrestled with in international trade journals was the so-called 'Chinese Question'. This related to the importation of Chinese labour to countries such as the US, Australia and South Africa to service unskilled and semi-skilled roles mainly in mining, engineering and railway construction. The subsequent backlash against Chinese immigrant labour was harnessed for maximum political effect first in the US from the 1850s onwards, then in mining labour struggles in South Africa between the 1880s and 1910s, and subsequently as a significant card played in 'white labour' Australian Federation politics from 1901 onwards. As Mae Ngai has mapped out in a wide-ranging study of Chinese diasporic migration across the US, Australian and South African regions between 1850 and 1910, major influxes and absorption of Chinese 'coolie labourers' at key historical junctures in these three countries were fraught with complications and bound up in social panics over racial dilution and perceived external community threats (Ngai 2021).

The resulting debates over cultural, national and racial identity, and the casting of Chinese emigrants as a minority group to be feared and rejected, would lead to the passing of major legal restrictions on Chinese citizens in these countries. These included a rolling and increasingly restrictive set of Chinese Exclusion Acts enforced in the US from 1875 into the twentieth century, which drew admiring columns and recirculation of US commentary and news in colonial typographical trade issues of the period. One such example, drawn from the *Australasian Typographical Journal*, noted the 1902 battles over reconfirmation of the Chinese Exclusion Act (the so-called Geary Act) of 1892. It approvingly reprinted an American source announcing the following call to arms on the matter: 'Make it your business to see that the congressmen and senators from your state or district are pledged to vote for the re-enactment of the Geary law, or a more stringent one . . . If the officials at Washington understand that the workers – the men with votes – are in earnest in this matter, the passage of proper legislation on the Chinese question is assured' ('American Item' 1902: 6–7). Australian rulings from similar periods culminated in the newly constituted Australian Federation's Immigration Restriction Act of 1901, which added policies aimed at excluding non-whites and all potential Chinese arrivals (not just labourers) through application of a fifty-word dictation test in a European language (Ngai 2021: 182). When Chinese migrant workers were brought in to work South African diamond mines in the early 1900s, organised labour groups warned of the 'horrible nightmare' of the 'yellow agony' invading such colonial labour spaces. The *South African Typographical Journal*, like many trade sources in the region, featured such terms in strongly worded editorials, articles and letters, warning of the threat of 'coolie' labour on local wages, and demanding strong political action to exclude Chinese from South African labour markets (Anon. 1903a, *South African Typographical Journal*: 6; Anon. 1903b, *South African Typographical Journal*: 10).

Indian Print Labourer Communities

Similarly, the supposed threat to white printers posed by Indian and Native print artisans was closely commented on, particularly when they were workers educated and trained in religious mission schools such as the Lovedale Missionary School in South Africa, founded by the Glasgow Missionary Society. A beady eye was cast over colonial examples of Indian print labourer intrusion, such as the importation into Australia in the 1850s of Indian compositors from Madras to set type for the *Empire* newspaper (Neame 1907: 71). L. E. Neame, a prominent Johannesburg journalist for the *Rand Daily Mail*, editor for a period of the *Times of India*, and high-profile advocate of exclusionary white policies, noted with concern in 1907 that such initiatives, alongside South African examples such as the 1896 importation into Natal of Indian indentured artisans, including compositors, were mere preludes to an overwhelming future deluge of clever, ambitious and successful brown- and yellow-skinned artisanal disrupters of the white colonial status quo. 'No one can possess a greater admiration for India and the Indian peoples,' he claimed disingenuously, but 'A decision against Asiatic immigration in the Colonies is in no way due to a lack of appreciation of Asiatic virtues—it is rather a testimonial to Asiatic capacity for succeeding' (Neame 1907: viii).

Such exceptionalism was also woven into views of Indian subcontinent print labourers, particularly when the examples offered reflected well on white overseers and managers seen to be raising the typographic standards in non-white colonial spaces. A *Scottish Typographical Circular* notice in 1887, for example, drew attention to printing work in the form of handbooks and published specimens of type received from the Calcutta-based Central Printing Office of India. The Indian printing office staff of 1,830 members, overseen by two white superintendents, were locally based and trained, with the compositors 'nearly all Hindus, the readers East-Indians, and the pressmen Mahomedans' ('General News' 1887: 448). The samples proffered, journal commentators concluded, were equal to that produced by British printers, with great credit to the white superintendents 'for the manner in which they have trained their native subordinates'. 'On the whole,' it was grudgingly admitted, 'even taking into account the extra care which would doubtless be taken in doing specimen work, we have to congratulate our Indian typographical brethren on their knowledge and ability in the "Art preservative of all Arts"' ('General News' 1887: 448).

Though integration of such efficient workers into unions might have defused and rectified such imbalances, racialist policies led many print union sections to restrict Indian compositor access to local union branches in South Africa and Australia. Indian members were allowed to join in small numbers in South Africa after the First World War. Prior to that, requests were frequently turned down or deferred for discussion at annual typographical conventions, and then left unactivated.

While not allowed to join unionised spaces, Indian-focused printers and printing enterprises in South Africa were generally left to their own devices. The International Printing Press, started in Durban in 1898 by Mohandas K. Gandhi, made an appearance in union records in one such case. A South African Typographical Union member was hired in 1899 to help with its printing needs, and sought special permission to join the non-unionised Indian print concern. 'In his report to a general meeting in October,' the relevant journal issue recorded, 'the Branch Secretary refers to an application from the proprietor of an Indian printing office to employ a Union member, which was granted, and an unemployed member secured a situation on satisfactory terms' (Downes 1952: 99; see also Hofmeyr 2013: 50).

Printers' journals in India, on the other hand, spoke of the importance of training, educating and closely supporting indigenous compositors in the complexities of typographical composition. As these were journals emanating from engaged indigenous printers, the language used was strongly invested in proselytising for positive change in approach and labouring direction, as well as displaying keen awareness of a need to present Indian printing in best form to the outside world. 'We have been at a considerable expense in getting together well-trained men in their different departments, from some of the best offices in India,' the first issue of the *Indian Printers' Journal* trumpeted in October 1895, 'and soon we hope to present to our readers a Journal which will reflect credit upon our Indian Printers' ('Editorial Notes' 1895: 5).

Black Print Labourer Communities

Indian and Chinese labour may have been partially acceptable but sidelined or ignored on the basis of racial views of competence and potential in some colonial spaces. Black African print labourers were accorded no such privileges in South Africa. Vocal South African Typographical Union members made that clear in repetitious reports and letters to the journal, denying agency to such print labourers, and calling out those who employed them. Despite their frequent and successful presence in non-unionised print establishments, Black and Coloured print workers were classed as mere 'hewers of wood and drawers of water', fit mainly for unskilled work, not precise compositor tasks. One 1899 correspondent argued that those proprietors who supported equality in workspaces were to be discouraged, for their actions damaged the cause of the white labouring classes. 'I hope one day', the correspondent concluded, 'to see the Union throw itself full force against this class of proprietor, who makes white and black stand side by side as equals, and endeavour to bring him to reason by promoting a more generous feeling in his greedy heart' (Anon. 1899, *South African Typographical Circular*: 13; Anon. 1902, *South African Typographical Circular*: 9).

When Native workers attempted to join the dominant unions, they were denied access. An example noted in the *South African Typographical Journal* concerned the Union conference in Durban in April 1902, when the East London branch, represented by Harry Sampson, subsequently to leave for Johannesburg and then to become head of the South African Typographical Union, petitioned for 'a subsidiary union for Natives to be formed'. It was batted away for consideration the following year, then quietly dropped (Downes 1952: 175). When a printer at the mission station in Natal applied for Union membership in 1903, the March 1903 issue of *South African Typographical Journal* recorded that he was advised to go and organise a Native trade union instead (Downes 1952: 106).

Such views remained prevalent in subsequent colonial trade journal contributions. A February 1909 article in the *South African Typographical Journal* entitled 'The Evils of Missions' featured strenuous pronouncements on the threat to the status quo of mission print centres and Native print workers. 'The practice of certain mission stations in running printing plants on low-paid Native labour is condemned as a danger to the standards of living of the white worker,' it declaimed in shrill terms (quoted in Downes 1952: 200). Such individuals, recruited to work for wages significantly below those laid down by union negotiations in key districts, threatened white labour interests. 'The fundamental creed of the white man', concluded the piece, 'is to maintain the supremacy of the race: the teaching of trades to the negro tends to place him on an equal footing with the white man. This must not be – and the solution? Segregation' (quoted in Downes 1952: 200).

When there was cultural interaction, strict racial barriers were in place to prevent mixed social connections outside workspaces, and these were reported in such terms. Thus, we find reports of a Wayzgoose, or day social outing, organised by employees of the Kimberley-based *Diamond Fields Advertiser* in October 1903, notice of which was reprinted in the November issue of the *South African Typographical Circular*. The news item informed readers that objections had been raised at the inclusion of Coloured workers in the proceedings. 'It was therefore decided', the summary noted, 'that they should hold one of their own, the Company kindly granting them a sum of money and providing them with prizes, and accordingly some four or five set out for the picturesque banks of the Modder. Athletic sports were held, and, I am told the most interesting event of the day was the veteran's race' ('Advertiser Outing' 1903: 5–6).

Trans-Imperial Colonial Discourse and Identity

These and other examples offer insights into the colonial capitalist discourse present in key colonial print trade journals. Such journals shared locally grounded views on generalised labour questions. They purported to support the transnational circulation of trade information, filtered through recognised artisanal identities, and drawing on shared trade language and themes to connect directly to intended audiences. In colonial periodical press arenas, international social identity, labour and trade capital was strongly linked to colonial intentions, and viewed through the lens of colonial trade agendas. Thus indigenous artisanal print labourers were invariably framed within a 'white labourist' racial discourse of unequal status, serving as lesser skilled backdrops and threats to white hegemony and labour aspirations. Typographical journals representing mainstream print labour union consensus fed into wider, trans-imperial discourses of colonialism. Trade identity was enmeshed in a broader, collective, transglobal British settler identity, what Donald Denoon identified in the 1980s as instances of 'settler capitalism' (Denoon 1983), marking the imprinting of trade and labour structures on colonial soil, with attendant social constructs and racial boundaries hedging what was proffered in the pages of colonial trade journals.

Notes

1. See Bartrip 1990; Bynum et al. 1992; Finkelstein 2018a; Kynaston 1988; Broks 1997; Cantor et al. 2004; Martel 2018; Mussell 2007.
2. See Franks 2001: 30; Anon. 1871a, *Australasian Typographical Circular*; Anon. 1871b, *Australasian Typographical Circular*.
3. See Bowerman 1903; 'General News' 1903: 11; 'Industrial America' 1903: 6; 'English and American Workmen' 1903a, 1903b; 'President's Page' 1903: 23; Anon. 1903a, *South African Typographical Journal*: 6; Anon. 1903b, *South African Typographical Journal*: 10.

Bibliography

'Address' (1840), *Compositors' Chronicle*, 7 September, 1.
'Address' (1854), *Typographical Circular*, 1, New Series, 1.
'Advertiser Outing' (1903), *South African Typographical Circular*, 6.61, November, 5–6.
'American Item' (1902), *Australasian Typographical Journal*, 356, May–June, 6–7.
Anon. (1871a), *Australasian Typographical Circular*, 1.9, July.
——— (1871b), *Australasian Typographical Circular*, 1.10, August.
——— (1858), *The Australian Typographical Circular*, January, 1.
——— (1864), *Scottish Typographical Circular*, 38, 1 October, 32.
——— (1899), *South African Typographical Circular*, September, 13.
——— (1902), *South African Typographical Circular*, March, 9.
——— (1903a), *South African Typographical Journal*, June, 6.
——— (1903b), *South African Typographical Journal*, October, 10.
——— (1900a), *Typographical Circular*, 1 July, 26.

—— (1900b), *Typographical Circular*, 15 July, 69.
Bartrip, Peter W. J. (1990), *A Mirror of Medicine: A History of the British Medical Journal*, Oxford: Clarendon Press.
'Book Notices. The Australian Typographical Circular' (1858), *Scottish Typographical Circular*, 4, New Series.
Bowerman, C. W. (1903), 'Report by Mr. C. W. Bowerman, of the London Society of Compositors', in *Mosely Industrial Commission to the United States of America, Oct.–Dec. 1902: Reports of the Delegates*, London: Cassell & Company, 221–32.
Broks, Peter (1997), *Media Science before the Great War*, Basingstoke: St. Martin's Press.
Bynum, William F., Stephen Lock and Roy Porter (eds) (1992), *Medical Journals and Medical Knowledge: Historical Essays*, Abingdon: Routledge.
Cantor, Geoffrey, Gowan Dawson and Graeme Gooday (eds) (2004), *Science in the Nineteenth-Century Periodical: Reading the Magazine of Nature*, Cambridge: Cambridge University Press.
Denoon, Donald (1983), *Settler Capitalism: The Dynamics of Dependent Development in the Southern Hemisphere*, Oxford: Clarendon Press.
Downes, A. J. (1952), *Printers' Saga: Being a History of the South African Typographical Union*, Johannesburg: S.A.T.U.
'Editorial Notes' (1895), *Indian Printers' Journal*, 1.1, 28 October, 5.
'English and American Workmen' (1903a), *The Examiner*, 24 April, 4.
'English and American Workmen' (1903b), *The Examiner*, 25 April, 4.
Farrell, Jack (1902), 'South Africa', *Australasian Typographical Journal*, 360, October, 4.
Finkelstein, David (2018a), *Movable Types: Roving Creative Printers of the Victorian World*, Oxford: Oxford University Press.
—— (2018b), 'Scottish compositor poets and the typographical trade press, 1850–1880', special issue, 'Scottish Political Poetry and Song 1832–1918', *Scottish Literary Review*, 10.2, Autumn–Winter, 47–69.
—— (ed.) (2020), *The Edinburgh History of the British and Irish Press, Volume 2: Expansion and Evolution, 1800–1900*, Edinburgh: Edinburgh University Press.
Finlay, Hugh (1876), 'Salutatory', *Printer's Miscellany*, 1.1, July, 2.
Fitzgerald, R. T. (1967), *The Printers of Melbourne: The History of a Union*, Melbourne: Sir Isaac Pitman & Sons Ltd.
Franks, Peter (2001), *Print and Politics: A History of Trade Unions in the New Zealand Printing Industry, 1865–1995*, Wellington: Victoria University Press.
'General News' (1887), *Scottish Typographical Circular*, 11.305, 1 January, 448.
'General News' (1902), *Australasian Typographical Journal*, 360, October, 8.
'General News' (1903), *Australasian Typographical Journal*, 369.1, 19 July, 11.
Hofmeyr, Isabel (2013), *Gandhi's Printing Press: Experiments in Slow Reading*, Cambridge, MA: Harvard University Press.
Hyslop, Jonathan (1999), 'The imperial working class makes itself "white": White labourism in Britain, Australia, and South Africa before the First World War', *Journal of Historical Sociology*, 12, 398–421.
—— (2010), 'Scottish labour, race, and Southern African Empire c. 1880–1922: a reply to Kenefick', *International Review of Social History*, 55.1, April, 63–81.
'Industrial America, The Report of the Mosely Commission' (1903), *The Sheffield Daily Telegraph*, 18 April, 6.
'J. Farrell: First President of S.A.T.U.' (1902), *South African Typographical Journal*, 4.39, January, 13–14.
Katz, Elaine N. (1976), *A Trade Union Aristocracy: A History of White Workers in the Transvaal and the General Strike of 1913*, Johannesburg: African Studies Institute, University of the Witwatersrand.

Kenefick, William (2010), 'Confronting white labourism: Socialism, syndicalism, and the role of the Scottish radical left in South Africa before 1914', *International Review of Social History*, 55.1, April, 29–62.

King, Andrew (2020), 'The trade and professional press', in David Finkelstein (ed.), *The Edinburgh History of the British and Irish Press, Volume 2: Expansion and Evolution, 1800–1900*, Edinburgh: Edinburgh University Press, 558–84.

Kynaston, David (1988), *The Financial Times: A Centenary History*, London: Penguin.

Markus, Andrew (1979), *Fear and Hatred: Purifying Australia and California, 1850–1901*, Sydney: Hale & Iremonger.

Martel, Michael (2018), 'Participatory government by journalism: Class periodicals and the local state, 1880–1914', *Victorian Periodicals Review*, 51.1, Spring, 18–47.

Martin, D. E. (2020), 'Bowerman, Charles William (1851–1947)', *Oxford Dictionary of National Biography*, https://doi.org/10.1093/ref:odnb/47327 (accessed 16 September 2021).

Mitchell's Newspaper Press Directory (1846–1900), London: Mitchell's.

Mussell, James (2007), *Science, Time and Space in the Late Nineteenth-Century Periodical Press: Movable Types*, Aldershot: Ashgate.

Neame, L. E. (1907), *The Asiatic Danger in the Colonies*, London: George Routledge.

'News' (1869), *Scottish Typographical Circular*, 94.

'News from Glasgow' (1871), *Scottish Typographical Circular*, 1 October, 524.

'The New Union' (1898), *South African Typographical Journal*, 1.1, 1.

Ngai, Mae (2021), *The Chinese Question: The Gold Rushes and Global Politics*, New York: W. W. Norton & Company.

'Notes of Interest' (1900), *Typographic Journal*, 17.7, 1 October, 283.

'Our First Issue' (1895), *Indian Printers' Journal*, 1.1, 28 October, 5.

'President's Page' (1903), *Typographical Journal*, 23.1, 23 July, 23.

Rastus (1901), 'Notes', *Typographical Journal*, 18.6, 15 March, 245.

Sharma, Rajendra Kumar (1998), *Social Disorganisation*, New Delhi: Atlantic Publishers and Distributors.

Visser, Wessel P. (2004), '"To Fight the Battles of the Workers": The emergence of pro-strike publications in early twentieth-century South Africa', *International Review of Social History*, 49.3, December, 401–34.

25

THE ANGLO-ZULU WAR IN THE *FRIEND OF INDIA*: MEDIATION, MEANING AND AUTHORITY

Andrew Griffiths

'KING CETEWAYO WILL of course be vanquished in the long run', the *Friend of India and Statesman* reported on 21 February 1879, 'but the contest will be tedious, costly, and inglorious' ('Notes' 1879a: 167). Printed shortly after news of the annihilation of an imperial force some 1,700 strong at Isandhlwana reached India, this assessment of events is both accurate and unsparing. It combines a confidence in British power with a sense of unease at the moral and material cost of the conflict. The remainder of the piece amplifies the sense of unease: 'The army has suffered a grievous reverse, and England has on her hands a war which will cost more than the profits of all the piece-goods which Manchester can hope to sell in South Africa for the next twenty years' ('Notes' 1879a: 168). The imputation of purely commercial motives to colonial policy in Southern Africa is striking in its bluntness. This article is by no means an outlier in the *Friend of India*'s coverage. The newspaper maintained a steady assault on key decision makers for the duration of the 1879 Anglo-Zulu War. The editorial line leaves little room for doubt about where responsibility for the war lies. 'Sir Bartle Frere', readers are informed, 'has hurried us into a bloody and costly, and we must add, wicked, war' ('The Zulu War' 1879b: 270). Criticism of Frere, Governor of the Cape Colony and High Commissioner for South Africa, became a dominant theme in the *Friend of India*'s reporting of the war.

The tone, content and focus of the *Friend of India*'s coverage offers insight into the ways in which information circulated in the Indian Ocean region in the late nineteenth century. By exploring its highly critical coverage of the conflict and its particular focus on Frere's role, this chapter illuminates the ways in which connections between Southern Africa and India, personal relationships, and the challenges of newsgathering shaped the *Friend of India*'s rhetoric and perspective. A rich body of scholarship delineates the networks and systems of imperial news circulation. System- and network-based models imply linear flows of information, regulated or limited by news agencies, commercial interests, governments and the capacity of the available technology.[1] Other influential analyses focus primarily on the relationship between metropole and colony (Kaul 2003). By focusing on an Anglo-Indian publication, this chapter gives an insight into the process of reporting major events from the periphery of those news networks and communication systems, with a focus not on the relationship between metropole and colony but on the relationship between two colonies.

In doing so, the chapter challenges analysis that places undue emphasis on networks and systems. It argues that the *Friend of India* ran an informal newsgathering and analysis operation outside mainstream news networks, which nonetheless competed for authority with better-connected publications. By contesting authority in this way, the *Friend of India* promoted a highly critical position on the Anglo-Zulu War. To make this case, and to understand the *Friend of India*'s distinctive perspective on the war, it is essential to consider the nature of the Anglo-Indian press and the *Friend of India*'s place within it. The articles quoted above fit uneasily with the conventional understanding that the Anglo-Indian press 'rarely challenged the status quo' (Finkelstein and Peers 2000: 9). As Priti Joshi explains, 'The standard account of Anglo-Indian newspapers . . . that they were belligerent bullhorns for empire' is an over-simplification (Joshi 2021: 11). This is a view that recent work by Joshi, Amelia Bonea and Priyamvada Gopal complicates in highly suggestive ways (Joshi 2021; Bonea 2016; Gopal 2019). The emphasis placed by these authors upon resistance, dissent, borrowing (or appropriation) and failures of circulation influences this chapter. One reason why the language of systems and networks fails to describe adequately the *Friend of India* is its exclusion from (and occasionally resistance to) the connections that might have brought it fully into an imperial system of communication.

The *Friend of India* and the Anglo-Indian Press

The earliest publication carrying the title *Friend of India* appeared in 1818 and was published monthly by Joshua Marshman and his son, John Clark Marshman. The press that they operated at the Baptist mission in Serampore is significant – in 1818 the Marshmans also launched the first Bengali-language daily newspaper, *Sumachar Durpun*. The *Friend of India* was relaunched in 1835 as a weekly (Hamilton 2004; Boase 2006). The middle decades of the nineteenth century were a period of steady growth in circulation, which rose from 500 subscribers in 1839 to 3,500 in 1860, by which time the newspaper reached readers 'throughout the subcontinent, in Britain, [and] even the Strait Settlements' (Joshi 2021: 14). It changed hands in 1853 and 1859 before being purchased by Robert Knight in 1875. As editor-proprietor, Knight merged the weekly *Friend of India* with the daily *Statesman* in May 1875, formally combining them as the *Statesman and Friend of India* in 1877. Following the merger in 1875, the daily edition achieved a circulation of around 9,000 copies, 'almost phenomenal by the standard of the time'; by November 1876 daily circulation was second only to Allahabad's *Pioneer* (Chanda 2008: 166).[2] After the merger, the *Friend of India* title continued to appear in compound form (*Friend of India and Statesman*) on a separate weekly edition for several years (see Figure 25.1). This weekly edition was aimed at subscribers overseas and in the more remote regions of India. It is the coverage of the Anglo-Zulu War in these weekly editions that this chapter examines (Hirschmann 2004: 150). Though *Friend of India* was subsequently dropped from the title entirely, the *Statesman* remains in publication today.

As proprietor of the *Friend of India* throughout the period under discussion, Robert Knight is a significant figure for the argument of this chapter. He might readily be interpreted as a 'cultural broker' with a perspective 'informed by . . . migration between metropole and periphery' (Finkelstein and Peers 2000: 15). The high-water mark of his career arguably came in the early 1860s as editor and part-owner of the *Times of India*. When he stepped down in 1864, 'A delegation of grateful Indian

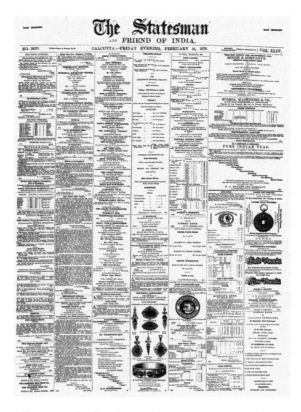

Figure 25.1 The *Friend of India and Statesman*, 14 February 1879, p. 1.
Courtesy of the British Library.

businessmen ... presented a cheque for Rs 1500' (Hirschmann 2008: 79). Over the next two years, Knight would contrive to lose almost all of his fortune. Rs 50,000 disappeared when the Bank of Bombay crashed, while another large sum was lost to the 1866 'Black Friday' panic in England (Hirschmann 2008: 99). Significantly, Knight held Sir Bartle Frere responsible for his losses in Bombay; on his return to the city at the end of 1866, Knight published a biting leader 'charging the retiring governor with irresponsible neglect of the fiscal danger' (Hirschmann 2008: 99). Knight's criticisms were not confined to Frere, however. He proved willing to challenge imperial policy in a number of areas, including the application of economic doctrine in famine relief, the Anglo-Afghan war of 1878–80, and various attempts to regulate the press in India. Indeed, Knight purchased the *Friend of India* in 1875 following a brief period in government employment, which ended in a dispute over his freedom to publish articles critical of government policy (Hirschmann 2008: 127).

Knight was never quite 'a part of the imperial establishment', a fact perhaps rendered inevitable by his critical views (Hirschmann 2008: 93). Both his outsider status and his political stance were determined to a large degree by Knight's particular conception of the role of the press in India. He articulated his views on the press most fully in an 1876 letter to Owen Tudor Burne, Private Secretary to the Viceroy, Lord Lytton. Describing the Government of India as 'a despotism, tempered only by the character of the men who administer it', Knight argued that

> the only right conception of the office of the Press is that of Her Gracious Majesty's Opposition, and whether that opposition shall be well-informed and loyal or the reverse, depends wholly on the relations established therewith by the Government. (Hirschmann 2008: 245–6)

Knight's language anticipates later debates about the role of the press: where W. T. Stead famously called for 'Government by Journalism' in Britain, Knight – a decade earlier – was calling for opposition by journalism in India (Stead 1886: 653–74). Knight's view of the constitutional function of newspapers gave the editorial line of the *Friend of India* a distinctive character. That character remained apparent even when Knight took an extended period of leave from the editorial chair.

Knight spent the years 1878–83 in England, where he sought to establish a London edition of the *Statesman*. During this period, he left editorial control of the *Friend of India* in the hands of William Riach. Little information is available about Riach, though Ram Gopal Sanyal describes him as 'a great friend of the natives, whose cause he advocated with . . . warmth and ability' and draws attention to his 'brilliant articles' opposing press restrictions (Sanyal 1894: 170). Those articles drew official criticism for the way in which they 'ridiculed Mr. C. E. Buckland, the Press Commissioner' (Sanyal 1894: 170). Riach had described official press releases as 'fatuous flapdoodle' (Hirschmann 2008: 193). Sanyal also records that, like Knight in 1864, Riach was honoured with an 'Evening Party' attended by '150 native gentlemen, representing different sections of the educated community' (Sanyal 1894: 171). Prior to his departure, Riach resolved a financial crisis at the newspaper by soliciting an investment by a wealthy Indian, Indra Chandra Singh. This seems to have provoked a rift with Knight, who may have been anxious at appearing to be placed in 'a position subordinate to a "native"' and thus violating 'a prime law in Anglo-India' (Hirschmann 2008: 195). Despite this rift, the available evidence suggests that Riach followed in Knight's editorial footsteps, championing similar causes in a similar tone.

The interactions between Knight, Riach and an affluent, educated Indian community underline the fact that the *Friend of India* was part of a literary world that, while connected, was 'distinct from . . . Britain and Britons' concerns' (Joshi 2021: 123). The roots of the Anglo-Indian newspaper press extend back at least as far as the 1780s, with publications appearing in Calcutta, Madras and Bombay before the end of the decade. By the middle of the nineteenth century, the Anglo-Indian press was well established and newspapers were as much a part of everyday life for the expatriate community as they were for the British population at home (Finkelstein and Peers 2000: 9). As noted above, recent work has challenged the consensus that Anglo-Indian publications were always vocally supportive of the conduct of British rule in India. In particular, Priti Joshi's *Empire News* emphasises synergies with the vernacular-language press, while Julie F. Codell and David Finkelstein and Douglas M. Peers have highlighted the hybrid nature of Anglo-Indian publications (Joshi 2021: 11; Codell 2003: 17; Finkelstein and Peers 2000: 15). By the second half of the nineteenth century, Anglo-Indian publications existed in a print culture that included

'Indian-owned and -edited newspapers' which 'assumed an increasingly anti-colonial and largely nationalist stance' (Joshi 2021: 10).

Collaboration and exchange were also features of the relationship between the Anglo-Indian press and Fleet Street, with London newspapers depending on the staff of Anglo-Indian publications for their news from the subcontinent (Kaul 2003: 42–3). For example, George Smith, editor of the *Friend of India* from 1859 to 1875, also acted as Indian correspondent of *The Times* (Bonea 2016: 221). His predecessor at the *Friend of India*, Meredith Townsend, had combined his role as editor-proprietor with roles on the *Calcutta Quarterly Review*, the *Annals of Indian Administration* and a vernacular journal, *Satya Pradip* – all of which he combined with correspondence on Indian affairs for *The Times* (Morris 2008). The *Friend of India* existed in a complex context defined by relationships of influence, exchange and borrowing.

Those complexities cannot readily be accounted for by histories of the press which foreground the role of systems and networks. Simon J. Potter has characterised British imperial communications in this period as a system 'dominated by a restricted number of powerful organisations, whose interests dictate more formal, entrenched and limited patterns of interconnection' (Potter 2007: 622). While this accurately describes flows of information via London, the Anglo-Indian press was, to a considerable degree, excluded from this imperial communication system, even to the extent of struggling to gather information about the decisions and policies of the Indian administration (hence Riach inveighing against the 'fatuous flapdoodle' of press briefings). In gathering news, therefore, the *Friend of India* had to operate differently to metropolitan newspapers, more often improvising to fill gaps by 'rereading ... and reframing' information borrowed from other publications (Gopal 2019: 64). Such limitations necessarily shift the newspaper's selling point away from its ability to source and disseminate news and on to its distinctive analysis of the news.

Reporting the Anglo-Zulu War

The *Friend of India* framed its coverage of moves towards war in Southern Africa in highly distinctive personal and regional terms. Throughout the Anglo-Zulu conflict, the major foreign news item in the *Friend of India* was the British invasion and occupation of Afghanistan, which spanned the period from 1878 to 1880. Comparisons between the situation in Afghanistan and the emerging situation in Southern Africa feature regularly. 'The parallel between the course pursued by Sir Bartle Frere towards the Pondo chief, and the treatment of the Amir Shere Ali by Lord Lytton, is curiously exact,' readers were informed on 13 December 1878. The article continues with several personal attacks: 'Sir Bartle Frere is one of the counsellors most responsible for this Afghan war'; the Viceroy, Lord Lytton, 'has been the pliant, unscrupulous diplomatic tool of other men and can claim no credit for originating anything'; British diplomacy has been 'Machiavellian' ('Sir Bartle Frere' 1878: 1,087–8). Even before the British invasion of Zululand, the contours and the tone of the *Friend of India*'s coverage of imperial affairs are apparent. Frere had, of course, been Governor of Bombay during the banking crisis that had seriously damaged Robert Knight's finances and it is reasonable to infer Knight's influence here. Comparisons to policy on Afghanistan and personal knowledge of Frere become claims to authoritative judgement on the Anglo-Zulu conflict.

On 20 December 1878, just days before the British force moved into Zululand, an article under the title 'Cape Affairs' set out the case against Frere in detail:

> We need not conceal that our own misgivings as to the [Cape] colony, arise largely from the fact that Sir Bartle Frere is the Governor. The ruin of the Bombay community by the share *mania* of 1864–65 was very largely the work of this amiable but weak man. Those who remember the later years of his Indian career, can want no reminder from us of the fatal weaknesses of his character. A popularity hunter of the most pronounced type, and morbidly afraid of being thought behind his age on any subject, we can hardly imagine a man less fitted to deal with great emergencies. As a ruler he is at once rash and weak, possessing no moral courage and ready to adopt any plausible *doctrinaire* folly that may be in the air or casual accordance round him, at the moment. ('Cape Affairs' 1878: 1,108)

The whole article has little to say about 'Cape Affairs', but a great deal to say about Frere. The grievance about the Bombay financial crash is thoroughly aired as part of a sustained attack on Frere's character. The article concludes with the statement that 'To send him to India as Viceroy, would be to court calamity'. The attack was renewed frequently in the *Friend of India*'s columns (see, for example, 'Notes' 1879c: 208–13).

As the conflict developed, the *Friend of India* offered a running comparison of Frere's African policies with those of the Viceroy, Lord Lytton, in Afghanistan. The military campaign in Afghanistan ran almost parallel to the Zulu conflict, from 1878 to 1880, and was, geographically at least, much more pertinent to readers in India. Making the link suggests the interconnectedness of empire, as well as an awareness of the need to sell news to a specific audience. Readers were informed on 3 December 1878 that 'it is curious that just as we learn that it is Sir Bartle Frere's policy that is being carried out by Lord Lytton, we should learn that Sir Bartle Frere's diplomacy in South Africa offers an exact parallel to Lord Lytton's' ('Sir Bartle Frere' 1878: 1,087). This parallel is one to which the *Friend of India* recurs frequently, and critically. 'It is an "Imperial" policy that is producing mischief at the Cape,' we read in an article of 21 February 1879, 'and the parallel with Affghanistan [sic] is positively startling' ('The Cape' 1879: 156). Indeed, for the *Friend of India*, a part of the significance of the British defeat at Isandhlwana is that it 'will ... attract so powerfully the interest of the English public, that our further proceedings in Affghanistan [sic] will hardly be attended to, and government will probably be left to carry out its plans, whatever they may be, with little question and no parliamentary control' ('General Summary' 1879a: 156). South African events are viewed through a distinctively Anglo-Indian lens.

Connections between colonial India and Africa shape the coverage, whether at the level of micropolitics in a personal antipathy to Bartle Frere or at a macropolitical, regional level. This personal and regional framing of the news suggests two conclusions. First, it seems clear that a personal grudge against Frere colours the *Friend of India*'s approach. Indeed, it appears that news of the war is secondary to a campaign to ensure that Frere does not succeed Lytton as Viceroy of India. Secondly, the focus on Frere and the implications for the Indian political landscape also mask an absence of up-to-date news about events in Southern Africa.

Shortage of news was certainly a factor shaping coverage. The contents list on the front page of the 20 December 1878 issue indicates that there were no significant developments in Southern Africa. In fact, Lord Chelmsford's forces were in an advanced stage of preparation for an invasion of Zululand, which took place on 11 January 1879, just three weeks later. Sir Bartle Frere was waiting for a response to an ultimatum sent on 11 December to the Zulu king, Cetewayo (variously rendered as 'Cetewayo', 'Cetchwayo' or 'Cetywayo' in the *Friend of India*). South Africa was poised on the edge of conflict, and the *Friend of India* had no definite news. When news came, it was derived from several source types. In a case study of the Anglo-Indian press's coverage of the Austro-Prussian War, a little over a decade earlier, Bonea divides sources into two main categories: 'postal news sent via the overland mail that consisted of regular digests of "Home News", letters from correspondents, and articles clipped from various European newspapers; and telegraphic news' (Bonea 2016: 292). In 1879 the *Friend of India* depended on just these sources.

By 3 January 1879, the editors of the *Friend of India* seem to have received no further news; another 'Affairs at the Cape' column shows awareness of peripheral unrest in the region but gives no hint of the imminence of a major invasion. Despite the lack of clear news, the author confidently asserts:

> Some of our contemporaries appear to be awakening to the fact, that affairs at the Cape are becoming serious, and Reuter sometimes condescends to furnish us with valuable information, which has, however, been generally anticipated by our own correspondents. ('Affairs' 1879: 6)

This assertion is fascinating for what it reveals about the *Friend of India*'s sources. Telegraphed news is evidently in short supply, and the point about Reuters' condescension implies that the *Friend of India*'s editors felt that they were not receiving all the information that they might have done. The identities of 'our own correspondents' are not made clear, despite the claim that they offer insight unavailable from the wider imperial news system. The challenges of a conflict in Southern Africa demanded ad hoc arrangements to secure news, just as earlier crises had done.[3]

The effectiveness of those arrangements is as unclear as their precise nature. On 31 January 1879, the *Friend of India* was still unaware of the details of Frere's ultimatum: 'The contents of Sir Bartle Frere's ultimatum are not yet known, but it is supposed to have demanded a general disbandment and disarmament of the Zulu army' ('Miscellaneous' 1879a: 103). By this time, an invasion had taken place and the British Army had already suffered a major defeat. Indeed, definite news of the outbreak of fighting did not reach the *Friend of India* until the receipt of telegraphed news of 'A great disaster at the Cape' on Tuesday 11 February (the same day the news appeared in the London press), in time for a leading article in the issue of Friday 14 February (see Figure 25.2). Even then, there were no details and the focus was substantially on Frere ('a thorough Jingo' and 'the man to bring a calamity upon us') ('The Cape Disaster' 1879: 136). The disaster to which the article referred was the complete defeat and destruction of a force of around 1,700 men at Isandhlwana on 22 January. Even such urgent telegraphed news was delayed by several weeks and entailed seaborne transport: the first telegraph cable linking sub-Saharan Africa to the global network would not reach Durban until later in 1879 (Wenzlhuemer 2012: 113; Beckett 2003: 181). The *Friend of India*'s weekly publication schedule served to add to the delays.

Figure 25.2 The *Friend of India and Statesman*, 14 February 1879, p. 136.
Courtesy of the author.

The challenges this produced were freely acknowledged at times. For example, a report on developing tensions in Southern Africa published in August 1878 had explained that 'By some mistake our Cape papers to 31st May have been forwarded *via* Southampton, and we are unable, in the meantime, to keep our readers as well posted up as usual'. In the absence of those official papers, the author depends on 'letters from the Transvaal' ('The War at the Cape' 1878: 691). The report acknowledges a delay in excess of two months in the circulation of information. In such circumstances, the *Friend of India* gleaned its news from a variety of sources. The nature of those sources is not always readily apparent. For instance, on 10 January 1879, the article on 'Cape Affairs' was informed by 'information, dated Cape Town, October 26th from a valued and reliable correspondent' ('Cape Affairs' 1879: 36). Elsewhere the newspaper relies on 'extracts from a letter by a young officer . . . dated Fort Weeber, 31st July'. This is 'the latest reliable direct intelligence we have received from that very remote portion of her Majesty's dominions' ('Letters' 1878: 954). The article sets the officer's account of a frontier action peripheral to the oncoming conflict alongside a brief extract from a letter received from 'a gentleman of high standing at Cape Town, dated 25th September'. That letter refers to a build-up of imperial troops in

Natal. Through the late autumn and winter of 1878–9, the *Friend of India*'s staff were struggling to comprehend unfolding events with inadequate and obsolete information.

That struggle is all the more striking when compared with the ability of Fleet Street publications to gather news, and the detail and insight provided by the special correspondents they could afford to employ. Archibald Forbes, special correspondent of the *Daily News*, rode through the night after the war's decisive battle at Ulundi on 4 July 1879, covering over 100 miles to reach the nearest telegraph station ahead of his rivals. Forbes recalled that his report on the battle, the first to reach London, was read out by ministers in both Houses of Parliament (Griffiths 2015: 36–7). That was on 23 July. Forbes's employers at the *Daily News* published his account of the battle the following day ('Latest Telegrams' 1879: 5). With its weekly publication schedule, a further five days elapsed before the *Friend of India* was able to report that 'We have also heard of the success obtained at last by Lord Chelmsford at Ulundi' ('General Summary' 1879b: 654). The issue carries little direct description of the battle, in contrast to the London papers, which all published substantial first-hand accounts in the coming days. As was the case earlier in the war, the weekly *Friend of India*'s selling point is analysis rather than reportage; as earlier in the conflict, that analysis is blunt in its criticism of imperial policy: 'Though the decisive battle had been won in January rather than July, the war would still have been unjustifiable.' Reinforcing this stance, the adjacent column sets out evidence of alleged British atrocities, excerpted from letters published in the *Cape Mercury* ('Notes' 1879d: 660–6). It is important to note that news of British victory, while a major item in the Fleet Street papers, had a far lower priority in the *Friend of India*. Very limited space was devoted to news from Africa, with routine reports from India and bordering regions (especially Afghanistan) taking priority.

Faced with such difficulties in securing information directly, the *Friend of India* did not seek to offer up-to-the-minute reportage of the war. Instead, the paper offered commentary on the political issues and, notably, on the coverage offered by other newspapers. By assessing the information provided by other newspapers against its own sources, the *Friend of India* vigorously asserted its own authority as an arbiter of truth. For example, on 28 February 1879, readers were informed that 'The letter of the *Times*' correspondent from Utrecht, Transvaal, dated 14th December, on our relations with the Zulus, is interesting and suggestive. It confirms the opinion we had already gathered from other sources, that till we annexed the Transvaal, the Zulus were always our warm friends' ('Notes' 1879b: 185). This strategy of analysis and editorial comment entails those processes of 'rereading' and 'reframing' identified by Gopal as typical strategies deployed by publications opposed to imperial policy (Gopal 2019: 64). A very wide range of publications was subject to reassessment in the *Friend of India*, including regional publications in Britain and Southern Africa.

On occasion, the *Friend of India*'s rereading and reframing could be highly critical. On 7 March 1879, the 'Notes of the Week' column selected an excerpt from *The Scotsman* for discussion:

> If Sir Bartle Frere can induce the Zulus to abandon any of their barbarous customs, it is most desirable that he should do so. At the same time, *there is a strange feeling here* that we have no right to make war upon the Zulus in order to compel them to adopt a more humane system of government. Is it really 'a strange feeling,'

or a reasonable one, that we have no right to make war upon the Zulus to force social changes upon them at the point of the bayonet? Nothing could justify the demands Sir Bartle Frere made, but power to enforce them *without the sword*. ('Notes' 1879c: 208)

That gives a clear impression of the *Friend of India*'s editorial voice and political position. In the absence of up-to-the-minute news, Frere's decision-making takes centre stage. Indeed, readers are reminded once again in this article that his policies 'plunged [Bombay] into a sea of financial difficulties' ('Notes' 1879c: 208). The attack on Frere has a secondary function here. Like the direct challenge to *The Scotsman*'s editorial position, it is a means to claim an authoritative perspective. This distracts from the fact that the *Friend of India* is dealing in second-hand news. Several other articles follow this pattern of extensive quotation and analysis of items from the British press. As a strategy by means of which both content and authority are appropriated from the source material, this scissors-and-paste journalism is effective.[4]

Whatever advantages this approach might have afforded, it also introduced considerable scope for misinterpretation and error. On 14 February 1879, the same day that news of defeat at Isandhlwana reached the *Friend of India*, the newspaper's 'Miscellaneous' column reported that 'British soldiers will find themselves fighting with regiments of women, in this Zulu war'. The source for this information is the *Manchester Guardian* which, the writer notes, 'is not very clear on the subject' ('Miscellaneous' 1879b: 145). The imaginary female soldiers emerge from the *Friend of India*'s misinterpretation of a quotation from the *Manchester Guardian* outlining the regimental organisation of Zulu society. In April 1879 a further error emerged in relation to material reproduced from the London *Daily News*. The article, 'Dr. Colenso on the Zulu War', reproduces a long letter, justifying the lengthy quotation as follows:

> The following letter from Bishop Colenso deserves a prominent place, and must have the greatest weight with the English people, it being well known that no man knows the Zulus better, and perhaps no Englishman so well as the Bishop. ('Dr. Colenso' 1879: 339)

John William Colenso was Bishop of Natal, resident on the border with Zululand and a leading advocate for the Zulu people in their dealings with imperial authority. The bishop's views on empire and on theology had made him a controversial and well-known figure in Southern Africa and Britain. The letter published in the *Daily News*, however, is clearly signed 'Robert J. Colenso, Royal Infirmary, Windsor'. This Colenso, a doctor of medicine rather than of divinity, was the son of the renowned bishop. Clearly, the *Friend of India* was keen to align itself with a prominent critic of imperial policy in Southern Africa – one who may well have shared his son's views on 'irresponsible alarmists and stay-at-home Jingoes' ('Dr. Colenso' 1879: 340). Equally clearly, scissors-and-paste journalism of this sort brought its own risks. Despite the best efforts of Riach and the staff of the *Friend of India*, exclusion from the imperial news system was a very real handicap.

Robert J. Colenso (doctor, not bishop) makes the case for the Zulu king, Cetewayo: 'During the whole of Cetewayo's reign, we have had no quarrel with him, or any other feeling than that of friendship . . . During this time Englishmen have travelled through and hunted over the length and breadth of his kingdom, and have met with kindness and courteous hospitality from him and from his people' ('Dr. Colenso' 1879: 339). By publishing his letter, the *Friend of India* establishes an inter-continental axis of resistance to British policy in South Africa. That resistance is pressed still further by the decision to devote a significant space in the edition of 10 March 1880 – over six months after the decisive battle at Ulundi in July 1879 – to Cetewayo's own narrative. The article describes and analyses the now-captive Cetewayo's personal history of the war, as published the previous month in *Macmillan's Magazine*. It is stretching the point to say that Cetewayo is given a voice in the *Friend of India* – his words came via an interpreter (one Mr Longcast), a military liaison officer (Captain J. Ruscombe Poole, Royal Artillery) and the editorial staff at *Macmillan's* before being re-digested in the *Friend of India* ('Cetywayo's Story' 1880: 273–95).[5]

Still, Cetewayo is given a hearing of sorts and the *Friend of India* comes down decisively on the side of opposition to the policy of annexation in South Africa. Of the pretext for war, for example, we read that 'The ultimatum sent to him, by which he was called on to disband his army and alter all Chaka's institutions, came like a thunderbolt from a clear sky' ('Cetewayo's Narrative' 1880: 206). Unlike *Macmillan's*, which devotes twenty-two uninterrupted pages to Cetewayo's history of the Zulu nation, the *Friend of India* offers considerable commentary on the deposed king's narrative. The final paragraph of the report concludes the discussion of the conflict in the *Friend of India* with a damning summation of the motivations of imperial policymakers:

> Our kindness has come to this, that, finding two small states quarrelling, we have destroyed both to keep the peace. We had no quarrel with the Transvaal, and our agents had express orders not to annex it without the consent of the Government. They coveted such honour as is to be got by murdering an infant republic about the size of a Bengal police outpost, and with three regular armies defeating these terrible Zulus, who cannot use fire-arms; and now they have got it. England has only to reward them for their disobedience and their distinguished effect in the field, paying always the little bill for glory.
>
> ('Cetewayo's Narrative' 1880: 206)

This is an unusual instance of an opponent of empire, a non-European who actively resisted imperialism, being offered any sort of hearing in the English-language press. It is still more striking that Cetewayo receives a broadly positive reception while imperial expansion is condemned. Compared to the original article in *Macmillan's*, the criticism of Cetewayo as a narrator has disappeared, to be replaced by vigorous criticism of 'our agents' and the locally decided policy of annexation.

This approach differs from that adopted by *The Times*, for example, which criticised the 'peremptory orders of Sir Bartle Frere' and described the war as 'ill-advised' but defended the conduct of the soldiers and commanders involved (Anon. 1879, *The Times*: 9). Criticism of Lord Chelmsford was 'most ungenerous and uncalled-for', in the judgement of that newspaper. He and his officers had been 'labouring most gallantly under enormous disadvantages to carry out a scheme which was none of their seeking' ('The Zulu War' 1879c: 8). For *The Times*, then, the war was an inexpedient act of policy. For the *Friend of India*, by contrast, it was a wholly unjustifiable act of imperial violence. Indeed, the *Friend of India* later went so far as to argue that 'few things would give more satisfaction to Englishmen than the restoration of Ketchewayo' ('Ketchewayo' 1879: 1,069). Nor did the *Friend of India*'s contributors stint on criticism of the adulation afforded to returning officers: 'That young fellow, Lord Gifford, who the other day brought home dispatches . . . and saw no fighting at all, was met with triumphal arches and a greeting generally which might have been deemed appropriate for Wellington on his return from Waterloo.' By these means, the *Friend of India* asserts, a whole country 'does its "level best" to believe in him as a hero' ('Notes from London' 1879: 1,003). In highlighting the importance of an imperial conflict to Britain's sense of identity, the *Friend of India* anticipated present-day debates about the commemoration of imperial figures.

That alternative perspective on the Anglo-Zulu War was a product of several factors. The *Friend of India*'s location on the periphery of the imperial communications network meant that it relied on a process of rereading news published elsewhere. Its weekly publication schedule shifted the emphasis further away from reportage and on to political commentary. Lacking a special correspondent to provide the authority of an eyewitness, the *Friend of India* asserted authority by drawing on experience of Sir Bartle Frere's career in India and by reinterpreting reports from the British press. The newspaper's regional perspective emphasised parallels with events in Afghanistan. If events in Southern Africa were viewed through an Indian lens, that lens was coloured by the financial losses suffered by the proprietor, Robert Knight, in the Bombay banking crisis of the mid-1860s – losses for which he blamed Frere. Those factors overlay one another and operate by means of influence as much as direct connection. Information did not always transfer smoothly to the newspaper, which was constantly seeking strategies to work around blockages in the flow of information. For all of these reasons, the *Friend of India*'s coverage is highly distinctive, presenting outspoken criticism of imperial policy in Africa.

Notes

1. For examples of such system- and network-based studies of colonial communications, see Potter 2007: 621–46; O'Hara 2010: 609–25; Lester 2006: 121–41.
2. Those figures are based on claims made in the *Statesman* and should be treated with some caution. It is reasonable to infer that circulation of the weekly edition considered in this chapter was significantly lower than for the daily paper; separate figures are not available.
3. Joshi describes a more acute disruption to newsgathering during an emergency during the rebellion of 1857–8; the same principles apply in 1878–9 (Joshi 2021: 142, 144).
4. The archive incidentally created in reportage of this type also offers a way to gauge the varying interpretations of events in different regions of the British Empire. See Gopal on the way in which this type of journalism constitutes 'an archive of sorts' (Gopal 2019: 64).
5. Undermining its own prize source, *Macmillan's* adopts a patrician tone, advising readers that 'it must not be supposed that Cetywayo is capable of giving a long consecutive narrative such as appears in the following pages' ('Cetywayo's Story' 1880: 273). Nevertheless, Cetewayo's narrative, running from the birth of Chaka to the end of the Anglo-Zulu War, covers twenty-two pages and is interrupted only by footnotes triangulating his account with other sources.

Bibliography

'Affairs at the Cape' (1879), *Friend of India and Statesman*, 3 January, 6.

Anon. (1879), *The Times*, 24 July, 9.

Beckett, Ian F. W. (2003), *The Victorians at War*, London and New York: Hambledon & London.

Boase, G. C. (2006), 'Marshman, John Clark', revised by Michael Laird, *Oxford Dictionary of National Biography*, https://doi.org/10.1093/ref:odnb/18162 (accessed 5 January 2022).

Bonea, Amelia (2016), *The News of Empire: Telegraphy, Journalism, and the Politics of Reporting in Colonial India, c. 1830–1900*, Oxford: Oxford University Press.

'The Cape' (1879), *Friend of India and Statesman*, 21 February, 156–7.

'Cape Affairs' (1878), *Friend of India and Statesman*, 20 December, 1,108.

—— (1879), *Friend of India and Statesman*, 10 January, 36.

'The Cape Disaster' (1879), *Friend of India and Statesman*, 14 February, 136–7.

'Cetewayo's Narrative' (1880), *Friend of India and Statesman*, 10 March, 205–6.

'Cetywayo's Story of the Zulu Nation and the War' (1880), *Macmillan's Magazine*, 41.244, 273–95.

Chanda, Mrinal Kanti (2008), *History of the English Press in Bengal, 1858–1880: With List of Papers Published in India (Including Burma and Ceylon)*, Kolkata: K. P. Bagchi & Company.

Codell, Julie F. (2003), 'Introduction: Imperial co-histories and the British and colonial press', in Julie F. Codell (ed.), *Imperial Co-Histories: National Identities and the British and Colonial Press*, Madison, NJ: Fairleigh Dickinson University Press, 15–26.

'Dr. Colenso on the Zulu War' (1879), *Friend of India and Statesman*, 18 April, 339–40.

Finkelstein, David, and Douglas M. Peers (2000), '"A Great System of Circulation": Introducing India into the nineteenth-century media', in David Finkelstein and Douglas M. Peers (eds), *Negotiating India in the Nineteenth-Century Media*, Basingstoke: Macmillan Press, 1–22.

'General Summary' (1879a), *Friend of India and Statesman*, 21 February, 155–6.

—— (1879b), *Friend of India and Statesman*, 29 July, 653–5.

Gopal, Priyamvada (2019), *Insurgent Empire: Anticolonial Resistance and British Dissent*, London: Verso.

Griffiths, Andrew (2015), *The New Journalism, the New Imperialism and the Fiction of Empire, 1870–1900*, Basingstoke: Palgrave.

Hamilton, Thomas (2004), 'Marshman, Joshua', revised by Michael Laird, *Oxford Dictionary of National Biography*, https://doi.org/10.1093/ref:odnb/18163 (accessed 5 January 2022).

Hirschmann, Edwin (2004), 'The hidden roots of a great newspaper: Calcutta's "Statesman"', *Victorian Periodicals Review*, 37.2, 141–60.

—— (2008), *Robert Knight: Reforming Editor in Victorian India*, Oxford: Oxford University Press.

Joshi, Priti (2021), *Empire News: The Anglo-Indian Press Writes India*, Albany: State University of New York Press.

Kaul, Chandrika (2003), *Reporting the Raj: The British Press in India, c. 1880–1922*, Manchester: Manchester University Press.

'Ketchewayo' (1879), *Friend of India and Statesman*, 5 December, 1,068–9.

'Latest Telegrams' (1879), *Daily News*, 24 July, 5.

Lester, Alan (2006), 'Imperial circuits and networks: Geographies of the British Empire', *History Compass*, 4.1, 121–41.

'Letters from the Cape' (1878), *Friend of India and Statesman*, 1 November, 954.

'Miscellaneous' (1879a), *Friend of India and Statesman*, 31 January, 103–4.

—— (1879b), *Friend of India and Statesman*, 14 February, 144–5.

Morris, A. J. A. (2008), 'Townsend, Meredith White', *Oxford Dictionary of National Biography*, https://doi.org/10.1093/ref:odnb/36542 (accessed 5 January 2022).

'Notes from London' (1879), *Friend of India and Statesman*, 14 November, 1,002–5.

'Notes of the Week' (1879a), *Friend of India and Statesman*, 21 February, 165–70.
—— (1879b), *Friend of India and Statesman*, 28 February, 185–92.
—— (1879c), *Friend of India and Statesman*, 7 March, 208–13.
—— (1879d), *Friend of India and Statesman*, 29 July, 660–6.
O'Hara, Glenn (2010), 'New histories of British imperial communication and the "networked world" of the nineteenth and early twentieth centuries', *History Compass*, 8.7, 609–25.
Potter, Simon J. (2007), 'Webs, networks and systems: Globalization and the mass media in the nineteenth- and twentieth-century British Empire', *Journal of British Studies*, 46, 621–46.
Sanyal, Ram Gopal (ed.) (1894), *Reminiscences and Anecdotes of Great Men of India, Both Official and Non-Official for the Last One Hundred Years*, Calcutta: Wooma Churn Chukkerbutty.
'Sir Bartle Frere at the Cape' (1878), *Friend of India and Statesman*, 13 December, 1,087–8.
Stead, W. T. (1886), 'Government by Journalism', *Contemporary Review*, 49, 653–74.
'The War at the Cape' (1878), *Friend of India and Statesman*, 6 August, 691–2.
Wenzlhuemer, Roland (2012), *Connecting the Nineteenth-Century World: The Telegraph and Globalisation*, Cambridge: Cambridge University Press.
'The Zulu War' (1879a), *Friend of India and Statesman*, 7 March, 201–2.
—— (1879b), *Friend of India and Statesman*, 28 March, 269–70.
—— (1879c), *The Times*, 18 September, 8.

26

British Anarchism and the Colonial Question: The Case of *Freedom*, 1918–62

Ole Birk Laursen

Introduction

T HIS CHAPTER EXAMINES the history of British anarchism and the colonial question in the post-World War I period until the onset of decolonisation across Africa and the Caribbean in the early 1960s. It looks specifically at the London-based paper *Freedom* (1886–present) – and its temporary successors *Spain and the World* (1936–8), *Revolt!* (1939) and *War Commentary* (1939–45) – and how British anarchists and anti-colonial writers in *Freedom* approached the question of colonialism. The chapter also explores how anti-colonial activists engaged with anarchism – or travelled in Britain's anarchist circles – and the extent to which these ideas filtered back to the colonial world. By exploring *Freedom*, the chapter brings anarchism's core impetus for freedom into closer conversation with colonial subjects' aspirations for freedom from empire. Debates in the periodical raise important questions about the true meaning of freedom and open a window on to anarchism's reach into the colonial world. At the same time, such conversations illuminate the ways in which anti-colonial resistance influenced British anarchist thinking about freedom.

The failure of the Wilsonian moment in the wake of the First World War, challenged by the Bolshevik promise of self-determination for subject and colonial nations, set in motion new forces and movements for independence across the colonial world and within European metropoles (Manela 2020: 11–15). But for many anarchists, the Russian Revolution and Civil War exposed the Bolshevik dictatorship of the proletariat as another authoritarian regime that oppressed its own subject nationalities and offered colonial peoples no true liberation but only uncritical devotion to Moscow. Anarchists principally viewed nationalist movements as elitist, and they were wary of native rulers replicating colonial structures of oppression in the postcolonial context.

An Unruly History of *Freedom*, 1886–1918

Freedom was founded in October 1886 by Charlotte M. Wilson and the Russian anarchist Peter Kropotkin, who had arrived in London in March 1886 at a time when the broader socialist movement in Britain was flourishing, with the Social Democratic Federation, the Fabian Society and the Socialist League all very active alongside the Labour Party and the Independent Labour Party (ILP) (Shpayer-Makov 1987: 373–90).

In 1895 Wilson left the reins to Alfred Marsh, who then edited *Freedom*, supported by Max Nettlau and with Thomas H. Keell handling the financial affairs, until 1913. Keell then assumed editorship, and throughout the next two decades, he and his partner, Lilian Wolfe, were the driving forces behind *Freedom*, printing around 1,000 copies of each issue, until it was suspended in 1932 (Ray 2018: 53). The periodical was revived in 1936 at the outbreak of the Spanish Civil War – now with the title *Spain and the World* – under the editorship of Vernon Richards and Wolfe. At the end of 1938, *Spain and the World* was incorporated into *Revolt!*, which then became *War Commentary* when the Second World War broke out, before reverting to the name *Freedom* again after the war.

Anti-Colonialism and Anarchism in the 1920s–30s

In the early 1920s, Nathalal Jagjivan Upadhyaya, an Indian lascar who had arrived in London from Bombay in 1922, contributed to *Freedom*. The struggle for harmonious solidarity between western workers and colonial subjects, Upadhyaya argued, was crucial to freedom from slavery:

> Slavery can only be abolished by the united effort of Indians, assisted by the sympathetic action of comrades in all parts of the world. Let them not be afraid that by elevating the worker of India harm will befall them. Freedom never harms anyone. If, however, Capitalism is allowed to make India and Chinese coolies the hewers of wood and drawers of water for the white races, then danger will assert itself. But let them be free men, and lo! they will render free service for free service in the shape of raw material in exchange for labour-power. Comrades! You who are free from the poison of patriotism and race hatred, my hope is to see you busy studying the problems of the Indian working class – one fifth of the world's population. Then only will India rise. (Upadhyaya 1925: 2; see also Upadhyaya 1924: 44)

But Upadhyaya soon abandoned anarchism, becoming active in the Comintern-backed Indian Seamen's Association, and eventually veering towards Trotskyism (Sherwood 2004: 438–55).

A more important interlocutor was the Indian anarchist M. P. T. Acharya. Then living in Berlin and active within the international anarchist community, Acharya approached Keell in August 1925 and asked for copies of *Freedom* that he could send to India, South Africa and Turkey. They needed an English-language paper, he emphasised, and Acharya soon became a conduit for anarchism in India. At the time, however, Acharya did not write for *Freedom*, but through his efforts *Freedom* was distributed across India. 'Such literature is unknown in India,' he assured Keell, 'and they are very pleased to get such stuff' (Acharya 1925; Laursen 2020: 241–55). Aside from Upadhyaya and Acharya, there were no contributors from the British colonial world to the periodical during this time, but the British anarchists still devoted attention to the colonial question.

Throughout the late 1920s, the Indian-born British anarchist William C. Owen, who had worked with the Indian revolutionaries in the Ghadar Party in North America in the 1910s, frequently wrote about broader issues of imperialism (Zimmer 2015: 106). The onset of the Chinese Civil War in 1927, Owen argued, demonstrated the urgency of anarchism's impetus for complete freedom – not just in China but also in India. 'Do we realise that, thanks to the great struggle going on in China, the thought of all the world is now becoming concentrated on one single issue, and that this is *our* issue; the one that we, through generations, have made most specially our own?' Owen asked. 'That men and women, whether individually or in those groups to which we give the name of nations, should be masters of their own lives and destinies, has always been the very cornerstone of Anarchism, and to this we have held all else subordinate' (Owen 1927: 16).

Though supportive of Gandhi's civil disobedience movement, *Freedom* noted, 'We have no illusions about the future welfare of India's teeming millions of peasants under native rulers, but their awakening has been stimulated by the agitation for self-government' ('The Revolt' 1930: 3–4). Instead, Keell warned that, 'If the Indian movement is to have our full sympathy, it must show its intention to make the alleviation of the misery of the people a first consideration and to do away with the abominations of the caste system' (Keell 1930: 3). In other words, throughout the 1920s, British anarchists such as Owen and Keell generally supported anti-colonial struggles for self-determination but also remained critical of the nationalist, autocratic tendencies of anti-colonial movements.

Spain and the World: Anti-Fascism and Anti-Colonialism

With the periodical published only sporadically since 1932, Vernon Richards picked up the torch from *Freedom* and started *Spain and the World* when the Spanish Civil War broke out in July 1936 (see Figure 26.1). While the editorial line was anarchist, the publication drew in other British radicals such as ILP members Reginald Reynolds and F. A. Ridley (Goodway 2006: 127–9; Gopal 2019: 370–2). While the first part of the title of the periodical revealed its editorial focus, the second part – 'the world' – suggested an international outlook. However, a look at the location of subscriptions about a year and a half into its life reveals that the periodical circulated primarily in North America, Australia and Britain, thus not reaching the colonial world ('Our Balance Sheet' 1938: 3).

The Italian invasion of Abyssinia in October 1935 preceded the outbreak of the Spanish Civil War, revealing Mussolini's fascist-imperialist ambitions, but initially anarchists in Britain rarely connected the two events, except for a few brief remarks.[1] However, the Spanish Civil War became a pretext to reassess the situation in Abyssinia – and colonialism more broadly – through anti-fascist, anarchist eyes. For instance, an editorial pointed out that the British labour movement, in working with the League of Nations, had shirked its responsibility towards 'Spain and Ethiopia by stressing the possibilities of an international war' and precluded international solidarity amongst the working classes (Editorial 1937: 1). Indeed, the British government, argued the anarchists, was no different from the fascists: 'If anything it is worse than the blatant Fascists, for under the guise of democracy and its love for peace it can bomb the civilian populations of Palestine and India and prevent Spain and Abyssinia from obtaining the arms required to defend themselves against continued air-raids and the consequent loss of life' ('British Imperialism' 1938: 2).

While *Spain and the World* remained focused on the Spanish Civil War, the Arab Revolt in Palestine also attracted great attention and soon caused tensions within

Figure 26.1 *Spain and the World*, 13 October 1937, p. 1.
Courtesy of the British Library.

the international anarchist movement.[2] For Reynolds, British rule in Palestine was 'a regime comparable to that of Hitler and Mussolini', and Arab claims to self-determination should be supported indiscriminately. While condemning Arab anti-Semitism, Reynolds argued that 'it is and has been the avowed intention of the Zionists to make Palestine a Jewish country with the help of British imperialism and in spite of the wishes of the Arab population'. Ultimately, Reynolds concluded, 'The very reasons which make one pro-Jew and anti-Nazi in Germany lead logically to the pro-Arab, anti-Zionist position in Palestine' (Reynolds 1939a: 2). What is more, commenting on the 1917 Balfour Declaration, Reynolds argued that British support of a Jewish state in Palestine risked driving Arab nationalists into the hands of Hitler and Mussolini (Reynolds 1938a: 2, 4).

Reynolds's article caused uproar among certain anarchists. Most notably, Emma Goldman, then living in London, criticised Reynolds's views, though defending him against accusations of anti-Semitism. While Goldman conceded that she had 'for many years opposed Zionism as the dream of capitalist Jewry the world over for a Jewish State with all its trimmings, such as Government, laws, police, militarism, and the rest', she criticised Reynolds for suggesting that Zionists were the only advocates of Jewish resettlement in Palestine. Goldman also criticised Reynolds for defending Arab land monopoly – even as a strategy against British imperialism – and for neglecting to welcome persecuted Jews in the era of Nazism (Goldman 1938: 2).

Reynolds's response framed his argument in relation to British imperialism:

> But just as Anarchists realise that Fascism is worse than 'democratic' capitalism, so most of them will agree with me that imperialism is worse, and for the same reasons. Those who cannot see this as a matter of common sense should study and compare conditions – say – in India and the British colonies with conditions among British workers. (Reynolds 1938b: 4)

Disagreeing with Goldman's anarchist view, Reynolds argued that 'I am not ... interested in nationalism for its own sake, but only where it is an expression of revolt against imperialism' (Reynolds 1938b: 4). In other words, where Goldman upheld the right of Jewish resettlement in Palestine on grounds of standing with persecuted Jews as well as the denial of a 'just' right to land and the rejection of borders, Reynolds defended the right to self-determination for colonial subjects. Moreover, he feared that the growing enmity between Jews and Arabs would lead Arab nationalist leaders into dangerous collaborations with fascist leaders Hitler and Mussolini. Richards agreed with Reynolds: 'The persecution of Jews in Europe to-day is in our opinion but one problem, and their treatment is not a greater travesty of justice than Mussolini's murderous attacks on the Abyssinians or on the Italian workers who still fill his gaols, nor of British Imperialism's policy in India, nor of International Fascism's campaign of extermination in Spain.' Abandoning the scales of comparison between fascist and colonial atrocities, Richards urged that 'The Jewish workers must now unite with the Arab workers, before hatred and suspicion create an unsurmountable barrier, which will make it virtually impossible to rid Palestine of British Imperialism and Arab and Jewish Capitalism, for many years to come' (Richards 1938: 5). By the end of 1938, *Spain and the World* was saddled with debt and went into abeyance, but for two years it had been an important platform for debating colonial questions in relation to fascism.

Revolt!, 1939: 'Our aim is a world of free men'

Picking up the torch from *Spain and the World*, *Revolt!* appeared in February 1939, and the young Albert Meltzer soon made his voice heard. Having attended the Workers' Empire Conference in London in January 1939, he wrote admiringly about the speakers, who included Jomo Kenyatta and George Mansour, many of whom 'emphasised the fact that "democracy" and Fascism were synonymous terms to the colonial worker', while criticising the conference resolution. A passage stating that 'The Indian National Congress and other colonial organisations have declared that they will refuse to support any war waged by the British Government until they are politically free' irked Meltzer (Meltzer 1939a: 2). This passage, to Meltzer, suggested that 'the colonial workers should support British Imperialist War IF they were given their freedom'. Such promises of 'freedom to colonial workers', Meltzer noted, 'are broken as easily as they are made', and he concluded: 'Where we differ from the Conference is that we do not intend to tell the colonial workers that it is their duty, in certain circumstances, to support their enemies' (Meltzer 1939c: 4).

On the question of Palestine, Meltzer put it clearly: 'Every movement against British Imperialism must be welcomed as the rulers of this country rule (or, synonymously, misrule) the larger part of the world's colonial peoples.' He compared British imperialism to Zionism and Zionism to Fascism: 'The Zionist leaders, keeping up a pretence that they are struggling against Fascism, have been the motivators of Fascism in Palestine.' While supporting the Arab masses, he did not support a bourgeois nationalist government but demanded a three-part strategy: 'The struggle must be against imperialism first, against Zionism secondly, and lastly against the bourgeois nationalist government when created' (Meltzer 1939b: 2).

Such 'divide and conquer' policies could also be seen at home. As Ridley pointed out,

Today, therefore, the British proletariat is not a proletariat in the classical sense of the term as employed by Marx and his disciples. Contrarily, that proletariat is today a hybrid: it turns towards its masters in England the face of an exploited class; but towards the colonies that of a class of exploiters, one united front with its class brethren, the capitalist class of the metropolis. Hence, at home it will wage class struggles via the agency of a highly organised Trade Union movement. But when the Empire is in danger, it stands side by side on the imperial front with the very men whom *at home* it denounces as exploiters. (Ridley 1939: 3, 5)

During the few months between the end of the Spanish Civil War and the onset of the Second World War, the likes of Meltzer and Ridley pulled no punches in exposing the brutalities of British imperialism as well as of bourgeois nationalisms.

War Commentary: World War II, Anti-Colonialism and Anarchism, 1939–45

When the Second World War broke out, the majority of the international anarchist movement assumed an antimilitarist stance, including *War Commentary*. Indeed, Britain had dragged its colonies into the war without consultation. Britain's record of massacres – such as the 1919 Amritsar Massacre – compared 'favourably' to Nazi methods: 'The destruction of whole Arab villages, the Palestine concentration camps, the shooting in cold blood of Jamaican workers, all these crimes are typical, not only of "Nazism" but of BRITISH and FRENCH IMPERIALISM too' ('What Are We Fighting For?' 1939: 14). According to Meltzer, *War Commentary* initially had a readership of a little more than 2,000, later reaching 4,000 (Ray 2018: 68).

India's role in the war filled the pages of *War Commentary*. Reynolds continued his critique of British imperialism, which was supported by Indian princes, as well as of Indian communists and the Indian National Congress. Only the 'Congress Socialist Party has declared for "*unconditional* resistance to war"', Reynolds stated. 'Thus the peasants, the industrial workers, and the best of the Indian "intellectuals" (who are mostly in the Congress Socialist Party) are united in a policy of vigorous and uncompromising resistance' (Reynolds 1939b: 3). Kenyatta's friend and staunch anti-imperialist Dinah Stock reflected on Gandhi's struggles against British imperialism and characterised Gandhi as the great unifier of all castes and religions in India, who brought the masses into the struggle (Stock 1941: 7; Maloba 2018: 63–4). However, while giving space to Stock's views and recognising Gandhi's achievements, the editors of *Freedom* dissented from her praise and stated: 'Gandhi calls for unity of all classes in India against the British on the grounds that such "unity" will bring strength; in effect, however, it is this substitution of "unity" for the workers' fight for their own class interests against all exploiters that will destroy the movement's strength at the very moment when the issue is most seriously joined' (Editors 1941: 7).

War Commentary also gave space to anti-colonialists such as Kenyatta, George Padmore and Chris Jones ('Chris Braithwaite'), all members of the International African Service Bureau (IASB) and the ILP. As Leslie James argues with reference to a letter from Padmore to W. E. B. Du Bois, 'the main focus of political aspiration at that point was for self-determination of individual colonies', so those who subscribed to different political ideologies – socialism, communism or anarchism – did so out of 'practical politics' (James 2014: 61).

In his analysis of the effects of nine months of war on Britain's colonies, Padmore summarised British colonial oppression in Africa, India and the West Indies and noted that 'The Emergency Powers Act, passed immediately after the declaration of war by the National Government, with the approval of the Labour Party, ostensibly against Nazi activities in Britain, is now being used by Colonial authorities to tighten the yoke of Imperialism around the necks of the natives' (Padmore 1940: 7). The purpose of the arrest of his friend I. T. A. Wallace-Johnson, a Sierra Leonean trade union leader, in 1939, Padmore argued, was 'to intimidate those who have the courage to take the initiative in organising the downtrodden native masses. The imperialists hope that by arresting and imprisoning such native leaders they will sow terrorism among the workers and thereby frustrate the development of trade unionism in the colonies' (Padmore 1940: 7). While *War Commentary* gave space to Padmore, they did not always agree with his politics. In his review of Nancy Cunard and George Padmore's *White Man's Duty* (1942), written in response to the Atlantic Charter, George Woodcock conceded that 'Padmore exposes the major defects of British rule and shows that only when this rule has been withdrawn will the native people of the colonies live reasonable lives, without poverty and enslavement', but also criticised that 'Where he fails is that he foresees this coming about by parliamentary means', which would only allow local elites 'to take the place of the white exploiters and crawl to power on the backs of their countrymen' (Woodcock 1943: 15). This did not deter Padmore from associating with the Freedom Group. For instance, on 1 April 1945, he gave a lecture on 'Constitutional Changes in the British Empire' in the Freedom Press lecture series at Holborn Hall in London ('Freedom Press Lectures' 1945: 2).

Described by Meltzer as an 'intolerant man' but with 'good reasons for his bitterness', Kenyatta also wrote for *War Commentary* (Meltzer 1976: 23). Summing up the brutality of British rule in Kenya and the hypocrisy of defending British 'democracy' during the war, Kenyatta painted a utopian picture of African tribes before the arrival of European colonisers:

> Cut off as they were from the outside world, they lived in their isolation with natural contentment, each group acting independently and satisfying its immediate needs and desires with material near at hand. As to their own mode of government, they managed their own affairs as best they could, through democratic tribal organisations formed according to the local customs and the stage of development which the

particular tribe had reached. Tribal affairs were in the hands of several groups or councils which every tribesman had the right to join. (Kenyatta 1941: 13)

Kenyatta's description of Africa's tribal system of land tenure, as self-governing 'masters of their destiny', chimed with anarchist ideas.

Meltzer described Padmore's friend Chris Jones, a Barbadian seaman, as 'certainly one of the most effective' speakers on anti-colonialism (Meltzer 1976: 23). At a 1941 May Day meeting organised by *War Commentary* at Conway Hall, 'the platform welcomed Chris Jones, who turned up at the last minute to convey a message of solidarity from the coloured workers all over the globe'. Jones told the 'audience just what "democracy" means for the 400 odd million coloured wage-slaves of the British Empire' ('May Day' 1941: 8). On 23 August 1942, British anarchists held a rally at Conway Hall in support of the Indian struggle against British rule. On behalf of the IASB, Jones spoke on 'the position in India from the point of view of the oppressed coloured workers all over the world'. Jones advocated international anti-colonial and class solidarity and 'stressed the fact that the interests of the working-class, whatever its race, colour or creed, was everywhere the same, and he appealed to the British workers to support the struggle of the Indian people, and the coming struggle of the workers in other parts of the Empire' ('Indian Freedom Rally' 1942: 16). Jones continued his involvement with the British anarchists, and on 12 March 1943, he was billed to speak on 'The Colonial Blacks are on the Move' at the weekly Friday lectures at the Freedom Press Rooms at Belsize Road, and on 14 May 1943, he gave another lecture on 'Life in H.M. Colonies' at the Freedom Press Rooms.[3] His premature death in September 1944 was also noted. The Irish-born veteran anarchist Mat Kavanagh wrote: 'All revolutionary workers will share in our sorrow at the death of our militant fellow worker, Chris Jones.' Describing Jones as the 'best coloured open-air speaker', Kavanagh referenced his speech for their Indian rally at Conway Hall and noted: 'His work amongst his coloured comrades made him loved and respected by them all, for these the true spirit of Internationalism shone out. His death is a great loss for the militant labour movement' (Kavanagh 1944: 7).

When the Bengal famine began in 1943, British anarchists were quick to connect it to British colonialism and wartime policies. Perceived as a deliberate tactic of the British government to break any anti-colonial resistance, *War Commentary* noted that leftist pressures to free Nehru and Gandhi from prison and calls for unity were meaningless: 'How can there be unity between workers who oppose the imperialist war on class grounds, and supporters of the war who only want to see India free so that the Indians can fight Britain's battles against the Japanese?' In typical fashion, *War Commentary* posited: 'We refuse to have anything to do with such misleading calls for an illusory "unity". We deride this conception of "freedom for India" which in fact means only Indian National Independence, and merely wishes to see Indian politicians instead of British ones ruling over the impoverished Indian workers.' From an anarchist point of view, the notion of 'Freedom for the Indian workers means freedom to work the land and the factories for the good of all and the production of abundance, instead of slavery and starvation for the enrichment of property owners, bureaucrats and investors' ('British Rule' 1943: 2). As the Bengal famine claimed millions of lives throughout the following years, *War Commentary* continued to cover the devastating atrocities stemming from imperial rule, while also criticising any calls for independence without freedom from governmental tyranny.[4]

In the final months of the Second World War, British authorities arrested four of the leading anarchists behind *War Commentary*: Vernon Richards, Marie Louise Berneri, John Hewetson and Philip Sansom. The arrests caused an uproar across the broader radical left, and the Freedom Press Defence Committee (FPDC) led by Herbert Read was established in March 1945 (Honeywell 2015: 257–84). At a 15 April 1945 protest meeting at Holborn Hall, Padmore 'brought messages of solidarity from the International African Service Bureau and from the Sierra Leone Trades Union Congress, making it clear that the struggle for freedom of the white and the coloured workers was identical' (Freedom Press Defence Committee 1945: 2; '800 Express Solidarity' 1945: 1). His sympathy for the anarchist cause commanded great respect: 'Such an action goes far beyond what one could imagine from the British T.U.C.,' one anarchist commented ('Who Are the Backward Races?' 1945: 4). In appearing at the protest meeting, Padmore connected the global nodes of anti-colonial and anarchist movements.

Return to *Freedom*: Independence and Decolonisation, 1945–62

In August 1945, *Freedom* incorporated *War Commentary*. The Labour Party had won the election in July, and the British left now veered more towards parliamentarianism than anarchist ideals of freedom, although the cause of the FPDC had brought public attention to the anarchists (Finn 2020: 159). At the same time, there were tensions with the British anarchist movement, leaving the Freedom Group somewhat diminished and challenged by new publications such as the *Anarchist Federation (London Group) Bulletin* and *Direct Action*. However, *Freedom* remained the most prominent international anarchist periodical in Britain at the time.

The end of the Second World War inaugurated the era of independence and decolonisation. Indian independence, Partition and violence soon became widely debated topics in *Freedom*. For anarchists, it was clear that independence would mean nothing to Indian workers: 'National independence can mean nothing to these people, for it will only give them new masters in the same conditions of exploitation. The only satisfactory struggle for colonial peoples, if they will only realise it, is that which means an end to native as well as foreign masters' ('Behind Indian Political Circus' 1947: 5).[5] Criticising the communist-led trade unions in India, M. P. T. Acharya, now a frequent contributor to *Freedom*, concurred: 'without an anarchist movement, this country will go to the dogs – in spite of the labour leaders trying to adapt themselves to capitalist-Fascism, which is the wage system' (Acharya 1947: 5). Furthermore, the communal violence of Partition was a direct outcome of British colonialism and religious differences. British anarchists condemned the violence and the poison of religious hatred and factionalism fanned by imperialism ('Religious Massacres' 1947: 1, 4; 'Indian Riots' 1948: 1).

In the early 1950s, *Freedom* still covered Pan-Africanist struggles for independence. In addition to commenting on the arrest of Gold Coast (now Ghana) trade union leader Kwame Nkrumah in January 1950, the Gold Coast government's ban on Padmore's *Africa: Britain's Third Empire* (1949) drew criticism in *Freedom* ('Who Is Free?' 1950: 3; Libertarian 1950: 3). However, in his review of *Africa: Britain's Third Empire*, Charles Humana criticised Padmore for – despite noting the effectiveness of boycott of British goods, strikes and decentralised communities –

advocating parliamentarian politics and 'constitutional approaches to the British' (Humana 1950: 2).

Beyond the Gold Coast, struggles against racism, colonialism and segregation in Rhodesia and apartheid South Africa attracted great attention. The South African president Daniël François Malan's introduction of apartheid laws drew criticism from the anarchists.[6] The brutality of Britain's colonial rule in Africa became evident during the Mau Mau uprising in 1952. Led by the Kenya Land and Freedom Army (KLFA), it was one of the longest anti-colonial uprisings against British rule in Africa. Referencing a speech by the London-based South African author Peter Abrahams, *Freedom* noted that 'European settlers, small in number but influential, . . . are conscious of the instability of their domination of Kenya' ('Mau Mau' 1952: 1, 3). Condemning the white settlers and British authorities for the developments in Kenya, *Freedom* stated that their attitude 'on the events in Kenya is not an extravagantly extreme one, but is based on facts which are recognised in reformist quarters'. However, the anarchists differed from reformists in their solution to the violence: 'The Kenya situation is inherent in imperialist economic and social structure. But the grievances of Africans could be solved by the application of revolutionary principles of social economy and human relations' ('Kenya: The Basic Question' 1952: 1, 4).

The arrest of Kenyatta and others in October 1952, ostensibly for leading the uprising and taking orders from Moscow, as Meltzer observed, was blatantly false. In fact, Kenyatta, as Meltzer put it, 'belonged always to the group of African anti-imperialists whose concern was the African people always, and who fell out with the Communists' (Meltzer 1952a: 1, 4). In the following months, the arrest and trial of Kenyatta was covered extensively in *Freedom*, which even reprinted Kenyatta's article from *War Commentary*.[7] However, *Freedom* also made it clear that this did not 'by any means imply an uncritical support of whatever is done by those opposing imperialism in Africa'. In fact, as they stated, '*Freedom* has made it clear in the past that anarchists have little sympathy with the nationalistic aspirations of Mau Mau, still less with the nationalistic brutality with which their resistance is punctuated' ('The Mau Mau Massacre' 1953: 1).

In the early 1960s, across Africa and the West Indies, Nigeria (1960), Sierra Leone (1961), Tanzania (1961), Uganda (1962), Trinidad and Tobago (1962) and Jamaica (1962) gained independence from Britain. However, as anarchists saw it, independence did not necessarily mean freedom for the workers and peasants across the colonial world. As Richard J. Westall asked rhetorically after Nigerian independence: 'Why is it that lovers of freedom, the anarchists, show such slight enthusiasm – if any at all? We have been crying for the end of colonial rule for many years, and yet when Nigeria is independent of this rule, we are not interested.' Westall answered, 'A black elite is taking over from a white elite to suit the "liberal" policy of Conservatives', but hoped that 'Nigerians realise that the European Africans are dangerous and unpleasant men – soon' (Westall 1960: 2).

As independence from British rule swept across the colonial world in the early 1960s, anarchists around the Freedom Group took an unwavering stance: support for anti-colonial struggles for freedom, but not the establishment of native, elitist, totalitarian regimes. In this sense, British anarchists stood out compared with other left-wing activists and ideologies. At the same time, however, *Freedom* no longer attracted the voices of anti-colonialists as the periodical had done in previous decades. In some ways, this discrepancy embodied the contentious relationship between anarchism and anti-colonialism. Anti-colonial anarchists and sympathisers such as Acharya, Jones and Padmore had died by the late 1950s, and Kenyatta had assumed the role of native ruler upon Kenya's independence in 1963, thus confirming anarchists' suspicion of supporting anti-colonial nationalism (see Meltzer 1976: 23).

Towards Freedom in *Freedom*

An examination of British anarchists' relation to the question of colonialism through the lens of *Freedom* reveals that, from the 1920s onwards, these issues were frequently debated in this periodical. True internationalism extended to the colonial world in that sense, but the periodical struggled to reach activists across the British Empire due to the predominantly nationalist character of anti-colonial movements. Indeed, throughout those years, there was an important position running through the anarchist school of thought: support for anti-colonial struggles for self-determination in the name of freedom for workers and peasants but refusal to support nationalist movements that sought to replace an imperialist oppressor with a native oppressor. At the same time, while assuming this position, *Freedom* gave space to divergent opinions and voices. From the Indian radicals Upadhyaya and Acharya to Pan-African anti-colonialists Padmore and Jones, from anarchist sympathisers Reynolds and Ridley to Owen, Meltzer and the renowned Goldman, *Freedom* and its temporary successors provided a forum for debating the true meaning of freedom. While the Freedom Group's periodicals often struggled to survive, they offered a sense of continuity of British anarchist thought as well as a platform for radical anti-colonial voices. As the most important British anarchist periodical, *Freedom* continuously demonstrated a serious and substantial engagement with the colonial question from the 1920s to the onset of decolonisation in the early 1960s.

Notes

1. See, for example, 'Mussolini Admits Defeat' 1937: 2; 'Malaga and Beyond' 1937: 2.
2. See, for example, Richards 1937: 3; Almoni 1938a: 2; Almoni 1938b: 2, 4.
3. For articles in *War Commentary* reporting on lectures by Jones, see 'Lectures' 1943a: 5; 'Lectures' 1943b: 2; 'Lectures' 1943c: 2. For a discussion of Jones's contributions, see Høgsbjerg 2011: 57, n. 93.
4. Articles in *War Commentary* on the Bengal famine included 'India: Famine Smothers Unrest' 1945: 1; 'Business as Usual' 1945: 3; Pittock-Buss 1945: 2.
5. See also 'What Next in India?' 1947: 1; 'India: A Problem We Leave Behind' 1947: 5; 'India – A Change of Masters' 1947: 1.
6. On *Freedom*'s coverage of the early years of apartheid, see R. 1950: 3; C. 1951: 3; N. C. 1951: 3; 'Racial Segregation in South Africa' 1952: 1; 'Central Africa and the Shadow of Malan' 1952: 3; 'Dr Malan and the World' 1952: 3; Libertarian 1952: 1.
7. For *Freedom*'s extensive coverage of the Mau Mau in Kenya, see 'Mau Mau: Symptom of a Sick Society' 1952: 1, 3; 'Kenya: The Basic Question' 1952: 1, 4; 'Facts Emerging in Kenya' 1952: 1, 4; 'Smouldering Africa' 1952: 1; Meltzer 1952b: 4; Kenyatta 1952: 3; 'Issues in the Pritt Case' 1953: 1; 'The White Men's Solution for Kenya' 1953: 1; Meltzer 1953: 1; '"Third Degree" in Kenya' 1953: 1; '2,800 Detained in Kenya Raid' 1953: 1; 'Africa and Kenyatta' 1953: 1, 4.

Bibliography

'800 Express Solidarity with Arrested Anarchists' (1945), *War Commentary*, 6.13, 21 April, 1.
'2,800 Detained in Kenya Raid' (1953), *Freedom: Anarchist Weekly*, 14.13, 28 March, 1.
Acharya, M. (1925), Letter to Thomas H. Keell, 15 October, Freedom Archives, Amsterdam; International Institute of Social History, ARCH00428.435-438.
—— (1947), 'Labour Splits in India', *Freedom: Anarchist Fortnightly*, 8.11, 31 May, 5.
'Africa and Kenyatta' (1953), *Freedom: Anarchist Weekly*, 14.16, 18 April, 1, 4.
Almoni, I. (1938a), 'Facts Concerning Palestine', *Spain and the World*, 2.28, 21 January, 2.
—— (1938b), 'Facts Concerning Palestine', *Spain and the World*, 2.29, 2 February, 2, 4.
'Behind Indian Political Circus' (1947), *Freedom*, 8.2, 18 January, 5.
'British Imperialism in Action' (1938), *Spain and the World*, 2.36, 24 June, 2.
'British Rule in India' (1943), *War Commentary*, 4.6, January, 2.
'Business as Usual While Indians Starve' (1945), *War Commentary*, 6.8, 10 February, 3.
C. (1951), 'Rhodesia: Setting the Scene for the Race War', *Freedom: Anarchist Fortnightly*, 12.7, 31 March, 3.
'Central Africa and the Shadow of Malan' (1952), *Freedom: Anarchist Weekly*, 13.26, 28 June, 3.
'Dr Malan and the World' (1952), *Freedom: Anarchist Weekly*, 13.36, 6 September, 3.
Editorial (1937), 'The League Will Not Stop the Massacre of the Innocent in Spain, China or Abyssinia', *Spain and the World*, 1.21, 13 October, 1.
Editors (1941), 'Indian Nationalism against the Indian Revolution', *War Commentary*, 2.9, July, 7.
'Facts Emerging in Kenya' (1952), *Freedom: Anarchist Weekly*, 13.46, 15 November, 1, 4.
Finn, Mike (2020), *Debating Anarchism: A History of Action, Ideas and Movements*, London: Bloomsbury.
Freedom Press Defence Committee (1945), 'Freedom Press Defence Committee', *War Commentary*, 6.12, 7 April, 2.
'Freedom Press Lectures' (1945), *War Commentary*, 6.11, 24 March, 2.
Goldman, Emma (1938), 'Palestine and Socialist Policy', *Spain and the World*, 2.38, 26 August, 2.
Goodway, David (2006), *Anarchist Seeds beneath the Snow: Left-Libertarian Thought and British Writers from William Morris to Colin Ward*, Liverpool: Liverpool University Press.
Gopal, Priyamvada (2019), *Insurgent Empire: Anticolonial Resistance and British Dissent*, London: Verso.
Honeywell, Carissa (2015), 'Anarchism and the British warfare state: The prosecution of the *War Commentary* anarchists, 1945', *International Review of Social History*, 60.2, 257–84.
Humana, Charles (1950), 'Africa: Can Constitutional Methods Help the African Worker?', *Freedom: Anarchist Fortnightly*, 11.12, 10 June, 2.
Høgsbjerg, Christian (2011), 'Mariner, renegade and castaway: Chris Braithwaite, seamen's organiser and Pan-Africanist', *Race and Class*, 53.36, 36–57.
'India – A Change of Masters' (1947), *Freedom: Anarchist Fortnightly*, 8.17, 23 August, 1.
'India: A Problem We Leave Behind' (1947), *Freedom: Anarchist Fortnightly*, 8.12, 14 June, 5.
'India: Famine Smothers Unrest' (1945), *War Commentary*, 6.6, 13 January, 1.
'Indian Freedom Rally' (1942), *War Commentary*, 3.19, September, 16.
'Indian Riots' (1948), *Freedom: Anarchist Fortnightly*, 9.2, 24 January, 1.
'Issues in the Pritt Case' (1953), *Freedom: Anarchist Weekly*, 14.2, 10 January, 1.
James, Leslie (2014), *George Padmore and Decolonization from Below: Pan-Africanism, the Cold War, and the End of Empire*, Basingstoke: Palgrave Macmillan.
Kavanagh, Mat (1944), 'Chris Jones', *War Commentary*, 5.23, October, 7.
Keell, Thomas H. [Editor's comment] (1930), 'Thoughts on India', *Freedom*, 30 October, 3.
'Kenya: The Basic Question' (1952), *Freedom: Anarchist Weekly*, 13.44, 1 November, 1, 4.

Kenyatta, Jomo (1941), 'How Kenya is Governed', *War Commentary*, 2.11, September, 13.
────── (1952), 'How Kenya is Governed', *Freedom: Anarchist Weekly*, 13.50, 13 December, 3.
Laursen, Ole Birk (2020), '"Anarchism, pure and simple": M. P. T. Acharya, anti-colonialism and the international anarchist movement', *Postcolonial Studies*, 22.3, 241–55.
'Lectures' (1943a), *War Commentary*, 4.7, February, 5.
'Lectures' (1943b), *War Commentary*, 4.8, March, 2.
'Lectures' (1943c), *War Commentary*, 4.12, May, 2.
Libertarian (1950), 'Attacks on Press Freedom', *Freedom: Anarchist Fortnightly*, 11.8, 15 April, 3.
────── (1952), 'Fascism in S. Africa', *Freedom: Anarchist Weekly*, 13.22, 31 May, 1.
'Malaga and Beyond' (1937), *Spain and the World*, 1.6, 19 February, 2.
Maloba, W. O. (2018), *Kenyatta and Britain: An Account of Political Transformation, 1929–1963*, Cham: Palgrave Macmillan.
Manela, Erez (2020), 'Foreword: Plotting the anticolonial international', in Michele Louro, Carolien Stolte, Heather Streets-Salter and Sana Tannoury-Karam (eds), *The League against Imperialism: Lives and Afterlives*, Leiden: Leiden University Press, 11–15.
'The Mau Mau Massacre' (1953), *Freedom: Anarchist Weekly*, 4 April, 1.
'Mau Mau: Symptom of a Sick Society' (1952), *Freedom: Anarchist Weekly*, 13.42, 18 October, 1, 3.
'May Day, 1941' (1941), *War Commentary*, 2.8, June, 8.
Meltzer, Albert [A. M.] (1939a), 'Workers' Empire Conference Fiasco', *Revolt!*, 3.1, 11 February, 2.
────── (1939b), 'Anarchist Tactic For Palestine', *Revolt!*, 3.3, 25 March, 2.
────── (1939c), 'Workers' Empire Conference', *Revolt!*, 3.3, 25 March, 4.
────── [Internationalist] (1952a), 'Military Adventure in Kenya', *Freedom: Anarchist Weekly*, 13.44, 8 November, 1, 4.
────── [Internationalist] (1952b), 'Bolshevik Methods in Kenya', *Freedom: Anarchist Weekly*, 13.49, 6 December, 4.
────── [Internationalist] (1953), 'Armed Rebellion of Kenya Whites', *Freedom: Anarchist Weekly*, 14.5, 31 January, 1.
────── (1976), *The Anarchists in London, 1935–1955*, Sanday, Orkney: Cienfuegos Press.
'Mussolini Admits Defeat' (1937), *Spain and the World*, 1.5, 5 February, 2.
N. C. (1951), 'The Coloured Franchise in S. Africa', *Freedom: Anarchist Weekly*, 12.14, 2 June, 3.
'Our Balance Sheet' (1938), *Spain and the World*, 2.36, 24 June, 3.
Owen, William C. (1927), 'Imperialism the Issue', *Freedom*, 41.441, March, 16.
Padmore, George (1940), 'Nine Months of War', *War Commentary*, 1.8–9, June–July, 7.
Pittock-Buss, Geoffrey (1945), 'The Atrocity of Authority', *War Commentary*, 6.15, 19 May, 2.
R. (1950), 'White Man's Paradise', *Freedom: Anarchist Fortnightly*, 11.22, 28 October, 3.
'Racial Segregation in South Africa' (1952), *Freedom: Anarchist Weekly*, 13.13, 29 March, 1.
Ray, Rob (2018), *A Beautiful Idea: History of the Freedom Press Anarchists*, London: Freedom Press.
'Religious Massacres in India' (1947), *Freedom: Anarchist Fortnightly*, 8.19, 20 September, 1, 4.
'The Revolt in India' (1930), *Freedom Bulletin*, 10 July, 3–4.
Reynolds, Reginald (1938a), 'Palestine and Socialist Policy', *Spain and the World*, 2.38, 29 July, 2, 4.
────── (1938b), 'Reg. Reynolds Answers', *Spain and the World*, 2.40, 16 September, 4.
────── (1939a), 'The Situation in Palestine', *Spain and the World*, 2.32, 18 March, 2.
────── (1939b), 'Watch India!', *War Commentary*, 1.2, December, 3.
Richards, Vernon [V. R.] (1937), 'Terrorism in Palestine', *Spain and the World*, 1.22, 27 October, 3.
────── (1938), 'Palestine – Idealists and Capitalists', *Spain and the World*, 2.45–6, 3 December, 5.
────── (1939), 'The Problem of Nutrition in the Colonies', *Revolt!*, 3.5, 1 May, 3.
Ridley, F. A. (1939), 'What is a Proletariat? A Study of Contemporary Imperialism', *Revolt!*, 3.5, 1 May, 3, 5.

Sherwood, Marika (2004), 'Lascar struggles against discrimination in Britain 1923–45: The work of N. J. Upadhyaya and Surat Alley', *The Mariner's Mirror*, 90.4, 438–55.
Shpayer-Makov, Haia (1987), 'The reception of Peter Kropotkin in Britain, 1886–1917', *Albion: A Quarterly Journal Concerned with British Studies*, 19.3, 373–90.
'Smouldering Africa' (1952), *Freedom: Anarchist Weekly*, 13.48, 29 November, 1.
Stock, Dinah (1941), 'Gandhi and the Indian Revolution', *War Commentary*, 2.6, April, 7.
'"Third Degree" in Kenya' (1953), *Freedom: Anarchist Weekly*, 14.8, 21 February, 1.
Upadhyaya, N. J. (1924), 'The Indian Press', *Freedom*, 38.422, September, 44.
—— (1925), 'Chattel Slaves v. Indian Wage Slaves', *Freedom*, 39.426, January, 2.
Van der Walt, Lucien (2011), 'Anarchism and syndicalism in an African port city: The revolutionary traditions of Cape Town's multiracial working class, 1904–1931', *Labor History*, 52.2, 137–71.
Westall, Richard J. (1960), '"Independent" Nigeria', *Freedom: Anarchist Weekly*, 21.42, 15 October, 2.
'What Are We Fighting For?' (1939), *War Commentary*, 1.1, November, 14.
'What Next in India?' (1947), *Freedom: Anarchist Fortnightly*, 8.12, 14 June, 1.
'The White Men's Solution for Kenya' (1953), *Freedom: Anarchist Weekly*, 14.4, 24 January, 1.
'Who Are the Backward Races?' (1945), *War Commentary*, 6.14, 5 May, 4.
'Who Is Free? In the Gold Coast' (1950), *Freedom: Anarchist Fortnightly*, 11.4, 4 March, 3.
Woodcock, George (1943), 'How is It with the Empah?', *War Commentary*, 4.18, mid-July, 15.
Zimmer, Kenyon (2015), *Immigrants against the State: Yiddish and Italian Anarchism in America*, Urbana: University of Illinois Press.

27

The Atlantic Charter in British Colonial Periodicals

David Johnson

Introduction

The Atlantic Charter was a statement issued on 14 August 1941 following a secret meeting between Franklin D. Roosevelt and Winston Churchill in Placentia Bay, Newfoundland. Formally known as 'Joint Declaration by the President and the Prime Minister', the Atlantic Charter set out the United States and Britain's shared vision for the post-war world and was endorsed on 24 September 1941 by the governments-in-exile of Belgium, Czechoslovakia, Luxembourg, the Netherlands, Poland, Norway, France and Yugoslavia, with the Soviet Union also adding its assent. Further ratification of the Charter followed on 1 January 1942 with the Declaration by United Nations. Looking back, commentators have placed the Atlantic Charter in the tradition of iconic documents like the Ten Commandments, the Magna Carta and the US Bill of Rights, and, looking forward, have credited it with inspiring the charters of the United Nations, Nuremberg and Bretton Woods (Borgwardt 2005: 5, 44).

Synthesising elements of Woodrow Wilson's 'Fourteen Points' (1918) and Roosevelt's 'Four Freedoms' (1941), the Atlantic Charter laid down eight pledges aimed at securing a new international order free from Nazi tyranny: (1) no territorial gains would be sought by the United States or the United Kingdom; (2) territorial adjustments would be in accord with the wishes of the peoples concerned; (3) all peoples would have a right to self-determination; (4) trade barriers would be lowered; (5) global economic cooperation and advancement of social welfare would be pursued; (6) signatories to the Charter would work for a world free of want and fear; (7) signatories would work for freedom of the seas; and (8) the aggressor nations would be disarmed, extending to a common disarmament.

The Charter immediately provoked controversy, with the main bone of contention the third clause: '[The US and UK] respect the right of all peoples to choose the form of government under which they will live; and they wish to see sovereign rights and self-government restored to those who have been forcibly deprived of them' (quoted in Brinkley and Facey-Crowther 1994: xvii). The earliest interpretation of Clause Three was delivered the very next day by Clement Attlee, Britain's Deputy Prime Minister, who reassured West African students in London that the Atlantic Charter's principles 'will apply, I believe, to all peoples of the world' (quoted in Reeves 2018: 262–3). Very soon afterwards, however, on 9 September 1941, Churchill contradicted Attlee's interpretation, first declaring that 'at the Atlantic meeting, we had in mind, primarily, the restoration of the sovereignty, self-government and national life of the states and nations of Europe now under the Nazi yoke', before insisting that the Charter did not constitute a promise of self-government to Britain's colonies: '[Liberating occupied European nations from Nazi rule] is quite a separate problem from the progressive evolution of self-governing institutions in the regions whose peoples owe allegiance to the British Crown' (quoted in Borgwardt 2005: 30). Churchill reiterated this interpretation more bluntly in a speech on 10 November 1942: 'Let me, however, make this clear, in case there should be any mistake in any quarter. We mean to hold our own. I have not become the King's First Minister in order to preside over the liquidation of the British Empire' (quoted in Simpson 2004: 181).

Roosevelt, by contrast, held to Attlee's interpretation of Clause Three. In his 1946 eyewitness account of the signing of the Charter, Roosevelt's son, Elliott, recalled his father saying, 'I think I speak as America's president when I say that America won't help England in this War simply so that she will be able to continue to ride roughshod over colonial peoples' (quoted in Venkataramani 1974: 18–19). In public pronouncements, unsurprisingly, Roosevelt expressed this view more diplomatically, as on 23 February 1942, when he declared in a speech commemorating George Washington's birthday that 'The Atlantic Charter applies not only to the part of the world that borders the Atlantic but to the whole world; disarmament of the aggressors, self-determination of nations and peoples, and the four freedoms – freedom of speech, freedom of religion, freedom from want, and freedom from fear' (quoted in Venkataramani 1974: 26).

These contending interpretations of Clause Three set out by Churchill, on the one side, and by Attlee and Roosevelt, on the other, were repeated, elaborated and contested in periodicals in Britain and across the Empire. For subject peoples in Britain's colonies, the prospect of being able to 'choose the form of government under which they will live' reverberated in a variety of distinctive ways. This chapter attempts to convey the wide range of competing interpretations of Clause Three that appeared in colonial periodicals in the years immediately after its promulgation. These interpretations are grouped into three sections: the first, those aligned with Churchill's imperial reading; the second, those reiterating Attlee and Roosevelt's interpretation; and the third, those rejecting the terms of the Charter, and demanding more radical post-war settlements.

The British Colonial Empire Is Not Coming to an End

Australian periodicals of the early 1940s provide an instructive snapshot of the sympathetic reception of Churchill's contribution to the Atlantic Charter, as they reproduce the views not only of Australia's leaders, but also of politicians in Britain and the other settler colonies. The most widely read Australian periodical, the *Bulletin*, published a hagiographic article on Churchill's efforts to draw the United States into the war, quoting from his speech on the Atlantic Charter of 24 August 1941 before concluding, 'In Mr Churchill's grand words, is the story of the evolution of American foreign policy . . . a record of the most amazing singlehanded feat in the whole brilliant history of British diplomacy' ('Uncabled Additions' 1941: 18).[1] Such sentiments were echoed in reports in the Australian Foreign Office's official periodical, *Current Notes on International Affairs*, which reproduced Lord Cranborne's speech to the House of Lords of 3 December 1942:

> Of one thing I am quite certain – the British Colonial Empire is not coming to an end. The work we have done is only the beginning. We, the citizens of the British Empire, whatever our race, religion or colour, have a mission to perform, and it is a mission which is essential to the welfare of the world. It is to ensure the survival of the way of life for which the United Nations are fighting, a way of life based on freedom, tolerance, justice and mutual understanding in harmony with the principles of the Atlantic Charter. It is that great mission, we must not, and shall not fail. ('Colonial Policy' 1943: 18)

Reinforcing Cranborne's message, *Current Notes* also published the views of the South African leader – and confidant of Churchill – Jan Christian Smuts, quoting his article in the December 1942 edition of the US magazine *Life*: the post-war world, Smuts argued, will 'be governed by the Atlantic Charter and similar international instruments . . . [I]t would be unwise to disturb the existing administrative relationship between mother countries and their colonies. Mother countries should remain exclusively responsible for the administration of their colonies and interference by others should be avoided' ('Colonial Policy' 1943: 19). Echoing Smuts's worries about the threat to the Empire posed by the colonised majorities, the Australian Broadcasting Corporation's magazine, *ABC Weekly*, argued, 'The white peoples of the world must settle their disputes quickly if they desire to retain their prestige in China and India. A long war will result in arming the masses, and the white race will be in the minority' (Carley 1942: 39).

Sympathy for Churchill's pro-imperial interpretation of the Charter was by no means confined to the public spheres of the settler colonies. Periodicals and newspapers in British colonies in East Africa, West Africa and the Caribbean all reported favourably on Churchill's role in drafting the Charter and remained silent about the potentially radical implications of Clause Three. The *Tanganyika Standard*, the English-language daily newspaper owned by the East African Standard Corporation in Nairobi and aimed at the colony's white readership, recorded that 'the general opinion in political circles is that the eight points form the basis of an international New Deal' ('Anglo-American Statement' 1941: 1), and that the Charter 'will find its place in history side by side with the Magna Carta and the Declaration of Independence' ('Three-power' 1941: 7). Another settler-owned publication, the *East Africa and Rhodesia* periodical, quoted in full the Charter's eight points, observing that 'most of [them] have direct East African application' ('Charter' 1942: 811), but never going on to elaborate, focusing instead on the Allied campaign in Ethiopia.

In West Africa, the *Ashanti Pioneer* embraced the Allied cause and the spirit of the Charter, declaring, 'Fortunately for the world, Britain and her Allies have unsheathed the sword to cry halt', and exhorted West Africans 'to enter the fray with all our might – body, soul and spirit to fight to rid the world of what had hitherto nursed strife and confusions' ('The Cause' 1942: 2). Begun in 1939 by John and Nancy Tsiboe, the *Ashanti Pioneer* in its first years prioritised keeping its black readership up to date with war news of direct concern to West Africans (Hargrove 2019: 29–32). For its editors, sustaining a united front against Nazism superseded any thoughts of challenging British rule. Gandhi's anti-colonial struggle therefore came in for harsh criticism: 'In the grim struggle for liberation of humanity from Nazism, we have been betrayed by Gandhi and his misguided followers . . . *The Ashanti Pioneer* counsels all our fellow Indian subjects of the Crown . . . to maintain a sober attitude and remain loyal' ('Gandhi's Failure' 1942: 2).

In the Caribbean, an article in the mainstream *Trinidad Guardian* published the day after the Charter also emphasised the priority of defeating Hitler: 'The German Fuehrer seeks world domination for himself and the enslavement of the rest of mankind; the heads of the two great democratic nations desire that all men should live under their own vine and fig tree in freedom from fear and want' ('Principles' 1941: 6). Applauding Churchill's diplomatic efforts, a later article contrasted the Atlantic Charter with the Treaty of Versailles, concluding, 'A new Versailles will inevitably bring new Hitlers for us to destroy. Let us destroy Hitlerism once and for all and begin to build a real New Order' ('No Room' 1942: 6).

Mr Churchill Must Think Again

At the same time, many newspapers and periodicals across the Empire rejected the Churchill interpretation of Clause Three. The Australian *Current Notes on International Affairs*, for example, juxtaposed the pro-imperial sentiments of Cranborne and Smuts with those of Walter Nash, New Zealand's Minister in Washington, who argued that the Attlee/Roosevelt interpretation of Clause Three should prevail:

> Freedom should and must be universal. So that the war we are fighting is, from New Zealand's point of view, a war to secure for all nations – large or small – strong and weak – old and new – the same freedom that I believe will rightfully come to ourselves and to the other countries of the United Nations when the conflict is over . . . Our relations towards dependent, backward or colonial peoples and territories must be governed by a spirit of trusteeship and not, as so often in the past, a desire to exploit and to profit. Our only consideration must be the well-being, education and development of these peoples with a view to their being entrusted at the earliest possible moment with the responsibilities of government. ('Colonial Policy' 1943: 19)

Nash's views were shared by Herbert Vere Evatt, the Australian Minister for External Affairs, whose many speeches on the Charter were scrupulously reported. In an address in New York, for example, Evatt reiterated, '[T]he declaration is universal in its scope and application. It follows that in the future the regions of the Pacific are to be covered by the broad principles of the Atlantic Charter' ('The Post-war Settlement' 1943: 146). Both Nash and Evatt, however, tempered their universalist rhetoric with a discourse of trusteeship, thus leaving space for the extension of the rights to self-government to be delayed until the colonies were 'ready for independence' – a decision which remained at Britain's discretion.

Such hesitations over the appropriate timetable for independence were absent in the Lagos publications, the weekly magazine, the *Comet*, edited by Duse Mohamed Ali, and the *West African Pilot*, edited by Nnamdi Azikiwe.[2] Both publications targeted black readers and were committed to accelerating Nigeria's journey to freedom from colonial rule. The *Comet*'s political allegiances were expressed in exorbitant praise for Roosevelt, who was applauded as certain to 'outlive many succeeding generations. George Washington fought for American independence. Abraham Lincoln secured freedom for the enslaved Africans. Franklin Delano Roosevelt has proved himself to be the Champion of Democracy!' ('American Neutrality?' 1941: 1). Azikiwe in the *West African Pilot* singled out Attlee as the decisive authority on the meaning of Clause Three, reporting that 'Africans, too, have been assured by Mr. C. R. Attlee ... that Anglo-American War aims apply to Africa. Africans also will enjoy these things promised for the new world to come', but concluding with the anxious thought, 'We hope that the Eight Points Declaration will not fizzle out in the end to be mere platitudes' ('Africans' 1941: 2). In contrast to the respectful coverage of Churchill in much of the colonial press, the *West African Pilot* republished with an approving preface an extended quotation from the British left-of-centre *News Chronicle*, which emphasised Churchill's role in pursuing Britain's interests in India, and challenged him to reverse his colonialist interpretation of the Charter:

> He never wholly eradicated from his mind the early bias of a subaltern in India who was convinced of the superiority of the Rule of the English Sahibs. In Indian eyes, his intentions are, therefore, doubly suspect. But he is a big enough man to cut out the past and deal honestly with present realities. The coloured races of the Empire have supported Britain in her hour of need, with money, men, and materials. They have earned the reward which reason and justice should have given them long ago. Mr Churchill must think again. Otherwise, the Atlantic Charter will become, for hundreds of millions, a symbol of hypocrisy. ('The Atlantic Charter' 1941: 3)

Azikiwe's words in the *West African Pilot* in 1941 were translated into action, as two years later he travelled to London with a delegation to submit a memorandum entitled 'The Atlantic Charter and British West Africa' to the British Secretary of State for the Colonies, demanding self-government along the lines promised by the Charter, and insisting that by 1958 all West African colonies should be independent and sovereign nation states.[3]

News of Azikiwe's memorandum and delegation soon reached Southern Africa, with Dr A. B. Xuma, the leader of the African National Congress (ANC), inviting Chief Sobhuza of Swaziland in November 1943 to a conference on post-war reconstruction, noting, 'This document should be an inspiration to all of us and we are trying to draw up ... a similar document for South Africa and the British Protectorates of Southern Africa' (quoted in Neame 2015: 180). The ANC accordingly discussed the Charter at its annual conference on 16 December 1943, concluding with the publication of *African Claims in South Africa*, which comprised two documents – 'The Atlantic Charter from the standpoint of Africans within the Union of South Africa' and the 'Bill of Rights'. In his preface to the first document, Xuma explicitly endorsed Roosevelt's interpretation, insisting that for fascism to be 'uprooted from the face of the earth', the Atlantic Charter 'must apply to the whole British Empire, the United States of America and to all the nations of the world and their subject peoples' (Karis and Carter 1973: 209–10). Like Azikiwe, the ANC Committee emphasised Clause Three: 'It is the inalienable right of all peoples to choose the form of government under which they will live and therefore Africans welcome the belated recognition of this right by the Allied Nations' (Karis and Carter 1973: 214).

The ANC's adoption of the Atlantic Charter was extensively covered by *Inkundla ya Bantu* [People's Forum], the leading African nationalist newspaper which was edited by Govan Mbeki from 1938 to 1944 (Switzer and Ukpanah 1997: 215–20). In his regular column, Khanyisa applauded the efforts of 'shrewd, short-statured Congress President-General, Dr A. B. Xuma of Sophiatown, Johannesburg, and grey-haired, learned Professor D. T. Jabavu of Fort Hare, President of the Convention', declaring *African Claims* to be 'an impressive document [which] has won admiration from widely different quarters' (Khanyisa 1943: 3). Although the overwhelming weight of *Inkundla*'s coverage of the ANC's adoption of the Charter was sympathetic, dissenting views were also published. An article by Sceptic, for example, points out, 'Problems of Labour will be inextricably bound with problems of land distribution and this fact [*African Claims*] does not face squarely' (Sceptic 1944: 2), and an open letter by the Communist Party member Edwin Mofutsanyana attacks *Inkundla*'s obeisance to the ANC, characterising Khanyisa as 'a pen prostitute ... whose love of the African National Congress has forced him into a political controversy with every organisation' (Mofutsanyana 1944: 2).

As had been the case in the other colonies, so too in India news of both the Charter and Attlee's speech in London explaining its import was reported within twenty-four hours. The front-page headline of the pro-Congress *Hindustan Times* of Delhi on 15 August 1941 was 'Churchill and Roosevelt Meet', and Attlee's London speech was on the front page of Bombay's *Illustrated Weekly of India* on 17 August 1941 under the heading '"Democracies Fighting War for All People". Peace Principles Applicable to Every Country'. Both publications reproduced in full Attlee's words framing the Charter as a commitment to reversing Britain's racist colonial legacy:

> We ... have always been conscious of the wrongs done by the white races to the races with darker skins. We have been glad to see how with the passing of years the old conception of colonies as places inhabited by inferior people, whose function was only to serve and produce wealth for the benefit of other people, has made way for juster and nobler ideas. Yesterday I was privileged to announce a declaration of principles which apply, I believe, to all the peoples of the world. ('Principle' 1941: 1; '"Democracies"' 1941: 1)

Notwithstanding Attlee's reassurances, the *Hindustan Times* noted Britain's long record of false promises: 'In India we are so accustomed to the process of unexceptionable principles being whittled down to the point where performance denies their very existence that this Joint Declaration is not likely to arouse the least enthusiasm' ('The Eight-Point Plan' 1941: 6).

Indian cynicism about the fine phrases of the Atlantic Charter was expressed in both the Indian and the British public spheres (see, for example, Figure 27.1). In an interview published in *The Hindu* in November 1941, Mohandas K. Gandhi declared, 'I am not able to envisage in the Atlantic Charter the emergence of a non-violent new world order of my conception', and in a second interview published in the British *Spectator* in March 1942, he repeated his doubts about the Charter's capacity to hasten Indian independence: 'What is the Atlantic Charter? It went down the ocean as soon

Figure 27.1 'Cartoon: Freedom for All', *Hindustan Times*, 18 August 1941, p. 1. Courtesy of the British Library.

as it was born! ... Mr [Leo] Amery denies that India is fit for democracy, and Mr Churchill states that the Charter could not apply to India' (Gandhi 1999, vol. 81: 60, 348). In a third interview published in May 1942 in his own weekly newspaper, *Harijan*, Gandhi asked, 'Can we depend upon Britain and America, both whose hands are stained with blood? India's name can be found nowhere on the Atlantic Charter ... I have been thinking of a new mode of life. But it is impossible unless Britain withdraws to let the Indians and the Negroes be free' (Gandhi 1999, vol. 82: 285). Reinforcing such sceptical views in the colonial periodicals were widely circulated pamphlets, like Jawaharlal Nehru's *What India Wants* (1942), which observed, 'The Atlantic Charter is again a pious and nebulous expression which stimulates nobody, and even this, Mr Churchill has told us, does not apply to India' (Nehru 1942: 8).

For anti-colonial nationalist leaders like Azikiwe in Nigeria, Xuma in South Africa, and Gandhi in India, the Atlantic Charter provided an opening to press their claims for independence from colonial and segregationist rule. Responding to the Charter's binary juxtaposing Nazi tyranny and Anglo-American liberal democracy, Azikiwe's 'The Atlantic Charter and British West Africa' and the ANC's 'The Atlantic Charter from the standpoint of Africans within the Union of South Africa' imagine liberated postcolonial national communities modelled upon the Charter's eight principles. Such visions of freedom from colonialism and segregation inspired by the Charter were widely reported and debated in periodicals across the Empire, with *Inkundla ya Bantu* in South Africa and *Harijan* in India both embracing its possibilities, while noting its silences and limitations. Receiving arguably even more coverage than the Charter itself, the fracas over the meaning of Clause Three exposed the gulf between the Charter's universalist rhetoric and Britain's post-war imperial ambitions. The established lines of communication between periodicals in Britain and its colonies ensured that the post-war shape of imperial rule was discussed extensively in the overlapping metropolitan and subaltern public spheres, with charges of hypocrisy and bad faith levelled at Britain's rulers in the pages of (for example) the *News Chronicle* and the *Spectator* in London, as well as in the pages of the *West African Pilot* in Africa and the *Hindustan Times* in India. Periodicals in the different parts of the Empire might not always have been in direct dialogue with each other, but the Charter nonetheless provoked similar arguments from anti-colonial nationalists alive to the opportunity Clause Three provided to press their claims for freedom.

The Biggest Fraud of our Time: The Atlantic Charter

Refusing the alternatives of Anglo-American democracy versus Nazi tyranny proffered by the Atlantic Charter, several articles imagined post-war dispensations independent of these starkly opposed Euro-American models. One of the earliest disavowals of the Atlantic Charter was an article by George Padmore published in the Independent Labour Party's paper, the *New Leader*, in January 1942. First summarising Attlee's expansive interpretation of the Charter of 16 August 1941, which 'aroused tremendous enthusiasm among the 500 million colored peoples in the Empire', and then Churchill's insistence of 9 September 1941 that the Charter only applied to European nations, Padmore concluded, '[Churchill's] statement made it obvious that the Tories envisaged a perpetuation of imperialism and a continuation of their domination of colonial peoples after they had got rid of their German imperialist rival' (Padmore 1942a: 3). Demonstrating an up-to-date knowledge of anti-colonial politics across the Empire, Padmore summarises the angry responses to Churchill's words in Nigeria, Burma, India and Malaya. The subject peoples in the colonies, Padmore argues, see through 'all the [Atlantic Charter's] talk about democracy and freedom'; from their perspective, the Second World War is no more than 'a quarrel between imperialist bandits for a re-division of their countries' (Padmore 1942a: 3). Padmore thus reframes the fundamental opposition of the Atlantic Charter by insisting that 'the old-established democratic "peace-loving" imperialism [of Roosevelt and Churchill] . . . is indistinguishable from [Hitler and Mussolini's] fascist authoritarianism' (Padmore 1942a: 3). The congruence Padmore identified between fascism and colonialism therefore demanded a postcolonial solution that transcended the Atlantic Charter's spurious binary: 'only a Socialist Europe can offer to these millions of brown, yellow and black races the possibility of freedom, in order that, as free peoples, they may voluntarily take their place as equals in the community of the World Federation of Socialist countries' (Padmore 1942a: 3). Padmore repeated such arguments (often verbatim) not only in other British radical publications (see Padmore 1942b), but also in articles published in newspapers and periodicals across the Empire – in the *African Morning Post*, the *Ashanti Pioneer*, the *West African Pilot*, the *Barbados Advocate*, the *Bermuda Recorder* and the Jamaican *Public Opinion* (James 2016: 56) – as well as in the pamphlet co-written with Nancy Cunard, *The White Man's Duty: An Analysis of the Colonial Question in Light of the Atlantic Charter* (1943). Padmore emphasised that the honouring of Clause Three was but the first step towards securing economic self-sufficiency; self-government would enable colonial peoples to pass laws 'to protect the native industries, which would prevent them from being systematically thwarted by monopoly interests' (Cunard and Padmore 1943: 36).

Padmore's determination to root his objections to the Atlantic Charter in a critique of capitalism was shared by influential writers in the two major Indian periodicals, Kolkata's *Modern Review* and Mumbai's *Indian Social Reformer*. Publishing its first issue in January 1907 under the editorship of Ramananda Chatterjee, the *Modern Review* swiftly became the pre-eminent forum for nationalist debates about India's future, earning the exorbitant praise of historian Jadunath Sarkar, who compared the *Modern Review*'s contribution to India's freedom struggle to the *Edinburgh Review*'s thirty-year duel with Lord Elden's Tory bureaucracy in early nineteenth-century Britain, declaring, '"the first forty years of the twentieth century in India were marked by a still longer duel between the *Modern Review* and the Tories in power over India's destiny"' (quoted in Bose 1974: 37).[4] Several contributors to the *Modern Review* published opinion pieces well to the left of the official Congress line. Shriman Narayan Agarwal, for example, insisted that capitalist economic models packaged in duplicitous phrases could never dupe the poor of India:

> If the capitalist structure is allowed to remain intact after this war, life will not be worth living, and the world will be again overwhelmed by a greater tragedy before long. The orthodox economists, however, cannot think in terms of anything save a modified system of capitalism. They wish to pacify the revolting masses by using fine and suave phrases and throwing a few crumbs of rights and privileges here and there. The well-known Atlantic Charter is, more or less, an attempt in this direction. All such efforts are wholly futile and will lead us nowhere. (Agarwal 1942: 258)

In a similar spirit, D. K. Malhotra complained that the declarations and charters by western leaders 'are good enough in their own way, but they hardly stir the imagination'; what is needed instead, he argues, is 'to break the power of entrenched privilege wherever and in whatever form it appears – whether as a monopoly, a cartel or discriminatory trade treaty' (Malhotra 1942: 466). Instead of the eight broad commitments of the Atlantic Charter, India requires 'a charter of man's economic rights – right to work, right to leisure and right to a decent wage' (Malhotra 1942: 466). Like Padmore and Nehru, Agarwal followed up and expanded upon the arguments he first outlined in periodicals in a series of pamphlets. In *The Gandhian Plan of Economic Development for India* (1944), for example, he quoted Harold Laski to bolster his vision of an anti-capitalist postcolonial India based upon the principles of 'simplicity, decentralisation and cottage industrialism' (Agarwal 1944: 15).

The radical objections to the Atlantic Charter which circulated in Britain's *New Leader*, the *West African Pilot*, Jamaica's *Public Opinion* and India's *Modern Review* were echoed in two quite different South African periodicals. *The Guardian*, the newspaper written and run by members of the Communist Party of South Africa (CPSA), enjoyed a surge in circulation figures through the war years, rising from 8,000 sales in 1939 to 50,000 in 1945.[5] *The Guardian* was cynical about the Atlantic Charter. Quoting Clause Three, the columnist Vigilator remarks, 'A fine sentiment. But does anyone imagine that it will be applied to India?' (Vigilator 1941: 5), and an editorial published a week after the Charter's arrival argued that only the Soviet Union provided a meaningful alternative to the hypocritical proclamations of the capitalist Allies:

> The Soviet Union is proving that only a free and equal association of nationalities can develop the human and natural resources needed to resist successfully the robber aims of aggressive imperialisms. The Soviet Union is succeeding where others have failed, precisely because she has rooted out imperialism without withering her own frontiers. ('Editorial' 1941: 6)

In contrast to Padmore, who had broken with the Comintern in 1935, and to Agarwal, who looked to autochthonous forms of Indian socialism for inspiration, *The Guardian* embraced Stalin's Soviet Union as the model society which would lead the way in '[establishing] the world of free men and nations, drawn together in peaceful co-operation, [in which] imperialism must be rooted out and complete freedom granted to all subject peoples' ('Editorial' 1941: 6).

The second Cape Town periodical, the *Bulletin*, was published by the Anti-Coloured Affairs Department (Anti-CAD) movement between 1943 and the early 1950s. A bi-weekly two-to-four-page newsletter, the *Bulletin* published opinion pieces, anonymously and without titles, which criticised segregationist South Africa and global capitalism with equal vigour. The likely author of many if not all of the issues of the *Bulletin* was Ben Kies (Lee 205: 42), who attacked repeatedly what he saw as liberal hypocrisies paraded on the world stage, pre-eminently the Atlantic Charter. Arguing that the strategic liberalism of Smuts during the Second World War paralleled Roosevelt and Churchill's bogus liberalism embodied in the Atlantic Charter, Kies exposed the abuse of the word 'freedom':

> No doubt this veteran-son of Imperialism and servant of Finance-Capital [Smuts] has made invaluable contributions to the biggest fraud of our time: the Atlantic Charter . . . What are these Four Freedoms? The Freedom of Capitalism to exploit Labour. The Freedom to restrict production and create scarcity, wherever it is profitable for Capitalism. The Freedom to create monopolies, trusts, cartels, to corner markets and divide the world into spheres of influence. The Freedom to plunder the Colonies, to oppress and exploit the Colonial peoples in order to obtain raw materials for their industries. These are the Four Freedoms which the Atlantic Charter seeks to preserve. (Anon. 1943, *Bulletin*: 2)

In contrast to the ANC's endorsement of the Atlantic Charter, Kies believed that the Charter was a false dream peddled by the Allied leaders. Accordingly, he attacked the ANC leaders who 'still clung pathetically to the illusion that the Churchill-Roosevelt Atlantic Charter . . . would usher in the Four Freedoms for the oppressed'; rather, he observed, they should register that 'while they may dream, the ruling class does not dream. The ruling class sells dreams' (Anon. 1944, *Bulletin*: 1).

Critical of the CPSA's reverence for Stalin's Soviet Union, Kies looked for inspiration to other successful anti-colonial struggles, notably China, which he praised for turning the words of the Atlantic Charter against its western progenitors: 'the Chinese people took the Atlantic Charter seriously and started a Civil War' (Anon. 1945, *Bulletin*: 1). In a similar vein, he praised black South African workers for appropriating the words of the Charter to serve their own struggles for 'houses and jobs and African trade unions and fundamental human rights for all' (Anon. 1945, *Bulletin*: 1). Finally, Kies insisted upon a fundamental distinction between anti-colonial political leaders who exploited the Charter's words in their efforts to extract concessions from their rulers, on the one hand, and the collective struggle of the exploited and oppressed masses, on the other:

> Now we have never concealed from the people the fact that both the Atlantic Charter and the preamble to the World Charter are just plain frauds. But we must also make it quite clear that there is a fundamental distinction between those honest, working people who may not know anything about politics but who are turning the ideas contained in those documents into weapons for use in their direct fight for liberation, and on the other hand, those so-called political leaders who hope to obtain freedom by reminding the rulers of the words of the Charter. (Anon. 1945, *Bulletin*: 1–2)

Kies concludes that the oppressed will never win their freedom 'by holding up the Atlantic Charter or chanting snatches of the preamble'; they will only prevail if 'they stand up and fight' (Anon. 1945, *Bulletin*: 2). Not the platitudes of western leaders, but rather the collective struggles of the colonised, will deliver freedom.

Conclusion

During the Second World War, British colonial periodicals hosted furious debates over the meaning and significance of Clause Three of the Atlantic Charter. The widest range of interpretations of Clause Three circulated, with the imperfect flow of traffic between colonial and metropolitan public spheres ensuring that pro-Churchill, pro-Attlee/Roosevelt and more radical interpretations appeared in periodicals from Accra to Cape Town to Dar es Salaam to Delhi to Kingston to Kolkata to Lagos to London to Mumbai to Port of Spain and to Sydney (the list could be extended). Although no global communication network existed for the accurate and efficient intercommunication of these arguments across a single coherent 'British colonial public sphere', arguments were nonetheless waged in multiple parallel and overlapping colonial public spheres, with instances of trans-colonial connection and solidarity, as well as possibilities of dialogue frustrated by failures of communication or lack of access to the publications of other colonies. That so many articles critical of the Churchill interpretation appeared across the Empire might give hope to Nancy Fraser's contemporary aspiration to 'connect the historical experience of postcolonials with those of the Global North [because both] resent subjection to arbitrary, unjustified power to which one has not been asked to consent' (Fraser 2014: 148). However, as the locally inflected, widely scattered attacks upon Churchill's interpretation of Clause Three demonstrate, communication across national and colonial boundaries in the 1940s was far from coordinated. At the same time, after the war, throughout the Empire, anti-colonial ideas circulated to the extent that successful independence struggles proceeded to refute Churchill's interpretation.

Recent histories recounting the rise of global human rights discourse since the Second World War allocate an honourable place to the Atlantic Charter but consign a subsidiary role to the contributions of anti-colonial intellectuals to its reception and impact. In Joseph R. Slaughter's terms, the story of human rights is 'chiefly a Euro-American tale [which] tends to present European and American actors as the pioneers and primary agents of human rights discourse and law – rather than as, say, reactive and defensive double-agents against populist desires in the Third World' (Slaughter 2018: 756). By excavating the many compelling criticisms of the Atlantic Charter expressed by anti-colonial intellectuals in the early 1940s in the pages of colonial and metropolitan periodicals, the Eurocentric account of the Atlantic Charter's promulgation and legacies founders. In particular, the demands by Padmore, Agarwal and Kies to redress the economic hardships occasioned by colonial rule under capitalism highlight the inadequacy of liberal definitions of postcolonial freedom. By taking advantage of the publishing possibilities afforded by the anti-colonial periodicals circulating in the counterpublic spheres of the 1940s, these writers inspired their readers with radical alternatives to the Atlantic Charter, visions of post-independence futures invariably anti-capitalist, in some cases anti-Stalinist, and in other cases rooted in collectivist non-western political traditions.

Notes

1. The Sydney-based *Bulletin*'s satirical and irreverent mode of address mediated a racist and masculinist settler ideology which was consistent with Churchill's pro-imperial stance (see Chapter 7 by Tony Hughes-d'Aeth and Chapter 8 by Sam Hutchinson).
2. On the histories of the *Comet* and the *West African Pilot*, see Chapter 33 by Marina Bilbija.
3. Azikiwe's anti-colonial politicking during the Second World War is discussed by Idemili 1978: 87; Sherwood 1996: 139–40; Ibhawoh 2014: 842–3, 850–1; Reeves 2018: 272–80.
4. On the *Modern Review*, Chatterjee's editorship and the other anti-colonial periodicals circulating in India in the 1940s, see Israel 1994: 194–215; Chatterjee 2020: chapter 4. On Hindi-language periodicals in the same period, see Orsini 2002: 52–68. On the socialist strands in Congress ideology of the 1940s, as well as varieties beyond the Congress umbrella, see Sherman 2018: 485–504.
5. On *The Guardian* during the war years, see Zug 2007: 37–69; Switzer 1997: 266–330; Pinnock 1992: 69–88. The CPSA also published a monthly periodical, *Inkululeko* [Freedom].

Bibliography

'Africans and Anglo-American War Aims' (1941), *West African Pilot*, 20 August, 2.
Agarwal, Shriman Narayan (1942), 'Gandhian Socialism', *Modern Review*, 72, September, 258–60.
—— (1944), *The Gandhian Plan of Economic Development for India*, Bombay: Padma Publications.
'American Neutrality?' (1941), *Comet*, 27 September, 1.
'Anglo-American Statement of Joint War and Peace Aims' (1941), *Tanganyika Standard*, 15 August, 1.
Anon. (1943), *Bulletin*, 13 October, 1–2.
—— (1944), *Bulletin*, 20 December, 1–2.
—— (1945), *Bulletin*, 7 November, 1–2.
'The Atlantic Charter' (1941), *West African Pilot*, 13 November, 3–4.
Borgwardt, Elizabeth (2005), *A New Deal for the World: America's Vision for Human Rights*, Cambridge, MA: Harvard University Press.

Bose, Nemai Sadhan (1974), *Ramananda Chatterjee*, New Delhi: Ministry of Information Publications Division.
Brinkley, Douglas, and David R. Facey-Crowther (eds) (1994), *The Atlantic Charter*, London: Macmillan.
Carley, Stephen (1942), 'Tomorrow's World', *ABC Weekly*, 7 March, 39.
'The Cause Reiterated' (1942), *Ashanti Pioneer*, 4 August, 2.
'Charter of World Freedom' (1942), *East Africa and Rhodesia*, 21 August, 811.
Chatterjee, Kalyan (2020), *Media and Nation Building in Twentieth-Century India: Life and Times of Ramananda Chatterjee*, London and New York: Routledge.
'Churchill and Roosevelt Meet' (1941), *Hindustan Times*, 15 August, 1.
'Colonial Policy' (1943), *Current Notes on International Affairs*, 15 January, 17–21.
Cunard, Nancy, and George Padmore (1943), *The White Man's Duty: An Analysis of the Colonial Question in Light of the Atlantic Charter*, London: W. H. Allen.
'"Democracies Fighting War for All Peoples"' (1941), *Illustrated Weekly of India*, 17 August, 1.
Editorial [Jack Simons] (1941), *The Guardian*, 21 August, 6.
'The Eight-Point Plan' (1941), *Hindustan Times*, 17 August, 6.
Fraser, Nancy (2014), *Transnationalizing the Public Sphere*, Cambridge: Polity Press.
Gandhi, Mohandas K. (1999), *The Collected Works of Mahatma Gandhi*, New Delhi: Publications Division Government of India, https://www.gandhiserve.net/about-mahatma-gandhi/collected-works-of-mahatma-gandhi/ (accessed 19 January 2024).
'Gandhi's Failure' (1942), *Ashanti Pioneer*, 14 August, 2.
Hargrove, Jarvis L. (2019), '*Ashanti Pioneer*: Coverage of growing political developments in the Gold Coast, 1946–1949', *Journal of West African History*, 5.2, 29–56.
Ibhawoh, Bonny (2014), 'Testing the Atlantic Charter: Linking anticolonialism, self-determination and universal human rights', *The International Journal of Human Rights*, 18.7–8, 842–60.
Idemili, Sam O. (1978), 'What the *West African Pilot* did in the movement for Nigerian nationalism between 1937 and 1957', *Black American Literature Forum*, 12, 84–91.
Israel, Milton (1994), *Communications and Power: Propaganda and the Press in the Indian Nationalist Struggle, 1920–1947*, Cambridge: Cambridge University Press.
James, Leslie (2016), 'Transatlantic passages: Black identity construction in West African and West Indian newspapers, 1935–1950', in Derek R. Peterson, Emma Hunter and Stephanie Newell (eds), *African Print Cultures: Newspapers and their Publics in the Twentieth Century*, Ann Arbor: University of Michigan Press, 49–74.
Karis, Thomas, and Gwendolen M. Carter (eds) (1973), *From Protest to Challenge: A Documentary History of African Politics in South Africa, 1882–1964*, vol. 2, Stanford: Hoover Institution.
Khanyisa (1943), 'South African Political Commentary', *Inkundla ya Bantu*, 30 December, 3.
Lee, Christopher Joon-Hai (2005), 'The uses of the comparative imagination: South African history and world history in the political consciousness and strategy of the South African left, 1943–1959', *Radical History Review*, 92, 31–61.
Malhotra, D. K. (1942), 'The Economic Prospect', *Modern Review*, 72, December, 464–6.
Mofutsanyana, E. T. (1944), 'S. A. P. Commentary', *Inkundla ya Bantu*, 29 February, 2.
Neame, Sylvia (2015), *The Congress Movement: The Unfolding of the Congress Alliance 1912–1961*, vol. 3, Cape Town: HRSC Press.
Nehru, Jawaharlal (1942), *What India Wants*, London: The India League.
'No Room for Another Versailles' (1942), *Trinidad Guardian*, 28 August, 6.
Orsini, Francesca (2002), *The Hindi Public Sphere, 1920–1940: Language and Literature in the Age of Nationalism*, New Delhi: Oxford University Press.
Padmore, George (1942a), 'Atlantic Charter Not Intended for Colonies. Colonial People are Told to Have No Illusions', *New Leader*, 24 January, 3.

—— (1942b), 'Atlantic Charter Not Intended for Colonies. Colonial People are Told to Have No Illusions', *The Militant*, 14 March, 3–4.

Pinnock, Donald (1992), 'Writing left: Ruth First and radical South African journalism in the 1950s', unpublished PhD thesis, Rhodes University.

'The Post-war Settlement in the Pacific' (1943), *Current Notes on International Affairs*, 15 May, 145–52.

'Principle of Joint Declaration to Apply to Asiatics and Africans' (1941), *Hindustan Times*, 17 August, 1.

'Principles for a Post-war World' (1941), *Trinidad Guardian*, 15 August, 6.

Reeves, Mark (2018), '"Free and Equal Partners in your Commonwealth": The Atlantic Charter and anticolonial delegations to London, 1941–1943', *Twentieth-Century British History*, 29.2, 259–83.

Sceptic (1944), 'Comment on Atlantic Charter Statement', *Inkundla ya Bantu*, 17 February, 2.

Sherman, Taylor C. (2018), '"A new type of revolution": Socialist thought in India, 1940s–1960s', *Postcolonial Studies*, 21.4, 485–504.

Sherwood, Marika (1996), '"Diplomatic platitudes": The Atlantic Charter, the United Nations and colonial independence', *Immigrants and Minorities*, 15.2, 135–50.

Simpson, Brian (2004), *Human Rights and the End of Empire: Britain and the Genesis of the European Convention*, Oxford: Oxford University Press.

Slaughter, Joseph R. (2018), 'Hijacking human rights: Neoliberalism, the new historiography, and the end of the Third World', *Human Rights Quarterly*, 40.4, 735–75.

Switzer, Les (1997), 'Socialism and the resistance movement: The life and times of *The Guardian*, 1937–1952', in Les Switzer (ed.), *South Africa's Alternative Press: Voices of Protest and Resistance, 1880s–1960s*, Cambridge: Cambridge University Press, 266–330.

—— and Ime Ukpanah (1997), 'Under siege: *Inkundla ya Bantu* and the African nationalist movement, 1938–1951', in Les Switzer (ed.), *South Africa's Alternative Press: Voices of Protest and Resistance, 1880s–1960s*, Cambridge: Cambridge University Press, 215–51.

'Three-power Supply Conference in Moscow' (1941), *Tanganyika Standard*, 22 August, 7.

'Uncabled Additions. Churchill's Winning Way' (1941), *Bulletin*, 10 December, 18.

Venkataramani, M. S. (1974), 'The United States, the colonial issue, and the Atlantic Charter hoax', *International Studies*, 13.1, 1–28.

Vigilator [Harold Baldry] (1941), 'Behind the Overseas News. The Churchill-Roosevelt Meeting', *The Guardian*, 21 August, 5.

Zug, James (2007), *The Guardian: The History of South Africa's Extraordinary Anti-Apartheid Newspaper*, Pretoria: UNISA Press.

28

CITATION AND SOLIDARITY: REPORTING THE 1955 ASIAN-AFRICAN CONFERENCE IN AFRICAN NEWSPAPERS AND PERIODICALS

Christopher J. Lee

In April 1985, *The Ethiopian Herald* published an editorial with the title 'The Spirit of Bandung' to mark the anniversary of the 1955 Asian-African Conference held in Bandung, Indonesia (see Figure 28.1). 'Thirty years ago, leaders of the newly liberated African and Asian countries met in the Indonesian city of Bandung in a historic conference that heralded the emergence of former colonies as an effective political factor in international relations,' it began. 'What made the Bandung Conference possible was the collapse of the colonial system in Africa and Asia under the blows of the liberation forces. Bandung also epitomised the dawn of a new era which opened new vistas for the young states to bring their political weight to the future course of international relations' ('The Spirit' 1985: 2). The editorial went on to describe how the atmosphere at Bandung 'was overshadowed with suspicions and uncertainties' due to ongoing imperialist interventions, though this was 'to be expected since the Bandung Conference passed a death sentence on a trend in international relations largely dominated by the former colonial powers' ('The Spirit' 1985: 2). Still, the diplomatic principles agreed upon at Bandung, including 'respect for sovereignty, territorial integrity and non-interference in the internal affairs of other countries' ('The Spirit' 1985: 2), had continued to shape the international landscape, particularly through the Non-Aligned Movement (NAM) established in 1961. The NAM served as 'a living refutation' of western imperialist ambitions. The editorial concluded with a statement about Ethiopia's role in this history. 'As a founding member of the Non-aligned Movement, Revolutionary Ethiopia believes that the spirit of solidarity that animated participants of the Bandung Conference thirty years ago has to be given a new lease of life to put the ideals of South-South cooperation into practice,' the editorial summarised. 'This would indeed break the deadlock in the North-South dialogue and open new perspectives for the future. The spirit of Bandung has indeed to be kept alive' ('The Spirit' 1985: 2).

The spirit of Bandung has been a subject of attention in recent scholarship on global decolonisation published over the past two decades. Perceived as a pivotal moment during the high point of decolonisation after the Second World War, the Asian-African Conference, as it was formally named, of April 1955 has garnered notice due to its timing, intercontinental involvement, and its political ambiguities that have generated competing interpretations of its historical significance. Co-sponsored by Indonesia,

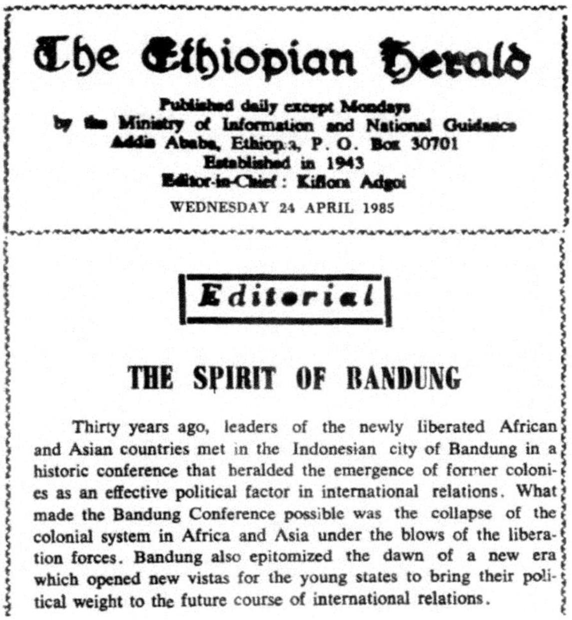

Figure 28.1 'Editorial: The Spirit of Bandung', *The Ethiopian Herald*, 24 April 1985, p. 2. Courtesy of the author.

Burma (Myanmar), Ceylon (Sri Lanka), India and Pakistan, who were referred to collectively as the Colombo Powers, delegations from twenty-nine countries in Africa and Asia convened in Bandung from 18 to 24 April to address pressing issues their respective continents faced during the early Cold War period.[1] Though the countries present were not all independent – Sudan would achieve its independence in 1956 and the Gold Coast (Ghana) in 1957 – the meeting initiated a new period of postcolonial diplomacy and Third World internationalism. What is striking about this editorial in *The Ethiopian Herald* is the citation of Bandung as a reference point three decades after its occurrence and, furthermore, the connection made between the Bandung moment of the 1950s and a later political terminology of the 1970s and 1980s regarding South-South alignments and North-South tensions (Prashad 2013). It consequently underscores how the Asian-African Conference remained a source of inspiration and a means of understanding international history even after the failure of a number of its ambitions.

In contrast to accounts that have dwelled primarily on the diplomatic repercussions of the event (Ampiah 2007; Phillips 2016; Tan and Acharya 2008), this chapter addresses how the Bandung Conference was reported in African newspapers and periodicals over an extended period of time – indeed, how Bandung became mythologised in the global public sphere following the event itself (Prashad 2007; Pham and Shilliam 2016; Lee 2019). It examines in particular reporting from a geographic spectrum that highlights the wide-ranging symbolic circulation of the event across Africa, including such venues as *The Ethiopian Herald* (Ethiopia), the *Daily Nation* (Kenya), *Africa*

South (South Africa) and *New Age* (South Africa). Though based in urban areas with largely small readerships due to the limited reach of such locales, these newspapers and periodicals nonetheless reveal perspectives from countries that sent delegations to Bandung (Ethiopia), countries recently independent (Kenya), and countries still in the midst of revolutionary struggle (South Africa). Indeed, though not examined in this chapter, the citation of Bandung would occur in liberation periodicals like *Sechaba*, an organ of South Africa's African National Congress (ANC), and *The African Communist*, published by the South African Communist Party (SACP), in the years ahead. In summary, the Bandung Conference became a recurrent topic of reference and discussion during the long period of decolonisation and the Cold War in Africa. Though situated in Southeast Asia, the Bandung meeting and its ethos of self-determination became iconic in the popular imagination for decades. This chapter argues for the crucial role that newspaper and periodical accounts had in producing and sustaining this political vision of intercontinental solidarity and anti-colonial internationalism that would last in idea and spirit until the end of the Cold War.

The Bandung Moment

In December 1954, upon returning to Paris from a research trip to Spain, an intellectual interest which would eventually result in the book *Pagan Spain* (1957), the African American novelist Richard Wright (1908–60) picked up a newspaper that announced a forthcoming conference of twenty-nine Asian and African countries to be held in Indonesia the following year. As recounted in the opening pages of *The Color Curtain* (1956), his narrative of the 1955 Bandung Conference, the news struck him with a sense of astonishment. His underlying western-centric worldview was tempered by a strong desire to connect with the wider world that came into focus through the magnitude of this conference and its participants. As Wright put it, a 'stream of realizations claimed my mind' regarding this emergent postcolonial world, with 'colored' peoples who had experienced different forms of European colonial rule now determining their own destiny (Wright 1995: 11). Wright had already visited a part of this world, having toured the British Gold Coast, which would become independent Ghana in 1957. His account of this experience, *Black Power: A Record of Reactions in a Land of Pathos* (1954), had been published earlier that year. Though unplanned, his eventual trip to Bandung expanded his sense of decolonisation and its meanings. The inventory of leaders he recalled that night in Paris – with the names Jawaharlal Nehru (1889–1964), Kwame Nkrumah (1909–72), Ali Sastroamidjojo (1903–75), Zhou Enlai (1898–1976) and Ho Chi Minh (1890–1969) being brought to attention – highlighted his sense of wonder and his limited familiarity with the world at hand. Indeed, his ultimate motivation for attending was not based on expertise, but his own life experience and the consequent emotional sensitivity he could bring to bear on the event. Wright, too, had 'a burden of race consciousness' and, as he summarised, 'These emotions are my instruments. They are emotions, but I am conscious of them as emotions. I want to use these emotions to try to find out what these people think and why' (Wright 1995: 15).

Though Wright's journey to Bandung continued to have ambiguities, among them the fact that his trip was funded by the Congress for Cultural Freedom, a CIA-supported organisation, *The Color Curtain* remains the most influential account of the Bandung Conference.[2] This status can be attributed to Wright's stature as a Black writer and intellectual who had achieved exceptional international prominence by the 1950s. It can also be attributed to the compelling confluence of political commentary and travel reportage that inhabits his book. Wright's trip to Bandung was motivated by an immediate curiosity about the event as described, but the conference's themes touched upon deeper issues that Wright had grappled with for decades, among them the function of race and racial identity in the modern world, the role of class politics, and, not least, the possibilities of freedom at individual, community and global levels. The moment of global decolonisation as symbolised by Bandung intersected with Wright's own attempts at individual self-determination, signalled in part by his forays into travel and non-fiction during the 1950s.

Nonetheless, the scale and importance of the conference as described by Wright should also not be overlooked. It was the largest summit of its kind, ostensibly representing 1.4 billion people, or almost two-thirds of the world's population by some estimates (Lüthi 2020: 278). Only the United Nations (UN), which had seventy-six members in 1955, was larger in numeric representation and in terms of geographic and political magnitude. Of the delegations in attendance, twenty-three, including the five sponsors, represented countries in Asia. These included the People's Republic of China (PRC), Turkey, Japan, Lebanon, Jordan, Syria, Iran, Iraq, Saudi Arabia, Yemen, Afghanistan, Nepal, Laos, Cambodia, Thailand, North and South Vietnam, and the Philippines. The remaining deputations from Africa represented Egypt, Libya, Ethiopia, the Gold Coast, Sudan and Liberia. As Wright's title underscored, this group of emergent nation states highlighted a racialised, postcolonial 'Color Curtain' in world affairs beyond the more well-known 'Iron Curtain', which separated western liberal democracies from the Soviet Union and the communist Eastern Bloc. Furthermore, Wright's phrasing also echoed W. E. B. Du Bois's famous declaration from *The Souls of Black Folk* (1903) that 'The problem of the twentieth century is the problem of the color-line, – the relation of the darker to the lighter races of men in Asia and Africa, in America and the islands of the sea' (Du Bois 1986: 372). Wright's project can consequently be understood as counterposing the Bandung meeting against an American foreign policy framework and placing it within a genealogy of Black American thought.

Yet the importance of Bandung was not limited to an American worldview. Coverage of the event was global, with Africa no exception. Indeed, it is important to note that the Bandung Conference was reported even before its occurrence. On 17 March 1955, the leftist South African newspaper *New Age* addressed its planning with an article titled 'Two Important Asian Conferences' along with the subheading 'Against Colonialism, For Peace' ('Two' 1955: 8). Published without authorial attribution, the article described two meetings, the first being 'the great African-Asian conference' in Bandung – an erroneous, continental reversal of the conference's formal name that is nonetheless suggestive of how African activists perceived the event. The second meeting reported was 'the Asian Countries Conference', formally known as the Conference of Asian Countries on the Relaxation of International Tension – an event that historian Carolien Stolte has called 'the People's Bandung' due to its broader inclusion of popular participation (Stolte 2019: 126). This meeting was held in Delhi in early April prior to the Indonesian conference.

Regarding Bandung, the article enumerated specific details, including how it 'is estimated that more than 1,000 delegation members, staff and correspondents will attend' and how 'more than 40 hotels with a total of 1,200 beds have been earmarked ... to accommodate the delegates and others' ('Two' 1955: 8). It further added that 'Special postal and telegraphic facilities will be provided to handle the additional traffic, as well as a simultaneous translation system for the conference itself' ('Two' 1955: 8). Specific to the trade unionist readership of *New Age*, it was also reported, 'The All-Indonesian Central Organisation of Trade Unions branch in West Java has issued a statement appealing to all labouring people and other sections of the population in West Java to give unreserved support to make the conference a success' ('Two' 1955: 8). The article concluded that the agenda would be shaped by 'the five principles of peaceful coexistence' agreed to by India and the PRC through the Panchsheel Treaty of 1954. More specific agenda items included military alliances, military bases by foreign powers, the PRC's membership in the UN, the reunification of the Korean peninsula, and, of particular interest to South Africa, 'the abolition of racial discrimination' ('Two' 1955: 8).

It appears the editors at *New Age* had a preconceived sense of the Bandung Conference. Expectations were high – a reflection of a number of elements, among them the emerging dynamics of decolonisation and the Cold War in places like South Asia and Korea which had unfolded during the late 1940s and early 1950s. Not least were local conditions of anti-apartheid activism in South Africa. The ANC had become the most effective political organisation of the period through its broad-based resistance to apartheid, which had been established as official government policy in 1948. Under the leadership of Chief Albert Luthuli (c. 1898–1967), the ANC had implemented the Defiance Campaign during the early 1950s, which, if not triumphant in rolling back apartheid measures, had succeeded in foregrounding the ANC and escalating its membership enrolment. More significant in this context, however, is the approach Luthuli took by fostering local Afro-Asian solidarity during the campaign. His political career began in the province of Natal, where South Africa's sizeable Indian community largely resided, and he played a critical role in allying the ANC and the South African Indian Congress as one component of the ANC-led Congress Alliance. Historian Robert Trent Vinson has written that, after April 1955, Luthuli viewed the ANC's struggle and the Congress Alliance as 'part of a global anticolonial, anti-imperialist, anti-white supremacy coalition in the spirit of the recent Afro-Asian solidarity campaign in Bandung, Indonesia' (Vinson 2018: 62–3).

This global perspective for situating the anti-apartheid struggle can be seen in two more articles on Bandung in the pages of *New Age*. On 21 April 1955, during the midpoint of the diplomatic meeting, a piece entitled 'Kotane and Cachalia Arrive for Asia-Africa Conference' discussed how '[t]he oppressed millions of South Africa have a special interest in the great Afro-Asian conference, which opened in Bandung, Indonesia, this week' ('Kotane' 1955: 3). The attendance of Moses Kotane (1905–78) and Ismail Cachalia (1908–2003) as unofficial observers proved significant. The apartheid government was not invited to send a formal diplomatic delegation, given its entrenched racism, though the internationalisation of the anti-apartheid struggle had already begun. Kotane served as secretary general of the SACP, which arose from the ashes of the Communist Party of South Africa (CPSA) that had been banned by the Suppression of Communism Act in 1950. Parallel to Luthuli's revival of the ANC, Kotane played a vital role in rejuvenating the SACP during the 1950s and aligning its interests with those of the ANC. Despite different political outlooks, at least on the surface, Luthuli and Kotane forged a close relationship. Cachalia, also known by his nickname 'Moulvi', had been a member of the Transvaal Indian Congress and became active with the ANC during the Defiance Campaign. Cachalia and Kotane's joint diplomatic presence at Bandung consequently symbolised the collaborative working relationship between the ANC and the SACP that would continue in the decades that followed. The ANC-SACP alliance reflected, respectively, the nationalism and socialist internationalism of the anti-apartheid struggle.

The immediate task at hand, however, concerned the need to publicise what was happening in apartheid South Africa for an international audience. *New Age* described the mission of Kotane and Cachalia as defined by the intention to outline 'the realities of the "police slave state" which is South Africa' ('Kotane' 1955: 3). It further explained how 'all the delegates must be the official representatives of the governments of their countries' and '[i]n the case of all those countries and peoples who have not yet won their freedom, representation is on an unofficial basis' ('Kotane' 1955: 3). The written and distributed 'Kotane-Cachalia memorandum' was subsequently designed to appeal to official conference participants in order that they might 'use their good offices internationally to persuade other civilised and freedom-loving nations of the world to prevail on the Government of the Union of South Africa to abandon its unjust and disastrous policy of apartheid and racial discrimination' ('Kotane' 1955: 3). 'We are convinced and confident that the Government of South Africa could be forced to reconsider its reactionary and inhuman policy,' the memorandum declared, as reported by *New Age*, 'if all the nations who do not approve of policies and practices of racial oppression and discrimination, particularly the Governments of the United States and Britain, would boldly take a firm stand against such practices' ('Kotane' 1955: 3). What is fascinating in this instance is the entreaty to the US and Great Britain, who were not present at Bandung, to intervene in South African affairs. Their invocation as past and contemporary global powers undercut, at a certain level, the anti-colonial spirit cultivated at the Bandung Conference. Nonetheless, this appeal underscores the gestures of realpolitik also present at the meeting.

A third article published in *New Age* during the same period summarised the essence of the event, beyond the priorities of the South African liberation struggle. Entitled 'Moses Kotane Reports from Indonesia', this piece was published after the conference on 5 May 1955. Though the article suggests that Kotane composed it, 'writing on the opening day of the Asian-African conference' ('Moses' 1955: 3), the piece itself consists mostly of facts about Indonesia and the purpose of the diplomatic meeting. It conveys the impression of publicity material reutilised as journalism. For example, beyond a brief introduction of particulars about the country of Indonesia, the article discusses the purposes of the conference, including to promote 'goodwill and cooperation among the nations of Asia and Africa' and to address 'problems of special interest to Asian and African peoples, e.g., problems affecting national sovereignty and of racialism and colonialism' ('Moses' 1955: 3). The article goes on to discuss the exclusion of South Africa – 'South Africa was disqualified by her racial and discrimination policies' ('Moses' 1955: 3) – as well as former and declining imperial powers like Britain, France, Spain, Portugal and Belgium. The article also quotes President Sukarno (1901–70) of Indonesia and his address to the conference at length: 'But what harm is in diversity when there is unity in desire? This conference is not to oppose each other, it is a conference of brotherhood' ('Moses' 1955: 3).

The article concludes with the idea of world peace as promoted by the summit. 'No task is more urgent than that of preserving peace. Without peace our independence means little,' stated Sukarno, as quoted in the article. 'The rehabilitation and upbuilding of our countries will have little meaning. Our revolutions will not be allowed to run their course' ('Moses' 1955: 3). Sukarno again: 'We can demonstrate to the minority of the world which lives on the other continents that we, the majority, are for peace, not for war, and that whatever strength we have will always be thrown on to the side of peace' ('Moses' 1955: 3). These excerpts point to the benevolent nature of the meeting and how South African activists viewed themselves as part of such an endeavour. Indeed, two separate articles published in the leftist newspaper *Fighting Talk* in May 1955 – entitled '"Without Peace Our Independence Means Little"', by Sukarno, and 'Seeking Common Ground for Peace', by Chinese Premier Zhou Enlai – also emphasised the aspiration of world peace promoted at Bandung.[3] Similar to the report by Kotane, these articles reprinted the words of Sukarno and Zhou rather than providing secondary analysis. Nonetheless, these articles captured the intentions of the meeting for a South African audience, while also establishing a common idea and perspective that would foster the mythology of Bandung and its principles in the years and decades ahead.

Mythologising Bandung through Newspaper Accounts

The Final Communiqué was the general agreement reached among the delegates in April 1955. The fact that it was a 'communiqué' or statement, not a formal treaty or institutional arrangement as such, conveys the ambiguity of what was accomplished diplomatically at the conference. It consisted of ten principles, known as the *Dasasila Bandung*, which included the right to self-determination, the importance of sovereignty and the doctrine of non-interference, the need for economic assistance and cultural exchange, the affirmation of human rights, and the abiding aspiration of world peace discussed above. Yet, despite this largely rhetorical outcome, the impact of Bandung reverberated throughout the postcolonial world. As indicated at the beginning of this chapter, the Bandung Conference continued to gain publicity and clout through articles and commentary published in African newspapers and periodicals. Much of this post-1955 journalism cited Bandung as a reference point for the escalating politics of decolonisation and Third World internationalism. This emergent politics of citation had much to do with the Final Communiqué, despite its principles that appeared more abstract than concrete. Indeed, it is this declamatory quality of the communiqué that contributed to the birth of the Bandung Spirit. Postcolonial journalism further fostered this ethos, contributing consciously and unconsciously to new networks of political solidarity by circulating and sustaining its principles. If the Bandung meeting itself was relatively limited in its achievements, the idea of Bandung remained important by pointing to the possibilities of a new world order through its growing mythology.

An example of how this politics of citation performed two purposes – networking and mythmaking – can be found in an article from 1958. In a contribution to the journal *Africa South* on the First Conference of Independent African States held in Accra, Ghana, the South African journalist Colin Legum (1919–2003) reported on the meeting's activities that at times reflected the earlier Bandung Conference and the continuing shadow it cast over Third World diplomacy.[4] He recounted in one instance how the foreign minister of the United Arab Republic (today Egypt and Syria), Dr Mahmoud Fawzy (1900–81), described his country as 'Asian as well as African' and how, as a consequence, it symbolised 'the sprawling and regenerated Afro-Asian existence that was given resonant expression in Bandung and is now, here in Accra, having its say again with perhaps a particularly African accent' (Legum 1958: 86). Legum later noted on 21 April, a day before the conference's end, amid deliberations over concluding statements, that,

> To judge by the preliminary drafts of resolutions, it appears that the African States are basing their policies on two basic programmes, which are becoming the political scripture of Africa. For [an] Old Testament, they are taking the Ten Points of the Bandung Declaration. And for [a] New Testament, the United Nations Charter. (Legum 1958: 90)

Though the ordering of the latter two references is perplexing from a chronological standpoint – the 1945 UN Charter preceded the Bandung Final Communiqué by a decade – Legum's commentary highlights the continued influence that Bandung had on diplomatic meetings and the political atmosphere that followed. Indeed, the unusual ordering he employs suggests a conscientious decentring of the UN, an organisation under Euro-American influence, in favour of a new, postcolonial worldview. The Declaration of the Conference of Independent African States ultimately avowed that, 'We, the African States assembled here in Accra ... hereby proclaim and solemnly reaffirm our unswerving loyalty to the Charter of the United Nations, the Universal Declaration of Human Rights and the Declaration of the Asian-African Conference held at Bandung' (Legum 1958: 92).

This type of invocation of the Bandung Conference as symbol and intellectual substance continued in the years ahead, especially at anniversary moments that enabled reflection and the marking of a new post-Bandung chronology. This chronology provided a means of organising the diplomatic conferences and summits that followed and the varying ideas – such as Third Worldism, non-alignment and Tricontinentalism – that evolved with them. In April and May 1960, for example, *The Ethiopian Herald*, which was based in one of the original Bandung delegate countries, reported on the meeting's fifth anniversary in two articles. The first article, from April, entitled 'Soviet-Chinese Press Greets Bandung Five Year Anniversary', noted 'the fifth anniversary of the 29 nation Afro-Asian "non-alignment" conference at Bandung' and how the Soviet and Chinese press had mutually declared that 'the [past] five years had seen an enormous increase in the influence of its members and their agreement' ('Soviet-Chinese' 1960: 3). The article quoted the Soviet paper *Pravda* as saying that Bandung was 'a vivid symbol of the national resurgence of the peoples of the great continents of Asia and Africa' ('Soviet-Chinese' 1960: 3). Furthermore, '[i]t was now impossible to settle international problems without the participation of China, India, Indonesia and the other African and Asian countries' ('Soviet-Chinese' 1960: 3). *The Ethiopian Herald* similarly reported how, in Peking (Beijing), the All-China Federation of Trade Unions 'sent messages to 18 trade unions in other "Bandung" states' and how the Chinese newspaper *Ta Kung Pao* argued that 'the Asian and African peoples had realised ever more clearly that United States imperialism was the arch enemy not only of the course of peace in Asia, Africa and other parts of the world, but also "the most vicious and dangerous enemy of the national independence and national democratic movements in Asia, Africa and Latin America"' ('Soviet-Chinese' 1960: 3).

The second article published in *The Ethiopian Herald*, from May 1960, titled 'The Bandung Anniversary', further celebrated the fifth anniversary of the Bandung Conference, in this instance by reporting on a commemoration of Bandung held in Prague, Czechoslovakia (in today's Czech Republic), on 20 April. The chairman of the Czechoslovak National Assembly, Zdenek Fierlinger (1891–1976), who was a former diplomat, delivered the main address to an audience that included diplomats from countries that had participated at Bandung. 'The voice of the Bandung Conference has met with wide response not only in colonial and former colonial countries, but wherever people have realised that the advance of the peoples of Europe and America and their peaceful coexistence cannot be isolated from the fate of the peoples of Asia and Africa,' he professed. 'We, Czechs and Slovaks, even though we are in the centre of Europe, are at one with the Asian and African peoples. We reject the superiority of the white race; we openly and fully endorse the humane principles of equality and fraternity of all peoples, which alone can provide a safe basis for a new, truly peaceful international policy' ('Bandung Anniversary' 1960: 2).

What is important about these two articles is how they highlight the broader political geography that the Bandung Conference and its meaning had quickly accrued over time. While it was natural for Bandung to retain resonance among those countries that had directly participated at the meeting, like Ghana, China and Ethiopia, it is remarkable how non-participants like the Soviet Union and Czechoslovakia made concerted efforts to indicate their support of the historic meeting in its aftermath. Indeed, it is noteworthy how this internationalism through the escalating symbolism of Bandung placed the Soviet Union and China in the same diplomatic court, if not exactly aligning them, at a time when the Sino-Soviet split was unfolding. The dual effects of mythologising and diplomatic networking in print media can therefore be seen once again and in a more expansive frame. The Bandung Conference became an event that was more than a moment of Afro-Asian solidarity or an articulation of the evolving notion of non-alignment. It became a key reference for an emergent world order that was anti-imperial and anti-western in orientation and, thus, an indicator of new political possibilities that appeared tangible and forthcoming but were still yet to be fulfilled. Newspapers and journals like *The Ethiopian Herald*, *Africa South*, *Pravda*, *Ta Kung Pao*, *New Age* and *Fighting Talk* collectively, if without self-conscious coordination, contributed to this global sensibility through its generation of journalism that reported on and cited Bandung and its legacies. This growth in symbolism continued in the build-up to the anticipated second Bandung meeting, to be held on the first's tenth anniversary in 1965.

Toward a Second Bandung

Reporting on a possible second Bandung started in earnest in 1964, though anticipation of such an event in African newspapers can be traced to at least 1959.[5] In September 1962, *The Ethiopian Herald* announced, via Reuters, that Indonesia was planning a 'Second Bandung' and had 'invited Asian and African nations to meet' to discuss this possibility, 'this time to include Latin American nations' ('Indonesia Plans' 1962: 1). This brief mention followed an article approximately a week earlier that indicated

India's involvement in the preparations for a second meeting ('India Consents' 1962: 1). By 1964, the *Daily Nation* (Nairobi) published a short piece discussing how President Muhammad Ayub Khan (1907–74) of Pakistan, one of the original host countries, had expressed 'the urgency of holding a conference of Afro-Asian countries on the model of the first Bandung conference' since he believed 'the emerging African countries needed help from Asian countries in their efforts to stand on their own legs' ('President Wants' 1964: 5). Yet strategic moves toward a reprise of Bandung faced new diplomatic headwinds due to shifting Cold War politics. An organisational meeting of 'sixty Afro-Asian countries' held in Geneva, Switzerland, to plan for a second Bandung in March 1965 encountered declined invitations from the Soviet Union and Eastern European countries due to the presence of China ('Afro-Asians Meet' 1964: 1). Furthermore, conflict was anticipated between delegations from North and South Korea, which had not been invited to the original Bandung Conference due to the then recent denouement of the Korean War (1950–3) ('Afro-Asians Meet' 1964: 1). The intervening years had sustained the Bandung Spirit as highlighted earlier, but the sense of confidence and solidarity that had once existed, however spectral initially, confronted an evolving and competitive geopolitical landscape that continued to test the possibilities and limits of Afro-Asian solidarity.

Indeed, the aim of holding a second Bandung, to be held symbolically in Africa, ultimately failed. African newspapers like *The Ethiopian Herald* and the *Daily Nation* reported on the multiple factors that informed the breakdown and disappointment of this ambition. Central among these factors was the role of China and its rivalries with the Soviet Union and India. Beyond the Sino-Soviet split touched upon earlier was the 1962 Sino-Indian War, a conflict based on shared border concerns and the fact that long-standing tensions had existed between the countries in relation to China's expansionist takeover of Tibet during the early 1950s. The 1954 Sino-Indian Agreement, also known as the Panchsheel Treaty, mentioned earlier, had promoted the Five Principles of Peaceful Coexistence – mutual respect for territorial sovereignty, non-aggression, non-interference, cooperation and peaceful coexistence – which directly influenced the Final Communiqué of the Bandung Conference. But the effects of this agreement proved short-lived, with India going on to promote the idea of non-alignment, which was not universally accepted at Bandung, in the years that followed to coalesce by 1961 the Non-Aligned Movement, formalised in Belgrade, Yugoslavia, that year. This iteration of Third Worldism involved Indonesia, Egypt, Ghana and Yugoslavia, in addition to India, but notably excluded China. The falling out between China and the Soviet Union only added to the complexity and uncertainty of what future Third World solidarity might hold, given the escalation of Soviet support for international decolonisation and postcolonial sovereignty. The upshot is that the diplomatic coalition and principles affirmed at the Bandung Conference appeared to be unravelling less than a decade later, even if the myth of Bandung was still being actively sustained.

This growing tension and paradox between diplomatic pragmatism and continued mythmaking can be witnessed in the reporting of African newspapers in 1965. Against a backdrop of broader Cold War rivalries that were aggressively reshaping the legacies of Bandung, *The Ethiopian Herald*, for example, recounted how China was aiming 'to set up a "rebel" United Nations Organisation' according to the British newspapers *The Times* and *The Guardian* ('British Papers' 1965: 4). 'Presumably this scheme will be tried out at the meeting of Afro-Asian Governments (the "second Bandung") to be held in March,' the article concluded. 'The Chinese Government is anxious that non-revolutionary countries like Malaysia and the Soviet Union shall be excluded from this conference – the latter on the convincing grounds that it is not an African or Asian power' ('British Papers' 1965: 4). Though the article did cast doubt on the potential of this new organisation, it highlights the types of manoeuvring and diplomatic characterisation, however fanciful, taking hold at the time. Similarly, in April, an anniversary event was held in Bandung – not to be confused, however, with the proposed 'second Bandung' – during which President Sukarno criticised US intervention in Vietnam and the parallel involvement of Britain in Malaysia. Feeling an escalation of regional pressure and the need for a new breakthrough, he affirmed that 'the Second Afro-Asian Conference to be held in Algiers in June would be "a second Bandung"' ('Sukarno Attacks' 1965: 6). The relative sense of diplomatic freedom that countries had in 1955 – to make a world anew, to paraphrase Sukarno at that time – faced increasing obstacles.

The brief momentum between April and June 1965 ultimately took a turn, however, that upended the hopes for a second meeting. In a lengthy contribution to the *Daily Nation* in June 1965 entitled 'From Bandung to Algiers', the Sri Lankan journalist Tarzie Vittachi (1921–93) provided an insightful overview of what was at stake, writing that the 'Second Bandung' to start on 29 June in Algiers would be 'a very different affair' from the first, given that the relative coherence of the Three Worlds – a liberal democratic West, a Communist bloc and an emergent Third World – had radically changed since 1955 (see Figure 28.2). 'The Communist bloc has proved to be as fissionable as the "decadent West",' Vittachi remarked, while 'The West also has

Figure 28.2 'From Bandung to Algiers', *Daily Nation*, 17 June 1965, p. 6. Courtesy of the author.

experienced a few dangerous breaches in its Atlantic fortress, but has found peaceful coexistence possible in the balance of terror. Asia and Africa have learned the hard way that the problems of resurgent nationalism must be overcome before a common regional philosophy can be achieved' (Vittachi 1965: 6). He went further to comment that the preparations for the Algiers meeting had been 'bedevilled by these forces of change', with the 'prime movers' of the Bandung Conference being 'India, Indonesia, Burma, Ceylon and Egypt' while those for the Algiers summit were 'Indonesia, Communist China and Algeria' (Vittachi 1965: 6). India, at odds with China, had urged the inclusion of the Soviet Union at Algiers, which was supported by Egypt but rejected by China and Indonesia. The latter's attempted withdrawal from the UN and Sukarno's 'intention of persuading the Algiers meeting to establish a separate world organisation' met with further disagreement and disapproval (Vittachi 1965: 6). Many African countries planned not to attend. 'Participants at Algiers fall broadly into three categories: the "left" led by Indonesia and China; the "middle" to which the majority belong; and the "right" led by Japan, Turkey and Iran,' Vittachi concluded, less than two weeks before the Algiers conference. 'The issues are so wide-ranging and the relationships between some of the major participants so bitter that the boundaries between these three groups will certainly be constantly crossed and straddled' (Vittachi 1965: 6). On the eve of a second Bandung, its myth and meaning had reached a limit.

Conclusion

On Friday, 25 June 1965, a bomb exploded at the assembly hall at the Club des Pins, a beach resort west of Algiers that was to serve as the site for the second Asian-African conference. Algeria had been chosen to host the summit during the July 1964 meeting of the Organisation of African Unity held in Cairo. Given Algeria's recent status as a beacon of postcolonial revolution following its independence from France in 1962 (Byrne 2016), its selection seemed a natural one to emphasise the transformative changes that decolonisation had brought to the African continent since 1955. Nonetheless, as cited earlier, debates and outright conflict ensued as to which countries would be invited, testing not only Afro-Asian solidarity, but also Asian solidarity and African solidarity – a situation that persisted up to the final weeks before the meeting. Indeed, the government of President Ahmed Ben Bella (1916–2012) of Algeria was overthrown by Defence Minister Col. Houari Boumédiène (1932–78) in a coup on 19 June, resulting in confusion about whether the summit would continue. The hotel bombing almost a week later merely confirmed the tensions animating the meeting – a symbol of the charged disarray at hand.[6] Despite the presence of Asian and African delegations in Algeria in the days immediately prior to 29 June, when the conference was still scheduled to start, and the urgent diplomacy of countries like China to move forward with the meeting, the second Afro-Asian conference was postponed. As reported by the *Daily Nation*, this moment was a decisive 'setback for the Communist Chinese' ('Algiers Setback' 1965: 8). Though plans moved forward for a summit several months later on 5 November, the conference was cancelled once more, with an article in *The Ethiopian Herald* summarising the debacle with the title 'Afro-Asian Summit Postponed Indefinitely' ('Afro-Asian' 1965: 6). The article further noted that, in the words of Boumédiène, 'a guiding idea which will galvanize our energies and strengthen our solidarity' was currently missing ('Afro-Asian' 1965: 6).

Yet this failure to organise a second Bandung did not diminish the 1955 Asian-African Conference and its meanings. Indeed, an argument can be made that the inability to convene a second iteration of the conference only contributed to its enduring mythology and *sui generis* nature as indicated at the start of this chapter. Unlike other diplomatic summits of the post-Second World War era, the Bandung Conference did not establish an institution, movement, ideology or diplomatic routine. The Bandung Conference began as an idea and, ultimately, it returned to being an idea – one fostered and sustained in part through African newspaper accounts. Indeed, in many respects, it remained more useful as an idea. The idea of Bandung was not necessarily singular, comprising instead a polysemic intersection of Third Worldism, non-alignment, anti-imperialism and Afro-Asian solidarity. As a result, it persisted as a reference point for these complementary ideas, with emphasis dependent on the author, region and time period. African newspapers played a vital role in this long-term evolution of Bandung – from its early pre-beginnings through to its contemporary status as a Third World myth.

Notes

1. On the Colombo Powers and their motivations, see Ewing 2019: 1–19.
2. For an in-depth analysis of his trip, see Roberts and Foulcher 2016.
3. For further discussion of the politics of *New Age* and *Fighting Talk*, see Pinnock 1992 and Zug 2007.
4. On the history of *Africa South*, see Daymond and Sandwith 2011.
5. See, for example, 'Present Afro-Asian Tension' (1959) and 'Afro-Asian Confab' (1959).
6. For an overview of these events, see Pauker 1965: 425–32.

Bibliography

'Afro-Asian Confab Response Lacking' (1959), *The Ethiopian Herald*, 1 December, 1.
'Afro-Asian Summit Postponed Indefinitely' (1965), *The Ethiopian Herald*, 7 November, 6.
'Afro-Asians Meet to Evaluate Results of Trade Conference' (1964), *The Ethiopian Herald*, 17 June, 1.
'Algiers Setback for the Chinese' (1965), *Daily Nation*, 29 June, 8.
Ampiah, Kweku (2007), *The Political and Moral Imperatives of the Bandung Conference of 1955: The Reactions of the US, UK and Japan*, Leiden: Brill/Global Oriental.
'The Bandung Anniversary' (1960), *The Ethiopian Herald*, 3 May, 2.
'British Papers Write on China's Idea of Another UNO' (1965), *The Ethiopian Herald*, 27 January, 4.
Byrne, Jeffrey James (2016), *Mecca of Revolution: Algeria, Decolonization, and the Third World Order*, Oxford: Oxford University Press.
Chou En-lai (1955), 'Seeking Common Ground for Peace', *Fighting Talk*, 11.3, 8–9.
Daymond, M. J., and Corinne Sandwith (eds) (2011), *Africa South: Viewpoints, 1956–1961*, Scottsville: University of KwaZulu-Natal Press.
Du Bois, W. E. B. (1986), *Writings: The Suppression of the African Slave-Trade, The Souls of Black Folk, Dusk of Dawn, Essays and Articles*, ed. Nathan Huggins, New York: Library of America.
Ewing, Cindy (2019), 'The Colombo Powers: Crafting diplomacy in the Third World and launching Afro-Asia at Bandung', *Cold War History*, 19.1, 1–19.
'India Consents to Second Bandung' (1962), *The Ethiopian Herald*, 15 September, 1.
'Indonesia Plans Second Bandung' (1962), *The Ethiopian Herald*, 23 September, 1.

'Kotane and Cachalia Arrive for Asia-Africa Conference' (1955), *New Age*, 21 April, 3.
Lee, Christopher J. (ed.) (2019) [2010], *Making a World after Empire: The Bandung Moment and its Political Afterlives*, 2nd edn, Athens: Ohio University Press.
Legum, Colin (1958), 'Ghana: The Morning After (III): The Accra Conference', *Africa South*, July, 82–93.
Lüthi, Lorenz M. (2020), *Cold Wars: Asia, the Middle East, Europe*, Cambridge: Cambridge University Press.
'Moses Kotane Reports from Indonesia' (1955), *New Age*, 5 May, 3.
Pauker, Guy J. (1965), 'The Rise and Fall of Afro-Asian Solidarity', *Asian Survey*, 5.9, 425–32.
Pham, Quynh N., and Robbie Shilliam (eds) (2016), *Meanings of Bandung: Postcolonial Orders and Decolonial Visions*, London: Rowman & Littlefield.
Phillips, Andrew (2016), 'Beyond Bandung: The 1955 Asian-African Conference and its legacies for international order', *Australian Journal of International Affairs*, 70.4, 329–41.
Pinnock, Donald (1992), 'Writing left: Ruth First and radical South African journalism in the 1950s', unpublished PhD thesis, Rhodes University.
Prashad, Vijay (2007), *The Darker Nations: A People's History of the Third World*, New York: New Press.
——— (2013), *The Poorer Nations: A Possible History of the Global South*, London: Verso.
'Present Afro-Asian Tension [sic] Require New Afro-Asian Meeting Leader Says' (1959), *The Ethiopian Herald*, 24 November, 4.
'President Wants Second Bandung' (1964), *Daily Nation*, 8 February, 5.
Roberts, Brian Russell, and Keith Foulcher (eds) (2016), *Indonesian Notebook: A Sourcebook on Richard Wright and the Bandung Conference*, Durham, NC: Duke University Press.
Soekarno (1955), '"Without Peace Our Independence Means Little"', *Fighting Talk*, 11.3, 8–9.
'Soviet-Chinese Press Greets Bandung Five Year Anniversary' (1960), *The Ethiopian Herald*, 19 April, 3.
'The Spirit of Bandung' (1985), *The Ethiopian Herald*, 24 April, 2.
Stolte, Carolien (2019), '"The People's Bandung": Local anti-imperialists on an Afro-Asian stage', *Journal of World History*, 30.1–2, 125–56.
'Sukarno Attacks UN and the US' (1965), *The Ethiopian Herald*, 25 April, 6.
Tan, See Seng, and Amitav Acharya (eds) (2008), *Bandung Revisited: The Legacy of the 1955 Asian-African Conference for International Order*, Singapore: NUS Press.
'Two Important Asian Conferences: Against Colonialism, For Peace' (1955), *New Age*, 17 March, 8.
Vinson, Robert Trent (2018), *Albert Luthuli*, Athens: Ohio University Press.
Vittachi, Tarzie (1965), 'From Bandung to Algiers', *Daily Nation*, 17 June, 6.
Wright, Richard (1995) [1956], *The Color Curtain: A Report on the Bandung Conference*, Jackson: University Press of Mississippi.
Zug, James (2007), *The Guardian: The History of South Africa's Extraordinary Anti-Apartheid Newspaper*, Pretoria: UNISA Press.

29

Non-Alignment and Maoist China: *Eastern Horizon* in the Era of Decolonisation, 1960–81

Alex Tickell and Anne Wetherilt

Asia is awake. Africa is on the move. People in many lands are opening their eyes to these changes. To get to understand one another – that is the urgent need of our times.

Liu 1960a: 6

Introduction

IN JULY 1960, Liu Pengju, a Hong Kong-based journalist, launched the first issue of his – initially – monthly journal *Eastern Horizon*, with the aim to 'present Asia in the widest possible way and so contribute to a better appreciation of Asian life and culture' (Liu 1960a: 5).[1] The journal's commitment to its readers was summarised under five headings, announcing that *Eastern Horizon*

(1) Seeks to present the best writing on Asia, with articles on Art, History, Science, Archaeology, Philosophy, Literature, Theatre, Music, Dance, Folklore, etc., as well as Poetry and Short Stories.
(2) Has especially invited many of the best known Eastern and Western writers and scholars to give you their views on the great changes in Asia.
(3) Is a popular cultural magazine designed to give the general reader a comprehensive understanding of Asian life and culture; at the same time it will provide stimulating reading for the expert.
(4) Aims to serve as a forum for an independent exchange of views – and so contribute to a better appreciation of the fast developing East with its divers [*sic*] cultures and peoples.
(5) Will be illustrated with drawings and photographs. (Anon. 1960, *Eastern Horizon*: 2)

Fourteen months later, Liu reflected further on *Eastern Horizon*'s aims, adding that the magazine sought to '[speak] for the underdogs, for the generous sharing of the fruits of the earth rather than monopolies, for peace rather than for war' (Liu 1961b: 5). Noting the positive encouragement received from its readers, he reaffirmed the magazine's founding commitments, underlining its apparently reconciliatory intercultural goals, and adding: 'Today, Asia has changed, and is developing fast. The East has rediscovered itself. It's time that East and West meet in peace and understanding before the common altar of humanity. The twain CAN meet now!' (Liu 1961b: 5).

But Liu's editorship was short-lived and terminated by his tragic early death in July 1962. After a brief interval, the editorial role was taken up by fellow journalist Lee Tsung-ying. Lee steered the magazine during the remainder of its history, until the final issue in September 1981. It is unclear why publication ceased.

In a volume on the British colonial press, the journal *Eastern Horizon* (1960–81) is something of an outlier: both contextually colonial, drawing on contributors who were part of the anglophone colonial world and published from the British crown colony of Hong Kong, and yet also boldly anti-colonial in its editorial line, its politics and its commitment to international solidarity and decolonisation. Not only did *Eastern Horizon*'s editors and contributors recognise the receding power of British colonialism, they also responded positively to the spring tide of global decolonisation, as numerous former British colonies in Africa, the Caribbean and South/East Asia gained independence in the late 1950s and throughout the 1960s.[2] *Eastern Horizon* was editorially positioned to celebrate these changes through calls for mutual solidarity and understanding. At the same time, it did not refrain from calling out the unequal economic relationship between East and West as the material legacy of western imperialism.

From its inauguration in 1960, *Eastern Horizon* also bore witness to the mounting global dramas of the Cold War, as they intersected with the coming-to-independence of former European colonial territories. The journal's broadly eastern (South, Southeast and East Asian) focus – although other parts of the world were covered too – located it in one of the most conflicted regions of the Cold War. More than any other factor, the journal's geographical and political proximity to Mao's China shaped *Eastern Horizon* through most of its publication run: China became an abiding focus soon after its inception, and especially during the Cultural Revolution. *Eastern Horizon*'s editorial policy appeared to be directed in part at international readers who might also be sympathetic to Maoism as a global revolutionary export, and in part at those who might hold sceptical or negative views about Mao's China.[3]

Eastern Horizon appeared as a 'monthly review' and had a broadly cultural agenda with an emphasis on the arts, but the journal also carried articles on scientific, medical and technological developments in the service of forms of Asian political identity. Indeed, with its eclectic cultural emphasis, the journal echoed the national cultural priorities of a time which, in the view of theorists like Frantz Fanon, promised to reconnect newly decolonised peoples with collective identities devalued and damaged by colonial rule. Hence, in its early years, the journal's wider global agenda registered the optimistic internationalism of the period, which saw new solidarities being forged between emergent postcolonial states regionally and pan-continentally, and resonated with the non-aligned movement inaugurated only five years before – in 1955 – in the appropriately eastern location of Bandung, Indonesia.

As noted already, the brightest star on the journal's eastern horizon was China, and this would become its principal focus for much of its lifespan. The nation's response to the non-aligned movement had been variable, but by 1960 Chou En-lai stated that China and the new non-aligned nations had common objectives and should strive for peaceful cooperation in response to imperialism and American aggression (Chou 1960:

7–9). Coinciding with this new idiom of solidarity between China and its neighbours, *Eastern Horizon* followed a strongly pro-Chinese line (in the March 1964 issue, for instance, the journal's contents included a pictorial feature on Chinese calligraphy, an article by Kao Mi on Chinese calligraphy, annotated translations by Wong Man of poems by Mao Zedong, and a short travel feature on 'Old Chingchow' by Rewi Alley). As the cultural politics of Maoist China during the Cultural Revolution were increasingly perceived in the West as radically self-destructive, the corresponding emphasis of *Eastern Horizon* turned to a more consistent defence of Maoism. Indeed, after 1966, the magazine became more overtly political in its coverage, celebrating first the successes of the Cultural Revolution, and later criticising the 'Gang of Four', while expressing cautious support for Deng Xiaoping's modernisation policies.

In their common commitment to correct inaccurate and/or biased representations of China permeating western discourse, both editors and the many contributors also participated in a tradition of western critical writing, which contested orientalist representations of China.[4] As such, the journal built on earlier efforts of western journalists and novelists, such as Edgar Snow, Agnes Smedley and Pearl Buck, whose writings had attempted to explain Chinese history and culture to their western audiences.[5] Yet, today, *Eastern Horizon*'s rich history is largely forgotten. Admittedly, Elaine Ho covers its early years, locating the periodical in the literary-cultural field of 1950s Hong Kong, whose writers are associated with either China or western-sponsored publications. She identifies two poles of Hong Kong writing in the 1950s – an internationalist agenda and a colonial cosmopolitan culture – and associates *Eastern Horizon* with the former (Ho 2009b: 99–100). Ho also views the magazine as the 'material expression' of the Bandung legacy (Ho 2009a: 85). This chapter broadens the scope and offers the reader an overview of *Eastern Horizon*'s entire publication history. Our overall aim is to demonstrate its wider relevance, both as a contemporary record of two decades of political developments in China and as a reflection of the evolving international outlook of its long-term editor and several of its regular western contributors.

The chapter is organised chronologically, covering, first, the early years (1960–5), second, the Cultural Revolution (1966–76), and third, the years of reform following Mao's death (1977–81). Each section starts with a discussion of the editorials and continues with an exploration of selected contributors. The chapter concludes with a reflection on *Eastern Horizon*'s impact and relevance for contemporary scholars.

The Early Years (1960–5)

Initially conceived as a monthly review, *Eastern Horizon* was remarkably consistent in its commitment to 'present the best writing on Asia', even as its editors and contributors responded to the changing times. At the time of the journal's inauguration, China was just emerging from the Great Famine (1959–61) – an event which was not registered in *Eastern Horizon* and has since been attributed to the economic reforms associated with the Great Leap Forward (1957–8) (Dikötter 2011: xi–xiii). On the international scene, China was keen to promote its anti-colonial and anti-capitalist revolutionary message, while projecting its status as a non-interfering superpower amongst the non-aligned nations (Lovell 2019: 137–41, 147).

Eastern Horizon's founding editor, Liu Pengju, was born in 1918 in Chengtu, Szechuan. Liu lectured in the Foreign Languages faculty of Szechuan University and later obtained a British Council scholarship to pursue postgraduate studies at Leeds University. Returning in 1950, he joined the communist Chinese newspaper *Ta Kung Pao*, then transferred to the *New Evening Post*. Under his direction, *Eastern Horizon* quickly established its cosmopolitan reputation, as his obituary explains: 'From the original aim of a magazine dealing in Chinese Culture, it soon became the mouthpiece of South-Eastern Asian civilisation. Then in the short space of twelve months it had welcomed into its fold the voices of Asia, of Africa and Latin America' ('Obituary' 1962: 3).

Liu's tragically early death, aged forty-four, in a plane crash in Thailand in 1962 brought the first phase of *Eastern Horizon* (from 1960 to 1962) to an abrupt, shocking end. Appropriately for the cosmopolitan, intercultural editorial position he espoused, Liu had been flying to Cairo to attend the tenth anniversary celebrations of the United Arab Republic when his United Arab Airlines Comet crashed in mountains north of Bangkok. As the Belgian-Chinese author Han Suyin wrote in her obituary letter to *Eastern Horizon* after Liu's death: 'As Editor of *Eastern Horizon*, he worked incredibly hard to create a magazine which might give writers in Asia a chance to express themselves, and give readers all over the world an opportunity to know Asian ways of thought and living better than through the usual distortions, antedated viewpoints or profit motives' (Han 1962: 5).

Liu created a format which would undergo relatively few changes. Each issue started with an editorial, entitled 'Eastern Diary', followed by articles from both Asian and western contributors, many of whom would be part of the journal's established writing stable for many years. The internationalism of *Eastern Horizon* was compounded, especially in its early years, in a vibrant letters section, with responses on topical issues and praise for previous articles.[6] These were complemented in most issues by a commissioned piece of foreign correspondence – a longer 'Letter from' feature – which sought to record the political and cultural temperature in key locations (Peking, Tokyo, Bangkok, London, Havana, Algiers) around the globe. In addition, the journal published book reviews, short stories and poems. Each issue usually included illustrations and at least one 'pictorial feature', initially in black and white, but from new year 1961 colour plates were included. As we shall see, Liu's successor retained most of these elements, even though some of the early diversity was lost during the Cultural Revolution.

Reflecting his commitment to shining a light on what he called the 'rediscovery of Asia' and 'the great changes happening in this area' (Liu 1960c: 5), Liu used his editorials to engage with a variety of topical issues, but usually avoided taking an explicit political position. Yet his pithy remarks and rhetorical questions revealed his disappointment with western-centric thinking. As an example, in 1960, he reproduced and reframed a *Time* headline to comment on the American presence in Laos: 'U.S. INTENSIFIES INTERVENTION IN LAOS BY SUSPENDING MILITARY AID ... Well, aid or no aid, it seems intervention has been intensified. Mind your own business – yes, *they* do!' (Liu 1960b: 4–5).

From 1962 onwards, he became more explicit in his commentary on developments in Vietnam, questioning whether the US strategy could win the war. Early editorials also covered developments in Africa. Thus, in July 1960, Liu commented on the independence of Congo and Somalia, concluding: 'On the old "Dark Continent" a new world is taking shape. We are happy to see rightful aspirations fulfilled. The day is not far off, we believe, when all African people will become again masters of their own beloved land' (Liu 1960a: 6). Liu was worried too about the 'strings attached' to foreign aid, acknowledging newly independent nations' need for technical and economic assistance, but advocating a more equitable approach: 'Let us start anew by sharing all the fruits of the good earth' (Liu 1962: 5). In a veiled attack on American consumerism, he questioned whether 'Men from Karachi to the Congo' want to follow the American example and buy American consumer goods (Liu 1961b: 6). Similarly, he denounced America's wasteful use of resources, asking, 'Cannot the rest of the world, co-inheritors of the earth, demand some measure of control?' (Liu 1961a: 2).

Hence, *Eastern Horizon*'s initial editorial agenda was informative and sought to bridge a perceived knowledge gap between East and West. It thus represented a corrective postcolonial impulse: countering what its editors and many contributors saw as a persistent ethnocentrism and political misrepresentation in metropolitan accounts of South/East Asian culture. In some cases, such as in the involvement of British academics like Joseph Needham, Edmund Blunden or Keith Buchanan in New Zealand, the critique issued from partisan figures from within the (expatriate) western academy.

Other articles were commissioned from recognised experts, including freelance journalists, travel writers and western expatriates based in Asia, as well as one-time visitors. In its first years, the journal relied heavily on a group of trusted high-profile western contributors to lend critical weight, supplemented by a diverse range of occasional contributors, and including works serialised from longer publications. Many of these articles took the form of travel accounts – of note are the regular contributions from the New Zealander Rewi Alley, which covered his extensive travels in China; the reports from the British journalists Stuart and Roma Gelder, who were the first westerners to visit Tibet after its annexation by China in 1950; and several short pieces by Han Suyin on her travels in China and Cambodia. Han also wrote an early commentary on the newly created communes and praised China's efforts to give women 'a new sense of liberation and an unfolding of potentialities now which were never within her reach before' (Han 1960: 16). Notably the coverage of creative writing and literary criticism from decolonising Asia and Africa was also strong, perhaps reflecting nascent 'Commonwealth Literature' influences during Liu's time at Leeds University.[7] The magazine provided a platform for major writers and critics such as Ahmed Ali, Mulk Raj Anand, Khwaja Ahmad Abbas, Amrita Pritam and Kofi Awoonor (writing as George Awoonor-Williams).[8]

After Liu's death, Lee Tsung-ying took over as editor. Lee too was a former journalist on *Ta Kung Pao* and had witnessed the fall of the Kuomintang in 1949, reporting from Shanghai (Lee 1979: 1). Initially, he made relatively few changes to the journal, with 'Eastern Diary', the 'Letters from', book reviews, short stories and photographic features continuing as standing items. He was able to draw too on the existing contributors, whilst adding some new names. Yet despite this commitment to continue in his predecessor's footsteps, Lee's early editorials took on a more critical anti-American and pro-Chinese tone. He wrote longer pieces, putting forward his own views on selected foreign policy topics. As we shall see in the next section, over time, he increasingly used 'Eastern Diary' to pen his own political opinion pieces, resulting in a reduction of the diversity of the early years, both in terms of geographical coverage and in terms of viewpoints.

During Lee's early years, most contributors covered travel and culture in Asia, but from 1964 onwards, westerners such as the British economist Joan Robinson, the

British Marxist David Crook and the New Zealanders Douglas and Ruth Lake communicated their favourable impressions of the changes they were witnessing in China. The 'Letters from' became less frequent from 1965 onwards – even though they didn't disappear altogether – and we start seeing a marked bias towards articles on China, travel and culture in particular.

For most of the period, though, the magazine maintained its international outlook, with both Lee and the various contributors conveying their criticism of American foreign policy and underlining persistent neo-colonial inequalities in East–West relations. Thus, in his first editorial, Lee reaffirmed his commitment to the magazine's original aims, but wondered whether, three years after its first issue, Asia was any better understood by the West (Lee 1963a: 3). Referring to (then) senator John F. Kennedy's call to 'open more windows between the peoples of China and the peoples of America', he requested 'no window smashing please', adding: 'What we need now is more understanding and less meddling in the affairs of others' (Lee 1963a: 3–4). Hence, we see a marked shift from Liu's enthusiastic commitment to mutual understanding to a weary critique of American interventionism. Lee was preoccupied too with US military intervention in the region, stating that 'if the Asians were left alone . . . they would certainly be able to make their own peace much more easily without outside help – or, rather, meddling' (Lee 1964a: 6). He further commented on China's nuclear programme, dismissing western distrust and putting forward the view that 'China is up to the present the only nation that has put on record her pledge not to be the first to use the bomb' (Lee 1964b: 3).

Lee and his fellow authors were critical too of the role of foreign aid in exacerbating the poverty gap between the so-called developed and underdeveloped worlds. In Lee's view, 'The problem of hunger . . . can only be tackled by the people who themselves are hungry . . . But they can tackle it effectively only when they have proper leadership, a government of their own choice' (Lee 1963b: 5). Similarly, Han Suyin characterised foreign aid as 'giving with one hand and taking away with the other, *and taking away much more than is given*' (Han 1963: 13; italics in original). Finally, Liu and Lee shared an interest in language and the arts, particularly Chinese. In addition, the magazine had regular contributions from the British orientalist Husein Rofe, as well as short stories from South Asian authors, as noted above.

The Cultural Revolution (1966–76)

Eastern Horizon appeared without interruption during the Cultural Revolution, albeit on a bi-monthly basis. Lee continued to write his 'Eastern Diary', which appeared alongside articles by many of the regular contributors. Towards the end of the period, some new faces appeared, including western students and visitors who had been granted access to China. There was, however, a reduction in geographical diversity, particularly in the 'Letters from' feature. As this section explains, while at first sight the magazine remained committed to its original aim – to promote western understanding of Asia – in practice this amounted to a more partisan endorsement of Mao's policies, both at home and abroad. Hence, the earlier commitment to 'present Asia in the widest possible way' (Liu 1960a: 5) appeared to have made way for a concerted effort to educate the western reader in the aims and achievements of the Cultural Revolution.

Continuing the trend seen in the previous period, Lee's own editorials were largely focused on developments in China and an expression of his own political views. As early as December 1966, he used 'Eastern Diary' to applaud the achievements of the Cultural Revolution, pointing to the increases in agricultural and industrial production (Lee 1966: 5). On later occasions, he was keen to correct western reports of a power struggle within the Communist Party, of excessive violence by the Red Guards, and of chaos throughout the country, claiming instead that a new revolutionary order had been established:

> a revolution such as the world has never seen before, a revolution launched in the framework of a proletariat dictatorship and waged by practicing mass democracy under the guidance of Chairman Mao to make China, and for that matter the whole world, safe for socialism and communism. (Lee 1967b: 4)

Lee frequently revisited the achievements of the Cultural Revolution in the areas of agriculture, industrial production, medicine, science and technology. Likewise, he commented on the revolution in the arts and was particularly interested in the discovery of ancient tombs and artefacts (see, for example, the cover of the December 1967 edition; Plate 3). Here, he was keen to counter western reports of the destruction of archaeological sites at the height of the Cultural Revolution. Instead, he praised Chinese workers and peasants for the care taken when coming across new sites (Lee 1972: 5). In later years, however, he started sharing his concerns about factionalism in the Communist Party, devoting long editorials to the 'Gang of Four', whilst continuing to express his support for Mao's teachings.

Consistent with the lines taken in the magazine's editorials, *Eastern Horizon*'s regular contributors focused primarily on developments in China. For example, Rewi Alley, David Crook and Han Suyin used their travel reports to reflect on the impact of Mao's policies, describing the visible successes of the Cultural Revolution. There was strong interest too in the communes and the lives of rural women, as seen for example in the reports by Barbara Mututantri (a British teacher in China), who also interviewed Chinese peasants, factory workers and students.

A common theme was the western misrepresentation of the Cultural Revolution. Thus, in February 1967, Wong Siu Kuan, manager of the Eastern Horizon Press, accused western critics of approaching the Cultural Revolution with 'mental blinkers ... prevent[ing] themselves from seeing the truth' (Wong 1967: 14). Similarly, in early 1968, Han expressed her annoyance at 'the "great wall" of ignorance and fear' that the western press had created (Han 1968: 20). Reporting on lectures and interviews held in the first half of 1967, she was eager to convey the interest shown by young Americans and Europeans, who were aware that 'the Cultural Revolution in China, Vietnam, and their own fates were interlinked' (Han 1968: 21). She further remarked how this younger western generation easily grasped the meaning of the Cultural Revolution 'because it corresponds to their own desires and wishes and search for a change of attitude and an explanation, in scientific terms, of the problems of their own age' (Han 1968: 22). The influence of Maoism for a radical intellectual avant-garde was also apparent in this period in the ideological turn taken by journals such as *Tel Quel* in France (Wolin 2018: 4, 16).

In addition to these regular contributors, the magazine also featured occasional pieces from western visitors to China, including a number of university students. All shared their positive impressions of the country and repeatedly pointed to the West's lack of understanding. These ad hoc pieces became more regular after 1970, but their presence in the early years of the Cultural Revolution is of interest, as they described the changes in material conditions witnessed by these visitors, whilst also recording their personal evaluations of what one student calls 'an ideological revolution . . . an essentially peaceful propaganda and revitalising campaign' (Pearson 1967: 51).

Hence, during the early years of the Cultural Revolution, *Eastern Horizon* endeavoured to give its foreign readership a detailed and up-to-date picture of events in China (for an idea of the extent of the readership, see the list of distribution centres on the back cover of the December 1967 edition; Figure 29.1). Combining the personal and the political, regular and occasional contributors had a common agenda: to provide fact-based analysis in order to convince a sceptical western readership of the positive changes brought about by the Cultural Revolution. Yet, despite their contributors' extensive travels, western access was tightly controlled by the Chinese authorities (Lovell 2019: 87), and the correspondents' personal sympathies with the Maoist agenda is likely to have influenced their reporting.

Figure 29.1 Distribution list, *Eastern Horizon*, December 1967, back cover. Courtesy of the authors.

After 1970, regular contributors continued to provide their perspectives on the Cultural Revolution, emphasising the presence of counter-revolutionary elements and the need for continued commitment to the class struggle. Criticism was rare during this period. For example, in 1973, David Crook discussed the party struggle between Lin Piao and Mao, adding that the conflict between their respective commitments to capitalism and socialism was not over yet, even as he was in no doubt that socialism would prevail, 'based on his [Mao's] boundless confidence in the common people' (Crook 1973: 42). In 1974, the American academic William Sewell acknowledged the pain involved in the loss of old traditions, remarking, 'It is the goal, now clearly unfolding, that makes the price worth paying, the burden light' (Sewell 1974: 44).

Yet, for both new and old contributors, the achievements of the Cultural Revolution were manifest. For example, in 1973, the British journalist Felix Greene wrote that China's 'achievements are very great ... a milestone in the history of human development' (Greene 1973: 52). Also in 1973, the Cambridge academic Joseph Needham reflected on the changes in China since his last visit eight years earlier, remarking that China was 'leading the world towards the humanisation of human beings' (Needham 1973: 8), while praising the dismantling of class barriers and emphasising the minimal destruction of 'cultural values and cultural objects' during the Cultural Revolution (Needham 1973: 14).

Conversely, the magazine's primary interest in China's domestic policies implied reduced coverage of international developments. This was apparent in Lee's 'Eastern Diary' notes, which became more one-sided, as he praised China's role on the global scene, compared with the imperialism displayed by the United States and the Soviet Union. Echoing the earlier Bandung Spirit, he emphasised that China's foreign policy was 'based on solidarity with the working class of the world and nations fighting for their own freedom and independence' (Lee 1969: 2). Lee further corrected the notion of non-proliferation as 'being a step forward', arguing that it served American and Soviet interests only. Instead, he endorsed China's proposal for a worldwide ban on nuclear weapons, since 'all nations are equal and ... a handful of big powers should not be given the exclusive right to this most destructive weapon' (Lee 1967a: 2). Lee's editorials also discussed the normalisation of international relations, including the readmission of China to the United Nations, and the 1972 visits of US President Nixon and Japanese Prime Minster Tanaka.

At the same time, Lee's coverage of countries outside Asia was much reduced, with only a handful of mentions. For example, in 1976, he praised a joint railway project in Zambia and Tanzania as an example of China's cooperation with Africa (Lee 1976a: 4). In the same issue, he reported on the Non-Aligned Countries' Fifth Summit in Colombo and denounced Soviet tactics as 'typically imperialist divide-and-rule' (Lee 1976a: 4–5). Later that year, he expressed his support for the Summit's declarations, highlighting 'its unity of purpose' and noting that 'the continuous deterioration of the economic situation in the developed countries ... has once again shown that the present economic structure dominated by the big powers is detrimental to the developing countries', concluding that 'a new international economic order is of the utmost importance' (Lee 1976b: 7).

Reflecting the altered editorial outlook, there were fewer articles too on foreign politics, apart from a series of reports by Han Suyin on her trips to the United States (1966), Australia (1970) and Algeria (1971), and the occasional piece on Vietnam (e.g. Felix Greene on China and the war in Vietnam in 1966, and Wilfred Burchett on the American campaigns in North and South Vietnam in 1968). The 'Letters from' continued, albeit with reduced frequency and much narrower geographical coverage. Some were sketches of local life, whilst others touched on political developments, such as the regular 'Letter from Peking' and 'Letter from Tokyo', by A. Li and David Conde, respectively. At the same time, there were remnants of the Bandung ideal of the earlier period, revealing *Eastern Horizon*'s continued interest in Afro-Asian matters and the global politics of non-alignment. Of note are two articles in 1966 and 1967 by the anonymous 'N. S. C.', considering the 1967 Afro-Asian writers' conference held in Peking, and the role of literature in the struggle against (American) imperialism. In 1968, the American writer and activist Shirley Graham Du Bois reported on political developments in Ghana and Sierra Leone, whereas in 1969 and 1970, Tom Tsekie wrote a number of articles that were deeply critical of the South African apartheid regime.[9]

Perhaps reflecting the greater breadth of Lee's editorials from late 1971 onwards, there was a corresponding increase in the range of topics covered by the magazine's contributors, in particular science and technology, medicine and population control. While most articles continued to focus on China's domestic policies, the 'Letters from' featured more prominently again, and their geographical scope expanded, with letter writers reporting from San Francisco, London and Paris, as well as Peking, Hanoi and Khartoum.

As in the previous period, the magazine featured regular articles on Chinese culture (opera, ballet, cinema, arts and crafts), which was customarily associated with the 'Great Proletarian Revolution'. Others shared Lee's interest in archaeology, covering findings of ancient burial sites and relics, as well as the warrior figures of Sian in 1974. Besides offering detailed descriptions of the ongoing excavations, the various authors related the findings to the historic suffering of China's labouring classes, asserting that they reflected 'the intelligence, ingenuity and great creative power of the Chinese labouring people' (Hsinhua News Agency 1972: 25). In their view, archaeology, consistent with Mao's teachings, would 'help clarify the long sweep of China's civilization in terms of politics and class struggle', correcting existing historical records which reflect the outlook of the ruling classes (Shuman 1975: 11–12). And finally, although the diversity of the earlier period was lost, the reader was given the occasional glimpse of cultural developments outside China, with articles on Middle Eastern art and literature by Husein Rofe; a short series on literature in Latin America, Africa and South Asia by Keith Buchanan; and a few short stories by Mulk Raj Anand and Bhabani Bhattacharya, amongst others.

Eastern Horizon after Mao (1977–81)

After Mao's death in 1976, *Eastern Horizon* resumed monthly publication, although issues were typically shorter and featured fewer articles. For both Lee and the regular contributors, the events preceding Mao's death were of paramount importance. But they also reflected on the longer trajectory of the Cultural Revolution and its place in China's history. In his editorials, Lee remained committed to its overall aims – 'to revolutionize people's ideology and as a consequence to achieve greater, faster, better and more economical results in all fields of work' (Lee 1977a: 1). However, his first critical assessments appeared in April and May 1977, when he asked, 'what is now left of the Cultural Revolution?' (Lee 1977b: 1). While admitting that the mass revolutionary movement had led to some 'shortcomings' and 'disorders' (Lee 1977a: 1), he attributed these to a minority, adding, in a gloss on Mao's famous saying, that 'Modernization will go ahead. A hundred flowers will blossom and a hundred schools will contend' (Lee 1977a: 2). Lee further believed that the new leadership would continue the 'Great Proletarian Cultural Revolution' whilst also promoting the 'four modernisations' in agriculture, industry, national defence, and science and technology, a topic he would revisit in subsequent issues.

Despite a decline in the number of contributors, some of the regulars – Alley, Crook and Han – continued to publish their travel reports, commenting on the events after Mao's death and the subsequent period of readjustment. On the whole, *Eastern Horizon*'s regular contributors appeared to follow closely the editor's direction: expressing their dismay at the Gang of Four; emphasising their confidence about China's future; and voicing their satisfaction with the newly created opportunities for debate. These regular contributors also looked back on the period of the Cultural Revolution, continuing to celebrate its significant achievements, even as they acknowledged some of its shortcomings. There were fewer new contributors during these final years. Of note are retrospective pieces by the American Margaret Stanley, who visited Mao's base in Yenan in 1947 and returned to China in 1972 and 1978. In addition, there were new contributions on the Chinese diaspora, with for example a series of articles on Chinese living in Australia and New Zealand, and a short series featuring a Chinese family in London's East End.

During this period, Lee appeared primarily interested in domestic developments. On occasion, he discussed education and the arts, emphasising their political role. There was some limited coverage too of international issues, but it was relatively unvaried and invariably viewed through a Chinese lens. But the earlier interest in the 'Third World' was absent from both Lee's editorials and the wider set of articles, suggesting a departure from *Eastern Horizon*'s original commitment to cover 'the great changes taking place in Asia and Africa', as 'All men within four seas are brothers' (Liu 1960a: 6).

Finally, most issues contained a few cultural pieces, as well as short stories, now almost exclusively by Chinese authors. Archaeological findings continued to attract the interest of both western and Chinese writers, and were appreciated as exemplifying the class struggles of the past (Dwight 1977: 15). Of interest is a piece in 1980 by the American journalist Robert Friend, covering a Peking exhibition of young Chinese artists, whom he termed 'rebels' as they gave expression to the fears and traumas of the Cultural Revolution, caused by 'the errors of the Communist Party in which they had been taught to have so much respect' (Friend 1980: 23).

Conclusion

The twenty-year archive of *Eastern Horizon* affords some startling insights for readers who make the time-warp journey into its pages, and back to the pivotal decades of global decolonisation. Initially the journal's very existence reveals that remarkable political latitude allowed in late British colonial outposts such as Hong Kong, where *Eastern Horizon* was able to flourish as an international publication critical of old and new imperialisms and supportive of the revolutionary Maoism of neighbouring Communist China. More subtly, the developing editorial line of *Eastern Horizon* – broadly from non-aligned internationalism to defensive Maoism – also reminds us of the political complexity of this period, in which both postcolonial intellectuals and radical allies in the West sought political answers from China and the developing world. With the benefit of historical hindsight on Mao's humanitarian crimes, the sympathies of *Eastern Horizon*'s contributors can now seem naïve and misguided, but they are also valuable in providing a forgotten view of China's radical international influence long before its emergence as today's global superpower.

Notes

1. The article employs the Wade-Giles system for Chinese names, as used in *Eastern Horizon*.
2. There is no evidence that *Eastern Horizon* upset the colonial government in Hong Kong, and a number of publications espousing views from across the political spectrum operated in the crown colony. Nevertheless, the government had wide-ranging powers to intervene if the local press 'overstepped the mark' and was judged to have put the security of the colony at risk (Ng 2022: 60). These powers were used extensively in the immediate post-war period and again during anti-government riots in 1967, but rarely so in later years (Ng 2022: 119–21, 157, 161–2).
3. *Eastern Horizon* carried advertisements for other radical journals, such as the Paris-based *Revolution*, which presented 'first-hand reports on all the world's revolutionary struggles'. These adverts appeared in multiple issues. There were regular adverts too for the English weekly published by *Ta Kung Pao*.
4. Western views of China underwent several changes during the twentieth century, with a dominant negative narrative after the creation of the People's Republic of China in 1949 replacing the largely sympathetic response to Chiang Kai-shek's regime of the 1930s. In the 1950s and 1960s, the dominant narrative in the West was heavily influenced by anti-communist sentiment in general, and American containment policies in particular. See, for example, Klein 2003; Lowe 1991; Mackerras 1989; Mackerras 2000.
5. Edgar Snow's *Red Star over China* (1937) and Pearl Buck's *The Good Earth* (1931) were particularly influential. Early accounts of the developments after 1949 include Edgar Snow, *The Other Side of the River* (1962) and *The Long Revolution* (1970), and Han Suyin, *China in the Year 2001* (1967).
6. Correspondents hailed from all four corners of the globe and included celebrities such as Bertrand Russell and Simone de Beauvoir (both sent a congratulatory letter on the magazine's launch), as well as regular contributors, academics and librarians, alongside British expatriates and Britons with an interest in the East.
7. His time at the university would have preceded the inaugural conference on Commonwealth Literature held in 1964.
8. As an example, the magazine carried the short stories 'The Gold Watch' by Mulk Raj Anand; 'The Boy Who Moved a Mountain' by K. A. Abbas; 'A Moment of Eternity' by Bhabani Bhattacharya; and 'Just to Buy Corns' by George Awoonor-Williams.
9. We were not able to establish the identity of Tom Tsekie.

Bibliography

Abbas, K. A. (1960), 'The Boy Who Moved a Mountain', *Eastern Horizon*, 1.3, 47–52.
Anand, Mulk Raj (1969), 'The Gold Watch', *Eastern Horizon*, 8.5, 55–64.
Anon. (1960), *Eastern Horizon*, 1.1, 2.

Awoonor-Williams, George (1964), 'Just to Buy Corns', *Eastern Horizon*, 3.7, 57–62.
Bhattacharya, Bhabani (1962), 'A Moment of Eternity', *Eastern Horizon*, 2.1, 51–5.
Chou En-lai (1960), 'On the Current International Situation and China's Foreign Relations', *Peking Review*, 3.15, 12 April, 7–9.
Crook, David (1973), 'Two Line Struggle Travel Notes', *Eastern Horizon*, 12.6, 37–42.
—— (1974), 'Two Line Struggle Travel Notes', *Eastern Horizon*, 13.4, 44.
Dikötter, Frank (2011), *Mao's Great Famine: The History of China's Most Devastating Catastrophe, 1958–1962*, London: Bloomsbury.
Dwight, Alan (1977), 'The Past Serves the Present', *Eastern Horizon*, 16.5, 12–15.
Friend, Robert C. (1980), '"Rebel" Artists Finally Recognized in Beijing', *Eastern Horizon*, 19.11, 23–31.
Greene, Felix (1973), 'Free to be Human', *Eastern Horizon*, 12.6, 52–5.
Han Suyin (1960), 'Social Changes in Asia', *Eastern Horizon*, 1.2, 12–18.
—— (1962), 'From Han Suyin', *Eastern Horizon*, 2.8, 4–5.
—— (1963), 'Relations Between East and West', *Eastern Horizon*, 2.11, 9–15.
—— (1968), 'The Cultural Revolution Abroad', *Eastern Horizon*, 7.2, 20–3.
Ho, Elaine Yee Lin (2009a), '"Imagination's Commonwealth": Edmund Blunden's Hong Kong Dialogue', *PMLA*, 124, January, 76–92.
—— (2009b), 'Nationalism, internationalism, the Cold War: Crossing literary-cultural boundaries in 1950s Hong Kong', in Elaine Yee Lin Ho and Julia Kuehn (eds), *China Abroad: Travels, Subjects, Spaces*, Hong Kong: Hong Kong University Press, 85–103.
Hsinhua News Agency (1972), 'Two-thousand-year-old Tomb Found in Perfectly Preserved Condition', *Eastern Horizon*, 11.4, 16–25.
Klein, Christina (2003), *Cold War Orientalism: Asia in the Middlebrow Imagination, 1945–1961*, Berkeley: University of California Press.
Lee Tsung-ying (1963a), 'Eastern Diary', *Eastern Horizon*, 2.9, 3–7.
—— (1963b), 'Eastern Diary', *Eastern Horizon*, 2.11, 3–5.
—— (1964a), 'Eastern Diary', *Eastern Horizon*, 3.4, 5–7.
—— (1964b), 'Eastern Diary', *Eastern Horizon*, 3.12, 2–5.
—— (1966), 'Eastern Diary: China in Revolution', *Eastern Horizon*, 5.12, 2–5.
—— (1967a), 'Eastern Diary', *Eastern Horizon*, 6.2, 2–5.
—— (1967b), 'Eastern Diary', *Eastern Horizon*, 6.10, 2–4.
—— (1969), 'Eastern Diary: China's Foreign Policy', *Eastern Horizon*, 8.5, 2–4.
—— (1972), 'Eastern Diary', *Eastern Horizon*, 11.6, 2–6.
—— (1976a), 'Eastern Diary', *Eastern Horizon*, 15.4, 2–5.
—— (1976b), 'Eastern Diary', *Eastern Horizon*, 15.5, 2–7.
—— (1977a), 'Eastern Diary', *Eastern Horizon*, 16.4, 1–4.
—— (1977b), 'Eastern Diary', *Eastern Horizon*, 16.5, 1–5.
—— (1979), 'Eastern Diary', *Eastern Horizon*, 18.5, 1–4.
Liu Pengju (1960a), 'Eastern Diary', *Eastern Horizon*, 1.1, 5–6.
—— (1960b), 'Eastern Diary', *Eastern Horizon*, 1.4, 4–6.
—— (1960c), 'Eastern Diary', *Eastern Horizon*, 1.5, 5–7.
—— (1961a), 'Eastern Diary', *Eastern Horizon*, 1.11, 2–5.
—— (1961b), 'Eastern Diary', *Eastern Horizon*, 1.14, 5–7.
—— (1962), 'Eastern Diary', *Eastern Horizon*, 2.3, 5–6.
Lovell, Julia (2019), *Maoism: A Global History*, London: Vintage.
Lowe, Lisa (1991), *Critical Terrains: French and British Orientalisms*, Ithaca and London: Cornell University Press.
Mackerras, Colin (1989), *Western Images of China*, Hong Kong: Oxford University Press.
—— (2000), *Sinophiles and Sinophobes: Western Views of China*, Oxford: Oxford University Press.

Needham, Joseph (1973), 'China Revisited After Eight Years', *Eastern Horizon*, 12.2, 6–14.
Ng, Michael (2022), *Political Censorship in British Hong Kong: Freedom of Expression and the Law (1842–1997)*, Cambridge: Cambridge University Press.
'Obituary: Liu Peng-ju' (1962), *Eastern Horizon*, 2.8, 3.
Pearson, Kent (1967), 'The Cultural Revolution as a New Zealand Student Sees It (concluded)', *Eastern Horizon*, 6.6, 47–51.
Pickowicz, Paul (2019), *A Sensational Encounter with High Socialist China*, Hong Kong: City University of Hong Kong Press.
Sewell, William (1974), 'Without Bitterness', *Eastern Horizon*, 13.4, 42–4.
Shuman, Julian (1975), 'Archaeology in China', *Eastern Horizon*, 14.3, 11–15.
Wolin, Richard (2018), *The Wind from the East: French Intellectuals, the Cultural Revolution, and the Legacy of the 1960s*, 2nd edn, Princeton: Princeton University Press.
Wong Siu Kuan (1967), 'Why the Cultural Revolution? (illustrated)', *Eastern Horizon*, 6.2, 14–23.

Part V

Anti-Colonialism in the Colonial and Postcolonial Public Sphere

30

For Illustrative Purposes: Nana Sahib, Jotee Prasad and Representation in British and Anglo-Indian Newspapers

Priti Joshi

IN 1863, THE *Homeward Mail from India, China, and the East*, a bi-weekly compendium of news, reported that 'A joke at the expense of the London press is circulating through the Indian journals' (Anon. 1863, *Homeward Mail*: 553). This was scarcely the first time 'Indian journals' – by which the *Homeward Mail* meant papers run by Britons in India, or Anglo-Indians, as they were referred to – mocked the British press. In 1857, as the metropolitan press was scrambling for copy on the insurrections in India, the *Madras Athenaeum* ridiculed Dickens for his gullibility in believing that the lotus was a symbol of the mutiny and upbraided Disraeli for 'confound[ing] lotus and lotas' in a speech in Parliament (Anon. 1858, *The Mofussilite*: n.p.). This chapter explores the traffic between the British and Anglo-Indian press following the Uprising of 1857 to analyse representation on multiple registers: visual, textual, judicial and sovereign. The *Homeward Mail*, a steamship journal that gathered news from the colonial press and reprinted it for readers in Britain, was metaphorically located between London and Calcutta; it thus serves as a useful entry into matters of transit and circulation that are the focus of this chapter.

The joke the *Homeward Mail* refers to occurred in 1857 when *sipahis* (anglicised as sepoys) of the British East India Company's army mutinied. Initially, Britons were disconcerted but not overly perturbed; that changed as word of the Satichaura Ghat and Bibighar massacres at Kanpur (Cawnpore) trickled into London in August and September 1857.[1] The man behind the massacres was believed to be Nana Sahib, who, like many Indians, had reasons to be dissatisfied with the government. Prior to the massacres, Nana Sahib was virtually unknown in Britain. As the British press learned of the massacres, it scrambled for information on Nana Sahib and relied on two sources: Anglo-Indian newspapers arriving on steamships and 'India hands' who had returned to Britain. The earliest references to Nana Sahib in the British press date to mid-August, when *The Times* quoted reports from the Calcutta-based *Englishman* (Anon. 1857a, *The Times*: 8), while the *Liverpool Albion* cited the Serampore-based *Friend of India* (Anon. 1857, *Albion*: n.p.). These reports required a degree of translation; *The Times* had to follow the excerpt from the *Englishman* with an explanatory 'Bhitoor is a little place a few miles . . .' (Anon. 1857a, *The Times*: 8). Consequently, British newspapers leaned on local 'experts' who filled in explanations. *The Times* carried a report from a Mr H. F. Gibbons, of Brick-court, Temple, who confidently announced:

> Nana Sahib, the wretch who is reported to have committed the wholesale murders at Bhitoor ... is not ... as represented, the adopted son of the ex-Peishwa Bajee Rao, nor does he pretend to be so, Dhoondo Punt being the adopted son of that Prince. He is the eldest son of the ex-Peishwa's Soubedar, Ramchunder Punt, and is, as natives go, tolerably well educated. (Anon. 1857b, *The Times*: 10)

Gibbons was wrong in almost every particular: Nana Sahib *was* an adopted son of Baji Rao II, and his name *was* Dhondu Pant; moreover, a 'Peishwa' was not a Prince but Prime Minister in the Maratha court.[2] The challenges British newspapers faced – boots on the ground, reliable sources, speedy transmission – were compounded by Britons' sizeable ignorance about almost every facet of their colonial holding.

In September 1857, the man who was now referred to in the press as the 'butcher of Cawnpore' acquired a face. On 26 September, two London newspapers, *The Illustrated London News* (*ILN*) and the *Illustrated Times* (*IT*), published images of Nana Sahib (see Figures 30.1 and 30.2). The *ILN* and *IT* had a long-standing rivalry: Herbert Ingram started the *ILN* in 1842 with Henry Vizetelly as art editor. Within a year Vizetelly broke with Ingram and started a rival newspaper, the *Pictorial Times*, which Ingram bought out in 1845. A decade later, Vizetelly started another rival, the *Illustrated Times*, this one more successful, and by 1857, it was challenging *The Illustrated London News*'s market-share. In September 1857, both newspapers

Figure 30.1 'Nana Sahib', *The Illustrated London News*, 26 September 1857. Courtesy of the author.

Figure 30.2 'Nana Sahib (From a picture painted at Bhitoor, in 1850, by Mr. Beechy, Portrait painter to the King of Oude.)', *The Illustrated Times*, 26 September 1857. Courtesy of the author.

managed the scoop of the season: an image of Nana Sahib. The trouble was that the images they published were of two patently different men. Though one man is in profile, the other front-facing, their differences are legion. The *ILN*'s Nana Sahib has a long, angular face, straight and sharp nose, large, almond-shaped eyes, a wide mouth and full lips; the *IT*'s Nana Sahib, on the other hand, is portly, has a small mouth with slightly puckered lips, a wide nose and small eyes. The former is quite dark, the latter quite fair. Both images include a number of 'oriental' ornaments: an onion dome, minaret, arches, stone wall and palm trees behind the *ILN*'s Nana Sahib, a hookah, sword and upturned slippers in front of the *IT*'s Nana Sahib, who is seated on the floor on a patterned carpet.

Andrea Kaston Tange (2021) and Brian Wallace (2015) attend to these differences to sort out the genuine from the fake. At the close of this chapter, I will turn to questions of authenticity and identification as well, but I begin my analysis with Peter Sinnema's caution that as we analyse images in newspapers,

> We should not become obsessed with the idea of an original scene, an empirical site which finds its full expression in the representation. Images do not simply reflect a pre-existing reality which can function as a standard of judgment. Rather the representation . . . is *constructed* out of desire; it is not the mimetic reproduction of an original, breathing being . . . Behind the picture . . . we find lurking . . . a series of politically interested significations. The [image] is a material distillation of these interests. (Sinnema 2018: 47)

Attending to desire and context over mimesis, as Sinnema advocates, ensures that attempts to identify the 'real' Nana Sahib are embedded in a broader social and political analysis. One element of that context appears on the page itself: the text surrounding an image. Brian Maidment writes: 'Studying illustration requires first of all an awareness of the physical relationship between type and image on the printed page and an understanding of the ways illustration comments on, re-enacts, or rewrites the text which it accompanies' (Maidment 2016: 107). Within the wider context of the circuits of exchange between the British and Anglo-Indian presses, my discussion of the images and their accompanying text will illuminate the 'significations' that produced the Nana Sahib Britons needed.

The *ILN*'s image of Nana Sahib appears in a supplement to its 26 September number, adding eight pages to its standard sixteen. The supplement consists of: a full-page triptych of generic Indian scenes in the picturesque mode; a page-plus of reprinted reports from India; a John Leech illustration of families at Scarborough; a page of advertisements; and, on the final page, the image of Nana Sahib which occupies the upper half of the page and is approximately two columns wide. The text alongside the image is a pastiche of *The Times*'s now-discredited assertion by Gibbons of Brick-court that Nana Sahib was not the adopted son of Baji Rao, a lengthy passage from the Calcutta-based *Bengal Hurkaru* fuming that 'no sentimental sympathy' or 'maudlin regard' should be shown to the 'demon' Nana Sahib, and 'a translation of a proclamation posted by Nana Sahib at Cawnpore' (Anon. 1857, *ILN*: 326, 328). This hodgepodge of text underscores that the *ILN* had no 'news', a factor that beset illustrated newspapers in particular and nineteenth-century newsgathering generally. The *ILN*'s contemporaries expressed doubts that an illustrated newspaper could offer both 'fresh' news and illustrations (Sinnema 2018: 15–19); indeed, the paper flourished only because it relied on the culture of reprinting that pertained in the industry for much of the nineteenth century (Slauter 2019). While the text surrounding the *ILN*'s image of Nana Sahib was entirely cobbled together from borrowed material, the image itself claimed novelty: 'The accompanying Portrait is from a sketch of Nana Sahib recently received from India by Major O. Gandini' (Anon. 1857, *ILN*: 328).

The *Illustrated Times*'s sixteen pages on 26 September were largely devoted to developments in India. On its cover was an image of Havelock, the general who led the British recapture of Kanpur, riding a black stallion. Of the paper's remaining five spreads, three pertained to India: two of British troops fighting in Delhi, and the image of Nana Sahib. The latter appears on page nine, takes up virtually the full page, and is captioned as 'a picture painted at Bhitoor, in 1850, by Mr. Beechy, Portrait painter to the King of Oude'. The accompanying text occupies almost two-thirds of page ten. In contrast to the *ILN*'s regurgitation of the story that Nana Sahib is not the adopted son of Baji Rao, the text in the *IT* begins, 'Nena Sahib is the adopted son of the late Peishwa Bajee Rao, who ... lived at Bhitoor ...' (Anon. 1857b, *IT*: 217). Following a report of his attempts to reinstate his father's denied pension, the paper explains that 'Nana Sahib' is a nickname and that the 'patch upon the forehead is the "tilluck," a piece of white clay, the thickness of a wafer' (Anon. 1857b, *IT*: 218). The text includes two testimonies: from 'the gentleman to whom we are indebted for the accompanying portrait' and who refers to Nana Sahib as 'one of the best and most hospitable natives in the Upper Provinces', and that of a 'correspondent' who met Nana Sahib in 1853. Neither had appeared elsewhere and both indicate a measure of independent sourcing on the part of the *IT*.

In contrast to the *Illustrated Times*'s coverage, *The Illustrated London News*'s looks slapdash and hurried. The *ILN* was probably prompted to rush to print an image of Nana Sahib by a notice in the previous week's *IT* promising in its next number 'A finely engraved full-length Portrait of nena sahib ... by Mr. Beechy, Portrait Painter to the King of Oude' (Anon. 1857a, *IT*: 202). The notice was Vizetelly waving a red cape before the bull(y) Ingram – who charged. Though the *ILN*'s text may have been stale and cobbled together, the image Ingram printed was 'recently received' by Major O. Gandini. The battle of Beechey versus Gandini was on. In the world of portraiture, George Duncan Beechey was blue-blood, the son of Sir William Beechey and Anne Jessop, portrait painters at the Royal Academy. Though Gandini lacked such credentials, he had a military title in a conflict that at that point was still considered a 'mutiny' and he operated in an age when sketches by men on the battlefield were desired commodities in the marketplace of illustrated journalism (Sinnema 2018: 63–5).[3] Moreover, Beechey's image, as the *IT*'s caption noted, was from 1850, while the *ILN*'s was fresh, 'recently received from India'. The round appeared a draw.

In the coming months, however, the *Illustrated Times*'s seated Nana Sahib – the Beechey image – seems to have gained the upper hand. Two months later, on 28 November 1857, *The Lady's Newspaper and Pictorial Times* (*LN&PT*) carried on its cover a three-quarter-page image of the *IT*'s portly Nana Sahib – with a few variations (see Figure 30.3). The text surrounding the image was, like the *ILN*'s in September, entirely borrowed: the *LN&PT* describes the 'tulluch' on Nana Sahib's forehead as 'composed of a piece of white clay, about the thickness of a wafer', and explains the

Figure 30.3 'Nana Sahib', *The Lady's Newspaper and Pictorial Times*, 28 November 1857. Courtesy of the author.

origins of his nickname (Anon. 1857a, *LN&PT*: 337). This copy is lifted verbatim from the *Illustrated Times*'s 26 September number, but neither quoted nor attributed; even in the culture of scissors-and-paste journalism that flourished at the time, such wholesale plagiarism exceeded the acceptable. The *LN&PT* also quotes – without attribution, but this time surrounded with quotation marks – the account of a 'writer of a very talented periodical [who] gives to the world the account of a day which he spent with the demon, Nana' (Anon. 1857a, *LN&PT*: 337). The 'talented periodical' this account is pillaged from is *Household Words*.

Before we turn to Dickens's weekly, a few words on the *LN&PT*. Though only press insiders would have known it at the time, *The Illustrated London News*, the *Illustrated Times* and *The Lady's Newspaper and Pictorial Times* were entangled in a ménage. The *LN&PT* was born when Ingram, a businessman who had perfected the art of undercutting rivals, bought out Vizetelly's *Pictorial Times* in 1845 and merged it with another newspaper he owned to create *The Lady's Newspaper and Pictorial Times*. A decade later, in 1855, Vizetelly started the *Illustrated Times*. In his self-aggrandising memoir, *Glances Back through Seventy Years*, he writes that this rival paper was so successful that within a year Ingram confessed to him that the *Illustrated Times* was a 'great thorn in his side' and tried to buy it. Ingram succeeded in acquiring a third of its shares but 'no power of interfering in its management' (Vizetelly 1893: I, 425–6). In short, in 1857 Ingram owned the *ILN* and the *LN&PT* and held shares in the *IT*, which however eluded his control and remained independent and a rival to Ingram's empire.[4]

In the mid-nineteenth century, as questions of copyright were simmering, the rivalry between these newspapers acquired a legal face. Not a week after the *LN&PT*'s image of Nana Sahib appeared on its cover, *Vizetelly v. Johnson* accused the proprietor of the *LN&PT* of 'piracy' of the 'engraving and sketch' of Nana Sahib, calling for the *LN&PT* to refrain from printing or publishing any further copies of the image and sketch (Anon. 1857d, *The Times*: 9). The suit claimed that 'the right to make and publish a wood engraving from the original picture of Nena or Nana Sahib was purchased by the plaintiff from the owner of such original picture, an officer in the Indian army, and that the plaintiff afterwards procured a competent person to write a sketch of his life and character, which engraving and sketch were in the month of September published in the *Illustrated Times*' (Anon. 1857d, *The Times*: 9). The court granted the stay, and the *LN&PT* was prohibited from printing further copies of the purloined image.

The court offered no commentary on the *LN&PT*'s textual description of Nana Sahib, copy that was lifted from Dickens's journal. A week earlier, *Household Words* had carried in its leading position 'Wanderings in India', the narrative of 'a wanderer in the East' who visits 'Nena Sahib' at Bithoor (Lang 1857: 457). Significant portions of this account were reprinted, without source attribution, in the *LN&PT* alongside the pirated illustration of Nana Sahib. In *Household Words*, that 14 November account was followed by another eleven parts, all relating the journey of an insouciant traveller through the central plains of the subcontinent. As with all pieces in *Household Words*, 'Wanderings in India' was unsigned. The identity of the author, however, was soon revealed, as Dickens permitted authors to republish works after a short period. In August 1859, *Wanderings in India and Other Sketches of Life in Hindostan* by John Lang appeared in London. In the Preface, the author thanks Dickens for 'sanctioning a reprint' of material that first appeared in *Household Words*.

Lang is the lynchpin of this case study of the circulation of materials between the British and Anglo-Indian presses. He was an Australian who was called to the bar in London in 1841, had resided in India since 1842, and was the owner and editor of *The Mofussilite*, an English-language newspaper he began in 1845. Lang embodies the transit and press traffic between Britain and India. In 1857, he was on furlough from *The Mofussilite* and attempting to break into the London literary scene when *sipahis* in Meerut, the town he had relocated his newspaper to in 1847, mutinied. Dickens had in 1853 published several of Lang's stories and travelogues. At this news-hungry juncture, Dickens turned to Lang, a man not connected to the Company or government but resident in India for over a decade who happened to be in London. Dickens commissioned the twelve-part 'Wanderings in India', and Lang, an 'India hand', landed the best contract of his life.

Lang had spent a good part of the previous dozen years critiquing the Government of India (at the time the East India Company). His newspaper *The Mofussilite* was but one avenue for these criticisms; in 1851, Lang, the London-trained barrister, briefly abandoned his pen and donned legal robes to challenge the Company in the courts. The sensational trial of *East India Company v. Jotee Perhsad* took place in Agra and it made Lang a minor celebrity. He represented Jotee Prasad, a banker and commissariat contractor who had provisioned the Company in its many wars of aggression and conquest. The Company owed Prasad some £570,000 for services dating back to its Afghan and Sikh campaigns of the 1840s, but in 1850, they accused him of fraud and perjury (Joshi 2021: 98–117). Against long odds, Lang secured an acquittal for his client and embarrassed the Company and its judicial system. As the British and Anglo-Indian presses reported with shopkeeper-obsession, Prasad paid Lang handsomely for his services – to the tune of Rs 3 lacs (approximately £30,000).

Dickens turned to Lang for copy on India in 1857, but Dickens was not the only editor to hit up Lang that autumn: Ingram and Vizetelly did as well. In 1863, long after the appearance of the images in the illustrated weeklies, Lang's *Mofussilite* carried an account on the 'gullibility of the British public' (Anon. 1863, *The Mofussilite*: 340). Though the text leaned into the editorial 'we', it was clearly Lang's writing and recounts how 'the portrait of Jooteepersâd once did duty for Nana Sahib'.

> We were called upon, in London, by a personal friend, the late Mr. Ingram, the proprietor of the *Illustrated London News*, who asked us if we could put him in the way of getting a portrait or sketch of 'the fiend of Cawnpore'. Pointing to a good sized portrait in oils, and a life-like likeness of Jooteepersâd, taken by Mr. Roods, we were asked, 'Who is that?' We told him it was the likeness of the great contractor in India. 'By Jove,' he exclaimed, 'could it not duty [sic] for the Nana?' We were tickled with the suggestion, and responded, 'well it might, in *this* country'. 'That is all we want,' said Ingram. 'Will you lend me that picture?' 'By all means,' said we, and within a week the Lallah's [Prasad's title] likeness was all over the United Kingdom, and shipped to every part of the civilized world. (Anon. 1863, *The Mofussilite*: 340)

In short, *The Illustrated London News*'s 'Nana Sahib' (Figure 30.1) was not Nana Sahib at all, but Jotee Prasad, Lang's client whom he exonerated in 1851. The originator of the fraud says so himself. *The Mofussilite*'s account of the deception got some traction in metropolitan and colonial papers, largely as an amusing anecdote: the *Times of India* and the Melbourne *Herald* reported it, and the *Homeward Mail* cited

Lang's account as a 'joke at the expense of the London press' (Anon. 1863, *Times of India*: 3; Anon. 1863, (Melbourne) *Herald*: 4; Anon. 1863, *Homeward Mail*: 553).

Trouble arises, however, in the next lines of *The Mofussilite*'s account of the prank when Lang describes the image he shared with Ingram: 'It was supposed to be the Nana holding a Durbar. There was the sword, the nosegay, the gold slippers in the foreground, and a magnificent hookah on one side' (Anon. 1863, *The Mofussilite*: 340). The image Lang describes handing to Ingram – the purported image of his former client – is not, of course, the one that appeared in Ingram's *Illustrated London News* but instead in Vizetelly's *Illustrated Times* (later pirated by *The Lady's News and Pictorial Times*). As he proceeds, Lang's account muddies the waters further: the image in Ingram's *ILN* 'attracted the attention of Madame Tussaud, who paid a visit to Ingram', who directed her to Lang, who loaned her the same oil painting, and before long Madame Tussaud's was exhibiting an image of Nana Sahib (Anon. 1863, *The Mofussilite*: 340). The wax image of the man 'whose death the whole mass of Englishmen throughout the world thirst with a deadly longing' (Anon. 1857e, *The Times*: 10) was well attended. One newspaper reported that the wax Nana Sahib 'is represented in a white Hindoo dress, such as is worn by men of rank in the East. He is occupied in smoking his hookah, composed of silver and silver-gilt, which is of very elegant workmanship' (Anon. 1857b, *LN&PT*: 374). The white-robed, hookah-smoking Nana Sahib is, of course, from Vizetelly's *Illustrated Times* (and the *LN&PT*), not Ingram's *ILN*. To disentangle this increasingly tangled skein: Lang claims he passed on to Ingram and Madame Tussaud an image of Jotee Prasad as Nana Sahib. But the image he describes sharing is not the one that appeared in Ingram's paper (indeed, Ingram's Nana Sahib and Madame Tussaud's were not the same). Meanwhile, the image Lang claims he handed over to Ingram appeared in Vizetelly's – Ingram's rival's – paper. The 1863 'clarification' by an ailing Lang – he was a heavy drinker and died in August 1864 at the age of forty-eight – only complicates the picture and adds a puzzle: which is the image of Prasad, and which Nana Sahib?

When Lang's *Wanderings in India* appeared in 1859 in London, it included a frontispiece image of several men in a coach; one has a feather in his headdress and rests his hands on his sword (see Figure 30.4). The text below it reads 'Nena Sahib's Turn-out.--p. 115'. (Though the European seated beside the ornately dressed 'Nena Sahib' is not named, the letterpress indicates it is Lang.) This is a technically cruder woodcut of the image that appeared in the *ILN*. The inclusion of this image in Lang's travelogue would suggest that the dark, aquiline-featured man in the *ILN* – the image Lang in 1863 was to claim was Jotee Prasad – was in fact Nana Sahib. Are we to credit the frontispiece of his 1859 volume or his 1863 account that the painting he loaned Ingram was a hoax, an image of his client Jotee Prasad, not Nana Sahib? Given these wild inconsistencies, Lang makes, in the parlance of his profession, a poor witness.[5]

In 1893, Vizetelly of the *Illustrated Times* offered his account of acquiring the image, and this too features Lang:

> Nana Sahib was one of Lang's especial friends and had presented him with his portrait—a large oil-painting—for which he had sat to the European portrait painter to King of Oude. This portrait Lang lent me for reproduction on a large scale in the 'Illustrated Times,' and its publication excited a good deal of curiosity at the time. (Vizetelly 1893: II, 9)

Figure 30.4 'Nena Sahib's Turn-out.--p. 115', frontispiece of John Lang's *Wanderings in India and Other Sketches of Life in Hindostan*, 1859. Courtesy of the author.

In short, the painting of Nana Sahib by Beechey – 'the European portrait painter to King of Oude' – had come into Lang's possession; this image of the portly man seated on the floor he loaned to Vizetelly, who reproduced it in the *Illustrated Times*. One is inclined to credit this straightforward report – though Vizetelly's pile-up of errors about Lang gives one pause:

> He had practised at the Indian bar, and been editor of the Bombay 'Mofussilite;' and some millionaire begum [lady] had presented him with £10,000, it was said, for successfully pleading her suit against John Company, then the ruling power in India, in the native courts. Owing to this circumstance, Lang's fame spread far and wide among the native princes, and . . . the Ranee of Jhansi, when her territory was about to be annexed and more than half her income confiscated, sent him a letter, written on gold paper, urging him to come and advise her on the subject. (Vizetelly 1893: II, 8)

There are slivers of truth here mixed in with many inaccuracies: Lang did become a celebrity after the trial against 'John Company' and the Rani of Jhansi did consult Lang – he wrote about the encounter in *Wanderings* with much the same orientalist flourish as Vizetelly does (Joshi 2021: 209–11). But *The Mofussilite* never published in Bombay – it was a provincial paper that appeared from Meerut and Agra – and Lang never successfully pleaded the suit of a 'begum': Jotee Prasad was a male banker, who paid Lang handsomely to the tune of £3,000. Vizetelly's account telegraphs an offhand attitude towards the colony. Noteworthy for our purposes, however, is that Vizetelly never mentions a swap of Jotee Prasad-Nana Sahib images, and that he refers to Lang as 'especial friends' with Nana Sahib.

In 1857–8, when 'Wanderings in India' appeared in *Household Words*, the very hint that one was the 'especial friend' of the most reviled man in Britain would have been career suicide. By 1859, when *Wanderings* came out, the Uprising had been crushed and many leaders exiled or killed, but Britons were not satiated, particularly as Nana Sahib remained fugitive. This makes the inclusion of the frontispiece in *Wanderings* somewhat curious, as seated beside this supposed-Nana Sahib is Lang. It is possible that Lang did not sanction the inclusion of the image in the book: he had returned to Calcutta on 4 March 1858 and signed off his copyright to Routledge on 28 June 1858. The inclusion of the image of the men in the open carriage may have been a marketing decision made at the press and not approved by Lang. His papers have not survived, and though this suggestion is speculative, it is bolstered by another curious detail: the 1861 edition of *Wanderings* – also published by Routledge – does not include the frontispiece.

What are we to make of this excision? Possibly when Lang saw the image, he objected for it indicated greater intimacy with Nana Sahib than was prudent. Another possibility is that the image in the frontispiece (and the *ILN*) was not of Nana Sahib after all but (as Lang claimed in 1863) of Jotee Prasad – and the prank was up. This possibility is supported by the 1893 memoir of William Forbes-Mitchell, a former sergeant in the Company's army. *Reminiscences of the Great Mutiny, 1857–59* relates the now-familiar tale of Lang passing off to the *ILN* the image of his client Jotee Prasad as Nana Sahib. Much of the narrative echoes Lang's 1863 account in *The Mofussilite* – his protestations that Jotee Prasad and Nana Sahib did not look alike, his visitor's retort that it did not signify – with one new detail and one alteration. Forbes-Mitchell writes that after the image of Jotee Prasad appeared in the *ILN*, '[w]hen those in India who had known the Nânâ saw it, they declared that it had no resemblance to him whatever, and those who had seen Ajoodia Pershâd declared that the Nânâ was very like Ajoodia Pershâd' (Forbes-Mitchell 1893: 159). Thanks to Lang's joke and the global reach of the *ILN*, Jotee Prasad, a wealthy but innocuous Marwari banker, had become Nana Sahib, a Maratha nobleman.

That the knowledge of 'those in India' did not make its way to Britain is significant for the threads – sometimes threadbare – of print circulation this paper tracks and to the silence newspapers relied on as they produced 'truth' about India. The one difference between Forbes-Mitchell's and Lang's accounts is significant in this regard as well. Lang had ended his 1863 'confession' on a jovial note: 'There is no one who can relish this true story of "gullability" then [sic] did Jooteepersâd himself, when we told it to him' (Anon. 1863, *The Mofussilite*: 340). Forbes-Mitchell, by contrast, recounted: 'To the day of his death John Lang was in mortal fear lest Ajoodia Pershâd should ever come to hear how his picture had been allowed to figure as that of the arch-assassin of the Indian Mutiny' (Forbes-Mitchell 1893: 159). That the image of the supposed Nana Sahib was removed in the 1861 edition of *Wanderings* suggests that the 'mortal fear' Forbes-Mitchell mentions had come to pass.

This fear appears to have materialised on a register Lang would grasp: the legal. In 1861, the Bombay-based *Times of India* reported that there are no less than three suits for libel pending against the celebrated John Lang [*The Mofussilite*] alone – 1st, said to be brought by Major Goad, 2nd by the Dhera-Dhoon Tea Company, and 3rd, of which we have just heard, by an equally celebrated individual as J. L. Lalla Jotee Pershand. It appears that the 'great contractor' has filed a bill of complaint against Mr. Lang, in which he has set forth a whole lot of alleged wrongs and grievances, but upon which, though conveyed to us in a 'leader' cut and dried, we shall by no means enter, having no inclination just now to go in perchance for another libel ourselves. (Anon. 1861, *Times of India*: 2)

Starting in 1860, the judiciary in India was in the process of reorganisation, and details of this case have been impossible to track. But the timing suggests that Prasad's charge potentially related to the image in *Wanderings* that represented him as Nana Sahib; this would explain the expunging of the frontispiece from the 1861 edition. The irony here is thick: the client sues for libel – a charge of misrepresentation – the man who had represented him in 1851 against fraud, itself a species of misrepresentation. In 1851 Lang had represented Prasad in the courts; in 1857 he did so in newsprints. In the former case, Lang facilitated Prasad's acquittal and cleared his name; in 1857, by contrast, Lang stole Prasad's face and misrepresented him as the arch-villain of the Uprising.

Three cases – Jotee Prasad's trial in Agra in 1851, Vizetelly's against the *Lady's Newspaper and Pictorial Times* in 1857 in London, and Prasad's against Lang in Calcutta in 1861 – bring into relief multiple forms of representation that coalesce around what would otherwise be an innocuous case of misrepresentation. Lang's representation of Prasad in 1851, the first case against an Indian that the Company lost, gave shape and voice to the dissent of the colonised. On its surface, it was about an individual, his unpaid invoices and an accusation of fraud. But as the *Bombay Times* grasped at the time of the trial, it represented larger stakes. Referring to the government's 'long career of past misconduct', the newspaper drew an analogy between the charges of fraud against Prasad and the Company's acquisition of territory by fraud and 'dishonest means' (Anon. 1851a, *Bombay Times*). Matching fraud for fraud, the *Bombay Times* lamented that in bringing its case against Prasad, the Government of India had 'convinced . . . the natives . . . that our intention was to perpetuate a stupendous fraud by form of law' (Anon. 1851a, *Bombay Times*; Anon. 1851b, *Bombay Times*). For those willing to look, the case shed light on the deception that undergirded the colonial regime. The case also signalled resistance, an Indian using the courts to clear his name.

In 1857, Vizetelly used the courts in ways familiar to print history scholars: for copyright purposes. Though the property in copyright is not tangible, copyright hinges on matters of ownership not dissimilar to those at the heart of colonial questions. Who owns the image of Nana Sahib is to 'who owns India' as intellectual property is to tangible property. Which is to say they are analogous questions, brought together in the court of law by extending the principle of physical property to intellectual products. (The blind spot of this copyright case, as the blind spot of colonialism, was that neither attended to the colonised subject himself.) The final case, Prasad's charge of libel against Lang in 1861, closes the circle. By claiming that Lang misrepresented him in the frontispiece of *Wanderings*, Prasad disaggregates the legal representation a barrister provides a client from an individual's right to a non-distorted representation.

Prasad's charge against his former counsellor points towards an act of reassertion or budding self-representation.

Coda

Which is an image of Nana Sahib, and which Jotee Prasad? My informed view is that the *Illustrated Times*'s image of the man seated on the patterned carpet is most likely that of the historical figure Nana Sahib. Tange appears to think otherwise: taking up a throwaway comment by Forbes-Mitchell that Nana Sahib would never be caught in the clothing of a 'Marwaree banker', Tange concludes that the 'stiffly embroidered tunic with epaulettes and weapons' – the *ILN*'s image – better fits Nana Sahib's 'militaristic' background than that of the 'merchant-banker' Jotee Prasad (Tange 2021: 212). The assumption here is that as a Maratha – typed as a 'warrior people' (Fordham 2008: 84, 68n) – Nana Sahib would be in 'militaristic' clothing. This reading is, in fact, erroneous. The white dress-like garment – an *angarkha* – worn by the man in the *IT*'s image is in the style of Maratha clothing. A 1792 oil painting, *The Maratha Peshwa with Nana Fadnavis and Attendants* by James Wales, depicts the peshwa who preceded Nana Sahib's father dressed in a similar *angarkha*. (In Wales's painting, both peshwa and his minister also have a *tilak* or mark on the forehead, as the *IT*'s Nana Sahib does.) The saucer-shaped *pagri*, or turban, in the *IT*'s image is also closer to what Ritu Kumar, the pre-eminent historian of royal clothing in India, refers to as 'the distinctive Maratha "cartwheel" *pagri*' (Kumar 2006: 78).

The attempt to settle the question by coming from the direction of 'merchant-banker' that Forbes-Mitchell posits presses up against our own stereotypes and attempts to read a social position that was in flux in the mid-nineteenth century. Jotee Prasad, as Ellenborough, former Governor-General of India, said in the House of Lords, came of a family 'who held as conspicuous a station in India as the Barings and the Rothschilds' (Hansard 1851). The ornate clothing and headdress of the *ILN*'s Nana Sahib would have been fitting for an Indian Rothschild, a man whose work with the new masters opened doors to immense wealth. By contrast, the setting and mise-en-scène of the *IT*'s seated Nana Sahib is more in keeping with a Maratha peshwa and the work of a Royal Academy-trained artist, Beechey, than that of a young artist just arrived in India, as Thomas Roods was.[6] In my estimation, the image of 'Nana Sahib' that appeared in the *ILN* in September 1857 and in the frontispiece of *Wanderings* in 1859 was most likely based on the painting of Jotee Prasad by Roods and remediated by the *ILN*'s and Routledge's in-house artists. The image of the front-facing, seated man in the *Illustrated Times* is, I venture, of the historical figure of Nana Sahib based on an oil painting executed by George Duncan Beechey in 1850.[7]

The images of 'Nana Sahib' that appeared in three illustrated London newspapers serve as a case study to illustrate the considerable ignorance, even indifference, in Britain about its colony. Steamship journals such as the *Homeward Mail* attempted to bring the two locales closer by building a print-bridge, as it were, and Anglo-Indian newspapers served as adjutants in the process. That bridge had all the constraints of its architects, engineers and contractors. If, as Ingram purportedly told Lang, the differences between Indians did not signify for Britons, that indifference is replicated in the prints: one man could stand in for another without comment. Lest we repeat the indifference and bifurcation that allowed such stereotyping – of reproductive technology and of typecasting the Other – to flourish, it is crucial that we study the British and Indian presses simultaneously and in active conversation with one another. In doing so, we may not be able to represent Indians with a voice, but we can prevent them from misrepresentations that held for over a century.

Notes

1. The massacre at Satichaura Ghat took place on 27 June when Europeans, promised safe passage, were fired upon and almost 300 men were killed. The women were taken to the Bibighar and held as bargaining chips in wretched conditions for almost three weeks until 15 July, when the 200 women were massacred as a relief column advanced.
2. At the conclusion of the Third Anglo-Maratha war in 1818, Baji Rao II, the Maratha peshwa, was pensioned and relocated to Bithur, near Kanpur. When he died in 1851, the government refused to extend his £80,000 annual pension to his son, Dhondu Pant – nicknamed Nana Sahib – on the grounds that he was adopted.
3. The identity of Gandini remains murky. In the 1850s, letters commenting on continental politics from an O. Gandini appeared in British newspapers. In 1855, the *Morning Advertiser* printed a signed opinion by O. Gandini whom it identified as an 'Italian Liberal, who fought bravely at Venice' and 'in the Australian service' (Anon. 1855, *Morning Advertiser*: 3).
4. In 1859, Vizetelly sold his share of the *IT* to Ingram, who now had the controlling interest in the paper, though Vizetelly continued to edit it for another five years (Vizetelly 1893: II, 60).
5. Even prior to his 1863 account, Lang's credibility was called into question: a letter by 'An Old Indian' in the Adelaide-based *South Australian Register* proclaimed Lang's account of meeting Nana Sahib as 'bear[ing] evidence of random recollection, written off with culpable haste', the visit 'simply a draft upon imagination to amuse readers' (Anon. 1859, *South Australian Register*: 3).
6. In his 1863 account, Lang mentioned Roods as the artist of the image of Jotee Prasad that he palmed off on Ingram. Thomas Roods was a portrait painter who worked in oils, who arrived in Calcutta in March 1851 and set up a studio shortly thereafter (Anon. 1851, *Bombay Gazette*: 560). That Roods, a relative newcomer to India, would paint Jotee Prasad upon his acquittal is plausible; that he would paint Nana Sahib, a claimant to the Marathas' grandeur, seems unlikely. Roods barely survived the Uprising – he took shelter in the Agra Fort, along with the city's Europeans and the mofussilite presses – and returned to Britain in 1864.
7. Beechey lived in India from 1828 to 1852, the bulk of his professional life. In 1851, the ship carrying his paintings to Britain sank, with the result that few paintings identified as his work survive (Beechey 1994: 123–5). That Beechey would have gifted his portrait of Nana Sahib to the man himself, and that Nana Sahib would have passed that painting on to Lang, is within the realm of plausibility, especially if Nana Sahib considered Lang an 'especial friend'.

Bibliography

Anon. (1857), *Albion*, 17 August, n.p.
—— (1851), *Bombay Gazette*, 7, 560.
—— (1851a), *Bombay Times*, 28 April, reprinted in *Bengal Hurkaru*, 8 May, 510.
—— (1851b), *Bombay Times*, 28 April, reprinted in *Bengal Hurkaru*, 8 May, 511.
—— (1875), *Chicago Daily Tribune*, 21 March, 5.
—— (1863), *Homeward Mail*, 6 July, 553–4.

—— (1857), *The Illustrated London News*, 26 September, 326, 328.
—— (1857a), *Illustrated Times*, 19 September, 202.
—— (1857b), *Illustrated Times*, 26 September, 217–18.
—— (1857a), *The Lady's Newspaper and Pictorial Times*, 28 November, 337.
—— (1857b), *The Lady's Newspaper and Pictorial Times*, 12 December, 374.
—— (1863), (Melbourne) *Herald*, 18 July, 4.
—— (1858), *The Mofussilite*, 9 March, n.p.
—— (1863), *The Mofussilite*, 29 May, 340.
—— (1855), *Morning Advertiser*, 3 September, 3.
—— (1894), *The Saturday Review*, 12 May, 499.
—— (1859), *South Australian Register*, 31 October, 3.
—— (1857a), *The Times*, 14 August (second edition), 8.
—— (1857b), *The Times*, 19 August, 10.
—— (1857c), *The Times*, 22 August, 9.
—— (1857d), *The Times*, 4 December, 9.
—— (1857e), *The Times*, 28 December, 10.
—— (1861), *Times of India*, 18 September, 2.
—— (1863), *Times of India*, 16 July, 3.
Beechey, G. D. S. (1994), *The Eighth Child: George Duncan Beechey 1797–1852, Royal Portrait Painter to the Last Four Kings of Oudth*, London: Excalibur.
Forbes-Mitchell, William (1893), *Reminiscences of the Great Mutiny, 1857–59: Including the Relief, Siege, and Capture of Lucknow, and the Campaigns in Rohilcund and Oude*, London: Macmillan.
Fordham, Douglas (2008), 'Costume dramas: British art at the court of the Marathas', *Representations*, 101, 57–85.
Hansard, HL Deb. vol. 117, col. 1,124, 24 June 1851, https://hansard.parliament.uk/lords/1851-06-24/debates/89b9cb54-8229-438a-8678-e3db319da89e/JoteePershaud#1124 (accessed 10 January 2024).
Joshi, Priti (2021), *Empire News: The Anglo-Indian Press Writes India*, Albany: State University of New York Press.
Kumar, Ritu (2006), *Costumes and Textiles of Royal India*, Woodbridge: Antique Collectors' Club.
Lang, John (1859), *Wanderings in India and Other Sketches of Life in Hindostan*, London: Routledge, Warne & Routledge.
Maidment, Brian (2016), 'Illustration', in Andrew King, Alexis Easley and John Morton (eds), *The Routledge Handbook to Nineteenth-Century British Periodicals and Newspapers*, London: Routledge, 102–23.
Sinnema, Peter (2018), *Dynamics of the Pictured Page: Representing the Nation in the Illustrated London News*, Brookfield: Ashgate.
Slauter, Will (2019), *Who Owns the News? A History of Copyright*, Stanford: Stanford University Press.
Tange, Andrea Kaston (2021), 'Picturing the villain: Image-making and the Indian Uprising', *Victorian Studies*, 63.2, 193–223.
Vizetelly, Henry (1893), *Glances Back through Seventy Years: Autobiographical and Other Reminiscences*, 2 vols, London: Kegan Paul, Trench, Trübner & Co. Ltd.
Wallace, Brian (2015), 'Nana Sahib in British culture and memory', *The Historical Journal*, 58.2, 589–61.
'Wanderings in India' (1857), *Household Words*, 14 November, 457–63.

31

THE INDIAN NEWSPAPER REPORTS OF BRITISH INDIA: 'A KIND OF PERIODICAL PRESS'

Sukeshi Kamra

Introduction

ALONGSIDE THE INDIAN and Anglo-Indian press of mid- to late-Victorian India, there was a third form that looked to some suspiciously like a periodical press. Producing weeklies, titled 'Native Newspaper Reports', it claimed to present political views of the Indian-owned periodical press, had an editor, bearing the official title of government translator, and a distinct class of reader, the colonial government (see Figure 31.1). In reality, it was a genre powered by substitution, standing in for the Indian-owned press, in a thinly veiled act of surveillance of the latter. These and other facts did not escape some Indian and Anglo-Indian newspapers and periodicals of the time,[1] who subjected the structure, function, objective and readership of the Reports to scrutiny. Their concerns were far from misplaced, as this chapter hopes to prove. From the 1870s on, the Newspaper Reports are a key contributor to a discourse in the making – of an incendiary Indian press and readership steeped in superstition and emotionalism. Focusing on the 1870s to 1890s, decades during which the Indian press and readership expanded rapidly,[2] as did technologies of control (including especially the surveillance represented by the Newspaper Reports), this chapter considers the role played by the Newspaper Reports in the legal and political history of the time.

The chapter opens with a discussion of reactions to the genre found in the periodical press of the 1870s to 1890s. These set the stage, so to speak, for approaching the Newspaper Reports as a far from inert, routine text and discursive act. The discussion of the latter, which follows, focuses on a four-year period that is bookended by an 1888 report on the Indian press at one end and, at the other, legal proceedings against an Indian newspaper charged, in 1891, with seditious libel under section 124a of the Indian Penal Code.[3] The exchanges that take place within government over the four years are revealing, to say the least: they describe the solidification of a particular image of the Indian press via repeating vocabularies. Without exception, the supporting evidence claimed in each instance is the Indian press of the Newspaper Reports, not the Indian press itself. The former, which is normalised as that which it is not (the latter), via an extensive citational afterlife, is thus authoritative in a process that produces a legal fiction of the Indian press as the leading site for the production of 'seditious propagandism' in the colony (Proceedings of the Home Department January 1890: prog. 319).

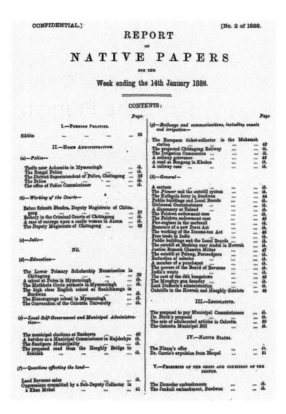

Figure 31.1 Title page of a 'Newspaper Report', p. 1 of report, IOR/L/R/5/14. Courtesy of the British Library.

The Indian Newspaper Reports: A Topic in the Periodical Press of the 1870s–90s

On 2 August 1874, the Bombay-based Indian newspaper *Native Opinion* published an article headed 'The Native Press' on the Newspaper Reports that it attributed to the Anglo-Indian *Indian Daily News* of 15 July 1874.[4] Hailed as a 'system', the Newspaper Reports, the *Indian Daily News* editorial article maintains, are a kind of 'periodical press':

> In every country the officers of Government are sharply criticised in the press, and have some cause to feel irritated at the comments, which are being incessantly made on their conduct and character. But we believe that it is only in India that officials retaliate in kind. Our system of official reports, regularly published, and forming not the least valuable or permanent literature of the country, is in itself a kind of periodical press. Magistrates and Commissioners are encouraged to deal in these productions with every subject of public interest, and in particular to describe the tone and influence of the native journals. ('Editorial' 1874: 2)

Why, in the view of the *Indian Daily News*, is an administrative genre that government was wont to describe as balanced and objective more correctly classified as a periodical press?[5] What 'kind of' periodical press is it? The answer is embedded in descriptions, such as this paragraph provides, of the workings of the genre: the Newspaper Reports are the source of government opinion on the Indian press, not the Indian press itself; and their objective is to present the 'tone' of the Indian press (the article's disapproval of a term lacking in clarity is visible later when the article suggests 'tone' translates into the equally vague 'feelings of the people on subjects of importance'). In essence the paragraph correctly intuits political emotion (not thought) is, by government definition, the exclusive concern of the Reports ('Editorial' 1874: 2–3).

In another key paragraph, in which the article focuses on the figure of the government translator, a rather more vivid description, of the meaning on the ground of a genre focused on its subject's (the Indian press's) 'tone' and 'feeling', indicates the kind of periodical press the *Indian Daily News* has in mind.

> We think that the Government Translator is as much to blame as any one for the hostile feeling, which would seem to exist between officials and the press. He has to select the articles which are to be brought to the notice of Government and indirectly to that of the English public, by being put into something resembling our language, and printed at the cost of the State. He invariably chooses all the most abusive passages, and strings them together, without any of the decent padding with which they are surrounded in the original. This is not the way in which he should pick out the plums. ('Editorial' 1874: 2)

The figure of the Translator – strategically employed, it would appear, to deflect critique away from the government as a whole – is described in terms reminiscent of an expanding demotic Victorian press, with some segments considered to be trafficking in sensationalism. In the government translator's hands, the Indian press devolves into decontextualised 'abusive passages' that are reconfigured ('strings them together') in the pages of the Newspaper Reports to a particular effect – magnification of hostility in the Indian press toward the government. Adding another layer to an already distorted product, there is the unstable domain of linguistic translation. In sum, the forthright critique suggests the typical Newspaper Report is more correctly identified as a newsrag with its ideological function hiding in plain sight: comprising decontextualised 'abusive passages', in translation, it is informed by a directive that renders any shade of reasoned opinion irrelevant. The article comments, with some irony, that such a provably unstable site is a government expense, attacks the local administrator-reader (for an over-reaction to criticism), and expresses concern over its reach, which, in its opinion, extends to the English public.[6]

The kind of periodical press the *Indian Daily News* article will recognise in the descriptions it provides of this government genre, I am suggesting then, is the range of popular print genres described in their time as a destabilising site of sensational rhetoric and content.[7] Indeed, the subject of respectability, as it relates to the periodical press, is a routine topic in the Indian press of the time, no doubt in part due to the Anglo-Indian press's majority view of the Indian press as immoderate, emotive and lacking in political knowledge as well as judgement, a view it made only too public in post-1857 British India.

It is, then, more than likely that readers of the *Indian Daily News* and the *Native Opinion* would have caught the intertextual reference to the Victorian sensational press in the article on the Newspaper Reports. One might even speculate that a deflection of the accusation of rhetorically excessive political emotion, from the Indian press on to the Newspaper Reports, in an article such as the one which appears in the *Indian Daily News* and is republished in the *Native Opinion*, would have held much appeal for the Indian press. Not infrequently, Newspaper Reports present just such an Indian press in excerpts of Indian newspaper articles complaining of the misrepresentation to which it, the Indian press, is subject in the Reports. Consider the following excerpts:

> In the course of a long article on the Bengal Administration Report for 1874–75 the same paper [*Bharat Sangskaran* of 28 January] makes the following remarks on the observations made in the report on native newspapers:-- . . . The Government weekly reports are often a mockery of the native papers, and there is very little likelihood of the authorities being correctly informed of their meaning from these reports. (Bengal Newspaper Reports 1876; week ending 5 February, para. 11; *Bharat Sangskaran* 28 January)

> The *Dharwar Writt* [of 24 January 1877] . . . reiterates the old and often-repeated complaint of the Vernacular Press, that the vernacular newspapers get no opportunity to see the weekly reports submitted by the Reporter on the Native Press to Government, and are thus kept in the dark as to whether the important matters they contain for the information and notice of the authorities, are properly noticed or not in these summaries. If Government will kindly exchange these summaries with the vernacular newspapers, the latter will be enabled to see whether the Official Reporter performs his work rightly; and if he errs now and then, to point out and complain of his errors.
> (Bombay Newspaper Reports 1877; week ending 3 February, page 5 of report; *Dharwar Writt* 24 January)

In the Newspaper Report excerpts cited above, the genre is accused of disrespect as much as misrepresentation, quite openly in one ('mockery of the native papers') and more circumspectly in the other ('if he errs now and again'). It is of course difficult to see past the mediation represented by the Newspaper Report excerpts to original articles of Indian newspapers. We can, however, be reasonably certain that such excerpts contain something of the widespread concern in the Indian periodical press over a genre in which misrepresentation is actively encouraged by an ambiguously worded directive (to report on the 'tone' of the press), an unreliable figure (editor-translator) charged with interpreting this directive, and a readership (government) hostile to the Indian press. Indeed, a similar critique, I will suggest, is packed into the following remark, which takes cognisance of the transformation of the Newspaper Reports from a transparent, if mediating, forum to one of surveillance:

> Over here, we have no means of knowing at all what the official reporter says of ourselves and our purely vernacular brethren. Time was when the reports were available to the public, but the illiberal spirit which induced the Director of Public

Instruction more than four years ago, still seems to sway that department. ('The Native Press' 1874: 2)

The Indian Newspaper Reports of the 1870s–90s: Characteristics and Effects

Critiques of the sort described above encourage us to question the style and content of the Newspaper Reports. Do the excerpts look anything like the *Indian Daily News* article, for instance, would have us believe? Of the Newspaper Reports across the provinces and territories of British India, the Bengal Newspaper Reports are not only the most voluminous but also the most cited in government commentaries on the Indian press. The chapter thus focuses on these Reports, which are, in the 1870s–90s, liberally peppered with affective excerpts in which the government is directly or indirectly an object of critique. Here are some instances:

> If the English really desire to hold us in eternal subjection, let their rule be yet more severe; and the sooner the Hindu race disappears from the face of the earth, the better it will be for them. Let plagues infest the country, and the earth thus be freed from the yoke of slavery. (Bengal Newspaper Reports 1875; week ending 6 February, para. 8; *Amrita Bazar Patrika* 28 January)

> Even a dangerously sick man speaks out his mind in a delirium, and in broken and indistinct language, if not in an intelligible and methodical way. But India has no life, no capacity of feeling. For if she had, we would not have become, for all time, the sport of others, an instrument of their will, to pander to their pleasure; nor would the Secretary of State have been able to sell India in the Manchester market. (Bengal Newspaper Reports 1876; week ending 18 March, para. 5; *Bharat Mihir* 8 March)

> You will not understand our hearts' language, you will not hear our hearts' cries. If you hear our hearts' language, you will excommunicate us; if we give expression to our hearts' language, you will take up the punishing rod, and yet you will attempt to force, in the fullest measure, your own hearts' language into the heart of our hearts. (Bengal Newspaper Reports 1891; week ending 12 September, para. 89; *Dacca Gazette* 7 September)

While over-represented, emotive excerpts that border on melodrama are by no means the only style of political comment filling the pages of the Newspaper Reports. The latter typically include, also, excerpts in which argument and reasoning are the dominant mode of engagement. Consider the following representative excerpts:

> The gradual growth of a public opinion in this country, gaining strength year by year, is a hopeful sign. The educated classes are not now, as before, indifferent to public matters; and politics, the acts of public men, and the merits and demerits of the administration, are all discussed in the columns of the newspapers. It is, however, a matter of regret that Government has not, in the slightest degree, given heed

to, or assisted in, the formation of this public opinion; nay, acting upon improper counsel, it is manifesting an attitude of bitter hostility to the press. (Bengal Newspaper Reports 1876; week ending 9 December, para. 7; *Bharat Mihir* 30 November)

The loyalty of the people would not be shaken if Mr. Stephen had not enacted his law of sedition. Were it not for the rigors of the Penal Code, the increase in the number of such crimes as perjury, fraud, forgery, murder, and suicide would not otherwise be easily accounted for; while Government itself would never have found its way so thickly strewn with thorns, if it had not sought to humble the natives of India by a rigorous system of administration. (Bengal Newspaper Reports 1875; week ending 18 December, para. 4; *Amrita Bazar Patrika* 9 December)

Remarkably, such excerpts, as indeed any acknowledgement of the presence in the Indian press of an intellectual engagement with political and social topics, are missing from government commentaries on the Indian press. Affective excerpts, on the other hand, structure them. From this process, which flattens out a heterogeneous press into a homogeneously inflammatory one, the Indian press emerges as a legal fiction, fitted to the language of the (seditious libel) law. Thus while the *Indian Daily News*'s article may have overstated the case when it comes to the Newspaper Reports themselves (given the reports are confidential, as the *Native Opinion* complains, one has to wonder where the periodical press gets its information – possibly leaks and possibly via annual administrative reports),[8] it is an accurate gauging of the legal and political effects of the Newspaper Reports.

1888–91: A Case in Point

A key moment in this storying of the Indian press unfolds over 1888–91, culminating in the Bengal government's decision to charge the *Bangavasi* under sections 124a and 500 of the Indian Penal Code. It provides us with insight into the administrative context within which affective Newspaper Report excerpts acquire force, as and when they are assimilated to commentaries on the Indian press. An undated report, produced some time before 6 November 1888 by 'the Committee appointed to consider the question of the enlargement of the functions of the Provincial Councils', advises the government of India to balance the proposed 'enlarging [of] Provincial Councils and liberalizing their proceedings and functions' with 'a more effective criminal law against libel and seditious propagandism' (Proceedings of the Home Department January 1890: prog. 319). Evidence of a runaway Indian press, which the report offers as both cause and evidence of widespread 'seditious propagandism', comes in the form of a lengthy appendix comprising Newspaper Report excerpts. Titled 'Extracts from some of the Vernacular and Anglo-Vernacular Newspapers in India' (prog. 320), the appendix includes about forty excerpts excised from the Newspaper Reports of Punjab, Bengal, Bombay, Madras, and North West Provinces and Oudh. Excerpts date from 1886 to 1888 and are organised by theme, under headings such as 'Foreign Politics' and 'Political' (headings that, incidentally, duplicate headings found in the Newspaper Reports) (prog. 320). The excerpts themselves have titles such as 'Tyranny borne by the Hindus' (*Khair-khwah-i-Kashmir* 10 July 1888; cited in prog. 320) and phrases such as 'harrowing acts of oppression and cruelty' (*Bangabasi* 7 July 1888; cited in prog. 320).

The report on the Indian press (titled 'Note'), which is forwarded by the government of India to the secretary of state for India on 6 November 1888, is characterised by overstatement such that a homogeneously sensational Indian press and its audience appear a given. The latter is, the report maintains, 'an ignorant and credulous population containing elements of superstition, lawlessness and fanaticism' (prog. 319) – one easily swayed, that is, by an irresponsible Indian press:

> When no questions calculated to arouse angry feelings are discussed, the newspapers exercise an influence on probably two millions of people. But when such questions are discussed – and now-a-days they are discussed with growing frequency and increasing virulence – the influence exerted is of course much greater and more widespread. (prog. 319)

If the Indian audience – a flattened category – is ridiculed in phrases such as 'angry feelings', 'ignorant and credulous', 'superstition' and 'lawlessness', as well as 'fanaticism' and 'increasing virulence', so too is the Indian press, which stands accused of trafficking in political hostility; and reader and press are together encompassed in superlative adjectives ('much greater' and 'more widespread') that describe an alarmingly indefinite horizon of public hostility toward the government. Elsewhere in the report, the Indian press acquires legal-sounding, political definitions: the press, the report claims, is responsible for spreading a 'propagandism of disorder' (prog. 319). What is meant by the latter is indicated in an equally imprecise legal phrase, 'doctrines dangerous to law and order' (prog. 319). Not unexpected, but nonetheless worth emphasising, is the fact this report (as all such reports on the Indian press) presumes that 'tone' and influence of the Indian press are what is of interest to the authorities. In the process, the committee's report effectively erases evidence contained in the source it cites, the Newspaper Reports, of an intellectually engaged Indian press, making it (the report) look very much like the *Indian Daily News* article's claims of the genre.

Reading against the grain, it is clear that the committee report traffics in stereotype, simultaneously categorising and arresting the Indian character in emotionalism and irrationalism. The stereotype thus identifies affect (the body) as a site of political resistance, marking it as a potential site of sedition ('disaffection' in the language of the law). The consequence of the report is a restoration to local governments of the right to prosecute newspapers of the Indian press, but not as immediately as one might think. The secretary of state for India's memo to the government of India conveying the decision is dated 28 March 1889 (prog. 321), while the latter's memo to local governments granting the right to prosecute is dated 31 January 1890 (progs. 322 and 323).

Not surprisingly, a little more than a year later, on 20 April 1891, the Bengal government submits a report for the government of India on the Indian press, and readership, in the province. In the opening remarks, the report claims the weight of previous opinion for legitimising its own conclusions. The lieutenant-governor, it states, 'thinks it will not be superfluous to re-state the main arguments which have been used', even though he is 'aware that the mischief and danger of allowing writings of this kind to be published unchecked have been frequently brought before the Government of India with the greatest possible weight and emphasis' (Proceedings of the Home Department October 1891: prog. 260). The 'main arguments' (prefaced with the kind of emphasis a superlative adjective such as 'greatest' provides) describe an irresponsible, inflammatory periodical culture, spreading misinformation, in a society constituted of 'an ignorant and credulous population among whom only a small minority can read or write' (prog. 260). Lacking the moderating influence that a responsible press provides, the Bengal government claims, regional governments in India find themselves in a bind. That the argument itself is structured by contestations taking place within the Victorian press is apparent in the comparison which the memo draws in an attempt to impress upon the government of India that press and readership in the colony represent a deviation from the norm. In the words of the report,

> It has often been pointed out that in enlightened Western countries misrepresentation, written or oral, of the acts or intentions of Government or its servants may be safely left to exposure in the columns of newspapers which support the Government, or to the speeches of public men, but that no such safeguard or resource is available in India, where the Government is daily exposed to slanders and misrepresentations. (prog. 260)

Elsewhere the report puts a legal spin on the same conclusion, while pointedly bringing the entire Indian press into the scope of its claim: 'it is hardly an exaggeration to say that at the present time the tone of the Native Press as a whole is one of uncompromising disaffection and dis-content, qualified only here and there by expressions calculated to open a door of escape from the danger of a prosecution under the Penal Code' (prog. 260). Seven affective passages excised from articles of Indian newspapers (and translated of course) are included in the report as evidence, while in the margins of each cited excerpt the Bengal Newspaper Reports are identified as the source. The fact that claims about the 'tone of the Native Press as a whole' are based on excerpts from the Newspaper Reports, not the Indian press of Bengal, is nowhere acknowledged, nor is the array of excerpts (see Figure 31.2).

In June 1891, substantially the same argument is urged yet again upon the government of India in another lengthy communication (prog. 261) and, once again, Newspaper Report excerpts are attached as evidence. The strategy by which the argument is made, though, is somewhat more complex. The report, which, like previous ones, describes an alarmingly unstable public culture, made so by the Indian press, is set up as a rebuttal of a more moderate, balanced reading of the Indian press which the report includes as an attachment. Both claim the Newspaper Reports as evidence. The attachment is titled 'report on the Vernacular Newspapers published in the Lower Provinces and in Assam in 1890' (prog. 263). An annual report, it is submitted by the government translator to the office of the director of Public Instruction on 14 March 1891, who in turn forwards the report to the government of Bengal on 25 March 1891, who in turn incorporates it into the June 1891 memo to the government of India. The attached translator's annual report describes an Indian press that spans a range of styles in its political comments and holds a diverse set of opinions on social, economic and political facts of colonial rule. This view is inscribed as much in enumerative as in narrative components of the report. For instance, in the usual tabular statement by which the newspapers of the Indian press are made trackable – columns note the proprietor, printing press, frequency of publication, language of publication – under the final column, titled 'Tone, politics, &c, of the paper' (prog. 263), the report observes about one newspaper, 'Gives much attention to local matters and discusses social questions from the

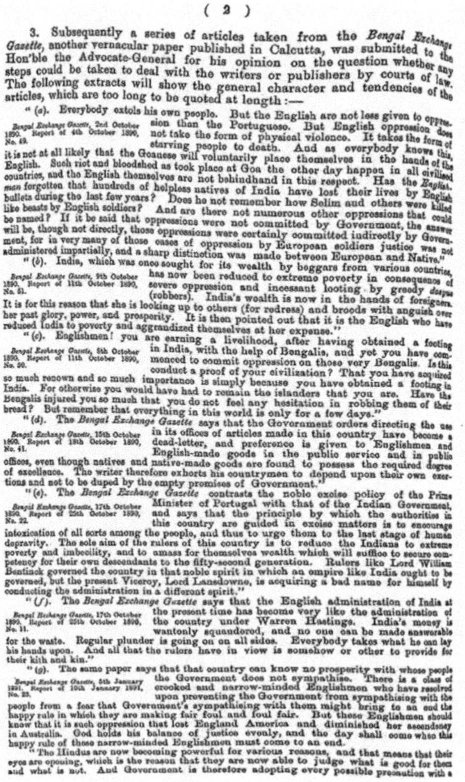

(2)

3. Subsequently a series of articles taken from the *Bengal Exchange Gazette*, another vernacular paper published in Calcutta, was submitted to the Hon'ble the Advocate-General for his opinion on the question whether any steps could be taken to deal with the writers or publishers by courts of law. The following extracts will show the general character and tendencies of the articles, which are too long to be quoted at length :—

Bengal Exchange Gazette, 2nd October 1890. Report of 4th October 1890, No. 49.

"(*a*). Everybody extols his own people. But the English are not less given to oppression than the Portuguese. But English oppression does not take the form of physical violence. It takes the form of starving people to death. And as everybody knows this, it is not at all likely that the Goanese will voluntarily place themselves in the hands of the English. Such riot and bloodshed as took place at Goa the other day happen in all civilised countries, and the English themselves are not behindhand in this respect. Has the *Englishman* forgotten that hundreds of helpless natives of India have lost their lives by English bullets during the last few years? Does he not remember how Selim and others were killed like beasts by English soldiers? And are there not numerous other oppressions that could be named? If it be said that oppressions were not committed by Government, the answer will be, though not directly, those oppressions were certainly committed indirectly by Government, for in very many of those cases of oppression by European soldiers justice was not administered impartially, and a sharp distinction was made between European and Native."

Bengal Exchange Gazette, 9th October 1890. Report of 11th October 1890, No. 51.

"(*b*). India, which was once sought for its wealth by beggars from various countries, has now been reduced to extreme poverty in consequence of severe oppression and incessant looting by greedy *dasyus* (robbers). India's wealth is now in the hands of foreigners. It is for this reason that she is looking up to others (for redress) and broods with anguish over her past glory, power, and prosperity. It is then pointed out that it is the English who have reduced India to poverty and aggrandized themselves at her expense."

Bengal Exchange Gazette, 9th October 1890. Report of 11th October 1890, No. 50.

"(*c*). Englishmen! you are earning a livelihood, after having obtained a footing in India, with the help of Bengalis, and yet you have commenced to commit oppression on those very Bengalis. Is this conduct a proof of your civilization? That you have acquired so much renown and so much importance is simply because you have obtained a footing in India. For otherwise you would have had to remain the islanders that you are. Have the Bengalis injured you so much that you do not feel any hesitation in robbing them of their bread? But remember that everything in this world is only for a few days."

Bengal Exchange Gazette, 15th October 1890. Report of 18th October 1890, No. 41.

"(*d*). The *Bengal Exchange Gazette* says that the Government orders directing the use in its offices of articles made in this country have become a dead-letter, and preference is given to Englishmen and English-made goods in the public service and in public offices, even though natives and native-made goods are found to possess the required degree of excellence. The writer therefore exhorts his countrymen to depend upon their own exertions and not to be duped by the empty promises of Government."

Bengal Exchange Gazette, 17th October 1890. Report of 25th October 1890, No. 22.

"(*e*). The *Bengal Exchange Gazette* contrasts the noble excise policy of the Prime Minister of Portugal with that of the Indian Government, and says that the principle by which the authorities in this country are guided in excise matters is to encourage intoxication of all sorts among the people, and thus to urge them to the last stage of human depravity. The sole aim of the rulers of this country is to reduce the Indians to extreme poverty and imbecility, and to amass for themselves wealth which will suffice to secure competency for their own descendants to the fifty-second generation. Rulers like Lord William Bentinck governed the country in that noble spirit in which an empire like India ought to be governed, but the present Viceroy, Lord Lansdowne, is acquiring a bad name for himself by conducting the administration in a different spirit."

Bengal Exchange Gazette, 17th October 1890. Report of 25th October 1890, No. 11.

"(*f*). The *Bengal Exchange Gazette* says that the English administration of India at the present time has become very like the administration of the country under Warren Hastings. India's money is wantonly squandered, and no one can be made answerable for the waste. Regular plunder is going on on all sides. Everybody takes what he can lay his hands upon. And all that the rulers have in view is somehow or other to provide for their kith and kin."

Bengal Exchange Gazette, 5th January 1891. Report of 10th January 1891, No. 23.

"(*g*). The same paper says that that country can know no prosperity with whose people the Government does not sympathise. There is a class of crooked and narrow-minded Englishmen who have resolved upon preventing the Government from sympathising with the people from a fear that Government's sympathising with them might bring to an end the happy rule in which they are making fair foul and foul fair. But these Englishmen should know that it is such oppression that lost England America and diminished her ascendency in Australia. God holds his balance of justice evenly, and the day shall come when this happy rule of these narrow-minded Englishmen must come to an end.

"The Hindus are now becoming powerful for various reasons, and that means that their eyes are opening, which is the reason that they are now able to judge what is good for them and what is not. And Government is therefore adopting every possible precaution with a

Figure 31.2 Typical page of a Newspaper Report with (translated) extracts from multiple Indian-language newspapers. Proceedings of the Home Office (Oct 1891, prog. 260), P/3880, IOR. Courtesy of the British Library.

orthodox standpoint'; 'Tone less sensational than before [*sic*] cynical and not quite liberal in politics, extremely orthodox in its views on social and religious questions' (prog. 263) (see Figure 31.3). In other words, the government translator (whose name, incidentally, identifies him as a Bengali, Babu Chunder Nath Bose) appears careful to impress upon readers of his report that the Indian press culture in the province is a complex and varied one, with identifiable political leanings from liberal to conservative, political positions that, moreover, are fluid.

The report, in which the attachment is an embedded text, sets itself up as the counter-argument to the nominally authoritative report on the Indian press, produced as it is by the office constituted for the surveillance of the Indian press. The government translator's report, the report asserts, 'fails to show, what is at least as important for the Government to ascertain, which papers are conspicuous for violence in their denunciations of the Government policy, and what causes have led them to adopt this attitude' (prog. 261), to which it, the report, is thus a corrective: 'The Lieutenant-Governor therefore thought it desirable to place before the Government of India a further exposition of the information he has received from various quarters regarding

No.	Name of paper	Place and press at which published	Language and character in which published		Period of publication	Circulation	Name, profession, or status, &c., of the Proprietor	Name, profession, or status, &c., of the Editor	Tone, politics, &c., of the paper
			Language	Character					
1	"Ahmadi"	The Ahmadi Press, Delduar, Tangail, Mymensingh.	Bengali	Bengali	Fortnightly	600	Moulvie Abdul Hamed Khan Eusofzai.	The same as proprietor	A well-written paper. The professed object of the conductors is to promote social union between Hindus and Musulmans. Displays no religious bigotry.
2	"Hitakari"	Kushtea	Ditto	Ditto	Ditto	800	Mir Mosaraff Hossein	Ditto ditto	An indifferent paper, written from the Brahmo standpoint, and treating of local matters.
3	"Kasiporo Nibasi"	The Kasiporo Press, Burrisal.	Ditto	Ditto	Ditto	280	Protap Chandra Mukerjea	Ditto ditto	Not a political paper.
4	"Navamihir"	Printed at the Basanti press, Mymensingh, and published at Ghatail, Mymensingh.	Ditto	Ditto	Ditto	500	Durga Chura Roy	Ditto ditto.	
5	"Sahayogi"	The Hitaishi Press, Burrisal.	Ditto	Ditto	Ditto	342	Monoranjan Guha	Ditto ditto.	
6	"Uluberia Darpan"	Printed at the Somprakash Samiti Press, Calcutta, and published at Uluberia.	Ditto	Ditto	Ditto	700	Monimohan Ghosh, Pleader and Surendranath Roy, Medical Practitioner.	Surendranath Roy	Gives much attention to local matters and discusses social questions from the orthodox standpoint.
7	"Arya Darpan"	11, Simla Street, Calcutta.	Ditto	Ditto	Weekly	102	Jaya Govinda Shom, M.A., B.L., Vakeel, High Court, a Native Christian convert.	Ditto ditto.	
8	"Bangavasi"	The Bangavasi Machine Press, Calcutta.	Ditto	Ditto	Ditto	20,000	Jogendra Chandra Bose, formerly Sub-Editor of the Saddharani newspaper; a tenure-holder.	Indra Nath Banerjea, B.A., B.L., a distinguished Bengali writer, and a successful pleader of the Burdwan Judge's Court.	Tone less sensational than before cynical and not quite liberal in politics, extremely orthodox in its views on social and religious questions. Advocate of the ryots and tenure-holders. Its columns often contain humourous sketches and poetry, and are at times illustrated by cartoons.
9	"Bangonibasi"	The Commercial Steam Machine Press, Calcutta.	Ditto	Ditto	Ditto	8,000	Mahesh Chandra Pal, a publisher of Sanskrit philosophical works.	Bam Deb Dutt	An orthodox paper, exceptionally violent in tone.
10	"Burdwan Sanjivani."	The Burdwan Press, Burdwan.	Ditto	Ditto	Ditto	335	Jogesh Chandra Sarkar	The same as proprietor	Moderate in tone and liberal in politics. Treats often of local matters.

Figure 31.3 Example of the standardised tabular statement of Newspaper Reports. Among information produced by the table is 'tone' of the Indian-language press. Proceedings of the Home Office (Oct 1891, prog. 263, IOR). Courtesy of the British Library.

the spirit and the motives which influence the leading vernacular papers in Bengal' (prog. 261). Included in an already unclear statement of an alternative body of expert knowledge is a vague and sweeping generalisation: '[t]he weekly reviews prepared by the Translator have also led the Lieutenant-Governor to believe that a change for the worse has recently come over the Vernacular Press; that some papers which were neutral have become more or less hostile; that the hostility of others has assumed an aggravated and malignant form' (prog. 261). Finally, descriptive phrases such as the following, spread throughout the report, act to re-enforce the conclusion: 'noxious tone'; 'malignant and irreconcilable spirit'; 'misrepresentation and abuse of the Government' (prog. 261). The fact that the government of Bengal proceeds to charge the *Bangavasi* is evidence, if one needed it, of the ease with which views that are interruptive of the government narrative are co-opted even as they are acknowledged.

The attempted assimilation of the singular narrative on the Indian press to the law on sedition, in 1891, is where the peculiarity of the process by which the Newspaper Reports are normalised as the (Indian) press is quite spectacularly visible. Legal advisors to the Bengal government, to whom Newspaper Report excerpts from the *Bangavasi* are sent, build their legal reading of the 'tone' of the newspaper on the basis of these excerpts. The 17 July 1891 memo, sent to the Bengal government by the advisors (three in number), advises:

> Throughout these articles there is an attempt to excite in the minds of others the same feeling of fierce hatred of the English Government of India as animates the

writer, to represent that Government as the persecutor of the Hindoo religion, the cause of all poverty and distress and famine of imminent ruin, moral and material to the people. (prog. 271)

Thus political topics (which the trial would identify as objective facts of colonial rule in India) and national character are identified as the site of seditious libel, based on translations of slivers of Indian articles contained in the Bengal Newspaper Reports. That excerpts, not the *Bangavasi* itself, are the source is an openly acknowledged fact: a letter from the government of Bengal to the government of India dated 28 July 1891 identifies the *Bangavasi* excerpts of the Bengal Newspaper Reports, page and volume number included, as the 'articles' submitted by it for legal advice (prog. 267).

As for the reading provided of the press and public, there is little further that can be said other than to note the presence, yet again, of a practically hyperbolic vocabulary. The articles, the memo claims, are

> addressed to 250 millions of superstitious people whom experience shows can be moved to forcible resistance by religious excitement must we think be taken to be attempts to excite feelings which if fully aroused would not only be incompatible with a disposition to obey and assist the Government but are compatible only with a disposition to disobey and to use force when occasion offers in order to subvert a tyranny of so odious and intolerable a character. There runs throughout this seditious intent. (prog. 271)

'[S]uperstitious' and 'religious excitement' are, here, made continuous with 'forcible resistance', which is, in turn, equally seamlessly linked with disobedience and the latter with 'seditious intent'. By this imposition of causal logic on a disparate set of (claimed) traits, 'superstition' and 'religious excitement' are declared political emotions and intention, of the seditious sort.

At the trial, which takes place on 19 August 1891, contesting translations of the articles for which the *Bangavasi* is charged (some translations are by the high court translator and some by the government translator), the introduction of additional articles by the Crown counsel and defence suggests that the original newspaper articles surface, for the very first time, in a process until then dependent entirely on the Newspaper Reports. In the case made by the Crown counsel, a seamless continuity between the Newspaper Report excerpts and the full articles, in translation, is presumed, judging by the vocabulary employed to make its case. The articles, the counsel claims, are 'directed to inflame the prejudices of people of the lower classes by appealing to their superstitious feelings. With this object the British Government [are] compared to revolting characters in the Hindu mythology' (Indian Law Reports Calcutta Series 1892: 38). In an equally familiar idiom, separating thought and emotion, the counsel declares, 'in these articles no attempt at a reasonable discussion of the Age of Consent Bill is to be found. There is nothing but vituperation and invective' (38).

There are of course moments of a potential undermining of the stereotype of the Indian press and reader in the Crown counsel's arguments that are admitted, briefly, only to be declared inadmissible in trials for seditious libel. When articles refer to 'famines and high prices', which are, to cite the presiding judge, 'undoubted fact[s]' (Proceedings of the Home Department October 1891: prog. 279), for instance, the Crown counsel directs the jury's attention to the intent behind the presentation of the facts – 'to make people discontented and dissatisfied' (Indian Law Reports Calcutta Series 1892: 38). In the arguments of the defence there is a more sustained attack, as we would expect, on the stereotype: the defence points to the Crown counsel's stabilising of the inherently unstable site of translation; its absenting of articles showing signs of 'reasonable discussion' (43); and disregard of cultural difference ('native modes of thought' (43)), evident in its act of reading the *Bangavasi* articles. Thus, the defence concludes, the articles 'contained no direct incitement to rebellion or the use of force, and did not exceed the bounds of legitimate criticism, when allowance was made for the difference between European and native methods of thought and the conservative character of the paper' (43).

The verdict, in this juried trial, appears to have taken the governments of Bengal and India by surprise, judging by the rationalising that sets in when it is announced. Given the importance of this first, and thus precedent-setting, trial of an Indian newspaper under section 124a, the presiding judge insists on a unanimous decision, which the jury fails to deliver, and the charge against the *Bangavasi* is dropped. It would appear that for a brief moment in the law court the concerns expressed by the periodical press (over the Newspaper Reports), which are echoed in the arguments of the defence, receive a measure of legitimacy. On the other hand, the government view, of an Indian press full of disaffection (not critique), a view that is not disturbed in the slightest by the verdict in this trial, finds a subtle confirmation in the interpretation given to the vague language of the law of sedition: in this trial, 'disaffection' is given a (basic) dictionary meaning of 'absence of affection', legitimising the focus, in reports of the Indian press, on emotive texts. Indeed, it predicts the successful prosecutions of Bal Gangadhar Tilak's *Kesari* in 1898, and many newspapers as well as other printed materials (pamphlets, calendars, posters, leaflets, articles of clothing) from 1906 to the 1930s.

Conclusion

The most striking fact in this story, of the transformation effected by the colonial administration of an increasingly anti-colonial Indian press, one that devises strategies for surviving law force in its subtle and not so subtle forms, is not the vocabularies (which are overstated and overplayed) so much as the fact of (their) circulation. While we may not have access to facts and figures about the circulation of the Newspaper Reports (no such study exists), in the numerous reports on the Indian press that are written by multiple levels of government in the colony we do have a scrupulous recording of producers and receivers of reports on the Indian press to which the Newspaper Report excerpts are, inevitably, appended. These include forwardings of such reports from one level of government to another, from a regional government to its legal advisors and back, and so on. As this chapter has demonstrated, vocabularies remain remarkably static throughout this process. The circulation is such that, in the India Office Records archive, in addition to the voluminous Proceedings of the Home Department, we discover Newspaper Report excerpts appended to, and sometimes pasted into, correspondence between the government of India and the secretary of state for India, on the Indian press, usually in the context of parliamentary questions (the Public and Judicial Department Records); in European Manuscripts such as F 86, a box of print materials in a bound volume with the title 'Native Opinion/Vernacular Press/India 1867–1877' that includes copies of some pamphlets presenting anti-colonial arguments along with print pages of Newspaper Reports; and in Law Reports, as abbreviated summaries of arguments made in previous reports. One cannot, of course, rule out the possibility that the circulation and repetition are of a formulaic sort, with no one paying particular attention as vocabularies take on a life of their own in multiple reports on the Indian press, producing the reality of which they speak. In this instance, it is vocabularies saturated with contestations taking place elsewhere that misread the Indian press as the Victorian sensational press writ large, with race standing in for class. The effects of such a map of misreading are, however, undeniable. The stereotype which circulates is the stage on which government legislates a move from a dependence on pre-censorship, in its attempt to check the politically astute and tactical Indian press, to a deployment of criminal law/censorship. This same juncture, political and legal, provides a mobilising Indian periodical-reading public with a historic opportunity – to transform the legal courtroom of seditious libel trials of Indian newspapers into the (very first) symbolic space, of resistant nationalism – which it seizes, with alacrity.

This chapter has hoped to show that this process – of circulation and repetition – and the product, a stereotypical Indian press spewing 'seditious propagandism', depends profoundly on the Newspaper Reports. The point is made also when we take note of the fact that the singular story of the Indian press that develops within the confines of government reporting culture, confidential in nature, is not the sum total of government discourse on the Indian press. There is a markedly different public view presented in volumes, some produced annually, with titles such as 'Administration Reports of the Government of India, Bengal, 1888–1889', and the India Office's *Statement Exhibiting the Moral and Material Progress and Condition of India*. Lest we think public documents might also be constituted by a level of bureaucratic perfunctoriness, it is worth noting that much thought appears to have gone into the content and style of at least one, the *Statement Exhibiting the Moral and Material Progress*, the report that is submitted to both houses of parliament. A handwritten memo dated 17 March 1881 from the secretary of state for India to the government of India, which contains instructions for the preparation of a decennial volume of the *Statement Exhibiting the Moral and Material Progress*, charges the latter to 'be particularly careful to refrain from any expression of opinion as to questions of policy or administration and to confine [missing word] to a lucid statement of facts' (Public and Judicial Department Records 1881: file 926). This is, of course, in direct contrast to the culture that is encouraged in the confidential conversations on the Indian press, in which interpretation of the 'tone' of the Indian press is an expectation. A short citation from a *Statement Exhibiting the Moral and Material Progress* shows the stark difference between public and confidential narratives of the Indian press:

> The principal English newspapers published in Bengal during 1890–91 remained the same as before. There were in all 29 English newspapers and 17 periodicals published during the year, 13 vernacular newspapers came into existence, and 24 were discontinued. The total number supplied to the Bengali Translator's Office was 63 as against 74 in the previous year. (India Office 1892: 206)

It remains to be said that while I do not wish to overstate the case for considering the Newspaper Reports as a colonial iteration of the Victorian sensational press, in function and effect, approaching the genre as such brings visibility to the emergence in British India of the (Victorian) sensational press as a floating signifier of sorts. In government employ, it is assimilated to the 'discovery', in commentaries, of an Indian press that is uniformly sensational; in the periodical press it is a vocabulary that turns the tables, so to speak, on the government, identifying the Newspaper Reports as a sensational press, not the Indian press which the genre purports to represent, fully and impartially.

Notes

I would like to take this opportunity to thank David Finkelstein for recognising in the Newspaper Reports signs of functions, characteristics and forms that are, in the nineteenth century, usually claimed for the periodical press. It is this peculiarity, of something that mimics the periodical press but takes on a life that leads to prosecutions of the 'real' periodical press, that this chapter has hoped to explore. Thanks are due, also, to him and David Johnson for their valuable feedback on an early draft of the chapter.

1. The 1835 Registration of the Press Act does not distinguish between periodicals and newspapers, placing '[any] printed periodical work whatever, containing public news or Comments on public news' under the jurisdiction of the Act (quoted in Basu 1979: 118–19). The 1867 Press and Registration of Books Act maintains this definition (Roy 1915: 1).
2. Histories of the Indian press have documented the rapid growth of the Indian press in the second half of the nineteenth century (Barrier 1974; Kaul 2003; Natarajan 1962) and in the readership, literate and aural (Basu 1979; Bayly 1996; Chandra et al. 1989; Dasgupta 1977; Finkelstein and Peers 2000).
3. In the colony, the crime described in section 124a is 'disaffection'. Until it was amended in 1898, the substantive part of the statute read: 'Whoever by words, either spoken or intended to be read, or by signs, or by visible representation, or otherwise, excites, or attempts to excite, feelings of disaffection to the Government established by law in British India, shall be punished' (Mayne 1896: 65). 'Disaffection' is defined in the 'explanation' as 'an attitude incompatible with the requirement of rendering obedience to government' (Mayne 1896: 65). This was not the first time the Bengal government attempted prosecution of an Indian newspaper under section 124a. In 1873 the *Halishahar Patrikar* and in 1875 the *Amrita Bazar Patrika* were identified for prosecution by the lieutenant-governor of Bengal. The governor-general at the time, the Earl of Northbrook (1872–6), dismissed the request on the grounds that 'the law was vague' (quoted in Dasgupta 1977: 272).
4. The *Native Opinion* was founded in 1864 by Vishvanath Narayan Mandlik (1833–89), a public figure of the Bombay Presidency, as an English weekly. He managed it till 1871. Subsequently the newspaper turned into a bi-weekly and was printed in Marathi and English. The *Indian Daily News* was a Calcutta newspaper owned by David Yule (1858–1928). Among the 'lesser Anglo-Indian journals', it was moderate in its views on the colony (Dasgupta 1977: 40).
5. The standard government view is one expressed by John Edgar in June 1891. The Newspaper Reports, he writes, are 'full and impartial' in their reporting of the vernacular press (Proceedings of the Home Department October 1891: prog. 261).
6. While critical of the government in this article, the *Indian Daily News* shares with the majority of the Anglo-Indian press an assumption about the beneficial nature of British colonialism in India. The concluding comment in a 15 July 1874 editorial article, for instance, describes the colony as 'a people who have been crushed for centuries, and are now for the first time enjoying protection under foreign arms' ('Editorial' 1874: 2).
7. See Conboy 2001; Conboy 2010; Jones 2008; Kamper 2003; Koss 1990; Lee 1976; McWilliam 1998; Williams 2009.

8. The *Indian Daily News*, for example, identifies 'the volume of selections from annual reports of 1872–3' as its source of information on the Newspaper Reports ('Editorial' 1874: 2).

Bibliography

Administration Reports of the Government of India (Bengal) (1888–9), India Office Records, V/10/60.
Agathocleous, Tanya (2018), 'Criticism on trial: Colonizing affect in the Late-Victorian Empire', *Victorian Studies*, 60.3, 434–60.
Barrier, Gerald (1974), *Banned: Controversial Literature and Political Control in British India, 1907–1947*, Columbia: University of Missouri Press.
Basu, Jitendra Nath (1979), *Romance of Indian Journalism*, Calcutta: Calcutta University Press.
Bayly, Christopher A. (1996), *Empire and Information: Intelligence Gathering and Social Communication in India, 1780–1870*, Cambridge: Cambridge University Press.
Bengal Newspaper Reports (1875), India Office Records, L/R/5/1.
Bengal Newspaper Reports (1876), India Office Records, L/R/5/2.
Bengal Newspaper Reports (1891), India Office Records, L/R/5/17.
Bombay Newspaper Reports (1877), India Office Records, L/R/5/132.
Campbell, George (1893), *Memoirs of my Indian Career*, ed. Charles E. Bernard, vol. 2, New York: Macmillan.
Chandra, Bipan, Mridula Mukherjee, K. N. Panikkar and Sucheta Mahajan (1989), *India's Struggle for Independence, 1857–1947*, Delhi: Penguin.
Conboy, Martin (2001), *The Press and Popular Culture*, London: Sage.
——— (2010), *The Language of Newspapers: Socio-Historical Perspectives*, London: Continuum.
Dasgupta, Uma (1977), *Rise of an Indian Public: Impact of Official Policy, 1870–1880*, Calcutta: Riddhi.
'Editorial' (1874), *Indian Daily News*, 15 July, 2–3.
European Manuscripts (n.d.), India Office Records, MSS/EUR/F 86/214.
Finkelstein, David, and Douglas M. Peers (2000), '"A Great System of Circulation": Introducing India into the nineteenth-century media', in David Finkelstein and Douglas M. Peers (eds), *Negotiating India in the Nineteenth-Century Media*, Basingstoke: Macmillan Press, 1–22.
India Office, *Statement Exhibiting the Moral and Material Progress and Condition of India During the Year 1890–91* (1892), London: Eyre & Spottiswoode.
Indian Law Reports Calcutta Series (1892), India Office Records, V/22/19.
Jones, Aled (1996), *Powers of the Press: Newspapers, Power and the Public in Nineteenth-Century England*, Brookfield, VT: Scolar Press.
——— (2008), 'The press and the printed word', in Chris Williams (ed.), *A Companion to Nineteenth-Century Britain*, Hoboken: Wiley, 369–80.
Kamper, David Scott (2003), 'Popular Sunday newspapers in Late-Victorian Britain', unpublished PhD thesis, University of Illinois at Urbana-Champaign.
Kamra, Sukeshi (2011), *The Indian Periodical Press and the Production of Nationalist Rhetoric*, New York: Palgrave Macmillan.
Kaul, Chandrika (2003), *Reporting the Raj: The British Press and India, c. 1880–1922*, Manchester: Manchester University Press.
——— (2016), 'Researching empire and periodicals', in Alexis Easley, Andrew King and John Morton (eds), *Researching the Nineteenth-Century Periodical Press: Case Studies*, London and New York: Routledge, 175–91.
Koss, Stephen (1990), *Rise and Fall of the Political Press in Britain*, London: Fontana Press.
Lee, Alan J. (1976), *The Origins of the Popular Press in England, 1855–1914*, London: Croom Helm; Totowa, NJ: Rowman & Littlefield.

McWilliam, Rohan (1998), *Popular Politics in Nineteenth-Century England*, London and New York: Routledge.
Mayne, John D. (1896), *The Criminal Law of India*, Madras: Higginbotham.
Moir, Martin (1988), *A General Guide to the India Office Records*, London: The British Library.
Natarajan, Swaminathan (1962), *A History of the Press in India*, London: Asia Publishing House.
'The Native Press' (1874), *Native Opinion*, 2 August, 2.
Palmegiano, Eugenia M. (2013), *Perceptions of the Press in Nineteenth-Century British Periodicals: A Bibliography*, London and New York: Anthem.
Proceedings of the Home Department (January 1890), India Office Records, P/3650.
Proceedings of the Home Department (October 1891), India Office Records, P/3880.
Public and Judicial Department Records (1881), India Office Records, L/PJ/6/99.
Rosenkrantz, Susan (2005), 'Breathing disaffection: The impact of Irish nationalist journalism on India's native press', *Southeast Review of Asian Studies*, 27, 17–35.
Roy, Gouri Kant (1915), *Laws Relating to Press and Sedition*, Simla: Station.
Williams, Kevin (2009), *Read All About It! A History of the British Newspaper*, Abingdon: Routledge.

32

THE ANTI-COLONIAL PERIODICAL BETWEEN PUBLIC AND COUNTERPUBLIC: *THE BEACON* AND *PUBLIC OPINION* IN THE INTERWAR YEARS

Raphael Dalleo

During the 1930s and 1940s, a new type of periodical began to emerge in the colonial Caribbean that found novel ways to combine literary aspirations with a critique of colonialism. While these publications were neither the first to protest colonial rule nor unique in their inclusion of literature, the way those features came together was part of the emergence of a particular type of literary intellectuals who sought to distinguish themselves from the colonial bureaucracy and business class who had monopolised political and economic power in the region. Newspapers such as *The Beacon* in Trinidad and Tobago and *Public Opinion* in Jamaica sought to use this fusion of politics and art to overcome the contradictions of middle-class anti-colonialism, even as an examination of these publications shows how the tension persisted between speaking in the name of a national public and occupying the space of oppositional critique.

Local publication of creative writing in the anglophone Caribbean certainly did not begin in this period.[1] Yet despite many predecessors, the periodicals of the 1930s and 1940s occupy a special place in the story of West Indian literary history because of their connection to the group of middle-class intellectuals who became the first successful nationalist leaders during the era of decolonisation. Critics have been drawn to these publications as an idealised version of the alliance of literature and politics. Kenneth Ramchand discusses *The Beacon*, *Kyk-over-al*, *Focus* and *Bim*, which all began publishing between 1931 and 1945, as periodicals where 'the new spirit [of nationalism] showed itself' alongside the emergence of the West Indian novel (Ramchand 1983: 71). Victor Ramraj, writing of the development of short fiction in the English-speaking Caribbean, lists 'the most prominent . . . literary magazines' as '*Trinidad*, and its successor *The Beacon*, *Kyk-Over-Al*, *Focus* and *Public Opinion*' (Ramraj 2001: 199). Edward Baugh's history of West Indian poetry lists the same journals as well as Barbados's *The Forum* (Baugh 2001: 238–9). More recently, Katerina Gonzalez Seligmann names *Trinidad*, *The Beacon*, *West Indian Review*, *Focus* and *Bim* as crucial to 'the enterprise of making Anglophone Caribbean literature possible' (Gonzalez Seligmann 2021: 103). Scholars thus continue to emphasise the importance of these periodicals to the development of a locally published literature, and place them in the context of the rise of nationalist political movements and the explosion of literary outlets throughout the region. That alliance was never easy or untroubled.

Jürgen Habermas's theory of the public sphere provides a useful framework for understanding the relationship of writers to this complex matrix of social forces – from political structures and audience to the institutions of publication and dissemination – but translating this framework to the Caribbean context requires modifying his most basic assumptions.[2] Habermas's vision of the public sphere is not designed to address the racial hierarchies of the plantation or the transnational nature of power characterising a colonial or postcolonial site like the Caribbean. In the light of a history where slavery restricted personhood to a small elite, and modern colonialism meant the removal of local power from a population where the proportion of nonwhites made representative government seem terrifying to these elites, the Caribbean public sphere could not possibly develop as the bourgeois public sphere Habermas describes arising in Europe. In the story Habermas tells in *The Structural Transformation of the Public Sphere*, the European literary public sphere emerged as a space of rational debate independent of the institutions of the state, yet claiming the right to critique and intervene in the functions of the state on behalf of the citizenry. Once this public sphere – physically grounded in salons and coffee houses but also articulated in newspapers, pamphlets and other early literary forms – broke the church and state's monopoly on power during the seventeenth and eighteenth centuries, public debate becomes theoretically available to all: unlike the feudal model, in which a person's status in society determined how his or her ideas would be received, a public sphere 'governed by the laws of the free market' (Habermas 1991: 79) means that 'the authority of the better argument could assert itself against that of social hierarchy and in the end can carry the day' (Habermas 1991: 36). This newly organised public, where arguments could appeal only to reason rather than rank, thus established itself as a counterpoint to the power of the state: 'By the turn of the nineteenth century, the public's involvement in the critical debate of political issues had become organised to such an extent that in the role of a permanent critical commentator it had definitively broken the exclusiveness of Parliament and evolved into the officially designated discussion partner of the delegate' (Habermas 1991: 66). Crucial to Habermas's definition is the way that the western European bourgeois public sphere could be a critic of the parliamentary government, but an officially acknowledged one invested with the power to keep the state in check by its ability to speak in the name of the public. With access to discursive expression severely limited under plantation slavery, and a lack of representative political institutions in the Caribbean during the period of modern colonialism, the idea that local appeals might be heard by those in power could not inspire intellectual projects as it did in Europe.

Attending to the blockages in Caribbean access to the public sphere also serves as a reminder of the reality that even in Europe this bourgeois public sphere did not actually give voice to all of the elements of what was in fact a diverse and conflicted public; the European public sphere was restricted in terms of access to its institutions, by what it would recognise as rational debate, and thus by race, class and gender. Saidiya Hartman in *Scenes of Subjection* makes the point that enslaved people were excluded not only from the public, but also from the private: 'If the public realm is reserved for the bourgeois citizen subject and the private realm is inscribed by freedom of property ownership and contractual transactions based upon free will, then in what space is the articulation of the needs and desires of the enslaved at all possible?' (Hartman 1997: 89). She offers 'everyday practices' as attempts at 'the creation of a social space in which the assertion of needs, desires, and counterclaims could be collectively aired' (Hartman 1997: 89). Hartman therefore asks us to 'take seriously Jean Comaroff's observations that "the real politik of oppression dictates that resistance be expressed in domains seemingly apolitical"' (Hartman 1997: 64), suggesting how various forms of black culture became places where aspirations to 'create social space' were located.

In the Caribbean, periodical publication especially has been tied to these aspirations even as it has resided at a site of tension between a nationalist position allowing it to speak in the name of a public and a subaltern space of critique and Hartman's 'counterclaims'. In a special issue of the journal *Public Culture*, the editors, calling themselves the 'Black Public Sphere Collective', wonder if Habermas's description of the bourgeois public sphere could be adapted to theorise a black public sphere, which, in their words, has 'sought to make Blackness *new* and remove it from the pathological spaces reserved for it in Western culture' (Black Public Sphere Collective 1994: xiii). In other words, the creation of black narratives and cultural forms and their consumption by a black public is part of 'a more general process of diasporic world-building' (Black Public Sphere Collective 1994: xiii). In the issue's first essay, Houston Baker critiques Habermas's monolithic construction of the bourgeois public sphere as 'overdetermined both ideologically and in terms of gender, overconditioned by the market and by history, and utopian in the extreme' (Baker 1994: 8). Such a bourgeois public sphere, Baker shows, depended precisely on the exclusion of enslaved people, the poor and women as non property owners. Building on the work of Nancy Fraser and Bruce Robbins, Baker argues against mourning the decline of this exclusionary bourgeois public sphere, and in favour of conceiving of public space as made up of a 'plurality of spheres' (Baker 1994: 10), among them a 'subaltern, black American counterpublic' able to 'recapture and recode all existing American arrangements of publicness' (Baker 1994: 12).

The anti-colonial movements that emerged in the Caribbean may have had features in common with the black American counterpublic Baker describes, yet the Caribbean's colonial context created a distinct tension between the aspiration towards speaking in the name of a public versus a counterpublic. In *Publics and Counterpublics*, Michael Warner defines a counterpublic as a public that 'maintains at some level, conscious or not, an awareness of its subordinate status' (Warner 2002: 56). Publication by Caribbean people, in which participants were constantly reminded of their subordinated position in relation to European literature and political debate, would in this way resemble a counterpublic. On the other hand, Warner goes on to add that 'a counterpublic in this sense is usually related to a subculture' (Warner 2002: 56). A counterpublic thus serves a different function than the theoretical 'larger public'; whereas the counterpublic is marginal, the 'larger public' claims to express 'public opinion' (Warner 2002: 56) and for that reason has been instrumental historically in national projects of imagining a common identity. The Caribbean public sphere that I describe arising during the modern colonial period is a counterpublic marginalised from and thus opposed to (rather than a legitimising check upon) the true centres of power, but at the same time aimed to serve the function of Habermas's idealised European bourgeois public sphere in claiming to represent the hopes and aspirations of the majority of the populace. In the Caribbean, anti-colonial writers authorised themselves as spokespeople for the nation by imagining themselves speaking for a marginalised counterpublic outside the circuits of power as well as a public representing the nation and aspiring to take control of the state.

My main thesis is that the shifting tension between these two demands – of being oppositional to power yet representing the nation – is crucial to understanding Caribbean periodical publication from the late colonial period. Two of the most important colonial periodicals in the formation of Caribbean literature and nationalist politics were the Trinidadian *Beacon* (1931–9) and the Jamaican *Public Opinion* (1937–74). While *The Beacon* was initially published as a monthly and *Public Opinion* as a weekly, they occupied similar spaces in the colonial public spheres of their respective islands: both presented themselves as alternative sources of news and opinion to the colonial *Trinidad Guardian* and Jamaica's *Daily Gleaner*, and both became closely associated with nationalist political movements (with the editor of *The Beacon*, Albert Gomes, eventually becoming the Chief Minister of Trinidad and Tobago during the 1950s, while an editor of *Public Opinion*, Edna Manley, was married to one of Jamaica's prime ministers and mother to another). While their focus on intervening in current events led to their presentation as newspapers rather than literary magazines, these periodicals also published poetry and short fiction that departed from outsiders' representations of the region and became incubators for their islands' literary development. As much as the goals and interventions of these publications overlapped, their titles also point to the breadth of their aspirations, from the representational politics of *Public Opinion* to the vanguardism of *The Beacon*. Examining these two publications shows how both projects remain present if in tension in each publication, just as literature and politics coexist sometimes complementarily and sometimes uneasily alongside one other.

The Beacon and *Public Opinion* deployed publication and the literary in a way that shaped the development of both Caribbean literature and politics.[3] Both newspapers figure their political project as indistinguishable from publication itself: the newspaper is meant to challenge the discursive monopoly of the region's established newspapers and create a robust debate about the future of the nation.[4] This political project establishes the importance of writing – especially literary writing – in governance. The format of the newspaper itself demonstrated the desire to map out the nation and include literary work as part of that nation-building process. *The Beacon* featured articles, poetry and fiction that brought all of its various settings and ethnic groups under the banner of the nation: it is no surprise that the immediate predecessor to *The Beacon*, which included many of the same participants, was titled simply *Trinidad*, as if its pages were the space of the nation (see Figure 32.1). The July 1931 issue (1.4) begins with an essay by Gomes titled 'Black Man', followed by Henry Alexis's historical piece 'The Water Riots of 1903', and later includes 'The Diary of a Naturalist' that describes flora and fauna from the island. The next month (issue 1.5), an article on Shouter Baptists sits alongside news from South Africa and C. L. R. James's book review of *Mahatma Gandhi: His Own Story*. These articles explore the histories, cultures and landscapes of Trinidad and Tobago, while positioning the colony as a crossroads of transnational currents, connected by the British Empire and multicultural migration to the region.

The fiction included in *The Beacon* emphasises even more directly the many kinds of people who make up Trinidad and Tobago: the poor barrack-yard blacks and East Indians of C. A. Thomasos's 'The Dougla', published in issue 2.10 of *The Beacon*; the Venezuelan exile residing in Trinidad in C. L. R. James's 'Revolution' from issue 1.2; the Portuguese small landholder and Chinese merchant in Alfred Mendes's 'Pablo's Fandango' from issue 1.1; the rural East Indian labourers and English planters of

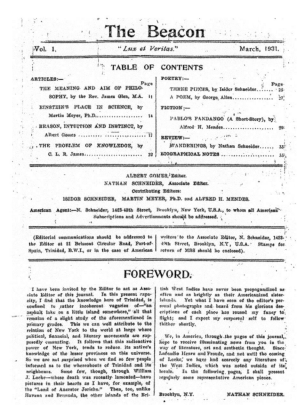

Figure 32.1 *The Beacon*, March 1931, p. 1. Courtesy of the University of the West Indies Library.

Mendes's 'Boodhoo', published serially in issues 1.11, 1.12 and 2.1. This diversity raises particular challenges for the consolidation of the nation – the inclusion of Indo-Trinidadian contributors is especially inconsistent – but the literary newspaper appears to be a space where the project can be attempted.

The stories themselves elaborate on the idea that the sensitivity possessed by the literary class makes them best suited to the task of understanding and speaking for the various elements of the nation. Mendes's 1932 story 'Boodhoo' lays out the challenges of knowing and representing the subaltern. The story focuses primarily on Minnie Lawrence, a white Englishwoman described as 'a recent arrival in Trinidad', and her experience of 'accustom[ing] [her]self to the strange surroundings' (Mendes 1978: 142). Throughout the story, the impossibility of learning to understand these 'strange surroundings' becomes a dominant theme, as Mrs Lawrence must ask her husband or servants the names of the island's flora and fauna that she doesn't recognise. The opening scene, in which Mrs Lawrence meets her social peers at a tea-party, emphasises how these upper-class women don't know much about their servants' lives or beliefs. That phrase – 'I don't quite know' or 'I don't know' (Mendes 1978: 142, 143) – appears repeatedly in their conversations, and sets the stage for the introduction of

Boodhoo, the East Indian servant with whom Minnie eventually has an affair. From the first description of this character – 'he was strange' – the narrative always returns to the ways in which Boodhoo is unknowable to Mrs Lawrence: he is 'enigmatical', he speaks 'a strange language' that she cannot understand, and his face has a 'nonchalant air that told her nothing' (Mendes 1978: 144, 154, 145, 156).

'Boodhoo', like many of Mendes's stories, features different levels of deception and secrecy. Until the end of the story, the husband remains unaware that his wife is having an affair with a servant. At the same time, the story involves the unfolding of a mystery in which the reader, like the main character, is blind to a secret hidden right in front of them – in this case, that Mrs Lawrence's lover, Boodhoo, is the illegitimate son of her husband and one of his former servants. One of the main obstacles to these white elites understanding the island is their insistence on racist ideology rather than close attention to reality: at the tea-party, for example, one lady advises Mrs Lawrence to 'be firm with [her servants] and they are like domesticated animals. No trouble at all', even while the narrative notes that 'she didn't add, however, that she changed her maids and cooks as often as there are months in the year' (Mendes 1978: 142). The implication here and throughout the story is that attempting to force the local setting to conform to a preconceived ideology prevents these characters from being able to truly understand or control it. The husband's inability to imagine his wife's infidelity means that these characters' lack of imagination and their failure to closely read the situation lead to their downfalls. 'Boodhoo' – like other stories from Mendes such as 'Her Chinaman's Way', published in *Trinidad*, where Maria fails to anticipate Hong Wing's cruel revenge, or 'La Soucouyante', in which the husband continues to cheat on his wife despite various warnings – suggests that Trinidad's complex mix of cultures and classes requires an attentive and sensitive reader equipped for listening to and understanding all of its competing interests.[5]

At the same time that the stories of the *Beacon* group emphasise the Caribbean poor as virtually unintelligible or unknowable, they show an equal desire to catalogue the various ways in which these groups do express themselves. The standard readings of yard fiction focus on how it is popular culture that these writers emphasise as that unique form of subaltern knowledge that distinguishes the Caribbean nation from its European master. Along these lines, Patricia Saunders describes obeah and picong in C. L. R. James's 'Triumph', published in *Trinidad* in 1929, as 'Trinidadian counter-cultural knowledge' deployed to 'fashion national identities and nationalist politics' (Saunders 2007: 32, 30). As important as music or religious practice is for representing alternative systems of belief and expression, critics have largely overlooked another form of 'counter-cultural knowledge' that dominates yard fiction and all of the writing of the *Beacon* group: the presence of gossip as a counterpublic where working-class people construct and transmit the kinds of knowledge or debate traditionally excluded from the dominant public sphere, but that a Caribbean literary public sphere seeking to be inclusive and representative must find ways to incorporate. Saunders and Leah Rosenberg make a strong case for the importance of calypso to the structure of 'Triumph'; I would add that gossip functions as an even more everyday form of expression, with the narrator describing how 'in Trinidad, when His Excellency the Governor and his wife have a quarrel, the street boys speak of it the day after' (James 1978: 92). At the same time that gossip provides these sorts of links and serves as a public sphere allowing a critique of those in power, it also creates division within the community:

the main conflict in the story, the jealousy and competition between Mamitz and Irene, comes from their gossiping about one another. One of the defining characteristics of yard fiction, whether it is 'Triumph' or Mendes's novel *Black Fauns* (1935), is the exploration of the potential and dangers of gossip as this sort of counterpublic.[6] The barrack-yard appears to interest these writers not only as a site of an authentic urban folk subject, but as a setting where public and private are not easily distinguished.

Just as *The Beacon* sought to critique and create alternatives to the limitations of the colonial public sphere, *Public Opinion* in Jamaica explicitly positioned itself as a solution to this problem. The first issue of *Public Opinion* in February of 1937 (see Figure 32.2) begins with a front page explaining the 'reason that *Public Opinion* has appeared' in terms of an 'abundance of ineffective discussion at present'; it urges instead 'an *effective* public opinion on topics of importance' ('New Wine' 1937: 1). Rather than just gossip, then, *Public Opinion* is meant to be this sort of formalised public sphere that can provide a space for writers and intellectuals to debate 'topics with a direct bearing on the welfare of Jamaica' ('New Wine' 1937: 1). A few issues later, another piece further teases out the value of this kind of rational discourse, urging the reader: 'once you have made up your mind what should be done, talk about it . . . Don't be misled by the cant which says that talk is just talk: it depends on whether there is any thinking behind the talk. Democracy is government by discussion instead

Figure 32.2 *Public Opinion*, 20 February 1937, p. 1. Courtesy of the British Library.

of government by brute force' ('You' 1937: 2). For the editors of *Public Opinion*, talk is more than just talk, and publication is the institution upon which a just, responsive and open government can be built.

Public Opinion is much less dominated by literary work than *The Beacon*, with more of the articles taking on explicitly political topics. The early issues from 1937 feature sections defining words like 'fascism' and 'communism' or discussing the Spanish Civil War, as well as debates between Amy Bailey and Una Marson over education or the place of women in politics. But all of these early issues give prominent place to the literary: fifteen of the first twenty issues feature a short story and almost every issue includes book reviews as well as a section called 'literary snapshots'. Even in the columns, a creative orientation is visible, with surrealist sections such as A. E. T. Henry's essays 'Hitler and I' and 'Mussolini and I', or the column appearing in each issue under the byline 'The Philosopher'. The importance of the literary in governance is perhaps best understood through the political vision articulated in the article 'Bureaucracy', which critiques government functionaries for lacking connection to creativity:

> Jamaica is largely governed by officials: those officials have routine work to do: and the pressure of routine is usually so great that the head of a department has no time for constructive thinking. It is for this reason that bureaucracy has been condemned so often all over the world – that it cannot see beyond the walls of its office. ('Bureaucracy' 1937: 1)

These issues show a clear desire to give the political and the literary – the public and the counterpublic – equal roles within the movement towards a Jamaican nation.[7]

The early issues stake out a public role for creativity, but the relationship between literature and politics was always tenuous. The stories published in *Public Opinion* during 1937 frequently engage in political commentary through mockery of the professional middle class, like the politicians in Peter Wayne's 'Supernumeraries' from issue 1.4, or the shade-obsessed 'average middle-class home in Jamaica' of Frank Hill's 'The Family' in issue 1.3. A story from issue 1.11 titled 'The Mad Tea-Party' transports Lewis Carroll's Alice to Jamaica's Headquarters House to protest the 'selfish' behaviour of officials who offer her only 'vocational training' and refuse to share their bread and butter.[8] This mockery of the professional middle class is not coupled by an idealisation of folk characters that would later come to define anti-colonial writing; in fact, working-class occupations are often depicted as just as lacking in creativity as the professional class. Dorothy Barnes's 'The Poincettia Bush' from the first issue, for example, describes the anxiety its main character, Miranda, feels in 'becom[ing] a factory worker' and 'shed[ding] her individualism' (Barnes 1937: 5). The story contrasts the 'dreary monotony' of Miranda's vocation with the beautiful poinsettia bush with which she shares her hopes and dreams; when Miranda leaves and the bush droops, the story opposes scientific explanation with poetic: 'probably the prosaic would put it down to the fact that the weather was too hot, the rainfall too scanty ... but the poets and the wind said that all this was due to the missing Miranda' (Barnes 1937: 5). Miranda's death at the end of the story, as she dives into the picturesque pool next to the poinsettia bush, shows the ornamental beauty and private sentiment associated with poetry as an ultimately unsustainable escape from the rationalised public world of factory work.

In both *The Beacon* and *Public Opinion*, then, this balance between the political and the literary is never easy. The editorial statements from issues 2.11 and 2.12 of *The Beacon* on 'The Literary Club Nuisance' show a surprising hostility to the mixing of literature and politics, attacking 'Bohemians' and their amateurist literary clubs, complaining that 'the majority of them will in time become subsidiary political bodies, whose prime function will be to supply the Legislature with idiots' (The Literary' 1933: 2). *Public Opinion*'s longer publication history makes these sorts of tensions more noticeable. For example, the founding of the People's National Party (PNP) during the second half of 1938 occurs at the same time that no literary works appear in twelve consecutive issues during October, November and December. In 1940 and 1941, the newspaper experiences a revival of literary publication, with authors like George Campbell, M. G. Smith and Roger Mais becoming very active. These writers would become known as founding figures in Jamaican national literature.

During this high point of publication, almost every issue also included a folk tale: 'A Brer Nancy Story, as told by Dorothy Clarke' became a regular feature throughout 1939 and 1940. The presence of these stories appears to give a space to the voices of the rural Jamaican peasantry. Yet in emphasising their translated nature – with Dorothy Clarke as the middle-class collector and curator of the folk tales – their inclusion shows the middle-class positioning of these publications, similar to how Belinda Edmondson reads the performances of Louise Bennett as 'both class ventriloquism – this is how *those* working-class Jamaicans speak – as well as class representation: this is the way *we*, middle-class, people speak, too, particularly when we are at leisure' (Edmondson 2009: 98). Janelle Rodriques describes 'Anancy stories' as 'among the most easily recognisable (and acceptable) forms of Caribbean folk culture among the middle classes' (Rodriques 2019: 16) and thus understands their promotion as co-optation that seeks primarily to domesticate the culture of the folk. She argues that African-derived religious practices were less easy for middle-class writing to assimilate than Anancy, and thus featured less frequently. When they did, as in Archie Lindo's story 'Pocomania' from a 1941 issue of *Public Opinion*, Rodriques sees evidence of the newspaper's 'anxiety' about Afro-Jamaican culture: 'The spectre of Africa, in other words, at once proved that we had a culture worth defending and a nation worth developing, and inspired deep anxiety, if even shame, about the elements of this lost culture that could not be "civilised," that is, subsumed and contained within a coherent "realist" narrative' (Rodriques 2019: 17).

During the mid-1940s, *Public Opinion* became more the official newspaper of the PNP and showed much less interest in giving a place to literary work. In 1943, as the PNP begins to contest the island's first elections, creative writing drops off the agenda, as it had during the PNP's founding: while in 1940 sixty-four stories and sixty-one poems ran in the pages of *Public Opinion*, and 1941 featured thirty-nine stories and sixty-six poems, in 1942 that output dropped to twenty stories and forty-two poems, and in all of 1943, only half a dozen stories appeared and only a handful of poems. This change provides a context for understanding Edna Manley's launch of a literary journal: having left the board of *Public Opinion*, Manley edited a collection of literary work and issued the first edition of *Focus* in December 1943. *Focus* is a very different publication from *Public Opinion*: it features fiction, poetry, drama and creative essays but does not publish news or political debate. The writings are still framed as nationalist and political: Edna Manley's Foreword explains this context, that 'it is, we feel the first collection of works to be published, that have sprung directly out of the great changes that have been and are still taking place' (Manley 1943: 1). But Manley presents an idea of how literature can be political that is overtly against instrumentality, as an entry in her diary from 25 January 1940 explains:

> the creative artist has only one contact with reality and that is through his highly sensitive and delicately adjusted sensory system approach. He trains it to register every nuance of change and impression. . . . Now what happens to me in the political world is what happens when I step out of my sphere into any other world. I start getting emotional experiences crammed down my throat through entirely foreign and wrong channels and the result is that the creative artist in me starts stifling and struggling most frightfully for air and the means of life. (Manley 1989: 7)

Edna Manley here expresses the idea of literature as a counterpublic form, and indeed, *Focus* separates out literary works from the other kinds of more overtly nationalist writing seeking to speak in the name of a public that appeared in *Public Opinion*. While *Public Opinion* sought to use the pages of the newspaper as a public sphere aimed towards governance, *Focus* emphasised literariness as a mode of opposition to the instrumentality of capitalist colonial culture.[9] The idea of literature as political but also non- or anti-governmental proved productive for anti-colonial writing, even if keeping this critical vision of the literary attached to party politics was often impossible.

The Beacon and *Public Opinion* thus illustrate the challenges that colonial status posed for periodicals from the 1930s and 1940s that aspired to speak to and for their local context. Colonial periodicals faced a tension created by their marginalised location within the British Empire: even as editors and contributors aspired to articulate the nation, they remained well aware of their dominated position in the global system. In response, colonial periodicals attempted to occupy the space of avant-garde aesthetics as a counterpublic site of marginality and critique alongside a more bourgeois political project that can claim to speak for the nation. *The Beacon* and *Public Opinion* show how successfully literary intellectuals were able to bridge these activities as part of an anti-colonial movement, even as these tensions were never resolved and resurfaced even more forcefully in newly founded nation states.

Notes

1. After slavery's abolition opened up literacy to more people, newspapers such as *The Mirror* in Trinidad and Tobago and *The Jamaica Times* began to provide places for literary work to be published locally at the end of the nineteenth and beginning of the twentieth century; Selwyn Cudjoe (2003) and Leah Rosenberg (2007) have uncovered the significant contributions these sorts of early publications made. Alison Donnell's *Twentieth-Century Caribbean Literature* (2006) provides some context for why the nationalist publications of the 1930s and 1940s have become so privileged in Caribbean literary history at the expense of these other predecessors.
2. On Habermas's relevance to the Caribbean counterpublic sphere, see Dalleo 2011a: 2–8.
3. For a discussion of the deployment of literature as the 'ideology of the literary' in relation to *The Beacon*, *Public Opinion* and *Kyk-over-al*, see Dalleo 2011b: 609–15.
4. Patricia Saunders mentions this aspect of *The Beacon* in her discussion of how the newspaper sought 'through public debates . . . to formulate their own systems' and 'fashion their national identities and nationalist politics' (Saunders 2007: 30).

5. Reinhard Sander has called attention to how Mendes's 'Commentary' from the second issue of *Trinidad* makes a case for the writer's heroic role as 'moral conscience of his community' (Sander 1988: 48).
6. Ana Rodríguez Navas examines in greater detail how 'gossip plays a crucial part in the negotiations through which Caribbean nations forge their societies and their public and political lives' (Rodríguez Navas 2018: 19).
7. The desire to distinguish the literary intellectual from the bureaucrat also appears in another 1930s text from Jamaica, Claude McKay's *Banana Bottom* (see Dalleo 2008: 54–67).
8. See Hobnailes 1937: 5. In an unpublished interview conducted on 17 November 2008, former *Public Opinion* editor John Maxwell informed me that Hobnailes was one of the pseudonyms used by H. P. Jacobs.
9. For further discussion of *Focus*, see Dalleo 2010: 67–9.

Bibliography

Baker, Houston A., Jr. (1994), 'Critical memory and the black public sphere', *Public Culture*, 7.1, 3–33.
Barnes, Dorothy (1937), 'The Poincettia Bush', *Public Opinion*, 1.1, 20 February, 5.
Baugh, Edward (2001), 'A history of poetry', in A. James Arnold (ed.), *A History of Literature in the Caribbean*, vol. 2, Philadelphia: John Benjamins, 227–82.
Black Public Sphere Collective (1994), 'Editorial comment: On thinking the black public sphere', *Public Culture*, 7.1, xi–xiv.
'Bureaucracy' (1937), *Public Opinion*, 1.2, 27 February, 1.
Cudjoe, Selwyn (2003), *Beyond Boundaries: The Intellectual Tradition of Trinidad and Tobago in the Nineteenth Century*, Amherst: University of Massachusetts Press.
Dalleo, Raphael (2008), 'Bita Plant as literary intellectual: The anticolonial public sphere and *Banana Bottom*', *Journal of West Indian Literature*, 17.1, 54–67.
—— (2010), 'The public sphere and Jamaican anticolonial politics: *Public Opinion, Focus*, and the place of the literary', *Small Axe*, 32, 14.2, 56–82.
—— (2011a), *Caribbean Literature and the Public Sphere: From the Plantation to the Postcolonial*, Charlottesville: University of Virginia Press.
—— (2011b), 'The ideology of the literary in the newspapers and little magazines of the 1930s and 1940s', in Alison Donnell and Michael Bucknor (eds), *The Routledge Companion to Anglophone Caribbean Literatures*, New York: Routledge, 609–15.
Donnell, Alison (2006), *Twentieth-Century Caribbean Literature: Critical Moments in Anglophone Literary History*, New York: Routledge.
Edmondson, Belinda (2009), *Caribbean Middlebrow: Leisure Culture and the Middle Class*, Ithaca: Cornell University Press.
Gonzalez Seligmann, Katerina (2021), *Writing the Caribbean in Magazine Time*, New Brunswick: Rutgers University Press.
Habermas, Jürgen (1991) [1962], *The Structural Transformation of the Public Sphere: An Inquiry into a Category of Bourgeois Society*, trans. T. Burger with the assistance of Frederick Lawrence, Cambridge, MA: MIT Press.
Hartman, Saidiya (1997), *Scenes of Subjection: Terror, Slavery and Self-Making in Nineteenth-Century America*, Oxford: Oxford University Press.
Hobnailes (1937), 'The Mad Tea-Party', *Public Opinion*, 1.11, 1 May, 5.
James, C. L. R. (1978), 'Triumph', in Reinhard Sander (ed.), *From Trinidad: An Anthology of Early West Indian Writing*, New York: Africana Publishing Company, 86–103.
'The Literary Club Nuisance' (1933), *The Beacon*, 2.11, May, 2.
Manley, Edna (1943), 'Foreword', *Focus*, 1.
—— (1989), *Edna Manley: The Diaries*, ed. Rachel Manley, London: Andre Deutsch.

Mendes, Alfred (1978), 'Boodhoo', in Reinhard Sander (ed.), *From Trinidad: An Anthology of Early West Indian Writing*, New York: Africana Publishing Company, 142–72.

'New Wine in New Bottles' (1937), *Public Opinion*, 1.1, 20 February, 1.

Ramchand, Kenneth (1983) [1970], *The West Indian Novel and its Background*, 2nd edn, London: Heinemann.

Ramraj, Victor J. (2001), 'Short fiction', in A. James Arnold (ed.), *A History of Literature in the Caribbean*, vol. 2, Philadelphia: John Benjamins, 199–226.

Rodríguez Navas, Ana Belén (2018), *Idle Talk, Deadly Talk: The Uses of Gossip in Caribbean Literature*, Charlottesville: University of Virginia Press.

Rodriques, Janelle (2019), *Narratives of Obeah in West Indian Literature: Moving Through the Margins*, New York: Routledge.

Rosenberg, Leah (2007), *Nationalism and the Formation of Caribbean Literature*, New York: Palgrave Macmillan.

Sander, Reinhard (1988), *The Trinidad Awakening: West Indian Literature of the Nineteen-Thirties*, New York: Greenwood Press.

Saunders, Patricia Joan (2007), *Alien-Nation and Repatriation: Translating Identity in Anglophone Caribbean Literature*, Lanham, MD: Lexington Books.

Warner, Michael (2002), *Publics and Counterpublics*, Cambridge: Zone Books.

'You' (1937), *Public Opinion*, 1.10, 24 April, 2.

33

'NOT A NEWSPAPER IN THE ORDINARY SENSE OF THE TERM': THE GEOPOLITICS OF THE NEWSPAPER/MAGAZINE DIVIDE IN THE NIGERIAN *COMET*

Marina Bilbija

Introduction

ON 22 JULY 1933, the Egyptian-born, Pan-African editor Duse Mohamed Ali launched his third and final journal, the Nigerian *Comet* (see Figure 33.1). His previous paper, *Africa* (1928), published in the US, had folded after only one issue. The venture before that, the London *African Times and Orient Review* (1912–20), had been a critical success, but a commercial liability.[1] Of all his journals, the *Comet* would enjoy the longest uninterrupted run. In 1934, it reported sales of 4,000 copies weekly, but estimated that it was reaching 16,000 actual readers (Newell 2022: 57). Though its sales numbers dropped to 3,000 by 1938, it remained in print even after Ali's death in a somewhat new reconfigured form (Duffield 1971: 743). In 1944, the elderly and ailing Ali sold the journal to Nnamdi Azikiwe's Zik Press. Soon after, it was rebranded the *Daily Comet* and relocated to Kano.[2] Perhaps no one was more surprised by the *Comet*'s longevity than Ali himself, who had chosen this title after musing on the unpredictable course of his career and life. In his 1937 autobiography *Leaves from an Active Life*, he reasoned that 'Had the *Comet* news-magazine disappeared after a month; a year; even two years, my friends and those who were not, would have asked 'What! Has the *Comet* died?' the answer was to be found in the title "Comet" which appears only for a space! But it is not lost' (Abdelwahid 2011: 195).

If, for Ali, the titular comet figured fleeting but memorable occurrences, for another contributor, 'S. O. N.', it was a celestial harbinger of 'the advent of some great worldwide event, a change of the old order or the dawn of a new era' which though unstoppable was ultimately positive (S. O. N. 1934: 23). His selective interpretation of the comet as 'a spectacle of an immensely interesting character calculated to work together for the good of humanity' is hardly surprising seeing as it doubled as an account of the *Comet*'s effects in Nigeria. According to S. O. N, the comet/*Comet* transmitted its power not only to those who beheld this phenomenon, but also to those who focused their thoughts on it. Therefore, 'to think of the Comet' was 'to become Comet-minded', that is, 'to expect a change in the direction of world progress and advancement' (S. O. N. 1934: 23). From S. O. N.'s effusive disquisition on the benefits of meditating on comets, we can infer that to read the *Comet* was also 'to expect a

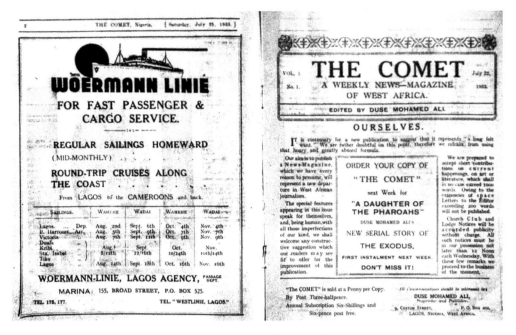

Figure 33.1 The *Comet*, 22 July 1933, p. 1. Courtesy of the author.

change in the direction of world progress and advancement', and thereby to become comet-minded (S. O. N. 1934: 23).

Given that the *Comet* was established in the 1930s, a decade marked by the rise of Nazism and Fascism, imperial aggressions in Ethiopia, Asia and Europe, and a global economic crisis, S. O. N.'s elision of the more ominous interpretations of a comet's sighting seems all the more jarring in hindsight. Nevertheless, his broader inferences about the characteristics of a comet-minded disposition ring true for the *Comet*'s general ethos. If becoming comet-minded meant learning how to read for signs of change, whether in the sky or on the page, then this was certainly an accurate description of the magazine's didactic project of identifying news of 'importance to the West African communities' from the reams of incoming reports the world over (Ali 1933b: 4).

In histories of the West African press, the *Comet* is best known for its detailed coverage of Italy's invasion of Ethiopia.[3] According to Fred Omu, 'of all West African newspapers at the time, the *Comet* probably most exemplified the sense of outrage at Italian aggression' (1978: 258). Omu's passing reference to the *Comet*'s editor as 'the Egyptian-born Nigerian nationalist Duse Mohamed Ali' reveals that neither Ali's emigrant status nor the *Comet*'s internationalist focus was incompatible with Nigerian nationalism. To understand how the Sudanese-Egyptian Ali came to also be known as a Nigerian nationalist, we need only to examine his editorial practices in the *Comet*. In both his editorials and his strategic juxtapositions of Nigerian and global news stories, Ali framed local events in relation to shifting political alliances everywhere (the schisms within the League of Nations, the Rome-Berlin axis) and in the contexts of rising world movements (Communism, Fascism, Pan-Africanism).

This chapter examines how Ali repopulated the imagined maps of places and events affecting West Africa under the banner of news reporting befitting a magazine, which he argued was categorically different from the styles and scopes of newspapers. Pointing to the *Comet*'s weekly publishing schedule, magazine format and literary orientation as interlocking features that distinguished it from 'a newspaper in the ordinary sense of the term', Ali set a new geopolitical agenda for a new kind of journal (Ali 1933b: 4). By touting the novelty of his magazine, Ali created a niche for himself in the Nigerian periodical market from which he could categorically claim what kinds of news and items went into magazines and which into newspapers. I argue that by sorting different styles and scopes of news coverage according to the length of a periodical's publication schedule (dailies versus weeklies) and its format and genre (magazines versus newspapers), the *Comet* reconfigured what ultimately counted as 'current events affecting the interest of the community' (Ali 1933b: 4).

In scholarship on West African print culture, moments of formal and genre experimentations are recognised as both symptoms and effects of social and demographic changes. Recognising the experimental function of the *Comet*'s taxonomy of print genres illuminates the Nigerian press's changing strategies for representing 'the time-space' of late-colonial Nigeria, to use Leslie James's formulation (James 2018: 570). When in 1937 Nnamdi Azikiwe launched the *West African Pilot*, he introduced a series of innovations into the Nigerian daily press that would cut across Ali's newspaper/magazine divide and render many of his claims about the time-space of the daily 'newspaper in the ordinary sense of the term' a moot point (Ali 1933b: 4). James thus points to the *West African Pilot*'s introduction of a new print persona of the flying news reporter, demonstrating how 'location, space, and time were simultaneously grounded and overcome' in his news reports (James 2018: 570). So suggestive was this fantastical figure to journalists seeking to comment on late-colonial Nigerian modernity that by the 1940s, the daily instantiation of the *Comet* introduced its own pseudonymous flying newspaperman. Between 1938 and 1949, James argues, these 'flying newspapermen' occasioned new ways of representing the 'time-space' of colonial Nigeria at a time when political alliances, international borders and the imperial world order were in flux (James 2018: 570). Viewed together, the *Comet*'s performative print taxonomies and the pseudonymous flying reporters of the late 1930s and early 1940s come into view as the Nigerian press's different imaginative responses to the 'absurd reality' of late-imperial decay, shifting geopolitical allegiances, and – in the wake of Ethiopia's occupation – the increasing difficulty of concealing the barbarism underpinning conceptions of western civilisation (James 2018: 572).

'Our object is to deal with the larger issues affecting West Africa rather than the minor issues of Nigerian politics'

When, on 22 July 1933, Duse Mohamed Ali first introduced his new journal to the anglophone Nigerian public, he declared it to be a 'new departure in West African journalism', and invited readers to adjust their expectations accordingly (Ali 1933a: 3). Ali's choice to establish a weekly newsmagazine rather than a daily that would be in direct competition with papers like the *Nigerian Daily Times* was both a prudent business decision and a sign of his being attuned to the way different periodicals gave a 'tempo to things', as Derek Peterson and Emma Hunter aptly put it (Peterson and Hunter 2016: 2). But, by his second 'Men and Matters' editorial, Ali was already complaining that some of his readers were lamenting 'the absence of Local News in this publication', and had therefore 'failed to understand the real purpose of "The Comet"' (Ali 1933b: 4). He thus directed readers seeking 'lengthy dissertations [on local news]' to the pages of the daily press, noting how this was 'their province upon which we have no intent to encroach' (Ali 1933b: 4). As the *Comet* was 'not a newspaper in the ordinary sense of the term', he reasoned, it would only print 'news of importance to the West African communities' (Ali 1933b: 4).

In this mission statement, Ali embedded a discussion of scopes and forms of news reporting into a schema of periodical genres in which newspapers 'in the ordinary sense' and magazines served different functions (Ali 1933b: 4). A third dimension of this schema was time, or, more specifically, what Mark Turner has called 'periodical time' (Turner 2002: 184). Ali's pronouncements on the *Comet*'s differences from other Lagos publications made newspapers interchangeable with dailies, and rendered local news their purview, and weeklies with magazines, and stories 'affecting West Africa' (and thus presumably not only occurring in West Africa) their focus. Consequently, his definitions of the local, topical and newsworthy became entangled with discrete periodical genres and publishing schedules (Ali 1933b: 4).

In his desire to demarcate the *Comet* from newspapers 'in the ordinary sense', Ali acted as if the distinctions between newspapers, magazines, reviews and periodicals were not notoriously slippery (Ali 1933b: 4).[4] Equally slippery were those between features of dailies, weeklies, bi-weeklies and monthlies on the one hand, and magazines and reviews on the other, as scholars of periodical culture repeatedly remind us. Weeklies in particular occupied a liminal place between newspapers and periodicals such as magazines and reviews.[5] The daily/weekly divide that Ali metonymically invoked to place his magazine in a different class from existing Nigerian newspapers made sense in the historical conjuncture of the 1930s, but it would not have registered in the same way for previous generations of Nigerian readers. Seven months prior to the *Comet*'s launch, the special Christmas issue of the *Nigerian Daily Times* (which Ali spearheaded) featured an essay entitled 'At Work and Play: A Day at the "Nigerian Daily Times" Office', which recounted how the shift to daily publishing schedules had transformed the Nigerian press. Its unnamed author described how the daily *Nigerian Daily Times* 'squeezed its weekly bright foster-father "The African Messenger" . . . out of existence' and thereby imposed a new rhythm of news reporting ('At Work' 1932: 57). As he tells it, the leisurely, '"plenty-of-time-to-do-it-in" days of the weekly papers' suddenly gave way to the '"hurry-up," "do-it-now" means by which, to score a success, a daily journal had to be served' ('At Work' 1932: 57). In the *Comet*, Ali would reclaim the leisurely pace of the weekly as the appropriate rhythm for a newsmagazine, availing himself of the longer lag between each number to follow events through, synthesise news at home and abroad from a greater critical distance, and cultivate the literary tastes of a magazine-reading public outside the dizzying daily news cycle. The *Comet*'s pace may have been slower, but it was still very much a commercial venture that relied on the business of big companies like Ovaltine, Bata and Kingsway (see, for example, Figure 33.2).[6]

However, the *Comet*'s mission statement produced the very categories it sought to demarcate: local news suited to daily papers, on the one hand, and news affecting West

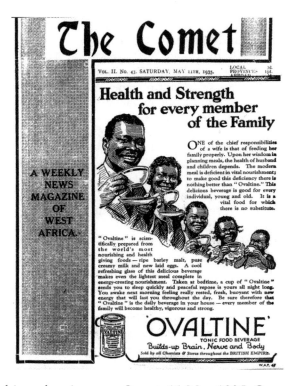

Figure 33.2 Ovaltine advertisement, *Comet*, 11 May 1935. Courtesy of the author.

Africa befitting magazine-style reporting, on the other. It was not as if, prior to the *Comet*'s arrival, West African papers had ignored world affairs. As Stephanie Newell reminds us, from its very beginnings, the West African press reported on 'Home Rule campaigns in India and Ireland, the activities of the Ku Klux Klan in North America, Japan's economic transformation and the emergence of racial segregation in South Africa' (Newell 2011: 28). English-language newspapers across West Africa enabled readers living in different colonies to draw 'comparisons between themselves and others' and thus instantiated 'trans-colonial "networks" of articulation' premised on competition and solidarity alike (Newell 2011: 28). Had West African papers historically only concerned themselves with local controversies, their publics would not have known what to make of an emigrant editor like Ali or the *Comet*. A more accurate assessment of the *Comet*'s intervention into the Lagos and West African press is that it rearticulated and condensed pre-existing trans-colonial 'networks of articulation' (Newell 2011: 28). But who decided which events occurring locally, regionally and internationally qualified as relevant to West Africa? The *Comet* did. On its pages, Ali made this into a category of news in its own right. Moreover, by virtue of their appearance in the *Comet*, stories about occurrences elsewhere were either explicitly or implicitly presented to Nigerian readers as events directly concerning them. Seen from this perspective, the *Comet*'s putative disinterest in the local comes into view as a reframing of the distinctions between the local and non-local, and an attempt to mediate between them. The *Comet*'s unsettling of these categories was perhaps its most powerful intervention into news reporting in 1930s Lagos.

If Ali's invocation of the local and West African do not align neatly with their instantiations in contemporary scholarship, it is because their meanings were not easily generalisable beyond the *Comet*'s specific schema. When Ali defined the *Comet*'s scope of action as distinct from the dailies, and explicitly removed 'local news' from its area of coverage, he was, de facto, extracting himself from a rivalry which he deemed to be a distraction from other events affecting the lives of people in West Africa (Omu 1978: 236–40; Zachernuk 2000: 94). As Duffield notes, 'in relation to Nigerian affairs, the *Comet* was cautious; it never identified itself totally with any of the Nigerian political parties, and apart from one lapse, a hostile obituary of Sir Kitoyi Ajasa, avoided personal mud-slinging of the type traditional in the Lagos press' (Duffield 1971: 754). Ali's separation of the category of local news from 'news of importance to the West African communities' is therefore yet another example of the complexity of discourses on the 'local' in West African print culture that Newell has observed in her studies of Ghanaian and Nigerian newspapers (Newell 2001: 339; Newell 2011: 30–2). Elsewhere, she has argued that whether used adjectivally or nominally, '"local" is a great deal more complex than is implied by its conventional usage as the marker of lesser – narrower, more parochial – cultural concerns in opposition to global or cosmopolitan people and ideas' (Newell 2022: 57). In the *Comet*, the category of 'events affecting West Africa' was provisional and arbitrated by Ali, whereas the category of local news encoded controversies between his colleagues at the Lagos daily press (Ali 1933b: 4). This partly explains why, in the *Comet*'s mission statement, the daily paper was metonymic for local events, and why Ali was framing his own publication in contradistinction to everything that the dailies were doing.

The encoded meanings of 'local news' were not lost on the *Comet*'s readers. In his 23 September editorial, Ali reported being 'importuned by many of our readers to express our views on the local political situation' and reminded his readers that 'it is not our intention to encroach upon the activities of the daily press' (Ali 1933d: 3). He explained:

> were we to express any definite views we should not only be engaging in a thankless task, but we should also be accused by the opposition of meddling with a matter which was no special concern of ours, thereby creating unnecessary enmity without serving any useful purpose. (Ali 1933d: 4)

This response only solicited more complaints. Two weeks later, in his 7 October editorial, Ali acknowledged the receipt of a 'remarkable' letter by a Mr Johnson-Pratt of Kaduna, who questioned the *Comet*'s ability to

> serve any useful purpose in Nigeria by adopting the principle of neutrality, especially at this time when the atmosphere of Lagos is charged with party bickering obstructing all attempts to effect an amicable settlement between the opposing parties, whereby peace may be established in the land. (Ali 1933e: 3)

Below these accusations, Ali printed a response that reiterated and fleshed out the founding principles of the *Comet* as follows:

We have frequently stated that our object is to deal with the larger issues affecting West Africa rather than the minor issues of Nigerian politics. And as such large issues include Nigeria it naturally follows the greater good must ultimately be derived by Nigeria through our humble effort and we hope to be pardoned if we fail to consider Nigerian politics to be a major issue. (Ali 1933e: 3)

Ali's conceptual separation of 'minor issues of Nigerian politics', which he relegated to the daily press, from the 'larger issue affecting West Africa', which he claimed for the *Comet*, was premised on the idea that there were two separate categories of events (Ali 1933b: 4). The minor issues were those that unfolded locally, in Nigeria, but had no major reverberations beyond their particular context. Larger issues indexed more systematic problems affecting the entire region.

Given his commitment to identifying the underlying global shifts driving changes in the region, it is unclear why Ali did not consider analysing the local Lagos party divisions plaguing the daily press as manifestations of larger issues affecting West Africa. Therefore, the *Comet*'s representation of local matters was limited insofar as it excised swathes of conversations about Lagos politics from its purview. However, it reconfigured conceptions of the local and regional in ways that cut across the periphery/metropole divide by framing events in West Africa and those affecting it as equally important for understanding Nigeria's place in the turbulent political landscape of the 1930s.

As we can see, in the *Comet*, foreign events were compressed into a West African frame and editorially domesticated. From Ali's repeated efforts to disentangle the *Comet*'s domain, 'news affecting West African communities', from that of the dailies, we can discern two different chronotopes: one in which analyses of Nigerian events were funnelled, on a daily basis, through the disputes of the Lagos press; the other in which news items from across the world were sorted and synthesised according to their purchase for West Africa (Ali 1933b: 4).

'Current events affecting the interest of the community . . . will be dealt with editorially'

Ali's taxonomy of Nigerian periodicals differentiated not only between types of journals, but also between the styles and forms of their respective news coverage. The dailies thus printed 'lengthy dissertations' on local news, while the *Comet* would deal with news 'of importance to the west African companies and communities editorially' and in 'a condensed form' (Ali 1933b: 4). The function of condensation exceeded narrative pithiness; it was a mapping strategy of sorts that shrank the globe into a West African frame. In this new frame, trends and patterns that would otherwise be dismissed as tangential to West Africans suddenly appeared in high relief as urgently germane. These condensed forms thus are world affairs transformed into those 'affecting West Africa' (Ali 1933b: 4).

The *Comet*'s condensed news reporting might have looked familiar to West African readers old enough to remember Ali's first journal, the *African Times and Orient Review*. Tanya Agathocleous has referred to Ali's editorial efforts to 'pack layers of allusion and criticism into tiny amounts of space, thereby training [the journal's] readers to pay attention to the way racism works economically, culturally, symbolically, and transimperially' as 'critical compression' (Agathocleous 2020). Whereas in the *African Times and Orient Review*, critical compression was the principle subtending both the composition of an individual page and that of an entire issue, in the *Comet*, editorials and review articles took on this function, in miniature.

Ali thus carried over the *African Times and Orient Review*'s method of compression while softening its critical edge. While Duffield has argued that the *Comet* was less radical in its politics than the *African Times and Orient Review*, he also concedes that the later Ali was no more consistent in his conservatism than in his earlier radical period (Duffield 1971: 735). He attributes this shift to both Ali's age and the more intense scrutiny that the African press was subjected to in the late-colonial period. Moreover, since Ali was an Egyptian rather than a British subject, there was a higher risk of deportation from the colonies if he published anything too critical of the British government than there would have been in London.[7]

Though Ali's condensed form may have lost some of the 'bite' of the *African Times and Orient Review* era, it nonetheless retained a critical function. Even if it did not articulate explicit challenges to British colonial rule, it created the conditions for global, intra-diasporic and paracolonial comparisons (Newell 2001: 350). Some examples of compressed reports merely concatenated events. Others included an editorial voice that reframed copy from foreign papers as West African events and outlined their future implications for readers at home. We find examples of the former in the recurring 'Here and There' column by the pseudonymous A. K.

Across the magazine's first four issues, this column included the subtitle 'Unemployment'. It took up two pages, and was divided into further subsections according to continents, regions and countries. A. K. did not directly comment on the purchase of his digests for West Africans in his column, another contributor did: a G. A. Sawyerr, author of 'The Unemployment Problem: Practice versus Theory', published in the 7 October 1933 number. Sawyerr began by referencing A. K.'s column, from which, he noted, 'we have been gleaning from time to time from the pages of the *Comet* the efforts of the various governments in the world to cope with the present worldwide depression and unemployment' (Sawyerr 1933: 11). As the newest examples of these world trends, he listed Nazi Germany and Fascist Italy's campaigns to lure women away from the workplace by offering 'marriage bonuses . . . to help prospective husbands set up homes' and in doing so free up jobs for men. While Sawyerr was unconvinced by the efficacy of this tactic in Europe or in Africa, he also noted that there was no use in armchair theorising either. The only way forward was to 'get busy', he wrote, citing this phrase as Ali's favourite 'American slogan' (Sawyerr 1933: 11). His two practical suggestions for solving Africa's unemployment problem were to invest in the modernisation of local industries and to reintroduce the Cowrie or introduce a similar new currency 'for want of a currency of a lower denomination than the half-penny' (Sawyerr 1933: 11).

Sawyerr's combination of references to A. K.'s column, Ali's editorial, German and Italian economic schemes, and potential solutions to African problems do not add up to a critique of capitalism or colonialism per se. Even as he explained Africa's unemployment issues in relation to a global crisis, his solutions reduced the problem to a lack of entrepreneurship and hard work. His recommendations were consistent with Ali's, who frequently turned to Booker T. Washington's industrial and agricultural solutions to economic, social and political problems. As Duffield notes, 'what is missing from the *Comet* is the advocacy of any overall plan, economic or political, whereby the "darker races" could confront their enemies in unity and advance along the road to freedom' (Duffield 1971: 758). Perhaps the function of the *Comet*'s condensed reviews and editorials was to map global political and economic trends and underline recurring issues as they related to West Africa, rather than posit blueprints for future action. This seemed to be Sawyerr's aim, given that immediately after outlining Germany and Italy's 'marriage bonus' proposal, he added, 'those who are able *to read between the lines* should agree that their path is beset with many pitfalls' (Sawyerr 1933: 11, emphasis mine). Given the article's expository aim, why invite readers to 'read between the lines'? In the same paragraph, Sawyerr digressed from the topic at hand by launching into his own opinions on women's place in the labour market, before stopping to remind himself that he was veering too far from the article's original topic. These two rhetorical moves highlighted places in the article where the reader could pause, read between the lines, and insert their own commentary rather than having interpretations 'fed' to them. Moments like these loosened the article's packed references from a didactic frame precisely by suggesting that readers could make inferences of their own.

In the *Comet*'s condensed representations of world affairs as they impacted West Africa, some crisis zones and kindred places were featured more prominently than others. In 1933 and 1934, the US and African America loomed large; in 1935 and 1936, news, articles and even historical essays on Ethiopia dominated its pages. Arguably, the proliferation of comparisons between West Africans and Americans in 1933 and 1934 helped set the stage for Ali's later discussions of the implications of Ethiopia's occupation for West Africa. Take, for instance, Ali's 5 August 1933 editorial on the death of an eighty-year-old African American educator by the name of Dinah Watts Pace. He devoted three paragraphs to Pace's legacy in the US, before delving into the relevance of this story to his readers. According to Ali, 'the life and labors of the ex-slave woman is an example to Africans at large and *West Africans* in particular', as she knew that 'mere "book learning" in an agricultural district would not supply her orphan pupils with a future, so she taught them the dignity of labor on a farm . . . in order to enable her charges to be useful members of society' (Ali 1933c: 3, emphasis in original).

Presented in the *Comet*'s leader, Ali's recurring 'Men and Matters' editorial, this obituary of an African American educator framed a larger conversation about the future of Black education and industry worldwide. Therefore, Ali's commemoration of Pace's career was not only a testament to his enduring support for Booker T. Washington's stance on African American industrial education, but it was also a provocation to Black intellectuals in the US and Africa who continued to advocate for liberal education models. Ali thus enlisted Pace's example to argue that wherever Africans lived, whether on the continent or in the diaspora, 'in each country he has regarded agriculture as his natural economic background' (Ali 1933c: 3). This, according to Ali, was something that Pace understood, but Black intellectuals in the US and West Africa alike failed to grasp. Articulating between the lessons of Pace's story and those gleaned from reports on farming initiatives in East Africa, Ali observed how in the latter context 'the gentleman farmer is to be found solving his economic problem' (Ali 1933c: 3). He suggested that West Africans follow the East African example and re-evaluate their own solutions for rising unemployment numbers and a depressed economy. He further reminded his readers that a 'Gentleman farmer' class had once been the 'backbone' of the English nation, noting how it had gradually disappeared thanks to its failure to introduce modern agricultural methods and the 'younger generation migrat[ing] to the cities to fill the ranks of an already overstocked market of unskilled labor' (Ali 1933c: 3). Having linked Africa's future to a gentleman farmer class, he urged his readers to ensure that they, rather than white European settlers, fill its ranks.

Ali had other motivations for spotlighting Pace's life story, besides applying her ideas about agricultural education to West Africa and Africa more broadly. His glowing account of her career provided a segue into a broader discussion of intra-diasporic relations. As someone who had overcome many obstacles to better not only her own life conditions but also those of countless others, Pace challenged the 'average West African's . . . assumption of superiority when he hears of, or comes in contact with, one whose forebearers were enslaved, overlooking the fact that for the most part, good fortune or fate was responsible for his escape from the similar condition' (Ali 1933c: 3). In defence of 'the descendants of African slaves under Anglo-Saxon or Latin rule', he argued that they had 'made greater strides along cultural and economic lines during the last hundred years than the non-slave population of Africa' (Ali 1933c: 3). Some of the conclusions that Ali draws from his diasporic comparisons point to the conservatism that Duffield has observed in his later career. Firstly, Ali places the onus of economic 'advancement', whatever that might look like, on people of African descent (Ali 1933c: 3). Secondly, in his attempts to educate his West African readers about the admirable achievements of the descendants of enslaved Africans, he ultimately reinscribes a hierarchical relation between them, only this time with the hierarchy reversed. But despite the conservatism of his final analysis, the comparative frameworks brought slavery, 'Anglo-Saxon' and 'Latin' rule and colonisation into high relief as the points that simultaneously separated and connected West Africa to the African diaspora (Ali 1933c: 3).

When the editorial's comparative frameworks brought different parts of the Black world into a single plane, they transvaluated the death of an African American educator (and her subsequent commemoration) into a 'current even[t] affecting West Africa' (Ali 1933b: 4). At first glance, Ali's discussion of a figure that probably no one in West Africa had ever heard of appears more like a dilation of a single event than a condensed review of world occurrences in the vein of A. K.'s recurring 'Here and There' column. But in his editorial framing of the event, Ali thickly layered additional African American and West African references, including, by the end of the piece, British and East African ones too.

If in 1933 Ali chastised West Africans for their condescending attitudes towards the descendants of enslaved Africans in the Americas, in 1935 he was condemning an unnamed new Nigerian weekly for 'going out of its way to "prove" that the Abyssinians are not Negroes' (Ali 1935a: 3). He drily observed that 'on this question the publication is absolutely correct for the very obvious reason that there is no such person as a "Negro"' in the sense of a 'Negro tribe' or ethnicity (Ali 1935a: 3). He went on to explain that the term was 'indiscriminately applied in the first instance to the black African slaves by the French, the Portuguese and Spaniards, without reference to the ethnic origin' and that, subsequently, it came to be 'generally applied to all Africans in that section of the "New" world' (Ali 1935a: 3). The stakes of these classifications were politically charged given Italy's occupation of Abyssinia, and the resounding calls across the Black world for solidarity with its peoples.

The Ethiopian crisis marked a turn in the *Comet*'s discussions of imperialism. In the 2 November 1935 number, Ali argued that 'someday the whole question of the right to possessions in Africa may be contested by those who shall place international morality above material advantage' (Ali 1935b: 22). Ali's criticisms of Italy's actions in Ethiopia extended to those of the League of Nations. In April 1936, Ali decried the League's blatant disregard for 'the inhuman sacrifice of innocent lives by poison gas and those other horrors of modern "civilised" warfare' (Ali 1936: 5). Almost every week that year, Ali published the same plea for financial support for the people of Ethiopia:

Ethiopia stretches her hands to God for Help through His People.
Help! Help Help!
Ye just and generous People of Nigeria please stop the murder, massacre and slaughter of innocent and defenceless People of Ethiopia! By helping them to acquire proper means of defending themselves and fighting on equal terms against their fully armed and condemned aggressor let bravery and justice have a chance against brute force through you! ('Ethiopia!' 1936: 13)

Ali's serial appeals to the Nigerian public to assist the people of Ethiopia were accompanied by weekly analyses of the Italian aggression's implications for the 'non-European world, subject and independent' (Ali 1936: 5). As Adom Getachew has argued, the invasion made it impossible to deny the 'unequal integration and racial hierarchy that had structured the league since its founding' (Getachew 2019: 62).

While Ali was spearheading the *Comet*'s Abyssinian Relief Fund, the Nigerian Youth Movement was gaining momentum. One of its founders, Eyo Ita, regularly contributed to the *Comet*. Ali's decision to publish dozens of Ita's essays on contemporary Nigerian politics did not necessarily contradict his earlier claims that Nigerian party politics were outside the publication's area of focus since Ita's writing also jumped scales between Nigerian political issues and global ones. For example, in an article published in the 7 November 1936 number, Ita condemned Italy's aggression against Ethiopia as a symptom of 'a belated and impotent imperialism', contending that this event spelled out 'the doom of modern imperialism . . . and in its vast ruin Italy and all the nations that maintain themselves by it must perish' (Ita 1936: 14). He predicted that 'the executors of judgment' on the imperialists would be oppressed colonised people and 'the proletariats of Europe, Japan, and the US' (Ita 1936: 14).

Ita's article on Ethiopia speaks to the *Comet*'s role as a Pan-African mediator between different African national movements. In his biography of Ali, Duffield cites Chief Enahoro's account of the 1930s in *Fugitive Offender*, where he recalls reading about Ethiopia in his 'favourite newspaper, the *Comet*' (Duffield 1971: 767). Through the *Comet* he had become more attuned to 'fellow-feeling with other Africans', which, he explained, was a 'newly awakened Sentiment' for him (quoted in Duffield 1971: 767). As people in Nigeria registered their disappointment with England's neutrality in the war, and raised money for the Abyssinia fund, 'the seeds of nationalism were being sown' (Duffield 1971: 767). For Duffield, Chief Enahoro's recollections of the *Comet*'s role in sowing the seeds of Nigerian nationalism suggest that the magazine was not Ali's only monument in Nigeria, so to speak, since 'more intangibly, he had influenced a whole generation of Nigerian "youngmen", among whom were some of the most prominent future political leaders of the country' (Duffield 1971: 730). Enahoro's account of Ali's influence on a younger generation of Nigerian nationalists is all the more interesting given that this peripatetic editor moved to Nigeria late in his life and only resided there for fourteen years. On the one hand, this is a testament to the hospitality that interwar Lagos showed to Black emigrants; on the other, it is an indication of Ali's success in calibrating his recognisable style of Pan-African journalism to a new West African context, after having built his career in England and the US.

Conclusion

As one of the longest consecutively running journals in colonial Nigeria, the *Comet* provides insight into Nigerian responses to the occupation of Ethiopia, the Liberian crisis, the rise of Hitler and Mussolini, and the outbreak and course of the Second World War. To be sure, the *Comet* is a record of news coverage by West African anglophone elites that is additionally informed by the idiosyncratic selection criteria of a foreign editor. But its Anglo-provincialism is in and of itself a worthy object of study. Attending to the anglophone print culture which mediated Azikiwe's and Ali's access to different diasporic and paracolonial networks also sheds light on their Nigerian papers' extensive engagement with African American news and political debates.

After all, mutual anglophone legibility not only made it possible for an emigrant like Ali to join the West African press, it also enabled Nnamdi Azikiwe to contribute to African American and Ghanaian papers before his return to Nigeria. If, as Derek Peterson and Emma Hunter remind us, African newspapers 'took shape in an economy of textual circulation through which material and stories moved laterally, without respect for geography', it is also true that they were shaped by the circulation of Black editors within but also beyond the Black Atlantic (Peterson and Hunter 2016: 2). Ali's and Azikiwe's transatlantic careers made them uniquely equipped to comment on the changing migration patterns of Nigerian students abroad, who by the late 1920s were as likely to be studying at US universities as at British ones.

Finally, as a journal edited by an 'Egyptian-born Nigerian nationalist', the *Comet* provides glimpses into a late-colonial anglophone Nigerian literary culture that flourished in periodicals but was not subsequently collected and 'institutionalized as history', as Newell aptly puts it (Omu 1978: 258; Newell 2022: 60). As a result, many of these texts remain unknown to students of this period in Nigerian literary history, even though periodicals were the primary site in which most of its literature was published. Newell has addressed this lacuna in West African literary history with a call for the reconceptualisation of the term 'ephemera' beyond its associations with fleetingness and disposable print to a 'mode of historical thinking' and an analytical category for studying 'experiments with form and genre that did not "become institutionalized"' (Newell 2022: 60). Doing so, Newell argues, 'helps us to appreciate the work of writers and local intellectuals for whom newsprint enabled the expression of topics and temporalities that are often tangential to the core concerns of later literary historians, for whom such material may be regarded as disposable' (Newell 2022: 60). The method Newell describes is a transvaluation of literary and journalistic 'comets', which, as Ali mused, 'appear only for a space!' but are not lost (Abdelwahid 2011: 195).

Notes

1. In its last year of publication – between January and December 1920 – it was published under its new, revised title *The Africa and Orient Review*.
2. For a discussion of the Zik Press's purchase of the *Comet*, see Duffield 1971: 730–48. For an account of the *Daily Comet*'s history in Kano, see Azikiwe's *My Odyssey* (1970: 368–72, 395).
3. See Duffield 1971 and Omu 1978.
4. Laurel Brake reminds us 'how slippery, ungainly, dynamic, competitive and resistant to categorisation periodicals and newspapers are' (Brake 2017: 48).
5. For discussions of periodical time, see Turner 2002 and 2006. For discussions of periodical genres and the elusiveness of periodical categories, see Beetham 1990, Brake 2017 and Schoenfield 2009.
6. Though the *Comet*'s cycle was longer than that of the dailies, its more leisurely publishing schedule and reading tempo were not congruent with the 'slow print' practices that Isabel Hofmeyr (2013) and Elizabeth Carolyn Miller (2013) ascribe to anti-colonial and radical papers. Ali's penchant for slower-paced literary magazines over newspapers did not entail a rejection of the genres and business models of print capitalism.
7. On the controversies surrounding Ali's claims to Egyptian and Sudanese heritage, see Duffield 1971 and Dorman 2023.

Bibliography

Abdelwahid, Mustafa A. (ed.) (2011), *Dusé Mohamed Ali (1866–1945): The Autobiography of a Pioneer Pan African and Afro-Asian Activist*, Trenton, NJ: Red Sea Press.

Agathocleous, Tanya (2020), 'Critical compression in the *African Times and Orient Review*', unpublished paper, British Periodicals Online Workshop, 3 July, Milton Keynes, Open University.

Ali, Duse Mohamed (1933a), 'Ourselves', *Comet*, 22 July, 3.

—— (1933b), 'Men and Matters', *Comet*, 29 July, 4.

—— (1933c), 'Men and Matters', *Comet*, 5 August, 3.

—— (1933d), 'Men and Matters', *Comet*, 23 September, 4.

—— (1933e), 'Men and Matters', *Comet*, 7 October, 3.

—— (1935a), 'Men and Matters', *Comet*, 5 October, 3.

—— (1935b), 'About It and About It', *Comet*, 2 November, 22.

—— (1936), 'About It and About It', *Comet*, 18 April, 5.

'At Work and Play: A Day at the "Nigerian Daily Times" Office' (1932), *Nigerian Daily Times*, December, 57.

Azikiwe, Nnamdi (1970), *My Odyssey: An Autobiography*, London: Hurst & Company.

Barber, Karin (2007), *The Anthropology of Texts, Persons and Publics*, Cambridge and New York: Cambridge University Press.

—— (2012), 'Introduction', in *Print Culture and the First Yoruba Novel: I. B. Thomas's 'Life Story of Me', 'Segilola', and Other Texts*, Leiden: Brill, 3–83.

Beetham, Margaret (1990), 'Towards a theory of the periodical as a publishing genre', in Laurel Brake, Aled Jones and Lionel Madden (eds), *Investigating Victorian Journalism*, London: Palgrave Macmillan, 19–32.

Brake, Laurel (2017), 'Periodical formats: The changing review', in Joan Shattock (ed.), *Journalism and the Periodical Press in Nineteenth-Century Britain*, Cambridge and New York: Cambridge University Press, 47–65.

Dorman, Jacob S. (2023), '"Western Civilization through Eastern Spectacles": Duse Mohamed Ali, Black Orientalist imposture, and Black Internationalism,' *The Journal of African American History*, 108.1, 23–49.

Duffield, Ian (1971), 'Duse Mohamed Ali and the development of Pan-Africanism, 1866–1945', unpublished PhD thesis, University of Edinburgh.

'Ethiopia Stretches her Hands to God for Help through His People!' (1936), *Comet*, 25 April, 13.

Getachew, Adom (2019), *Worldmaking After Empire*, Princeton: Princeton University Press.

Hofmeyr, Isabel (2013), *Gandhi's Printing Press*, Cambridge, MA: Harvard University Press.

Idemili, Samuel Okafor (1980), 'The *West African Pilot* and the movement for Nigerian nationalism, 1937–1960', unpublished PhD thesis, University of Wisconsin-Madison.

Ita, Eyo (1936), 'A Belated and Impotent Imperialism', *Comet*, 7 November, 14–18.

James, Leslie (2018), 'The flying newspapermen and the time-space of late colonial Nigeria', *Comparative Studies in Society and History*, 60.3, 569–98.

Miller, Elizabeth Carolyn (2013), *Slow Print: Literary Radicalism and Late Victorian Print Culture*, Stanford: Stanford University Press.

Newell, Stephanie (2001), '"Paracolonial networks": Some speculations on local readerships in colonial West Africa', *Interventions*, 3.3, 336–54.

—— (2011), 'Articulating empire: Newspaper readerships in colonial West Africa', *New Formations*, 73, 26–42.

—— (2022), 'Local authors, ephemeral texts: Anglo-scribes and Anglo-literates in West African newspapers', in Grace Musila (ed.), *The Routledge Handbook of African Popular Culture*, London and New York: Routledge, 56–73.

Omu, Fred I. A. (1974), 'Review: *Pan-Africanism and Nationalism in West Africa 1900–1945 (A Study in Ideology and Social Classes)* by J. Ayodele Langley', *Journal of the Historical Society of Nigeria*, 7.3, 594–7.

—— (1978), *Press and Politics in Nigeria, 1880–1937*, Atlantic Highlands, NJ: Humanities Press.

Peterson, Derek R., and Emma Hunter (2016), 'Print culture in colonial Africa', in Derek R. Peterson, Emma Hunter and Stephanie Newell (eds), *African Print Cultures: Newspapers and their Publics in the Twentieth Century*, Ann Arbor: University of Michigan Press, 1–48.

Sawyerr, G. A. (1933), 'The Unemployment Problem: Practice versus Theory', *Comet*, 7 October, 11.

Schoenfield, Mark (2009), *British Periodicals and Romantic Identity: The 'Literary Lower Empire'*, London: Palgrave Macmillan.

S. O. N. (1934), 'The Gist of It: Becoming "Comet-Minded"', *Comet*, 26 May, 23.

Turner, Mark (2002), 'Periodical time in the nineteenth century', *Media History*, 8.2, 183–96.

—— (2006), 'Time, periodicals, and literary studies', *Victorian Periodicals Review*, 39.4, 309–16.

Zachernuk, Philip Serge (2000), *Colonial Subjects: An African Intelligentsia and Atlantic Ideas*, Charlottesville and London: University of Virginia Press.

34

AFRICA IN JAMAICA: W. A. DOMINGO, GEORGE PADMORE AND *PUBLIC OPINION*

Myles Osborne

THE AFTERNOON OF 15 March 1957 saw thousands of Jamaicans filling lower King Street in Kingston's downtown. The crowd moved slowly along the west-east thoroughfare, their route taking them parallel to the sea several blocks to the south. In the centre, cheered on by all and sundry, was Jamaica's Chief Minister Norman Manley. Given the 'greatest welcome ever accorded to any Jamaican', enthused his party's mouthpiece *Public Opinion*, Manley had just returned from Ghana where he had represented Jamaica at the fledgling nation's independence celebrations. Carried on the shoulders of his 'jubilant supporters', the account continued, Manley then silenced the crowd and began to speak. Linking Ghana's historical experience to that of Jamaica – still a British colony though self-governing – Manley lamented how his political opponents had delayed Jamaica's freedom: 'we could have been there now!' he cried ('The Spirit' 1957: 1; see Figure 34.1).

Tying the Jamaican experience to that of African nations was, by 1957, a common trope of Manley, his People's National Party (PNP) and *Public Opinion*. It was a politically astute tactic in a colony where a significant proportion of the population had come to feel a direct and powerful connection to Africa and its inhabitants. The origins of these Pan-African links are deep and complex, and historically refracted through Jamaica's divisions of class and colour. Marcus Garvey and his Universal Negro Improvement Association had played a leading role during the 1920s and 1930s, and after the end of the Second World War, other groups ranging from Rastafari to the Ethiopian World Federation to the Afro-West Indian Welfare League had taken up the mantle in varying ways.[1]

Following the war's end, two voices rang loudest in foregrounding Pan-Africanist ideas in the colony's mainstream press: those belonging to the Trinidadian intellectual George Padmore and his Jamaican counterpart W. A. (Wilfred Adolphus) Domingo. Both were members of the PNP – founded in 1938 – and both wrote frequently in *Public Opinion*, founded the year before. *Public Opinion* was at the same time the colony's most radical mainstream newspaper which enjoyed a wide readership, second only to the more conservative *Daily Gleaner*. This chapter considers the ways that the two men – and other more peripheral figures including Roger Mais and Paul Robeson – represented Africa in Jamaica. Each brought African issues into discussions about Jamaica's present, as well as its future: should the island be an African satellite, a wholly independent nation or part of the West Indies Federation? And what role should larger, global movements like Pan-Africanism or socialism play, with

Figure 34.1 *Public Opinion*, 16 March 1957, p. 1. Courtesy of the British Library.

their promises to leave the nation behind in search of a brighter future? While *Public Opinion* was the venue for these discussions, the newspaper itself had a still larger role to play. Though it was never ostensibly aimed at lower-class Jamaicans, its news of Africa – and its function as a source for connecting and informing those interested in the continent – was crucial.

The Second World War inspired a seismic shift in the British Empire. The war laid bare the reality that the imperial system was unsustainable, a status catalysed by powerful movements of protest and activism that had spread across the colonies during the 1930s. Moreover, the Atlantic Charter document agreed upon (though never signed) by British Prime Minister Winston Churchill and United States President Franklin D. Roosevelt in 1941 had seemed to promise freedom for colonised peoples, widely viewed as a reasonable exchange for their sacrifices during the war (see also Chapter 27 by David Johnson). In 1945, millions of people of colour returned from foreign theatres with new views on the world. They possessed a burgeoning confidence and determination to change their personal circumstances, as well as those of their homelands.[2] It was in this context that Padmore and Domingo released volley after volley of articles to the Jamaican populace in the pages of *Public Opinion*.

Though George Padmore is often viewed as the most prominent Pan-Africanist writing in the Caribbean press after the war's end, in Jamaica, that role was shared with W. A. Domingo. Domingo had serious Pan-Africanist chops: he was the first editor of

Garvey's *Negro World* in 1916. Two decades later, in 1936, Domingo and W. (Walter) Adolphe Roberts had founded the Harlem-based Jamaica Progressive League (JPL). It was an organisation for expatriate Jamaicans to contribute to – and press for – freedom on the island itself. Both Domingo and Roberts had been heavily influenced by the Harlem Renaissance, a cultural revolution whose influence in literature, art, fashion and more spread far beyond New York City's borough of Manhattan. Importantly, as Birte Timm has shown, the JPL's demands for the end of colonial rule were often more powerful than much of the discourse in Jamaica itself (Timm 2016). Their opinions and viewpoints were often awkward for mainstream Jamaican politicians like Manley and his political competitor (and first cousin) Alexander Bustamante, who could come across as out of touch and relative moderates.

It was, therefore, a crucial moment when Domingo decided to return to Jamaica in 1941 following three decades living in the United States. Before he could set foot on Jamaican soil – when he was still on board ship in Kingston harbour – Domingo was summarily arrested. As Timm explains, 'This drastic decision of the Governor shows how much power and influence Domingo was believed to have exerted on the already destabilized society in Jamaica' (Timm 2016: 271). Domingo's arrest reflected a Jamaica in which free speech was curtailed by wartime Defense Regulations in the guise of the Undesired Publications Law. A wave of arrests of additional journalists followed. The arrest was certainly overreach, and protests swept Jamaica and the United States. To be sure, Domingo was a socialist who believed in the power of black unity across the globe; but he also supported Britain in the war and wished for Germany's defeat, a relatively uncommon position for black peoples in New York (Timm 2016: 280–1). On his release after twenty months, Domingo became an influential member of the PNP, an organisation he viewed as the successor to Garvey and the JPL which would surely take Jamaica to independence (Timm 2016: 304).

For Domingo, the Jamaican experience was tied to the experience of black West Indians in London, or indeed the independence of the African colonies. He expressed these views at the war's end in the daily *Public Opinion*, writing several columns per week between 1945 and 1947 (and at the same time contributing many articles to the *New Negro World*). Roughly half of these columns appeared under the title 'Sparks From My Anvil'. For Domingo, the black experience in Jamaica was inextricably linked to that in the United States, Britain or Kenya. But unlike Padmore – who, as discussed below, continued to think in broad, Pan-Africanist terms – Africa could light a pathway to true national independence in Jamaica undiluted, Domingo would come to argue, by plans for a West Indian federation.

One of the first major domestic episodes Domingo addressed in several columns was an incident at the Springfield Beach Club in Kingston's Corporate Area. On a Friday night – 30 November 1945 – a well-known journalist of 'dark complexion' had attempted to enter the club. Despite having frequented the club on previous occasions, he was informed that he could not enter as a non-member. Several hundred US servicemen, however – almost certainly non-members – were present. The manager was later overheard reminding the doorman of his instructions: 'not to let in anyone looking like me [the doorman]' (Mais 1945: 3). This was, noted Domingo, a 'condition' that Jamaicans 'are loth [sic] to face honestly' – that of discrimination in Jamaica based on skin colour. Linking this episode to a recent United Service Organizations (USO) advertisement which sought to hire a white person, and an episode of discrimination at Pan-African Airways, Domingo expressed his fear about a United States-style racism in Jamaica. Jamaicans, he thought, were quick to attack such discrimination in the United States but stayed silent at home. But if the Jamaican experience might be understood in the context of the United States, then the experience of African Americans also provided an example for Jamaica to follow: 'If New York and Chicago are virtually free from discrimination in public places it is because Negro Americans of every shade and complexion fought together and broke the colour line' (Domingo 1945b: 3).

Domingo took on the events at Springfield in a formidable alliance that he formed with Roger Mais. A journalist and writer of short stories, Mais would soon become one of Jamaica's most celebrated novelists with his depiction of poor, black Jamaicans. Mais took a stronger line against Britain than Domingo. In 1944, *Public Opinion* had published an article by Mais entitled 'Now We Know'. In it, he had lambasted Churchill's government for having no interest in giving up 'her exclusive prerogative to the conquest and enslavement of other nations' (Mais 1944: 1). For Mais, the war was fought to preserve empire. Following its publication, police had raided *Public Opinion*'s offices as well as Mais's home, and charged the City Printery, Mais and the newspaper's managing director O. T. Fairclough for contravening Defense Regulations. While Fairclough was acquitted, Mais was detained for four months (Watson 2012: 183–4). The offices of *Public Opinion* were then 'besieged' with requests for the piece (Watson 2012: 191).

On the adjoining page to his article on Springfield, Domingo followed his excoriation of race relations in Jamaica with an imperial event: Nigeria's new draft constitution. The House of Commons had recently debated the document with none other than George Padmore in the audience, Domingo's source for his piece. Explaining how educated Nigerians had rejected the draft, Domingo lauded the activism of expatriate Nigerian students in the United States. Skilfully utilising the press, wrote Domingo, they had publicised their demands in African American newspapers using 'facts, figures and logic', in an effort that had successfully won over 'anti-imperialist white Americans'. Unlike West Indians, Domingo asserted, West Africans 'are not influenced to any great extent by imperial patriotism', and this therefore provided an instructive model (Domingo 1945c: 3–4). The colonial system was, after all, a common one that both Jamaicans and Nigerians were battling, something that would have been profoundly obvious to people in both colonies: Sir Arthur Richards – Jamaica's governor from 1938 to 1943, who was responsible for detaining Domingo – had moved to Nigeria at the culmination of his service, where he had immediately set to work on that colony's constitution.

If Domingo tended to fuse West Indian with African issues, George Padmore's gaze was firmly set on the international scene. The war catalysed Padmore's intellectual development. As Leslie James has shown, Padmore came to view German fascism as not unique but a global custom also practised by the colonial powers. Moreover, Padmore was convinced that Britain had no intention of returning its colonies at the war's end. The veneer of protecting democracy as a justification for the conflict rang hollow given that democratic voting rights were denied to millions of colonised peoples (James 2015: 47–9). Padmore used his wartime writing to 'prepare the ground for a post-war battle for independence' (James 2015: 56). That preparation was most clearly manifested in the central role he played in organising the Pan-African Congress (PAC) meeting in Manchester in October 1945. Coming a little more than a month and a half after the war's end, Padmore viewed it as a critical moment in spreading and pressing the Pan-African case.

Padmore introduced his writings on the PAC with a series of pieces designed to draw local attention to the indignities and apparent weakening of the wider colonial system. He informed his readers about potential strike action in Nigeria, changes in Ceylon's governing structure, and political developments in Uganda (Padmore 1945a: 2; 1945b: 2; 1945c: 2). Ever-aware of debates in parliament and official government publications, Padmore leapt at the opportunity to inform his readers about the publication of the Moyne Report in 1945. The report detailed the results of a royal commission sent to the West Indies in 1938 to investigate social and economic conditions there. It was damning with its 'revelation of widespread disease-ridden hovels, malnutrition, squalor and poverty', wrote Padmore, and had 'shocked the British people'. 'Colonialism indicted,' he summarised (Padmore 1945d: 2).

With the groundwork laid, Padmore commenced a series of articles on the fifth meeting of the PAC. (*Public Opinion* would be the only publication in Jamaica to devote significant space to the PAC, something Domingo would lament directly in print (Domingo 1945a: 3).) Without doubt the most significant of the PAC meetings, coming at the end of the war, the meeting passed the torch from African Americans as leaders of the global black struggle to Africans. Future African presidents and prime ministers Jomo Kenyatta, Kwame Nkrumah and Hastings Banda attended alongside luminaries such as W. E. B. Du Bois. Padmore proudly labelled the PAC as the 'united federation of organisations of African Peoples and Peoples of African descent throughout the world' (Padmore 1945e: 2). Reflecting his sympathies with socialist thought, however, Padmore described the PAC's aims as 'an attempt to link up the nationalistic feelings and aspirations of the African peoples of the world with the vital economic, political and social needs of the working classes, peasantry and middle classes' (Padmore 1945e: 2). That balancing act – between Garvey and socialism, as Padmore put it – would be one of the major challenges facing the attendees of the PAC, as well as being the central part of his intellectual agenda for the following decade (Padmore 1945e: 2).

Padmore invoked Garvey twice during his introductory article: once as noted above, and once in a quite different manner. In describing the PAC's programme, Padmore drew it in contrast to Garvey's agenda which was 'purely propagandis[t]ic and emotional' (Padmore 1945e: 2). With this statement, Padmore drew a line in the sand: he was unafraid to attack the popular Jamaican whom he would later describe as 'a man of inordinate conceit' (Padmore 1956: 88). Padmore rejected Garvey's political approach which fused a capitalist agenda (in contrast to his own Marxism) with what Padmore viewed as 'racial fascism' (Padmore 1956: 97). Padmore also represented the view – best aligned with the middle and upper classes in Jamaica – that constitutional change in an orthodox nationalist framework was the route to freedom. For ultimately, as James argues, Padmore believed that the end of empire would come only 'through the will of the imperial power', though it could be forced to act (James 2015: 124). As I have argued elsewhere, this was in striking contrast to many of Jamaica's Garveyites and lower classes, black men and women who viewed the violent discarding of the colonial order as the only prescription for the island (Osborne 2020). The PAC demonstrated the reality, as Simon Gikandi puts it, that 'the men and women who met to plot the future of Pan-Africanism were also the most westernized of colonial subjects' (Gikandi 2000: 3).

Domingo, by contrast, took a more direct line. By 1945 he was perhaps best described as a Garveyite: he was editor of the *New Negro Voice*, a publication which took Garvey's life and teachings as a prescription for editorial policy. When he wrote about the PAC, Domingo opened his article by listing the PAC's most prominent attendees with short descriptions of them, including Learie Constantine, W. E. B. Du Bois, Sylvester Williams, Padmore and more. But he devoted his greatest attention to Amy Jacques Garvey, the Jamaican Pan-Africanist, journalist and second wife of Marcus Garvey.[3] Domingo – twice – described the central role Garvey played in arranging the conference, going so far as to attribute much of its success directly to her effort and skill. She had undertaken this work 'patiently and self-effacingly', he noted, as she was a lynchpin for negotiations and discussions with 'coloured leaders in all parts of the world' (Domingo 1945a: 3). Marcus Garvey, then, received accolades by association with his second wife. The contrast between Padmore's and Domingo's depictions of the Garvey name could not have been more striking.

Domingo also devoted a small though significant number of column inches to writing about topics of interest to Jamaica's lower classes. They often appeared under the pseudonym 'Ognimod' ('Domingo' spelled backwards). One of the first examples took on western Kingston's iconic Coronation Market. The market was a vibrant space of trading for poorer Jamaicans, and would soon become one of the first spaces in which Rastafari were welcomed and mixed with those who were not members of the faith.[4] Domingo wrote that the market demonstrated the 'industry and ingenuity of our people', who had created items such as sandals made from discarded car tyres. But, he argued, these people were forced to work in 'vile', unsanitary conditions (Ognimod 1946: 15). A second piece was entitled 'Back to Africa', a movement usually associated with Rastafari but one with which many poor Jamaicans sympathised. The notion promised a brighter future in which Jamaicans could return to their ancestral lands to live more prosperous lives. In his piece, Domingo quoted a Nigerian author named Mbonu Ojike who had criticised his fellow Nigerians for their 'indiscriminate aping' of European ways. Heralding an approach practised by Rastafari and others, Domingo informed his reading public how Ojike had called for Nigerians to 'forsake eating European food' and 'abandon European clothes'. He explained how J. E. Casely Hayford, the Fante journalist and lawyer, had attended court in 'African robes', a practice of sporting traditional clothing also undertaken by Mohandas Gandhi and Jawaharlal Nehru (Ognimod 1947: 8). It is easy to imagine cuttings of this piece being exchanged and discussed in Kingston's yards for months if not years to come.[5]

Turning to *Public Opinion*, the Jamaicans O. T. Fairclough, Frank Hill and H. P. Jacobs founded it in 1937. Raphael Dalleo has outlined the orientations it moved through during its early years. Before the founding of the PNP in 1938 it was 'uneven' and struggling for a clear identity. Into the early 1940s it enjoyed a 'golden age' of drawing together literature and politics in its content, before, after 1943, literature fell away and into the pages of *Focus* (Dalleo 2010: 57). True to its roots, *Public Opinion* remained largely aimed at the middle classes, though certainly the more radical and progressive among them. Since its founding the editors had consistently published articles by a wide range of authors both national and international (Post 1978: 215–19). This was characteristic of the era: as Leslie James has shown, whether publishing syndicated pieces, reprinting authors' articles from other media, or simple plagiarism, the black Atlantic was characterised by a rampant exchange of text (James 2015).

(The *Daily Gleaner* – more staid, and with writer H. G. de Lisser as editor – had stuck more to news from Europe (Dalleo 2010: 59).) This chapter has already mentioned Padmore, Domingo and Mais; soon, Paul Robeson's name began to appear in *Public Opinion*'s pages.

By 1946 Robeson was a household name for people of African descent. Known initially for his artistic abilities, he had become a powerful voice for change in global black communities. Robeson represented a more radical vision of African American and black independence that seemed to hint that violence might be a pathway to freedom and redemption. *Public Opinion* had introduced Robeson to its readers in 1946 by recounting a meeting between him and President Truman. Robeson was part of a delegation that visited the president following an anti-lynching demonstration in Washington that drew 3,000 people. *Public Opinion* recounted how Truman had stated that Secretary of State James F. Byrnes required unequivocal support for his foreign policy objectives. Robeson had firmly disagreed: 'I'm sorry to disagree Mr. President . . . How can Secretary Byrnes stand up in the Council of Nations as the representative of a land of freedom when lynchings and discrimination are common occurrences in that land?' (Robeson 1946: 6, 8). He continued with fiery words:

> The temper of the Negro is changed, Mr. President . . . Negro war veterans, particularly, who fought for freedom want to know that they can have freedom in their own country. If they can't have protection from VIOLENCE AND INTOLERANCE on the local level then they want to know they have federal protection. (Robeson 1946: 6, 8)

The article then continued: 'At this point the President accused Robeson of threatening', and soon after ended the meeting (Robeson 1946: 6, 8).

Robeson was the inspiration for a noticeable ratcheting up of *Public Opinion*'s rhetoric against Britain and its empire. On 8 November 1946, the newspaper took on the question of slavery. It ran the following headline: 'Slavery Exists in South Africa' (though self-governing, South Africa remained part of the British Commonwealth). At the head of the page, it described Robeson as a 'great artist . . . [but also] a great human being, socialist and internationalist' ('Slavery' 1946: 15). Because he believed in the 'essential equality of men and women', it was an extraordinary affront that Britain was 'one of the greatest enslavers of human beings' ('Slavery' 1946: 15). The article on Robeson was accompanied by a reprinted editorial from the British *Socialist Leader*. It described the 300,000 'slaves' toiling in South Africa's gold mines, and the appalling conditions in which they worked ('Slavery' 1946: 15). To use its history of slavery as a way to attack the British Empire was part of a longer historical trajectory that spanned the globe across several hundred years (Peterson 2010). It was an effort both to attack the colonial system, and also to shock the British conscience at home into taking action. The latter, in particular, was a common tactic to sow discord in Britain and expand awareness there regarding indignities in the colonies.[6] But in Jamaica, this was an important moment: *Public Opinion* had brought the topic of slavery into middle-class discourse, a rare event indeed, for it was a topic that was historically the bailiwick of lower-class Jamaicans.

In Jamaica, the history of slavery – and raising it in public – was tremendously powerful. The all-encompassing experience of slavery sat at the core of Jamaican society, with its population over 90 per cent black. The cultural theorist Stuart Hall – aged fourteen in 1946 – remembered the institution and its successor, colonialism, as 'dominating, [and] recurring' in the Jamaican worldview (Hall 2017: 65). In the 1920s and 1930s, supporters of Marcus Garvey had brought the experience of slavery into public discourse, fusing that history with contemporary activism in a way that pre-dated the other Caribbean islands. Rastafari – some of whose leaders were voracious readers – had derived inspiration from Garvey's ideas, long using the term 'slavery' to describe their bondage in 'Babylon'. They viewed themselves as the children of Egypt, who would soon undertake exodus to Africa. By the early 1960s, Rastafari groups were writing letters to the British monarch and prime minister describing their forcible removal from Africa in previous centuries as slaves. This removal, they argued, meant that the British Crown had a responsibility to 'repatriate' them to Africa.[7] It was into this heady rhetoric that *Public Opinion* tapped.

By 1947, Robeson was writing more regularly in the newspaper, providing a foil of sorts for George Padmore. Robeson appears to have authored a proportion of his articles for *Public Opinion* alone which were not syndicated or borrowed from other publications. Both Robeson and Padmore devoted at least half of their columns to discussing global movements of workers and the possibilities of change driven by strikes or labour protests (Robeson 1947: 9). Both Robeson and Padmore sympathised with communism to some degree and shared a fascination with the Soviet Union. Robeson's interest in (and visits to) the Soviet Union, indeed, would soon lead to his blacklisting in the United States. Both men saw the potential for racial equality that the Soviet system possessed, though Padmore had long broken with the Comintern and Robeson was aware of its shortcomings. Both men had been shocked by the Soviet Union's violent acts, but appreciated that it was also a vocal opponent of colonialism.[8]

But Pan-Africanism and worker movements could be fused, subjects thought through at length in Padmore's *Pan-Africanism or Communism?* (1956). This was made emphatically clear in 1947 when the Pan African Labour Conference met in Dakar under the umbrella of the recently created World Federation of Trade Unions (WFTU). News of the meeting was accompanied in *Public Opinion* with an article by Robeson: 'African Workers are Least Privileged of All Mankind,' raged his headline. Its contents included descriptions of difficulties facing South African mine workers, a general strike in Nigeria, strikes in Northern Rhodesia, and mentions of workers in Uganda, Belgian Congo and French West Africa. It was these troubles, explained Robeson, that had inspired the WFTU to gather the first Pan-African labour meeting (Robeson 1947: 9).

Robeson's writings helped drive a more direct advocacy of Pan-Africanist doctrine in the pages of *Public Opinion*. In late 1946, the newspaper had begun producing articles authored by – or about – prominent Africans.[9] These were accompanied by discourses on the origins of black music, poems by Langston Hughes and Louise Bennett, and profiles of luminaries such as Richard Wright. And before leaving Jamaica, Domingo had informed his readership about *Pan-Africa*, a monthly magazine which began publication in January 1947. It was created and produced by T. Ras Makonnen – the Guyanese Pan-Africanist, then based in London – and featured Padmore on the editorial board and as a frequent contributor. Domingo provided specific instructions to his Jamaican readers for how they might order copies. He introduced the new magazine by reminding his readers of a story *Public Opinion* had covered closely over the past several months. A Jamaican-born Royal Air Force airman, Donald Beard, had been accused of murder. Norman Manley had travelled to England to defend him successfully in a case that was widely viewed as representing the racism Jamaicans faced in Britain. 'Negroes in England are organized for self-defense and to represent the cause of their people,' noted Domingo, echoing the language of Paul Robeson (Domingo 1947: 5).

But for George Padmore, anti-colonialism and at times even Pan-Africanism could include other non-white peoples of the world beyond those of African descent. The colonial system was, of course, a global issue. In 1947, *Public Opinion* began a series of articles about the Indonesian anti-colonial battle against the Dutch. One was reprinted from Makonnen's *Pan-Africa*, which blamed colonialism for the conflict (Ali 1947: 6). And when Padmore joined the fray, he suggested that the 'Coloured World' should unite to attack colonialism in all its manifestations (Padmore 1949: 5). Pivoting between the global/anti-colonial and the Pan-African meant that Padmore was straddling two worlds. The following decade, St. Clair Drake drew Padmore's attention to this distinction after he read *Pan-Africanism or Communism?* 'I looked at his book,' remembered Drake, 'and the first whole part of it was about Marcus Garvey.' 'Look, you're talking about blackness throughout the whole first part,' he told Padmore, but then in the second part, 'now you're saying that an African is anybody who believes in "one man one vote"' (Shepperson and Drake 2008: 49).

The following decade, Padmore's mixed approach was most clearly manifested through the lens of Mau Mau. During the 1950s, the Kenyan conflict pitted Mau Mau guerrillas in a vicious war against Britain and its allies. Padmore seemed unsure how to respond. He devoted chapters 13 and 14 of *Pan-Africanism or Communism?* to explicating the causes and events of Mau Mau, but maintained that among colonial systems, the British provided 'the greatest possibility for dependent peoples to attain self-determination along constitutional lines' (Padmore 1956: 186). He wrote 'Mau Mau!' on a Christmas card to Drake in 1955, showing his 'approval' of the movement, noted the African American scholar, while consistently lauding Gandhi's non-violence (James 2015: 125; Shepperson and Drake 2008: 39). Padmore knew the British were likely to grant independence and power to non-violent nationalist movements, and sympathised with Kwame Nkrumah's non-violence in Ghana. But he also saw the power that movements like Mau Mau possessed for marginalised peoples around the world. Empires, he knew, could be pressured into action and change.

While Padmore's inclusive approach was broadly encompassing of the Caribbean's population diversity, it was problematic for many in Jamaica. As I have argued elsewhere, *Public Opinion*'s Pan-Africanist vision – however radical for middle-class Jamaica – was roundly rejected by many poorer, black Jamaicans. Marginalised Jamaicans had emphatically sided with the Mau Mau cause, while middle- and upper-class people had wanted little to do with the movement. Mau Mau's violent, underdog struggle had resonated deeply with those Jamaicans who had rejected and attacked moderate Pan-Africanist viewpoints such as those expressed by Padmore or radio commentator and author Peter Abrahams (Osborne 2020: 733–6). For many Garveyites and their children, who would soon join the Black Power movement, men like Padmore were simply too moderate for their taste.

But though *Public Opinion*'s stance was too moderate for some, it remained a vital source of news on Africa for the Jamaican public. During the 1940s and 1950s, Jamaica's government had on several occasions investigated the possibilities of formal migration to Liberia and other regions of Africa.[10] It was *Public Opinion* whose editors informed its readers about Liberia's history; about potential settlement plans; and how to reach out to the Universal Negro Improvement Association for additional information ('Liberia' 1948: 9). (Liberian President V. S. Tubman's visit to Jamaica in 1954 was in some ways a dress rehearsal for the extraordinary arrival of Haile Selassie in 1966.) While Liberia was arguably the most viable option for emigration, Ethiopia remained the crown jewel of the continent for Rastafari and other Africanists alike. Editors at *Public Opinion* – aware of the fascination Jamaicans had held for Ethiopia since Mussolini's invasion in 1935 – kept it constantly in *Public Opinion*'s pages. Authors typically recalled Ethiopia's ancient history as a way to lend weight to its geopolitical claims, from access to the sea to international recognition ('Ethiopia Now' 1947: 5). Ethiopia's well-known 3,000-year-old empire – of an 'Ancient African Civilization' – gave it a historical authority that far superseded even the colonial powers ('Ancient' 1950: 3).

By the mid-1950s, W. A. Domingo could note in a guest column for the *Star* that 'It used to be fashionable for Jamaicans of colour to boast of their European connections, however slight, while deprecating or completely ignoring their ties with . . . Africa' (Domingo 1954: 4). But by 1954 Jamaican politicians had begun to realise that playing up African connections was a way to gain traction with the colony's youth. Notions of Africa and Pan-Africanism were raised and debated across the island, with *Public Opinion*, Domingo and Padmore playing a central role in bringing the topics to mainstream debate after the war's end. There is sometimes a sense in the historiography of the black Atlantic that the heady years of Garvey were followed by something of a lull before the explosion of Black Power swept the Caribbean. But as this chapter demonstrates, the reality was quite different. Jamaicans read, debated and discussed socialism and Pan-Africanism; considered the future of their nation and the black race; and contributed to a vibrant discourse about what the future should hold at the twilight of empire.

Notes

1. For an accessible biography of Garvey, see Grant 2008. Robert Hill's edited collections featuring over 30,000 documents on Garvey and the UNIA are unparalleled (Hill 1983–2016).
2. For one classic exposition of this theme by soldier Waruhiu Itote, see Osborne 2015: 41–6.
3. On Amy Jacques Garvey and other related black female activists, see Blain 2018.
4. In May 1959, market workers threw stones at a policeman who had attacked a Rastaman (Osborne 2020: 740).
5. Barry Chevannes (1994) has discussed the importance of texts and reading for Rastafari.
6. See, for instance, the article by *Public Opinion*'s new editor Claude Robinson (1947: 8).
7. For examples of how adept Rastafari were at utilising colonial institutions to press their cause, see Rastafari Brethren 1961; for further discussion, see Osborne 2021.
8. For a longer discussion of Padmore's thinking on the Soviet Union, see James 2015: 99–119.
9. See, for instance, 'African Calls' 1946: 13.
10. See the evidence contained in Ministry Paper 1961.

Bibliography

'African Calls on World to Give His People a Voice' (1946), *Public Opinion*, 16 November, 13.
Ali, M. (1947), 'The Historical Facts Behind the Indonesian Struggle', *Public Opinion*, 25 October, 6.
'Ancient African Civilization: Buried Towns Found in Ethiopia' (1950), *Public Opinion*, 1 November, 3.
Blain, Keisha (2018), *Set the World on Fire: Black Nationalist Women and the Global Struggle for Freedom*, Philadelphia: University of Pennsylvania Press.
Chevannes, Barry (1994), *Rastafari: Roots and Ideology*, Syracuse: Syracuse University Press.
Dalleo, Raphael (2010), 'The public sphere and Jamaican anticolonial politics: *Public Opinion*, *Focus*, and the place of the literary', *Small Axe*, 14.2, 56–82.
Domingo, W. A. (1945a), 'Speaking Out Loud', *Public Opinion*, 31 October, 3.
—— (1945b), 'Sparks From My Anvil: Here at Home', *Public Opinion*, 5 December, 3.
—— (1945c), 'What Imperialists Fear Most', *Public Opinion*, 6 December, 3–4.
—— (1947), '"Pan Africa": A New Monthly Magazine', *Public Opinion*, 25 January, 5.
—— (1954), 'Jamaica's Share in Liberia', *Star*, 31 December, 4.
'Ethiopia Now Has Her Ships And Flag On Sea' (1947), *Public Opinion*, 27 December, 5.
Gikandi, Simon (2000), 'Pan-Africanism and cosmopolitanism: The case of Jomo Kenyatta', *English Studies in Africa*, 43.3, 3–27.
Grant, Colin (2008), *Negro with a Hat: The Rise and Fall of Marcus Garvey*, Oxford: Oxford University Press.
Hall, Stuart (2017), *Familiar Stranger: A Life Between Two Islands*, Durham, NC: Duke University Press.
Hill, Robert (ed.) (1983–2016), *The Marcus Garvey and Universal Negro Improvement Association Papers*, 13 vols, Berkeley: University of California Press; Chapel Hill: University of North Carolina Press.
James, Leslie (2015), *George Padmore and Decolonization from Below: Pan-Africanism, the Cold War, and the End of Empire*, New York: Palgrave Macmillan.
'Liberia: Land of Promise' (1948), *Public Opinion*, 24 April, 9.
Mais, Roger (1944), 'Now We Know', *Public Opinion*, 11 July, 1.
—— (1945), 'Incident at Springfield', *Public Opinion*, 3 December, 3.
Ministry Paper (1961), Mission to Africa, Jamaica National Archives, 1B/5/76/4/403/xlii.
Ognimod (1946), 'Make the Coronation Market Sanitary', *Public Opinion*, 14 December, 15.
—— (1947), 'Nigerian Notes', *Public Opinion*, 5 April, 8.
Osborne, Myles (ed.) (2015), *The Life and Times of General China: Mau Mau and the End of Empire in Kenya*, Princeton, NJ: Markus Wiener Publishers.
—— (2020), '"Mau Mau are Angels . . . Sent by Haile Selassie": A Kenyan war in Jamaica', *Comparative Studies in Society and History*, 62.4, 714–44.
—— (2021), 'Rites, rights, Rastafari! Statehood and statecraft in Jamaica, c. 1930–1961', *Journal of Social History*, 55.1, 207–25.
Padmore, George (1945a), 'Nigerians Threaten Strikes Unless Richards Recalled', *Public Opinion*, 12 October, 2.
—— (1945b), 'African Plan to Overthrow British Rule Discovered', *Public Opinion*, 20 October, 2.
—— (1945c), 'British Plan Self Government for Ceylon', *Public Opinion*, 22 October, 2.
—— (1945d), 'Royal Commission's Report Startles British Public', *Public Opinion*, 23 October, 2.
—— (1945e), 'Pan-African Congress to Rush Negroes' Uplift', *Public Opinion*, 24 October, 2.
—— (1949), 'Background to Indonesia: Dutch Attack Unifies Coloured World', *Public Opinion*, 15 January, 5.

—— (1956), *Pan-Africanism or Communism? The Coming Struggle for Africa*, London: D. Dobson.
Peterson, Derek R. (ed.) (2010), *Abolitionism and Imperialism in Britain, Africa, and the Atlantic*, Athens: Ohio University Press.
Post, Ken (1978), *Arise Ye Starvelings: The Jamaican Labour Rebellion of 1938 and its Aftermath*, Boston: Martinus Nijhoff.
Rastafari Brethren of Jamaica (1961), Letter to HRH Queen Elizabeth II, 14 April, National Archives of the United Kingdom, CO 1031/3995.
Robeson, Paul (1946), 'Paul Robeson Rubs Truman in Long Lynching Interview', *Public Opinion*, 30 September, 6, 8.
—— (1947), 'African Workers are Least Privileged of All Mankind', *Public Opinion*, 3 May, 9.
Robinson, Claude (1947), 'Why Don't Englishmen Tell Their People the Truth About the Colonies', *Public Opinion*, 6 December, 8.
Shepperson, George, and St. Clair Drake (2008), 'The Fifth Pan-African Conference, 1945 and the All African Peoples' Congress, 1958', *Contributions in Black Studies*, 8, 35–66.
'Slavery Exists in South Africa' (1946), *Public Opinion*, 8 November, 15.
'The Spirit of Freedom Abroad' (1957), *Public Opinion*, 16 March, 1.
Timm, Birte (2016), *Nationalists Abroad: The Jamaica Progressive League and the Foundations of Jamaican Independence*, Kingston: Ian Randle Publishers.
Watson, Roxanne (2012), '"Now We Know": The trial of Roger Mais and *Public Opinion* in Jamaica, 1944', *Journal of Caribbean History*, 46.2, 183–211.

35

CITIZENSHIP, RESPONSIBILITY AND LITERARY CULTURE IN THE UNIVERSITY PERIODICAL IN EASTERN AFRICA: SPACES OF SOCIAL PRODUCTION IN *BUSARA* AND ITS NETWORKS

Madhu Krishnan

THIS CHAPTER EXPLORES the case study of *Busara*, a students' literary magazine based at University College Nairobi (later the University of Nairobi), which began its life in 1967 under the name of *Nexus* before changing to *Busara* in 1969. Despite some increasing interest in the periodical, *Busara*, like most student magazines of the time, remains relatively understudied compared with the larger and more visible East African publications, such as *Transition*. Yet, as this chapter will explore, *Busara* remains important as a platform firmly situated within the larger intellectual and creative networks of its era, displaying a deep entanglement with the broader debates around post-independence identity and the role of art and creativity in the forging of national, regional and international African identities. To date, the most significant scholarly work on *Busara* remains Mwangi Macharia's archival research into the publication. As Macharia, writing on *Busara*'s origins, notes:

> In an apparent response to the politics of cultural production in East Africa at the time, the magazine only published four issues in 1967 and 1968 using the name *Nexus*. According to Awori wa Kataka and Richard Gacheche, the first editors of *Busara* after this change of name, the choice of the new name was in step with other publications which adopted Kiswahili names around the same time. *Penpoint* and *Darlite* changed their names to *Dhana* and *Umma*, respectively. (Macharia 2021: 229)

From the outset, then, *Busara* must be situated within the wider political and cultural context from which it appeared and to which it contributed. In particular, as Macharia notes, the very fact of its name change in the late 1960s, contemporary with that of its sister publications in Kampala and Dar es Salaam, also coincided with the call for the abolition of the English department in favour of an Africa-centred Department of Literature in 1968 by Ngũgĩ wa Thiong'o, Taban Lo Liyong and Henry Owuor-Anyumba, in what is now known as the Nairobi Revolution (Amoko 2010). Within its pages, *Busara* contained essays, fiction, reviews and poetry, which often took the form of long debates on a single text or provocation which persisted across multiple issues. Where, in its guise as *Nexus*, the periodical was primarily focused on creative writing and book reviews, *Busara*, in its new incarnation, would deliberately position itself as a platform for critical interventions and debate, a shift indicative of the broader movement towards self-analysis and criticality at the University and via the Nairobi Revolution more broadly. Like its sister publications in Kampala and Dar es Salaam, *Busara* was published under the auspices of the East African Publishing House and, from 1970–1, the East African Literature Bureau's Students' Book Writing programme, featuring writing from a wide range of authors including those who would go on to international acclaim and global visibility. By the mid-1970s, however, the publication's vitality began to wane, exacerbated by the fall of the East African Community (1977) and the closure of the East African Literature Bureau, leading to the termination of the publication.

It is difficult to ascertain the actual reach and circulation of *Busara*. Whilst the vast majority of contributions to the periodical came from within the University itself, featuring both staff – in early issues particularly expatriate staff – and students, a perusal of *Busara*'s table of contents shows pieces from writers outside of the University space, as far flung as the rest of the Eastern African community and its diasporas, particularly in the Americas. The question of circulation is further complicated by the extent to which issues of *Busara* would be shared amongst friends and classmates. *Busara* can thus be seen as a periodical which attempted to implicate itself within the larger struggle for the development of a distinctly East African, yet global, literary sensibility, despite its own material limitations. Due largely to challenges of marketing and infrastructure, the majority of *Busara*'s readership would have come from the University itself. At the same time, issues contained calls for subscriptions, and editorial essays demonstrate a felt desire to nurture wider readerships as part of a world-spanning critical-citational community. Gikandi argues that

> the identity of East African literature was to be determined in university departments and literary journals and was thus to reflect the interests and anxieties of a small elite. And since this elite was to manage the institutions of literary production after decolonization, their perspective on what was – or was not – literature was going to be seminal in the shaping of literary culture in East Africa. (Gikandi 2008: 427)

As a space, then, the university would prove to be a crucial node in the constitution of East African literature, both ideologically and as a market category. While the most significant location in this regard was Uganda's Makerere University, Nairobi remains a critical site through which to understand the development of East African literature and, particularly, the ideological push back against a curriculum and aesthetic landscape based on the 'Great Tradition' of European letters. In physical terms, *Busara* was a striking contribution to this struggle, with a bright yellow cover featuring a stylised human face and hands (see Plate 4). Text-based and without illustrations, the layout and organisation of contents shows a curatorial care in line with the publication's self-proclaimed interest in the development of intellectual social formations. Despite critical claims that early East African literature offered few outlets for women writers, moreover, *Busara*, from the start, featured a regular cast of contributors across genders.

As this volume makes clear, and as numerous commentators have noted, print cultures played an important role in the early years of independence. In their contribution to *The Novel in Africa and the Caribbean since 1950*, Simon Gikandi and Maurice Vambe suggest, following Watt's foundational work on the rise of the novel as a form, that the early European language novel in Africa can be seen as arising from a tripartite scheme defined as 'philosophical transformation', 'expansion of literacy' and the emergence of the 'modern individual' under 'the new capitalist culture' during the height of the colonial invasion in the mid-1800s (Gikandi and Vambe 2016: 3–4). As a form, then, the novel was – and arguably remains – inextricably intertwined with the anxieties of an imported post-Enlightenment order, one itself deeply implicated in the colonial project. If the novel remains an ultimately bourgeois form, in the larger world of print cultures (particularly periodicals) the status of literature appears more ambivalent. With its formal diversity, multitude of contributors from various corners of the world, and its nevertheless firm rooting in the University and region, *Busara*, like many of its contemporary publications, offers the potential, if not always the reality, for alternative modes of world-formation. Though less visible in public terms, such periodicals demonstrate lateral modes for negotiating the demands of so-called 'colonial modernity' and the quest for post-independence sovereignty.

Much has been written about the ways in which so-called 'popular' literature empowered ordinary individuals to negotiate the complexities and contradictions of everyday life, offering an outlet for agency under hegemonic domination and a medium against which to trouble simplistic notions of acculturation (Barber 2017: 1–2). Yet, as Richard Pierce notes in his study of Ghanaian popular literature, 'there is . . . another body of popular literature . . . that now has more sociological significance . . . : the creative writing that is published in newspapers and magazines' (Pierce 1997: 81). Because of its flexibility (in material terms), its relatively lower cost, and its more porous modes of authorship and circulation, periodical writing offers one means through which sustained, long-term and multivocal debate on the nature of the literary, the critical, the intellectual and the subject and society could be borne out. At the same time, much of recent scholarship has focused on the newspaper and the small (or little) magazine as sites through which publics and networks were forged in the post-independence period (Bulson 2017; Musandu 2018; Peterson et al. 2016). As Bulson notes, small magazines are significant for what they do 'individually to revolutionize literary production and consumption in their respective nations, regions, and continents [and] also about how together they [work] within and against an emerging literary network' (Bulson 2017: 2). Equally, following Musandu, the newspaper in East Africa can be seen as the staging ground upon which 'the political and economic elite of a colonized country, also en route towards capitalism from the end of the nineteenth century, utilized the print press to facilitate their entry and dominance within the emerging system' (Musandu 2018: 4).

By contrast, considerably less attention has been paid to the university periodical in particular, as a genre of its own. This is in no doubt due to the more obviously ambiguous nature of the university periodical as a material and institutional form. Unlike the small magazine – deliberately avant-garde and striving for autonomy – or the newspaper – largely institutionalised and often aligned with the state and elites – university periodicals held a place far less straightforward to define. In large part, of course, this is due to the very structure of the university in Africa, with its deep ties to the British higher educational system and the so-called 'civilising mission' of colonialism. In the case of *Busara*, for instance, no analysis of the periodical can neglect the importance of university faculty in its founding and running, particularly faculty from outside of the African continent. As Macharia observes, 'its founding editors were two students – Leonard Kibera and Amin Kassam – while the Editorial Board was constituted by James Stewart, the then Head of English Department at the University College, as well as fellow staff members, Adrian Roscoe and Angus Calder' (Macharia 2021: 230). Indeed, even the associated writers' club run initially by Taban Lo Liyong and later by Chris Wanjala was, as it has now been documented, based on Lo Liyong's experience of the Iowa Writers' Workshop, where he took an MA in Creative Writing. Following his return from Iowa, Lo Liyong founded the Nairobi Writers' Workshop, from which *Busara* sprang, featuring regular meetings at the Paa ya Paa art gallery and fostering a critical community. This is crucial background to the ethos of the periodical, shaped, as it were, by Lo Liyong's own concerns over the arrested development of East African literature – what Gikandi has characterised as 'the anxiety of influence' and 'the inferiority complex' of East African writing (Gikandi 2008: 426) versus that of West and Southern Africa – and a disdain for the straightforward nationalism of much nascent East African writing, on the one hand, and the vacuous nativism of the Négritude movement, on the other. Moreover, *Busara*, though originally published by the East African Publishing House, by 1970 was given over to the East African Literature Bureau, itself a product of the colonial publishing market.

It is crucial to recall, as Newell points out in her study of West African literatures, that though 'in the field of literature, these real economic imbalances between North and South have led African authors towards European and American publishing houses and away from their own national publishers' (Newell 2006: 5), it is equally the case that any 'emphasis on the "local" . . . is not intended to mark out a space of . . . African authenticity . . . against which international readings are judged to be true or false' (Newell 2006: 7). In the case of *Busara*, what comes to the fore is the tremendously complex ways in which literary networks operated, often traversing lines of connection, troubling simple dichotomies of local and global, as such. Within a single volume of the periodical, for instance, on which I will focus my readings in this chapter, contributor names span the canonical 'founders' of East African literature as a market category, emerging writers, students and more. Across the first issue of the third volume of the journal, published in 1970, for instance, are pieces by writers described variously as students at the University of Nairobi; lecturers from departments spanning the humanities and social sciences; graduate students based in the United States and Canada; an American Peace Corps volunteer based in Latin America; an established senior editor with Oxford University Press; established writers including one at the Iowa Writers' Workshop; a school teacher; and more. Other issues in that volume include contributions from working professionals, housewives, musicians, journalists and radio broadcasters. Unsurprisingly, a number of names reappear across multiple issues, indicating the existence of a literary network which, whilst diffuse, nonetheless retained a sense of a core team, many of whom were also notable for their editorial contributions to the publication (for an example, see Plate 5). In addition to this material diffusion, moreover, *Busara* shows a similar outward-emanating geographical orientation in its contents; though the majority of stories, poems and essays focus on the Eastern African region, within appear allusions to literary and intellectual traditions from China to Eastern Europe to the Soviet Union and beyond, constituting a world-spanning creative-critical landscape nonetheless firmly centred in its own place.

At the formal level, too, *Busara* explores a wide range of genres, with issues including fiction pieces, poems, book reviews and general criticism. While the main language of the journal was English, a significant minority of pieces across all genres appear in Kiswahili, particularly poetry and fiction, indicating a further linguistic complexity in the functioning of a Pan-Africanist literary network spread beyond the region and the continent. The following example illustrates the complexity within which *Busara*'s own intellectual and aesthetic formations emerged and shifted over time. Titled 'Editorial', this poetic text opens the first issue of *Busara*'s third volume, published in 1970, with the following stanzas:

> There was a general consensus that all should
> return to the shadows (with Robert Serumaga). That
> self-realization of creativity, of commitment
> and individualism, of the writer and the
> reader, of the singers and the audience –
> that was the foetus from Kampala.
>
> In the light of the present there is such a
> need, even of self-actualization, of
> intellectual honesty, and again of
> Commitment. As to what one should be
> committed to, honestly, I do not know, and I
> may not know in the farthest future. (Anon. 1970, *Busara*: 3–4)

Setting itself up as a search for commitment, for knowledge and for an understanding of the role of art and creativity in the forging of society, the speaker self-consciously positions themself as an interlocutor in a larger, more ambivalent debate on the nature of post-independence African identity. The piece continues with a self-reflective comment on the labours of its own work, presumably a reference to the complexities of forging an editorial identity in a context of fragmentation and negotiation:

> But then all these are no easy tasks!
> Okot has assayed to uncover the lid of the
> Village pot tried to show the van transporting
> People from the village citywards, of course
> Ocol is the pilot. (Anon. 1970, *Busara*: 4)

Setting up the metaphor of the journey between village and city, 'Editorial' continues to emphasise its larger themes of the struggle for understanding, foregrounding the difficulty of the task at the interstices of multiple social systems, modes of organisation and potential futurity. As it continues, moreover, the poem unspools a list of those unable to match this task:

> In the course of the journey things were bound
> to happen. And we knew it. Before we reached the
> first milestone someone dropped. He was the
> spare driver. He had to have

> some high level talks with colleagues at the Hilton . . .
> Some ladies dropped out to. The course was too
> hard or the change was too sudden. (Anon. 1970, *Busara*: 4)

Tellingly, the drivers of this 'van' are the central figures of Okot p'Bitek, Ngũgĩ, Okello Oculi, Philip Ochieng and Tejani, reinforcing the central metaphor as one about the struggle for culture, autonomy and society, whilst at the same time situating the editorial itself within its own kind of great tradition, distinct from the 'Great Tradition' of British literature and the official school curriculum. At the same time that the poem cannot be said to be experimental in any real sense, moreover, its use of lyric form in the first-person plural – a sort of lyric 'we' – indicates a desire for transformation, turning the introspective and individualist into something more collective.

What is striking, then, is how in this relatively small, localised literary magazine – one whose pages attest to the development of a literary consciousness rooted deeply in the place, or location, of the English department at one university in a particular time period, as well as within the larger institutional structures of the academy – comes a far larger statement about the role played by cultural production in the forging of a post-independence African reality, drawing in equal parts on the material and the symbolic in its constitution. *Busara* thus forms part of a larger network of literary magazines which developed in the region in this period, all of which in some way developed lines of literary and aesthetic production with links to the so-called 'Great Tradition' of anglophone letters, on the one hand, and yet striving for an indigenous idiom of their own, on the other.

Writing on the aesthetics of *Busara*, Macharia contends that 'The students' magazine created space for young and aspiring writers to experiment with form and content in creative and critical writing. These students either deliberately or inadvertently imitated the writings of the works they had read' (Macharia 2021: 231). Yet, as the example of 'Editorial' shows, a more complex formal picture emerges, one which draws on a broad range of reference, lyric form and metaphor and remains firmly rooted in an Eastern African intellectual tradition. What emerges, then, is less imitative or derivative and more indicative of what Stephanie Bosch Santana calls 'migrant forms'. For Bosch Santana, migrant forms 'necessitat[e] more flexible and culturally relevant understandings of literary form in order to account for them . . . since they are structured by, feature, and textualize such processes of continuous migration', both in the literal sense and in the sense in which narrative and textual forms themselves remain subject to varying and overlapping modes of circulation and adaptation (Santana 2014: 168).

Indeed, as this editorial poem demonstrates, a hybrid logic is evident within the pages of the journal, one which turns away from the colonial paradigm and its attendant geographies to seek a form of self-fashioning – or 'self-actualisation', as these brief stanzas state – even as it remains rooted within that same paradigm. This is a logic which strives to move beyond the boundaries of a normative Enlightenment-derived conceptual apparatus in order to re-map the topographies of literary commitment. Citing Robert Serumaga, the founder of Uganda's National Theatre and a writer whose works leverage a form of narrative absurdism to attest to the stagnation of the nascent Ugandan state under its post-independence leadership, the range of reference in 'Editorial' gestures toward the experimental, even as its formalism does not.

Later in the editorial, figures as varied as Grace Ogot and Okot p'Bitek and his fictional figures Ocol and Lawino are equally called upon, indicating an allegiance to a different kind of idiom or discursive tradition. The editorial may thus be read as invoking specifically localised images, figures and idioms inflected by the aesthetic forms of modernism under the purview of a specifically East African mode of transnationalism or black internationalism whose topographies gesture towards a longer history of interconnectivity and solidarity which colonialist paradigms of knowledge production cannot fully admit and which, as the uncertainty of the second stanza's last lines indicate, function through the future anterior of messianic time. Evoking the singularity of the creative practitioner in the same breath as their audiences, the editorial evinces the struggle against the forms of individualism championed in the earliest days of neoliberalist thought, rejecting the developmentalist bias towards the isolated and exceptional private mind in favour of a form of individualism whose appearance can only occur through a larger form of social embeddedness and commitment, reaffirmed in the editorial's closing lines:

> As we return to the shadows, singing songs of dead lambs,
> examining the Experience(s) we have brought forth and taking
> the Last Word(s) about them, we may
> falter, but I suppose it is O.K. for even when
> there is no bride price we still go, for even the
> old generator will start. Of course it will electrocute a
> few but that is fine. But since Africa is kind,
> let us allow Lawino to remain with her sages in
> the limbo, at least if she would not stand the city.
> After all, certain violinists still meditate down
> there (although these days I hear we can have
> limbos without graves!). (Anon. 1970, *Busara*: 4)

The fictional stories published in *Busara* are largely realist in form. With titles such as 'The Girl in the Green Cardigan', 'The Immortal Generation', 'Ngethe', 'A Dear Foe', 'Busara ndiyo Dawa Iliyomfaa' and 'The Child and the Giant', stories both in English (the majority) and in Kiswahili are largely didactic, often exploring themes of moralism, modernity and the tension between city and village life. A number of stories serve as cautionary tales, outlining the dangers of contemporary life, and still more emphasise conflict between the genders. Yet, particularly as it matured as a periodical, *Busara*'s contents were dominated less by fiction and more by critical writing, book reviews and commentary.

A significant feature of *Busara*, then, is its ambitions as a space for critical dialogue and debate. Across issues, pieces not only engage with more visible and widely circulated canonical texts through extended essays and book reviews, but articles both within and across subsequent issues also respond to, and often challenge, one another. A significant example of this appears in issue four of volume three, published in 1971. In this issue appears a longform essay by Atieno-Odhiambo (a graduate of Makerere and the University of Nairobi, whose contributor biography also lists him as a postgraduate student in Oxford), entitled 'The Dead End of Uhuru Worship'. A review of Okot p'Bitek's *Song of Prisoner*, the piece appears immediately after a short anthropological piece by the latter, 'Acoli Funeral', which provides an exegesis of Acoli burial rites.

Atieno-Odhiambo's review opens by situating *Song of Prisoner* within its larger material context, arguing that the work 'is too important to be discussed independently of some of the major political and moral issues symbolised by its very publication, nearly a decade after independence in East Africa' (1971: 51). Immediately, then, the review positions itself not merely as a literary exercise, but as an exercise in broader socio-political and cultural critique in a manner recalling Raymond Williams's assertions that 'it is often through art that the society expresses its sense of being a society' (2013: 50) and that 'art comes to us as part of our actual growth, not entering a "special area" of the mind but acting on and interacting with our whole personal and social organisation' (2013: 53). Atieno-Odhiambo's essay, then, sets out its central arguments through an extended analysis of the intersections between planning, development and independence, paying specific attention to the case of the Congo and Patrice Lumumba, to whom p'Bitek's work is dedicated. The essay, a detailed analysis of which is beyond the scope of this chapter, engages in a series of close readings framed by socio-political and historically informed polemics on the role of the intellectual, the question of the individual and the collective, and questions of power. With a range of reference that spans from Marx to Fanon, it ultimately seeks to foreground what it sees as the moral, intellectual and political weaknesses of its subject via an argument for the role of the writer as organic and engaged intellectual.

Critically, however, 'The Dead End of Uhuru Worship' is immediately followed by a second piece by Albert Ojuka, a columnist with the *Sunday Nation* newspaper, titled 'Futile Intellectualism: A Rejoinder to Atieno-Odhiambo'. The author of this piece, himself a subject of criticism in the original review essay, engages in a twelve-page, point-by-point refutation of the arguments in that piece, offering an oppositional position on the role of the intellectual, art and its implication in the larger socio-political organisation of the nation and region. Across these pieces, then, what emerges is a critical dialogue not just about literary value or quality, but about the ways in which literature, writing and intellectualism function as part of a larger whole. Tellingly, both pieces are highly personalised, critiquing specific individuals as well as texts, and occasionally falling into ad hominem attacks on their subjects. Polemical in tone, both nonetheless indicate a deep-seated engagement with a common sphere, if from diametrically opposed positions, which begins to unlock or uncover the traces of a structure of feeling. As Williams notes:

> This structure of feeling is the culture of a period: it is the particular living result of all the elements in the general organisation. And it is in this respect that the arts of a period, taking these to include characteristic approaches and tones in argument, are of major importance. (Williams 2013: 69)

Within the pages of *Busara*, then, what appears is a structure of feeling defined by intellectual and ideological struggle, where the specific role of the intellectual and their art serves major importance.

This is seen, too, in the first issue of volume three, where a piece by Ellen Mae Kitonga appears under the title 'Conrad's Image of African and Coloniser in Heart of Darkness'. The essay opens by situating itself as a response to an essay published in

Busara volume two, number two, 'The European Image of Africa and the African'. Mounting a defence of Conrad against the criticisms of racism in the older essay, Kitonga argues that any proposition of a 'distorted presentation' of Africans in *Heart of Darkness* 'must be regarded in artistic terms ... for Africa and the African serve both as a catalyst to the self-realization of Kurtz and Marlow and as a symbolic foil to the heart of darkness within the white man sent to "civilize" – and to exploit' (Kitonga 1970: 33). Of particular note is that this essay, published in 1970, seems to anticipate the by now well-known debates around Conrad's novella, spurred by Chinua Achebe's 1975 lecture, republished in 1988, 'An Image of Africa: Racism in Conrad's *Heart of Darkness*'. It is impossible to know whether Achebe himself would have read either Kitonga's essay or the one to which it replies, and yet a similar set of arguments and points of contention appear across these pieces (and, indeed, across responses to Achebe's own critique), an argument about intention, form, content and their wider socio-political implications.

Returning to volume three, issue one of *Busara*, Kitonga's piece is followed by Billy Ogana Wandera's 'A Word on the Last Word'. This piece critically examines Taban Lo Liyong's 'The Last Word' in order to construct an intervention into the ongoing debate around the relative merits of synthesism (or an African-inflected high modernism) and Négritude in the larger context of African philosophical thought, and is followed immediately by Amin Kassam's poem 'In Search of Knowledge'. As Moradewun Adejunmobi reminds us, 'publicness' operates across multiple levels, with differential levels of power:

> those subjects and objects that appear in public do so in a variety of ways: they are not all public in the same way. The different guises in which subjects and objects appear in public are often, though not necessarily, bound with a medium or conveyance that facilitates an encounter between a text or creative work and a public. (Adejunmobi 2020: 80)

In the case of a university periodical like *Busara*, 'publicness' might entail a smaller circulation or critical community, in material terms, while simultaneously functioning via wider, world-spanning intellectual networks in terms of its structure of feeling and its own ideological investments. In this manner, the kinds of critical and editorial discourse published in *Busara* demonstrate its larger entanglement in continent- and diaspora-wide debates around representation, responsibility and aesthetics. Taking the two examples of 'Conrad's Image' and 'The Dead End of Uhuru Worship', what begins to emerge is a sense of the university periodical not merely as a site of reductive or redundant imitation, nor as an inwards-looking institutional project, but as a crucial node in the constitution of a larger intellectual field of production. Tellingly, both examples demonstrate the ways in which *Busara* operated not through a single editorial ideology or orientation, but rather by positioning itself as a site of debate and inquiry, often in contentious terms. Though perhaps cut off from the larger and more visible intellectual networks of individuals like p'Bitek and Achebe, the younger writers and students published in *Busara* can nonetheless be positioned as part of a larger and more inclusive citational community engaged in rigorous and scholarly debates that are no less significant for their relative lack of visibility.

It is no coincidence that literary journals and magazines flourished in African universities in this period, particularly in Eastern Africa. A number of scholars have noted the ways in which universities functioned as crucibles for the development of intellectual cultures, literary trends and circuits of production, even as they were important sites for social production. Stephanie Newell notes the importance of what she terms 'paracolonial' networks – 'paracolonial' being used 'to describe the attitudes, aspirations and activities of non-elite readers who were neither the direct products of British colonialism nor the products of purely pre-colonial formations' (Newell 2002: 3) – in the production of structures of feeling and wider dispositions in the post-independence period. Certainly, the role played by university periodicals in this period acts as an apt exemplar of this phenomenon. Neither inevitably nor inextricably tied to the 'Great Tradition' of letters and British colonial curriculum, nor entirely autonomous in their forms, diction and preoccupations, university periodicals such as *Busara* demonstrate the complex networks, both discursive and ideological, through which different models of modernity and selfhood were being articulated at both the individual and collective levels. Moreover, they also demonstrate the deeply intertwined relationship between the more visible 'literary fiction' of the post-independence era and the wider and more diffuse intellectual and social networks with which they remained in dialogue. As the example of *Busara* shows, the university periodical was far more than an imitative version of 'high' literature, but rather an important, dynamic and often-contradictory platform and network for the creation of social forms and intellectual life.

Bibliography

Adejunmobi, Moradewun (2020), 'Abiola Irele and the publicness of African letters', *Journal of the African Literature Association*, 14.1, 72–89.

Amoko, Apollo Obonyo (2010), *Postcolonialism in the Wake of the Nairobi Revolution*, Basingstoke: Palgrave Macmillan.

Anon. (1970), 'Editorial', *Busara*, 3.1, 3–4.

Atieno-Odhiambo, E. S. (1971), 'The Dead End of Uhuru Worship', *Busara*, 3.4, 51–65.

Barber, Karin (2017), *A History of African Popular Culture*, Cambridge: Cambridge University Press.

Bosch Santana, Stephanie (2014), 'Migrant forms: *African Parade*'s new literary geographies', *Research in African Literatures*, 45.3, 167–87.

Bulson, Eric (2017), *Little Magazine, World Form*, New York: Columbia University Press.

Gikandi, Simon (2008), 'East African literature in English', in F. Abiola Irele and Simon Gikandi (eds), *The Cambridge History of African and Caribbean Literature, Volume 2*, Cambridge: Cambridge University Press, 425–44.

—— and Maurice Vambe (2016), 'The reinvention of the novel in Africa', in Simon Gikandi (ed.), *The Novel in Africa and the Caribbean since 1950*, Oxford: Oxford University Press, 3–19.

Kitonga, Ellen Mae (1970), 'Conrad's Image of African and Coloniser in Heart of Darkness', *Busara*, 3.1, 33–5.

Macharia, Mwangi (2021), '*Nexus/Busara* and the rise of modern Kenyan literature', *Social Dynamics*, 47.2, 228–42.

Musandu, Phoebe (2018), *Pressing Interests: The Agenda and Influence of a Colonial East African Newspaper Sector*, Montreal: McGill-Queen's University Press.

Newell, Stephanie (2002), *Literary Culture in Colonial Ghana: 'How to Play the Game of Life'*, Manchester: Manchester University Press.

—— (2006), *West African Literature: Ways of Reading*, Oxford: Oxford University Press.

Ojuka, Albert (1971), 'Futile Intellectualism: A Rejoinder to Atieno-Odhiambo', *Busara*, 3.4, 66–78.
Peterson, Derek R., Emma Hunter and Stephanie Newell (eds) (2016), *African Print Cultures: Newspapers and their Publics in the Twentieth Century*, Ann Arbor: University of Michigan Press.
Pierce, Richard (1997), 'Popular writing in Ghana: A sociology and rhetoric', in Karin Barber (ed.), *Readings in African Popular Culture*, Bloomington: Indiana University Press, 81–91.
Williams, Raymond (2013) [1961], *The Long Revolution*, Cardigan: Parthian.

Contributors

Tanya Agathocleous is Professor of English at Hunter College and the Graduate Center, CUNY, where she teaches classes on Victorian literature and on colonial and postcolonial studies. She is the author of *Urban Realism and the Cosmopolitan Imagination* (2011) and *Disaffected: Emotion, Sedition, and Colonial Law in the Anglosphere* (2021) and has edited Joseph Conrad's *The Secret Agent* for Broadview, a Penguin enhanced edition of *Great Expectations*, and Rokeya Hossain's *Sultana's Dream and Padmarag* for Penguin Classics.

G. Arunima is Professor at the Centre for Women's Studies, Jawaharlal Nehru University, New Delhi, and is at present the Director of the Kerala Council for Historical Research, Trivandrum, Kerala. Her research examines both the historical and the contemporary Kerala and India, focusing on cultural, visual and material texts, and the politics of the contemporary. Her publications include *There Comes Papa: Colonialism and the Transformation of Matriliny in Kerala, Malabar, c. 1850–1940* (2003); *The Hijab: Islam, Women and the Politics of Clothing* (2022); *Love and Revolution in the Twentieth-Century Colonial and Postcolonial World: Perspectives from South Asia and Southern Africa* (2021); and *He, My Beloved CJ*, a translation of Rosie Thomas's biography of C. J. Thomas (2018).

Karin Barber is Visiting Professor in Anthropology at the London School of Economics and Emeritus Professor of African Cultural Anthropology at the University of Birmingham. She taught and researched for many years in western Nigeria. Her research focuses on Yoruba oral literature, popular theatre and print culture, and she has also done wider comparative work on popular culture and the anthropology of texts. She was a founder member of the African Print Cultures Network. Her most recent books are *Print Culture and the First Yoruba Novel* (2012) and *A History of African Popular Culture* (2018).

Marina Bilbija is an Assistant Professor of English at Wesleyan University. Her research focuses on the role of print culture, more specifically, magazines and newspapers, in the making of Black internationalist publics in the nineteenth and early twentieth centuries. Together with Alex Lubin, she is the editor of the critical edition of Duse Mohamed Ali's 1934 novel *Ere Roosevelt Came: A Record of the Adventures of the Man in the Cloak* (2024). She is currently at work on a book on Black editorial practices in the Atlantic world.

Raphael Dalleo is Professor of English at Bucknell University. His book *American Imperialism's Undead: The Occupation of Haiti and the Rise of Caribbean Anticolonialism* won the Caribbean Studies Association's 2017 Gordon K. and Sibyl Lewis Award for best book. *American Imperialism's Undead* was completed with the support of an NEH-sponsored residency at the Schomburg Center for Research in Black Culture. His other books are *Caribbean Literature and the Public Sphere*, *Caribbean Literature in Transition, 1920–1970* (co-editor), *Bourdieu and Postcolonial Studies* (editor), *Haiti and the Americas* (co-editor), and *The Latino/a Canon and the Emergence of Post-Sixties Literature* (co-author).

Jonathan Derrick gained his PhD from the School of Oriental and African Studies. He has worked in Nigeria and elsewhere as editor, translator, indexer and academic, including a period as Lecturer in History at the University of Ilorin (1977–80). Besides contributing journal articles, he is co-author with Ralph Austen of *Middlemen of the Cameroons Rivers* (1999), and author of *Africa's 'Agitators': Militant Anti-Colonialism in Africa and the West, 1919 to 1939* (2008), *Africa, Empire and Fleet Street: Albert Cartwright and 'West Africa' magazine* (2017), and *Biafra in the News: The Nigerian Civil War Seen from a London Newsdesk* (2022).

Ruwanthi Edirisinghe is a PhD student at the Graduate Center, CUNY. Her research examines the historical and contemporary displacements of certain groups within the South Asian diaspora under liberal capitalism and its collusions with western and non-western nationalisms. Her interests span across postcolonial theory and literature, postcolonial South Asian diasporas, and Transnational Studies.

Michelle Elleray (Pākehā/white settler) is Associate Professor at the University of Guelph, Canada, and has published on queer film, settler literature, and Victorian literature of empire with a focus on Oceania. She is the author of *Victorian Coral Islands* (2020) and is currently researching English-language periodical accounts of Pacific Islanders who travelled to Britain in the mid-nineteenth century under the auspices of the London Missionary Society.

Chantelle Finaughty is a graphic designer and social media manager from Pretoria, South Africa. She studied Cultural History and Visual Studies. Her contribution to this book is from her master's study in Cultural History obtained from the University of Pretoria on the topic of 'Victorian Design and Visual Culture in the *Wesleyan Missionary Notices*, c. 1880–1902'.

David Finkelstein is a cultural historian who has published in areas related to print, labour and press history. Recent publications include *Movable Types: Roving Creative Printers of the Victorian World* (2018) and the edited *Edinburgh History of the British and Irish Press, Volume 2: Expansion and Evolution, 1800–1900* (2020), winner of the 2021 Robert and Vineta Colby Scholarly Book Prize for its contribution to the promotion of Victorian press studies.

Andrew Griffiths is Senior Lecturer in English Literature at the Open University and has previously taught at Plymouth University and Exeter University. He researches Victorian and Edwardian popular culture and empire. His current work explores the circulation of news through the British Empire during the nineteenth century. He is the author of *The New Journalism, the New Imperialism and the Fiction of Empire, 1870–1900* (2015).

Tony Hughes-d'Aeth is the Chair of Australian Literature at the University of Western Australia. His books include *Like Nothing on this Earth: A Literary History of the Wheatbelt* (2017), which won the Walter McRae Russell Prize for Australian literary scholarship, and *Paper Nation: The Story of the Picturesque Atlas of Australasia* (2001), which won the Ernest Scott and W. K. Hancock Prizes for Australian history. He is also the Director of the Westerly Centre, which publishes *Westerly Magazine*, a literary journal founded in 1956.

Emma Hunter is Professor of Global and African History, University of Edinburgh. She is the author of *Political Thought and the Public Sphere in Tanzania: Freedom, Democracy and Citizenship in the Era of Decolonization* (2015). She was a co-editor, with Derek Peterson and Stephanie Newell, of *African Print Cultures: Newspapers and their Publics in the Twentieth Century* (2016) and, with Leslie James, co-editor of a special issue of *Itinerario* on 'Colonial Public Spheres and Worlds of Print' (2020).

Sam Hutchinson received his PhD from the University of Western Australia in 2015, researching late nineteenth-century Australian colonial and British imperial history and print culture. He has since worked as a professional historian with the Waitangi Tribunal in Wellington, New Zealand, and as a researcher with the Western Australian Parliament. He is the author of *Settlers, War, and Empire in the Press: Unsettling News in Australia and Britain, 1863–1902* (2018).

David Johnson is Professor of Literature in the Department of English and Creative Writing at the Open University. He is the author of *Shakespeare and South Africa* (1996), *Imagining the Cape Colony: History, Literature and the South African Nation* (2012), and *Dreaming of Freedom in South Africa: Literature between Critique and Utopia* (2019); and the co-editor of *A Historical Companion to Postcolonial Literatures in English* (2005), *The Book in Africa: Critical Debates* (2015), and *Labour Struggles in Southern Africa* (2023). He is the General Editor of the Edinburgh University Press series *Key Texts in Anti-Colonial Thought*.

Priti Joshi is Distinguished Professor of English and Susan Resneck Pierce Professor at the University of Puget Sound in the US. She is the author of *Empire News: The Anglo-Indian Press Writes India* (2021), as well as articles on history and the essay in Indian periodicals; on exchanges between British and Indian newspapers; on the biography of Nana Sahib in the periodical press; on advertisements in Indian newspapers; and on the India exhibit at the Crystal Palace. Her current work is on the shifting technologies of image reproduction used by Indian newspapers and periodicals of the nineteenth century.

Sukeshi Kamra is Professor Emerita in the Department of English Language and Literature, Carleton University, Canada. Her research interests include anglophone South Asian literature and culture; postcolonial theory; historiography of nationalist India with a particular emphasis on revolutionary nationalism, the periodical press and pamphleteering culture; censorship; and Partition literature. She is the author of *The Indian Periodical Press and the Production of Nationalist Rhetoric* (2011) and *Bearing Witness: Partition, Independence, End of the Raj* (2002), and has published on the legal trials of periodicals in British India, the rhetoric of violence in 1947, Partition and collective memory, and the war of images in the press in 1947.

Paul Keen is Professor of English at Carleton University, Canada. His research focuses on the connections between eighteenth- and early nineteenth-century print cultures and broader debates about the revolutionary politics and the public sphere, commercial modernity and the professional author, and, most recently, emerging ideas about the humanities in modern institutional form. He is the author of *The Humanities in a Utilitarian Age: Imagining What We Know, 1800–1850* (2020), *Literature, Commerce, and the Spectacle of Modernity, 1750–1800* (2012), and *The Crisis of Literature in the 1790s: Print Culture and the Public Sphere* (1999).

Lize Kriel is Professor of Visual Culture Studies in the School of the Arts at the University of Pretoria. She is interested in the production of historical knowledge, with a specific focus on the intersections between oral art, image and text in African–European missionary encounters, more specifically, in Southern Africa. She is the author of *The Malaboch Books: Kgalusi in the 'Civilisation of the Written Word'* (2009) and co-author of *Ethnography from the Mission Field: The Hoffmann Collection of Cultural Knowledge* (2015).

Madhu Krishnan is Professor of African, World and Comparative Literatures at the University of Bristol. She is author of *Contemporary African Literature in English: Global Locations, Postcolonial Identifications* (2014), *Writing Spatiality in West Africa: Colonial Legacies in the Anglophone/Francophone Novel* (2018), and *Contingent Canons: African Literature and the Politics of Location* (2018). She is currently working on an ERC-funded project on literary activism in twenty-first-century Africa.

Ole Birk Laursen is a Researcher in the Department of History at Lund University, Sweden. His research focuses on South Asian history and literature, anti-colonialism, and anarchism in the late nineteenth and early twentieth centuries, focusing on political networks, representations of exile, and pacifism/terrorism. He is author of *Anarchy or Chaos: M. P. T. Acharya and the Indian Struggle for Freedom* (2023), editor of *Lay Down Your Arms* (2019), *We Are Anarchists* (2019), *Networking the Globe* (2017), and *Reworking Postcolonialism* (2016), and has published peer-reviewed journal articles and book chapters on the transnational intersections between anti-colonialism, socialism and anarchism.

Christopher J. Lee recently served as Professor of African History, World History and African Literature at The Africa Institute, Sharjah, UAE. He has published eight books on different aspects of African history, decolonisation and anti-colonial liberation struggles. His most recent book is an edited volume of essays, literary criticism, reportage and other non-fiction by the South African writer and activist Alex La Guma (1925–85) entitled *Alex La Guma: The Exile Years, 1966–1985* (2024).

Deborah Anna Logan is Emerita Professor of English at Western Kentucky University, where she has taught British Victorian and World Literatures and is editor of *Victorians: A Journal of Culture and Literature*. Logan's work on Harriet Martineau includes the literary biography *The Hour and the Woman* and twenty-one edited volumes of Martineau's writing and correspondence. Work on Victorian and colonial periodicals includes *The Indian Ladies' Magazine, 1901–1938: From Raj to Swaraj* (2017) and *The Life Literary* (2024), an anthology of Indian women's creative writing from pre-independence women's periodicals.

Jessica Lu is currently a doctorate student in the CUNY Graduate Center's English Program and adjunct lecturer at Brooklyn College. With a specialisation in Early Modern Literature, her research interests are primarily focused on race, gender and 'white femininity' in sixteenth- to seventeenth-century texts that include but are not limited to the works of William Shakespeare and Ben Jonson.

Athambile Masola is a lecturer in the Historical Studies Department at the University of Cape Town. Her research intersects Black women's historiography and literary studies with a focus on life writing and the newspaper archive. Her work analyses both English and isiXhosa texts. Her debut collection of poems written in isiXhosa, *Ilifa*, was one of the winners in the 2022 Best Fiction (Poetry) awards from South Africa's National Institute for Humanities and the Social Sciences (NIHSS). Her most recent collaboration is with award-winning writer Makhosazana Xaba, which is a compilation of Noni Jabavu's 1977 *Daily Dispatch* columns titled *Noni Jabavu: A Stranger at Home* (2023).

Katharina A. Oke is a postdoctoral researcher (Universitätsassistentin, post-doc) at the University of Graz, Austria. She has previously taught at King's College, London. Her research focuses on Nigerian English- and Yoruba-language print culture, political mobilisation, and social history. Her forthcoming book, *The Politics of the Public Sphere*, focuses on print culture in colonial Lagos, c. 1880–1940s. Currently, Katharina is a Marie Curie Global Fellow at the University of Graz and the University of Ibadan, Nigeria.

Myles Osborne is an associate professor of History at the University of Colorado Boulder. He completed his PhD at Harvard University in 2008. He is the author of *Ethnicity and Empire in Kenya* (2014) and *Africans and Britons in the Age of Empires, 1660–1980* (2015), with Susan Kent. He has edited two further collections: *The Life and Times of General China* (2015) and *Making Martial Races* (2024). He has published articles in journals including *Comparative Studies in Society and History* and the *Journal of African History*. Dr Osborne's current research explores connections between Africa and the Caribbean during the twentieth century.

Lachy Paterson is an Emeritus Professor in Te Tumu: School of Māori, Pacific and Indigenous Studies at the University of Otago, where he taught *te reo* Māori and Māori history. His primary research has involved *niupepa* (Māori-language newspapers) of the mid-nineteenth and early twentieth centuries, exploring the social, political and religious discourses promulgated within these publications. His publications include a monograph on nineteenth-century Māori-language newspapers, *Colonial Discourses: Niupepa Māori, 1855–1863* (2006); *He Reo Wāhine: Māori Women's Voices from the Nineteenth Century* (2017), co-authored with Angela Wanhalla; and a co-edited collection with Tony Ballantyne and Angela Wanhalla, *Indigenous Textual Cultures: Reading and Writing in the Age of Global Empire* (2020).

Jaïra Placide is a PhD student at the CUNY Graduate Center. She is the author of the young adult novel *Fresh Girl*, which won the Golden Kite Award from the Society of Children's Book Writers and Illustrators and was an American Library Association Best Book for Young Adults. Jaïra has written and self-published two poetry chapbooks: *Yellow Sky & Silhouettes* (2017) and *Drinks, Dreams & Kisses* (2019).

Janet Remmington is a Research Associate at the University of York, UK, and University of the Witwatersrand, South Africa. She was co-editor of *Sol Plaatje's Native Life in South Africa: Past and Present* (2016), which won the 2018 Edited Collection Prize from South Africa's Institute for Humanities and the Social Sciences (NIHSS). Recent publications include 'Rise of the 21st-Century Black South African Travelogue: Itineraries of Touring and Testing Freedoms' in *Research in African Literatures* (2022) and an essay on 'Olive Schreiner, Race, and Black South Africa' in *Olive Schreiner: Writing Networks and Global Contexts* (2023).

Honor Rieley is Lecturer in Victorian Literature at the University of Glasgow. Her work focuses on emigration literature and on the connections between regional, transatlantic and colonial periodicals. She recently received a BSECS-Northumbria Fellowship for a project on the literary content of local newspapers in Northumberland, which she is developing into a larger study of regional newspaper literature in Scotland and the North of England between 1820 and 1840. She has an article on reprinting in early Canadian magazines in *Studies in Canadian Literature*, and is currently working on a book on emigration and literary form in the early nineteenth century.

Corinne Sandwith is Professor of English at the University of Pretoria. She is the author of *World of Letters: Reading Communities and Cultural Debates in Early Apartheid South Africa* (2014) and co-editor with M. J. Daymond of *Africa South: Viewpoints, 1958–1961*. Her research interests include African print and reading cultures and the history of reading and cultural debate in early apartheid South Africa. Recent work focuses on the social lives of books and print materials, exploring questions such as the production of African literature and the circulation and citation of texts in disparate reading contexts.

Sarah Schwartz is an instructor at Barnard College and Queens College, CUNY. Her research sits at the intersection of modernist, postcolonial, and gender & sexuality studies. Her current project examines how queer and postcolonial novels refuse archival knowledge. An early version of this work was awarded the Paul Monette-Roger Horwitz Dissertation Prize by CLAGS.

Fariha Shaikh is Associate Professor in Victorian Literature at the School of English, Drama and Creative Studies at the University of Birmingham. Her research focusses on the multiple, complex relationships between literature, migration and settler colonialism in the context of the British Empire. She is the author of *Nineteenth-Century Settler Emigration in British Literature and Art* (2018) and co-editor (with Sukanya Banerjee) of the forthcoming *Routledge Companion to Global Victorian Literature and Culture*. She is an AHRC/BBC Radio 3 New Generation Thinker and the co-editor (with Rebecca Mitchell) of the journal *Victorian Literature and Culture*.

Graham Shaw is a Senior Research Fellow of the Institute of English Studies, School of Advanced Study, University of London. In 2010 he retired from the British Library, having been Head of Asia, Pacific and Africa Collections (APAC) for over twenty years. For the past forty years he has researched the history of printing and publishing in South Asia from the sixteenth to the twentieth century. Current projects include a book-length study of the production, distribution and reception of Christian literature in the subcontinent during the nineteenth century. His latest publication is *Subaltern Squibs and Sentimental Rhymes: The Raj Reflected in Light Verse: An Anthology Compiled with an Introduction, Notes and Glossary*.

Michelle J. Smith is an Associate Professor in Literary Studies at Monash University, Australia. She is the author of three books: *Consuming Female Beauty: British Literature and Periodicals, 1840–1914* (2022), *From Colonial to Modern: Transnational Girlhood in Canadian, Australian, and New Zealand Children's Literature, 1840–1940* (2018), and *Empire in British Girls' Literature and Culture: Imperial Girls, 1880–1915* (2011). She has also co-edited seven books in the fields of children's and Victorian literature, the most recent of which is *The Edinburgh History of Children's Periodicals* (with Beth Rodgers and Kristine Moruzi, 2024).

Philip Steer is Associate Professor of English in the School of Humanities, Media and Creative Communication at Massey University, New Zealand. He is author of *Settler Colonialism in Victorian Literature: Economics and Political Identity in the Networks of Empire* (2020) and co-editor with Nathan K. Hensley of *Ecological Form: System and Aesthetics in the Age of Empire* (2019). His research currently focuses on nineteenth-century settler writing as a form of environmental knowledge.

Cynthia Sugars is Professor of English at the University of Ottawa, where she specialises in early Canadian literature. She is the author of *Canadian Gothic: Literature, History and the Spectre of Self-Invention* (2014) and the editor of numerous collections including *Canadian Literature and Cultural Memory* (2014) and *The Oxford Handbook of Canadian Literature* (2015). She holds a Social Sciences and Humanities Research Grant for a project on Canadian print culture in the pre-Confederation period. She is currently the editor of the scholarly journal *Studies in Canadian Literature*.

Alex Tickell is Professor of Global Literatures in English at the Open University and Director of the OU's Postcolonial and Global Literatures Research Group. He specialises in the anglophone literary histories of South Asia and Southeast Asia and conjunctions of literature and politics. He is the author of *Terrorism, Insurgency and*

Indian-English Literature: 1830–1947 (2013). Tickell has published a guide to Arundhati Roy's *The God of Small Things* (2007) and edited an essay collection, *South-Asian Fiction in English: Contemporary Transformations* (2016). Tickell is the editor of *The Oxford History of the Novel in English, Volume 10: The Novel in South and South East Asia since 1945* (2019).

Annika Vosseler completed her PhD at Leipzig University, Germany, in 2022. Her research focused on the visualisation of Protestant missionary periodicals (Berlin Missionary Society and London Missionary Society) by tracing continuities and shifts in the use of visual motifs in the nineteenth and early twentieth centuries. She obtained her MSc in African Studies from the University of Edinburgh. Currently she is main investigator at the Museum of the University of Tübingen in a joint research project investigating the provenance of human remains from Africa's colonial past before 1919 in scientific collections of Baden-Württemberg, Germany.

Candace Ward is Professor of English at Florida State University, where she teaches early Caribbean and eighteenth-century British culture and literature. She is the author of *Desire and Disorder: Fevers, Fictions, and Feelings in English Georgian Culture* (2007) and *Crossing the Line: Early Creole Novels and Anglophone Caribbean Culture in the Age of Emancipation* (2017). Her work has appeared in *Journal of American Studies*, *Studies in the Novel*, *Studies in Eighteenth-Century Culture* and *Victorian Periodicals Review*. She is currently at work on a study of Emancipation-era print culture and creole identities, *The Creole Cosmopolis: Pan-Caribbean Identities in Early Nineteenth-Century Caribbean Print Culture*.

Anne Wetherilt is a PhD student at the Open University. Her thesis examines the work of British women writers, their fictional response to decolonisation and their location in the broader context of post-war middlebrow fiction. Her interests span postcolonial and global literatures, Cold War fiction and middlebrow culture more generally. She has published in the *Journal of Postcolonial Writing*, and her chapter 'Representations of the Malayan Emergency: Reading Han Suyin, Mary McMinnies and Anthony Burgess' features in *The Malayan Emergency in Film, Literature and Art: Cultural Memory as Historical Other*, edited by Jonathan Driskell, Andrew Hock Soon Ng and Marek Rutkowski.

Melodee H. Wood is a historian of migration and media at Loughborough University, specialising in the development of digital methodologies for transnational newspaper analysis. She is the author of *The Atlas of Digitised Newspapers and Metadata* (2020), multiple works on the development and spread of scissors-and-paste journalism in the anglophone world, and the forthcoming textbook *Digital History: An Introduction*.

Index

Note: *italics* indicate illustrations

Abantu-Batho, 344, 346, 350, 351
Abayomi, Oyinkan, 218
ABC Weekly, 420
Abdurahman, Abdullah, 165
Abrahams, Peter, 26–7, 413, 527
Abyssinia *see* Ethiopia
Acadian Magazine, 8, 39, 54
Acharya, M. P. T., 405, 412, 414
Acke, Hanna, 113, 114
Adarkar, Bhaskar Namdeo, 243, 248–9
Adejunmobi, Moradewun, 539
Aderinto, Saheed, 216, 217, 218
advertisements, 159, 206, 247, 249–50, 307–8, 349–50, 367
   calls for, 305–6, 308, 326
   for other periodicals, 61, 118, 202, 244, 334, 457n
   as source of revenue, 85, 86, 122, 155, 168, 170, 173, 178, 231, 326, 364, 508
Afghanistan, 84, 392, 394, 395, 401
African Claims in South Africa, 422–3
African Mail, 168–9
African Messenger, 332, 508
African National Congress, 346, 422–3, 424, 427, 434, 436–7
African Sentinel, 27, 214
African Times and Orient Review, 505, 511–12
African World, 7, 169
Africa South, 26, 31, 433–4, 438
Afrikaner Bond, 155–61, 164, 303–4
afterlives of periodicals, 67–8, 71–2, 296–8, 327
Agarwal, Shriman Narayan, 426, 427, 429
Agathocleous, Tanya, 511–12
Age, The, 206, 207
Aggrey, James Kwegyir, 171, 322, 351
Ainsworth, John, 326
Ajayi, Ronke, 214, 218
Akede Eko, 218, 332, 334, 337

Akintan, E. A., 332, 337–8
Algeria, 13, 442–3, 454
Ali, Duse Mohamed, 214, 332, 421, 505–17
Alley, Rewi, 450, 452, 456
Alston, Sandra, 38, 186
Amrita Bazar Patrika, 481, 482, 490n
Anand, Mulk Raj, 450, 455, 457n
anarchism, 404–14
Anderson, Benedict, 48, 67, 202
Anglo-Boer War, 143–4, 159–64, 169, 300, 305–9
Anglo-Zulu War, 390–1, 394–401
Annals of Jamaica (Bridges), 68–70
anti-capitalism, 17–18, 141–2, 165–6, 425–8; *see also* Communism
anti-Communism, 31, 213, 457n
anti-fascism, 234, 406–9, 421, 422
Aperaamo, 285–97, *286*
Arabic, 4, 84, 319
Archibald, J. F., 127–8, 130, 131, 134
Arista, Noelani, 295
Ashanti Pioneer, 420–1, 425
Asian-African Conference, 432–44, 448, 454, 455; *see also* Non-Aligned Movement
Asiatic Journal, 86, 88
Astley, William, 134
Athenaeum (London), 191, 192, 194, 195
Atieno-Odhiambo, E. S., 537–8
Atlantic Charter, 410, 418–29, 520
Attlee, Clement, 418–19, 422, 423, 425
Auckland Weekly Register, and Commercial and Shipping Gazette, The, 99
Australasian, The, 142, 143, 145–6
Australasian Typographical Circular, 379
Australasian Typographical Journal, 377–8, 382, 384
Australia
   Aboriginal people, 140, 145, 152n
   class, 147–52, 208–9

Federation, 127, 139–52, 201, 211, 384
fiction, 127, 135–7, 204–5, 207–8
gendered settler subjectivities, 129–31, 134–7, 143–4, 202, 205–11
history, 132–5, 145–7
missionaries, 117
publishing and distribution, 6, 127–8, 139–40, 202, 204
reporting on Empire, 419–20, 421
print trade, 376–9, 381, 382, 383–4
racism, 130, 131, 132, 136, 141, 143, 148–52, 384
women's education, 209–10
women's periodicals, 201–12
Australian Town and Country Journal, 128, 145, 208, 211
Australian Typographical Circular, The, 376–7, 377, 379
Avadh Akhbar, 3
Awati, P. R., 248
Awobiyi, E. M., 332
Awoonor-Williams, George [Kofi], 450, 457n
Azikiwe, Nnamdi, 222, 224, 421–2, 424, 505, 507, 516

Baker, Houston, 28, 29, 495
Baker, Pauline, 224
Bakhtin, Mikhail, 129, 131, 132
Ballstadt, Carl, 53
Bandung *see* Asian-African Conference
Bangavasi, 482, 486–8
Banks, George Linnaeus, 310
Bannerji, Himani, 229
Bantu World, 27, 343, 344–5, 348, 350–4, 354
Baraza, 327
Barbados, 66–8, 74–8, 175, 411, 425; *see also* Caribbean
Barber, Karin, 215, 305, 323
Barnes, Dorothy, 500
Barringer, Terry, 112, 114
Bashford, Alison, 251
Batchelor, Jennie, 190
Baugh, Edward, 493
Bayley, Diana, 190
Baynton, Barbara, 127, 129
Beacon, The, 493, 496–502, 497
Beattie, James, 100
Becker, Judith, 113
Bédard, Mylène, 193
Beechey, George Duncan, 466–7, 471, 474, 475n, 465
Beetham, Margaret, 190, 207
Belich, James, 22, 56, 98–9, 134

Belgium, 168, 178, 437
Bengal Hurkaru, 85, 92, 466
Bengal Monthly Sporting Magazine, 85, 87–8
Bentinck, William, 89–90
Berkeley-Hill, Owen, 247–8
Berwick Advertiser, 195–8
Besant, Annie, 16, 234, 236, 240
Best, Elsdon, 97, 106
Bharat Mihir, 481
Bharat Sangskaran, 480
Bhashaposhini, 272–3, 275–9, 281–3, 274
Blacker, C. P., 243, 250
Blair, William Newsham, 103
Blaize, Emily, 215
Bonea, Amelia, 391, 396
Bowerman, Charles William, 380
Bowness, Suzanne, 189, 193
Braithwaite [Jones], Chris, 410, 411, 414
Bratton, J. S., 288
Brennan, James R., 27
Bridges, George, 68–70, 72, 78n
Britain
anarchism, 404–14
newsgathering, 398–400, 466
periodicals published in, 168–79
print trade journals, 375–6, 377, 379, 380–1
racism, 173, 174, 527
readers of colonial periodicals in, 113–15, 118, 242
relationship with colonial press, 334–6, 394, 399, 463–75
British Emancipator, 73–4
British North American Magazine, and Colonial Journal, 38, 39
Brown, Mary Markham, 58
Browne, Thomas Gore, 260–1, 267
Bulletin (Cape Town), 427–8
Bulletin (Sydney), 127–37, 144, 150–1, 419, 429n
Bulson, Eric, 533
Busara, 531–40, *Plates 4 & 5*
Byfield, Judith, 214, 221, 222, 223, 224

Cabinet of Literature, 46, 47, 196
Cachalia, Ismail, 436–7
Calcutta Government Gazette, 82, 85
Campbell, Mavis, 68, 72
Campbell, Robert Calder, 88
Campbell Walker, Inches, 101
Canada
education, 39, 45
emigration to, 52, 55–7, 59–60
francophone culture, 193–5, 197

Canada (*cont.*)
  missionaries, 117
  national culture, 37–49, 51–63, 188–90
  newspaper publishing, 5, 361–7, 369, 371–2
  Patriote movement, 193, 361, 362
  print trade journals, 376, 379–80
  publishing and distribution, 5, 6, 38–9, 51–2, 54–5, 185–6
  reprinted content, 186, 188, 190–8
  women's periodicals, 185–98
Canadian Casket, The, 39, 40–1, 46, 47
Canadian Garland, The, 38, 41, 42–3, 47
Canadian Literary Magazine, 38, 43–4, 46, 48, 52
Canadian Magazine, The, 37, 39, 40, 41–2, 57
Canadian Magazine and Literary Repository, 38, 40, 44, 46, 53–4, 55–6, 198n
Canadian Review and Literary and Historical Journal, 53, 55, 198n
Canadian Review and Magazine, The, 47, 48
Canowindra Star and Woodstock Recorder, 206
Cape Argus, 121, 155, 164, 303, 305
Cape Mercury, 121, 156, 158, 303
Cape Times, 155, 157, 158, 164
Caribbean
  anti-colonialism, 27, 410–11, 493–503
  decolonisation, 71–2, 413, 447, 519
  fiction, 493, 496–503
  history, 68–71, 76–8, 496
  missionaries, 69, 117
  multicultural society, 496–8
  Pan-Africanism, 519–28
  slavery, 66–78, 365, 494–5
  see also Barbados; Jamaica; Trinidad and Tobago
Cartwright, Albert, 157–66, 169–75
'Cato', 68, 70, 72
censorship and press control, 1, 4, 27, 82, 85–6, 158, 159, 161–4, 213, 240, 250, 363, 482–90
Centlivres, Frederick James, 157, 161
Cetewayo, 390, 396, 399–400, 401n
Chamberlain, Joseph, 154, 160, 306
Champion, Allison, 347
Chanda, Mrinal Kanti, 391
Chang, David A., 288
Chapman, Henry, 361–7, 369–71
Chatterjee, Ramananda, 426
Chattopadhyaya, Kamaladevi, 230, 236, 240
Chelmsford, Lord, 396, 398, 400
children's periodicals, 39, 116, 118, 204–5, 285–93, 286, 296–7

China
  Civil War, 405–6, 427
  emigrants from, 128, 131, 132, 135, 148–9, 164, 251, 383–4
  Maoist, 439, 440, 441–3, 446–57
  nineteenth-century, 6, 117, 123
Chisholme, David, 53–4, 55, 62, 198n
Chou En-lai, 447
Christian Express, The, 118, 120–1, 122, 124n
Christianity, 115–18, 123, 160, 230, 235, 287–8; *see also* missionaries
Christie, Alexander James, 55–6, 62, 198n
Chronicle of the London Missionary Society, The, 115, 121–2
Churchill, Winston, 418–22, 425, 428, 522
Church Missionary Society, 4, 115, 326, 336
Clarke, Dorothy, 501
Clifford, Hugh, 214, 335, 336
Clifford, Lady, 214, 218
Codell, Julie F., 393
Coghlan, Timothy, 139
Coke, Thomas, 117
Colenso, John William., 115, 399
Colenso, Robert J., 399–400
Colenso, William, 101
Coleridge, Kathleen, 363
Collier, Patrick, 88
Colonial Reformer, 74
Colored American Magazine, 304
Comet, 214, 332, 421–2, 505–17, *506*, *509*
communications infrastructure, 4–7, 22, 146, 396–8
Communism
  Britain, 27
  China, 447–8, 451–57
  Comintern, 405, 427, 526
  India, 409, 412
  South Africa, 115, 122, 345–7, 423, 426, 427, 429n, 434, 436–7
  Soviet Union, 404, 526
  see also anti-capitalism
competitions, 203, 204, 205, 210, 214, 218, 337, 353
Compositors' Chronicle, 375, 376
Congo, 168, 178, 449, 538
Connolly, James J., 88
Conrad, Joseph, 7, 26, 538–9
Cooper, Frederick, 22
copyright, 54–5, 59, 63, 216, 468, 473
Cousins, George, 294
Cousins, Margaret, 234, 236, 240
cover design, 117–18, 235, 277, 350, 466, 467, 532

Cowan, Alexander, 169
Cowan, James, 105, 106
Cox, Jeffrey, 114–15
Cranborne, Lord, 420, 421
Crewe, C. P., 304
Crook, David, 451, 452, 454, 456
Crossman, A., 40–1, 46
Cunard, Nancy, 410, 425–6
Cunnabell, Jacob, 39
Cunnabell, William, 39–40
Current Notes on International Affairs, 419–20, 421

Dacca Gazette, 481
Dagblad, 158
Daily Advertiser, The (Montreal), 361–7, 371–2
Daily Gleaner, 496, 519, 525
Daily Nation, 433, 441–3, *442*
Daily News (London), 398, 399
Darwin, John, 22
David, C. D., 281, 282–3
Davidson, Charles James C., 94
Davis, Caroline, 31
Davis, Helen, 208
Davison, Graeme, 130
Dawn, The, 144, 201, 202, 215
Day, Patrick, 362, 363, 364, 370, 371, 372
Delisle, Jean, 194
DeLucia, JoEllen, 190
Deniga, Adeoye, 332, 335, 339
Denoon, Donald, 387
Denzer, LaRay, 215, 223, 224, 225n
Desai, Manilal Ambalal, 319, 320
Dharwar Writt, 480
Dhlomo, R. R. R., 353
Diamond Fields Advertiser, 155, 157, 386
Dickens, Charles, 4, 463, 468–9
Distad, N. Merrill, 364
distribution infrastructure, 5–6, 57, 67, 289, 294, 325, 332, 453
Docker, John, 131
Domingo, Wilfred Adolphus, 519–28
Donohue, Francis J., 134
Dougall, James W. C., 321, 323
Douglass, Millicent, 224
Dove Danquah, Mabel [Marjorie Mensah], 213–14, 216–19, 222–3, 224, 225n
Drake, St. Clair, 527
Dube, John Langalibalele, 345, 355n
Du Bois, Shirley Graham, 455
Du Bois, W. E. B., 410, 435, 523, 524
Dubow, Saul, 309

Duffield, Ian, 510, 512, 513, 514, 515–16
Duvernay, Ludger, 193

East Africa and Rhodesia, 420
East African Standard, 321, 325, 327, 420
Eastern Africa, 317–27, 420, 531–40; *see also* Kenya; Tanganyika; Tanzania; Uganda
Eastern Horizon, 446–57, *453*, Plate 3
East India Company, 81–3, 85–6, 89–94, 463, 469–73
East Indian United Service Journal, 85, 87
editorial paratext, 343, 346, 351–2, 355
Edmondson, Belinda, 501
education
    African American, 513
    Australia, 209–10
    Canada, 39, 45
    Eastern Africa, 320–1, 531–4, 539–40
    English-language, 17, 90, 230, 239–40, 281–3, 330, 340
    India, 17–18, 90, 228–30, 232, 234, 238, 239–40, 273, 281–3
    missionary, 171, 230, 256, 288–92, 301, 384
    Southern Africa, 311, 384
    Sunday schools, 115, 288, 289, 290
    universities, 165, 171, 178, 282, 330, 450, 531–4, 539–40
    West Africa, 170–1, 178, 215–20, 330, 332
    women's, 209–10, 215–20, 228–30, 232, 234, 238, 239–41
    see also literacy
Ẹdun, Adegboyega, 338
Eko Akete, 332–40, *333*
Eko Igbẹhin, 332, 338
Elder Dempster, 168, 169, 172–3
Eleti Ọfẹ, 332, 334, 335–6, 337, 339
Elliot, Henry Miers, 83–4, 86–90, 92
Ellis, Havelock, 242, 243, 244–5
Elphinstone, Mountstuart, 1
Enahoro, Anthony, 515–16
Englishman, 84, 85, 87, 88, 463
Etherington, Norman, 124
Ethiopia, 174, 406, 408, 506, 507, 513, 514–15, 528
Ethiopian Herald, The, 432–3, *433*, 439–41, 443
eugenics, 242–51
Eugenics Review, 243–4, 249, 250
Evans, George Essex, 139
Evatt, Herbert Vere, 421

Fairclough, O. T., 522, 524
Family Magazine, 192

Farrell, Jack 381–2, *381*
Fawzy, Mahmoud, 439
Fierlinger, Zdenek, 440
Fighting Talk, 438, 440
financing of periodicals
　black-edited/white-funded, 27, 302, 343–55
　by companies, 169, 172, 362, 367
　cross-subsidising, 87–8
　by governments, 31, 255–8, 267–8, 317–27
　by houses of agency, 85–6
　by individual supporters, 159, 302, 304, 393
　by unions, 375, 377–80
　see also advertisements; subscription
Finkelstein, David, 14, 62, 391, 393
Finlay, Hugh, 376
Firth, Josiah Clifton, 101
Fitchett, Thomas Shaw, 201, 202, 204–6, 208
Fitzroy, Robert, 258
Focus, 493, 501–2, 524
Fontaney, Antoine, 194–5
Forbes, Archibald, 398
Forbes-Mitchell, William, 472, 474
Foreign Field, 118, *119*
formal properties of periodicals *see* cover design; format; front page; illustrations; layout; mastheads; typography
format, 117, 195, 204, 212n, 256, 346, 507
France, 168, 178, 443, 452
Franklin, Stella 'Miles', 127, 129
Franklyn, Joseph Pitt Washington, 77
Fraser, Nancy, 428, 495
Freedom, 404–6, 412–14
Freeman, Joseph John, 285, 289–92, 293, 294
Freeman, William, 103
Fremantle, Henry, 165
Frere, Bartle, 390, 392, 394–6, 398–401
Friend, Robert, 456
Friend of India and Statesman, 1, 31, 390–401, *392*, 397, 463
front page, 27, 344, 353
Furphy, Joseph, 127, 129

Gadzekpo, Audrey, 214, 215, 216, 217, 218, 223
Galletly, Sarah, 202–1
Gambia, 168, 177; *see also* West Africa
Gandhi, Kasturba, 233
Gandhi, Mohandas K., 164, 230, 233, 236–9, 240, 241, 385, 406, 409–10, 411, 421, 423–4, 524, 527
Gandini, O., 466–7, 475n
Garner, Bill, 130
Garvey, Amy Jacques, 524

Garvey, Marcus, 345, 347, 519, 523–4, 526, 527, 528
Gaspé Magazine and Instructive Miscellany, The, 46
Gayll, Arthur, 134
Gelder, Ken, 204
Gelder, Stuart and Roma, 450
gender
　masculinism, 129–31, 136–7, 143–4
　pseudonyms to disguise, 66, 190, 215, 218, 224
　of readerships, 66, 249–50, 322
　sexuality and reproduction, 245–51
　see also women
Germany, 113, 174, 234, 242, 248–9, 280, 318, 320, 407–8, 512–13, 522
Gerson, Carole, 52, 59, 62, 190
Getachew, Adom, 515
Ghadar, 27
Ghana, 168, 171, 176–8, 420–2, 438, 440, 441, 455, 516, 519, 527; *see also* Gold Coast; West Africa
Gibson, John, 51, 58, 60–1, 63n
Gikandi, Simon, 523, 532, 533, 534
Godey's Lady's Magazine, 62
Gold Coast, 117, 123, 171, 174–8, 213–25, 333–5, 412–13, 433–5; *see also* Ghana; West Africa
Goldman, Emma, 407–8, 414
Gomes, Albert, 496
Gonzalez Seligmann, Katerina, 493
Gopal, Priyamvada, 27, 391, 398, 401n
Gosselin, Mary Graddon, 42, 47, 49, 185–98
Green, F. J., 122
Green, George A. L., 157
Greenbank's Periodical Library, 192–3
Greene, Felix, 454, 455
Grey, George, 257, 261, 268, 296
Grossmann, Edith Searle, 103
Guardian, A Monthly Magazine of Education and General Literature, The, 46
Guardian, The (South Africa), 426–7
Gundert, Hermann, 280–1
Gundy, Henry, 51–2, 54

Habari, 317–27, *318*
Habermas, Jürgen, 28, 494, 495
Hall, Stuart, 526
Hammill, Faye, 188
Han Suyin, 449, 450, 451, 452, 454, 456
Harber, Anton, 301
Harding, R. Coupland, 107
Hargrove, Ernest, 160

Harijan, 424
Harisharma, A. D., 273
Harris, Rutherfoord, 158
Harris, Thomas, 66, 75
Hartman, Saidiya, 494–5
Harvey, D. C., 38
Hau'ofa, Epeli, 292, 297n
Hawai'i, 288, 293, 295
Haynes, John, 127, 128, 131
Heath, Thomas, 285, 289–90, 296
Herald and Mail (Halifax), 379–80
Heuman, Gad, 68, 72, 78
Himes, Norman, 242, 244, 245, 250
Hindi, 230, 235, 272, 279
Hindu, The, 423
Hinduism, 232, 235–6, 246, 277, 279
Hindustan Times, 423, 424, 425
Hirschmann, Edwin, 392, 393
Hirst, John, 141
Ho, Elaine, 448
Hobhouse, Emily, 163, 165
Hobson, J. A., 160
Hobson, William, 363, 368–70
Hodges, Sarah, 243, 245, 251
Hofmeyr, Isabel, 301, 333, 340n, 383, 517n
Hofmeyr, Jan, 156, 157, 158, 164, 165
Holder, Julia Maria, Lady, 210
Homeward Mail from India, China, and the East, 463, 469–70, 474
Hong Kong, 446–57
Household Words, 4, 468, 472
Howe, Joseph, 38
Hudson, W. B., 97
Humana, Charles, 412–13
Hunte, George H., 175
Hunter, Emma, 508, 516
Hutchinson, Sam, 148, 149

Ieremia-Allan, Wanda, 294–5, 297
Ikoli, Ernest, 332
Ilanga lase Natal, 164, 305
Illustrated London News, The, 3, 464–70, 464, 472–5
Illustrated New Zealand Herald for Home Readers, 102
Illustrated New Zealand News, 102
Illustrated Times, 464–8, 465, 470–1, 474
illustrations, 3, 49, 62, 118, 121–2, 174, 186–8, 204–7, 231, 305, 339, 446, 449, 450, 464–75
Imvo Zabantsundu, 122, 155, 158, 161–2, 164, 300–6, 308, 309, 310–11, 314n
Indaba, 120, 344

India
    anti-colonialism, 1, 27, 230, 236–41, 245–6, 393–4, 405–6, 408, 409–11, 423–5, 426, 463, 467, 472–3
    Calcutta press, 84–8, 385, 463
    education, 17–18, 90, 281–3
    Kerala press, 272–5, 278, 283
    language and identity, 272, 278–84
    missionaries, 14, 230, 274
    mofussil press, 81–94
    newsgathering, 87, 390–1, 394–8
    reporting on colonial policy, 390–401, 478–90
    print infrastructure, 3, 86–8, 272–4, 385
    print trade, 376, 378, 384–5
    relationship with British press, 394, 399, 463–75
    sexology, 242–51
    vernacular press, 3, 5, 272–84, 477–91
    women's education, 228–30, 232, 234, 238, 239–41
    women's periodicals, 228–41
    see also East India Company; Indian National Congress
Indian Daily News, 478–80, 481, 482, 483, 490nn, 491n
Indian Ladies' Magazine, 228–36, 231, 238–41
Indian National Congress, 236, 237, 250–1, 408, 409, 423, 426
Indian Opinion, 164, 305
Indian Printers' Journal, 378, 385
Indian Social Reformer, 426
Indirect Rule, 170–2, 219
Indulekha (Menon), 282–3
Ingram, Herbert, 464, 467, 468, 469–70, 474, 475nn
Inkanyiso yase Natal, 122–3
Inkundla ya Bantu, 423, 424
Innes, James Rose, 157, 158, 159, 161, 163
Innes, Richard Rose, 157, 158
International Journal of Sexology see *Marriage Hygiene*
Irving, Helen, 141
Isigidimi Sama-Xosa, 120–1, 301, 305, 314n
isiXhosa, 120, 155, 158, 300–14, 344, 348–50, 353
isiZulu, 164, 344, 353–4
Italy, 174, 406, 408, 506, 512–13, 514–15
Iwe Irohin, 331
Iwe Irohin Eko, 333
Iwe Irohin Ọsọsẹ, 332
Izwi Labantu, 158, 162, 300–14, *307*, *312*

Jabavu, John Tengo, 122, 155–6, 158, 162, 164, 301–4, 306, 313, 345
Jackson, Thomas Horatio, 332
Jacobs, H. P. ['Hobnailes'], 500, 503n, 524
Jali, E. C., 352
Jamaica, 66–74, 78, 413, 496, 499–503, 519–28; see also Caribbean
Jamaica Journal, 68
James, C. L. R., 25, 27, 496, 498–9
James, Leslie, 352, 410, 507, 522, 524
Jameson, Leander Starr, 156, 162, 164–5
Jameson Raid, 156–7, 303
Jenkins, Paul, 113, 114
Jensz, Felicity, 113
Jinarajadasa, Dorothy, 228, 234
John Bull, 85, 334, 335
Jones, Aled G., 14
Jones, Chris [Braithwaite], 410, 411, 414
Jordon, Edward, 66, 67, 70–4, 77–8
Joshi, Priti, 82, 391, 393–4, 401n
Journal of the Polynesian Society, 106
Juvenile Missionary Magazine (LMS), 285–93, 286, 296–7

Kadalie, Clements, 347, 348
Kaffir Express, 120; see also *Isigidimi Samaxosa*
Karaitiana Takamoana, 263, 265, 266
Kavanagh, Mat, 411
Keell, Thomas H., 405–6
Kent, John, 43–4, 46, 48, 49, 52
Kenya, 170, 317–27, 410–14, 527, 531–40; see also Eastern Africa
Kenyatta, Jomo, 408, 409, 410–11, 413, 414, 523
Keralavarma, 277
Khamisi, Francis, 327
Khanyisa, 423
Kies, Ben, 427–8, 429
Kimball, Horace, 66, 74
Kiongozi, 318, 319, 320
Kirk, Thomas, 100
Kiswahili, 317–27, 531, 535, 537
Kitchener, Lord, 163, 164, 169
Kitonga, Ellen Mae, 538–9
Klausen, Susanne, 251
Klein, Thoralf, 113
Klinck, Carl F., 52, 58, 61
Knight, Catherine, 97
Knight, Robert, 391–4, 401
Kolbe, Frederick, 160, 161, 163
Koranta ea Becoana, 164
Korieh, Jimah, 224

Koschorke, Klaus, 123
Kotane, Moses, 436–8
Kratzmann, Mary Jane, 43, 48
Kropotkin, Peter, 404
Kumar, Ritu, 474
Kumaran, Murkoth, 280
Kuttainen, Victoria, 201–2

Lady's Magazine, 62, 190
Lady's Newspaper and Pictorial Times, The, 467–8, 467, 470, 473
Lagos Daily News, 216, 221, 334
Lagos Times, 215
Lagos Weekly Record, The, 214, 332, 334, 335
Lake, Marilyn, 149
Landon, Letitia Elizabeth, 58, 186, 191
Lang, John, 4, 468–75, *471*
language
  colonial policy, 17–18, 317–19, 326–7
  colonial publishing in vernacular, 255–8, 317–18, 323, 327
  cultural specificity of, 292–5, 337–8
  debates about, 279–82, 326–8, 337–8
  development, 278–82, 330–2
  education in English, 17, 90, 230, 239–40, 281–3, 330, 340
  and identity, 272, 278–84, 337–8
  linguistic interaction, 336–7, 339–40
  pidgin and non-standard, 332, 337
  standardisation, 272, 279–80, 319, 326–7
  see also multilingual content; translated content
Latai, Latu, 294
Lawson, Henry, 127, 129, 135–6
Lawson, Louisa, 143, 201
Lawson, Sylvia, 127, 128–9, 131
layout, 62, 117–18, 277, 344, 346, 351, 532
Ledbetter, Kathryn, 13
Lee, Chris, 135
Lee Tsung-ying, 447, 450–2, 454–6
Legum, Colin, 438–9
Lemire, Maurice, 191, 194
Leota, 285, 289
letters
  in missionary periodicals, 114, 121, 285–97
  'Notes to Correspondents', 343, 346
  overseas/regional correspondents, 160, 377, 381, 396–8, 449, 450–1, 455, 457n
  readers', 66, 171, 177, 193–4, 215, 222, 302–3, 307, 324, 327, 332, 335–6, 346, 347, 350, 353, 449
Leverhulme, William Lever, Lord, 168, 170
Liberal, The, 66–8, 74–8

Liberia, 174, 365, 516, 528
Liebach, Susann, 201–2
Limb, Peter, 311, 344
literacy (alphabetic)
   Africa, 353, 533
   Australia, 139
   Canada, 38
   Caribbean, 502n
   England, 287–8
   India, 93, 229, 232, 238, 240–1, 273, 283
   New Zealand, 5, 256, 258
   Pacific Islands, 285–97
   see also education
Literary Garland and British North American Magazine, The, 38, 39, 45–6, *45*, 47–8, 51, 54, 57–63, 185, 188
Liu Pengju, 446–7, 448–51, 456
Lochhead, Douglas, 60
Lochhead, Lynne, 98
Lo Liyong, Taban, 531, 534, 539
London Missionary Society, 115, 116, 120, 121–2, 124n, 285, 288–97
Lovell, John, 38, 45–6, 47–8, 58–62
Lugard, Frederick, 169, 170
Luthuli, Albert, 436–7
Lytton, Lord, 393, 394, 395

Macaulay, Herbert, 221, 224, 331, 334, 335
Macaulay, Thomas Babington, 90, 230, 239
MacDonald, Mary Lu, 38, 56, 186, 189, 190
McEldowney, Dennis, 99
McGill, Meredith, 188
McGregor, Hannah, 188
Macharia, Mwangi, 531, 534, 536
Mackay, Jessie, 106
McKenny, John, 116
MacLaren, Eli, 38, 186
McLean, Donald, 257, 260, 262–3, 268
McLean, Margaret, 210
Macleod, William, 127
Macmillan's Magazine, 400, 401n
Madras Athenaeum, 463
Mahoka a Becwana, 121–2
Maidment, Brian, 466
Mais, Roger, 501, 521–2
Maketū, 257, 259
Makonnen, T. Ras, 527–8
Malan, Daniël François, 413
Malan, François Stephanus, 156, 159, 160, 161, 163, 165
Malayalam, 272–84, 274, 276
Malayala Manorama, 278, 281, 282
Malhotra, D. K., 426

Maloy, S. H. 352
Malta, 4, 6
Mambo Leo, 317–25, 327
Manchester Guardian, 160, 399
Manley, Edna, 496, 501–2
Manley, Michael, 71
Manley, Norman, 519, 521, 527
Mantsayi, Robert, 303
Māori
   anti-colonial resistance, 98–9, 257, 260, 262–3, 267–8
   environmental knowledge, 98, 106–9
   Indigenous scholars, 292
   -language periodicals, 255–68
   mythology, 97, 106–7
   parliamentary representation, 255, 260–8
   see also New Zealand
Mao Zedong, 447–8, 451–7
Mapanya, Abner, 346–7, 351, 355n
Mappilla, Kandathil Varghese, 273, 276–7, 281, 282
Marais, J. S., 158
Marriage Hygiene, 242–51, *243*, *247*
Marsh, Alfred, 405
Marsh, George Perkins, 101, 108
Marshman, Joshua and John Clark, 391
Martin, Michèle, 272
Martin, Robert Montgomery, 85, 366
mastheads, 117, 202–3, *203*, 257, 308, 310
Maxwell, Gerald, 321
Mayer, Harold, 345, 355n
Mayo, Katherine, 246, 249, 250
Mba, Nina Emma, 224
Mbeki, Govan, 423
Meerut Universal Magazine, The, 81–94
Megill, Allan, 78
Melba, Nellie, 207
Meltzer, Albert, 408–9, 410–11, 413, 414
Mendes, Alfred, 496–8, 499, 503n
Menon, C. P. Achyutha, 274, 275
Menon, O. Chandu, 280, 281; see also *Indulekha*
Menon, P. Gopala, 275
Menon, Shungoonny, 277
Mensah, Marjorie see Dove Danquah, Mabel
Merriman, John Xavier, 157–9, 160, 161, 164, 165, 166, 303
Metcalfe, Charles, 85, 90
Mgqwetho, Nontsizi, 350
Michell, Lewis, 162
Milner, Alfred, 154, 155, 157, 159, 160, 164, 165, 169, 306
Milner, G. B., 292

missionaries, 4, 14, 69, 112–24, 171, 230, 256, 274, 285–97, 301, 305, 317, 344–5, 384
Missionary Magazine and Chronicle, 115, 122; see also *Chronicle of the London Missionary Society, The*
Modern Review, 25, 426
Mofussilite, The, 4, 83, 463, 469–73
Mokoena, Hlonipha, 350
Molteno, James, 156, 157
Molteno, John Charles, 157, 160
Monro, David, 100
Monthly Review, 107
Montreal Museum, The, 39, 42, 47, 49, 54–5, 185–98, *185*, *187*
Moodie, Susanna, 48, 49, 52, 54, 57, 59–62
Moore, Maurice George, 163
Morel, Edmund Dene, 168–9
Morning Journal, The, 72–3, 77, 78n
Mosely, Alfred, 380
Mother India (Mayo), 246, 249, 250
Mower, Nahum, 38, 40, 44, 46
Mqhayi, S. E. K., 304, 306, 311
Msane, Saul, 350, 355n
Muliyil, Joseph, 281
multilingual content, 27, 193–4, 218, 231, 235, 257–8, 300–14, 317–27, 330–2, 336, 339–40, 343–55
Murray, A. W., 288
Musandu, Phoebe, 321, 533
Mussell, James, 296

Nadkarni, Asha, 246
Nahe, Hoani, 266–7
Naidu, Sarojini, 230, 233, 236, 240
Nana Sahib, 463–75, *464*, *465*, *467*, *471*
Nash, Walter, 421
Nasson, Bill, 306
National Congress of British West Africa, 171, 219
Native Newspaper Reports, 273, 477–91, *478*, *485*, *486*
Native Opinion, 478, 480, 482, 490n
Nayyar, Abdur Rahim, 335
Neale, R. S., 361–2, 363, 365, 366, 371, 372
Neame, L. E., 384–5
Needham, Joseph, 450, 454
Negro World, 320, 334, 521
Nehru, Jawaharlal, 230, 250, 411, 424, 434, 524
New Age (Britain), 163
New Age (South Africa), 434, 435–7
Newell, Stephanie, 213, 216, 218, 222, 223, 347, 509, 510, 516, 534, 540

New Idea, 201–12, *203*
New Leader, 25, 27, 425
News Chronicle, 422, 425
Newton, Melanie, 77
New York Magazine, 273
New Zealand, *102*, Plates 1 & 2
 environmental knowledge, 97–109
 Kohimarama Conference, 260–1, 267, 268
 missionaries, 117, 256
 newspaper publishing, 361–4, 367–72
 politics, 255, 259–68, 421
 print trade, 377–8, 379, 381
 rapid growth of publishing, 5, 6, 97–8
 Treaty of Waitangi, 255, 261, 267
 women as readers, 202, 205, 210
 see also Māori
New Zealand Company, 361–3, 367, 368–71
New Zealand Gazette and Wellington Spectator, 259, 361–4, 367–72, *368*
New Zealand Illustrated Magazine, 103–4, 105, 106
New Zealand Tablet, The, 100, 104–5
Ngai, Mae, 384
Nigeria
 anti-colonialism, 170, 421–2, 424–5, 522
 class, 215–16, 217
 decolonisation, 176–7, 413
 Indirect Rule, 170–2, 219
 Lagos press, 173, 175–6, 330–41, 508, 510
 news weeklies, 168–79, 330, 505–17
 trading, 168–70, 177–8
 westernisation, 524
 women, 218–25
 see also West Africa
Nigerian Daily Herald, 215, 218
Nigerian Daily Telegraph, 332, 334
Nigerian Daily Times, 173, 175–6, 214, 334, 507, 508
Nigerian Evening News, 332
Nigerian Pioneer, 334, 335
Nkrumah, Kwame, 176, 177, 412, 434, 523, 527
Nokise, Uili Feleterika, 293
Non-Aligned Movement, 432, 441, 447–8, 454; see also Asian-African Conference
North New Zealand Settler: And Land Buyers' Guide, The, 104
Nova-Scotia Magazine, 38

O'Brien, George, Plate 2
Oceania, 287, 288, 292–6, 297n; see also Australia; Hawai'i; New Zealand; Pacific Islands; Sāmoa

Odendaal, André, 303–4
Ofori Atta, Nana, 171
Ojuka, Albert, 538
Oladejo, Mutiat, 224
O le Sulu Samoa, 287, 287, 293–8
Omu, Fred, 506
Ons Land, 156, 159, 161, 163, 164
O'Regan, John P., 17
Orsini, Francesca, 229
Osborn, Robert, 66, 67, 70–4, 77–8
Ostell, Thomas, 92
Owen, W. E., 326
Owen, William C., 405–6, 414
Oyerinde, N. D., 338

Pace, Dinah Watts, 513–14
Pacific Islands, 148–50, 288–90, 292, 297n; *see also* Hawai'i; New Zealand; Sāmoa
Padmore, George, 410, 412, 414, 425–6, 427, 429, 519–28
Palestine, 4, 406–9
Palmer, A. L., 73–4, 78nn
Palmer, Vance, 127, 129–30
Pan-Africa, 526–7
Pan-Africanism, 175, 322, 412, 505, 515–16, 519–28, 535
Papineau, Louis-Joseph, 361, 362
Paris; ou le Livre des Cent-et-Un, 194–5
Paterson, A. B. 'Banjo', 127, 129, 135, 143
Paul, Robert Benjamin, 172–3, 174, 175
p'Bitek, Okot, 535–6, 537–8
Pearl: Devoted to Polite Literature, Science, and Religion, The, 39–40
Pearson, Charles, 148
Pearson, Kent, 453
Peers, Douglas M., 14, 391, 393
Pelem, James, 302, 304
Pelewura, Alimotu, 222, 224
Pennycook, Alastair, 17–18
Penny Magazine, The, 192
People's National Party, 501, 519, 521, 524
Peterson, Derek R., 301, 508, 516
Phillip, Arthur, 132, 133, 145
Pierce, Richard, 533
Piesse, Jude, 52, 57
Pillay, A. J., 242, 243, 245
Plaatje, Sol, 164, 345
Ploetz, Alfred, 242
Porter, Andrew N., 113
Potter, Simon J., 22, 394
Prasad, Jotee, 469, 470, 471–4
Prescod, Samuel Jackman, 66, 67, 70, 74–8
Prescod, William Hinds, 74–5

Pringle, Thomas, 4
Printer's Miscellany, 376
print infrastructure 3–7, 52, 87, 272–4, 385; *see also* communications infrastructure; distribution infrastructure; print technology; print workers
print technology, 3–4, 5, 102, 118
print workers, 4–5, 60, 86–7, 215, 293–4, 301, 320, 375–87
Progress, 104
Progressive Party, 157–8, 164, 304
Provincial: or, Halifax Monthly Magazine, The, 43, 48
pseudonyms, 66, 190, 214, 215, 218, 219, 222–4, 323, 507
Public Opinion, 425, 426, 493, 496, 499–503, 499, 519–28, 520
public sphere, 7–9, 15, 17, 20–1, 25–8, 31–2, 66, 97–8, 100, 103, 106, 108, 215–16, 223–4, 272, 277–83, 303, 343–5, 355, 420, 423–5, 428–9, 494–6, 498–502
 anti-colonial, 423–5, 428–9, 433, 494–6, 498–502, 524–5
 colonial, 97–8, 100, 103, 106, 108, 214–16, 223–4, 303, 343–5, 355, 428
 literary, 39–48, 51–4, 57–62, 103–7, 272, 277–83, 450, 455, 493–4, 498–502, 524–5, 532–6, 538–40

Queenslander, The, 142–3, 144, 145, 146

Rafiki Yetu, 317, 326
Rakshit, Romeschandra, 246
Ramchand, Kenneth, 493
Ramraj, Victor, 493
Rand Daily Mail, 164, 165, 346
Randle, John, 335, 336
readers as contributors, 42, 47, 129, 130, 189–90, 205, 210, 216, 323–4; *see also* competitions; letters
Reddy, Muthulakshmi, 234, 236–7
Reid, Alexander Walker, 108
Reid, Ned, 103–4
Rentoul, Anne Rattray, 204–5
Rentoul [Outhwaite], Ida S., 204–5
reprinted content, 74, 88, 186–8, 191–3, 195–8, 244–5, 323, 333–4, 347, 365, 367, 380, 463, 466–8, 524; *see also* translated content
Revans, Samuel, 361–72
Revolt!, 404, 405, 408–9
Reynolds, Reginald, 406, 407–8, 409, 414
Rhodes, Cecil John, 155, 156–60, 162, 165, 166, 303–4, 305, 312, 380

Rhodesia, 156, 157, 162, 165, 413, 526; see also Southern Africa
Riach, William, 393–4, 399
Richards, Arthur, 522
Richards, Vernon, 405, 406, 408, 412
Ridley, F. A., 406, 409, 414
Roberts, W. Adolphe, 71, 73, 521
Robertson, Struan, 363–4
Robeson, Paul, 525–7
Robinson, Morgan, 327
Rock, Joseph, 76–7
Rodríguez Navas, Ana, 503n
Rodriques, Janelle, 501
Rofe, Husein, 451, 455
Roods, Thomas, 469, 474, 475n
Roosevelt, Franklin D., 418–19, 422, 425
Rosenberg, Leah, 498, 502n
Rubusana, Walter Mpilo, 158, 302, 304–5, 313
Rudd, Steele, 127, 129, 211n
Rudy, Jason, 52
Russia, 94, 404; see also Soviet Union

Saenger, André, 123
Saha, Jonathan, 22
Saklatvala, Shapurji Dorabji, 27
Salmigondis; Contes des toutes les couleurs, Le, 194, 195
Sāmoa, 285–97
Samoan Reporter, 296
Sander, Reinhard, 503n
Sanger, Margaret, 242, 247, 248, 250, 251
San Juan, E., 26
Santana, Stephanie Bosch, 536
Sanyal, Ram Gopal, 393
'Sarbah, Lizzie', 220, 225n
Sarkar, Jadunath, 426
Sastri, Mahadeva, 234
Sathyanatha Kahalam, 278
Satthianadhan, Kamala, 228, 230, 231–4
Saturday Review, The, 99
Sauer, Jacobus Wilhelmus, 157, 158, 161, 164, 303
Saunders, Patricia, 498, 502n
Sawyerr, G. A., 512–13
Schomburgk, Robert, 77
Schreiner, Olive, 157, 160, 162, 165
Schreiner, William Philip, 155, 157, 158–61, 165
Scotsman, The, 398–9
Scott, Rose, 210
Scottish Typographical Circular, 377, 379, 380–1, 385
Scotton, James, 319

Scribbler, The, 39, 47, 53, 56
'Scrutator' (*Eleti Ọfẹ*), 336, 339
Seibert, Johanna, 66, 68, 72, 73
Sekyi, Kobina, 171
Serumaga, Robert, 535, 536
Sesotho, 124n, 303, 308–10, 314n, 344, 353, 354
Setswana, 120, 121, 124n, 344, 348, 353, 354
Sewell, William, 454
Shakespeare, William, 336, 339–40
Sharpe, Christina, 68
Shaw, William, 116
Sibbald, William, 37, 40, 41–2, 49, 57
Sierra Leone, 117, 171, 174, 175, 177, 178, 330, 333–4, 337, 412, 413, 455; see also West Africa
Sifelani, Portia, 348, 355
Silva, Noenoe K., 295
Simpson, Thula, 309
Sinha, Mrinalini, 246
Sinnema, Peter, 465–6
Slaughter, Joseph R., 429
slavery, 66–78, 116–17, 123, 162, 330, 365, 405, 422, 494–5, 514, 525–6
Smiles, Samuel, 336
Smith, George, 394
Smuts, Jan Christian, 164, 165, 420, 421, 427
Smyth, Wyllys, 38, 41, 42–3
socialism, 130, 147, 304, 404, 425, 437, 523, 528; see also unions
Soga, Alan Kirkland, 158, 304, 313
Soga, Tiyo, 116, 304, 344
'S. O. N.', 505–6
South Africa
 African-language periodicals, 120, 121–2, 155, 158, 300–14, 343–55
 anti-apartheid struggle, 178, 413, 436–7, 455
 anti-colonialism, 27–8, 154–66, 343, 345, 347, 413, 422–5, 426–8
 Black activism, 301–14, 345–6
 Black editors and contributors, 27, 122–3, 155, 164, 300–14, 343–55
 Communism, 115, 122, 345–7, 423, 426, 427, 429n, 434, 436–7
 Dutch periodicals, 155, 156, 158, 159
 education, 311, 384
 growth of periodical publishing, 155–6, 164, 344–5
 immigration to, 164, 384–5
 missionaries, 115–16
 print trade journals, 376, 378, 381–7
 racism, 155–7, 158, 162, 164–5

see also African National Congress; Anglo-Boer War; Anglo-Zulu War; Southern Africa
South African Commercial Advertiser, 4
South African Native National Congress, 302–4, 308–9, 311, 313
South African News, 154–66, *154*, 169
South African Outlook, The, see *Christian Express, The*
South African Spectator, 164, 305
South African Typographical Circular, 386–7
South African Typographical Journal, 376, 378, *381*, 382, 384, 386
South African War *see* Anglo-Boer War
Southern Africa, 112–24, 169, 301–2, 305, 310, 390–401, 422–3; *see also* Rhodesia; South Africa
Southern Monthly Magazine, The, 99
Soviet Union, 244, 418, 427, 439–43, 454, 526; *see also* Russia
Spain and the World, 404, 405, 406–8, *407*
Spanish Civil War, 405, 406, 500
Spedon, Andrew Learmont, 58
Specimen of Printing Types and Ornaments, 60–1, *61*
Spiller, Peter, 362, 365, 366
Sprigg, Gordon, 156, 157–8, 161, 162, 164, 304
Sreenivas, Mytheli, 229
Stack, Frederick, *Plate 1*
Stafford, Jane, 102, 106–7
Stair, John Betteridge, 293–4
Standard and Diggers News, The, 155–6, 159
Stanley, Margaret, 456
Star, The (Johannesburg), 155, 157, 346
Star, Paul, 98, 105
Stead, W. T., 160, 163, 165, 393
Stenhouse, John, 100
Stephens, A. G., 136–7
Stern, Alexandra Minna, 247, 251n
Stevens, Siaka, 177
Stiles, Clark, 98
Stock, Dinah, 409–10
Stocqueler, Joachim Hayward, 84, 87–8
Stolte, Carolien, 435
Stornig, Katharina, 113
Stri-Dharma, 228–30, 233, 234–41
Studdert, Helena, 201, 204
Subrahmanyam, Sanjay, 22
subscription, 6, 54, 85–8, 202, 334, 367, 378–9
  appeals for, 74, 186, 235, 239, 532
  information about subscribers, 38, 83, 91–3, 406
  pricing, 231, 256, 308

Sukarno, 437–8, 442–3
Sun (Montreal), 366
Sun (New York), 128
Sundarayyar and Sons, 274
Sunday Times (Australia), 147
Suriano, Maria, 348, 355
Swahili, 317–27, 531, 535, 537
Switzer, Donna, 120
Switzer, Les, 120, 155, 344
Sydney Mail, 12, 141, 143, 144–5, 146–7

Tafawa Balewa, Abubakar, 177
Tagore, Rabindranath, 234
Ta Kung Pao, 439, 440, 449, 450, 457n
Tanganyika, 317–20, 322–5, 327; *see also* Eastern Africa; Tanzania
Tanganyika Standard, 420
Tangazo, 319, 321
Tange, Andrea Kaston, 465, 474
Tanzania, 413, 454; *see also* Eastern Africa; Tanganyika
Taonui, Rāwiri, 97
Te Karere Maori, 256–62, 267–8
Te Karere o Nui Tireni, 256–9, *257*
Te Punga Somerville, Alice, 292, 294
Te Rangitāke, Wiremu Kīngi, 260
Te Waka Maori series, 256–7, 262–8, *264*, 266
Te Whīwhī, Mātene, 261
Thampuran, Valiakoyi, 276–7
Thema, R. V. Selope, 351–2, 353
Theosophy, 228, 230, 234–5
Thomas, Isaac Babalola, 218, 332, 334, 336, 337, 340
Thome, James, 66, 74
Thuku, Harry, 319, 320, 326
Times, The (London), 3, 28, 163, 394, 400, 441, 463–4, 466, 468, 470
Times of India, 384, 391, 469, 472–3
Times of West Africa, 213, 214, 217, 220, 222
Timm, Birte, 521
Token, 190–1
Torrens, Henry Whitelock, 83–4, 86–90, 92, 94
Torrey, R. A., 209
Townsend, Meredith, 394
Tracey, Elizabeth, 185, 193, 198n
Traill, Catharine Parr, 48, 62
Transactions and Proceedings of the New Zealand Institute, 100–2, 105, 107
translated content
  from English, 196, 229, 231, 235, 259, 265, 326, 331, 336–7, 339, 348–9, 353, 355
  into English, 121, 191, 193–5, 291–5, 336–7, 339, 355, 448, 477–90

Triad: A Monthly Magazine of Music, Science, and Art, The, 102
Trinidad and Tobago, 27, 413, 496–9, 502n; *see also* Caribbean
Trinidad Guardian, 421, 496
Tsekie, Tom, 455
Tsiboe, John and Nancy, 421
Tucker, Maya V., 201, 211, 212n
Turner, Ethel, 204, 207–8
Turner, George, 296
Turner, Mark, 508
Twopenny, Richard, 139
Tyamzashe, George, 304, 347
Tye, J. Reginald, 98, 102, 364
Typographical Circular, 375, 376, 379–80
Typographical Journal (US), 379, 382
typography, 3–4, 60–1, 62, 117, 293, 308, 344, 347, 351

Uganda, 319, 413, 532, 536; *see also* Eastern Africa
Umhalla, Nathaniel, 302, 304
Umteteli wa Bantu, 319, 323, 343–50, *349*, 355n
unions
  print trade, 375–87
  students', 171, 173, 334
  trade unionism, *149*, 345, 346, 409, 410, 412, 428, 436, 439, 526
United Kingdom *see* Britain
United States of America
  African Americans, 495, 513–14, 522–3, 525, 526
  Atlantic Charter, 418–29, 520
  criticism of, 439, 442, 449–51, 455
  influence overseas, 31, 128, 243, 251, 288
  model of independence, 132–3, 422
  press censorship, 250
  print culture, 54–5, 59, 188, 190–3
  print trade, 376, 379, 380, 382, 383–4
  racism, 435, 522
  as source for reprinted content, 58, 188–9, 190–1, 204, 304
  women's periodicals, 202–4
Upadhyaya, Nathalal Jagjivan, 405, 414
Urdu, 3, 231, 279

Vambe, Maurice, 533
Varma, A. R. Raja Raja, 281
Veracini, Lorenzo, 134
Victoria Magazine, 61–2
Vidyavinodini, 272–83, *276*
Vincent, David, 287–8

Vincent, Thomas Brewer, 38, 186
Vinson, Robert Trent, 436
Vittachi, Tarzie, 442–3
Vizetelly, Henry, 464, 467, 468, 469, 470–2, 473, 475n
Vosseler, Annika, 122

Wakefield, E. G., 361, 363
Wakefield, William, 369, 371
Wales, James, 474
Wallace, Brian, 465
Wallace-Johnson, I. T. A., 174, 410
Walsh, Philip, 105–6
Wandera, Billy Ogana, 539
War Commentary, 404, 405, 409–12
Ward, Edmund, 38
Ward, Russel, 127, 129–30
Warne, Ellen, 210
Warner, Michael, 495
Warung, Price, 134
Washington, Booker T., 351, 512, 513
Watchman and Jamaica Free Press, The, 66–74, 77–8
Watchman: The Story of Edward Jordon, The (film), 71–2
Watkins, Elizabeth, 321
Watkins, Oscar Ferris, 321, 324–7
Watts, Michael John, 202
Weaver, Rachael, 204
Webby, Elizabeth, 140
Weeks, Jeffrey, 248, 251n
Welsh, 14
Wendt, Maualaivao Albert, 292
Wendt, Reinhard, 114
Wesleyan Methodist Missionary Society, 116, 117–18
Wesleyan Missionary Notices, 112, 117–18, 119, 122
West Africa, 168–79; *see also* Gambia; Ghana; Gold Coast; Nigeria; Sierra Leone
West Africa, 163, 168–79, 214, 334–5
West African Pilot, 217, 224, 421–2, 425, 426, 507
West African Review, 172–3, 175, 214, 225n
West African Times, 216, 218, 220
Westall, Richard J., 413
West Indies *see* Caribbean
Wickham, Chris, 22
Wilcocke, Samuel, 56, 62, 198n
Williams, David Morgan, 175, 176
Williams, H. Antus, 332
Williams, Mark, 102, 106–7
Williams, Raymond, 538

Wilson, Charlotte M., 404–5
Wilson, John Mackay, 195–8
Wolfe, Lilian, 405
women
  as compositors and printers, 215
  construction of female identities, 202, 205–11, 216–18, 234, 246–7, 250
  as editors, 13–14, 185, 188–91, 198n, 214–15, 228, 236–7
  education, 209–10, 215–20, 228–30, 232, 234, 238, 239–41
  gender reform, 229–30, 232–4, 246–8
  as mothers, 248–50
  as political actors, 210–11, 213–14, 218–25, 228–9, 232–41, 248, 524
  as readers, 62, 66, 144, 185–98, 201–12, 214, 228–41
  as writers, 13–14, 62, 189–90, 213–25, 228, 233, 532
  see also gender

Wong Siu Kuan, 452
Woodcock, George, 410
Wordsworth, William, 193
Work and Workers in the Mission Field, 118
Worker, The, 139, 144, 147–50, *149*, *150*
World War I, 169, 320–1, 404
World War II, 174, 221, 234, 409–12, 418–29, 516, 520, 522
Wright, Richard, 434–5
Wynn, Graeme, 97, 99

Xuma, A. B., 422–3, 424

Yoruba (language), 216, 218, 330–41
Young, David, 99, 103, 104

Zealandia: A Monthly Magazine of New Zealand Literature by New Zealand Writers, 103, 106
Zhou Enlai, 434, 438